The Kiss
That Changed Me

Kristy Nicolle

K Nicolle x

The Tidal Kiss Trilogy- Book 3

TRILOGY ONE IN THE
QUEENS OF FANTASY SAGA

First published by Kristy Nicolle, United Kingdom, December 2016

QUEENS OF FANTASY EDITION (1st EDITION)
Published December 2016 by Kristy Nicolle
Copyright © 2016 Kristy Nicolle
Edited By- Jaimie Cordall and Evelyn Summers

Adult Paranormal/Fantasy Romance

ISBN: 978-1-911395-04-1

www.kristynicolle.com

For Nanny,

I have put my world to rights.
Thank you for listening.

Prologue

ATARGATIS

My heels click against the coloured crystal floors of the Olympian Council chambers. Mist creeps in around my ankles, chilling my flesh as I stand in the middle of the foyer, Grecian pillars rising in diamond on either side. To my left, lapis lazuli flows artfully, interspersed with frothy flecks of quartz, mimicking the ocean waves over which I, and my fellow Gods, prevail. To my right the crystal fades to black, spitting specks of gold outward so the floor looks like a trampled milky way, providing passage to the Nexus Council chamber. Ahead, the stairs are diamond veined through with amethyst, rising upward into the Aetherial Court.

I sigh, troubled. Brushing my lilac hair behind my left shoulder and staring at the subject of my angst. Before me is a half pillar, upon which rests a set of golden scales. The Kindred Scales. I look at them, wavering under the weight of darkness and light, so close to tilting out of balance that it makes my spongy coral heart race within my chest. I watch it, thinking of the Necrimad, of the Psirens and of my Kindred, the mer. I stand a few more moments, watching it tremble ever so slightly with the passing of yet another Kindred soul, hopefully, I muse, that of a Psiren passing from the world below and back to the crucible of Gaia.

Mixing my magic with mortals had never seemed like a bad idea before, until now. Until I could see just how fragile it all was. I had taken my magic and imbued it in mortals. Emotional, fragile mortals. I had been cast down to the mortal world at the cost of their security against demon invasion. It was true my love for them had cost more than just me. With hindsight, if it had not been for my lover's rage, it all would have been perfect. I could watch the scales forever, but I know of several other Gods who have lost their minds over obsession with the Kindred Scales. Besides, I have other business to attend to, business which will do a lot better in restoring said balance than staring at a pair of old scales.

I take my usual left turn, walking with shoulders set firmly backward and steady in my long strides as my robes trail behind me in waves of sea blue. As I approach the mighty emerald doors of the council chamber, I hear whispers from within. I pause, wondering whether I should enter as I place my hand against the cool stone. Suddenly the door opens in a silent rush and a seemingly young man, who I haven't seen in a while, exits.

"Hercules." I nod to him and he looks surprised to see me here. I don't know why he should be. This is my domain.

"Atargatis… I mean, aunt. What a pleasure to see you here." He bows before me, his clothes pale in comparison to my own garment. He's wearing the signature black overcoat of the Nexus council. Black velvet, the back of which dons a white skeleton with vertebrae far too long for any human. They continue to fall down past the pelvis bone design all the way to the floor, following the line of the coat's long train.

"Thank you, visiting your uncle I presume?" I cock a violet eyebrow and he smiles, faltering only slightly.

"Why, of course. Looking for some advice. You know how father can be…" He begins, but I raise a hand to him, frowning.

"You'd do well not to slander your father beneath his own roof child. You know just as well as I why one should not tempt the temper of a God. Why on earth are you dressed for the underworld? Visiting more than one Uncle today?" I query him, suspicious.

"Of course. I must return this coat actually, awful thing. They barely had one to fit me, what with me being more than skin and bone. So bound by tradition down there as you might recall, wouldn't let me sit in on a meeting without one." He shrugs and I nod. Not reacting to his opinions of our family tree.

"Very well. Have a good day, Hercules." He bows his head once more and walks past me a little too quickly. I turn, calling after him, my voice like the cries of gulls carried on salt winds.

"Hercules…" He turns, looking to me expectantly. "Try not to get into any trouble…" I say, staring at him intensely. I watch as he becomes lost in the depth of my gaze, a side effect of my Goddess status. He starts, dropping his eyes suddenly, a sign of guilt no doubt.

"Of course, aunt. Thank you." He replies, bows once more and then turns on his heel and walks back down the walkway. He crosses the foyer and then disappears into the shadows of the black and gold marred chambers of the Nexus. I frown, feeling that something isn't quite right. With all my knowledge of the seas, the lives and whims of the others within these walls still evade me. I sigh, exhaling salty breath, before stepping through the emerald doors of the chamber, as I do, I'm greeted by the round table that holds a map of the human domain. It is divided by the spindles of a Ship's wheel, made of black marble, which separates each Circle member from the next. I see Poseidon at his usual position, right next to mine.

"Nice visit with your nephew?" I ask him, trying to sound casual.

"As ever Demi-Gods never cease to irritate. As you well know." He lifts his eyes, stormy as night, to mine.

"Yes I do." I admit, feeling the sting of his words. He knows I have a softness for humans, never letting me forget the man who had reeled me in and watched me turn to sand.

"I suppose you've heard the news about her then, our new niece?" I ask him, tilting my head and allowing my eyes to bear into his strong features.

"What Persephone? Of course. Another Demi-God. Just what we need." He looks angry, shaking his head from left to right and I wonder why he cares so much. I try to placate, to soothe his ragged temper once more.

"I hear she prefers to be called Sephy." I say, humanising her.

"Regardless of her name, Haedes should know better. Mixing blood with humans, it's a disgrace." He mutters under his breath. I sigh, deciding to change the subject.

"The Circle of Eight needs to assemble. As we near the assembly of the conduit we must look once again to the risks upon the walls of this world."

"You really think those mer can do it?" Poseidon laughs.

"I have never doubted them. Besides, Orion and Callie must succeed. Lest you forget the reason we are here, my love, is that you cannot control your temper. Just like your brothers." Poseidon stares at me for a moment, his white hair like sea foam, bouncing from his shoulders and falling from his face in the long white beard I love to tug and pull when I'm kissing him.

"Nothing wrong with a temper my dear. Without one we would all most certainly be doomed by now. Kindness and love doesn't always cut it. Particularly not with humans." I sigh, knowing I do not want to go over this again.

"It is not because of Orion and Callie I am here. It's Vex I'm concerned about." His eyes widen slightly and he gets to his feet. Towering over the table.

"My vessel? What of him?" His eyes spark, the lightning behind them evident. I wonder what it must be like for the people down below, suffering his wrath. I wonder this every-time we fight, praying silently I can remain calm, resist the storm within and prevent yet another natural disaster for the sake of our differences.

"He is losing faith. The darkness within him is waning and hopelessness is taking over. Solustus, that monster… he is torturing him and I fret that if he cannot escape, or hold strong, that all will be lost." Poseidon walks over to me, his stride threatening to crack the crystal floors with its heaviness.

"Come, we must go to the looking glass chambers… If Vex is losing hope, then I need to pay him a little visit and see to it that he toughens." Poseidon sounds so cruel in this moment I wonder how it is we haven't yet destroyed the worlds below, engulfed them in our differences and our wraths. I love him, and have loved him for my entire existence. Our souls were forged in the crucible of Gaia, made for one another, but I cannot fathom liking him one bit. I wonder how that can be.

"Very well, my love. Let us go." I take his hand and we walk from the room, our tempers placating.

Somewhere below I feel a stormy wind die and a cresting wave fall, leaving nothing beneath the surface but silence and bloodshed yet to pass.

1

Marcas

ORION

I watch his hands move around her body and his rusty looking blade press against the flawless alabaster of her neck. My breath catches in my throat, suspended in time along with the rest of me, unable to escape my body.

"And what, in the name of Loch Ness, is a pretty wee lass like you, doing in a place like this?" The words leave his lips and my mind races, trying to connect the pieces of what is going on. The man with Callie at his mercy is a hulking entity, taller than me by almost a foot. He has a messy orange mane of hair and a face that looks like it's been mauled by a bear. His eyes are limpet green and something I've not seen since I last encountered Caedes flickers behind them. Madness. His tailfin is a dark, bottle green and his body is captured within thick black tattoos that wrap around his torso like binding chains.

I want to move forward, to obliterate him, and yet I know if I try to defend her, we could start a war with this pod before we've even had a chance to identify ourselves. I suppose this is it then. Being a leader. Having to choose between what I love most and duty.

"Stop." My voice leaves me and I blink, re-entering the moment and allowing the hammering of my heart to bring me back to the urgency of the situation. I feel Cole move next to me, ready to launch forward, but I bring the arm that isn't raised to the attacker upward and across his chest, stopping him

1

in his tracks. I say nothing, not wanting to turn and lose the eye contact of the red headed man for even a second.

"Ah, a challenger? That what ye are, lad?" The man moves, and I blanche, petrified he will slit the throat of the woman I waited several lifetimes to find.

"Please. Don't hurt her. She is no threat to you." I repeat, holding out a hand, showing him I mean no harm.

"This here lass? A demon lad, that's what she be! Ain't no lassies around here. No sir." My eyes dart from left to right and I inhale. Trying to control my breathing. The water is a murky green, as though a fog has descended upon us and the kelp forests that surround us sway, soundless. The mood in the water is tense and silent as the seconds tick past. I can feel the pod of mer behind me with Azure at my side, unmoving, terrified. Suddenly, a voice breaks the silence.

"Marcas!" The voice is younger, higher pitched and entirely Scottish. I turn my head slowly, afraid to move too quickly and startle the man. Callie's eyes bulge as they bore into mine and I can tell she's been caught completely off guard. Moments later a young man, also sporting a jade green tail and a mess of red hair, parts the curtains of long kelp and emerges into the middle of the tense scene. At the sight of the mer and myself, of Callie within the clutch of the strange man, his eyes widen. I drop my hand, which I realised is still raised, just in case I have to make a dart to disarm Callie's attacker.

"Father! Let her go!" The young merman moves forward as his father turns to him. I exhale slightly as suddenly the light behind his eyes, the fire that had once resided there, so sure that Callie was a demon, diminishes. His irises seem to cloud over as he lets his arm slip from her torso and his hand drops.

"How did I git here, Conan? Ahm so muddled." Conan takes his hands in his own and I watch as he turns to me.

"Ah am sorry. My father, Marcas, he gits a wee bit confused sometimes. Who are you?" He looks confused as his eyes dart away from my own and toward Callie, and then Azure. Callie moves back to my side in a hurried wave of her fluke, rubbing her neck nervously.

"You okay?" I ask her, my heartbeat slowing.

2

"Yes. Thankfully. I thought he was you… I thought…" She stutters, clearly feeling foolish.

"It's alright. You're okay, that's what's important." I move my hand through the water and place it on her shoulder, giving her a little comfort. She smiles and I have to tear my eyes away from her, attending to the business of introductions.

"I'm Orion. The Crowned Ruler of the Children of Atargatis… I think you might know of my father, Atlas?" I hold out a hand to Conan and he takes it. His handshake is limp and weak like a dying fish. Now I think about it, the man in front of me is less of a man and more of a boy. He's scrawny and pale, his face marred by a spattering of freckles. His green eyes sparkle slightly as he looks up into my face and that's when I realise he's shorter than I am too.

"I never heard of anyone by that name."

"What about your father?" Callie asks him, eyeing Marcas with a nervous glance.

"He don't know his own shadow frae them demons. I doobt, even if he had met this Atlas, that he would remember."

I sigh at his response, taking a moment to absorb the astuteness of his attitude. He may very well seem like a young boy, and yet, despite his lack of confidence, he speaks with wisdom. Frowning, he takes up a wooden looking whistle, puts it to his lips and blows, causing it to emit a sound not unlike that of a pan-pipe. We float for a few moments, as a shoal of brown trout sway past us, shimmering dully with the murk of the water. Suddenly, I hear a whinny.

Horses?

I turn to stare at Philippe, but he stands, Azure atop his spine, still and calm. She stares at me, eyes wide, clearly alarmed. Her fists are clenched and her spine is poker straight. I pivot once more, just in time to see figures approaching through the fog.

"Conan, what is it? Marcas got himself intae trooble again?" The voice is thicker Scottish than both the men we've already encountered, and as the figure approaches on the back of what I can only describe as the oddest horse I've ever seen, I recoil slightly. His staggering gait and broadness make me feel

3

instantly uncomfortable and I back into the crowd of my people, wishing I had longer arms so I could protect them all.

"Domnall, this is Orion an' th' bairns ay Atargatis. My father, he attacked 'er." Conan points to Callie and my heartbeat accelerates.

"Bairns?" I cock an eyebrow, staring at Conan. He turns back at me, looking exasperated.

"Ay, wee littlun's." His gaze is unwavering, scrutinising me like I'm stupid and I exhale. I think he means children. I had thought the Scottish spoke English, but now I'm seeing that I'm going to struggle with their terms. The one he calls Domnall dismounts the horse looking creature. It is closer now so I can examine it more clearly. It's a mint green, and its body isn't like that of a horse at all, or at least the back isn't. The torso of the creature has two long legs, ending in hoofed feet like a normal horse, but it's back legs aren't there and its waist twists into an odd, curling tailfin. It's utterly bizarre, unnatural, but at the same time beautiful. Its mane is made of long green kelp and its eyes are brown and large, shimmering despite there being no concentrated light source. I'm distracted by its ugly beauty.

"Oi! You! Explain yerself! Whit brings ye tae these waters!"

"We're here to save our species. We need help. We're looking for a vessel, a person. We've been sent here by an old friend, Atlas, do you know of him?" These words do not fall from my lips, but from my maiden's as she rises slightly in the water to face Domnall at his full height. He's tall, with a navy-blue tailfin, much longer than mine. His body is stout and covered in tattoos that look like giant slashes across his chest. His hair is red, slicked back against his head and it looks like it's braided down his back.

"Atlas? Ah ne'er heard ay him." Domnall looks down into Callie's face. I watch them before saying anything more, intrigued. At her face his whole demeanour has altered, slackened and softened.

"Where did ye come frae?" Another man with a froth of curly red hair has dismounted one of the odd horse- mer hybrids and is now addressing me. His tail is indigo and his teeth are rotting in his mouth. His voices reaches out to me while his eyes also settle on Callie.

4

"The Pacific. We've just come from the Arctic. From the Adaro, do you know them?" I ask him, point blank, figuring honesty is the best way to go. They're no longer looking at me though, ignoring my reply and still transfixed by Callie. "Excuse me! Do you mind, she's spoken for!" I reach out and push Callie behind me, making one swift movement through the murk to protect what's mine, still raw from the idea of the tentacled clutch of Vex encasing her. I won't be cuckolded again.

"Sorry laddie, it's jist... we've ne'er seen a mermaid afore." The man with rotting teeth apologises and Domnall's hulking great mass shifts, breathing out in a stilted sigh.

"Fergus is right. This is a first fur us. Ye will find nae woman 'ere."

"What do you mean? There aren't any mermaids here?" Azure speaks, her voice less bold than I'm used to hearing it.

"Nae. Only lads." Conan replies to her. A curious expression crossing across his face as he moves towards her. It's then that I watch his gaze and realise it's not on her at all. It's on Philippe. Everyone stops as he approaches.

"That's my Equinox. You can approach if you like. Just stay where he can see you." I offer, keeping Callie behind me. I can feel her hand on my back and I turn to her. Looking her full on in the face her gaze grounds me, reminds me I'm here to do a job. "What are your horses called?" I ask them and they burst into laughter, a sound so deep that it rattles the water we're immersed in, disturbing tiny invertebrates and phytoplankton.

"These arenae horses, laddie. These are Kelpie. The pride ay Lir!"

"Lir?" I catch his final word and latch onto it.

"Aye, the grae' creator, ruler ay these waters." Domnall puffs out his chest, as though he's announcing someone who will actually appear through the distant fog of the jade waters.

So, the next god in the circle is Lir. I think.

"Where are we?" I hear someone ask from behind me, Rose is the first amongst the pod to speak, and her figure rises slightly in the water, singling her out as the speaker.

"Yae be in Moray Firth. Wit thae Selkies, Defender's o' Loch Ness." Fegus replies, giving her a rotting, gap toothed smile. I watch her recoil, as though his evident bad breath has already reached her. I laugh slightly under my breath. Then the impact of the information hits me.

Scotland. Well, that's not exactly what I was expecting.

I ponder this and then wonder what exactly it was that I did expect. Did I think I was going to pop up in the tropics and go on a jolly holiday with Callie? My mind wanders to thoughts of her waiting for me, naked on a beach... then I remind myself I am a ruler, I'm responsible. I can fantasise later.

"Well hello, I'm Orion." I reach out a hand to Domnall as his towering height throws shadows across my face. He reaches out with a tilted head, uncertain and takes my hand; shaking it so hard my arm feels like it may leave my shoulder socket.

"Domnall, Chief o' the Selkies."

"I didn't catch the name of your beautiful Kelpie there?" I compliment and Domnall smiles, his teeth in better condition than Fergus' by a long way.

"This 'ere be Magnus. And that there is Casanova." He points to his and then Fergus' Kelpies as they float, innocuous and without touching the sediment of the sea floor.

"Beautiful. You must be very proud of them!" I nod to him with a slight smile, seeing the clear love between Kelpie and rider.

"Yae, ain't no grae'er love than thit atween a man and his mount." Domnall nods and Fergus raises an eyebrow.

"Dom, dinnae say this in front ay th' lassies, they'll think we're uninterested." He winks with a crooked smile at the mermaids behind me and I feel a sudden inhale of water at their subtle backwards stroke. Clearly these men haven't been around women in quite a while. I look to Callie, her beauty more evident to me now than ever. I watch her from the corner of my eye as Conan coos to Philippe, whispering in horse tongue and Azure rolls her eyes. Callie's eyes haven't yet left Marcas, not for a second, despite the fact he's floating and his eyes appear glazed.

"Did he hurt ye, miss?" Domnall looks concerned as Callie rubs her neck slightly.

"No, it's fine. It was just an accident." She shrugs but the chief's eyes narrow.

"Conan! Yae need tae keep a better watch over that ravin' loonie! Cannae at least do that?" At this harsh decree, Conan becomes stiff in the water, his spindled form acute with tension. He turns, his face a contortion of misery, away from Philippe. As I watch him it's the first time I've noticed not only his pallor, but his lack of tattoos.

"Ah ahm sorry, Father can be difficult. He is sae large, and ah struggle to contain him to the Bùrn." He looks like he might cry and I pity him. I wonder what it must be like to become the caretaker to your own parent. My father died suddenly, too suddenly, but at least he didn't go mad and suffer.

"See that it doesnae happen again. Ah willnae compromise security fae that ol' codger. These folk could hae bin anyone, they could hae bin demons. Nae offence." Domnall looks to me with a slight frown. He's not wrong.

"No, I understand. Demons are a problem for us too. That's why we're here."

"Come to the Bùrn Kildrummy, we shall talk there." Domnall commands it with such complete authority that I dare not refuse. He's a much sterner ruler than I'm used to seeing. With Gideon falling head over heels in love with his daughter, as one would expect, I had seen a softer side to him. This type of leadership was something I hadn't come across yet. It is Domnall's extreme masculine air and the might of his physical presence that makes his followers respect him. Not a bad way to be. As I watch him sling his waist length, red braid over his shoulder and mount his Kelpie, I wonder if he's got it right, this ruler-ship thing. He beckons the rest of us forward from the clearing amongst the kelp forest, not one of whom, can refuse. I wonder if I might not even learn a thing or two from Domnall about leading. I look after them, admiring their odd Kelpies and their massive stature. Then, something happens. A high pitched, Scottish yelp travels to me, causing my heart to start hammering once more. I turn as Conan yells out and the Kelpie mounted Selkies pivot to find

7

the source of the commotion as well. Azure's eyes have turned white and she's screaming, something that I've never seen happen to her during a vision before. She tilts, unable to control her physical form, toppling in what appears to me to be slow motion. As Callie goes to aid her, with a quick glance back at me, Azure falls through the murk and fog of the highland waters from horseback and to the ground. Crushing Conan, who tries to catch her, flat.

AZURE

The vision that overcomes me is so agonising I can barely stand it. The pain within my skull pounds against my bones like angry fists of a monster trying to get free. I surrender to the agony, the only thing I can do. I feel myself slip from Philippe and conscious reckoning as the fog rolls in, but I can do nothing. Nothing to stop my body from falling, oh so slowly, through the cloudy waters of Moray Firth and to the ground as my soul is taken somewhere else, transported and transmogrified into something ethereal and fluid, slipping through the fingers of time.

The sound of water sloshing against sand greets my ears and something I haven't felt for hundreds of years bathes me with humid stickiness. The sunlight is falling on me, igniting my soul with something I wondered if I'd ever feel again. Joy. I feel the emotion, strange and warm coursing through my veins, followed by an unending tumult of guilt. I shouldn't be happy. My sister is dead. I failed her. She's gone. Then I realise I'm not alone. I turn, feeling the breathing of another prickle my skin. Vex is next to me, dressed in black jeans and no shirt. He looks confused which is hardly surprising.

"What the bloody hell are you doing here?" He looks to me, rolling his eyes. I shake my head. A nice vision killed by a smart mouthed Brit. Just what I need. Then I realise something is off. I've never had a vision like this before. I'm usually watching, not immersed. I've never been able to talk with someone

8

face to face before. After all, when Starlet had died, I'd been talking to her, but it was inside the deep recesses of her mind and I was trapped, helpless to move or act. Unable to save her.

"What's going on? Why are you here?" I look to him and he shrugs.

"I'll be damned if I know… oh wait…" His sarcasm is cut short by a booming voice. Both our heads turn simultaneously, and my eyes rest on a man walking across the sand toward me. Palm trees rustle with a cool breeze, and suddenly, for no reason I can discern, I know exactly who it is I'm looking at. I just can't work out why he's here.

"Vexus." His voice booms out, entangled with the sounds of crashing waves and stormy seas. I suppose from an angry God of the sea I should expect nothing else.

"Yes. Who the bloody hell are you?" Vex looks startled as he shifts on the balls of his naked feet, his muscles bulging as he tenses at the stranger's proximity. I turn to him, speaking in a harsh whisper.

"Vex… You might not want to piss him off with your sparkling personality. I don't really fancy getting burned to a crisp under his scorn. Play nice." I warn him and he lets out a low growl, like that of a feral dog.

"I am Poseidon, God of the Seas that you squirm in, son. I suggest you listen to what I have to say." His eyes spark, their depths lit by lightning forks just like that of his damned creation.

"Right…" Vex licks the front of his teeth with his long tongue, contorting his mouth into a pucker of distaste, but says nothing further.

"I am here to tell you to hold on. We need you, both of you. Vex, you're important. More so than you know. The fate of the world rests on your shoulders. There is no room for human weakness here. Pain, love, hate. It's all useless if you give in. If you stop breathing. Everything will perish. Do you understand?" Poseidon looks at him with a stern expression.

"So you need me?" He cocks an eyebrow and looks slightly amused. I want to roll my eyes, but I desist, feeling the power radiating from the man before me like heat off hot coals.

9

"No, Vex. You need me. But if you die then I can't help you. Do not mistake this request for weakness. You will find no weakness here." He looks furious but something behind his eyes holds that fury captive, keeping it from unleashing on its target. I wonder momentarily if Vex is right. Maybe Poseidon does need him. But for what I wonder?

"As for you, Azure, you are here merely by connection to Vex. He now holds your sister's aptitude for visions. You two are connected. In more ways than you know."

"So what, I'm just his sidekick now?" I spit, forgetting myself momentarily. I cringe slightly realising I just took out my frustration on a God. He narrows his eyes, but then smiles.

"You give me hope."

"Hope?" I let the word wrap itself around my tongue, so long departed from any relationship with the concept that I barely remember what it means, let alone what it feels like.

"Yes. Hope that I wasn't completely devoid of reason when I created the Psirens. Solustus and Saturnus, they are perhaps my greatest failures... what I did, what I unleashed; It was unforgiveable, not that I'd ever admit that to anyone else, particularly my beloved or my brothers. You however, you are something else. I see that there is darkness within you, and yet, it's not consumed you. Instead it's become you."

"Well, black is my colour." I suck in my cheeks, feeling like I'm sucking on sour lemon. I don't need anyone to tell me who I am. Particularly not some jackass with a God complex.

"Well, if you two are done with the therapy session I think I'd like to get back to being tortured. Preferable than listening to your life story and this idiot's oh so important cause. I'm sure you understand. As it is, mate, I don't really think I want to be taking advice on how to be human from the likes of you." Vex laughs and then puts his hands in his pockets, rummaging around. "Oh, and next time you bloody well step into someone's brain for a nice little chat can you at least provide some freaking smokes? I'm dying over here." He turns and walks away from Poseidon, disappearing into the blinding light of the distance and leaving only the cry of gulls and footprints in the sand behind. I let out a small sigh. Vex isn't the most likely candidate for someone I'd respect, but I can't deny he's fearless and I like that. He won't bend to be someone he isn't, not even for a God. I turn back to Poseidon's bearded face. He runs his hand back through his white hair and looks frustrated.

"Don't let him do anything stupid. Unfortunately, more depends on that idiot's choices than you know." Poseidon rolls his eyes and I look up at him, squinting against the sun. Suddenly I'm angry.

"You know what? How about... um no? I'm not your goddamn carrier pigeon, and I'm pretty damn sick of you lot up on the higher plains using my brain as your own personal walk in centre. How about you use your mightiness to do something useful, like saving my fucking sister? How about that? Did it ever occur to you that what you do to us mere mortals isn't fair? We're not pawns in your game. We're not chess pieces to be played. These are our lives, our hearts you're toying with. They're not worth less than yours, just because you happened to be born in different circumstances or on a different plain. Know what I think? I think you guys need a goddamn reality check. I'm done being your lap dog. All of you. I'm done. You want my respect? Put yourself at risk for once for this war you've got us all fighting for you. Want me to respect you? Fix your own damn problems. Vex is right. I don't owe you anything. What you did to Solustus, it was evil. You imbued him with darkness that he didn't want. Didn't ask for. He just wanted to be free of this pitiful fucking existence. So yeah, the darkness hasn't eaten me alive. It doesn't mean what you did was right. It wasn't. Want someone to do your bidding? Try Callie Pierce or someone who gives a shit. I'm freaking done." I'm panting, finally finished in my rant.

My anger is surging, coming forth from a depth in myself I hadn't known was overflowing. Poseidon looks affronted, offended, but after everything I've lost I really don't care. I turn on my heel, spraying up powdery white sand in my wake. I storm off into the distance, marching right on back to myself and my melancholia, leaving Poseidon and his stupid ego in the dust.

2

Sight

SOLUSTUS

His body squirms. Weak; mere flesh beneath my influence. It contorts as he cries out, his lungs sucking in air to ease the pain that I continue to inflict. Vex lets the metal of his restraints bite into his wrists, into each of the tentacles that stem from his waistline. Getting a restraint to hold a tentacled foe wasn't easy, but when you have the metal master of the mer within your grasp, nothing is too much to ask. Especially when you threaten to gut not only him, but also his soulmate the next time she comes calling.

"What did you see?" I bark, tired of his lip-lock. His eyelids flutter as he spits blood into the water. The globule floats a second before pluming outward and diffusing into the salty surroundings.

"I already bloody told you. I didn't see anything. It's just a lot of fog and darkness." He rolls his eyes, giving me attitude even though he's bound and completely at my mercy.

"Don't play me for a fool, Vexus! I was around Azure for eons. I know how visions work." I remind him of whom he's dealing with as I clench my fist around the handle of Scarlette. I bring her length up to his neck, watching his gills as they falter open then close, struggling to sustain him after the amount of blood I've wept from him.

"I'm not. I didn't bloody see anything!" He barks in reply. A lie, I'm sure. Time for another lesson I suppose. I pull Scarlette back and plunge her tip in between his fourth and fifth rib, penetrating him. I twist it, giving him another chance to speak.

"You're sure you saw nothing? You don't want to adjust that little statement?" I purr, rotating Scarlette inside of him and finding pure joy in the blood leaking from around the blade's narrowing circumference. Vex squirms, smashing his head into the wall of the armoury tower that curves behind him as though he wants to knock himself unconscious. His wrists twist inside the shackles that hoist his arms above his head, exposing his armpits and sides, leaving him completely vulnerable.

"Bloody hell!" He exclaims, screwing up his eyes and turning his head so his cheek rests against the sandstone of the wall. I wonder if it's coolness is giving him relief, so I withdraw Scarlette from his torso. Vex grunts, going limp and letting his head hang. I lift the blade, blood-stained with stickiness that refuses to be washed away by the salt water, bringing it up to his cheek and pushing the edge against his narrowed cheekbone.

"Vex, do not mistake me. I can do this for days, and you, well you're not exactly known for your stamina are you? Not enough of a goer to satisfy even Callie Pierce, always gagging for a fag or some rank spirit to release you from your miserable existence. If you tell me, it can be over, I can free you from this. You can be where you belong..." I taunt him with the promise of release, that same promise that had led me to the height of those cliffs near my childhood home, overlooking the sea. That very same wish to be free from life had clutched at my heart as I threw myself with reckless abandon onto the rocky shards at the frothing mouth of the ocean. Those rocks that had broken my body and released me... to this.

"Or, you could shut the bloody hell up and get on with it." Vex gestures to Scarlette with his head, spitting more blood. I feel rage rise through me like bile.

Perhaps a different approach. If he's trying to play the righteous victim.

I shift, making one quick flick of my swordfish-esque tail and move to the left, away from Vex and onto his roommate. Violet scales glisten dully, spattered with blood.

14

"Perhaps then, I will torture him until you yield. If you're so righteous." Oscar looks unconscious, but I will soon change that. I grow impatient.

"Go ahead, you'd torture him anyway." Vex bites out. I push the blade into Oscars stomach, poking holes in him like he's nothing more than fish fillet.

"So you're not going to talk? That's too bad. Ah well, I'm sure Caedes will be able to get something out of you. You know he's more brutal than anyone. You saw what he did to the sacrifice at our little ceremony." I remind him of that night, the night I had waited years to experience. I remember feeling the scythe releasing its energy from within my palms, its power flooding the seal along with that blonde harlot's blood like a key in a mystical lock. I remember the awestruck faces of the meaningless fodder, my army; their eyes experiencing something beyond their simple comprehension. I will treasure that memory for as long as I'm toting around this hideous skin sack.

"Bring it on." Vex coughs, his breath struggling to escape his body as his injuries spark raw impulses of agony around his nervous system. I withdraw my rapier from the metal master and he whimpers, semi-conscious. He has two black eyes and cuts, half-healed, all over his body from Caedes prior assaults. Whatever you say of my brother's mental competencies, he is none the less good at bloodletting, never cutting too deep.

"Very well." I admonish, turning in the water quickly and leaving the two of them hanging in the armoury tower, alone and bleeding. Caedes is outside the door, talking to himself. Something about fire. Next to him floats one of my pawns, the boy I had created to best Miss Callie Pierce, keeping guard.

Useless. I snarl internally, wondering why it is I've left him still breathing.

"Caedes, have your way with them. I want to know what he's seeing. I have business to attend." I wave my hand at him lazily, knowing that my words are lost on him. I move sideways, allowing his long, spine toting lionfish tail to pass by me. As he does, a cruel smile spreads itself across his face, like that one would expect to see the first time you take a child to the circus.

Outside the armoury I find myself bored. I had thought after showing my people I could raise such a powerful beast as the Necrimad they would treat me as a King. Kneel before me and serve me, love me and take care of my every whim. Instead I see the reluctance in their gazes, the fear behind their eyes. It's better than them laughing at me, but it's not the adoration that I am looking for. I look around at the city, at the ruins of the once opulent Occulta Mirum. It was dust now, dust and sand and shattered glass with grating edges. It wasn't like I had thought it was going be. I look down at myself, grey and dull in the acute sunlight from the surface. My skin looks slug-like and thin, flimsy. My spindled skeleton is bony, jutting out at sharp angles. My tail isn't interesting, it's not intimidating like Saturnus', it's not grand or terrifying, but merely useful.

As though he knows I am thinking of him, Saturnus' tones reach me, like noxious gas moving through the water. Silent, but always a most unpleasant experience.

"Solustus, I thought I might find you here. Vexus still not talking?" Saturnus assumes my failure, which irritates me more than I want to admit.

"No, he had another vision while I was in there with him. Then the boy has the gall to act as though he's seeing nothing but darkness." I fold my thin arms across my chest and feel my heart rate heighten, though I can't think of a reason why. "He won't talk."

"No, he just won't talk to *you*." Saturnus sighs, coming up next to me, his black and white King Crown Betta tail longer than mine by several inches.

"I've been torturing him for days." I remind my brother, turning to his dark features with a sneer. He may be my brother, but that doesn't mean I'll bend to his whim.

"Maybe you need to try a more… feminine touch." He waves a hand and I stare at him, no longer facing his dark eyes and spiky black mane, but rather the face of Alyssa. His body has been glimmered. He's been practicing with his powers; worrying to say the least.

"You think he'll talk for his mommy?"

"Yes, he doesn't know she's dead. A tragedy for sure, she was very good for the army's numbers. Regus confirmed this morning that her body was found in the throne room. Also, more worrying is that Titus' trident is gone."

"Titus' trident? That useless hunk of metal?" I turn on him, not needing to remind him of the pathetic aesthetic reasons for which Titus carried the weapon.

"Useless perhaps, but it's absence and lack of an explanation leads me to believe that the mer have been snooping around in the Necrocazar and I don't like thieves." Saturnus waves his hand again and his voice deepens back to its original tone mid-sentence. His glimmer drops and he returns, before my eyes, to his ominous self.

"That is true. I'd say then that they're responsible for Alyssa's demise." I muse. Saturnus' face remains impassive, but I can't help but wonder whether he's hiding the loss of his intended soulmate. Does he still feel for her? Or has all emotion been hollowed out of him?

A Psiren interrupts my thought, approaching gingerly beneath me from my left. His lower half is stout, red and green. It looks like a he might have merged with an odd piranha looking creature, but I care not, for without the teeth of a piranha and their vast numbers he's no more deadly than a sea slug.

"Yes?" I pivot to face him square on, looking down into his dark eyes and skin. His thick black hair is plaited in wide cornrows against his skull. This is when I notice that the darkness of his skin is marred by lighter patches, whorls of torment and pain, healed but not forgotten.

"Tiberius, Sir. I came to update you of the Necrimad's state. It's still causing us some problems with its ability to exhale boiling water. Feeding it now it's flesh… is causing some difficulty also. It's eaten seventeen of your men today alone…" He looks like he might cry, angering me further.

"Man up! For goodness sakes, Tiberius, your burns are victories, showing you survived something wanting to kill you. Wear them with pride and stop whimpering." I shake my head, sighing at his pathetic excuse for a report. He rises slightly through the water, coming out from beneath my shadow. That's when I notice half of his face is distorted from the heat of the boiling water too. He looks horrific. I smile.

"You must understand…" He begins to explain, but I cut him off, hearing Saturnus chortle beside me. I need to prove I can handle my men. I must not appear weak.

"I'll go and see for myself. It's my power inside that beast. I'll know exactly what it needs." I wave him away and I swear I can here Saturnus full on sniggering now. I turn to him, pivoting too fast and looking him straight in the face.

"Yes, Saturnus?" I round on him.

"Nothing, brother. Let us go and tend to the monster that has these children crying for their mother, shall we?" He rubs his hands together and we rise above the piles of rubble, what is left of this once great city. There are only a few buildings still standing now and the space around the seal where the Necrimad had been summoned is still covered in dried blood that refuses to be washed from its surface. I had watched as the Psirens became restless, pulling down buildings for fun and searching for any remaining mer they had left alive. It seemed unlikely, even to me, but it keeps them occupied so who am I to complain? I'm not a babysitter and their last guardian had found herself being eaten by molluscs, sea cucumbers and shrimp. She, who had given birth to so many monstrosities, is now being consumed and dismantled piece by piece. I twist my mouth, amused and enjoying the poetry of her rotting corpse, returning to the oceans she had so lovingly doomed.

"Solustus? Are you coming?" My internal reverie is broken and I catch up to Saturnus in one swift undulation, looking forward to seeing the Necrimad up close once more. I have been close to it so many times and yet it is never long enough. It wasn't just its giant scaled mass, or the fury behind its eyes. It was the fact that the fury had once belonged to me. It had been mine and would be again. I adored it in flesh as much as I craved it in substance, and proximity only increased my longing and impatience to grasp it once more.

The Necrimad crouches, it's giant talons gripping into the sand, causing the foundations beneath it to crack and allowing heat from deep within the earth's

18

core to escape. Its scales are a deep bloody aubergine and its eyes glow a piercing coral orange. The scales around its neck that cover the beast's gills part as it inhales water, causing the ocean around it to tremor and vibrate. I also note the hot flames that flicker beneath its flesh, more powerful than any undersea vent or volcanic eruption. I feel the heat from hundreds of feet away, washing over me in waves that make my stomach churn, fluttering at the idea of such concentrated power.

"It is hot today. The creature is irritable." Tiberius, who I had thought we had left far behind, speaks as I notice him catching up to us.

"I'm sure. If I had to put up with you morons I'd be irritable too. Oh, wait, I am." It's about as close as I'll ever get to cracking a joke, so I scowl at him and he retreats, leaving us alone in haste. I don't know why he followed us; Saturnus and I don't exactly need his meagre expertise. "The blood moon cannot come fast enough." I sigh, falling a little in love with the beast before me. I had never found myself aroused by the flesh of another, by the idea of limbs and organs, squirming and pulsating with need. But this attraction, this was different. I love everything about this creature because it represents no weaknesses. It represents power, control, and having one's desires fulfilled not for mere moments in a climax, but for generations. For eternity.

"We must tread carefully, Solustus. Be patient." Saturnus warns. I round on him.

"Don't you think I know that?" I bark, unimpressed. "I am well aware of how to wait, Saturnus, I waited centuries for Titus' demise." I remind him of the years I served under that imbecile ruler. He was weak and let his rage and desire fuel his actions, let them cloud his logical mind. I, however, will not be so stupid.

"I am aware of our history, brother. Do not forget that I too have waited. But the closer the ritual becomes the easier it will be to forget ourselves, to make mistakes. We need to make sure that we're ready for the mer's final stand." He speaks and I blink a few moments, surprised. He was right, though I disdain the fact, that I had forgotten what we must do to release my power from the Necrimad's flesh prison. We must bleed enough magic from them to

19

tip the scales of the higher plains in the favour of darkness. Only then would Poseidon's desire for the creature to wipe the face of the earth clean from its human scum be a reality.

As I'm pondering this final hurdle, the creature shifts before my eyes. It looks agitated by the chains we've used to harness its huge body. It shakes its spiny head, groaning and wailing in a sound more harrowing that a child's last breath to a new mother. I feel the urge to be close to it, to comfort it. Using my tail in a way that's now second nature to me, I push forward through the water, feeling the incredible heat of its body washing over me and causing my skin to sting. I grit my teeth, baring it with ease, as I move in as close as I dare. I hang, suspended before it's mighty mass as it halts, noticing my approach.

"Hush now." I hold up a hand and it comes closer, pushing forward toward me. It's two slit nostrils flare and its eyes widen as it takes me in, pushing its enormous muzzle against my hand. The moment is tense, lingering in the silence that suddenly falls around me as my palm burns against the creature's scaly flesh. I will not show the agony of its touch, I will remain impassive and calm. I can feel the surrounding Psirens watch me, in awe of my command of such a vast creature. Suddenly, the beast's head recoils and it balances back on its hind legs, before letting out an almighty roar. My thought processes are caught off guard, but my instincts remain rightfully intact as I bolt with one controlled and precise movement of my long tail, escaping the torrent of boiling water that the demon begins to blast toward me by mere inches. The creature shifts back onto all fours, the weight of it causing the ground beneath us to vibrate, and plumes of dust to rise like mushroom clouds. I pant, caught completely off guard, furious. Saturnus swims over to me, looking amused.

"Just because it's made from your power doesn't mean you have control over it, Solustus. That's sort of the point." He raises an eyebrow and looks down on me, becoming the complete and total focus of my rage in one careless phrase. I pounce, shifting into high speed and crossing the water between us before he even has time to exhale. I place my long fingers around his throat, clamping his gills shut. He looks shocked, his eyes widening and yet he doesn't struggle for breath. I wrap my tail around his, locking it in place.

"You're right, the power does belong to me. And only me. You'd do well to remember that, brother. If you don't I may lose my desire to share." I threaten him, bringing my face within centimetres of his yellow feline pupils. I examine him before letting go of his gills and allowing him to breathe. He doesn't collapse, or gasp, but rather resumes breathing as though I've done nothing more than lightly tickle him. I expect him to say something, retaliate, but instead he remains silent, gives a feline smirk and returns to the ruins of the once great city. I watch the beast for a moment, thinking back to the words of Tiberius. I ponder the issue with the fact the creature cannot be controlled. We may have chained its mass, but it still needs to eat, still needs sustenance. It is then that something unusual happens, something that I haven't seen in a long time. A shadow from above falls over me. I look up and smile, inspiration coming in a torrent of scarlet desire.

"Regus!" I call, viewing the bald headed strong man struggling below with a few other Psirens, trying to stop the creature from further cracking the foundations on which the city once stood. He looks upward at the mention of his name, undulating quickly, left to right as his hammer head form continues it's natural, ancient rhythm.

"Yes?" He says, not one for using more words than necessary. He'd never be a poet. But I suppose the bruises this man leaves upon flesh are artistic enough.

"Find me a cruise-liner." I command. He looks confused, not an uncommon look for him of course but none the less it pisses me off. I need not explain my decisions to a glorified brawler with fins. "Well, go!" I shoo him away and he nods, not asking for further explanation.

I look upon the beast, smiling to myself. I wanted its love, and much in the way master breaks a dog, I assume that feeding time will bring me its loyalty.

3
Manhood

CALLIE

Ripples form on the surface above, but little sunlight falls down onto Azure's haunting pallor in the green cloudiness of Moray Firth's waters. It's cool here, but not as chill as the Arctic, so I can't complain. The vision passes and her form goes limp. I've never seen her go unconscious from a vision before and it makes me worry more than I already am about the state of things. Ever since I entered the whirlpool and left my father behind, a kind of anxiety has taken root in my stomach and my heart hasn't quite managed to maintain its regular beat for more than a few seconds. I stare warily at Marcas, who has turned toward Philippe, also disturbed by Azure's high pitched and eerie screams.

Orion catches my hand as he moves from behind me where he was, only seconds ago, leading us along with the odd Scottish mer who call themselves Selkies. We swim together, approaching Azure as Conan struggles to get free of her weight. Orion reaches her before me and pulls her up, effortlessly, in his arms. He's so strong, and I can't help but admire the fact he's holding her limp body in his arms with nothing to keep him balanced but the muscle of his sinewy, royal blue tailfin. Conan rights himself and looks embarrassed as redness floods his white freckled complexion.

"Ah tried tae catch 'er but..." He begins to explain but I shake my head, silencing him.

"Don't worry, she just fell, you couldn't have caught her in time." I smile at him, trying to make him feel at ease. I dislike how Domnall had spoken to him about his father and I'm grateful that he saved my life. Regardless of whether he looks like a weakling or not, we can't all be strong men.

"Cheers." He takes a scrawny arm and rubs the back of his neck, glancing nervously up at Philippe. Orion moves toward me; well aware we're still being observed by the mer travelling with us along with the new Scottish individuals, he glances to me quickly. I watch Conan, and inspiration hits. I nudge Orion.

"Let him ride Philippe back." I whisper, looking up at him through thick lashes. He sighs.

"Alright." He looks to Domnall and contorts his mouth.

"Conan can take my steed." He orders and Domnall raises a ginger eyebrow, though his expression remains impassive.

"He is a stable boy efter aw, yer steed will be weel taken caur ay." His tone is flat, as though Orion has insulted or mystified him. Orion shifts Azure in his arms as Domnall and the rot mouthed Fergus turn their Kelpies toward the way they were travelling before Azure feinted.

"Any reason why I'm offending the nice giant Scotsman over that boy?" He whispers, cocking his lips to the side as though it'll stop the sound from travelling.

"I don't know. He just looks... well, like he might kiss that horse on the mouth. I've never seen anyone look at something like that unless they were, well... you looking at me." I smile slightly at the memory of his adoring gaze when I had danced with big blue and her baby.

"That's it?" He looks confused. I shrug, beginning to move my aquamarine scaled tail in time with his. Azure's head is falling back over his arm, leaving black tresses floating from her scalp like dark seaweed. I stare at her face, contorted and uncomfortable in its expression. I wonder what she saw. I want to reach out and touch her, try to absorb the vision for myself, but something deep within me flutters, call it gut instinct, and so I resist the urge. I look back over my shoulder, watching Conan swimming beside the Equinox. I stop, turning back.

"Don't you want to ride?" I ask him, watching his expression flush red once more.

"Ah dunnae…. Uh, ah dunnae know how." He looks so embarrassed I worry I've offended him.

"Oh. Don't you have a Kelpie?" I ask him, prying more than I probably should with someone I barely know. He flushes practically purple this time.

"Nae." Is his only answer. I sense I've overstepped and so straighten my spine.

"Philippe likes you. I can tell." I compliment him with a wink and he flushes even further. I wonder if soon his face might burst at the volume of blood coursing to the surface of his cheeks.

"He's a bonnie one." He replies and I cock my head, not sure of his meaning. I'm struggling with the dialect I have to admit. I didn't exactly take classes that one would expect for ruling over a city. I wish now I had asked about learning other languages. I hadn't thought I'd need it, but now I'm beginning to wonder.

"Uh, thanks. Look after him okay?" I say with a smile, turning away from him and moving to catch up with Orion. I glide through the fog of the water and over thick greenery that stems, lush and dense from the ocean floor. Everything is so alive here, crawling with tiny invertebrates, carnivorous bladderwort, pondweed and prawns. My mer vision picks up on the pulsations, the twitches and the vibrations of it all, an environment literally thrumming with life and a welcome cacophony compared with the silent waste of the Arctic.

"What do you think happened to her?" I ask Orion as I glide quickly past the length of his body, meeting his gaze side on.

"I don't know. I'm worried. I've never seen her like this." He looks concerned and I can tell that he knows only too well that she's his only surviving family.

"She'll be okay. She's a tough one." I smile, remembering all the occasions when I've thought Azure could actually do with being a little *less* tough.

"Oh, don't I just know that to be true." He laughs slightly and I can't help but join him. His face in all its statuesque flawlessness has become more than merely attractive. Looking into it I feel safe.

"What?" He asks me, suddenly self-conscious.

"Nothing." I blush slightly and suddenly my gaze is pulled from his features and onto a less comforting sight.

"If you two would stop making googly eyes at each other I think Orion should go to speak with Domnall. Don't you?" Rose has come up to Orion's side and is sticking her lovely nose into our business yet again. You'd think she wanted to be Queen for all her whining. I sigh and watch Alannah and Skye swim up level with Rose as she continues to undulate beside us. Their eyes flick between us, as always, loving the spectacle.

"As much as I hate to admit it, Rose has a point. We don't want to appear rude or uninterested. Even if Marcas did try to kill me on sight." I look to Ghazi, whose hand is clutched tightly by his wife Fahima, and notice he's watching Marcas like a hawk, who is swimming without the aid of a Kelpie a few meters in front of him. Fahima looks at me, as though begging me not to ask anything of him, I can tell she's scared after what Marcas tried to pull, not that I blame her. Cole, who is next to them, catches my gaze.

"I got her." He moves across the front of our paths, volunteering to take Azure, as we trail after the Selkies who are way ahead of us now with a speed advantage from their Kelpie steeds. Orion hands over Azure's unconscious form.

"Thanks." Orion smiles graciously at him.

"No problem." Cole nods, dipping slightly in the water under Azure's body weight. I look between the two men. Something has definitely shifted there. They're less King and Knight now than they ever have been.

"Orion, Callie, you two go ahead. We'll follow." Cole assures us.

Losing no time, we turn together and swim across the kelp fields that sway a chilled out hula in the calm tide. As we catch up to the group of Kelpies and their riders, it becomes apparent that the bottom of the Moray Firth is hilly. We reach the top of the rising peak's edge and the riders stop, allowing us to enjoy the view down into the vivacious underwater valley.

"It's beautiful." I breathe, sighing slightly. I feel eyes watching me, focusing in on my femininity. These men are surely starved of female company and I feel my skin prickle at the intensity of their gazes combined.

"Bùrn Kildrummy is doon there." Domnall explains. I smile up at his towering height and then take a moment to examine his Kelpie that shifts by my side. It really is extraordinary. My attention falters as I register what Domnall has just said, and I turn my gaze downward into the greenery at the bottom of the oceanic valley. I can't see anything but a sprawling ruin of an old castle and I have absolutely no idea what a Bùrn is either.

"You live in castle ruins?" Orion asks him and Domnall looks mildly affronted.

"Arnae ruins there laddie, it's jist weathered, like me." His sentence comes out in a low rumble, like thunder following a lightning fork. Orion frowns.

"Oh of course not, I just, I apologise. That was rude."

"Whit are ye a lassie? Ain't nae need fur apologies." Domnall condemns Orion's attempt at good etiquette and I can't help but be a little offended that he's using the word Lassie as an insult at all.

"I just didn't mean to offend." Orion tries to save the conversation, but Domnall clears his throat.

"You'd know if ah was truly offended laddie, fur you'd already be dead." He doesn't laugh, but instead commands his Kelpie to begin a measured descent toward that which they call Bùrn Kildrummy. I look to Orion whose expression is slightly alarmed. As the Kelpies swim away, he grabs my arm as I go to follow.

"I don't know about this. They're a bit…"

"We don't have a choice. We're here now." I bite out, frustrated.

"I can't… I can't lead these people into those ruins…" He looks like a scared horse that might bolt at any second. I breathe deep, seeing the fear behind the icy blue of his eyes. Inching forward I wrap my arms around him gingerly, careful to avoid the trident still pressed flat against his spine. Our armour clangs together and I sigh, all this duty getting in the way of our intimacy both physically and metaphorically. It's exhausting. Orion and I have only just

26

gotten back on solid ground with our relationship, and now we are trying to stop a race of Psirens, being led by two psychopaths, from destroying everything we hold dear. As usual, my life is just a little too much, but I've done my running. I can't outrun whatever the Goddess has in store for me, even if I was still trying. I run my fingers through Orion's stiff hair, trying to soothe him and myself for good measure.

"I know it's scary. I know you feel like what happened at the Occulta Mirum was your fault. But even if you'd have known Saturnus' true intentions what could you have done to stop him?" I look into his eyes deeply, trying to ground him. Trying to support him.

"I... I don't know." He looks surprised at his own response. I stare back over my shoulder momentarily, looking down to the Kelpies who are now reaching the bottom of their descent.

"It would have been a bloodbath either way Orion. You did the best you could at the time with the information you had. That's all anyone can ask. If anyone says differently, send them to me."

"You're my bodyguard now?" He cocks an eyebrow, amused.

"Think of me like your emotional bodyguard, yes. There's been enough hurt around the mer for several lifetimes. Everyone has lost. They're still grieving and so are you, but unfortunately we don't have time for that right now. All we have is Atlas' letter and a whole lot of ridiculous odds to compete with. So let's just take it one step at a time. The first step is talking to Domnall about the vessel. So let's take care of that." I look at him, feeling my gaze getting intense as he smiles.

"When did you get so... mature." He laughs at my mock offended expression.

"I have no idea what you're talking about, I've always been mature." I turn away from him, flouncing my long blonde hair over one shoulder and taking off down the hill toward the Selkies. My ears pop as I reach their depth. They've stopped a few hundred metres from the outskirts of the Bùrn Kildrummy and are looking up at us, bored. Yet as I get closer their expressions soften slightly, as though they cannot bear the thought of me thinking of them unkindly.

27

"Everythin' alright?" Fergus asks me, looking concerned as he shoots me a crooked and blackened smile.

"Yes, we've come a long way from home to find you. It's been a long journey. Everyone is tired." I make the excuse and they melt slightly, slouching atop their mer-horse steeds.

"Ahm sorry to hear that Lass, is a hardship being far awa' frae home." Domnall replies, though his sentiment seems slightly less than sincere.

As I wait for Orion and the rest of our pod to catch up, I hear another Scottish voice that I don't recognise calling. I look up, greeted by the sight of an approaching monstrosity. He's huge, even bigger than Gideon and his hair is swept back in a low ponytail. His tailfin is thick and dark in midnight blue and his entire body is covered in red tattoos that look like lightning forks, wrapping around his immense biceps. I swear these men just keep getting bigger. I had thought Orion was the biggest man I'd ever seen, then Regus and my father, but now, looking at this stranger, I am left wondering if I am to to meet giants in the near future.

"Flannery, son, come here." Domnall beckons the beastly man forward. As he comes closer I feel the water swell around me, his displacement of it something you just can't ignore.

"This is…" Flannery's eyes widen as they rest on me. I blush slightly, feeling more than a little intimidated from his broadness alone. "Sorry lass, what's yer name?" Domnall requests.

"Callie." I reply, smiling nervously. Flannery bows his head, unsure what to make of me.

"Where did she come frae?" He asks, wide eyed even still. Suddenly there's a cacophony at my back and I know Orion and the rest of the pod have finally made it down into the valley.

"Um…" I begin but Orion comes forth quickly, taking over the conversation.

"We're from the Pacific. The children of Atargatis at your service sir." He bows his head, staring up into the shadow of Flannery's face, eclipsed by the dull sunlight.

28

"Who are ye?" Flannery asks him.

"Orion." Orion puts his arm around my shoulder loosely, like we're hanging out in my little red vintage or something. He's being possessive, but with a man that size I don't blame him. If he wanted to harm me he'd only have to place both hands around my neck, give a good squeeze and I'd be a goner.

"Let's gie inside. We can hae a proper discussion in th' banquet hall." Domnall dismounts his Kelpie and beckons Conan forward. Conan passes me in the water, extending out a long fingered palm toward the thick ropes of dried seaweed that have been used to make the Kelpie's reigns. He takes them in hand, along with Casanova's and then retreats behind me, hanging his head as though he's ashamed of his mere existence in front of these giant, muscle-clad warriors. I pity him slightly; I don't know much about the Selkies, but I can already tell they value strength of body over strength of mind.

I go to begin my journey forward, but Flannery smiles, moving across my path.

"Where dae ye think you're gonnae?" He asks, amused as his thick lips form a smirk.

"To the banquet hall." I look up at him lazily, not wanting to give him any more control over me by meeting his gaze.

"Nae, Lassies do nae make th' decisions ay men." Domnall nods behind him in agreement and I frown, feeling suddenly angry at their lack of respect.

"I'd be careful, addressing a Queen like that." I snarl, feeling my spine straighten in defence of my legitimacy. Suddenly Orion stiffens at my side, placing a hand at the base of my spine as the men begin to laugh at me.

"Why don't you go with Conan to make sure Philippe is comfortable?" He looks back over his shoulder, catching my eye with an apologetic glance as he looks to the rest of the group. "Is there somewhere they can stay?" He queries Domnall, watching Marcas who lingers now at the back of our pod, swimming after an eel in the most docile manner imaginable.

"Aye, there be lodgings upstairs." He gestures with his chin to the castle ruins and I exhale, feeling frustrated. I don't want to give Flannery the satisfaction of seeing me defeated by their stupid misogyny and so turn, heading over to where Conan is hovering around the Equinox and two Kelpies, whispering to them in a small and measured tone.

"Let's go." I bite out, irritated still. I feel Orion's eyes on my spine but don't turn to look at him. I know it isn't his fault, I know that we need the Selkies to help try and find the vessel, to potentially help us build an army to take down the Psirens, but that doesn't mean I have to like it.

ORION

Flannery leads Cole around the crumbling corner of the Bùrn Kildrummy, Azure in his arms as though she were no more than a doll. He's taking my pod to the upstairs chambers of these ruins, giving them a place to regroup while I settle things with the chief for which I'm grateful, but his presence still makes me uneasy, particularly when he looks at Callie. I pivot to face Domnall.

"To business." I gesture forth with one arm as I had seen my father do a hundred times when in council with Saturnus. Domnall nods in consent and swims past me in a gush of bubbles, water displaced by his enormous mass. I follow him, nearly matching his speed. We come to two rotting wooden doors at the end of a long cobble stone laden path and Domnall swims forward quickly, pushing them open with about as much grace and poise as a rhinoceros.

"Come." He beckons as I follow through the dingy and derelict hallway. I wonder how the castle got here. How it came to be in this state. I suppose not all races of oceanic warriors were lucky enough to have a state of the art city at their disposal. A feeling of wonderment blooms within my chest as I ponder how they manage to thrive in such a place.

"The Bùrn is… lovely." I compliment, remembering his temper flaring at my prior comment. He doesn't respond, but rather sits down in a rotting wooden chair at the head of a long table. Now I've entered the banquet hall, I notice that the ceiling has fallen in and that the walls are covered in wooden plaques and moss, with vines of some kind growing between the cracks in its stone, the walls are covered in a lush green carpet. Each plaque holds the skull of a demon,

30

preserved in all their revolting infamy. I move over to one of the skulls as Domnall's eyes follow my motion, rising through the water and running my hand along the inside of one its eye sockets. "Demons?" I ask him.

"Aye." He responds, looking grave. I move away from the skull now, falling through the water whilst maintaining my forward momentum. I take a seat in the wooden chair at the opposite end of the table to Domnall, putting the length of it between us. Domnall strikes me as the type of man who likes his space, so I indulge him that.

"So…" I look around, feeling the echoes of my words, falling into silence within the large stone room, pushing in on me, creating a pressure upon me to speak. Domnall shifts in his seat, waiting for the rest of my sentence, which seemingly won't come. I breathe and pick the first question that I can think of off the top of my head. Finding yet more species of mer is overwhelming and I find myself neck deep in questions.

"So you were created by Lir? You're here to kill demons I assume, from your… collection." I look around at the demon skulls on the walls and floor, now noticing remnants of bones smashed to oblivion scattered across the cobblestones beneath me.

"Aye, the loch Ness, the trench deep within, it spawns demons often. We keep them frae escapin' it intae th' open sea and ontae land." He looks serious, his silver eyes dull and lifeless as he waits for my next question.

"How many Selkies are here?" I ask him, looking around at the hall. The Bùrn Kildrummy doesn't look that big.

"Abit fife hunder" He answers, looking around the room, uninterested as though he'd rather be pummelling something.

"Five hundred?" I repeat, making sure I heard him correctly. It's a surprising figure to say the least.

"Aye." He brushes his chin with the end of his fingers lightly, breathing outward and looking bored at the smalltalk. I inhale, deciding to cut to the chase.

"So, I'll get to the point, shall I? We're here looking for someone, someone who could be something called 'the vessel'. You wouldn't happen to know

31

anyone like that? They can usually absorb the magic of other Selkies, that kind of thing?" I ask him point blank and suddenly his expression contorts into one of interest.

"Nae. Yer won't find nae magic 'ere lad. Whit is this vessel? Whit dae ye need it fur?" He asks, pushing his long red braid back over one shoulder and leaning forward, curious.

"It's a part of something called The Conduit, it's a kind of failsafe against this one demon we have in the Pacific. It could even be a weapon. We don't really know. What we do know is that it's to do with having a connection to the Gods and Goddesses of the seas. So this person would have a connection with Lir. Something special about them."

"Aye, I know just the lad. My boy, Flannery. You've seen him. He's obviously close tae Lir wi' aw that muscle." He immediately falls in love with the idea and I realise my mistake. I should have explained it is not merely physical strength we are looking for.

"Wait, I think you misunderstand." I say, placing my hand on the rotting table before me. Tiny prawns squirm in and out of the wood, escaping the shadows of my hands.

"Nae, it has to be Flannery. Ye said it's a weapon, jist look at him. Any dunce can see he's blessed, he's a ruddy killer that lad."

"I said it *could* be a weapon. We don't know what it is. My father, his letter, it didn't really give specifics."

"How dae we fin' out if it's him, is there a test? I'll bet mah life he passes." Suddenly Domnall is once again erect in the murky water, disturbing the sediment floating within the room. He looks determined and I feel myself flailing, completely overshadowed by his enormous presence and authority. I breathe, trying to calm myself. Thinking back to Callie, her assurance atop the hill that we can do this. Do it together. I worry now that I dismissed her presence too easily. She wouldn't have taken this crap. I suppose I need to make a stand too.

"We need to test everyone; we can't just assume it's your strongest warrior. It's not about strength, it's about connection with Lir." My words come out

32

firm and I lean forward, making sure Domnall knows my intent isn't to back down. I have to be firm if I ever hope to command an army to war with the Psirens, to stop the Necrimad. Hardships must be endured to get there and that starts here. I grit my teeth and glare at him.

"Well then, if ye want a test, I'll show ye th' best test there is. Th' hightide games."

"That's not what I mean. We need to test more than just strength." I exclaim, getting irritated by this man's lack of listening skills. He's hearing what he wants to hear. He cocks an eyebrow and smirks once again, suddenly narrowing his eyes and giving a feral expression.

"Ye misunderstan' me lad. Thes isnae testin' fur th' vessel. Thes is testin' ye. Ye think ye can come intae mah Bùrn an' order me, chief ay th' selkies, tae dae yer biddin'? Ah willnae tak' 'at withit knowin' you're strong as ye look son. Nae sir." His voice is harsh and now completely Scottish in dialect. He's lost any type of English speech in his fury. His eyes blaze as we float, hands down on the wooden table, staring at each other intensely. I sigh, his temper is out of control, but I think that's just how he is. I guess in that case I'm going to have to play ball.

"Fine." I say, slamming my fist atop a prawn that's squirming across the table. "Let the games begin."

4
Stable Boy
CALLIE

The Kelpies whinny, swimming faster than Philippe can trot through the water. I move beside them, looking to Conan. I know he can feel me watching him, but is refusing to look at me since we left the crowds of people behind us. We've swum left of the Bùrn Kildrummy and are making our way slowly toward what I assume will be wherever they keep their Kelpies. Conan leads me out to the edge of the Moray Firth, passing an extraordinary creature on the way that I've never seen before, but that I've studied in books as I had become engrossed in the ocean in my early teens.

"A Basking Shark! I've only ever seen them in books! I didn't know they lived in Scotland?" I exhale, moving around the cluster of moving equines and toward the creature. Its gaping mouth opens, sucking in water and taking the nutrients that it requires from the surrounding plankton. It ignores me as I watch it pass, awed by it's odd anatomy. I savour the moment, knowing it will be one that stays with me.

Bye.

I hear the voice in my head and I take a sharp inhale of water, having forgotten that I can now hear marine life. I haven't experienced it since I had rescued Blue off the Gulf of Alaska, but I watch the Basking Shark disappear into the distance whispering "Bye." aloud and hoping it can hear me.

"Who are you talking to?" Conan asks, popping up behind me intrusively. He's suddenly seeming more interested in making small talk, so I take the opportunity to try and get to know him better.

"I can hear sea-life talk sometimes." I admit and his eyes widen.

"Really?!" He's so enthused at this news I wonder if he might burst above the surface and flip like an awkward dolphin. A grin spreads wide across his face as he grabs my hand and pulls me back toward Philippe, Magnus and Casanova.

"Whit ur they thinkin', tell me!" He demands. I look at him, exasperated.

"It doesn't always work like that. I can't just make it happen." I explain and his face falls. He looks down to the end of his jade tailfin, flicking it from left to right gingerly, almost like he's afraid of being in his own skin. He looks up with hopeful, forest green eyes.

"Please! Try! Please Callie!" He begs me, looking no more than twelve as his freckles and pale skin light up at the idea.

"Okay. I guess I can." I move toward the Kelpie closest to me, Casanova I think, and look into the creature's odd, slimy green looking face. Its black eyes are large and convex, protruding sideways from its long skull. I take them in, trying to connect with the animal. As I take several strokes backward with my aqua fluke, I give Casanova ample room to continue swimming forward, watching as the long strands of seaweed that make up his mane, float, innocuous in the water.

Mare. Colt needs.

I inhale again, somehow unable to get used to the feeling of telepathy. It's hardly surprising I'm feeling my heart hammer within my chest every time words of another reach me. When I think about it, my nerves are in tatters after the day's events and after Titus' intrusion of my psyche, I've had enough of odd voices in my head for a lifetime.

"Whit did it say??" Conan can tell immediately from my change in expression that I've heard something.

"You're not gonna like it…" I say, not sure whether I want to divulge the urges of a colt.

"Come 'en tell me? It's Casanova, sae it's likely tae be food."

"Um, not quite." I blush, keeping consistent in my backward strokes now.

"Well, whit is it then?"

"He wants a… um… lady horse. To um…" I feel so awkward talking with him about sex, I feel like I'm talking to a teenager about something they just aren't ready to hear.

"I shoulda known, it is Fergus' Kelpie efter aw." He laughs to himself, looking like he's genuinely enjoying this awkwardness. We reach the shoreline, though we are still far beneath the level of the land. At the bottom of the long even cliff that towers above us now, I see makeshift stables carved into the cliff-face, with crude wooden doors knocked in. I gasp, there aren't only a few, there are hundreds.

"How many Kelpies do you have?" I ask him, eyes wide at the prospect of this many steeds.

"A body fur every Selkie, Weel, except me ay coorse." He looks so forlorn at this explanation; my heart breaks a little.

"So where are all the other Kelpies?" I ask him. Looking up into the cave stalls, I can see a lot of them are empty.

"We donnae trap Kelpie haur. They run free, like Lir intended." He explains.

"But what if you have need of them?" I cock my head, trying to keep the conversation going while the young stable boy is out of his shell and willing. I don't know what it is about him, but I feel like I want to find out more. An anomaly of stature in this race of warrior strongmen, he intrigues me more than I want to admit.

"Pan-pipes. Each warrior is given a set at Conformation tae call their Kelpie." He doesn't look at me as he explains this, unbridling the Kelpies and patting their scaly hides. They race away, not wanting to be constrained to the stables, but rather to be elsewhere. Philippe finally catches up to us, his leathery wings beating a slow and steady rhythm. He whinnies, drawing my attention to him. Conan looks upon him and a smile graces his face. That seems to happen a lot when in the presence of horses.

"What's Conformation?" I ask, watching him as his face drops, the equine trance of Philippe broken once more.

"It's th' ceremony whaur a Selkie becomes a man. After he has killed his first demon alone. Lir tooches ye durin' th' ceremony an' ye git yer tattoos, like whit Flannery an' Domnall hae. An' ye can call yer Kelpie tae ye." His voice is wistful, his longing evident, as he approaches the Equinox and removes his bridle, slipping it over his soft face. He slaps his behind and Philippe rises through the water and into the closest cave to my left.

"That's why you don't...." I begin, but stop myself. I realise now why Conan doesn't have any tattoos. Doesn't have a Kelpie of his own.

"Yeah, laugh it up, ah ne'er killed a demon alright?" He looks so shamefaced in this second that I want to slap him as his cheeks blush beetroot.

"Hey! It's okay. Not everyone is a great warrior who can crush rocks into dust. Besides, you're amazing with these animals. I can tell how much they love you." I move toward him and touch his shoulder, but he shrugs me away, moving to fasten the makeshift wooden door on Philippe's stall for the night.

"It doesnae matter. Ah donnae hae a place here. Ahm jist a stable boy." He shrugs, a crestfallen expression taking over his face.

"Marcas, he needs you." I remind him, shuddering involuntarily at the thought of his father's breath against my neck.

"He needed me tae tak' over as chief. Ah failed him." He looks downward again as he pushes the wooden door shut, putting a hand on Philippe's face and cooing to him gently. The horse immediately stops stepping from one hoof to the other.

Rider.

I hear the word loud and clear but bite my lip, remembering how embarrassed Conan got about the fact he couldn't ride before. I shake my head slightly at the horse and he nods his head back. I smirk but the joke is utterly lost on all but me and the Equinox.

"Whit?" He asks, looking at me with an unsure and completely self-conscious expression.

"Oh, nothing." I say, brushing away Philippe's sentiment. "So if you don't have a Kelpie, why do you have the Pan-pipe?" I ask him, changing the subject.

"It was mah Father's. Ahm carin' fur his Kelpie, Thunderhoof, until he gets better." He explains and I nod, smiling, but inside I'm wondering whether or not Marcas will ever get better. It seems like it's a little too late for that. Then again, what do I know of the man? He tried to kill me sure, but it's not like we sat down to tea and braided each other's hair in the process. I hope for Conan's sake Marcas does get better, it seems like he could use a friend.

"There must be something you're good at. Other than with Kelpies I mean…" I question him and he crosses his arm, an obvious shiver running rampant down his spine.

"Ah can shoot, wi' a bow an' arrow, but sometimes Ah miss an'…" I watch him start to rip himself down again. This kid really needs a confidence boost. I quickly change the subject as the hideous blush he can't help but unleash every time I attempt a compliment starts to creep back across his cheeks.

"So, uh, tell me. How come Domnall is chief now? Did the rest of the Selkies vote?" I turn in the water, looking after the Kelpies that are now only specks, disappearing into thick kelp forests in the distance.

"Nae, it is determined by who has th' most demon kills." He looks up at me and watches as my eyebrows rise in surprise. That doesn't seem like a good way to isolate the best ruler to me. Conan watches me for a few moments before he sighs. "It's stupid. Domnall cannae rule. He's a reit dobber."

"A dobber?" I laugh at what I assume is meant to be an insult. Conan goes red again.

"Aye, he's as thick as a numpty atween two logs." He rolls his eyes again, clearly throwing caution to the wind.

"A numpty?" I question again, feeling a high-pitched giggle escape my lips. Conan begins to laugh too, and soon we're both howling and hysterical, closing our eyes against streams of happy tears. A cough from a foreign source breaks our happy reprieve and my eyes suddenly snap open before resting on the jackass who had stopped me from going into the Bùrn earlier.

"Ah hope ahm nae interruptin' whit is obvioosly quite a funay joke at mah faither's expense, but i've bin sent fur 'er." He doesn't address me, but rather keeps his eyes fixed on Conan, who shrinks away from the large, red haired man like his proximity is physically painful.

"Nae, Ah was jist..." He begins but Flannery speaks over him.

"Ah donnae caur whit ye were jist. Ye hud better go an fin' thit lunatic ye caa a father. Dornt want heem tryin' tae mudder anither innocent? Come 'en Miss." He almost spits this sentiment and it immediately makes me not want to go with him. Then again, I need to talk to Orion and find out what's going on, so I don't really have a lot of choice, and if Flannery is the son of the clan's Chief, then I don't want to offend him either. The mer aren't exactly in a strong position to bargain for support. So I breathe out and swallow my pride and resentment. I turn to Conan and give him a quick hug, pulling his scrawny and awkward body to my scaled breast and staring maliciously at Flannery.

"Thank you for showing me this. It's amazing." I whisper to him. He nods and smiles, blushing again. I move over to Flannery's side and look back at Conan who hangs there, defeated in the water.

"Go an' fin' Marcas!" Flannery barks, his pectorals bulging at the sharp exhale of his breath. Bubbles rise from his exclamation, breaking the calm mist of the surrounding water.

"You know you don't have to be so mean! He's not done anything to you!" I snap, turning to him and scowling.

"Whit dae ye know abit it?" He snaps back, taking off into the water with a single, abrupt flick of his stout, midnight blue tailfin. I gasp slightly as an array of bubbles flick up and hit me in the face, taking me by surprise. I scowl again, taking off after him. It's hopeless though, and in spite of my willing otherwise, I'm just not as fast as he is.

We arrive at the Bùrn Kildrummy and I'm out of breath, though I suck in the water, trying to steady myself, trying to remain composed and un-fazed by Flannery's speed.

"Guid day slowpoke." He is propped against the fallen remnants of some kind of wall, slanted in the water with a cockiness that I want to smack right out of him, though I doubt with his muscle I'd even make a dent. I don't say anything in retort. I don't even scowl. I choose instead to look completely contented. I shoot him a wide smile, fluttering my eyelashes.

"Should we adjourn inside?" I ask him, swaying past his body with my scaly hips and annunciating the sentence perfectly.

"Aye," is his blunt retort. He takes off again, not waiting for me and leaves the rotting wooden double doors that lead into the Bùrn open. I sigh, hoping that inside he's decided to let me find Orion myself. I don't need his misogynistic complex, or his bulging muscles. I am more than capable.

Swimming inside, I find that he is still waiting.

"I don't need an escort." I snap.

"Woah, lassie, wa sae hostile? Why can ye nae jist be sugar an' spice? Isnae 'at supposed tae be th' deal wi' ye lassies? Granted it's bin a lang time since Ah spoke tae one, but arenae ye burds supposed tae be sweet or something?" He folds his arms and I can't quite wipe the horror off my face. Sugar and spice? Birds? Was he looking to get slapped?

"Where's Orion?" I ask him, not wanting this to turn into a full-blown argument. It's taking all my newfound maturity, but I know it's better than starting a fight I can't win. I'm standing against hundreds of years of patriarchy here, or so it would seem.

"He's still 'speakin wi' th' chief, ye can wai' fur him wi' ye rest ay yer pod. Up th' collapsed stair case, second door oan th' right." He turns away from me before he's even finished speaking and disappears down the corridor laden with crumbling brick and algae. I turn, making my way toward the collapsed staircase that he spoke of, which I can see through a pair of adjoining arched windows that sit on either sides of the inner corner on my right. As I make my way up the crumbling remnants of what was once a thickset grey stone staircase, I wonder how the building got to be in this state. The mer clearly took for granted their circumstance and seeing how the other half live, though not as drastically different as the Cryptopolis, is clearly not as decadent as what the pod is used to. Even the Adaro had a vast city full of decoration and venues

40

formed from ice, and I wonder how such a large pod came to adopt these ruins as their home.

I finally arrive at the door that Flannery had directed me to and as I press down on the handle and I hear a slight gasp from inside.

Opening the door, I notice all the mermaid's eyes are fixed on me as they exhale.

"What's wrong?" I ask them. Seeing Sophia's wide eyes, I instantly feel my stomach drop as fear clutches at me in a way all too familiar.

"Oh, thank God it's you. We were worried that awful Fergus had come back to tell more stories of his bravery." Sophia swims forward as she speaks and the other mermaids nod, multiple heads of lustrous hair in every shade shaking in distaste at the thought.

"Have any of the other Selkies been up here?" I ask, fearing an over-amorous onslaught of men searching for more than just, in the words of Vex, *cookies.* These women had only just lost their soulmates and didn't need to be bombarded by lonely Scotsmen.

"No. Just Fergus. The big guy popped his head around the door, but I could barely understand what he was saying." Marina flips her long black hair over one shoulder and sighs slightly. The room is quite dark, with the only light source being a narrow arched window at the far end of the room opposite the doorway where I'm still suspended. There's a rotting wooden four-poster bed covered in a tartan bedspread, a wardrobe, an armoire and a large tapestry of the Scottish mainland which is hung on the wall to my left, but other than that the room is fairly basic. The mermaids are sitting on the bed and sprawled out across the floor with their backs to the stone walls. They look exhausted. I look around and I can't see any of the men.

"Where are Cole and Ghazi?" I ask them and they gesture behind me to the door on the opposite side of the narrow hallway. Nobody speaks, they just sit there in the gloom. I look behind me at the door to the room where the men and, I assume, Azure are resting. I contort my mouth, considering going to check on them too, but as I turn back and see the mermaids looking all but defeated, I decide they need cheering up instead. I close the wooden door behind me with a creak and turn to them. "You all look exhausted." I say and immediately the room erupts into a cascade of complaint. I move over to the edge of the four-poster bed and sit down. Listening to their worries and concerns. Knowing they need a chance to vent.

"When Marcas had you I was so scared Callie!" Alannah exclaims, almost in tears.

"I'm more scared about those men, Domnall and that other one, his son. They look like they could crush me to death with one hand!" Skye wails.

"What about those weird horse things, I mean that's not natural." Rose looks disgusted as is per usual for her.

"What about you Callie, you went off with that kid... what did he say?" Sophia asks me, and suddenly the whines and moans stop. Fahima's eyes find mine and though she has no voice to speak I can tell she's scared too.

"Conan was showing me where they keep the Kelpies. They're amazing animals and so fast in the water. I know the Selkies aren't exactly what you were all expecting, but I think they're going to be a great asset against the Psirens if they agree to fight with us."

"Fight? We're going to fight the Psirens?" Emma's voice is no more than a squeak but instantly the rest of the mermaids look terrified.

"Yes. We need to. It's what we were made for. Remember?" I remind them of their purpose and they look back at me with incredulous faces. I watch Fahima, rising from the floor where she's sitting with her tail spread out before her in a fabulous sun-kissed orange. She moves over to me, curling around one of the bedposts and brushing my arm lightly with her fingers. Five words dance across the forefront of my psyche. Melancholic in tone.

I don't want to die.

I look to her and my eyes widen as I see there are tears running down her cheeks.

"I won't lie to you. You could all die. There's no guarantee of any of us getting out of this alive. We spoke about this before. Before we left the Gelida Silentium, you remember that, don't you?" I look around to all of them.

"I thought the conduit, or whatever this thing is that we're trying to build would do the fighting for us." Alannah admits, looking down to her mint and peach tailfin with a guilty expression.

"It might. But there's no guarantee of that." I gulp slightly. I had been thinking about the conduit recently too. I couldn't deny I was scared of what it could be. I knew as the vessel I would be part of it. I didn't want to die either.

"I know it seems scary right now, but we're going to build the best army possible. I know you all feel alone, but you still have one another. You still have family. We can all support each other and get through this together. None of you are alone. We're all here. Like sisters. Okay?" I look to them and their precious eyes stare back into mine. Marina touches me on the shoulder gently and I turn to her. She's crying. I wrap my arms around her as she reaches across the bed to me. I bury my face in her thick black hair and inhale. She smells like the Occulta Mirum, making me miss it all the more. Before I know it the rest of the mermaids are rising from the floor too, coming over and joining us in a giant embrace that incorporates everyone. It might seem silly to anyone else, but I know that these women need to be each other's strength if they're going to get through what's to come.

I look over at their faces, which act as mirrors, reflecting my own terror back at me. I had been on edge ever since we'd left the Adaro behind us and entered the whirlpool. I'd been carrying that anxiety around inside me and so I let it go, exhaling and slumping under the weight of so many arms and faces looking to me for security. As much as Orion was my crutch, these women offer me a kind of comfort too. I'm responsible for each one of them and I know that they can fight. I know that within each one lies a uniqueness that can belong to no other. It's just about bringing that out and making them believe they can do it. Atargatis had known they have what it takes, and so do I.

After a few moments the hug disbands, leaving the mermaids relaxed and falling into their normal chatter, that which eases their frayed temperaments so often. I rise from the bed, realising that my work is done.

43

"You're going?" Marina looks to me and I nod.

"I have to go and check on Azure and the others." I remind her. She looks sad to see me go, so I add, "I know you have them taken care of. Thank you." I wink at her and she beams slightly, this perhaps the first time I've seen her smile since she lost Christian. I turn to exit the room and the rest of the mermaids watch me as I open the door coming face to face with Orion with his fist raised, ready to knock.

"Oh!" I exclaim, stopping myself from moving forward like I had intended to.

"I was just coming to find you. Everything alright ladies?" He asks, peering around my head and into the room.

"Yes thanks, we're fine." Marina shoos us out of the door and I shut it behind me, leaving them with the privacy they deserve in which to relax in this strange place that is so far away from home.

"Are you okay?" He asks me, stroking his fingers downward from my shoulder.

"I am. Are you? How did things go with Domnall?" I ask, he looks around nervously.

"Let's get inside." He ushers me to the door of the opposing room from whence I've just come and I push it open. The room opposite mirrors its adjacent twin backwards in decor. The only real difference is that Azure is lying, her eyes bloodshot and cracked a few millimetres with Ghazi and Cole watching her like hawks from two, three-legged stools that have been placed on the floor next to the wooden four poster bed.

"Are you okay?" Orion asks, his voice booming as he enters the room from behind me.

"Small voices or you die." Azure looks like she might murder her brother for daring to speak as she cringes, clearly in pain.

"What did you see?" Orion asks again, moving over to her bedside and lowering his voice.

"Poseidon. Vex. There was yelling. I'm thinking that's why this vision left me supernaturally spanked." She cringes at the sound of her own voice.

44

"You yelled at Poseidon?" I ask, seriously impressed.

"Hell yeah I did. That asshole has used my brain as a home cinema for the last time." Azure raises a hand above her in a thumbs up sign. I laugh and then quieten myself to merely a snigger as I watch her physically tense up at the sound.

"What did he say?" Orion asks and I watch him as he tries to keep his voice low and even in tone, but I can tell he's intrigued.

"Just about Vex being important blah blah. I don't think he even wanted me there. I was just a happy coincidence." She sounds completely unamused.

"So Vex is the vessel?" I look to Orion, my eyes wide and his expression has turned deadpan.

"That still doesn't mean I won't kill him for what he did to you Callie." He makes this dark promise and I almost want to laugh. The man would doom humanity to mass murder and demon invasion over the fact Vex and I got a little physical? It sounds ridiculous.

"What did Domnall say?" Cole asks, breaking Orion's gaze from mine.

"Well, he challenged me to something called the High Tide games. To prove that we're worth his time." He shrugs and I feel my brow crease.

"So what about the vessel?" I ask him, crossing my arms. Azure groans and everyone lowers their voices to whispers.

"Well, he insists it's his brute of a son, Flannery. He thinks because his son is strong that he's got a connection with their God. I can see why he'd think that, but he wouldn't listen to me when I told him that it's not just about strength." Orion looks irritated and I know he must have had a hard time negotiating.

"So these High Tide games, what are they exactly?" I ask him and he shrugs again.

"I asked and he said I'd see tomorrow, when I elect a champion. So I'm guessing I have to choose someone to compete for us." His eyes flick to Ghazi who instantly rises to stand erect, clamping his fist over his heart. "I thought of you instantly Ghazi. Thank you." He looks so grateful and his eyes sparkle with

45

pride for the two men who are still fighting alongside him after everything we've been through.

"This is crazy." I mutter, thinking about the Selkies and their obsession with physical strength.

"I know, what about you? Did you find out anything useful?" He queries me and I think back.

"They have a lot of Kelpies. I saw the stables. It would be useful if we didn't piss them off too much. They'd make great allies. Also, Conan is pretty much despised, which I think you already gathered." I say, pressing my lips together. I wish now I'd asked Conan more questions, but I hadn't wanted to push him.

"Yeah, Domnall said they're five hundred strong. It wouldn't hurt to have them on our side." Orion looks thoughtful for a moment.

"This is turning out to be more complicated than I thought." I admit and Orion catches my gaze.

"Isn't it always?"

5
High Tide
CALLIE

The loch extends out before us, deep and vast. The pod is at my back, and as they peer around into the green of the water, everyone is tense. Orion has my palm in his and Ghazi floats next to me, a stern and unwavering determination plastered onto his face. I smile at him but he doesn't return the gesture, keeping his focus for the Games ahead. I hadn't slept last night. Orion and I had sat against the wall of Azure's room whispering until the sun began its ascent over the horizon once more. Orion hadn't wanted to leave her and I didn't want to go back into the room where the mermaids continued to voice all of the fears I was still trying to quiet about the coming days.

The Selkies are in front of us, having led us down the river which takes the waters of Moray Firth inland into Loch Ness. I can't make out any kind of arena from here, but it's murky in the water, as it was outland, so I guess I'll see once we move further into the Loch. The Selkie pod has emerged in its hundreds, clearly intrigued by the challenger from a far off sea. We don't know for sure, but I'm pretty sure Domnall will name Flannery as his champion. Now I look at the rest of the Selkies, I can easily see the Chief's son, towering above the rest of the massive, muscled bodies that are topped with varying degrees of frothy red hair. Each body is covered in tattoos, and as I look at the different designs my mind flits back to Conan and his pale awkwardness. I wonder if he will be here.

The Selkies take off again and we follow them into the wide body of Loch Ness. I take in my surroundings and watch as the Kelpie mounted pod scatters wide to prepare for the events of the day. Domnall stays behind, looking to Orion as he turns Magnus to face us and gains height in the water, asserting his authority for a few moments before dismounting the Kelpie.

"Come, lit us tak' our seats. Yer pod can watch frae aroond th' arena." He gestures to three seats that are set atop giant wooden stands as we come toward the middle of the Loch, where it's at its deepest, and I realise he's had this set up so Orion and I can sit with him. I turn to the rest of the mer that follow in my wake with a calm smile.

"You guys get a good view from the ground. We're sitting with Domnall." I explain to them and they nod. Fahima looks wary as I next turn to Ghazi. "You ready?" I ask him and he gives me a determined glance, face stoic and hard in its expression.

"Thes is yer champion then?" Domnall laughs, a deep rumble shaking his pectorals and making the slash tattoos, that interrupt his pale skin, shudder.

"Yes. This is Ghazi." Orion replies, sucking in water and rising slightly so he's on eye level with the Chieftain.

"Doesnae look like much." Domnall smiles and Orion cocks an eyebrow, folding his arms and leaning back.

"He doesn't have to look like much. Ghazi is strong enough to handle your champion. I assure you." He annunciates his words again, coming off cocky, but Domnall seems to respect that kind of confidence. I watch the two men, jumping as Domnall exhales a sudden exclamation, startling the pod behind me who still haven't descended to get a place around the arena.

"FLANNERY LAD!" He barks. I watch as the large shadow of the champion grows closer, coming in through the slight fog of the water caused by dislodged sediment.

"Och aye father?" Flannery's voice reaches out as his full form grows defined in its proximity.

"Meit yer opponent. Ghazi." At these words Flannery's eyes jump quickly to Ghazi's stocky and, by comparison, short form. He looks like he may bust a gut.

"Wa didne he jist choose a lassie?" He inquires with a deep laugh. Ghazi frowns and narrows his eyes but, as usual, says nothing. "Whit, naethin' tae say tae that?"

"He's a mute." Orion explains and I sigh, these Scots are certainly asking for a good ass kicking. Flannery's expression turns slightly confused, like he doesn't know what a mute is, before saying,

"Time fur talkin' is over anyhaw! Let's dae thes!" Domnall claps his son around the back with a palm the size of a small dinner plate and smiles.

"Th' lad is reit. Lit th' games begin! Ghazi, go wi' Conan, he'll explain hoo things ur done." He commands before licking his bottom lip and putting two fingers to his lips. He exerts a high pitched whistle, like he's calling a dog, and sure enough Conan appears at his side within seconds, though not for looking out of breath and extremely flustered. "Tak' ghazi an' teel him what's expected while th' Fist ay Lir present themselves." He orders Conan. Ghazi moves over to him soundlessly and I hear Fahima behind me exhale bubbles into the water, probably worrying as usual. I can't say I blame her, the Selkies are huge and if Ghazi does beat Flannery, I wonder if the Selkies would harm him for defeating their strongest fighter. I think for a moment, wondering if perhaps Flannery really could be the vessel for Lir. We hang, suspended in the green waters of Loch Ness as Ghazi disappears with the scrawny stable boy. I watch as they grow smaller, moving downward before turning as I hear Orion inhale to speak.

"What's the Fist of Lir?" He asks, looking curious.

"It's th' army ay coorse!" Domnall gives this answer as if it's the most obvious thing in the world.

"Ah! I see!" Orion says, nodding and keeping himself level with measured strokes of his fluke. He opens his mouth to ask another question, but at the sound of multiple Pan Flutes his eyes widen.

"Enaw talkin'. Th' display will teel ye everythin' ye need tae know." The chief waves a hand and turns, revolving underneath himself in a half somersault and pounding his musculature against the water, climbing to the height of the chairs above the arena. Within moments everyone else has scattered too. Cole leads the rest of our pod downward, watching Flannery warily from the corner of one eye. Orion nods to him and something unspoken passes between ruler and knight before Orion turns to me.

"Come on, let's go." He takes my hand and we climb together to the top of the wooden beams holding up thickset, oak chairs. They don't look entirely stable but as Domnall takes the centre seat, we have little choice but to indulge the host and follow suit. Orion lets my hand drop, turning back to look me in the eyes momentarily before moving and taking his place on Domnall's left. I feel his reserve, his anxiety about what's going to happen. I wonder if we can reason with Domnall somehow if we lose, it doesn't seem likely, but we might not have any other choice. As I take my seat on Domnall's right hand side, I turn and study his face. He doesn't seem like he can be bargained with. He seems stubborn and arrogant. I wonder, as my eyes trace his bulky profile, if I had thought about the fact we were going to be dealing with people in the course of this quest to find the vessels. I realise I hadn't understood what a wild card each pod was going to turn out to be. These people owed us nothing, and yet we required everything of them. We need the Selkies trust and co-operation if we are going to make this work. As I'm pondering this, Domnall catches me staring and turns to me.

"Whit are ye starin' at?" He asks me, raising both his eyebrows. His eyes blaze, but it's not a threat that I find catching behind his irises. It's something else.

"You're just so strong." I whisper, deciding to go for something complimentary. Domnall looks taken aback at this and his cheeks flush slightly pink even. That's when I realise I have an in. The Chief opens his mouth to speak, but before he gets a chance a noise that makes me feel slightly nauseous erupts into the previously calm water.

The Fist of Lir come forth out of the murk, riding on Kelpie back with what look and, unfortunately for me, sound like bagpipes in mass force. I know I shouldn't really have expected anything else, but I was hoping I could avoid bagpipes all together on this trip. I sit back into the chair, letting the sound wash over me and seep into my bones. It's headache inducing for sure, but as I sit, hostage to a sound I absolutely hate, I cannot help but admire how smart the Fist of Lir appears. They're all moving forward in a giant shield-like wall, mounted completely erect upon their steeds, blowing into instruments I would quite like to smash to pieces. I contemplate this as I watch them move, each man as proud looking as the next. That's when something far below catches my eye. It's Ghazi, though he's not what I noticed first. It was a look. A look of longing so intense it looks like the bearer might combust with desire. Desire to belong. Conan is floating, looking up, as though he's seeing Lir himself, upon the army. He looks like he might even be counting the march they're working to in his head. I feel my heart plummet slightly in my chest at his face. The look he's giving is one of complete envy and love all at once. As I'm caught up in this thought I feel my body involuntarily relax. I draw my eyes upward and realise that the bagpipes have ceased torturing the cats trapped within. I laugh at the imagery and Domnall looks sideways at me, frowning. I realise I should probably act more like a Queen, he probably thinks I'm making fun of him.

"So what's involved in the High Tide games? Can you tell me more about them?" I turn to Domnall and reach over from my chair, it's in close proximity to his so I place my hand on his forearm gently. Orion perks up at this slight touch, leaning forward and turning his head to face me. He looks confused, but I glare at him quickly and he leans back once more. However, he need not worry about Domnall catching him staring, he's too busy staring at me instead.

"Weel, uh, they're based ay th' Heelain Games, a Scottish tradition. But we can only dae them when th' Loch's tide is high. Coz ay th' caber toss yer see." He looks more relaxed than I've seen him before and I take the opportunity to ask more questions.

"What's a... caber toss?" I ask him and he frowns.

"Ye huvnae ever heard ay caber toss?" He looks deeply shocked so I shake my head and blink rapidly, making my eyelashes flutter ever so slightly.

"No. I haven't." I breathe out in increments. I see Orion's head perk out again and he rolls his eyes. I try not look at him but I can't help but glance, amused. Domnall turns quickly and Orion smiles at him, looking innocent as the day he was born. Domnall turns slowly back to me as something below us in the rural arena starts to happen. I can see now that the arena he was talking about is nothing more than a large expanse of flat rock, free of Kelp and other vegetation. A fish passes by my left ear and I shudder as its tail tickles my neck.

"Th' caber toss is th' first event. Watch. it's now aboot to start." He gestures downward and I watch as Ghazi comes forward. A few Selkie I've never met move before him, carrying a large log about 10ft tall. It's huge and I wonder what he's going to do with it. Ghazi comes forward, swimming so he's erect in the water. He rubs his hands together, making a flurry of bubbles. I look over to the sidelines where Fahima floats, observing his every move. The crowd of Selkies are watching eagerly too, interested to see what the strange champion will be able to accomplish on their playing field. Ghazi takes a final deep breath and moves, pulling the log so his hands are both beneath it. He tilts, causing it to fly to a standing position in the water. I watch, amazed as I observe him balance with it, no legs beneath him. I can see the definition of his abdominals from here and watch as his biceps strain with keeping the log's position controlled in the water. He lets himself dip, but only slightly, before he lurches upward and tosses the log higher than I'd have ever thought possible. It shoots upward and touches the surface, flying like a wooden missile before beginning its descent back down. Selkies scatter as it hits the floor of the arena and Domnall inhales before turning to me.

"Isnae possible!" He looks shocked, his eyes wide.

"What? Is that good?" I ask him, pretending I have no idea what's going on. The shot was obviously impressive and a stunned silence has fallen over the crowd. I hear our small pod making some cheers, but beside them Flannery looks silent and furious.

52

"Ye waur reit, he's stronger than he looks." Is Domnall's only reply to my question. I look past him as Orion sits back once more with a smug smile.

Try not to look so damn pleased Orion, we need his help remember? I think to myself as I watch Flannery swim forward quickly to make his attempt at the Caber toss too. My eyes follow the red headed brute as he makes his attempt at the toss, my heart fluttering with anxiety as I observe. It's a good shot, but as I watch him I realise that Ghazi's shorter, stockier build is an advantage here. He has a lower centre of gravity and in this event it's given him the upper hand.

"What's next?" I hear Orion ask as Domnall clenches his fists on top of the armrest at seeing Flannery's throw fall short of Ghazi's.

"Tug-o-war." Domnall bites out, irritated. I lean over to him. Looking at the two men I think it's easy to predict that Flannery will win this one, because he has more mass than Ghazi. I sit back in the chair, thinking on this and contemplating how I can get to finding the real vessel. I watch as the two men begin to strain, swimming with their tailfins and adjusting their grips on the rope that's fraying at both ends. It ends quickly, as Flannery gives a final almighty tug and Ghazi falls, smashing his rear end into the rock at the bottom of the Loch with a defeated thud.

"OCH AYE! Gang oan Flannery!!" Domnall belts, rising, with a voice like thick Scottish thunder. I watch him as he sits back in his seat, flicking his tailfin with satisfaction. He reminds me of a man watching the Kentucky Derby with how into this he is. I sit for a moment as an idea hits me.

"What do you say we make this a little more interesting?" I request, placing my hand on his arm once more. His long red braid hangs limply over his left shoulder and he turns to me, making it shift as his once more blazing gaze burns into mine.

"Whit dae ye suggest?

"How about we make a little bet?" I goad him, knowing that a man with this much competitiveness will be unable to resist a wager.

"Sic' as? Ah dornt loch bettin' wi' Lassies." He says, narrowing his eyes, stroking his long beard with one hand and continuing to hold my gaze. I think for a moment before responding, choosing my words carefully.

"Well, what do you have to lose? After all, I'm a woman. I don't know anything about these games. Are you scared a woman will beat you?" I look at him and he suddenly looks angry. I know I've got him at a disadvantage. He'll look weak if he doesn't take me up on the offer.

"Braw! Whit ur th' terms?" He puffs out, clenching his fist once more on the armrest of his chair.

"How about, if Ghazi wins I get to choose the candidates to test as the vessel. If Flannery wins then…"

"Ah gie a kiss." Domnall's eyes sparkle maliciously and I hear a sudden falter in Orion's breathing. I almost want to laugh, but instead I hold out a hand to Domnall.

"Deal." I say and he looks surprised, almost shocked by my gall. I wonder if maybe he had expected I wouldn't accept after he had voiced his desire, especially in front of Orion. He takes my hand in his, crushing my bones in his vice like grasp. I smile through the pain and turn back to the games, my heart hammering. Ghazi better win.

The next event is the Stone Put, or I think that's what it is, I find it increasingly hard to decipher the meaning from the thick Scottish of Domnall.

"Go on Ghazi!" I yell, anxious. He looks up to me and I think I see a small smile cross his face. I watch him as he continues to keep me in his line of sight, moving up to the plate from which I assume he will make his throw. Selkies have lain twigs out, forming an acute angle which extends out from the plate. They hover and eyes watch, nervous as the men are now tied. Ghazi is handed a small stone and I smile, remembering the very first time I had met him, how he had made me attempt to lift boulder after boulder. I knew he was strong. The only question was whether or not he was stronger than Flannery and a better throw. I inhale, looking over to Domnall's mouth which is surrounded by red whiskers. I wonder if it'll be like kissing a bush. It certainly looks that way. I shudder.

My attention is drawn back to Ghazi as I sense his wind up. I watch him, placing the stone under the right side of his jaw, between his chin and his shoulder. He grips onto it as he turns from me, before winding his body around and releasing the stone in a loud exhale that is similar to the grunt a tennis player would exude. The stone flies and lands near the widest end of the area mapped for the event. He smiles and I wink at him, feeling cheeky. Domnall exhales, clearly agitated. Flannery swims forward to take his turn, taking the stone between his chin and shoulder and beginning to tense the muscles in his enormous form. I can feel the crowd inhale, anxious to see their champion beat the short foreigner.

"Gang oan Flannery!" He rises from his seat again, right as Flannery is about to throw. The exclamation is so harsh it startles him, faltering his momentum. He throws, the stone flying through the water and landing, perhaps half a metre short of his competitors. "GAH!" Domnall curses, returning to his seat. He's too competitive and it's making his son falter. I wonder what it must be like to have Domnall as a father, putting that much pressure on you. Momentarily I find sympathy for him, but then lose it once more as he tries to punch a nearby member of the crowd in his frustration.

I turn around to look at Orion and watch him, head in one hand, peering between his fingers and looking like watching this is the most pained experience he's had in his life. I scowl at him and he erects himself, scowling back. I know he can't be happy about the bet I made with Domnall, but then again, why shouldn't I use their penile measuring contest to my advantage? I turn my attention back to the games, feeling myself tire of the straining and the exertion. I wish we could have just sat down around a table and discussed this like adults. It's pretty obvious to me now, Flannery isn't the vessel for Lir. I just don't get that from him. I mean, I hadn't known Cage was the Adaro vessel right away, but once we'd discovered the truth with the help of Starlet, I'd felt something radiating from him I hadn't noticed before. A kind of energy similar to my own. I frown, feeling my forehead crease appear as I sit back in the chair. Frustrated.

The Games have passed slowly and it all comes down to one event. Flannery and Ghazi are still tied. We've seen them through multiple events and I watch as they bring out the equipment for the final one. In the event of a tie, Domnall explains to me, a final deciding event is brought forward. I watch the targets being placed on the flat of the arena's bedrock; they have three rings, the outermost blue, the middle ring red, and the bullseye yellow.

"Archery?" I ask with a cocked brow. He nods with a smile. I don't know if Ghazi is good with a bow. I don't even know if he's ever used a bow, I feel my heart start to race. I mean, kissing Domnall is better than the alternative of Fergus, and yet I don't quite want to have to stomach it. I watch as Flannery is handed a bow and a heavy duty looking arrow, I mean it would have to be to make its way through the water. It's the only high tech piece of equipment I've seen the Selkies bring out and I wonder where they get them from.

"Och aye, th' selkies ur some ay th' best archers' in th' warld." The water stirs my blonde locks around my ears as Domnall brags and I watch as Flannery positions himself sideways, so his body is facing toward us as I dig my nails into the wood of my chair. He inhales water, pulling the arrow back in the bow and taking a few seconds before he releases it. I watch as the arrow flies and hits the bottom of the blue circle painted on the target. It's not a good shot, but it could still beat Ghazi. Ghazi swims forward as Domnall begins to grind his teeth and I watch as Flannery passes him, tripping him with the end of his long midnight blue tailfin. Ghazi falls to the floor, his arms buckling underneath him as his face meets with rock and a shower of bubbles rises around him. I rise from my seat and swim downward to aid him with a pissed off glare at Flannery on the way.

"That wasn't fair! You tripped him!" I exclaim, furious.

"Son! whit hae ye dain?" I hear Domnall's thunderous roar. I pick Ghazi up from the floor, rolling him around. He looks like he's hurt his wrist.

"Well he can't shoot now! Look at that wrist! It's swelling already!" I hear Marina's horrified Italian tones as Fahima rushes to Ghazi's side. Domnall presents a fleeting expression, one of envy, as the women flutter around their fallen warrior.

"What do you propose we do?" Orion asks, coming around the left side of Domnall's body with one flick of his tail. He's far more graceful than any of the Selkies by far.

"Ah dunnae know. We dornt allaw cheaters haur!" Domnall looks at Flannery once more, his face the picture of disgust.

"Faither it was an accident ah swear." I look between the father and son but I can tell Domnall isn't impressed. His mouth is a firm angry line, unmoving in the water, he stands statue-esque.

"Seeing as how our champion is injured. I want to choose another." I demand, turning as I rise from the floor in one fluid rotation and crossing my arms.

"Ah dornt answer tae a Lassie." Domnall snipes, pivoting to face Orion.

"I do, and this 'Lassie' in particular is more than equipped to choose. We want another champion of our choice to take the final shot." He looks to me, nodding and I beam, grateful for his confidence in me. Then I feel slightly sick knowing I have to pick the next champion and the fate of my bet relies on this decision. I look around. Cole is practically itching to be chosen and the Maidens shrink from my gaze. That's when I catch Conan's eye. A shudder runs through me.

"Conan." I say, waiting for the kickback from this response.

"Whit? 'at pipsqueak?" Flannery turns to look at him with hostile distaste.

"Callie he's not even a member of our pod." Orion looks surprised as he speaks in a slow and measured tone.

"Nae laddie it's fin', I'll alaw it. Lit th' lass hae 'er choice." Domnall smiles and I wonder if he knows something I don't. I wonder what the hell I was thinking. I've never even seen Conan shoot. I don't even know if he *can* shoot.

Oh god why did I have to open my big mouth! I scold myself, wondering what possessed me to choose the pale stable boy with about as much upper body strength as a twig. The moment is tense as everyone falls silent, looking to Conan who has turned beetroot purple at the attention of so many eyes at once. He looks like he might puke, but instead he just nods. Unable to speak, but nonetheless accepting of my choice.

Oh crap now I've really done it.

I turn to move back to the raised seating, but Domnall shakes his head with a sly smile and places a hand on my shoulder, stopping me from returning to where I was previously sat.

"Nae, Ah want tae be ringside fur thes giant tossel up." He laughs and I narrow my eyes. I really hope that Conan hits that target and shows him what for. Someone this arrogant needs a good slap if you ask me.

"All right, let's resume." Orion says, moving to my side as we back out of the Arena and Ghazi rises, holding his left wrist in his right hand. He looks thoroughly irritated as Fahima comforts him with a slender arm draped around his huge shoulder.

"I hope you know what you're doing. You've seen him shoot before?" Orion whispers as we take our positions at the edge of the arena.

"Urm... not exactly." I admit and Orion sighs.

"What? Why on earth would you pick him? He's going to lose this and then I'm going to have to watch you kissing the ginger savage over there!"

"I didn't realise that was what he would want if he won. I couldn't exactly back out without looking rude now could I? We need these Selkies to help us and we need to find the vessel, this was the only way I could think of that he would let me pick someone else to test." I explain, I realise my voice is louder as in intended as someone in the crowd shushes me into silence. Orion doesn't respond, but he twists his mouth in a face that tells me he knows I'm right. There are more important stakes here than his ego.

Conan takes his place in front of the target and the crowd goes hushed apart from a few echoes of deep laughter from Selkies. I know they must think I'm mad. Nothing more than a woman who doesn't know any better. Maybe then, that's why I picked Conan. I want him to prove that things aren't always what they appear. I know he has strength and courage just like any of these other Selkies. I've seen him with Marcas, dealing with his parent falling apart in front and fading before his eyes. That takes an inner strength that he doesn't even

58

realise he possesses. I want to show him he's wrong about himself, as well as proving that his appearance is deceiving to these hulking great men.

He breathes in and pulls back the bow. I inhale too, my breath caught in my chest as I watch him hold the bow back for a few seconds. Everything is silent now. The moment hanging between me and victory is thick with tension. I hear it before I see it. The string of the bow let loose. I exhale as the arrow leaves the bow and he slumps, seeming not to know whether he's made the shot or not. I watch the projectile slice through the water like a knife through cream atop shortbread. Then, with the sound of splintering wood and the vibration of the arrow I stare. It's there, embedded and perfect, damn straight in the middle of the bullseye.

The crowd roars. Half in shocked joy and half in disbelief. I can't believe it. My ears are tuning out the noise as I look at the arrow, lodged perfectly in its target.

Oh my god he did it.

"Callie! Oh my god he did it!" Orion is bobbing up and down in the water, holding onto my shoulders and shaking me as I stare past him at Conan's shocked expression. He doesn't seem to know what happened. The mer pod are entering the arena, picking up Conan and patting him on the back, lifting him up above them and cheering his name. I move over to Ghazi, not forgetting for a second who got us to the tie break event.

"Thank you for what you did Ghazi. You were amazing." I put my arms around him and he winces as I nudge his wrist. Fahima smiles at me before she goes back to nursing him. I turn, moving from the couple and over to the gaggle of mermaids who are fussing over Conan and rubbing his red mane of hair with fondness.

"You did it!" I gush, moving through the mermaids as they part to let me through. Conan looks sheepish.

"It was a lucky shot. Nae big deal." His eyes fall to the floor and his face looks sad once more. His eyes dart behind me quickly and I turn. Flannery is standing there with his arms crossed.

"Aye. It was. Nae more than a lucky shot." He snaps, before turning and moving away from us in a flurry of angry bubbles.

"Nae, 'at was a true archer's shot. Yer Faither woods be prood." The voice rings out and Conan's eyes light up. I pivot to see Domnall approaching us. He actually looks impressed.

"Th… Thank ye." Conan stutters.

"Congratulations Lass." Domnall holds out a hand to me. I look at it, mystified.

"You're not mad I won?" I ask him, feeling bold from my victory.

"Nae, that's not th' spirit of th' games." He smiles, his face taking on a whole new demeanour. I smile back as he replies, "Ah am however disappointed abit 'at kiss." He admits, joking as he nudges Orion who laughs, looking relieved. The Chieftain's whole attitude seems to have changed at our victory. It shouldn't surprise me that a culture revering physical strength respects its competitors, but it does. Whatever the reason for this shift in attitude, I'm glad that the grudge he had against Orion seems to be gone.

"I want to pick someone to test as the vessel." I remind him that I won our bet and he sighs.

"Aye. Ye won. Hae at it." He turns to the rest of the Selkies, blowing his panpipe as they move closer. "These mer ay Atargatis ur lookin' fur th' vessel. You'll aw need tae be tested." He orders the command and the rest of the Selkies nod, some of them looking, with irritated stares, towards Conan. I catch their gazes and Orion notices too. He moves forward, squaring himself to Conan. He holds out a hand to him and smiles.

"Thank you for representing my people. You were amazing." Conan looks like he might cry as he takes Orion's hand.

Then, something unexpected happens. Orion is thrown backward, a gush of air moving him through the water and throwing him to the ground. My head snaps around, moving back to Conan's startled expression. He looks terrified.

60

A look I know only too well, a look that I held the first time I absorbed someone's powers by accident. Domnall stares at me, his gaze questioning and I nod my head, knowing we're thinking something similar. Silence falls, being broken only by Domnall's simple exclamation.

"Weel I'll be damned..."

6
Brawl

CALLIE

Back in Azure's chambers at the Bùrn Kildrummy, Orion closes the door behind him as I move past his glistening royal blue tailfin. I swim over to the bed to take a look at how Azure is doing. However, rather than finding her sleeping, I am met with a sodden and musty pillow in my face. I throw it back to where it had previously been shielding Azure's eyes from the light, which is now dim and streaming through the glassless window.

"Do you mind?" She grimaces with a crumpled expression, her voice is hoarse and her eyes are bloodshot even still.

"Mind what?" I ask, watching as she scowls at me.

"That door and its goddamn squeaky hinges. It's like someone's running their fingernails along the insides of my skull." She moans, pulling the pillow back over her head.

"So I take it you won't be coming to fling later?" Orion says with an amused expression. She tilts the tartan plaid pillow up at the bottom and peaks out from beneath, flicking her charcoal tailfin in restless motion.

"What did you just say to me?" She has a mock offended look on her face and I can tell it's taking everything within her to be funny. I know she uses humour to fight back the darkness raging within her and so I laugh. She looks like I've stabbed her as the sound hits the open water and I quieten myself as she exhales.

"The Selkies are celebrating Conan's shot and his connection to Lir. It's called a fling apparently."

"What that weedy little dweeb? The one I kersplatted?" She looks startled and halfway between laughing and crying as she sits up.

"That's the one." Orion rubs the back of his neck with a careless hand and I can tell he's not convinced either.

"It's not always about physical strength. Take a look at me. I'm not exactly the most muscular woman. I doubt I could beat Azure in a fight."

"Got that right, blondie." Azure says the words before she realises their implications, of whom she sounds like.

"You sound just like…" I begin but she cuts me off by talking across me.

"So Conan is the Vessel for Lir? We're sure?" She looks to Orion with a harsh stare and he stutters in his response.

"Yes. He stole my ability over air. He took it from me as I shook his hand. Still, he made one hell of a shot with that bow and arrow. Did you see that? All the hairs stood up on the back of my neck. I've never seen an archer hit a target like that." He is gushing all of a sudden, looking to me. I smile at his awestruck expression, what we'd witnessed had definitely been special.

"It was pretty amazing. It was like he was taking instruction from a higher power." I agree. Azure shrugs her shoulders.

"I hope this Circle of Eight knows what they're doing." She says, wincing again as she reaches up to touch her head. "Ugh, the Leprechaun has returned to tap dance on my temples again."

"Leprechaun?" I raise one eyebrow.

"Yes, we are in Scotland you know." She replies and I laugh.

"I'm pretty sure they're Irish Azure…"

"Oh whatever!" She huffs, pulling down the tartan blankets of the wooden four-poster to cover her, cocooning her like some sort of dark moth. Orion turns, moving toward me and taking my hands in his palms.

"Thanks for choosing the right champion for the job." He whispers, touching the side of my face with a ginger caress.

"It's okay. I just had a feeling." I admit, biting my bottom lip. I look up into the icy blue of his gaze, loving the pride in the look he's giving me. He makes me feel stronger than I had thought possible. I had been caged in his embrace for so long, I'm still trying to let my heart catch up with the fact that he has discovered he prefers me free, prefers me capable.

"Trust that feeling. Your instincts. They're from a higher power than you can comprehend. You're special. Trust yourself. I do." He leans in to kiss me and my heart leaps. I put my arms around his neck and let my tailfin wrap around his scales, creating a delightful friction that makes my heart hammer even harder. I let my lips trace across his lightly and he groans. I move in to deepen the kiss, only to feel something pillow-like hit the side of both mine and Orion's faces.

"Oi!" He turns and scowls at her. She crosses her arms.

"This isn't a frat house. Go make your star-crossed lover, bullshit, sucking face noises somewhere else!" She complains and Orion frowns.

"They only gave us two rooms Azure." He rolls his eyes and I pivot, folding my arms across my chest.

"Well, then I suppose you'll just have to wait until this headache kills me then." She flops back onto the bed once more in a flurry of slow moving bubbles and rolls onto her side, wrapping the tartan blanket around her once more.

"We had better make sure everyone is getting ready for the fling next door." I say, looking up at him with a mischievous desire filled gaze.

"Yes, I agree. Let's make sure everyone is briefed on what not to say." Orion suddenly looks nervous again, and I worry that our relationship will never find a rhythm of its own with all the responsibilities that come with the crown getting in the way. Then again, if we don't get through this we'll probably all be dead. So the point is moot. I sigh, feeling anxiety seeping into my gut again.

"I'd say making sure everyone knows Leprechauns are from Ireland and not Scotland is a start." I say, shooting Azure a look over my left shoulder. She rolls her eyes again and covers her face with the tartan pillow, her black hair so long it trails over the edge of the bed.

"Good plan." Orion cups the back of my shoulder with a strong hand and I breathe out, accepting my fate. Let's go fling.

"Ye loch lik' ye need a guid bevvy Lassie." Domnall bellows with a laugh. He's chewing on something, though I have no idea what.

"A bevvy?" I ask him with a cocked eyebrow, confused. We're sitting in the banquet hall, surrounded by crumbling brick, heavy wood furniture crawling with prawns and other small invertebrates, and the mounted skulls of demons. The fling is nothing short of a bar room brawl. There are Selkies that look drunk, but I have no idea how they can be. That, however, isn't why I look so uncomfortable. The reason I look like I'm being tortured is because of the band in the corner. Bagpipes, fiddles and an array of other instruments are being played haphazardly in an overly amorous and jovial cacophony that is making my stomach churn. I sit in the seat, my nails clawing into the wood, as I try to drown out the wailing bagpipes.

I watch the men, hovering above the long table that's central to the room, dancing the most ridiculous dance I've ever seen. They're all holding on to one another's arms, flailing their tails behind them and singing in an awful off pitch that makes my skin crawl. As I watch them, I notice that they're all wearing make-shift kilts over the top of their tailfins, which been woven from kelp in green, purple and yellow strands that interlock in traditional square, tartan-like patterns. Conan is, I now notice, in the centre of the ring of dancing men, rising and falling inside their miniature whirlpool with both arms over his head in a kind of gawky dance of his own. The joy on his face is the last thing I notice before Domnall slams down a large, metal tankard in front of me.

"What's this?" I enquire, peering into the depths of the cup. Green slime sits at the bottom and I frown, confused.

"Is seamead Lass! Ye chew it." He pats me on the back of the shoulder and puts a hand into the bottom of the cup, pulling out a strand of what he calls 'seamead'. I watch him place it in his mouth and chew happily. I stare, fascinated. Orion watches me from my right as I place my hand deep into the

65

tankard, displacing the water and gripping the green slime in my palm. I cup it in my fist and place it in my mouth, chewing a few times.

Holy Crap. This tastes rancid.

Domnall watches me as I chew on. It's like some kind of seaweed jerky, but there's something else… Domnall's expression turns amused at my face. My jaw begins to ache as the taste continues to diffuse throughout my mouth. My head gets fuzzy for a moment and I sit there, temporarily calm in spite of the grating squeal of bagpipes. Orion takes a handful from the bottom of the glass too and puts it in his mouth. His eyes widen.

"This has been…." He continues to chew, his expression half elated and half disgusted, "Soaked in some kind of alcohol?" He questions Domnall who laughs.

"Wa mead an' ale ay coorse!" Domnall makes this exclamation before spitting the seamead into a bucket next to his chair, that I hadn't noticed before, almost like he's been chewing tobacco.

"Ah of course!" Orion says, giving me a look of surprise. I spit my seamead out into my palm, as my head starts to fill with the happy haze of alcohol hitting my system, before tossing it into the bucket beside Domnall's chair. Now that I look around, I realise most of the men here are chewing on something similar to what I've just experienced. The seamead is strong and it took me only moments to feel the effects, so I can only imagine how drunk they must be by now. I watch as the mermaid's stay grouped together, floating from one side of the room to the other and trying to avoid getting the attentions of Fergus who is avidly following them like some sort of groupie. As I look away from them with a slight frown, my eyes fall on Flannery who is sulking in the corner.

"So, Domnall…" I begin, shifting my gaze to watch as the hulking red headed Selkie sinks back into the wooden seat at the head of the table. He looks relaxed.

"Aye Lass. Tha's me!" He plays with his beard, like a child who is far too easily amused.

"Your men are fine fighters. How would you feel about helping us fight the Psirens? I can't think of anyone stronger than you. We need that." I brush the red spattering of hair on his forearms and he looks to me.

"Ye want me tae leave th' loch tae help ye?" He looks surprised and I nod. Orion takes up the line of conversation. I sit back in my seat, looking between the two men.

"Yes. That's the other reason we're here. They obliterated our race. We need help taking them down. If we don't raise an army big enough, they're going to overrun the planet. Nowhere will be safe."

"But ah thooght ye jist wanted tae fin' th' vessel? Whit did ye think thes fling was fur? We're bludy glad tae be gettin' rid ay Conan." Domnall is now sitting upright and Orion's expression falls about a mile. What, did he think we were going to take Conan off his hands? This guy is unbelievable.

"Finding the vessel was a part of why we came, that's true. I don't think you quite understand the severity..." Orion begins but Domnall is suddenly upright and high above the table.

"Who'd protect th' loch while we're gain fightin' yer war?" He cocks an eyebrow and clenches his fists, making his muscles bulge and his throat's veins protrude.

"It won't matter about the Loch. If we lose this war, then there's no telling how far the infection of Dark magic will spread, not to mention you'll have the powers of the Necrimad to content with. You'll find the Loch crawling with Psirens just like the Pacific is right now. It's only a matter of time." Orion says these words clearly, but he doesn't shout, or even raise his voice. He looks tired if I'm honest.

"Wa dornt ye jist tak' Conan an' lae us aloyn?" Flannery moves forward from the shadows, rising through the water. He's slurring his words and his accent is thicker than I've heard it before, it's clear to me he's had far too much Seamead.

"Och sae ye dorn't caur if ah die?" Conan exclaims, sounding hurt. The room has gotten quiet and even the band has stopped playing in a sudden squeal of fiddle strings.

"That's reit pipsqueak. Yoo're naethin' mair than demon food." He slurs this sentiment and I have trouble discerning what he's saying, only just able to catch the gist. I watch as Conan straightens up and I notice he's chewing on Seamead too. I wonder if it might be filling him with confidence, or whether it's his vessel status that's doing the trick, because there's no way he'd have gotten this confrontational with Flannery yesterday. I look between the two men as they begin to turn in the water, rotating around one another like irritable bears.

Orion rises from his chair and moves across the hall in silence. I watch him edge around the looming brawl and over to the band, perhaps the only one who has noticed he's moved. Everyone else is too transfixed by the potential for violence. Orion speaks in a hushed whisper to the Selkie who's been murdering my nervous system in slow torment for the past few hours and then he takes the funnily coloured bagpipes before taking a long measured blow. The note is all wrong, but it gets the attention of the two men about to begin pummelling one another.

"Stop this! There's no need for violence!"

"Ye know 'at bagpipe is made frae sheep's stomach dornt ye laddie?" Domnall asks him with a cocked eyebrow and a wicked smile before exuding a guffawing laugh. Orion goes green. I sit, watching him look like he's going to vomit, musing that it makes sense they use sheep stomach, I can't imagine that fabric bagpipes would be as effective underwater.

"No, I did not know that." He admits, shaking his head and trying to clear his apparent nausea.

"Besides, that's nae hoo ye gie noise oot ay a bagpipe. THES is hoo ye gie noise oot ay a bagpipe!" Flannery moves over to Orion and I lean forward, enraptured by the scene unfolding before me. It's so much better than a soap opera, mainly because you couldn't find a scriptwriter in the world mad enough to make this stuff up. Conan floats before me atop the banquet hall table, still strong in his stance in spite of his lack of muscle. I admire him a little for that, the kid's got guts.

Flannery snatches the bagpipe out of Orion's fist and takes the pipe to his mouth. He inhales and blows hard, the sound emitting from the instrument more deafening and hideous than anything I've ever heard. I cringe, wanting to cover my ears, but at the same time not wanting to appear rude. Flannery rises, blowing into the bagpipes with everything he's got. His chest rising and falling like tectonic plates, hefty and immovable. He comes close to Conan, getting in his face and deafening him in one startling, final exhalation. Conan however, doesn't move, instead he takes his thin fingers and presses down on the sheep's stomach bag. Halting the sound. He's definitely my hero.

I'm watching them so intensely that I barely register someone's familiar and pissed off tones getting nearer. The double wooden doors slam open, smashing into the brick on either side of the back wall and revealing a sight more terrifying than I'd anticipated.

"Who. The bloody hell. Is playing. Bloody. BAGPIPES?!" Azure's voice rolls out from her in a staccato tsunami of wrath. I forget how scary she can be when she's pissed, I also can't help but notice how her vernacular is evolving, changing to match that of a certain tentacled menace.

Domnall turns, pivoting to face her, he recoils slightly, backing up in the water atop the banquet table. It's barely noticeable but I can tell even he's caught off guard.

Azure moves forward, eel-like in her stroke. She's more fluid when she's angry, when she's channelling the darkness, with an almost scary level of grace and speed. Her eyes are still bloodshot and her hair is flaring out around her like bolts of onyx electricity.

"WELL? WHERE IS THE OFFENDING PARTY?" She barks, making most of the Selkies in the room jump. I watch Flannery turn, slowly. Her eyes catch onto the bagpipes in his hands. Then, she's off like a bull seeing scarlet. She takes a few strokes before launching herself on top of Flannery. He crashes onto the table, smashing it into a million splintered pieces. I rise from my chair, backing up and watching the spectacle, eyes wide, unable to believe what I'm seeing. Azure is on top of Flannery. He's trying to get her off him but she's caught him off guard, winding him. She brings back her fist and then catches my eye as she breaks focus from her target. Her pupils are fully dilated, the darkness' hold on her clear, but something shifts. Her pupils retract at the sight of my horrified expression. Her eyes return to their prior bloodshot state and she looks down once more. I wonder if she'll go through with it, but instead of smacking ten bells of crap out of him, she unleashes her palm in the mother of all fish slaps across both sides of his face. Then she rises, turns, and swims to the doors. Upon reaching the open doorway, she turns back.

"So if you could keep it down... that would be great." She curls her snarl into a sweet girlish smile and then vanishes. I look around the room, my eyes jumping from Orion's shell shocked expression to Conan's, then to Domnall's and finally resting on the outraged look of Flannery who's sprawled at the end of my fluke.

"Whit th' heel! Faither did ye see 'at?" Flannery finally manages to find his words. Domnall looks down on him and the room is silent. He laughs. More than I've ever seen him laugh. He looks like he actually might cry from laughing too hard, or bust a lung.

"Ye got slapped by a lassie!" Domnall chokes out, rubbing oily tears from beneath his eyes. I watch them as they fall, waiting for them to turn to diamond but they don't. Flannery straightens himself, rising, and moves from the hall as his face turns red and angry, before slamming the wooden doors closed behind him. The rest of the Selkies are joining in, laughing in a tumult of deep voices at his absence, shaking at the ridiculousness of someone as large as Flannery getting slapped by a girl half his size. Now I think about it, it is quite funny.

"Ye got yerself an army. The Fist o' Lir is yours!" Domnall comes forward toward me and holds out a giant hand. He reaches out to me.

"Wait... I don't understand." Orion says, moving over so he's behind Domnall. The Chieftain turns, lowering himself over the remains of the table so he and Orion are on eye level with one another.

"Anythin' evil enough tae make a lassie lik' that run fur th' hills has got tae be bad." He whispers in a low voice, his Scottish accent straightening out under the weight of his words. His expression is still amused but something dark passes behind the whites of his eyes as he and Orion share a look. I shudder

70

slightly, the smile wiped from my face. He's not wrong. Azure is a force to be reckoned with and she's still not as evil as most of the Psiren army.

"Conan!" Domnall calls him over with a wave of his huge hand.

"Och aye?" Conan replies.

"Ye best be learnin' hoo tae barnie son. Yer gunnae need it." He looks to Conan with a deadly serious expression. I watch the two men with interest before Conan bows his head slightly.

"It woods be mah honoor." Conan says with a small smile. As he expresses this sentiment there's an explosion of sound to my left. A Selkie atop his steed with really red hair and a dark green tailfin like Conan's approaches.

"Dom, a demon!" The exclamation is short and sharp and the Selkies immediately jump to. There's a flurry of motion in the room and a mass sounding of Panpipes into the cloudy waters. I hear whinnying from afar, and soon, above the ceiling of the banquet hall, hundreds of Kelpies are coming to meet their riders. Among them I catch Philippe and I wonder how he got free.

"Orion!" I yell out, moving around the bodies of Selkies that are rising to meet their steeds. "Philippe!" I gesture upwards and catch his unmistakably light blue gaze as it moves to look above. He sees the Equinox and rises to meet him, ushering him down to the stone floor beside the previously long and unbroken banquet table. The Equinox moves from hoof to hoof, anxious at the surrounding din of cries for armour and swords. Domnall looks down to me from above.

"Come. See whit thes army is capable ay." He practically growls. Another Selkie rises through the water next to him, wrapping him in a thick chest piece that looks like it's made of some kind of kelp that been dried and braided. He's handed a broad sword by another Selkie before riding away in a stream of bubbles. The rest of the mer pod are heading over to us. I look to the worried expressions of the maidens.

"What should we do Callie?" Sophia asks me, swimming around Skye's lemon tailfin and toward the front of the assembly.

"Well, Orion and I are going to see this demon, to try to help. I'd say it's the least we can do." I shrug as the rest of them nod.

71

"We'll take the maidens here back to their room and perhaps begin to prepare for departure?" Cole looks to me, his impatience making me increasingly aware that every day we stay here after securing the Fist of Lir as our ally, is a day wasted. We've come to find the vessel, and he's been found. Also, I'm reminded that the blood moon, which Azure has prophesised will bring war, won't wait until we're ready. It will come whether we're prepared or not.

"Yes." Orion speaks my thought and gives a quick nod. He takes me in his arms in one fell swoop and pulls me onto Philippe. He wraps his arms around me tight and ushers Philippe to ascend with a click of his tongue.

"You know, I never get tired of flying through the water with you on a kickass, aquatic, magical pony." I sigh and he throws his head back in a laugh.

"Me neither."

It doesn't take us long to find the source of the alert that's been sounded. The problem is though, it isn't a demon at all, it's our ride out of here. Behind the assembled Fist of Lir, five hundred strong, the whirlpool has appeared once more, rumbling and disturbing local flora with its epic speed.

"Ah assume thes has somethin' tae dae wi' ye?" Domnall turns Magnus to face us with a bored expression, clearly disappointed that he won't be getting any demon action. We come closer, moving in so Philippe and Magnus are almost touching.

"That's how we got here." Orion admits. Domnall turns to the Selkie who had alerted us to the disturbance.

"Aedan ye stoatin moron! Diz thes loch lik' a demon tae ye?" He barks and Aedan shrinks backward, disappearing into the ranks of Kelpie with a shame faced look. Domnall shakes his head, rolling his eyes. He's clearly not a big fan of false alarms. "Naethin' tae see haur. Oan th' plus side, mair Seamead lads!" He raises his sword in the air, declaring more alcohol and the warriors behind him cheer like primal cavemen. The Selkies launch forward, stampeding toward us and away from the roaring cyclical waters, causing Philippe to falter, startled, as they rush past.

"I think this means it's time for us to move on." Orion says, dismounting Philippe and holding out a hand.

"Weel, aam nae gonna argue wi' 'at." Domnall laughs, giving the whirlpool a wary gaze.

"We'll head back and gather our things now." I add and Domnall looks upon me with fondness. He's not the brightest crayon in the pack, but he's at least honourable in some respect. Orion and I turn, and as we begin to move away with Philippe, Orion's eyes light up suddenly as I watch him swim beside me before his forehead creases in concern.

"But wait, Callie, we can't leave the Selkies here, they need to come with us." Orion whispers to me. I look at him, incredulous. I can't stomach the thought of toting around the Selkies while we're trying to be democratic. Who knows where we'll end up next. Having Azure in our pod is unpredictable enough without the added bonus of five hundred red headed and rowdy Scotsmen.

"We can't do that! They'll make us a massive target Orion! They're not exactly..." I turn my head away from Domnall so he can't read my lips, though I doubt he knows how, "a low key type of society. You know what I'm saying?" Orion ponders this for a moment, his royal blue tailfin swaying in the water, before he speaks.

"We need to talk to Azure. She had that vision about the blood moon, maybe she saw something about how it's all supposed to happen. You're not wrong about them being less than discreet though." I feel a sudden weight upon me. We had left the Adaro behind us too, and I had assumed they would meet up with us in the Pacific because of my father's loyalty to me. However, we don't have that luxury with the Selkies, and it makes me wonder if they'd be willing to make such a journey in exchange for little other than honour and duty.

"You're right. Let's go." I agree.

"Azure!" I crash in through the door of her room, feeling slightly out of breath and flustered. I had known this stay wasn't permanent, but the appearance of the whirlpool, a signal from the Circle that it was time to move on, had still caught me by surprise.

"Keep it down. My headache *just* went away." She mutters. This time she's not lying on top of the bed. Instead, she's drooped over the sill of the glassless window, staring outward into Moray Firth.

"Sorry... I..." She turns and looks back at me.

"You came about the whirlpool. I can sense it from here. Stupid thing." She sighs, looking tired. It's a lot different than how wound up she'd been in the dining hall.

"You okay?" I ask her, not really wanting to pry, but knowing without her co-operation it's going to be a long trip.

"Yeah. I'm just tired of the darkness." She looks worse than I've ever seen her. It's not the outright rage of the night Starlet had passed, which I know is still a gaping wound, it's something I've never seen in her before. Azure has always been angry, or sarcastic, or insulting to cover her pain and her struggle with the darkest parts of herself, but I'd never seen her actually *sad* before. I'd seen her angry and devastated, but never just sad. It seems like the emotion isn't strong enough for her to feel. Azure is an extreme person and I've never seen the in-between side of her, not soft or hard, just human.

"Do you want to talk about it?" I ask her. Her head snaps up.

"No! I don't want to talk about my crappy life with the one and only Callie Pierce, golden child of Atargatis and saviour of the Occulta Mirum, thank you very much!" Suddenly she's Azure again, snapping back like an elastic band from her depressed state and leaving me with whiplash.

"Right, well, Orion will explain..." I feel relieved as I hear Orion finally enter in behind me after tying Philippe up outside and then going to inform Cole and Ghazi about what's going on.

74

"Greetings your high and mightiness. What can I do for your oh so special self today?" She sneers, turning nasty. Orion is taken aback and I flash him a warning stare as he passes me by.

"I just wanted to know about your vision. The one you had at Aurora Sanctum?" He looks hopeful for a second, but Azure's face turns hateful in the extreme, her eyes dilating black.

"Oh, so you need something from me? Again? After you did nothing about saving our sister? That's funny." Her tone is dangerous. Orion moves with tenuousness, reaching a hand out to touch her shoulder.

"Don't touch me."

"Azure, what is this about?" Orion asks her with a serious expression. His pastel blue irises blaze with caring.

"You! The lot of you! You're all having a grand old time down there, I saw you! She's dead Orion! She's dead and you're having a party. She's dead and you're having a great old time, laughing. How can you do that? How can you laugh when she's dead? How can you do any of this when she's dead? She's gone…" Azure's facade is cracking and the blackness within her recedes as emotion rages through her like a storm, clashing and striking with paradoxical accuracy.

"Azure… I miss her too; it's painful for me too. Every day. I loved Starlet. I will always love Starlet, but life, life goes on…" Orion says these things, desperate.

"Why? Everything's changed. Everything is different. I'm broken inside and the world still looks damn peachy for you. Why?" She demands this of him, looking terrifying in her conflicting emotion.

"Because… life is awful. At times." Orion begins, turning to shoot me a *'what the hell can I say here'* type stare. I shrug as he pivots back to Azure. "If it wasn't awful at times then it wouldn't mean anything when it was good. Right? If people didn't die, nobody would appreciate life." Azure doesn't look him in the eye, staring out into the murky water once more. I can tell she's not satisfied with the answer, but she's done with the conversation. I know Orion is probably getting too deep for her to handle. She sucks at public displays of emotion.

"What did you want to ask?" She mumbles, changing the subject. Orion sighs, but whether it's frustration or relief I can't tell.

"I wanted to know if we need to ask the Selkies to join us on this jaunt to every corner of the earth." Azure looks confused.

"Uh no, that's not how this works."

"What do you mean?" I ask, feeling surprised at her lack of concern.

"The whirlpools, they're gateways right? Well, they're not just for us. They will open again when the time comes, and when that happens, the armies need to come through." She says it like it's common knowledge, like there was a news bulletin and we're all stupid. I start to feel my anger boil over at her lack of cooperation.

"Why the hell didn't you just *tell us* that Azure? That's actually useful! You get these visions to help us! You can't pick and choose what you tell!" I exclaim. She cocks an eyebrow all of a sudden, moving past Orion so she can face me head on.

"Look, *blondie,* I get the visions, I put up with the crap in my head, so I can do what I want. Got that?" She smirks at me; like this is something she's got to hold over me. I narrow my eyes but don't take the bait. Fighting with her won't solve anything, though it's becoming increasingly creepy that she's starting to talk like Vex.

"So all the armies will just come out in the middle of the Pacific or something?" Orion asks her, turning to face us both.

"I don't know." Azure bites out and I narrow my eyes.

"You don't know as in you really don't know, or you don't know as in you don't want to tell us?" I ask her, feeling the need to get a final dig in.

"Wouldn't you like to know?" She smiles, cocky. I try not to let it get to me, but the fact is we're all drowning trying to save the damn world and she's being a complete jackass.

"We better get ready to leave Orion." I say, looking to him. He gives me a pleading stare, like he knows I'm right but that he's helpless to do anything about it because Azure's his sister and grieving. I turn from the both of them and leave the room, heading over to the mermaids and readying myself to be thrown into the unknown once more.

Conan smiles to me as we float a few metres from the rushing waters of the whirlpool. Domnall is shortly behind him and Marcas is in close proximity too. The more I see this individual the more increasingly insane he appears. His hair is even more dishevelled than the last time I saw him and his eyes are glazed.

"I'll see ye suin." Conan vows. He stares to the rest of the pod, to the women who had lifted him up, the people who had believed in him for the first time in his life. He beams.

"Yes, now you know what to do right?" I ask him, feeling Philippe move in the water beside me. I almost feel Azure shifting and rolling her eyes from atop the Equinox, but I can't quite muster the will to care. I know I'm on show once more for the Selkies, who are gathered in full number behind the Chief.

"When th' whirlpool starts, we'll come." Domnall calls over Conan's shoulder. I see a sulking Flannery among the other men, towering above them as Fergus waves to the maidens who look, once more, horrified at the idea of his affections.

"Oh, and before I forget. Keep your eyes peeled for something called a 'Piece of Eight.'" Orion reminds me of this small detail I had forgotten, nudging the armour on my shoulder.

"Whit is it?" Conan asks me. I shrug.

"We don't know. But if you find anything or anyone by that description, hang onto them or it. Okay?" I ask him and he laughs slightly.

"Ye soond loch ye dornt know whit yoo're daein." He laughs and I feel suddenly uncomfortable. Conan's eyes widen. "Ye dae know whit yoo're daein' reit?" He looks fearful now, his white skin turning almost translucent.

"Um, yes." I say, trying to sound confident. Azure snorts next to me and I want to hit her.

"Ye know… Ye kno hoo aam th' vessel? Diz 'at mean aam gonnae survife? It diz reit?" He looks so scared and I don't know what to say. I lie before Orion can answer in my place.

"Yes. Of course." I plaster on a fake smile and look deeply into his eyes. Trying to make him trust me.

After about a minute I break the stare and turn, unable to regain eye contact with him again, he'll know I'm lying and I'm terrible at it. I don't know what being the vessel means. If it meant he was safe, then I wouldn't have almost been killed five months ago. If I'd have been safe I wouldn't have absorbed Titus' darkness and had it almost rip me apart inside for weeks. As I make my way into the mind-bending speed of the whirlpool once more, headed into the unknown, I know only one thing.

No one is safe anymore.

7
Ciao
CALLIE

We exit the rumbling torrent of cyclical current in a daze that is soon lifted as the richness of unknown waters coats my gullet. I'm less disoriented this time around, mainly because I knew what to expect upon exit, and have tensed my entire body for the duration of the crazy whirlpool journey, terrified of landing in the arms of a psychotic stranger again.

"That never gets less mind bending." I hear Orion's slightly irritated tones and turn to see him exiting behind me. He might sound irritated, but he doesn't look the least bit dishevelled, his armour isn't skewed and his hair is, as always, tousled to perfection. He catches me staring and smiles, blinding me with Hollywood white.

"You don't look worse for wear." I comment, raising an eyebrow as I watch Azure and Philippe come through the portal behind him. Seconds later the rest of the Pod follow. The mermaids look flustered as always, and yet they present themselves without a single hair out of place. I roll my eyes at their constantly maintained grooming habits.

I mean, we're in the middle of what could be the end of life as we know it, and they're concerned about whether their bangs look ruffled.

"I know this place." A feminine voice reaches out to me, diffusing through the vivacious clearness of the water, a welcome change after the cloudiness of Moray Firth.

79

"You do?" I ask as the owner of the voice moves, ethereal and weightless, past the other mermaids. Marina's eyes are wide and sparkling.

"Yes, this is near the Baiae Ruins. I'd know the taste of Naplean waters anywhere." She hums to herself.

Naplean? So we're in Italy?

"Italy?" I ask, my voice betraying my excitement.

"Yes... I'm home." She looks like she might cry, and as the other mermaids swarm around her in a fuss, Azure sticks her tongue out and places her index finger an inch away from her mouth, pretending to make herself sick.

"Well, well, well, the Children of Atargatis... We've been wondering how long it would be before you made your little house call to European waters." The voice makes me jump slightly and I strain the musculature of my tail, pivoting so I can face the stranger from which it has come. A merman with curly black hair slicked back into a ponytail and olive skin is only inches from my face. I move back, unnerved by his proximity and the intensity that lies behind his sapphire eyes. That isn't the only thing about him that's sapphire coloured though, as I scan him and realise that his tailfin is entirely encrusted with the stone. His eyes are surrounded by a few smaller droplet stones too, their facets reflecting the fire of the low hanging sun above. If I had thought Saturnus' tailfin had been heavy duty on the sparkle, I was wrong and this guy made him look like a badly painted garden gnome.

"Uh, hello."

"Oh my dear, hello? That is not how the Water Nymphs greet one another. Come, let me show you."

Well, he's forward I'll give him that.

His accent is thickly Italian but his English is extremely fluent none-the-less. I breathe a sigh of relief at that, casting my mind back to confusing Scottish dialect flying drunkenly left, right and centre. As I do so, the mysterious sapphire-clad stranger comes toward me, placing a kiss on both sides of my face and then placing both hands on my shoulders a moment as he looks deeply into my eyes. "Ciao. I, am Enzo. You, are beautiful. The name of this sweet water lily is?" He takes a leisurely stroke backward and puts my hand in his, raising it to his lips and placing kisses upon my skin before beginning to trace his lips up my forearm. My eyes bulge.

What the hell is this guy doing? Is this normal in Europe? This kind of open intimacy with complete strangers?

I turn my head to look at Orion. His mouth has popped open and his brows are knitted in a taken back and mildly horrified look. I shoot him a terrified glance, conveying my complete confusion as I suddenly hear Enzo clearing his throat. My head snaps back around to face the strange man, not wanting to appear rude in the face of his... well, rudeness.

"Your name, sweet water lily?" He asks me once again, persistent in his affections with an intense gaze and serious expression gracing his features. I can hear someone laughing behind me at the spectacle of it all, and I just know it's Azure.

"I'm Callie." I mumble, feeling my face flush at his over amorous response.

"How beautiful that is. Fitting for a fragrant aquatic flower such as thee." My eyes widen at this.

What the hell is this guy on? Like seriously, am I being punked?

I feel the water around me stir and I know its familiar displacement. Orion is coming to my aid, ready as always to defend what he feels belongs to him.

"I am Orion. Crowned Ruler." He places out a hand and Enzo lies back lazily in the water, looking at him from head to fin.

"I am Enzo. Consort to Queen Isabella." He repeats Orion's tone in mocking and Orion narrows his eyes.

"So you know of us then? Surely you remember my father, Atlas?" Orion stares at him with no trace of amusement, asserting his dominance.

"Oh, why of course. Atlas. Come, let us take you into our temple and give you rest. You are surely tired from such a long journey, are you not? Let us tend to your wary bodies and nourish your wilting souls. Come." He decrees this with a flourish of his hands and I look to Orion. What the heck is all this about? I feel like I've swum right into the Renaissance.

"That was easy?" I shrug to Orion and he looks at me, concerned.

"He certainly thinks you are at any rate. Sweet water lily? Please!" He cocks an eyebrow in disgust and I feel my forehead crease.

"Maybe it's a European thing?" I say, wondering if it's just a cultural difference.

"You might be forgetting Callie that I am from Europe originally, trust me, that is not cultural."

"Oh really? Mister, *some people believe they can hear the call of the Ocean you know?* And we can't forget my personal favourite, *the ocean is really beautiful, isn't it?*" I quote his own words back at him, remembering what feels like a lifetime ago, when I was just a human girl, sitting on a beach, and he was just a stranger who I was wildly and misguidedly attracted to. He shoots me a tired and not even slightly amused glance and Marina bursts past us, obviously curious to see where Enzo will lead us.

"We better get going." I say. He nods, somersaulting back on himself to address the others.

"Come on, let's get to this temple. It seems like these 'Water Nymphs' knew my father, so this one looks like it's going to be an easy sell." He says it to raise their morale, but I know he doesn't know what lies ahead. He lied to them. But that's the thing; it's a necessary lie. If there's one thing I know now about leadership, it's that showing your fear to those you are leading can cause panic and among other things, chaos. Orion is getting the hang of things, slowly but surely, but I know, more than anyone else, that I still have miles to go before I sleep.

We move in the crystalline water, over reefs teeming with mantis shrimp, cuttlefish and lobsters. The colours of the flora and fauna are luscious, but that's not the most stunning thing about the path we take. The most incredible thing is the Baiae Ruins, the mosaic floors of once great temples, lain out bare for all to see as they're reclaimed by nature. Statues host a flurry of tasselled nudibranch and black sea urchins fill the ocular cavities of once magnificent saints and humble martyrs. We finally catch up to Enzo, who waits beside a teeming rock face.

"This doesn't look very temple like to me." I say to Orion and he shrugs, not bothering to respond. I hear Azure tutting behind me in impatience as Enzo moves, the sapphires in his tail shimmering and flickering with captured light from the sun. His hand flourishes outward from his form as he addresses me once more.

"Patience, Bella."

"My name isn't Bella." I turn to Orion and he cocks his head, his expression unimpressed.

"It means beautiful in Italian, Callie."

"Oh." I blush scarlet and he rolls his eyes.

"He can call me Bella anytime he likes." I hear Cole mumbling from behind me and I almost want to turn around and offer him my place.

As I'm debating this, I watch as Enzo holds out a fist and knocks three times on the heavy rock formation before us, casual as though he's picking up a date. He mutters something in Italian and Marina behind me laughs.

"What did he say?" I turn to her and she purses her lips, suddenly embarrassed.

"He's just cursing." Is all she elaborates as her scarlet tailfin sways beneath her in gentle rhythm. I watch her form, realising it's the most relaxed I've seen her since the death of her soulmate.

After a few minutes more of silence, a sudden movement from beneath the sand of the ocean floor becomes visible. The sand and rock tremble, shifting and sliding away as the rock beneath it is moved aside and an entryway is revealed.

"Huh, didn't see that one coming." I admit, realising I had expected the rock wall itself to be some kind of doorway.

"There is beauty in the unexpected, yes sweet water lily?" Enzo asks me with a wink, before disappearing. My mouth is hanging open in silent retort as Orion looks at me with a nervous expression.

"Stick by my side alright. I don't like his attitude." He whispers, trying to be discreet, but Marina gives him a disgruntled stare.

"This is common practice in Italy. Women and their beauty are revered above all things Orion. Surely you have not found your soulmate's beauty diminished after so little time?" She queries him and Orion turns to face her, squaring his shoulders.

"Of course Callie is beautiful. A blind man can see that. I'd just rather *he* kept his opinions to himself." Marina smiles, watching my reaction as though she was only goading him into such a compliment for my benefit. Another voice interrupts the debate about my looks, causing us to look back to Enzo.

"Come along, come along!" Enzo's impatient tones beckon me toward the hole in the floor of the seabed. However, as I go to move, Orion pushes me behind him with one arm, taking the lead. I descend shortly after him, my tailfin beginning only inches from the final tousles of his mahogany hair.

"Isabella! My darling! Look who has returned to our waters!" I hear Enzo's over excitable tones bouncing from the walls of the temple as I turn a full three hundred and sixty degrees in awe. I can now see why we have entered from above, because the entire temple is buried beneath the sands of the Mediterranean Sea. Lost, for years.

As I reach the stone floor of the building I take in my surroundings. High arches and stained glass windows with pictures of a God, yielding a shield and trident. The floors are sand swept, but decadent in the fact that they are also littered with jewels. The precious stones increase in frequency and my eyes rise in pursuit of them until they rest on the centrepiece of the room. A golden throne clad in red velvet, with a woman seated within its plush hold. Her hair is a gold dusted raven and her face speckled with rubies. I look down at her tail, ruby encrusted just as Enzo's is with Sapphires, and stare, blown away by the decadence of her form. Her torso is clad in a corset of fine gold mesh, the bustier rising and forming coral stalks as the bottom of the piece flares out into a mobile of delicate golden jellyfish ornaments. She's the picture of materialism, her head adorned with a crown that makes the Crown Jewels of England look like

84

something you'd find at a garage sale for a dollar fifty. Her lips are a plush red and her throat is clutched by a choker of onyx and yet more rubies.

"Isabella. My love. Look." Enzo is before Isabella now, who is looking down upon him with something teetering between adoration and disgust.

"Atlas and his Queen have returned?" She asks, her voice high pitched and harsh, commanding the man in front of her with absolute authority.

"No, Atlas is dead. I am his Son. Orion." Orion comes forward and bows respectfully; it's an odd situation, a Crowned Ruler bowing before a Queen. You'd think they'd forgo the formality of it all.

"And what of Shaniqua, his Queen?" Isabella asks, her chin tilting back downward so her raven locks billow outward from her pale face.

"She is gone. Mourning the loss of her soulmate." Orion admonishes. The rest of our pod has now filtered into the temple chamber and watches from behind us with fascination. Azure enters last, without Philippe, clumsily knocking sand down over herself as she lowers herself through the ceiling entrance. She exclaims, swearing. Isabella looks upward with distaste, waving some of the falling debris away with one hand.

"Well, that's very disappointing indeed." I feel something stir behind me and Marina takes a few strokes toward me and then starts to speak fluid Italian. Orion looks slightly shocked that she's being so forward, but soon she's gesturing to me and I feel unable to stop shifting my gaze from his expression to the intensely dark gaze of the Queen before me. The two Italian women laugh suddenly, and Marina comes forth in a flurry of scarlet and pushes me before the Royal couple. Enzo now stares down upon me also from Isabella's left side and I feel my body tense under their scrutiny.

"Just say your name and hello. Be respectful." Marina whispers in a harsh tone. I'm surprised she's ordering me around, but then she's not the outsider here, not as much as the rest of us.

"Hello Your Highness, I'm Callie, Orion's Queen." I put myself into the possessive position. Isabella frowns.

"Oh no my darling, you are not Orion's anything. He is your consort." She tilts her chin upward again, looking down at me with a smile. I kind of want to

85

do a little happy dance, because someone is actually recognising me as my own entity. As much as I know Orion respects me as an authority equal to his own, I'm yet to feel that way about the rest of the Occulta Mirum.

"I know right?" I go for casual, trying to seem happy and upbeat. Isabella is silent, her lips pursed and eyes wide as everything gets awkward really quickly. I hang there, wondering if I've made the biggest faux pas before I've even begun.

Way to go Callie. You suck. I castigate myself. I can feel Orion stir at my back, ready to take over. Suddenly Isabella bursts out into a hysterical laugh.

"Oh my goodness! She's *American?* Oh darling! Tell us, tell us of Hollywood. Tell us of Ashton Kutcher. Please…" She's gushing, before she turns to Enzo. "Enzo, darling, go and get Daniella. She'd *love* to hear this. Go on! Go!" She shoos him away as he turns and reluctantly exits the main room, sulking away down one of the sunken hallways. Isabella turns to me, her eyes ecstatic. "You simply must tell us all of the American fashions, oh the shoes you girls wear are crazy! But the dresses, the red carpet, it's all just so, *bellissima!*" She is gushing, but Orion gives a small cough, looking at me.

"I will, I will tell you anything you want to know! But we're here for more than just a visit. We're looking for the vessel." At this reminder her eyes darken.

"Yes, I am sorry to say we've had little luck on that front. We have been looking ever since Shaniqua's visit a while ago. Nothing." She's back to the serious manner she had adopted on our entry, like I've flipped a switch, hardening her back into an untouchable and cruel ruler that won't be messed with.

"That's alright, we might have a way to find them." I explain, feeling hopeful that this visit will be brief.

"Oh? Well, it'll have to wait darling. We've got other important business to attend this evening." She rises from her throne moving forward in a flash of bloody sparkle.

"There aren't demons are there?" I ask, looking around and feeling the hairs on the back of my neck rise.

"Oh no! It's far more fun and pressing! My daughter's betrothal is being announced tonight! There will be celebrating second to none. No expense has been spared. Of course, I expect you'll all be attending. The more the merrier. We are nothing if not the most decadent of creatures. I'm sure you'd agree." She stares at me, expecting a response.

"Oh of course, your tail is beautiful." I compliment her and she smiles, cat-like in her feline satisfaction.

"Why yes, it is. Thank you for noticing." She winks and takes a stroke back to sit in her throne once more. Marina is beaming from ear to ear and the mermaids are beginning to whisper and shuffle behind Orion and Cole, excited at the prospect of a grand celebration.

"Is it a full moon tonight?" I ask, wondering if I'll actually be able to attend this party.

"No." Orion shakes his head.

"Fear not. We have something that will aid you with that." Isabella flicks her wrist as though what she's saying means nothing at all.

"What do you mean?" I ask, feeling my curiosity grow.

"Moonstone, is what I mean. Shaniqua brought them here and asked us to store them away from your city. She said they were for special occasions only. But I think this counts, don't you?" Isabella twists, with one flick of her deep red tail, so she is now behind her throne. I notice now that behind her, boxes, crates and valuables have been stacked high into a pile for all to see.

"Is that 'Portrait of a young man' by Raphael?" I hear Orion call out, incredulous in his tone. I move backward by a foot so I'm by his side once more.

"Yes, yes, it is. Good eye. The Camorra wanted it moved overseas, but I just couldn't let it go. Haunting don't you think?" Isabella's discussing this half-heartedly whilst throwing goblets made of gold, necklaces worth a fortune, and a long lost and probably priceless Fabergé egg behind her, where each item lands with a clatter, dislodging sand and the odd crystal with it.

"Yes, quite." Orion replies quickly, turning to me. He lowers his voice, covering his face with a hand. "The mafia? She moves stuff for the mafia?!"

He looks horrified and suddenly I realise what it is she's just revealed. My mind is pre-occupied by this, but before I can respond to Orion, Isabella is before him, inches from his face and with something clutched in her palm. She looks terrifying.

"Yes, the mafia is what assisted me in amassing the wealth of the Water Nymphs, part of which you can see here. Well, they were, before I had them all slaughtered for trying to start exporting parts of Water Nymphs for a pretty penny." She hands him a cluster of white looking stones and smiles, she could be the devil with the look she exudes, or a deadly temptress. Orion closes his palm around the group of stones, putting them into the satchel that's slung across his shoulder with Sedna's Codex inside.

"So we just hold them?" I ask Isabella, trying to distract from talk of the mafia.

"I don't know, Darling. Shaniqua didn't say." She's suddenly distracted as a young girl comes around the corner. "Daniella! Sweetheart! Come and greet our guests! Their Queen is an American you know!" Daniella's eyes widen at the news of my origins and she turns, looking like a rabbit in headlights at the number of people she's confronted with. She's the demurest young woman I've ever laid eyes on, her hair is a caramel waterfall and her eyes are dark and large like her mother's, but these come with a bambi-like innocence I've not seen since I last laid eyes on Kayla. Her tailfin is a pure white and encrusted with pearls which also surround her eyes in an utterly unique eye mask. She's so petite, sweet looking even, that it's a sudden wonder that her and Isabella are related at all.

"Ciao." She says, fluttering her lashes, shy.

"Hi." I reply, moving forward and taking her hand in mine. She reaches forward and kisses both my cheeks, her lips not actually touching me in the slightest. We are interrupted in the middle of this formality by the eruption of a trumpet. I watch her eyes widen and her lips spread back in a smile.

"Casmire!" She breathes his name like a lovesick school child and so I assume the man to whom she is referring is her betrothed.

Behind the pod of mer, a pair of double doors open. I don't know where they lead, but I see nothing other than shadow.

Maybe they lead into tunnels? I muse. After all, we are underground.

"Welcome returning warriors! Tell me, what of Venice?" Isabella calls out to them, her long fingernails flowing artfully from her outreaching fingertips in ruby red.

"The Canals are safe once more, Your Highness." A male Water Nymph with an emerald encrusted tailfin comes forth, followed by a woman clad in garnets with a group of warriors in tow. They're all absolutely encrusted with rich jewels, ranging from Tanzanite to Amethyst, which shimmer wildly as I watch them pile forth, all covered in a thick layer of shining gold armour which is adorned with yet more preciousness. It's a wonder they exist with such anonymity, especially when every single thing about them is the complete opposite of subtle.

"And what of the infrastructure Casmire?" She looks to him with an impatient tapping of her long nails on the armrest of her throne. The young man removes his golden helmet, putting it under his arm as his hair, blonde and curly, is unleashed into the water. I watch Daniella as he runs his hand through it and I fear she might faint. He pivots to glance at us, as though he's concerned about releasing confidential information, and I momentarily glimpse his attractive peridot coloured pupils before he turns away once more.

"The infrastructure has been maintained for now, but as you know the canals are an ongoing maintenance job, Your Highness." He bows his head slightly toward her and she smiles.

"Very good. Many demons this time?" She asks, cutting off Enzo as he moves to speak.

"You know how the canals can be, but fortunately for us this time they were fairly close together." The woman next to Casmire speaks this time.

"Well, look at you two, Claudia. Don't you make quite the pair?" This comment from Isabella makes me suddenly confused as I watch the look that passes between Daniella and Casmire, discreet but not enough so that it's not all I can look at. Daniella fingers a silver whale tail pendant that's held around her neck, not particularly precious by the standards of what her mother is adorned with, but none the less, she continues to play with the charm, twiddling it back and forth between her thumb and forefinger.

"So, what do you think of my warriors, Callie?" Isabella rises and beckons me up onto the steps where her throne resides. Orion clutches my hand, wanting to pull me back but I shrug it off, swimming from his protective stance. I glide over to The Queen and the small assembly whose eyes follow my every motion. I'm both intrigued and pleased to see that there are both women and men in the group.

"I think you all look wonderful. Particularly the women." I decree as Claudia gives a tight smile.

"Ciao Callie, I am Claudia, commander of this group of warriors." She takes her helmet off and swings her head around, tossing lustrous black hair behind her golden, armour-clad, shoulder. Her face is filled by deep brown eyes that are surrounded by garnets in princess cut gems that speckle around her eyes and forehead. I'm loving that, yet again, a woman is in charge.

"Ciao." I reply, feeling the foreign term roll off my tongue like a magic word. What is it about speaking another language that makes me feel like a sophisticate?

"This is my intended, Casmire." She introduces the blonde haired Water Nymph and his eyes blaze a lime green as I watch him tear his gaze from Daniella to stare at me instead.

Am I the only one noticing that he's totally unable to take his eyes off her? Apparently so.

"It's wonderful to meet you Casmire. Ciao." I say the word again as he pulls me in and kisses both cheeks. He's a large man, his biceps bulging against the gold of his armour as his hands rest lightly on my shoulders.

"My soulmate, Orion." I gesture to Orion who's still watching me toward the back of the room. The group of warriors part and Orion takes measured strokes forward.

"Well, isn't he quite the catch." Claudia fans herself with her hand, lacking any emotional subtlety just like the rest of the Water Nymphs. She doesn't even look at Casmire, though he's floating right next to her and very attractive in his own right. Enzo flutters behind us, watching me with interest.

"Yes, he really is." I blush, grabbing Orion by the arm and watching him, bewildered at being the arm candy for once.

"Now we're all here, I think it's time we ready ourselves for the festivities ahead. Warriors, go and make yourselves presentable for transport to the Castella Aragon." Isabella barks the order, though her Italian accent caresses the harsh tone, curving it smooth and dulling its edge like the sea wears glass.

"Castella Aragon?" I ask, looking to Isabella. I wonder if she can sense my excitement. I've never told Orion this, but Italy is somewhere I've secretly always wanted to visit. Much more so than Paris, for me Italy seems much more like romance, especially when I imagine the food. I start to drool slightly at the thought of garlic bread and pizza as Isabella replies, jerking me back to the moment after my marinara Reverie

"Why of course, we rent a Castle nearby on the island of Ischia. It's beautiful there, very romantic." She winks at Orion who looks surprised. I peek up at him through lashes, my gaze laden with intent.

"You hear that Orion? Romantic." I say, just to rub in the fact that I'm in the position of power here.

"Is that a challenge, Miss Pierce?" He growls, not caring about the fact we're surrounded by complete strangers. After all, everyone else is terribly overt, so why should he hold back?

"Depends if you think you can rise to the occasion." I purr back and Isabella laughs, clapping.

"I like her, she's sassy, so *American*." She emphasises the final word, leaning back into the hold of her throne. She drapes an arm over one of the rests and gives a hand to Enzo, who leans forward in the water and takes it in hold. He caresses her wrist, kissing it gently so she giggles. Daniella looks away, blushing.

"So you're getting engaged? How wonderful!" Orion turns to Daniella who shrinks back from him. She's such a tiny thing and Orion is huge in comparison.

"Yes… Paolo. He is my intended." She says it, but her eyes are watering with oily tears. Casmire looks away, turning back to the warriors and leading them slowly from the room and into the shadows of the sprawling ruins.

"How lovely." Orion says. "Let me introduce the rest of our pod!" He raises his arms, trying to get into the loose but happy spirit of our hosts. The rest of the mer come forward from the back of the room and I watch Enzo, his eyes falling across the mermaids one by one. A chill runs up my spine, and not in a good way. Azure, I notice, stays back in the shadows. I glide across the temple chamber, my tail flicking up emeralds and rubies mixed in with sand.

"You okay?" I ask her and she rolls her eyes.

"Yes I'm fine, I don't need a babysitter. I just don't fancy going and being quite so touchy feely yet. That's all." She shrugs and leans back against the stone of the temple wall.

"Suit yourself." I say, turning away. I've tried with her, I have. But there's a line. I know her sister just died, but I can't help her if she won't let me in.

I head back over to the group of mermaids who are all listening to Isabella like she's Atargatis herself. Marina is in animated conversation with Claudia who has remained in the throne room with us and Isabella is discussing the night's festivities

"Callie, Isabella says they have maids. Like actual maids!" Skye is babbling again as Alannah turns to me.

"There's going to be a feast, and dancing!"

"Callie, do you think they will have chocolate cake? I'm dying for a bite… just one!" Rose exclaims. Fahima and Ghazi stay in their usual solemn twosome to one side and Cole watches Enzo with an admiring eye. I get the impression though that Enzo is aware of, and uninterested by, Cole's fascination as he comes up behind Isabella and continues to watch over her every motion.

"Woah, okay, we're all excited! Just be polite and don't get drunk, no matter what!" I scold them. Isabella comes up behind me.

"Worry not Callie, I have many young male warriors, they will take care of your maidens, no problem. Women are held in the highest esteem here. And, if they wish to get a little tipsy, I have wine being imported by the gallon. A special Sinclair vintage, very expensive, very *bellissima*." She purrs and the girls suddenly look like they might burst with excitement.

For a moment, just a moment, as I turn and find myself in Orion's arms and kissing him deeply, as I hear him whisper promises of a night I won't forget in one ear, I do forget. I forget that we're almost at war, I forget there are demons in Venice and that its city is sinking into the oblivions of the water below. I forget that I'm a Queen and I let myself be lulled into his embrace and most of all into falling in love, oh so slowly, with Italy.

8

Bellissima

ORION

The night air is warm and thick as I float in the shallows of the bay of Naples. It's a highly populated area, one which I would usually stay away from while exiting the sea completely naked, but it's where Isabella decreed we will be picked up from, so here I float, Callie at my side and with a moonstone in my palm. There had been enough for one each, just, considering Azure didn't need one because she can phase. I look sideways to Isabella, who rises from beneath the surface in fluid silence.

"So I'm assuming you don't need the full moon either?" I ask her, raising my voice slightly above the crashing of the water onto the shore.

"No Darling, of course not! We are The Children of Neptune and governed only by our desires, that which as you well know are governed in themselves by the planetary alignment. I assume you're into Astrology no?" She cocks an eyebrow and I almost want to laugh, *governed only by their desires*? I snort to myself. *Oh shouldn't they be so lucky.*

"Uh no. Not really." I say, rubbing the water off the back of my neck as it begins to drop in cold slithers down my spine.

"Let me guess, you're an Aquarius?" She looks to Callie who shrugs.

"That reminds me, when is your actual birthday?" Callie looks to me, her breasts still covered in aquamarine scales, a look of complete disregard for where we are suspended plastered across her face.

94

"I'm over five hundred. I don't think it matters at this point." I shrug and Callie scowls. "We'll talk about it later." I brush her off, anxious of the stark stroll ahead.

"So how do these stones work?" Rose asks loudly, breaking through the din of chatter that has started up behind us as we wait.

"I don't know." I admit, shrugging. My father really ought to have thought of these things, of leaving better instruction, but he didn't. Instead I'm left bumbling around in the dark like a fool, a spectacle for all my people to observe and disappointing in every regard. I look to Callie as she turns the smooth milky stone over in her palm. She holds it up, closing one eye as though that will help things. Sometimes I find her so strange, but I suppose it's those quirks that make her one of a kind. All of a sudden, the moonstone catches the light of the waxing crescent suspended low in the sky. Then, as Callie jumps at the shock of it all, she almost drops the stone. I watch her eyes widen as it begins to glow in her shaking fingers.

"It's getting cooler." She says, fascinated. I hold my stone up, bathing it in the moonlight as well and the stone begins to glow too, cooling between my fingers. I feel a familiar tingle creep up my spine, before my legs return in a momentary fading of fin to flesh.

"Well, that was kind of awesome." Callie says, covering her breasts with her arms to protect her modesty.

"Where to?" I ask Isabella as I watch her beginning her climb up the shore, now naked and unashamed from the waist down.

"My men will attend you. Come, follow." She beckons me with a long limb and I can't help but take a male moment to appreciate the woman's physique, her form is willowy, pale and flawless. Her hips curve like that of a woman, not a girl, and the raven waves of her hair tumble down her spine in a flood of dark contrast, glistening gold in the moonlight.

"Come on, hurry." I grab Callie's hand and move up the beach, the sand clinging to my wet feet.

I really do hate sand, I think, cursing the grainy substance and its knack of ending up in completely odd places

95

As we approach the middle of the beach, which is blanketed by night, I see Isabella bend down and pick something up off the floor. She drapes it around her shoulders. A silken robe. As I step forward I see there's a stack of them. Then a glint of something catches the corner of my eye, or multiple somethings I should say, as I notice a fleet of men in black slim cut suits, handling shiny weaponry and posted at regular intervals around the beach's edge.

"Your men?" I question Isabella, who is saying something to Callie about how fine the silk of the robes is. I grab one quickly and throw it over my shoulders and Isabella pouts slightly before answering.

"Oh yes Darling, and why, you don't need to cover up on my account." She purrs as I roll my eyes. "Too much?" She asks me with a giggle, stepping a little too close to me and tracing her long nails around the curve of my shoulder and down my back. Callie watches her in amusement.

"Just nothing I haven't heard before." I say, going for cocky in the face of her outright sexual audacity. Isabella laughs once more as Enzo moves toward her, swooping up her long body in his arms and carrying her up the remainder of the sand. I watch as the rest of the pod get robed, the mermaids examining the quality of the fabric as though it's some sort of life or death type information they're gathering about the Water Nymphs.

"Definitely Mulberry silk." I hear Alannah mutter as she places the robe over her petite shoulders. As the group settles into calm chatter I take a moment to look around, turning on the spot and taking in the sprawling city that spreads back from the bay, the stars that twinkle overhead and the light breeze that ruffles my hair. This moment of calm is shattered only too fast as I hear Callie gasp as a roar erupts and lights flood the road that runs behind the bay.

Damn, what an engine.

Callie holds out her hand to me with a massive smile plastered on her face. We run, away from the pod and toward the edge of the sand, toward the beastly machines.

"Oh my god is that a Ferrari!?" I hear Callie exclaim above the roar, placing her hands up to her mouth in delight. I grin like a fool, loving being able to watch her like this.

96

"But of course Darling? What else?"

"Well, back home I have this little red vintage...." She begins with a nostalgic half-smile.

"Oh Darling no... you leave cars to the Europeans. The only two things that should be of vintage in my opinion are art and wine, and I hope you have noticed that one without the other is frightfully boring no? This red one here is mine..." She gestures to the vehicle in front of us, as I'm beginning to wonder how we're all going to fit in a two seater.

As if someone has read my mind, hundreds of roars erupt and headlights blind me as I lift my hand up, shielding myself from their unforgiving rays. That's when I realise; the entire beach is surrounded by hundreds of sports cars in every shade you could imagine. Isabella looks at Callie.

"How about you drive a *real* car Darling?" Callie looks like she might puke with excitement. "That one right there is yours. But no crashes darling, it's rented, and I hate paperwork." She tosses a key over her shoulder and Callie reaches out to grasp them. I watch her eyes ignite with a kind of feral power hunger I hadn't seen in her since she was infected with Titus.

What is it about cars that does this to women? I wonder as I look to her and she takes my hand.

"Oh no Darling, this one here is riding with me." Isabella purrs, grabbing me by the front of the robe and pulling me toward the shimmering, apple red, sports car. Enzo gets in his own deep blue Ferrari a few cars back, taking a sullen looking Azure with him as she rolls her eyes like she's unimpressed. He pulls out into the street quickly, passing Isabella and giving her a wink from his passenger side door, as I watch him pass I can't deny I'm relieved that Azure won't be driving one of these monsters.

"Will everyone be alright?" I ask Isabella, concerned as I watch the maidens climb into the variety of cars parked adjacent to the sand. They're perfectly equidistant in their spacing to one another and each one comes equipped with an armed driver.

"Of course Darling! They will have the times of their lives! I promise!" She's so over enthused I wonder if she actually knows what she's saying. I

97

know it would be easy to get caught up in all the glamour of the Water Nymph's world, but I can't forget I'm here with a job to do. I need to find the vessel, and I doubt they're inside the two seater Ferrari.

Isabella leans over and opens the door, waving her wrist for me to get in. "Get in darling, I'll put the heater on!" She exclaims as I take one last look at Callie as she lowers herself into the gold Ferrari behind me. I see Sophia in the passenger side, looking mightily uncomfortable. I know she doesn't like the human world, especially after the nightmare we had getting her soulmate back from Chicago all those many moons ago.

With those haunting memories banished once more, I reluctantly lower myself into the plush leather seating next to Isabella, who turns to me, placing her long nails on my leg.

"Ooh, the seat is warm!" I exclaim, feeling the heat seeping into my buttocks.

"Heated seats darling! It's a must I'm sure you'd agree?" She puts her seatbelt on and waits for me to do the same. "Buckle up darling, I don't want to have to watch my speed. These Naplean streets are like a rat race. It's far too exhilarating to be worrying about your little head going smoosh on the pavement now. Don't you think?" I don't answer, not one for enjoying a 'smooshed' head I begin to wonder about her driving capabilities.

Though, I muse, *she's probably better at it than me.* Driving wasn't really my forte; I far prefer a horse any day.

I hear the engine in the car behind us start before Callie pulls out and overtakes us, revving her engine far louder than I know is necessary. I'm so busy watching the gold car pass, that I don't even realise Isabella has started the engine of the car we're sitting in. She's at the front of the queue of parked cars, so takes off down the road like a bullet from the barrel of a shot gun. I feel the kick back of the turbo as I'm pushed back into my seat before being thrown to my right as she turns the car a sharp left and then presses down hard on the accelerator, cutting in front of Callie's car as she turns, proceeding to race down the far too narrow Italian streets. I can hear Callie behind us, frustrated by the sneaky inside turn and revving, longing to overtake again. I watch her frustrated hand signals in my side mirror and laugh as I see Sophia's terrified expression. She looks like she might be sick.

As Isabella tuts with impatience, a street cart, clearing away their day's market produce, moves in front of her full beam headlights. She fiddles with the radio and an Italian song, featuring an acoustic guitar and violin of some sort, comes on over the speakers.

"Oh I love this one!" She claps her hands, jumping up and down in her seat. The song continues and I catch the chorus.

"What does Volare mean?" I ask her, trying to make small talk as the cart finally disappears around the corner.

"Why darling, it means to fly." With that she pushes her small foot down on the accelerator and unleashes the power of the vehicle, full force. I'm crushed back into my seat with the force of the launch and as I hear revving I know Callie is tailing us closely. Isabella wasn't wrong about the streets either, as they twist and turn, making me feel like I'm in a kind of mouse maze. We slide around corners, Isabella tapping her fingernails on the steering wheel to the rhythm of the song, shaking her head to the beat as she twists the steering wheel to the left and then once again to the right. I let myself relax slightly and after a while it becomes apparent she knows what she's doing.

Callie turns off at another narrow junction and I wonder where she's going as my anxiety begins to niggle at me. Then I let it go. I breathe, remembering: *She can take care of herself.* I let my palms tap out the beautiful Italian melody on my knees as I lean back and let the speed clutch at me, making my stomach somersault and drop at sudden moments. I kind of like it, the speed, the excitement. Maybe I should ask Callie to teach me how to drive when this is all over… if we're both still around that is. The thought depresses me as the song comes to an end with a final few strums on the guitar.

We turn a final corner and the sides of the car which were previously surrounded on each side by white semi-detached housing opens up, leaving us on a narrow straight of road. Ahead of us, an old castle is perched atop an island, covered in greenery that obscures the building's full size. Isabella presses her foot down again, watching me as I gaze out of the window, seeing the flickering lights which light the nights of ordinary people's lives twinkling around the bay from which we've just come. We speed down the bridge which connects the island to the land, before twisting on what could be the head of a pin around the tight bends that lead up to the main building. As the trees become sparse the higher we rise, I see how close we've really gotten as we race up the final incline and up to the front of the castle. There's a red runner coming out from two wide open wooden double doors and lit sconces are on either side, mounted on the exterior of the brick wall and lighting the entrance.

Then, I notice something else and rush to remove my seatbelt, not waiting for Isabella to turn off the engine before opening my car door and hurrying out onto the gravel.

"Well how was I supposed to know which pedal was the brake? These European cars have THREE pedals!!! What the hell do you need three for??" Azure is yelling. I roll my eyes, looking at the beautiful blue Ferrari which is now wrapped around a lamp post in the gravel parking area.

"My beautiful Ferrari! You destroyed her!!!" Enzo has his hands on his head, running them through his hair in distress.

"Oh my goddess, what happened? Are you alright? You let her drive?" I exclaim, not knowing who is more to blame, Azure for crashing the car or Enzo for letting her drive it in the first place.

"Oh Si, we're fine! My car on the other hand… look what you did to my baby!" Enzo is yelling.

"I'm so sorry, I'll pay to have it repaired! Whatever you need." I make the promise and Azure is practically beside herself, laughing at the distress of Enzo over something made of metal and leather. I know she must be thinking there are far worse things to lose.

"What happened?" I hear Isabella coming up behind me.

"I'm really sorry. My sister here didn't realise European cars were wired… differently. I'll cover the damages." I sigh and turn to her, she throws her head back in a huge laugh.

"Darling, it's a rental. We're insured against act of American. Do not worry your pretty little head over it." She flicks her wrist and extends out her fingers, brushing away the problem as though Azure's no more than spilled champagne on the interior. I turn to look at the smouldering wreck. The lamppost has made a giant crumpled dent in the hood of the once pristine vehicle and it smokes a little where the metal pole has hit the engine.

Jesus Azure. You're killing me. I think to myself. *What is she trying to do, make sure the world is doomed?*

I hear the rumble of another engine approaching and turn to see the Gold Ferrari that belongs to Callie pulling into the castle parking lot. She must have taken a detour to test out the car for a bit longer, I deduce, watching as she leads in the rest of the convoy of beautiful Italian cars into the Castle courtyard. As her vehicle pulls in she turns the engine off and steps out, her blonde hair having dried and sprung into curly ringlets in the heated interior of the car. Her smooth legs and bare feet come out first, slender and gorgeous. Then her body moves up and out, graceful in a way I had not noticed she has become. She stands on the gravel, her bare feet exposed to its torment. As I watch her I can't bare that thought, so I forget the fact that I've got a job to do, I forget that I'm stood next to Isabella and I stride forward, my own bare feet scraping against the gravel. Callie turns to me as I approach her, surprised and expectant with her face lit up from the rush of the drive.

I sweep her up, kissing her and move over to the red velvet carpet, running my hand through her curly hair as her arms snake up around my neck. She giggles against my lips, once again eighteen. How she does this I'll never know, making me feel as though it is us alone, with nobody watching. I set her down reluctantly, breaking whatever spell she has cast over my better judgement.

"Um… What was that for?" She says, stumbling slightly, off kilter from my kiss.

"I didn't want you to hurt your feet." I mumble turning to look at the rest of the pod. The mermaids are staring at me with odd expressions, like they're surprised and jealous all at once. "Can I help you ladies?" I ask them, tilting my head as Isabella strides over and they erupt into giggles.

"Come on lover boy. Let's get you suited up and your Queen dressed in a manner appropriate for a grand celebration. Daniella!" She suddenly turns from me and exclaims her daughter's name. Daniella moves forward from behind the crowd of my people, her face red as beetroot. She had arrived in a white Ferrari I think, accompanied by a gun toting driver dressed in all black who remains close to her. I'm not too sure he had been in the car with her though, I had been too busy ogling my soulmate.

"Yes. That would be lovely. Thank you." I say, formal in my tone. Isabella strides forward, her long pale legs making short work of the distance between us.

"Enzo, take the boys and get them to Gordo. He'll know what to do!"

"Gordo?" I ask her.

"Yes, our tailor. You don't think I'd put you in off the rack do you? Ugh, darling. Just no." She waves me forward and I move through the door. I turn back, making sure everyone is following and see Fahima slapping Ghazi's arm, looking annoyed. He rolls his eyes and picks her up, though he's shorter than I am and he stumbles slightly under Fahima's weight. I close my eyes and laugh slightly, trying to keep it subtle. Poor Ghazi.

"Gentlemen, upstairs to our tailors. Though Enzo, the Crowned Ruler will see Gordo, yes?" Isabella commands and Enzo nods meekly. He looks so out of his element, as though he longs to be in control but isn't. Callie is a strong woman, but she wouldn't treat me like a lapdog either. I sigh as he begins to lead me upstairs before pivoting to catch Callie's eye. I also glimpse the lingering gazes of other mermaids and Water Nymphs who I've never met and I wish they wouldn't be so obvious. Turning away I head upstairs, no doubt to be prodded and poked by Gordo.

CALLIE

We're sitting in an elegantly decadent dressing room. It's expansive, bigger even than the parlour at the Lunar Sanctum and I'm behind a screen being fitted into what I can only be described as a highly ornate torture device. Marina is behind me, pulling the strings as tight as they'll go on the corset undergarment, but only because I refused to have one of the extremely pushy maids do it.

"Breathe in more, Callie."

"If I breathe in anymore, Orion will be taking a corpse to dinner, Marina. I can barely breathe as it is! Holy crap!" I complain and she pulls on the corset strings one last time.

"There!" She exclaims, finally satisfied.

"Oh Callie darling, come on out and let me see!" I hear Isabella's tones and I sigh, feeling only slightly like a Barbie doll. I step out from behind the screen and the mermaid's turn around to see me, their eyes wide and smirks on their faces. I'm not wearing anything except the corset, panties and high heeled, cream satin shoes. These girls have seen more of my naked body than most, so by this point I'm lacking the ability to feel shy or even attempt to cover my modesty.

"What are you all staring at?" I growl, slightly self-conscious despite myself. Azure is giggling in the corner.

"Just you complaining." Says Rose.

"Why? This is horrible! I can hardly breathe!" I exclaim, trying not to sound ungrateful, but feeling myself getting lightheaded.

"Callie, this is what all of us grew up with. Alannah and Rose in particular. They were ladies of high esteem." Skye reminds me. I gape at them, and Rose smirks.

"Seriously?" I cock an eyebrow and they both nod. I'm suddenly realising why it is that their priorities are so out of whack, they've clearly been starved of oxygen for far too long. Azure's eyes narrow suddenly. She rises to her feet.

"You know this is just a device to stop you being able to breathe enough to make a run for it right?" I ask them and they all snort. I'm about ready to rip this corset off.

"Well, Callie, I think Orion would like it." Azure comments. The mermaids and the other Water Nymphs turn, surprised to hear her speak.

"What do you mean?" I ask her, curious suddenly.

"Well, it might be a long time ago, my brother did love a girl in a corset. Something about ripping them off..." She says this wistfully, although caught in a memory none of us are privy to. It makes me think.

Orion was a man of old fashioned taste. Perhaps he would prefer me in something a little more old world...

As I'm lost in this reverie I see something pass between the mermaids as they look to each other. The other Water Nymphs go back to the making of their faces and gazing upon their reflections as maids go about taming their long dark hair. Daniella watches me with interest, but I don't look directly at her, for I know she's shy.

"What? Spit it out." I say, not feeling in the mood for messing around. Isabella pours a glass of wine and passes it to me, as though she knows I'll need it.

"It's just..." Rose begins, but then stops herself. Finally, I seek Sophia's eyes and she rolls them slightly.

"Fine, if none of you want to ask then I will. You do enough giggling about it. Why don't you just ask her?" She's snapping, still dressed in a robe and waiting for the maids to be done with the Water Nymphs and move on to her hair, which is still damp and ratty.

"What is it?" I ask, frowning. For them to be this nervous it must be serious.

"They want to know... what it's like, being with *him*." Sophia snaps, taking a giant slug of wine. She looks seriously cranky, but she did throw up out of the window of my Ferrari not an hour ago. Then again, maybe it's not such a good idea for her to be having alcohol.

"What? Orion?" I look at them, confused. Why is that a big deal?

"Yes. Oh Callie, he's so wonderful... I just..." Rose looks up at me and sighs. Then Skye starts up with another question.

"What's he really like? In private? He's just so rugged and... silent around us..." Then she trails off.

"Yeah, I bet he's sensitive, you know like in a really deep way..." Alannah sighs and they all lean in as I sit down on a red satin pouf, feeling the corset constrict, I take a sip of wine. This was a weird conversation already.

"I don't get why you didn't just ask me this earlier? Is it something you're really that interested in?" I look down into their enraptured faces. They nod. Even some of the Water Nymphs turn to each other and one of them whispers to the other, "Is that the *fine* Ruler?" she looks to me and giggles while her friend at the mirror next to her nods to her friend with flushed cheeks.

"Orion and I... it's complicated." I begin and Isabella laughs out loud.

"They're not asking about that Callie. They want to know about his... endowment." The other girls giggle and I roll my eyes at Isabella's joke, all of them looking to me.

"Orion waited a long time to meet me. I guess that's why everything is so intense with us. I'm still getting used to him. He really, just, takes my breath away sometimes."

"Like that fluttery feeling in your stomach?" Sophia asks me with a smile, her eyes glazed, clearly thinking about her own soulmate.

"Yes. All the time." I admit. The mermaid's get even closer to me, inching forward with a slight shuffle across the floor where most of them sit, cross legged. I take another sip of my wine.

"I remember when it was like that in the beginning with Oscar..." Sophia says in a small voice.

"You mean it's not now?" I ask her, interested. Was this flame between Orion and me going to flicker to embers?

"Oh Callie, surely you don't believe that your relationship will be this exciting forever?" Isabella splutters, laughing.

"What do you mean?"

"I see how he looks at you. Like you're the moon and the sun wrapped into one. That will diminish. Love becomes domesticated. Like all things." She says this like it's common knowledge. I feel my stomach tense in disappointment and my heart falter. I don't want this to end. The kiss he had given me when I had arrived here at the Castella Aragon had been so sweet, so tender. If I have to live eternity without another I think I might just go and sun bathe now.

"Especially now you and Orion are ruling over the mer. That is a lot of responsibility to balance with romance, don't you think?" Claudia speaks up from a nearby dressing table, her long raven locks being piled up onto her head by a bustling and curvy maid. Azure narrows her eyes as she watches the conversation, but doesn't say anything. She turns and eyes me from the mirror, brushing out her own hair because the maids are too scared to touch her, acting like she doesn't care.

"So you're saying he'll fall out of love with me, over time?" I ask them, hearing the waver in my tone. Rose frowns.

"I'm saying you have to keep a man like that interested. You can't just expect him to fall all over you when you don't make any effort to entice him." Her voice is making me want to slap her, but then I wonder... Is she right? Have I been lazy? Am I finding this new type of love with Orion so effortless because I'm not trying hard enough?

"So I should do what?" I ask her with a cocked head. She raises on eyebrow and gets up from the floor, walking on the balls of her feet and taking a sip of the champagne in her glass. She wheels out a rack of dresses, that look like they come from the renaissance period, from behind another giant vintage screen adorned with gold Fleur de lis.

"I say, we need to make you into what Orion loves, a part of his old world so to speak. So suck it up, Pierce. The corset stays."

9

Betrothed

ORION

I'm waiting again. Always waiting for something or other, that's me. This time it's for Callie, and once again I'm at the bottom of a staircase, waiting for her to descend. Everyone, including Daniella and her betrothed, Paolo, are already downstairs. Azure is at the back of the hall, purposefully not mingling and Isabella and Enzo are laughing ridiculously loud at something probably banal. The lighting is warm and the sconces dance a hearty flame on the walls. Tapestries hang and priceless antiquities stand on pedestals littering the space. The stone floor would usually sap the warmth from this place, but in this instance it doesn't, instead increasing the temperature and making me sweat.

I sigh, shifting from foot to foot. This suit is too damn tight. I don't know what Gordo thought he was dressing: me, or the lamppost that Azure crashed into. Either way, I think the lamppost would be more comfortable. The suit is skin tight, hugging me and making it so if I slouch the button on the jacket looks like it may bust because my pectorals are too wide for the cut. My biceps also feel like they've been bandaged to the point where they're losing blood circulation, bulging against the fabric in a way that's really quite obscene. The tailor had been pushy and I remember feeling slightly sick as Gordo told me over and over how amazing I supposedly look. If you ask me, he wouldn't have known how to measure my inseam properly if I'd had the pattern tattooed on my inner thigh. These trousers are something called 'skinny leg', whatever that means. I shuffle in them, claustrophobia creeping in against the expensive cotton, as I muse that perhaps it's a way for the women to assess the assets of a man before entering courtship. The leather shoes on my feet are designer apparently, but they pinch my toes as they narrow at the end, making me worry I'll trip over them.

As I stand, extremely uncomfortable and missing my tailfin, I realise that I'd much prefer armour any day, or even t-shirt and jeans as opposed to this Italian cut nightmare. Suddenly, I wonder…

Is this how women feel in heels and those tight dresses they wear?

I'm horrified at the idea of something this uncomfortable being daily routine, and vow to immediately ask Callie what clothes she wants stocked to the beach house for future visits. I've been dressing her for the past six months, but it's never actually occurred to me to ask what she feels comfortable in. She was right when she said I was trying to push her into a fantasy. I had almost forgotten she is a person too, with feelings and preferences. I vow, as the hallway quietens and people move through to the banquet hall, to always ask her what it is she desires. She has a right to those choices.

A gaggle of mermaids flutter down the stairs. Sophia is among them, wearing an ornate lilac gown with gold embellishments. She looks like something out of the old world from which I've come, and it startles me.

"Callie's now coming. She just needed a minute to catch her breath." She has a sly smile on her face and I wonder what she means. Everyone is here now, everyone except her and as I'm beginning to vibrate with impatience, I finally catch a glimpse of her. She's walking along the balcony corridor from where she's been dressed, flushed and hurried in her step. Her hand grips onto the polished balustrade and as she turns I see why. She's dressed in an expansive and ornate aqua and gold gown. The cut of the neck is square and I can tell she's got a proper corset on underneath making her waist look even tinier than usual. The gown has layers, lace and taffeta under the over garment. Her face is pained as she takes each step and I can tell she's struggling to breathe. Her hair is curly and piled up on her head like how women wore their hair long ago. I wonder what has prompted this look. I had seen the other girls dressed similarly, but I had never thought they'd wrangle Callie into one of those god

108

awful contraptions. She finally reaches the bottom of the staircase and smiles at me, her cheeks rosy and eyes wide.

"Hello, good Sir. Ready for dinner?" She asks me, fluttering her eyelashes.

"You look very... different." I whisper to her, smiling through my surprise.

"Good different?" She asks, batting those lashes again.

"Yes. Of course. Beautiful." I adjust my earlier compliment and she beams before exhaling and pulling me in for an overly amorous kiss. I'm not ready for it and I find myself out of breath.

"Come, we must join the others. It's time for dinner." I say sternly, wondering if she's forgotten we're here to do a job.

"Oh, okay." She looks sad so I change the subject quickly.

"Do you have any inkling as to who the vessel for Neptune might be?" I ask her and she shakes her head, ringlets bouncing.

"No, I can't say I have. I think we should ask Isabella. She might have some more information we don't know." Callie flutters her lashes once more, tempting me, before taking my arm as we proceed past the antiquities and lit sconces and adjourn into the banquet hall where the rest of the pod is waiting.

"Where have you been?" Cole asks me with a raised eyebrow. I don't know why, but something about this irks me slightly. I respect Cole deeply, but neither he nor any member of this pod have any claim to control how I manage my time.

"The fault is mine, Cole." Callie says smiling. "It took me a while to get dressed. I'm not used to all the finery." She makes the excuse for me and I turn, grateful to have her on one arm. In a way she's slowly becoming like armour, protection from the judgement of those closest to me. I know she won't agree with every decision I make internally, but she's not exuding displeasure toward them either. She is, in fact, becoming quite the confidant and necessary consort to the crown. I watch her as she says hello to a few of the Water Nymphs with long raven hair who I am yet to become acquainted, and admire her easy smile and way with people. I'm a lucky man indeed.

"Now that all of our esteemed guests have arrived, please be seated!" I hear Isabella command, her tones high pitched and demanding above the din of small talk. Enzo approaches me through the crowd, smirking slightly as he sees the cut of the suit in which I'm standing and how completely it doesn't suit my broad stature.

"Isabella would like you to join her at the head of the table please." He says this curtly and I wonder if he's still angry about the fact Azure ran his beloved car into a pole.

Probably, I muse, looking around to the corners of the room encased in a shadow that creeps, only to be banished by yet more lit sconces, searching for the sullen yet beautiful face of my sister. I spot her just behind me as I pivot slowly, feeling her gaze on my spine. She pokes her tongue out at me before striding forward to take her place silently at the table. Quickly realising that everyone is doing the same in taking their seats, I look now to Enzo, following his slim figure through the crowds of settling individuals and finding myself, with Callie in tow, moving toward the head of the hall. Isabella looks upon me fondly with a gracious smile, dressed in a deep merlot red, just as I expected. She's wearing another thick golden choker with a giant ruby held in its centre, surrounded by onyx stones woven in between the metal of the piece. It's eye catching for sure, and like everything else she does, just a little too much.

"Darlings sit! I'm about to make a toast to start the evening!" She demands. I do as she asks, sliding out the mahogany chair with red padding for Callie before seating myself beside her. As I bend at the waist to sit, the crotch on my trousers moves upward, making me blanch slightly.

This suit and I are going to have a problem. I curse, fidgeting and trying to make myself comfortable.

I look around, noting the heartily lit space and multiple fireplaces that blaze, creating a stifling warmth despite the cold stone walls. Each wall is covered in brightly coloured tapestries and art, making the room look truly regal in its standing. The table is solid mahogany with a scarlet runner down the middle. Each place, as you would expect, is set with far too many knives and forks alongside the alabaster and gold flatware. Isabella reaches out, ringing a bell that has been placed in front of her.

As if awaiting the sound like a pack of trained dogs, a swarm of butlers execute the most synchronised and blatantly organised serving of wine I've ever seen. I watch as the other members of the pod take it all in, the glistening silver trays, the sharp black suits and dapper white shirts, the tinkling of bloody red wine into clear cut crystal glasses. It really is the lap of luxury I'm sitting in, and yet something about it all makes me unable to relax. I don't know if it's because I'm tempted to get lost in the effortless materialism of the Water Nymph's world, or whether it's because I'm ruler and I know I cannot. As I sit, I find myself torn between enjoyment and terror, wondering if sitting down to silver service in the middle of the biggest war the mer have ever faced is quite what the doctor ordered.

"Are you alright?" Callie asks, placing a hand atop mine as she reaches for her wine glass with the other.

"I'm just anxious is all. We need to find the vessel!" I whisper harshly. As I do I'm caught unaware as the crowd silences and I watch Isabella get to her feet. I lean back so I'm upright, pretending I wasn't just whispering to Callie at all. The suit continues to cling to me, suffocating my skin with its tight python-esque grip.

"We are here tonight to celebrate the bringing together of two souls, those which have been so very blessed by Neptune and all his riches. It is with great pride that I would like to announce the engagement of my daughter, Daniella and her beloved Paolo!" Isabella gestures to the two supposed 'lovebirds', who are sitting directly opposite us.

So, Paolo is Daniella's intended? I wonder, confused at how such a match has been made. I mean, I'm not an expert, but I could have sworn Daniella had feelings for Casmire. I watch as the young woman before me sits, uncomfortable under the scrutiny of her people. She fiddles with a pendant hanging around her neck incessantly. My gaze shifts as Paolo gets to his feet and puffs out his chest. I examine his features; he has a slim face, light blue eyes and dark curly hair that falls to his shoulders in thick waves. His eyes catch mine observing him and he shoots me a smile that's just a little too white from across the table.

"I am just wanting to say, how blessed I am to have this beautiful angel beside me. I know you fell from heaven for me, Bella. For if you had not, why is it now that I cannot look at you without bringing myself to tears at your bellissima smile...." I wonder momentarily if he might burst into song, or a poem, or perhaps some sort of interpretive dance. Suddenly I wonder, is this how I look to outsiders when I'm lost in Callie's smile? Do I too look like a complete sap?

"Thank you Paolo. It is mine and Enzo's desire that you and Daniella go on to live the full and rich lives that you deserve. We are thrilled that you will be joining our family." With this she begins clapping and then the rest of the table join in. Daniella has Paolo's mouth thrust upon her as she sits stiffly in her seat. Her large brown doe eyes fall into her lap as it ends, a look of guilt and shame melding onto her innocent face. As the clapping continues, I watch as a member of my own pod rises and leaves the table quietly. I excuse myself, grateful for the distraction, as food is wheeled out promptly on silver trollies and run after the fleeing maiden.

"Marina!" I yell out. She falters momentarily in her hurried step as she moves across the hall from which we've all just come. She doesn't stop there though, she continues to moves hurriedly, taking off out of the open double front doors and into the night. I feel the suit chaffing but ignore it, breathing steadily and trying to ignore the encroaching sense of being shrink wrapped in my own clothes. "Marina! Stop!" I call out once more and watch as her figure slows.

As I exit the front doors of the Castle I catch up to her, grateful for the fresh night air. "What's wrong?" I ask her, confused as to her actions. She turns and there are tears running down her face, her red dress is covered in blotches of black mascara and she's hyperventilating heavily.

"I just... I couldn't..." She begins, but then stops, trying to catch her fleeting breath. I move over to her, placing my hand on her back and moving it slowly between her shoulder blades. Marina's dark eyes sparkle and she brushes her hair back from her face, weeping silently. I stand next to her, waiting for her to speak, giving her the silence. After a few moments she has calmed and so I sit her down on the front step before taking a seat next to her.

"You should go back in. You're Crowned Ruler." She smiles at me, acting fine when I know she isn't.

"I need to make sure you're okay. You're one of my people. Part of my job is taking care of you." I remind her. She shrugs, her lips full and red as they twist into a grimace of despair.

"Being an empath, it's just... it's terrible." She gasps slightly, taking in a deep breath and then exhaling once more.

"What do you mean?" I ask her, knowing what a burden it must be, but wanting her to talk it through for her own sake.

"I can feel everything that's going on inside those two couples. Daniella and Mister Lyrical Romance and those other two. Claudia and what's his name..." She admits placing her hands on her knees and sighing.

"Casmire?" I ask her and she nods.

"It's like something out of a Shakespearian tragedy." She says wiping her eyes.

"What do you mean?" I ask again, genuinely curious this time.

"Casmire and Daniella. They're in love. I could feel it before Casmire even entered the temple of Neptune this afternoon. And as for Paolo, that girl Claudia is falling hard for his overly amorous romantic side. It's all wrong. All wrong." She shakes her head as I lean back, placing my hands on the cold stone of the steps and exhaling.

"So you're saying they're betrothed to the wrong people?" I ask her and she nods.

"This would never happen to the Children of Atargatis. It's what made soulmates so special during those early days. You and I both know what it was like for a woman when we were alive. You didn't marry for *love*. You married for money and security. Marrying for love was like winning the lottery back then. Do you remember Orion?" She turns to me, still hunched over her skirt as I look her deeply in the eye. I do remember. I remember only too clearly how marriage had worked back then. It's only now that I realise I had almost trapped Callie into the same institution for selfish motives.

"I do." I say, feeling sour.

"It makes me miss Christian so deeply I feel like I might die. When you see this gaping wound in others who are being kept apart for no good reason, when you feel that longing coupled with your own grief. It's unbearable. I want to forget..." She begins but I interrupt her.

"Don't say that. You'll never forget. He was the love of your life." I remind her, stroking her shoulder.

"That's what is so terrible, Orion. He's gone. I'll never find another love like that. Not in a million years. Not if I lived until this planet was a burning hunk of ash and dust. My soulmate is gone. I'll never feel that kind of love again. It makes me feel like I'll never live again. Never be happy." She looks out and up to the sky.

"It might not be true love, or romantic love, but I know Callie loves you. I know I do. You were this beautiful energy to me when I was alone. You gave me hope. You still do." I remind her she's not alone. Though I fear it's hopeless.

"I gave you hope then. But you give me hope now. Hope that the Psirens will one day no longer be a threat. Hope that one day the seas will find their peace again. That's why I'm still here... I believe in this. What we're doing here. It's important." She stops and looks out past the trees that lightly sway and to the bay as her tears cease. I wait patiently, knowing that what she says next has been weighing on her for a while. "After this war, after this fight, I'm going to leave the mer, Orion. I'm going to go out into the world. I have to. For me. I need to know there's still something in the world worth living for now that he's gone." She looks at me, her once tearful gaze scorched dry with conviction.

"Okay. But you know, you'll always have a home. Wherever we end up." I remind her, smiling gently.

"I know, we're family." She looks like she might cry again.

"Come on, let's go and get some food. I bet it's really good!" I change the subject and she wipes her eyes.

"Okay, you go ahead, I'll be in once I've composed myself." She laughs at herself, cheeks tear stained as I give her one last look, narrowing my eyes and assessing whether or not she really is okay. "Go on! You're the one they're looking to. You need to be there." She laughs slightly at my reluctance, clearly finding my affection toward her endearing. It's odd, how I had known her for so long but had never realised how much she meant to me. Now I look back, I realise that she's been almost like a second mother to me. I twist my lips into a grimace, not wanting to leave her, but knowing my duty is once again at my back, pushing me toward everything I'd rather escape.

The smell of something light and zesty fills my nostrils with a tang as I walk back into the banquet hall, among the clatter of knives and forks and the moving of mouths, I take my seat next to Callie.

"Everything alright?" She asks me, cocking her head as a ringlet tumbles from her shoulder.

"Yes, Marina is just missing Christian I think." I acknowledge and she looks saddened, an empathy lying behind her aqua gaze that runs deep.

"Maybe I should go..." She begins but I shake my head.

"Short of bringing him back from the dead there is nothing you can possibly say." She smiles sadly, looking down into her lap knowing the truth of what I say. I turn to face Paolo who is offering something red on his fork to Daniella. She looks bored.

I stare down at my own plate, on which sits a solitary decapitated tomato, stuffed with grated zucchini, bacon and cheese. It looks divine as I sit back, feeling my stomach growl. I hadn't noticed I was hungry before, with more pressing concerns taking priority, but now that I'm sitting with food in front of me, I realise I'm ravenous. Callie watches me as I eat the stuffed tomato, shovelling in the food with less grace than an ice skating hippo.

"Hungry?" Isabella asks, placing her long fingers over my hand, which is clutching one of the many knives set out. I nod, licking my lips and letting the last of the rich vegetable juices and salty bacon coat my tongue before swallowing. Callie has only eaten half of her dish, so I turn to her.

"You're not going to eat that?" I ask her with a raised eyebrow.

"No, I'm feeling pretty constricted in this corset." She huffs out, but I sense she still hasn't fully exhaled.

"Can I..." I begin. She rolls her eyes.

"Have at it." At her permission I take the food from her and devour it whole just like I had with my own. I wonder if perhaps the moonstone's power to grace me with legs has interrupted my regular digestion, or lack thereof, as Callie looks past me and to Isabella.

"So you really have no idea who the vessel could be?" She asks. Isabella has finished her plateful and is sitting back, contemplative and watching over her daughter. Her head turns.

"No darling. None at all. No business talk tonight though, this is a time for celebration!" She leans forward and rings the bell once more as I place my knife and fork down. The fleet of butlers return with silver trollies once more piled high with more food. They begin serving as I turn to her. Enzo watches me from beside Paolo with interest.

"Isabella, you see we are on quite the tight deadline. A war is coming. A swarm of beasts more deadly than you can imagine and a demon with the power of a god running in its veins. This isn't a matter I can just drop you see. I need your help. Your people." I feel I must reiterate that I am asking for more than simply a vessel. I need to build an army with which to fight back.

"Fine. If you insist on ruining my dinner with talks of war, then I shall say to you what I said to your father all those years ago." She inhales, taking a large slug of wine in one fluid motion of her wrist. "You will have the Water Nymphs at your side..." I exhale. "Providing you can pay us what we are worth." She raises an eyebrow, challenging me and I feel the air around me still as the conversations of my pod members come to a falter down the length of the table, eager to hear what's being decided.

"What exactly was promised?" I ask, feeling my heart sink.

116

"Men, warriors… the usual kind of things we have need of here, that which cannot be bought or sold…"

"Our city was decimated Isabella, the Knights of Atargatis are dead. We have nothing other than what you see here. These are the only survivors." Callie says these words before they can fall from my lips.

"Well then I'd say the matter is resolved. I had hoped you had only brought part of the people for which you rule. I am not a charity Orion. Your father knew that, I thought he would have taught you the same. Clearly I was mistaken." Her tone is snide all of a sudden, berating and condescending all at once. I hollow out my cheekbones and I feel Callie's hand clutch mine.

"Very well." I breathe out, feeling the suit take the last ounces of my protest as it clutches around my chest as I move to try and reason one last time.

"This is why we do not discuss war over dinner. Look at that pout." Enzo taunts me and I suddenly feel the strong urge to hit him in the face.

"There'll be more to worry about than a pout if the Psiren army decimates what's left of the mer. If Saturnus and Solustus succeed in whatever it is they're planning with the Necrimad, we'll all be dead within a month." Callie says this haphazardly, seemingly unaffected by the realities of what she's just announced, as she reaches forward and takes a leg from the turkey which has been placed silently in the middle of the table by a white gloved hand. The entire golden carcass is steaming visibly and the platter is garnished with lettuce that looks a little too green. I lean forward, turning away from the scrutiny of the two royals at the head of the table and stare down the middle. I can see suckling pig, lobster, caviar, salmon, ratatouille, stews, spaghetti, meatballs, silver bowls of vegetable and similarly patterned gravy boats. It's enough to make a starving man lose his mind. My stomach rumbles once more, partly from hunger and partly from nerves. I feel like I'm being throttled by my own clothes and to top it off the thought of leaving here with neither a vessel nor warriors is making me anxious beyond what I'd thought possible. I can feel it all bearing down on me. Crushing me flat.

117

"Orion, are you okay? You've gone awfully pale." Daniella speaks to me directly for the first time this evening and Paolo turns to her with a surprised stare, as though he's forgotten she has a voice of her own.

"I'm sure you can understand I'm more than a little disappointed to hear you won't be aiding the cause. The matter of the vessel however is one I cannot so easily let go." I say the words, only semi-conscious of their intent. Somehow through the fog of my anxiety I can hear myself pushing my cause further.

"Worry not Orion, the vessel will be found. I can give you this much, no? But I cannot risk leaving the Canals and the rest of Italy defenceless. It would require great personal sacrifice to do so. Without the extra warriors promised I could not hope to control a swarm of demons on my return." Isabella explains this and I feel my mind clear a little, returning to a mere simmer at the stress of my father's promises that I cannot possibly keep.

"Thank you." I gush, slight relief clutching at me. Isabella looks surprised at the degree of gratitude I express and laughs.

"Look at him, he looks like I just gave him my still beating heart on a platter, no?" Enzo rolls his eyes and glares at me slightly as Isabella continues to giggle like a school girl. I look away, wondering what his problem is, before I decide not to care and reach for the turkey.

The meal passes slowly and as the dessert plates and tiny expresso cups are finally cleared away, Isabella stands once more.

"Please adjourn through to the great hall! Dancing and celebrations will continue right through the door at the end of the hallway!" She announces this and I hear a slow grinding of chairs against stone as guests rise, full from the decadent meal. I haven't eaten as much as I could of, mainly because I didn't want my suit to split at the seams but my appetite is none-the-less satiated. I take Callie by the hand as she rises, tilting slightly as her torso moves without flexibility. Enzo takes Isabella's hand and Paolo moves from the table as well. Daniella sits, still enjoying her coffee.

118

"I'll be one moment." She whispers, her voice meek. Paolo's eyebrows practically jump off his overly expressive face.

"Of course my darling angel. I shall wait for you…until we meet again." He strides, practically dancing from the room in flamboyant steps that would make a peacock blush.

"Oh for heaven's sake." I mutter. Callie looks up at me, surprised.

"Don't you think it's sweet? He clearly adores her!" She announces this and I can't help but laugh, cocking my head and wondering what it is she's been watching. I don't know exactly what it was I've been witnessing from Paolo during dinner, but I know it wasn't adoration for Daniella, but rather a show for everyone watching.

"Adoration isn't something one needs to constantly act out like a play Callie. It's intimate, shown in the tiniest motions…" I begin to move my hand up to caress her cheek, but Enzo calls out my name before I can, tearing my eyes from her expression and causing me to jump slightly.

"Come! Come! The dancing is about to begin!"

10
Zenith
SOLUSTUS

My body slices the surface of the pacific like a razor blade through a carotid. The air moves down my throat and into my lungs, a sharp and sudden dryness clutching at my ribcage. My body was not designed for this world, and yet I am still more suited to manipulating my surroundings than any human. Regus slides out of the water next to me, silent in tongue but unfortunately less so in body.

"Why do you insist on being such an insufferable brute Regus? Really, where is your finesse?" I demand this of him yet he doesn't say anything but merely looks at me, his green eyes dead in his fat head.

"Where's Saturnus?" He asks, either too stupid to know what 'finesse' means or ignoring my question all together. Either way his change of subject irks me as the Psirens swarm below, waiting for my command.

"Saturnus need not be involved in this." I reply in a harsh bite, feeling my lips sever the words, making them staccato and disconnected, just as I wish to see limbs from bodies.

The water's surface is calm, still and reflective of the empty darkness above. The night sky is void of stars and a crisp sensory edge overtakes me as its desolation looks back into my own as I stare upward, unimpressed, un-fazed and immune to any hint of sublimity.

"There!" It's a grunt, exclaimed in surprise from Regus. I look to where he points a stubby finger. Among the black, specks of light at organised intervals exude out into the dark. The cruise liner that I'd asked for. It is enormous, I grin.

More meat for the beast.

"You wait here Regus, prepare the Psirens for harvest, but know this: There can be no survivors. You understand me? I'm not ready for the world to know about our numbers yet. Not until I've got the power of the Necrimad coursing through my veins." I spit the words, gritting my teeth and feeling rage mount within my gut. I don't know why I'm suddenly so irrationally angry. Perhaps it's because I've been suppressing my urges for so long that as the power I've longed for nears me, I am losing control, ready to no longer need the restraint that binds my temper in blood soaked chains.

I watch as Regus ceases to reply, but instead sinks back into the depths of the ocean. I set my eyes on my target, ready for the opportunity to slash through the water at an unbridled speed. It has been only too long since I've been set loose in the water. I breathe in, narrowing my eyes and gritting my teeth. Quickly I launch upward, tensing my torso and allowing myself to arc, creating acute angles with my body. If I'm going to commit mass murder I might as well enjoy it after all.

I lash out, penetrating the water over and over, cutting through it mercilessly. The speed of the fluid, caressing my body, leaves an edge of light sensation, like a touch, making me feel sick at the thought of human hands stroking across my body. The darkness of the water makes me only more fatal to my surroundings as my silent speed carries me toward the bow of the hulking metal monster. Within seconds I am beneath its shadow, encasing myself once more in darkness as I prepare myself to board.

I look up, through the distorted image of the surface, spying my target with ease as I swim from beneath the hull so fast that as I break the surface I am launched about fifteen feet into the air. I grab the bottom rung of the ladder I have been aiming for, my body slamming, cold and sodden against the metal which assaults the sea's surface, carving its way through such a power. The seal skin sheath holding Scarlette slaps against my tailfin as I close my eyes, cleaving myself from the sea and feeling my naked human form return. With my disgusting legs dangling, pale and meagre, from my waist, I begin the climb, only taking a second to unsheathe Scarlette and bring her blade between my teeth, ready to be grabbed by my free arm should I need her. I hear chatter from above but I ignore it, the childish voices and screams meaning nothing to me. I climb, my shadow mere on the ship's metallic body. I pass large letters and turn my head to read the word. *Zenith.* That is the name of the ship I'm about to rip apart.

Once I've climbed over the railings I notice that there is a lot more light that I had first anticipated. It's glaring and harsh, unnatural to say the least. Luckily for me I have been spared its exposure and have climbed aboard under an awning, which is shrouded in shadow. I move a few steps forward, leaving the light behind me, pivoting as I spot a storage unit to my left and the scales fade in and out of existence over my naked lower half. I slam open the metal locker door, finding some stranger's jeans lying in wait.

Perfect. I purr, grabbing them and putting them on. They're baggy, not that I care. There's no shirt or shoes so I walk, barefoot along the fine pine deck, which is strewn with sea spray. I'm impressed; Regus had found me quite the juicy morsel, filled with the rich and gluttonous no doubt. Perfect for what I have in mind.

Slinking, invisible along the edge of the deck, I keep my wits about me as I recall what Tiberius had said, weighing in on something that didn't concern him as usual, but intriguing with the point he had made none the less.

You got to cut communications off first. All these state of the art cruise-liners are chocked full of technology. If an alarm sounds, tipping off the local authorities, we're dead.

He had been a little dramatic perhaps, underestimating my ability to get out of a tight bind with mere mortals. However, he was right about one thing, I don't know anything about technology. If you ask me it is just a way to make humans lazier than they already are.

As I peer around the corner I see what he meant when he had told me to look for a large rotating black disk, a satellite he had called it. I watch it from below, the spinning disk, the thing that makes these insects feel safe, feel like less than the fragile meat sacks they truly are. I narrow my eyes, slamming myself against the metal of the large upper-deck that rises above the main deck onto which I have slithered. Dangerous, a predator in the dark. Watching, biding my time, I let the disk spin a few more moments, concave and hypnotic in its motion as I take a few calculated leaps across the slick pine and launch myself with a power beyond what is human onto the ledge atop the room on which the disk is planted.

I stand, my chest bathed in the fluorescent lighting from above as I look down and out over the sardine-like crowds of pink, soft people. I feel its glare expose my pallor and so I hurry, keeping my focus, sharp and unwavering as I turn and crouch behind it, using Scarlette's quick and accurate point to sever several rubber tentacles that are connecting it to the metal roof of the room beneath. I bend, the jeans constricting my movement in ways I abhor, and bring my long arms under the disk as it's spinning ceases. I rip it, guts and all from the structure before sprinting to the edge of the metal platform and tossing it carelessly into the night, only waiting to hear its impact as it hits the sea below. I drop once more onto the deck and creep beneath an awning, as I do, I see a child coming toward me, running and lost.

"Mommy! Mommy!" The small boy cries, his fat arms and short stature irritating me already. I clutch the handle of my sword, my pulse heightening at the thought of blood.

I lick my lips, *fresh... young...* as he nears and I step forward, looking downward upon him from my mighty height. The child falters as the shadow is banished from my form, revealing my glory. "You're not my mommy!" The child cocks his small head, his brown eyes brimming and his nose running. He wipes the mucus onto his arm. In his left hand I notice he has a toy, a wooden

123

sword. For a moment I cringe, blanching as I'm taken back to the only good memory I have of my childhood.

Me and father, on the cliff where I had thrown myself to my death, play sword fighting with sticks… My blood curdles, rage forming in my gut. I turn from the child and slink back into the dark, not wanting to alert others to my presence by causing a scene with such a measly offering.

Hurriedly I move away, tired of dealing with menial distractions, *the satellite, the child, enough!*

I want to get to the killing. I think, inhaling to feel my ribs expand, to feel my chest grow larger and let my life force strain within my skin, reminding me that I am ready to ascend.

I reach the end of the deck and turn, making my way down a set of stairs in brisk fashion. I really have no idea where I'm going, all of these liners are so complicated with their layout and a million rooms that house a number of disgusting human habits. Drinking, gambling, fornication. I feel my stomach turn, the smell of spirits constantly burned into my memory like I've been branded with hot, whisky soaked, iron.

As I reach the midpoint of the flight of stairs, I hold my sword close to my body, resting the hilt against my hip as I push the blade inside the waistband of the jeans. I feel it push against my leg. A lethal appendage. As my foot hits the bottom step, I see a young man in a white uniform. He looks important, gold and black insignia shimmering across his shoulders and chest as he turns into the corridor in front of me, exiting a door on the left. He strides with entitlement, importance and so I slink, silent behind him as I let my fingers tickle Scarlette, readying her to strike.

Soon I'm practically pressed to his spine, silent as shadow as I still my breathing before gripping him across the collarbone with one arm and pressing Scarlette to his throat with the other.

"The Control Room. Now." I whisper into his ear, a deadly hush. He exclaims a gargle as he struggles against me. It is, of course, futile. "Now!" I feel my legs strain under his weight slightly as he bends backward, trying to make me crumple beneath him. He fails. Realising only too slowly that this is futile, he eventually begins to step forward as I push him, not having time for his mortal incompetencies.

Moronic bug.

"Which way?" I bark as we come to the end of the too bright, white walled corridor. The carpet is red at least, all the better for my sanguine intent.

"L… Left!" I feel his heart hammering within his ribcage, a trapped and pathetic bird, caged and incapable of anything useful. I observe my surroundings finding the corridor to my left is empty, thankfully I think I've managed to navigate myself to the part of the ship with the bridge. This makes me even more sure that I'm meant to do this. I'm meant to have this sacrifice for the beast.

Perhaps Poseidon is telling me he approves.

I smile at this thought, mainly because I know if it's true it'll mightily piss off my brother.

I stride whilst still restraining the man in uniform.

"Where now!?" I shake him, letting Scarlette bite into his neck ever so slightly. Giving her a taste of what's to come.

"Up those stairs! It's up those stairs! Please don't kill me! I have a baby on the way!" The man cries out. With this information, I falter. I breathe in the moment, and as I exhale I draw Scarlette across his throat and throw his body to the right in one seamless motion. He falls, blood spraying up the pristine white walls and ricocheting back onto the purity of his uniform.

I grin to myself; *I just did your child a favour.*

The barbed wire that has formed inside me constricts, cutting into the stone of my core, making grooves and dents, carving out the remnants of another life taken on the glorious monument my soul has become. I take not a moment's pause, not looking back, not caring to linger over the corpse. Striding forward I leap up, exerting myself for no other reason than the pure exhilaration that control of my muscles brings me. I take the entire staircase in this one momentum, landing like a panther on the balls of my feet without a sound. I see the metal door leading the control room; it's labelled 'Bridge' in block lettering carved into a metallic plaque. I stride backward, looking upon the alloyed frame of the door, it looks sturdy, but I know I'm sturdier. Inhaling once more I grit my teeth in a feral grin, feeling my soul ignite at the idea of such a test as I ram forward, smashing my full weight into the door at great speed. I'm aware that I'm not the most muscular brute, but I know how to use my body, with its acute jutting angles and immense speed capabilities, I can be just as dangerous as Regus, if not more so.

As I take a step back, admiring the dent I've made in the metal, I watch the wheel in the centre of the door begin to spin, opening from the inside. I dart to the edge of the door frame, lying in wait, my pulse still regular and droll.

A few moments later the door opens and silence falls as the echo of its metal mass shifting fades. I slide sideways across the carpet, pivoting and bringing the hilt of Scarlette up to hit the man, who has come looking for intruders, square in the jaw. Without a second's delay I bury my palms in his thick hair and twist his skull, relishing the severing of sinew and the crunch of vertebrae twisting against each other as I internally decapitate him before he crumples to the floor. I step forward and over his body, treading on his hand with my bare foot, which lies, still and cooling as the blood flowing around his body stills in its banal course. I move quickly now, knowing this next part will require fast and precise movement on my part. Luckily for me these are two things in which I am master.

"Hey, you can't be in here!" The first man comes at me as I enter the control room. It's large and littered with machines and equipment. I stride forward, gripping the man's raised fist in one palm, stopping him in his path. He struggles, his pupils dilating as I near him before I run Scarlette across his throat like his life is nothing more than a rope I'm severing.

"Who are you!?" Another man in uniform with an official looking hat comes toward, my reflection looking back at me from the shiny caps of his black shoes. I pivot, twirling, and slash open his gut with my lethal pirouette. As his body falls, his hands grasping for intestines that fall from him like rotten worms, I grab the hat off his head and place it on my own head.

I'm captain now.

126

I hear clunking footsteps nearing behind me, and so thrust my blood-strewn sword underneath my armpit, feeling the resistance of blood and flesh sheath the blade as the intruder attempts to tackle me from behind. Thrusting Scarlette forward and away from my core she exits the body as I hear it fall behind me. I turn now, looking over my shoulder with narrowed eyes, as I see another four men in uniforms coming toward me. I step back, relaxing into my stance before skewering the first man to my left and grabbing the assailant on my right by the throat, crushing his windpipe in my fist and raising him off the floor, causing his eyes to bulge in his skull. I remove the sword from the victim on my left and plunge it into the choking man I'm suspending on my right, gutting him from the groin upward like a fish. As I let the organs fall out onto the floor, a bloody, sloppy, mess that seeps between my toes, I turn to the remaining two men who had been trying to subdue me. They stand, eyes wide and trembling.

"You thought you could attack me?" I ask them, looking deeply into their faces as I tower over them, my shadow falling into their ocular cavities and making them ghostly, foreshadowing their fate. They both shake their heads and as they do I bring Scarlette down, catching beneath their jawlines in what looks like no more than a close shave. They're still shaking their head in faux innocence as their heads fall from their bodies and onto the floor like gaudy baubles. I look down at myself. I am covered in blood, drenched in organic wrath. I adore the feel of its warmth as it trickles down my chest and onto the tops of my feet. I look around at the blood spreading from the corpses, melding and twisting into a lake of luscious scarlet. I step through it, looking around for anyone who I've missed.

It's then I hear something, a tremble, a whimper, a scared breath caught in a windpipe. A figure with dark eyes and blonde hair, who looks no more than a child in uniform, is standing near the controls that back onto a window with a panoramic view over the decks below and beyond to the black of the sea. I lock eyes with him and he shakes slightly. Then his eyes dart sideways and before I can reach him his fist has slammed down on a red button on the console next to him. I launch over one of the work desks, catapulting my long limbs toward him as I skewer him multiple times, making his death painful and slow just for smiting me.

Stupid child. I spit in my head.

I feel his body turn cold as he slides to my feet and an extremely loud alarm begins to sound.

It wails, louder than anything I've heard in a long time, and only slightly less irritating that a Psiren's scream though far less lethal. I take a moment to collect my thoughts, trying to blank out the incessant noise. I stare around the room I've decimated. Rows of computers used to control the Zenith's course. I scan the area, my acute sight aiding me as it falls upon what I've been seeking, what I had hoped hadn't changed after all this time. The ship's wheel catches my attention. This is no wooden thing though; it's shiny, polished and metal. I stride over to it, stashing Scarlette inside the waistband of the jeans once more and I feel warm blood trickle down my leg from her length, pooling on the floor beneath me. As I reach it I notice that from this room I have a full circle view of the entire ship on all sides. If I turn I can observe the chaos I'm about to cause.

How marvellous.

I smile salaciously, contented with the bloodletting. I ignore the continual sirens that blare, trying to distract me from my course. I glimpse outward, trying to pinpoint where I know Regus will be raising rocks from the depths. I see a bubbling of the surface and turn the wheel, heading for that point, relieved that at least Regus seemed to be competent enough to follow orders.

As I keep one hand on the wheel, I hear an echo of the alarm emit. It's on the main deck now, so I turn, looking away from my destination and back to them. People are beginning to perk up, clueless as ever, from their activities. They stare up at the poles blaring sound like they're Gods. I chortle slightly to myself.

Pathetic.

I look to my left as I turn back and an equally shiny lever catches my attention. It calls to me, tempting me with its potential.

I wonder if... I think to myself as I touch it gingerly.

I take a few moments before giving in and pushing the lever forward. I feel a lurch from somewhere beneath and the boat seems to speed up.

Oh yes. I purr. *This is perfect.*

I watch on as I move from the wheel, the course for destruction now set. Below, groups of people are starting to move to the sides of the boat and they stand, pink and round, watching as I drive their lives onto the colossal shards of rock that are now protruding from the surface. I wait it out, the alarms blaring around me, knowing that by now my army of Psirens will be riding the waves beneath us, swarming like an angry hive, hungry for the kill. I have told them only to kill and not feed, no turning. These people are not destined for greatness; they are destined to feed the beast. Suddenly I feel the boat beneath me lurch.

Impact. I smile again, laughing with a glee that comes only from death. My chest is covered in drying blood and I watch from the control room as the insects below start to panic.

They flock to the edges of the boat as there is a groan from below, the ship is taking on water, it's hull punctured from the sharp shard of rock that Regus has procured from below to seal the Zenith's fate. It really was a genius plan on my part, a mass harvest.

The crowds of the wealthy and their mongrel offspring start to scream and shortly after, panic grabs them within its jaws, shaking them senseless and leaving them with one instinct; self-preservation. The size of the rioting crowd only grows as masses of guests flock from their cabins and onto the deck, having heard the alarm. The stampede of fear takes small children down and I watch on in fascination as these people, who the Gods claim to be so worth saving, trample their own friends and loved ones. They flock to the boats, fighting over who goes in first, and I cackle loudly, knowing they will only be lowering themselves to their doom faster. I feel the boat shudder beneath me once more, like a Psiren made earth quake. With this I know it's time to leave, to join in the underwater slaughter. I turn, treading through the puddles of coagulated scarlet without breaking stride and leaving bloody footprints and bodies as the only traces that I was ever the cause of such elegant mayhem.

I move up onto the deck, deafened by the continual alarm. Everything is tilting, people are screaming, children are crying. It's beautiful. Another tremor strikes and I continue to walk my path through it, watching as people cling onto the railings in a pathetic attempt not to fall to their deaths mere moments sooner. I rip the jeans off and grip Scarlette by the hilt before moving up and over the railing in one agile leap. I hit the water like lead, feeling the sting of its embrace against my pale skin as my true form returns in a ripple of scale and a binding of my limbs. I am in the middle of a feeding frenzy. Regus comes up behind me, his face dead of expression as usual.

"Beautifully done." I compliment him, looking to the shadows of the towering rocks that have pierced the hull of the ship clean through. It's amazing that a few holes made by Mother Nature can bring down a manmade structure that had taken such effort to build. "Come. We must make sure the bodies are preserved. We're here for meat." I exclaim and he nods.

I slice through the water, approaching the black mass of bodies, tentacles and tails that are writhing, hungry and murderous, close to the surface.

"STOP!" I exclaim, feeling the power of my actions fuelling my right to lead, my right to command. At the sound of my voice they turn, noticing finally that I have returned. "We need meat! I want clean kills. Drowning. Internal decapitation. Finesse. You are not mindless killing machines. You are murderers, skilled and concise. Take them all, children, mothers, daughters, sons and fathers, but save their blood for the beast. And NO turning!" I raise my sword into the water and exhale a high-pitched wail that I reserve for moments when I need them to feel my fury. Multiple pairs of eyes glisten at the thought of such evil. This wasn't urge, wasn't instinct, this was prepared and with purpose. This was an act that means something.

I watch as boats are lowered into the water one by one and my army rip them apart, pulling the bodies down into the ocean so deep that they will never see light again.

I see a familiar face enter the water from afar and dart, seeing the round doe eyes and chubby form hit the surface. Grabbing at his body I take him on a

130

ride of torment, letting him gasp for air for only moments before plunging him back into the depths once more. I feel his body still and add him to the pile of other meat. I look upon their faces, empty and I envy them for a moment. Released and free from this torment, not kept on this sick planet for a cause they didn't believe in. The water is littered with items, cameras, watches, jewellery, coins and sunglasses. Things clearly important enough to hold onto in the face of death. I circle through the water, watching them fall or float, examining them with minimal intrigue. What was it about these things that made them worth keeping I wonder? I look down to Scarlette and feel my rotting heart constrict. My sword was perhaps the only thing that mattered to me, more so than my brothers, more so than any woman, she had never failed me. I look back to the boy, the small child I had stolen from, from whom I had taken the years that spread before him. Something inside me shudders at his face, the remnant of a memory floating to the surface.

He had wanted his *Mommy.*

I feel myself snarl the last word and sink downward, ignoring the swarm above, ignoring the noise, the screams and the fire that has erupted on the surface where sparks of grating metal are meeting with something flammable and causing a final blow to the already dying vessel. She falls through the water finally and I watch as the entire mass plummets, sinking to the sea floor. People are trying to swim, trying to save themselves, but my army is pulling them down, pulling them under. Still I don't watch for long, it becomes boring after a while, instead I look down to the boy again, his face still and calm. I move through the water, staring into his porcelain face. It's then that something strikes me, something dark that stirs beneath the murky surface of my mind. It's not his face in particular that causes a memory to rise; it's his innocence, his fear. I had thought it beautiful. I recoil at this inclination, remembering how my father had too found that attraction with me. The memories of those nights, the memories of that act, those things, crawl across my skin like every sensation I've grown to hate, grown to know are wrong. I take my sword and gauge out the child's eyes, letting the urge pass and slicing up his small fragile body for good measure, blood plumes around me, baptising me and purifying me of my sins.

I rotate, turning away from my morbid mastery and watch as the Psirens that I've trained, that I've created from nothing but my imagination and will, slice across the planes of this world, this dark aquatic land that I've come to rule over, taking bodies for long and torrid joyrides, waiting until they go limp and then discarding them like a dog's old chew toy.

Then I see it from beneath, silhouetted against the dying flame of the world above.

It floats, wooden and juvenile. The child's sword remains after everything, unable to sink into the world of the dead and forgotten.

11

Puckish

CALLIE

Orion moves to follow Enzo through the banquet hall doors, which are still wide open from the bustling crowd. I pull on his arm, feeling my heart palpitate as his proximity threatens to diminish.

"What is it?" He turns back to me, his eyes blazing with something I don't recognise. He looks irritated, and all of a sudden I'm beginning to wonder if I've done something wrong. Is he angry I've been taking the lead with Isabella? Should I be taking a back seat and following his lead instead? It seems that Isabella prefers to talk business with me, but maybe I've offended him somehow. I hear Rose's words echo in the back of my mind:

You have to keep a man like that interested.

I frown slightly to myself, scrunching up my forehead and feeling my ribs pushing against the boning of the corset that's robbing me of breath.

"Nothing. Let's go." I say, taking a step toward him and wrapping my arm through the vacant bend in his elbow. I feel my heart sink as he doesn't reply, but guides me swiftly after Enzo who has taken off after his Queen as we've been stood here, staring at one another. As we turn the corner into the hallway I realise we're among the last to leave the banquet hall and something strikes me. A cunning plan. I halt again in my tracks, mind running away with me. Orion stops again, rounding on me once more.

"What is it?" He sighs; his forehead creasing and his icy blue stare making me inhale as much as I'm able. I saunter a few inches forward on the balls of my feet, twisting so my skirt sways, billowing out from left to right.

"I'm not in the mood for dancing." I bite my lip and watch as he sighs and puts his hand on the back of his neck, the way he does when he's guilty, and looks up at me. His eyes catch mine and I see they're dancing with an ambiguous flame.

Sucker. I think.

"I don't think this is the time or the place..." His sentence tails off as I grab his hand and pull his elbow, jerking it toward me. "Callie, wait!" He exclaims, pulling me back.

I sigh, *gosh when did the idea of sneaking off with me become such a chore?* I wonder, my heart beat continuing to pound frustrated at my own desire. I pucker my lips and flutter my lashes. I don't want to be Queen right now, I don't want to be responsible: I want to have fun.

"Orion, we've been given another night on land. Do you really want to waste it dancing the waltz? I'm sick of the waltz." I admit and he looks at me, narrowing his eyes.

"That's a low blow." He sighs, unable to control his lips as they curve.

"Did it work?" I cock an eyebrow. He breathes out heavily once more, defeated.

"I didn't stand a chance." He admits.

The glint of wickedness I'd been missing catches and sparks into life beneath his glacial irises as he grabs my arm, looking back over his shoulder as we hurry back up the stairs to the upper levels of the Castle. I feel my breathing increase in speed, but it's only coming in shallow wisps as the corset binds my torso flat.

As we reach the top of the staircase I trip and can't help but giggle, the sound high pitched and unexpected falling from my lips as I crash to the ornate rug beneath me. Orion looks back as I sprawl out on the landing.

"Oh for heaven's sake." He rolls his eyes and hurries back to me, sweeping me up in his arms like we're in a scene out of Gone with the Wind. He moves along the corridor that runs as a balcony around the top of the

134

entrance hall, rushing me away from the party and entering the first door he comes across. Putting me down on the balls of my high-heeled shoes he closes the door behind us and I turn to face the room, finding my breath caught once more in my throat.

"It's…"

"A library…" Orion finishes my exclamation in an equally surprised tone.

There are lit sconces illuminating the luscious space in a red and orange glow. I take it in as my eyes settle on ceiling high, glass, double doors leading out to a wide balcony that looks out to the sea. Around us shelves line every wall, filled with thickly bound books and leather volumes that look older than Orion. Desks litter the space and plush armchairs that are upholstered in plum velvet, the same plum velvet adorns the curtain rails that hang around the doors and across shelves that have been cordoned off, preventing dust from settling on the books.

I feel hands curl around my waist and I exhale as much as I can, letting Orion's embrace envelop my senses as I melt back into him and I feel his chin rest in my shoulder. The flames lighting the room flicker, making the space feel cosy and inviting as well as decadent. It's perfect, and I don't want to wait to be with Orion anymore. Desperation overtakes me, fuelled by the fear that I'll never have him again. I spin in his arms, turning to face him as I trace my fingers across his lips. He moves to speak but I lurch forward, pressing my lips to his and making sure every part of my body possible is in contact with his mighty stature. I feel him still as I force the kiss to continue for as long as possible, keeping my eyes closed and savouring every second. My head starts to feel light, and my stomach flutters as the sconces crackle into the silence. I open my eyes and he's staring directly at me. Suddenly his frozen pupils blur, multiplying in their beauty as I fall, breathless, into the dark.

I don't know how long it's been before I come to, but when I do I feel a light breeze moving my ringlets, causing them to tickle my shoulders.

"Callie, wake up." Orion whispers, shaking me lightly.

"Huh..." I say, groggy. Opening my eyes, I'm greeted by his face, statuesque and ruggedly handsome as always. As I stare at him he exhales, slumping back onto his butt on the floor of the balcony on which I am splayed. I notice his fly is undone and his jacket has been discarded to his left. I look down at myself and I'm partially dressed, the corset torn wide open and broken.

"What... what happened, I don't remember anything. I didn't drink that much wine..." I stutter.

"You fainted Callie." Orion rolls his eyes again and sits back, stretching his legs out in front of him. I notice he's taken off his shoes too. Why is he half-dressed if I fainted? I crease my brow trying to work it out, but my head is pounding.

"Why are you undressed?" I query him and he laughs.

"This suit and I have issues." He says, continuing to chuckle to himself.

"Why did I faint?" I ask him, suddenly confused again.

"Something to do with that monstrous contraption Isabella wrangled you into I'd bet." Orion says, looking at the corset that's been ripped open right down the middle.

"Isabella didn't wrangle me into it. I wanted to wear it." I say, feeling tears welling in my eyes. I'm so ridiculously emotional, probably because he's staring at me like he has no idea why I'd put up with such a painful piece of clothing. He doesn't know I did it for him.

"Callie, why on *earth,* would you want to do something like that? These things are abominations!" Orion looks horrified and I feel my eyes well with tears.

"I wore it for you." I sniffle, looking down at the skirt that is still wrapped around me in its many elaborate layers.

"Me? I don't understand." He shakes his head and comes closer, shuffling forward and wiping beneath my eyes with his dexterous fingers. I look up into his face, feeling embarrassed to say the least.

"The mermaids said... they said you liked women like this. From when you were younger." I start and he throws his head back in a laugh I've only heard a few times. He looks like he might actually get hysterical. "Don't laugh Orion! This is serious!" I say, wanting to stamp my foot. I can't because I'm

136

sitting, leaning against the railing of the balcony and bathed in the night air, so instead I slam my palm into his shirt-covered chest.

"That's the most ridiculous thing I've ever heard!" He continues to splutter and choke on his own breath. I slump against the railing feeling stupid.

"Orion stop laughing! This isn't funny!" I feel my sadness and my desperation clutch at me again and instead of moving to act on it I just sit and let tears roll down my cheeks.

"Oh don't cry!" He shuffles again, so his back is against the twisted iron bars as well. He stretches out his legs and cups my chin, raising it so my watery gaze has no choice but to meet his. "Now. Tell me. What is this about?" He narrows his eyes, like he's trying to tell if what I'll say is the truth.

"Isabella and Rose, they said that you and I... well, that we wouldn't be this in love forever. They said it would fade over time." I whisper the confession, like it's something criminal.

"Hmm... I see." He looks upward and to the side, exhaling.

"What?" I ask him, feeling my heart begin to pound again, afraid of what he might say next.

"Well, do you want that?" He queries me with a cocked eyebrow, putting his hands into his slack pockets after tucking a stray hair behind my ear. I let my head fall sideways toward the railing and look down. Beneath us, green luscious gardens spread down a hill to the sea and then drop off in a sudden natural abandon to the ocean. A path zig zags through the green, making miniature looking hills at equidistant points.

"No! Of course not!" I say, not looking at him as I stare out to the ocean.

"Well then, what's the problem?" He is curious now and I move my gaze so I'm watching him out of the corner of my eye.

"What if this thing... what if it doesn't last forever? What if it's not always this exciting?" I speak my fears aloud still not wanting to look him in the eye. He responds with a surprised intake of breath.

"Well, to be honest I'd quite like a little less excitement. This whole saving the world bit is getting a bit old. I'm getting grey hairs from the stress." He frowns and I slap his arm, finally turning to him.

137

"That's not what I mean Orion! I mean with us! What about if you get bored of me? Or stop finding me attractive… or…" He's laughing again.

"I wouldn't worry about that Callie. Honestly." He looks me up and down and coughs, tearing his eyes from my breasts, which are spilling from the open corset.

"ORION! I'M SERIOUS!" I yell now, sick of him laughing and making fun of me. I want some goddamn support and he's laughing? *Really?*

"Okay, I'm sorry, it's just a little hilarious. We're about to head into a war we might not survive and you're worried I don't find you sexy? I guess you're more prone to the everyday woman's worries than I thought." He looks deeply into my eyes, serious. I'm taken aback by his candour. Am I being silly? Unreasonable? I am silent for a few moments and he grabs my hands in his, bringing them up to his lips and kissing my knuckles.

"Might I remind you Miss Pierce that I proposed to you? I'm ready to have you be my wife. I've been ready since the day we met. It is you who is not ready. Not I." He leans forward and kisses my forehead before finishing the sentiment "I am sure. The question is, are you?" He stares at me, his face earnest and waiting. Then I realise, he wasn't doubting me at all. He was sure. It was me doubting myself, doubting my ability to be happy, my ability to rule, my ability to love him in the way he needed. To be loved in the way he had been trying to love me all along. I sit back.

"I shouldn't have listened to Rose and Isabella, you're right." I avoid the really important question he's asking me.

"No, you shouldn't. You and I have our own melody, our own rhythm. It works for us. It's nobody else's business. If we want to be ridiculously romantic and make everyone around us nauseous, it's our goddess given right. Atargatis knows we've given more than anyone can ask." He sighs.

"This ruler-ship thing is hard." I admit, biting my lip.

"I know. You're doing pretty good at it though." Orion sits back against the balcony edge again and looks up to the stars.

"Thanks, you too." I giggle, wiggling my feet beneath the skirts that are fluttering in the light breeze.

"I know mermen can't really sleep properly. But I feel like I want to for a million years." He admits, not looking at me.

"Me too."

"I'll get you a separate bed, a big one. I know how you like to spread out when you sleep." He winks and I slap his arm again.

"Alright Mr. Snore-head. You're worse than a walrus!" I exclaim, remembering the times we had slept together in the months before the coronation.

"At least I don't talk in my sleep.... *Oh Orion...*" He makes a high-pitched sexy sigh, pretending to be me and I get to my feet.

That's it! The boy's going down! I take off one of my shoes and throw it at him, taking off the other one in case I need more ammo.

"Oh no you didn't!" He gets up too, leaping after me. I flee, dropping the shoe in my hand and enjoying freedom in being able to move fully before I reach the other end of the library and realise I have nowhere to go. I twist on the spot, my back pressing into the spines of the books behind me. Orion towers over my body with a salacious smile, like a tiger trapping its next meal. "Did you just hit me with a shoe?" He asks me with a cocked eyebrow before biting down on his bottom lip.

"No. I would never do that." I slowly raise my gaze, trying not to laugh.

"I think you did. I think you *maliciously* attacked the Crowned Ruler, Callie... that's, well it's... reason enough for me to torture you..."

"You would never do that. You would never cause me pain." I say, swallowing hard.

"Who said anything about pain?" He asks me, sinking to his knees. As he finds himself beneath the many gossamer layers of my skirt I'm surrendering, my head falling backward in abandon to Orion's soft touch. My hand reaches out to clutch at the shelf, seeking support and I knock a volume onto the floor in my excitement. 'A midsummer night's dream' by William Shakespeare falls to the floor with a clunk and I glance the title page as a moan escapes my lips. As Orion and I find our own melody, our own rhythm, the shelves buckle against my trembling body, and the love stories of years gone past fall down around us like hot and heavy rain.

139

AZURE

The 'happy' couple begin to swirl around the dance floor and I feel a similar sensation begin in my gut. I ate my weight in salmon, so it's really no wonder I feel so sick, but I can't deny that Paolo in particular causes violent urges and nausea all in one. It really is quite the achievement on his part.

I saunter back into the double glass doors that tower high toward the gaudy painted ceiling.

Cherubs and clouds, how original, I sneer to myself, as I knock the handle of the door down with my bony hip before moving out into the gardens to skulk.

I hear giggling and look up; above me Callie and Orion are laughing about something on the external balcony of the upper level, most probably the fact they have managed to sneak away together. I have to admit, it's out of character for Callie's oh so perfect act that she's been peddling lately. The gardens of the castle spread out in endless and annoyingly-perfect green. The grass has been cut recently and the smell of it lifts off the floor in a pungent wave that makes my stomach turn again. I hate the smell of freshly cut grass; it's far too... lively. I glide forward and down the garden path that cuts through the slope of the garden in a hair pinned zigzag. It abruptly ends before the sea in a sheer drop. There are no guard rails and I momentarily debate launching myself off the side in the hope that I might knock myself unconscious until this group effort at 'saving the world' is over.

As I take a turn down the path that seems to be there merely for display, with no functional reason I can discern, I come to a fountain that is hidden behind the curving miniature rise of the garden. I move over to it, sitting down on the mosaic-covered ledge and looking down into the still water. The fountain isn't actually working, not even moving. It's just a pool of stagnant water really. A rose bush is growing in predestined confinement and pruned to perfection behind me. As I turn to examine it, bored, I note that the buds on it are closed.

Even the flowers want nothing to do with me. I huff, turning from them as quickly as I had moved to examine them.

I'm brought back to my reflection, my black hair pulled off my face for once, not falling in cascades of darkness around me as I usually prefer. The gown I'm wearing is black with silver veins running through it. I had been impressed Isabella had owned something to my taste, and it makes me think about where I've come from, making the absence of Starlet, my life's companion, crackle with fresh and raw pain like a wire in a broken circuit that keeps sparking off, trying to find a way to complete itself. Everything here is so old world mixed with the modern materialism the Water Nymphs seem to enjoy. It's scary how much everything has changed from when I'd been a child. Things had been so much simpler. As I bend forward my neck twinges, no doubt whiplash left over from the small accident I'd had in Enzo's Ferrari. I wasn't stupid, I knew how to drive, I mean I've been ashore far more than any mer in the last hundred years. The thing I hadn't wanted to tell Orion was that I'd crashed the car because Enzo had started to wander up my inner thigh with his fingers. He was lucky his car was the only thing that I'd lost control of, or he'd be dead and we'd be at a loss with these people.

That's the thing with me though. I never get any credit; nobody sees how much control it takes me not to rip out windpipes and crush bones into dust. Enzo thought his car looked bad? He should see some of the men who'd crossed me before Titus had died. Their bodies were the real car wrecks now, and there wasn't a mechanic in the world that could repair that kind of damage.

As I'm sat, lamenting my violent tendencies and remembering a spectacular array of bruises that I'd mentally mapped like sick star constellations, a rustle in the nearby greenery alerts me that I'm not alone. I ready myself to be intruded upon and dragged back to the party to be civil and genteel, all the things I am not. Then again, Callie and Orion clearly didn't feel the need to be there, so why the hell should I?

"Hello?" I call out, standing with my fists balled. Suddenly the patch of bushes rustles once more and a small donkey reveals itself. I sigh out, relieved to find myself still alone in the darkness. I am so sick of people, of their company and ridiculous habits. Travelling in this pod was getting old fast, especially since everyone seemed so damn sure we are going to win and come out the heroes. I mean, don't they know what we're up against? Don't they realise that what we're talking about here has Gods scared?

The donkey moves closer and I reach out to touch it. It's kind of cute, in a fluffy and completely pointless in its existence type way. I mean, what do animals even do other than eat and be eaten?

"Nice ass you got there." I hear the Italian accent wrap around the words like a vice and bend them into something that makes my heart rate heighten, spiking adrenaline through my system. I'm not scared for myself though; I'm scared for him.

"What are you doing here?" I ask him as he strolls around the bend of the garden path, lowering himself onto my level with just a few strides. His black hair is greasy and reflective of the half moon as his face turns smug.

"I thought, seeing as how you crashed my car, I might get a dance?" He asks me, a creepy smile passing across his lips. Oh god, is he serious? I really don't dance, and if I did, it wouldn't be with this smarmy bastard.

"No thank you." I get to my feet, ready to walk away. Then he does it, the thing I know he'll regret, the thing I was trying to avoid. He grabs my arm.

"You owe me a dance." He demands and I feel my blood curdle. He's pushing it.

"I don't owe you shit." I spit at him and he laughs.

"You think you're the first woman who thinks you're better than me? You think I don't know you all think I'm whipped? A little butler boy for Isabella? Well, think about this. If you don't dance with me I'll tell her you came onto me, and then your people will never get what you want. What do you think about that?" He snarls, suddenly speaking in straight English, his Italian flamboyance lost in a wave of disdain. His response irks me slightly. Does he think I really care about all this? About the army, about the vessels? I have nothing left to live for, nothing left to lose. I care about all this about as much as I do about Daniella and Paolo's engagement.

"Fine." I snap, suddenly feeling a wicked urge. He takes a step back.

"Thank you for seeing sense." He replies with a satisfied grin, the bastard. I put his hands on my waist, smiling pleasantly through gritted teeth. Placing

142

my hand on his shoulder and taking the other in my palm I hear the music drifting down from the castle up the hill. I listen, counting beats. We begin to waltz as the donkey begins to trot up the hill; smart enough to know trouble is imminent.

We sway together and I keep my features passive, the night calm around us. I can hear the music from above and the sloshing of the waves below as I turn, keeping my muscles tense in his grip. We waltz the traditional beat, circling down the garden path. I lead him unknowingly, making my forward steps a little longer and my backward motions slightly shorter, my heart rate remaining steady, controlled and precise as I wait, feeling his hand move down from my waist to rest on my ass.

Oh I'm going to enjoy this, I vow, feeling my pulse heighten once more and a violent spark ignite my raging temper. I quell the urge as Enzo's eyes catch mine and his mouth begins to move, emitting sounds I will soon silence.

"You really are a beautiful woman… but there's something about you, something different than the others."

Well, he's right about that. I think, taking another long stride forward. I stare into his eyes, distracting him from our course.

"Yes, I'd say you're right there."

"And you've come so far, a beautiful woman like you shouldn't be fleeing in fear from some monster…" He lands himself in a verbal bear trap as we reach the edge of the gardens, the water frothy below.

"Ah, but you see I'm not fleeing Enzo. *I'm* what we're all running from." I smile, my eyes diluting black as a salacious smile pulls my lips back over white teeth. Enzo's eyes widen and he stutters, his foot reaching the edge of the cliff and dislodging rocks that fall into the still Italian waters below.

What is it about me, jackasses and cliffs? I wonder internally as I recall a similar situation not a few months back with Vex. I feel the darkness kick in as my muscular arms vein over with darkness. I pick up the creep by his collar, hanging him over the edge. He doesn't speak, only stutters in horror.

"Still want to dance?" I ask him, cocking my head to the left with a grin as I laugh.

143

"What are you?" He asks me, his Italian accent now completely dissolved in fear. I wonder if it's not in fact an act at this point.

"No, no, no. That's not how this works. I ask the questions. How many woman have you bullied into your 'affections'?" I ask him, my eyes still diluted onyx. He doesn't respond so I take a half a step forward. He's now completely suspended above nothing but thin air. He cries out in fear, though I don't know why. He's probably strong enough to survive the fall.

What a whimp.

At least Vex had taken it like a man.

"How many? And no lying! I can tell!" I shake him once more. His eyes lock on mine as they move hesitantly away from the destination of his impending fall.

"I don't know. Lots!" He exclaims, his arms hanging limp. He's not as equipped in fighting as I had expected, I sort of hoped he'd fight back a little so I'd get to hit him.

"So you're saying that you've forced other Water Nymphs into being with you?" I say, wanting to be clear. I want a good explanation, based on fact, to give Orion later. This guy deserves a short drop and a sudden stop, but I doubt Orion will see it that way unless I have something other than the fact he's been coming onto me with no witnesses and no one to back me up on my claim, I need something more.

"Yes! Now put me down!" He cries out, struggling against me with futile motion. I stand on the edge of the grass-covered cliff with a choice to make.

I could put him down right now and walk away... I ponder this for exactly one second. *Nah.*

I let him go, my fingers slipping from under the collar of his shirt only too easily.

"Whoopsie. Hands slipped!" I yell after him, holding my hands up as a sign of apology as he plummets toward the water below. He lands with a beautiful *plop* sound and I smile, happy with my decision as I turn on the ledge, ready to walk back up to the party and deal with the rest of this ceremonial rubbish.

I momentarily ponder having to explain Enzo's disappearance to Isabella, but decide I'll worry about it later. After all, I don't have anything to lose. So why shouldn't I have a little fun when I can?

Then it hits, the mist. It's another vision. Before I have the chance to take even a step I'm falling backward off the cliff and the only words I can think are:

Oh crap.

12
Worth

CALLIE

I'm on the floor of the library, breathless and content. Moonlight streams in through the window, and a light breeze rustles the tapestries that hang surrounding the doors, the only space on the walls that aren't covered in shelves. Speaking of books there are hundreds scattered about the floor, pages crumpled and open at random chapters.

"Well I think I capitalised on the opportunity of the moonstone... wouldn't you say?" Orion asks me. We're both splayed out, clammy and flush against the now empty shelves.

"Speaking of opportunities, where is my..." I begin, suddenly feeling my heart drop. Orion senses my concern and pulls the white stone from his pocket.

"It fell out of your cleavage when you uh, fainted." He places it into the centre of my palm as I exhale, calming myself.

"I thought I had lost it. Phew. I don't want to be sprouting a tail." I vocalise my concern and Orion nods.

"I guess we should have them made into pendants or something... it's so odd don't you think, that father never mentioned the fact that Moonstones trap the moonlight and let us..." I interrupt him.

"Yeah, I was thinking that. I guess he didn't want Saturnus using it, then again if he's a Psiren he can phase like Azure, I guess. Maybe it was more than that. Maybe it was about you." I feel the pieces fall into place. I know Orion had been flighty, 'a lone wolf' I'd heard him called before. It would make sense if Atlas had wanted him to stay close.

"Me?" Orion asks, getting to his feet and raising a hand to run through his ruffled mahogany hair.

"Yeah, if Atlas wanted you close by, giving you this wasn't going to help." I shrug and Orion sighs out. His eyes are filled with sorrow.

"Hey, are you okay?" I ask him, getting up off the floor myself.

"I guess I'm just learning that father had more in mind for me than I'd thought. He's made promises I can't possibly keep, and I don't think he's really given us that much to go on either... I mean we don't even know what The Conduit does. Or what the Pieces of Eight are none the less." He walks across the wooden floor of the room, his feet padding like that of a large cat, each step carefully placed. I look down at myself, my breasts are exposed and I flush slightly, realising I'm not wearing anything on my upper half, and only the large skirt of my outfit remains, though it is skewed. I twist it around my hips, correcting the way it hangs as Orion moves back toward me from the balcony. In his hands are the rest of my clothes and the shoes I had been wearing.

"Turn around." He demands, lifting the upper part of the dress over my head. I place both arms into it and he pulls it around my torso, lacing it up, with no undergarment beneath, at the back.

"You know for someone who thinks corsets are abominations you're awfully good at lacing up the back of this dress." I say, suspicious. He snorts at my comment, kicking the broken corset aside after he's finished lacing up the overgarment. He turns me to face him.

"Anything that causes you pain is an abomination. I grew up making fishing nets Callie, tying knots on my father's boat and learning to throw a line. That's why I'm good at lacing up corsets." *Oh...* I think, wondering how I'd gotten it so wrong.

"You've seen the women I've been with now. How can you think I'd prefer anyone other than you?" He asks me the question and I realise I've been stupid; I let the mermaid's get to me. *The mermaids.* I really need to have better confidence.

"I shouldn't have listened to the mermaids." I admit and he nods, kissing me on the forehead.

"No, you shouldn't have. Besides, they're all utterly green with envy." He smiles and my forehead creases. Orion places my shoes back on my feet and I sit on top of a wooden table that holds a lit sconce and a few scattered papers.

"Envy?" I ask him as I let my feet dangle and swing, enjoying my last few moments of casual behaviour before I'm once again thrust under the scrutiny of our hosts.

"Yes, I saw how they looked at you when I kissed you outside."

"But they all had soulmates. I don't see what there is to be jealous of?" I reason as he shrugs.

"Me neither. But we're not going to listen to them, regardless. We're going to live our lives how *we* want to. I want us to experience everything this world has to offer, Callie. I want to shower you with affection while I'm at it, and I want to laugh. A LOT." His eyes blaze with the possibility of our future and I start to feel excitement clutch at me too, but then the reality of it all hits me.

"After this war is over, let's do that world trip we talked about, a real holiday, okay?" I ask him and he nods with a grin. As my feet hit the floor, I hear the door behind me open. I pivot, wondering whom they've sent to find us, but instead I'm surprised to see Paolo stumble into the room with his arms around Daniella. I stand, frozen to the spot, especially when the light hits the couple and I realise the woman isn't Daniella at all. It's Claudia.

"Oops!" I hear Claudia giggle, realising quickly that she's clearly had too much wine. The couple stand still, staring at us and unsure of what to do. Then I see Paolo's expression turn curious at my discarded corset that lies on the floor, and the shelf that has also clearly been disturbed. Orion leans toward me, grabs my hand, and we march past the couple, who are still obviously intending to do whatever it is they came up here for. Paolo and Claudia slam the library door behind us as we exit, leaving only the echo of their erupting slurred laughter as we walk down the corridor.

"Did that actually just happen?" I ask Orion, stunned, as he looks at me with a concerned glance.

"Not a word of this Callie. You hear me? This could really mess things up for us." He looks worried and I frown. I can't say I had expected to see Paolo wrapped up in someone who wasn't his '*beautiful angel*', but my first instinct certainly hadn't been to think what it would do to our relationship with the Water Nymphs. Orion is right of course, but it proves that his time as the son of a ruler has given him more political inclination than my American high school education.

"I wouldn't have thought of that. You're right. I won't say anything." I whisper and he squeezes my hand. I kiss him on the cheek as we walk across the hall swiftly, brushing a little gloss from his face and readying myself to be on show. I reach up to touch my hair, which I know must be ruined, and Orion smiles.

"You look perfect. Come on. Let's get in there." He opens the large double wooden door and we slip inside.

AZURE

Sodden, cold and pissed off I crawl onto the shoreline of the Bay of Naples, my dress dragging up sand around me. Luckily for me the vision was quick or I probably would have drowned, not being able to phase mid vision and all. I suppose the vision would be short considering the point the Gods and Goddesses were trying to make was one a deaf mute could grasp. Psirens feeding dead bodies to the Necrimad, death and bloodshed is imminent yada yada yada!

Not really worth drowning over though, was it? I roll my eyes at this thought. Wouldn't that have just summed up my stupid existence, the Psiren that freaking drowned.

Absolutely hilarious.

The dress hasn't helped, weighing me down so when I had woken I was lying on the sea floor, running out of air and gill-less.

149

Stupid visions. I curse, hating them more and more. Ever since Starlet had passed, they'd morphed, changing into something more like a partial paralysing seizure from the Gods, having their goddamn intent stuffed into my head. It makes me sick, or maybe that's all the seawater I'm coughing up.

Ugh, I spew fluid that's not been filtered through my gills, like I've been taken hostage and penetrated by the sea. Next to me a slimy crustacean, a being less than human, a sea slug in fact, crawls up, sodden and angry looking. Stupid Enzo flops down onto the sand, the pain on his face giving me a kind of sick glee.

"I'm going to make you pay for that you little..." He starts, but I know now what I must do. I've had enough of men and their entitled bullshit. I'm going to Isabella, and then we'll see who will be paying.

The realisation that I have nothing to lose, the epiphany which I have been on the cusp of since the death of that which I had loved most, has freed me and I feel the sparks of electricity fire through synapses within my brain, making me reckless as darkness shortly follows. I don't care about the vessels; I don't care about the Psirens. I have done nothing but try to play nice and behave ever since the destruction of the Occulta Mirum. What had it gotten me? Nothing. My sister is dead and my brother doesn't seem to care. The Psirens destroyed The Knights of Atargatis in spite of my best efforts, and they also used my sister's blood to raise the thing that will kill us all because of her innocence, not in spite of it. Anything pure in this world is crushed, like flower petals made into potpourri, leaving only sickly sweet scent and nostalgia behind of what was once thriving. It doesn't matter how good I am, how moral I have become, or how much I try to hide the darkness of what I truly am. None of it matters. After everything, after trying to save her, after trying to do good, all that any of us are guaranteed is more loss, more pain, more suffering.

I suppose that's it then, some of us, the Callie Pierces of the world, are destined to succeed, to love and to be shrouded in the divine light of those who rule over us like pawns. While others are the discarded pieces, those who are used as bait, those who are put out as nothing more than fodder for a greater cause we don't believe in. That won't be me. Not me. Not I. Not today.

I storm through the town on foot, leaving a trail of wrath and puddles in my wake. I am sodden, the dress soaked and heavy, hanging off my body like a dead wet thing that's been run over by a Ferrari.

As I reach the front steps of the castle, I take a moment to stop as I'm slightly out of breath. I want to appear terrifying when I enter, so flawless composure is necessary. Taking one final deep breath and ignoring the cold that is seeping into my bones from the completely over the top garment I'm wearing, I whip my hair backward so it lays down my back, slimy and cold like rat's tails since it has lost any semblance of style. I take the steps two at a time, my feet bare as my shoes are now lying at the bottom of the ocean and make my way through the entrance hall at a sprint. I see wait staff staring at me, looking curiously from the banquet hall where they're cleaning up. I turn back at them, my eyes diluted and they high tail it out of reach, obviously realising I don't want to be questioned.

Finally, I reach the double doors of the hall and make my entrance, reaching forward and throwing both doors outward from me. They fly forward, letting a rush of cold air in at my back as I step forward into the room, where all eyes have turned to me.

"Azure! What on earth?!" Orion comes forward, giving me a warning glance, trying to tame me into something civil and good. That which I am not.

"I need to speak to *her.*" I point rudely toward Isabella, who is sitting in another throne at the head of the stone dance floor. Her eyes widen as she sees my attire, my wet hair and probably mascara-smeared eyes.

"Whatever happened to you? Ugh, you look simply… ugh!" Is all she can exclaim. My eyes dilate as Orion comes closer, trying to block my path but I shove him away with a snarl.

Not today, big brother. I muse internally as I dodge past him, nimble and fuelled by my rage toward Isabella's sorry excuse for a consort.

I think about his hands on other women who were not so strong as I, women who had not wanted them there. It makes my rage morph, growing larger and uncontrollable by the second. Casmire steps forward, sensing my threat, but before I can get even close to Isabella my foot catches on the

151

underside of my waterlogged dress and I fly forward, tumbling and furious, toward him in his overly tight Italian suit. We clatter to the floor in a heap and I feel something I haven't felt in a while, something unexpected. I feel like someone is sucking the air from my lungs and into their own. Casmire is beneath me, trembling, and the last thing I see is his confused expression as his eyes turn a glacial white and he inhales in surprise like it's his very first breath.

"He's the vessel!" I hear someone cry out as I feel the vision being pulled to the front of my psyche once more, the Psiren's swarming, killing, murdering the victims of the Cruise Liner accident that Solustus had instigated. Bodies being fed to the Necrimad.

Delightful. I'm blunt in this thought, pissed off that I'm having to witness this crap *again.*

The vision passes from him, the little thief, and he goes limp beneath me like a dead fish as I get to my feet, wiping my hands on the front of my skirt and wincing slightly where my knees have hit the unforgiving stone of the floor.

Now where was I? Oh yes. Her.

I stride over Casmire's collapsed figure, stepping toward Isabella and trying to rekindle my rage.

"What is the meaning of this?" Isabella asks, getting to her feet with an outraged expression.

"Your *consort* just tried to assault me!" I yell out, watching her expression. I expect shock, or maybe even disbelief, but her features are impassive instead.

So she knows. I think to myself, pulling a disgusted grimace.

"Outrageous! Enzo would never do such a thing!" She exclaims, entirely false in her retort.

"Look lady, I don't care what deluded little fairy land you're living in with your fancy ass cars and ridiculously tasty wine, but you can't let him get away with this! What if next time it's not someone who can just throw him off a cliff? What if next time it's one of your friends? Or your daughter?" A gasp emits from the crowd and I watch as Daniella disappears into the corridor.

"You threw him off a cliff?" Isabella cocks an eyebrow and sits back down in her throne, frowning.

152

"He deserved it!" I exclaim. Orion has a hand on my shoulder and I turn once more, tearing my eyes away from the Queen who I am publicly shaming and onto the sodden and bruised figure of Enzo who is limping on Daniella's arm into the hall.

"Azure! What the hell are you doing! This isn't right? You can't just..." Orion starts but I cut him off.

"What? Defend myself from being assaulted? I don't care if he's the bloody King of England..." Callie comes forward, Marina at her side.

"Isabella, please, just listen." Callie implores her and Marina smiles weakly.

"What? What is it you could possibly say that would justify this kind of rudeness in the face of what generosity we have shown you?" Isabella snaps and Callie pushes Marina forward.

"Queen Isabella, I... I am an Empath. I can feel what other people are feeling you see..." She begins, unsure of herself.

Come on, hurry it up, hurry it up.

Isabella laughs like the ridiculous figurehead she is.

"How utterly absurd. Fine, what am I feeling?" She waves a hand before placing it back on her temple.

"Well, you're tired... and afraid. I think Enzo has done this before, but you turn a blind eye, to keep the peace. I can also feel fear coming off several of the women in this room, with a side of satisfaction at the fact he's been taught a lesson." She begins and Isabella's face goes slack in shock like she doesn't know how to respond.

Ha. I knew it.

"This is obscene." Enzo mutters as Isabella's eyes dart to him.

"Shut up." She demands and he drops his gaze like a puppy that's been spanked.

"I'll also tell you something else. The couple whose betrothal we are here to celebrate are not in love Isabella. Your daughter, she is not in love with Paolo. She is in love with another, the vessel." Marina speaks out and Isabella blinks a few times. She doesn't look happy, but at least she's not too stupid to listen.

153

"Go on."

"I wonder if perhaps you and Enzo were ever in love, or whether you were forced to marry as well?" Marina steps forward and Isabella sighs.

"Our pairings are decided now by what is most profitable for the pod as a collective. Long ago they were decided by the stars. But no longer. We are not here to always be happy; we are here to give security and protection to the people of Italy. We need money to do this. Not that it is your business, but Paolo has many links in high society and with organisations, that one does not speak of, which remain powerfully in control of today's world." Marina inhales slightly as Isabella gives us the clearly rehearsed speech.

"That's an awfully big price to pay. You know as well as I that our lives are not as fleeting as those who walk on land." Marina's pitifully large eyes are wide now and she looks like she might cry.

Oh for heaven's sake. Think about your credibility if nothing else. Cry baby.

I condemn her silently to status of a blubbering teenager. Isabella stands, her expression dead pan. She turns to me.

"Get out. All of you. Get out." She says the words calmly, but there's fierceness within her stare.

"No wait…" Callie stutters, pleading like the good girl she is, as her eyes dart to Casmire who's still strewn on the floor.

Isabella merely points to the door.

ORION

Out on the sands of the bay of Naples we sit, defeated and tired. I'd known this quest was going to be difficult, but I hadn't realised quite how much would be relying on the co-operation of others. Callie is sitting back in her dress, feet pushed out in the sand, letting the tide wash over them, but only just. Her forehead is creased and her eyebrows knitted together in concentration, trying to get some sort of clear handle on what to do next. Beside her I reach over and lay my hand on top of hers. She looks to me and smiles.

"So what, now we're just going to sit here and mope?" I hear Skye's tone caught up among the sloshing of the incoming tide.

"What else is there to do? They blew it." Rose replies, snarky as usual. I roll my eyes, a lump forming within my ribcage that won't shift. I'm angry, and suddenly it occurs to me why. I get to my feet in the early dawn, the wind ripping the shirt around my body in an uncoordinated cotton mess.

"Hey, why don't you just shut up, both of you." I know it's not the most democratic reply, but I've had enough of these two and their constant berating.

"What's that supposed to mean?" Rose asks, also getting to her feet. I straighten my spine and brush my fingers through my knotty tousles as I feel a speech coming on.

"It's supposed to mean that if you think you can do it better, why don't you? I mean all you seem to do is criticise everyone else, but I'm unable to remember a time when you've stepped forward to help us. You're only here because you're scared to be alone." I say the last sentiment with venom, aggravated that they're less than supportive in every respect.

"Well I'm sure I could…" Rose begins but I cut her off.

"Sure you could have what, Rose? What have you done to help except whine and stand around looking pretty? If you really want to help, you'd be trying to make connections with the other pods, or helping us to find the vessels. As far as I can see none of you have bothered doing any of this. Even you two…" I point toward Cole and Ghazi who are slumped in the sand, "have done nothing. The only person here other than myself and Callie who seems to give a damn is Marina." Azure looks up to me with a resentful stare. "Don't you look at me like that Azure, don't you dare, it's because of you we're in this mess. If you hadn't have stormed in there we'd probably be on our way to the next pod by now!" I'm ranting now and I know it. The pod look defeated, robbed of both my approval and our goals.

"Orion, I stepped up today, but I should have kept my mouth shut too, it's not like I've been much help either." Marina admits, looking guilty as well as heartbroken. Sophia pats her on the back and looks up to me with a frown.

155

"What I'm trying to say is that this isn't just something that Callie and I have to deal with because we're Crowned Rulers. This affects us all. If you don't want to continue on this journey with us then we understand, it's not going to be easy, but don't think you can sit back and take all the luxuries of the Water Nymphs and do nothing to help our cause. If you're not helping, you're just dead weight." I finish my speech, looking at them all. Nobody moves to get up or leave, nobody says anything. Callie finally leans forward, her blond hair falling around her face and exhales in a sigh.

"I know back in Moray Firth you all told me you're scared to die. I am too, but the truth is this is bigger than us. It's bigger than Orion and me, it's bigger than any single pod. It's about the world. It's about keeping the lives of millions safe from bloodshed and slaughter. You could run from this place, leave and never return, but that only makes us weaker, and that means that one day you won't be able to run from the bloodshed anymore. Because it'll find you if we fail. Sacrifice isn't supposed to be a walk in the park. It's about giving up something you want for the greater good, like that night you watched me die over the Occulta Mirum. You said you saw bravery in me. You believed in me. Now it's time for you to decide if you can make that sacrifice too, because without that, we really don't have much of anything." Callie looks at Sophia, looks at the mermaids, to Fahima and Emma, and I stare at her, slightly in awe. She never ceases to amaze me.

"We were put on this planet as mer to protect the world. This is what that means at the core, doesn't it?" Sophia asks and Callie nods.

"I'm afraid so." Skye puts her arms around Rose and Emma cuddles up to Alannah. Ghazi holds Fahima's hand and Cole holds my eye contact, a sign of his undying loyalty.

"The thing is, The Conduit is really the only lead we have on how to win this war. So if we don't get the vessels together, unite the military forces behind these pods and find the pieces of eight, we might as well not bother showing up at all. It'll be a bloodbath." I speak this terrifying thought aloud and the group look up to me, then to each other with determined faces. Marina stands, staring back at me as the early light of the sun begins to shine from beneath the edge of the glittering horizon. The bloody light catches in her eyes and she smiles slightly, an idea igniting her expression. Azure looks to me and rolls her eyes as Marina speaks.

"Let's get to the temple. I have a plan."

Inside the temple all is still and empty. I grab my satchel which is propped beside Isabella's throne where she had stored it for safe keeping, it's heavy on my shoulder as I haul it up, replacing my armour which lays beside it. We had managed to prize open the hatch from which we had first entered this sacred lost place, so I suppose you could say we are breaking and entering.

"Can you find anything that would indicate they have a supplier?" I look to Marina who is combing through the lost treasures that are piled high behind the throne.

"Not really, it's as I expected. I didn't notice any of them wearing anything that would indicate such ties either." Marina responds. Callie nods.

"I did think it was strange, the fact that they didn't have anything up in the dressing rooms now you mention it. Especially seeing as how everything else is completely over the top, you'd sort of expect it." Callie says this and suddenly I hear a rumbling from above, indicating that the Water Nymphs are returning.

"Quick, out there everyone! Marina you stay here with me." Callie darts away down the darkened corridor of the temple, hidden from view by the shadows cast from the roof that's falling inward. I stand up straight, erecting myself in the water and gripping Marina's arm with one hand. Light streams in as the recently closed rock hatch moves and in floats Isabella like a gush of overly perfumed air.

"Can you believe it?" I hear her exhale as she reaches the floor, sand pluming up around her as she turns, realising she is not alone. I put on a stern expression.

"Sorry to intrude. But I had to collect my things before leaving, I'm sure you understand. I also wanted to give Marina here a chance to apologise. I think we all know she overstepped." I look at her with mock disappointment plastered on my face, flicking my royal blue tailfin slightly and rising in the water so I may look down upon her.

"Well, that's very kind." Isabella seems meek for a moment and I wonder why, she had seemed so angry in the main hall of Castella Aragon. Perhaps now she realises she was a little rash.

"Marina..." I push her forward in the water. Marina bows her head and moves forward, sniffling. Her scarlet tailfin undulates and her overly shiny gold breastplate makes it clear she's never actually been in battle. When she gets close enough to Isabella, who is once again clad in the ornamental gold wired corset hung with starfish and jellyfish ornaments, Marina grabs her hands and looks upward, tears shining in her eyes.

"I am so sorry if I embarrassed you your highness. I was just so, so distraught. You see, I lost my own soulmate very recently. It's made me incredibly emotional." She begins to cry and I watch Isabella's gaze drop to the floor and her eyes widen as the teardrops start to crystallise.

Hook, line, sinker. Dammit Marina you're good.

The woman deserves an Oscar. And Isabella's concern for her suddenly takes on a life of its own.

"Oh Darling! Don't cry, it's okay. I've known about Enzo's infidelity for a long time. I didn't realise how bad it had gotten though. I also didn't see how unhappy my own daughter was, would you believe?" She cups Marina's chin in palm and I cock my hip to one side and cross my arms.

"I think you'd agree it's been an eventful evening all round. Especially considering Casmire has now been identified as the vessel for Neptune." I bring the conversation back around to where I want it to be. Marina wipes underneath her eyes and sniffles once more for extra-added effect. Isabella reaches down and picks up one of the diamonds now resting at the bottom of her tailfin in the sand sweeping across the temple floor.

"Indeed, I find it, interesting your father never mentioned you had the ability to cry diamonds..." She says, passing the stone between her fingers before holding it up to the light.

"He didn't mention it? I thought he would have for sure." I say, faux curiosity overtaking my demeanour.

158

"No, it wasn't mentioned. I would have remembered something like that." Isabella continues to examine the diamond as she floats backward through the water before settling in her plush throne. "The clarity is flawless..." She mutters, breathless, like she's about the faint or something. The diamond reflects its multifaceted rainbow in her eyes and it looks as though she's viewing a multi-coloured universe for the first time.

"Anyway, I think we had better go. We have other pods to be meeting with, and I also, if it's alright with you, would like to find Casmire to see if he's still happy to accompany us into battle with the Psirens. It is his calling after all..." I trail off and turn to leave. "Come on Marina." I call to her, looking back. She moves through the water, slowly as we both hold our breaths, waiting.

As she reaches me we move to the door and then suddenly the thing we've been waiting for happens.

"Orion, wait one moment..." The sound reaches me and my heart leaps. *Success.*

Before I turn back to make the deal I stare out into the corridor before me. From the shadow I see the unmistakable smile of the one I love, and I know that together, there is nothing we can't accomplish.

We hover before the rumbling cycle of the Whirlpool again, ready to move on. All in all, I can't complain, now clad in armour which isn't holding me hostage like my Italian tailored suit, and having secured the forces of the Water Nymphs as well as Neptune's vessel, I'd say we've been lucky at best. I look sideways to Azure, who's once more atop Philippe and sulking with a pursed face, black hair draped around her like a veil. She's a problem I can't ignore for long, with her outburst in front of the Selkies, and throwing the Queen's consort of a cliff, her rage and grief at losing her soulmate is out of control. I know I need to do something, but I'm not sure what I can do short of bringing Starlet back from a world beyond this one.

I turn away from her, facing forward and a more pressing engagement as I appreciate the crystalline and bright vivacity of the Mediterranean Sea. We could be anywhere in just a few moments, so I take it in, vowing to bring Callie back here one day for a real holiday, a vacation with dancing and drink and fine dining. Everything she deserves. Isabella looks kindly to me, her smile sweet and genteel.

So she should, I sigh internally, after all she's robbing me blind with the amount of diamonds she's requesting in exchange for her army's service. The deal isn't merely about amount of cargo either; she's got me on a schedule for delivering them in years to come as well.

"Thank you for everything." She comes forward to me, her daughter still meek at her side and fiddling with the whale pendant between her forefinger and thumb.

"You're most welcome, but before I forget, and now you're basically robbing me... I have a small request." I give a cheeky smile as I watch her partially melt.

"For you my darling, anything. You've made me an even richer woman than I thought possible. So what is it you desire? Tell me." Callie is staring at me, surprised in her expression, which I notice from the corner of my eye.

"I want you to let your daughter marry for love, Isabella. After all, I've just made you a very rich woman. You need not marry her off for wealth." I say it with a straight expression, my stare intense.

"What an odd thing to ask..." She begins, but I cut her off.

"Isabella, you see, I understand the value of choice. Callie has shown me that. No one should be forced to do anything that doesn't make them happy. We're fighting to maintain the freedom of the mortals who live in this world, so don't we deserve the same freedom we're giving them?" I ask her and she smiles, shaking her head.

"You're very cheeky darling, but yes... I yield to your request. Daniella may choose who she marries." She exhales, like a great weight has been lifted that she didn't know existed and Daniella's eyes widen behind her, staring directly into my face with more gratefulness than I'd thought possible. She doesn't, however, stay facing me for long. Instead she turns, rising in the water above the crowd, her hair swaying as a single word falls from her lips, dripping with long awaited emotion.

160

"Casmire?" He is back in the crowd somewhere, buried among the golden armour clad warriors of their army, all of whom have turned out to send us off. Their numbers are large, pleasing me, and I watch on as Casmire rises and moves forward in a rush of bubbles. Only moments later his hands are in Daniella's long hair and his lips are on hers.

I look to Callie, smiling and averting my eyes as I don't want to intrude on the moment. They remain in each other's arms, kissing, for longer than anyone expects.

"Well, uh. We'd better get going." I admonish as the couple part, breathless and flushed at the sound of my voice. Isabella looks truly happy at the look on her daughter's face. I look around for her companion Enzo, but find he is nowhere in sight.

"Where's Enzo?" I ask her, knowing the subject is sensitive but unable to help myself. Callie elbows me in the side and I wince, Isabella watches us with amusement, before replying without falter.

"He and I are having a little spat right now darling… As you can imagine, I am less than impressed with his conduct." She turns sideways with a frown, her ruby clad tail glittering in the deep sun of the afternoon, catching Casmire's gaze, which has travelled across her to the man who he is replacing.

"Paolo, I am sorry for this sudden change in arrangements. I hope you do not hold it against me…" She begins to apologise, but his relieved expression is already acceptance enough. His head turns, seeking out another individual in the crowd. Claudia bustles forward, armour clanking and he takes her hand in his. His eyes shine a light blue, surrounded by square cut tanzanite.

"I too have love for another, Isabella…" He begins. Isabella looks slightly taken back, her dark hair moving around her as she looks between the two now happily matched couples.

"All is well that ends well I suppose." She sighs, laughing in a highly melodic titter.

"I'm so glad everything worked out. It's time for us to move on though. Casmire, you know what to do, when this whirlpool starts up again, it is time to move." I remind him and he nods.

"I will not forget, Your Highness. Thank you for uniting my beloved and me. I owe my life's happiness to you." He reiterates the sentiment by moving forward with a single flick of his peridot encrusted tailfin and shaking my hand vigorously.

"Also, make sure to look out for anything termed as a 'Piece of Eight.' Okay?" Callie reminds him, moving forward and kissing him on both cheeks. She flushes slightly as I watch the gesture, surprised it's one she's maintaining.

"We'll see you on the battle field." I nod to Isabella and she shifts, cocking her hip and getting a sassy look on her face. I feel her army shift behind her as well, straightening their spines and adjusting their armour in all its golden glory.

"Oh don't worry darling, we'll be there. Those Psirens won't know what's hit them." She laughs dramatically and turns from us to view her forces. Daniella gives a shy smile and Claudia and Paolo begin kissing amorously. I look to my own soulmate, her eyes wet with happy tears.

"That was a lovely thing you did." She whispers.

"I realised how awful arranged relationships are. How trapped you must have felt by the whole soulmate thing. I'm sorry, I never realised how much pressure I put on you in the very beginning... I was just so..." I'm babbling, gushing all the emotions that have been welling inside me at observing the mismatch of Daniella and Paolo. Callie places her fingers to my lips.

"Shhh. No apologising. I just want to look to the future now. Okay?" She asks me and I smile. She's right as usual; I suppose looking to the past isn't any use. After all, the future has far more pressing concerns.

"Are you ready?" She queries, a gentle smile curving her lips. I feel comforted by her face, every single defining line of her features so well mapped in my mind that I know I better than any work of art. I nod, unable to tear my gaze from her aquamarine eyes, glad she is at my side through all of this, and scared at how close I've come to losing her in the past. I part my lips to answer her, but before I can say a single word Cole is already counting, signalling our entry into the whirlpool.

"One... two... three..."

My hand in Callie's, I am swept away once more, as though I am nothing more than sand at the bottom of a vast endless sea.

162

13
Ambush
CALLIE

The whirlpool is ravenous, coursing against my skin with a rabid bone deep clutch, pulling me apart. Suddenly everything halts and I'm hurled outward from the portal, thrust once more into the unknown.

I exit the whirlpool at the back of the pod this time, after the rest of the mer have moved from its transforming energy and out into the waters of our next destination. I watch as Orion swims ahead, having lost grip of me somewhere between Naples and here. He turns, his eyes searching for me. I take a stroke forward, reaching out to him through the water as the mermaids part to let me through. They watch me, tense as we hang in the open though I cannot discern why.

A sudden cry breaks the silence, a scream so high pitched and feral that it cuts through my current thought like a savage blade. I jump, my heart kicking into high gear as the dark sand beneath us begins to shift, mutating and falling away. A spear cuts through the water in a sudden and lethal jerk. It misses me by mere millimetres. Orion's eyes widen.

"GO CALLIE, GO!" He yells, his face contorting in horror. Before I can turn, transfixed by what lies beneath and with the whirlpool at my spine, another spear comes from nowhere, aiming for Orion. This time though, it's deadly in its accuracy.

"Orion! No!" I cry out, reaching out to him despite the knowledge that I'm risking everything by doing so. My hand is knocked back by something launching from my left, intersecting the path of the projectile and taking the blow, protecting Orion as he watches, dumbstruck.

"Cole!" I hear Sophia's scream as Cole's body contorts, arcing with deadly grace before my eyes. Blood plumes from him like ugly perfume in the water.

No! I scream internally.

"STOP! Show yourselves! We mean no harm! We're not demons!" I call out. Orion unsheathes the trident from his spine as he rotates silently in the water. He places his other hand in mine and yanks me close to him.

"Spread out in pairs. GO!" He orders. I watch the mermaids hang in the open water, useless and vulnerable. Azure is already half a mile away, atop Philippe who is moving in a full on gallop with all the speed he can muster.

So much for a little dark assistance. I roll my eyes. She's really not a team player.

"Sophia, come on!" I grab her hand and pull, moving her as far away from the site as possible. We flee, rushing through the water, which is now a dim red with the dying light from the setting sun. I glance back just in time to see Ghazi pulling Cole's body through the water with him, Fahima in tow.

"What do we do Callie?!" Sophia looks to me as I halt and her continued movement through the water causes her to jerk forward, pulling my arm. I stroke back with my tailfin, standing my ground.

"Wait! We can't leave them! This isn't happening! We have to go back!" I exclaim, my hair blooming out around me in a tangled mess.

"We can't go back there!" Sophia protests, looking frightened.

"Stay here!" I don't think about the consequences of my actions, I just act. I make a hairpin turn, gritting my teeth and lunging forward, letting the water caress my silken skin as my heart pounds within my chest. I dive deep, close to the ground, close to the source. Suddenly that's when I see it, nearing Orion from below. A mass of mounds are firing spears at regular intervals. Orion is using the trident to deflect them, but with shooting mounds on all sides, I know he won't be able to keep it up for long. I slither, like a snake along the sea floor,

165

parallel to sand and debris. I swim head first toward a mound readying yet another spear to launch, not thinking, only fearing for the safety of my people.

When I finally reach my target, I realise I'm not looking at a banal camouflaged weapon, I'm looking at a *person.* I grab the creature by the throat, raising it up as I slide, causing my body to erect against the seabed. My heart is racing, my pulse thrumming as my muscles strain to trap the assailant.

"What are you?" I demand. Orion looks to me from above as he turns, deflecting another spear. The creature suddenly opens its eyes, revealing a pair of light green irises that protrude in a grotesque fashion from the face of the person I've got in my grasp.

"You speak." The creature speaks and then something bizarre happens. A tailfin appears within the bottom of my field of vision, rippling into existence slowly as the hairs on the back of my neck rise in both fear and awe.

"What are you?" I insist, my grip tightening. Amid the chaos, I notice that the spears have stopped. Other creatures are rising from the seafloor, showing themselves. All eyes are on me. The person in my grip doesn't answer.

"WHAT ARE YOU?" I bellow, having had enough. This time I direct my anger not to the creature in my grasp, but instead to the group rising up behind her. Orion sinks slowly until he's level with me.

"We are Maneli." One of them speaks, wiping his hand across his face and removing his heavily applied make up. The face revealed is stunningly masculine with tanned flesh, dark eyes and a spattering of yellow and black scales across his hairline and down the side of his face. It kind of looks like a jaguar pattern.

"What is that?" I question them, looking up to the woman in my grasp.

"We are warriors of Ava. Who are you?" The man asks, coming forward in one stroke of his still camouflaged tailfin. He towers above me, his body large, well-muscled and powerful, as seems so common among warriors of the Circle.

"We are the Children Of Atargatis." I say, releasing the warrior in my hand. I don't know whether I can trust them not to start attacking us again, but I can't hold her captive forever; especially if I want a peaceful resolution with

166

these people. Orion is next to me and I breathe out, slowing my heart rate as his hand wraps itself around mine.

"We've come, searching for you." He bows his head, showing them he means no harm.

"You're trespassing here." The figure that I assaulted speaks, her voice feminine now I take a second to listen. She wipes the camouflage paint from her own face, revealing her black skin beneath. She's got short hair, matted with sand and debris, making her practically invisible against the seabed.

It's genius. I smile to myself, *these are definitely the kind of people we need fighting beside us. But first, we need to try and convince them not to kill us.*

"What was the whirlpool from which you came? Dark Magic?" The woman hisses, her tongue lizard like and direct, slicing up her words quick and fast.

"No, magic from the Goddess." Orion acknowledges, smiling a little. Everything is tense between us as more of the so-called Maneli wipe camouflage from their faces. None of them have the chameleonic tail of the woman who's just spoken, and I can't help but watch it, hypnotically changing colour from waist to tip as she undulates in the water.

"Ava?" Her eyes widen, watching me with curiosity.

"Atargatis." I say it and she holds her head back slightly, moving away from me and pursing her thick lips. I immediately regret naming my Goddess with such certainty; after all it was probably the entire Circle of Eight who were responsible. I shift, feeling uncomfortable once more.

"Blasphemy. Ava is the true goddess of the seas. Any whelk knows that." She blows out bubbles and tightens her grasp on the spear. I examine it, it's quite high tech really, a shiny metal pole ending in a barb that looks like it's been torn from some sort of marine animal. Not as gracefully put together as one of Oscar's pieces, but none the less it's savage in its intent.

"I see… I'm sorry I didn't mean to offend you. I'm Callie." I soften my expression, trying to placate them again, but the woman moves further away.

"Kaiya." She replies with a suspicious stare.

"Rourke." The hulking man doesn't reach out to take my hand either.

167

"Orion!" The call reaches me and I pivot on the spot. It's Azure. She's gathered the rest of the pod who had scattered, bringing them back with her on horseback. With the rest of the pod in tow and her aback Philippe she looks like some dark Goddess in the bloody red water of sunset. *The lone horsewoman of the apocalypse. How fitting.* I muse, watching as the rest of our pod comes forward. I am hit hard at the sight of Cole, his body limp in Ghazi's arms. The mute moves through the mermaids, soundless, but tears are streaming down his face. He touches my arm, his grip on me frightening.

Please, save my brother. I can't do this without him, Callie. I look into his expression. He's devastated.

"Okay, it's okay. We'll fix this." I say, looking to Cole, making promises I have no way of keeping. Ghazi holds his arms out wider, stretching out Cole's body in front of Orion and me. I move forward, brushing his hair from his face. His forehead is warm and I let my eyes scan across his form until they land on his wound. The site where the Maneli spear had cut through his body like he were no more than ribbon is festering and angry, still weeping blood. More importantly, blackish green lines radiate out from the wound.

"What was on the end of that Spear?" I hear Azure's tones, concerned, surprising me. I turn to Kaiya and the man named Rourke. They look surprised at her also, but as she dismounts the Equinox I can sense she isn't playing games. I worry she'll lose her temper and make the situation even worse.

"Is this poison?" I ask them, Kaiya nods, unapologetic.

"I don't know what we can do." I turn to Orion, whispering now. He narrows his eyes.

"Let me handle this." He squares his shoulders, raising the trident in his left palm and grasping it with his right also. He turns and I watch him, slightly afraid of what he'll do.

"You need to take us to wherever we can get this man healed immediately. If you have an antidote, anything that can help, I suggest you get hold of it right now. You wounded him when he was no threat to you. We aren't a threat and yet we were attacked. I don't think your Goddess would find that very satisfactory behaviour from her warriors. As far as I'm aware Goddesses don't condone unprovoked murder." His tone is one of non-negotiable rage and his

168

stare is serious, desperate even. I know he thinks highly of Cole, and seeing him limp in Ghazi's arms is harrowing to say the least. Rourke is obviously taken back, but crosses his arms, his look stern.

"What do you think Kaiya?" He doesn't look to her but she narrows her eyes, staring at Orion with her continually suspicious and unfriendly gaze.

"I think we need to ask Ava. They must stand trial before Akachi." She shrugs as if what's she's saying means very little to her and Rourke stays stoic at her side, not even moving to recognise she's spoken.

"Come." He says, his voice deep. I still can't pinpoint his accent, but his gaze makes me forget this. He's gorgeous, I can tell that much even though he's still covered in camouflage. I look back to Cole, who lies unconscious, breathing in and out in pained staccato. I feel my heart falter. He looks like he's in so much pain.

"Orion can we really do this? What if..." I start. Orion looks to me and his gaze is certain.

"Callie, I can't lose Cole. He's my best warrior, probably my best friend. If I have a small chance of saving him with these Maneli then I'll take it. No matter what." His gaze burns with a passion that's normally reserved for me. I knew he and Cole were close, but it's not until right now that I get quite how deep that friendship runs.

"For Cole." I agree. With that, we follow our camouflaged attackers into the fading bloody din of the twilight sea.

It towers above us, cutting out the light from the setting sun in its sublimity. I float beneath the surface, looking at it from beneath the churning waters of the ocean, flabbergasted by its size.

"What is that?" I ask Orion, feeling my curiosity get the better of me. We've travelled in silence, unable to speak at the prospect of voicing our fears about Cole. It's as though even mentioning the possibility of him turning to nothing more than sand makes it more likely. So we do not speak of it. Not a single word.

"Cape Point." The two words come from Rourke in an abrupt exhalation. His eyes narrow, watching me closely.

"Cape Point..." I say, turning the name over on my tongue, trying to remember if I've heard it before.

"As in near Cape Town?" Alannah asks from behind me. She moves forward slightly, a bold move for her.

"Yes. Why?" Kaiya asks the question like this is an interrogation, her chameleon-esque tailfin twitching as her body tenses.

"We're off the coast of South Africa?" Orion looks surprised and I hear a shallow exhalation coming from behind me, reminding me that once again I have no time to waste. Cole is getting weaker.

"So, where to next?" I push the conversation on as the Maneli look to me, my impatience growing. "Whatever poison he's been skewered with is working fast. Can we move on please?" I don't want to seem hostile, but as I straighten my spine under the gaze of our attackers, I can't help but wonder if I can be expected to be anything else. I mean, what kind of people attack innocents with no questions asked? What kind of people develop a poison that can kill a merman? They clearly aren't placid in the least, so I'm finding it hard to be in turn.

"Very well. Come." Kaiya commands. I expect her to rise to the surface, close to the beginning of the rocky peak's ascent into the sky, but she does not. Instead she dives deeper, skimming the side of the great peak and tracing its outline with her path through the water. I follow, diving and feeling my ears pop and my lungs expand. Orion grabs my hand as he moves in beside me, looking to me with nothing but anxiety filling the space behind his irises. I look away, my own anxiety reflected at me as the pod descends along with us. Azure overtakes us both, her black hair blooming out around her like a dark orchid as Philippe's weight causes her to fall like a stone.

Minutes later, the Maneli stop beneath us. They're almost invisible from above, their camouflage making them blend in with the sea bed far beneath us, and it is only the dark patches of skin that are uncovered on their bodies that make them distinguishable against the sand strewn sea floor.

"Stop." I hear the command, pushy and authoritative. I am already slowing my descent, and I can see the mermaids beside me getting a nervous look, like they're no more than students being scolded by a strict teacher.

As we halt, hanging beside the enormous rock mass that towers high beyond sea level above us, Kaiya moves forward and pushes a boulder away. The boulder is perched on an outcrop of rock, a natural ledge that would be invisible if you didn't know it was there. I feel Ghazi's mass behind me and a palm rests on my shoulder as I turn. It's Fahima.

He grows weaker. She whispers, the sentiment wandering through my mind, fleeting as a wisp of smoke.

"I know." I murmur. Rourke looks back to me, his eyes wide and angry.

"What was that?" He barks, his tone deep and threatening.

"Nothing. I was just muttering." I reply, setting my shoulders square again. He turns away without another word.

Well, how rude. I think to myself, my heart racing. I can't bear to turn to look at Cole again, and I know Orion feels the same as he hangs stiff in the water like a statue.

The boulder's absence reveals an opening into what looks to be a deep cave and the Maneli enter in silence. Orion looks to me and frowns, and I feel his anxiety transferring to me as well. We could be swimming into a trap. We could be leading everyone to their deaths.

Then a thought occurs to me.

If these really are a pod that belongs to a Goddess of the Circle of Eight, shouldn't we trust in that? I think about this for a moment, and as I look into the darkness of the tunnel before me, I can't quite find the belief to rely on pure faith. I'd never really thought about it before, but this fear, this anxiety that is within me is partly because I don't have faith in the Goddess. Not completely. Not enough to put mine and everyone else's lives on the line. My heart deflates in my chest at this thought, but before I can ponder on it anymore, Orion has grasped my palm in his and is leading me into the dark.

171

The tunnel is long and claustrophobia creeps in, making my skin feel hot as blood races close to its surface. Philippe cannot follow us, the passage is too narrow, so Azure whispers something softly in his ear and sets him free, allowing him to graze nearby among local flora. Her eyes aren't diluted black, but her attitude is none the less frosty as she overtakes me, pushing me up against the wall of the tunnel as her charcoal scales brush against my torso.

"Watch it!" She snaps at me. Orion rolls his eyes and sighs. The Maneli in front of us don't turn back, moving ever forward into the centre of Cape Point. All of a sudden the Maneli before us disperse and the tunnel opens up. Before me is a sight I couldn't have imagined, even if I'd tried.

The inside of the Triangular peak is half filled with water. Beneath the water line is an entire city, thrumming and vibrant. The architecture isn't fancy, or even pretty; it is crude, basic but functional. So functional in fact, the next part of the city that I notice leaves my forehead creased in confusion.

"Electricity? They have… Electricity…" I say, my mouth dropping so it's hanging open. Azure backs up to my side and closes my jaw for me.

"Wow, someone's easily impressed." She tosses her black hair behind her shoulder and Orion rolls his eyes again. I can tell he's getting annoyed with her, but he's also got far more pressing concerns.

Looking to the surface I can see the slanting V shaped peak of the rocky point above, and that the water level is sustained by several waterfalls, trickling through cracks that let in water from the outside. These cease above a certain point however, leaving the internal space of the hollow cliff only half full. Greenery hangs down from the high ceiling, and I can see its lush tangles, somehow having made their way through solid rock. It falls in cascades like the hair of Mother Nature, reminding me of the fact that all things in nature are connected. Even me.

"How is this possible?" Orion asks Rourke, unable to help himself. Rourke turns and sighs, his musculature slouching.

"Hydro-electric-power." He says in a simple monotone. It makes sense, and for a moment I can't help but ask myself how nobody has thought of this before. The mer have nothing in abundance if not sea water, so why not use it to power a city?

172

"That's genius." I say, trying to break down the divide of our deities.

"Thank you." Rourke nods to me, still stiff in his movement. "Come, we will take you to Akachi now." The group of Maneli move as one entity, their synchronicity uncanny and entirely supernatural. I had seen the Knights of Atargatis move before, but I'd never seen anything like these warriors. Every single motion is copied a dozen times over by each Maneli, even the slightest twitch, hand movements, everything. It's almost like they're of one mind, a hive mind.

We move forward too, lurching into the streets of the city before us. It's tightly packed, and full of tiny shanty town like huts which are roofed with corrugated metal that seems to come from boats that have met a nasty end. The whole place has a too bright glow, as crudely hung wires connect street lamps together via unorganised and tangled webs.

I can hear people talking within the huts, people humming, singing and praying. As we move toward the epicentre of the space, I notice a building that seems to be brand new, untouched. It has sweeping lines to it, curves, as it rises to a sharp point. I want to ask what the building is for, but the Maneli are too far in front of us for my questions to be heard.

"This is amazing. Who would have thought that this place would be inside a cliff?" I hear Rose say, enthusiastic. It's then as Ghazi overtakes me, Cole's form still limp in his arms, that I realise why we're here, and know my energies need to be on getting him help.

"Come on everyone." I call, hurrying them along. As we move quickly through one of the many narrowing streets of the city, I observe that it leads into a kind of central courtyard. I look around and notice that this focal point is definitely the centre of the city, with all roads leading toward it and the architecture surrounding it pristine. The Maneli disperse in front of us, moving to line the open circular space. Rourke pushes forward in the water, eclipsing the figure he is addressing with his massive stature.

"Akachi. I bring to the Oseaan Se Wieg, trespassers." His words ring out and I frown, my lips sagging at his tone.

"Oh?" I hear the voice ring out, deeper than thunder and more ancient sounding than rain hitting the savannah. Rourke turns and reveals us, floating

173

nervously in the street behind him. Ghazi leads us, Cole splayed out in his arms with black lines creeping slowly from his wound and toward his heart like slow moving bullets.

Orion swims up and over him, pulling me with him and leading me into the stark light of the centre space.

"Sir, please…" He begins, but the one they call Akachi rises from his throne and I inhale. I've never seen anything like it.

"No please, who are you?" He looks elderly and it alarms me. I'm not used to seeing older mer. Every single one of Atargatis' children are immune to time. I bow my head at his imminence, pulling Orion to his knees as well.

"What are you doing?" He whispers urgently.

"Bow!" I say, feeling Akachi's eyes fall onto my form.

"We're sorry to intrude. Your grace." I feel the words fall from me, instinctual and entirely unrehearsed. His gaze causes the hairs on the back of my neck rise, in both fear and awe.

"Rise." He orders, and I do, letting my eyes settle on him. One look upon him was all it had taken for me to fall on bended fin. When I study him in detail I know why he unnerves me so. He is blessed, blessed by the Goddess Ava. This was how I had felt the first time I had looked upon Saturnus, only this time it's real. It's too startling not to be, and where Saturnus had merely been an actor playing with makeup and glimmers. Akachi is not. Akachi is terrifying and awe inspiring all at once. I stare at him, his crocodile like eyes, blinking horizontally and revealing lime green irises that burn into me. His tail is long and scaled in crocodile hide too. His dark palm grasps a tall crooked staff, where higher up a small crocodile wraps itself, holding a glistening golden orb between its jaws. Akachi's age has no bearing on my assessment that he is strong. He rises from the throne of metal and bone on which he sits. Though where Solustus had once draped himself across a throne of bone like a damsel in distress, Akachi owns the chair. The bones it is consists of are not stolen, but given from the earth from whence they came.

"We are from the Pacific. We are the Children of Atargatis, Your Grace." I speak fluidly once more and Orion is staring at me. Akachi jerks through the

174

water, lightning fast and with only a sideways flicker of his crocodile-esque fluke. He is nose to nose with me.

"There is no such thing child. Ava is all there has ever been. All there ever will be." He breathes it out like it's a prayer he's speaking and the crocodile wrapped around his staff blinks at me, unfeeling.

"Please, listen. We have come from the Pacific. Whether it be by Ava's will or any other deity. We need your help." I say this and Orion's eyes widen.

"It is by Atargatis' will. I assure you. Our seer will attest to that." I cringe internally. Can't he see that these people are devout, that they are proud? I don't know where it's come from, but my newfound diplomacy drives me forward.

"Akachi, Ava's warriors have injured our friend. Please, he has been poisoned. Can you help him?" I ask him this, choosing my words carefully. This is not the place for me to pull sass, or Americanisms out of thin air. This is the time to put myself in the open-minded place where I can try to respect their culture.

"You are trespassers here. No more." Akachi waves a hand and Orion looks to me, his eyes wide. This is why we can't bargain with him.

We need him, and he needs nothing of us. These people aren't the Water Nymphs or the Selkies, they are someone new and entirely unknown to us. We really aren't in the position to insult them. I think internally, knowing that Orion's old world ways may just get Cole killed. I love Orion, but he's not always open minded when it comes to his Goddess.

"Please, Ava needs us to succeed. She is a part of a council, with many Gods and Goddesses. We need this man to live. He's our best chance at stopping the demons in our waters." I say the word demon and Akachi's head turns. His eyes blink sideways and his mouth turns downward in a sag. His dark hair is veined through with grey and lies in cornrows against his skull, before falling in long vines down his back.

"Demons?" He asks and I nod silently. Beside him a woman appears from the shadows beyond the stark light of the centre space.

"Amara, what do you make of this?" Akachi asks, turning to face her and keeping us at his back. The woman is gorgeous, but in the oddest way imaginable. Her skin is a lightly dusted bronze, like she's been bathed in dust

175

from the sun, and her body is covered in golden tattoos that contrast against her darker skin. Her eyes are yellow and vibrant in her face, which has feline features unlike anything I've ever seen. Her hair is a silken black waterfall that looks pristine and untouched and her tailfin looks like it's coated in black velvet. Black scales of the same velvet looking material wrap around her arms and around her neck, falling down over her breasts in a halter-top silhouette. Her arms are clad in gold bangles up to the elbow, and her ears hold falling chandeliers of gold vines.

"Bring the wounded forward." She demands, her voice high pitched yet malleable, like it could wrap around you and squeeze you to death, the boa constrictor of all sounds. Upon these words, Ghazi swims forward and lays Cole down before Orion and me. My heart falters when I see him. His skin is mapped with a mouldy green looking web of poison running through his veins and his gills open and close slowly. Too slowly. The wound looks dreadful as well, a puncture under his diaphragm, only narrowly missing his left lung. He took the spear for Orion, saved his life. He cannot die. He cannot.

Amara moves forward, diving slightly to reach him on the ground. Ghazi hovers, immovable, and stoic beside him, guarding him in case she tries to harm him further. The warriors who are still camouflaged float around us and the rest of our pod move forward. I turn to watch them pour in at our backs. We're surrounded and vulnerable.

"This is my fastest working poison. It's a wonder he's alive at all." She turns to Akachi as she says this.

"You have an antidote?" Orion asks, unable to help himself.

"Yes. But it is in short supply. Using it on someone I barely know from a demon..."

"I'll pay you!" Orion blurts. Akachi turns and his eyes blaze with lime fire.

"How dare you! The gifts of Ava cannot be bought!" He snarls and Orion leans backward. He moves in, teeth bared as I notice with horror that they're filed into points. In an instant and completely out of nowhere, Azure comes flying through the water, over me and Orion, who can only look on in horror, and into the chief. She holds her hand to his throat, covering his gills.

"Okay, Mr medicine man… I'm getting pretty sick of you people and your religious bullshit!" She begins a speech, but within an instant her arms are bound behind her back, her tailfin flailing and Rourke has his left hand in her hair, pulling her head back from her skull.

"You. Do. Not. Attack. Akachi." He says this with staccato, his voice deep like a gorilla's roar. I wonder momentarily how many words he actually knows.

"Take her to Callista for purification!" Akachi waves his hand and Kaiya moves forward, grabbing Azure's tailfin to stop her escaping.

"Orion! Aren't you going to do something?" I turn to him and he shrugs.

"Callie, I can't… My responsibility is to this pod. Azure will have to work it out on her own." He bites out and I feel my heart inflate slightly. I'm not saying he's right in letting them take her away, but she's not doing what's in the best interest of the pod right now. I watch her, struggling with wide eyes as we do nothing and she disappears down into the stark contrast of light and shadow in the narrow street behind us. Then I take a moment to think about what Akachi said.

They're going to *purify* Azure? I snort.

Well. They can try.

14
Blindside
SOLUSTUS

The beast leans back on its haunches, letting out an enormous roar as my army throw it the last of the bodies from what was a mass grave. It has devoured them all. Leaving nothing behind.

I feel him before I see him, his proximity known to me as the hairs on the back of my neck rise ever so slightly in uniform abandon of my conscious whim to ignore him. I turn in the water, but come face to face not with the eyes I am expecting, but with another pair, which I have not seen in so long.

"Titus? Really, Saturnus?" I cock an eyebrow, turning away from him, acting un-fazed. The snake-like tones of my predecessor creep around my neck and into my ear, slithering into my brain like a viper, unwelcome and slick.

"I thought you'd be pleased to see an old friend. After all, you are acting as though you know no better than he." Titus' voice it may be, but Saturnus' intent is dripping from every syllable like poison laced blood.

"How dare you!" I move to face him, my tail swinging behind me, compensating for my momentum.

"How dare I?" He laughs, Titus' gaunt face staring at me, his eyes dark and forked with lightning. "We are supposed to be a team! You're the one who went behind my back brother. You're the one who betrayed my confidence!" The glimmer falls away and Saturnus returns to himself, his voice fading from snake like to authoritative in a seamless dissolving of dark magic.

"I did what needed to be done. The beast is fed." I bark, turning away from him, ending the conversation. I will not be belittled or likened to someone as stupid or as blinded by rage as Titus.

"You disappeared with the entire Psiren Army Solustus! Tell me, exactly how incompetent are you?!" He barks again, moving in front of me now and eclipsing my view of the Necrimad's scaly hide.

"Not as stupid as you might think brother, I cut communications. There is no risk of discovery. You forget; I've been on land and among humans far more regularly than you. I know their world. You, do not." I reason and his eyes blaze. He snarls, baring his teeth in feral displeasure

"And what do you think these humans will deduce when they find a sunken cruise liner with no bodies, brother? What, that they just magically disappeared into the aether?" He says it calmly, but his voice shakes with tremors of irritation and loathing towards me. Then I realise he has a point. I had cut communications from the ship, but eventually someone would discover the fate of The Zenith. The lack of bodies could in fact be a problem... "Ah, I see you didn't think about that did you? Well I did, and had you come to me I would have notified you of your little miscalculation. We may have a vast array of disposable warriors, but you forget that without the powers of the Necrimad, the human race could still pose a threat. They have guns. Weapons. Children of darkness are no match for that. Certainly not from what I've heard about Japan..." He begins, reminiscing about the horror he had felt, the gut wrenching disgust at the thought of nuclear weapons. Of radiation poisoning. Men playing with magic they do not understand and calling it science.

"No matter, what's done is done." I brush away my own concern as though it were no more than a dead thing, limp and useless, cutting him off mid-sentence. His dark eyes shift and his flared tail sways as we both turn from the beast, beginning our journey back into the remnants of what had once stood tall and glittered in the sun. I can't help but smile. Now I am the sun, and everything and everyone revolves around me.

"I should say so. You should know better than to exclude me brother. We are stronger as a team. You used to know this... now I am not so sure." Saturnus

179

frowns and I narrow my eyes. Genuine concern, from the likes of him? I doubt it very much. So what's his game?

"I apologise. It won't happen again." I murmur and Saturnus nods, composed once more, a cold mask of unfeeling disdain sliding in behind his once feral expression. It's worrying how he does that, turns his rage off and on at will. I do it too, but to him it's so completely controlled it's as though his rage cannot be genuine.

"How are the prisoners doing?" I ask him, bored of talking about my faux inadequacies.

"Caedes is still with them." Saturnus replies, lazy as he exhales. He looks drained, weary.

"You look tired brother." I comment and he laughs, as though I could not possibly be correct in my assessment.

"I've been reading. Translating from the languages of old is not easy." He runs his hand through his black hair, looking the most human I've seen him in a while.

"What are you looking for?" I ask him, feeling my heart pick up its stagnant rhythm slightly. I ignore it.

"Oh, nothing. I'm merely looking into how the power can be shared between two. I'd like to know more specifics about that part of the ritual to release the Necrimad's power."

"I haven't really thought about it." I sigh, looking at the dirt beneath my long nails, uninterested.

"There are two powers the beast contains but only one it cannot utilise, that particular power is raising the dead from the ocean depths, the other as you know is strength, speed and the power to generate so much heat that one can boil the water around them, but remain impervious to harm. One ability for each of us." Saturnus continues.

"And what have you found?" I ask him, wanting to cut to the chase, I'd rather be ordering around my army, or sharpening Scarlette, anything but listening to him talk about the languages of old.

"Nothing yet on how to split the power between us."

180

"Ah, I see. So you've failed?" I feel like laughing, *wouldn't it just be perfect if he couldn't get half my power.* The darkness that is always so prevalent like a fine mesh, coating each thought and manipulating it to evil, snaps, forming the jaws of a rabid dog.

"I wouldn't..." Saturnus begins but my attentions waver. Suddenly I see Caedes floating, innocuous and hazy in his motions, through the rubble-strewn streets below.

"What's he doing out?" I wonder aloud. Saturnus, who previously shot me a look of hatred as I interrupted him, pivots as well, following my hawk like gaze as his tailfin coils with fluid momentum.

"I don't know. I thought he was with Vexus..." Saturnus begins. I'm no longer listening. I descend through the water, levelling off in a convex arc close to the ground, which is now spiked with shattered glass.

"Caedes." I say the word and my brother turns. His red hair blooming out around him like blood strewn seaweed.

"Solustussssss....." He says, his eyes glazed. The lionfish spines of his tailfin twitch, slightly on edge at my sudden appearance.

"What are you doing here little lamb?" I use my childhood nickname for him, remembering how pure and naive he had been at birth. His red face and chubby hands grasping out for life, afraid and squealing, fighting the world he had entered against his own desire. I know it's a strange thing to say by any normal adult standard, but he is not normal. He might be a savage killer, but he's also as mentally competent as a deer whose mother has just been shot in the forest; flighty, glazed and insane with the weight of his own inability to perish. The name calms him, taking him back to a time when our mother had still held him to her breast.

"Bored..." He snarls, slashing his tail sideways in a sudden and violent exertion. The rubble beside him moves, sea-glass shifting. He reveals something beneath, black and opalescent, it shimmers hideously, familiar and a welcome sight in spite of its glamour. I swim quickly downwards, pulling the whip from the remnants of the Occulta Mirum's destruction

"Azure's pearl whip..." Saturnus is by my side now, watching me as I release the length of pearl strung leather from its lost state.

181

"Caedes, why aren't you with the prisoners?" I ask him, suddenly realising why I'm down here. The whip feels heavy in my hand as I let it fall by my side once more. It's not as demure as Scarlette, or as pointed in its lethality, but it nonetheless might do some good in keeping my army in order.

"My dolls turned to sand…" He looks wickedly disappointed, his eyes flashing with anger and a certain unhinged melancholia that makes me pity him even more. I wonder a moment if he's killed Oscar and Vexus, but then remember that even if he had, Vexus wouldn't turn to sand. My brain works, slick cogs of reckoning grinding against one another. I must investigate further for myself.

"Alright brother, go on and find Regus. He'll give you something to amuse yourself with I'm sure." Saturnus looks at him affectionately, but the charred stare is also scorched through with disdain and pity. Emotions unchecked blaze within Saturnus as he narrows his eyes. Our brother's insanity is one thing he cannot cope with. He had failed him. So had I.

"What did he mean turned to sand?" I say, feeling my chest constrict. I didn't relish the idea of the metal master dying before I decree it. Saturnus' mouth shrivels, becoming a pucker of disapproval and I feel rage crest within me, replacing my fear that had taken over for but a moment.

I round in the water and shoot off through the streets. Psirens returning from the site of the Necrimad are joking, laughing among the shattered glass. I move like a lethal projectile, deadly in my accuracy and unamused with the idea of being slowed by their incompetence.

"GET OUT OF MY WAY BOTTOM FEEDERS!" I scream, my voice becoming sharp and high-pitched, Psiren-esque in its ability to make them cringe. Psiren song isn't pleasant, and I rarely used it because it's painful to the individual who projects it. However, needs must and these children need to learn who's boss. I let the sound of fingernails scraping down chalkboards mixed with the wailing of an incessant small child dissipate as the water tremors around me. The Psiren fodder don't move, shocked but still incompetent. I thrust my clawed fingers outward, slashing against their bare white flesh as I shove them out of the way and into the dirt below me. I snarl.

"Idiots."

182

I turn a corner, letting the water move over me as though it were no more of an obstacle in slowing me down than air. My tail tenses, slashing from left to right, erotic in its phallic supremacy. I let the fingers of my empty hand move back to where Scarlette lies pressed against my hip, exuding a shudder as they brush against my dirty grey scales. Within the blink of an eye I am in front of the armoury tower. I move through the door.

It's empty, and the manacles which restrained the prisoners hang, limp and useless, open against the wall. They haven't died. They have escaped.

No. The magnitude of this failure hits me full force. *Incompetents, Incompetents everywhere. But not a drop of useful anywhere.* The internal mantra reinforces my belief that the only people I can truly rely on are related to me.

I feel my blood curdle, hot and fierce through me, storming within and causing my synapses to fire, lightning strikes within my conscious. I know immediately what I must do. I must bring the thunder.

Turning away from the obviously empty tower and stirring up blood-spattered sand in my wake I move out into the street. Holding the whip low so it falls against the floor, trailing behind me as my eyes do something from which I often refrain, diluting to black and sparking through with lacklustre electricity. I relax, letting my muscles loosen before I look up to the heat of the midday sun that hovers above, lethal. Breathing in and looking into the light of the power for which I was so named I open my mouth and let it roll out from me.

The Psiren scream to end them all.

I bring the thunder in the storm that is my rule, the devastation in my wake, as glass bottles that remain whole shatter, becoming spectacularly broken and jagged. I see Saturnus, his eyes blazing with anger as he approaches, but I don't stop. Letting my mouth hang open as my long pointed tongue undulates, I bellow, the sound so high pitched, so deathly and so mind numbingly painful to hear that it would kill any passing human before I could gut them with my rapier. I let it out, as Saturnus stills before me, examining his nails and yawning. I feel my rage increase at the sight of him.

What the hell is he looking so irritated for? I wonder internally, as I finally let the scream fall into a silence more deafening than itself.

The Psirens have heard me and felt me as the water falls still, the vibrations of my wrath falling to a halt. They rise, settling on one level like pond scum, sensing unrest. They stupidly do not equate the sound with anger, for if they had, they would not be hovering there like oh so easy targets. I see the one individual I've been seeking, the one responsible for all this. The one who I had trusted with a very simple task. Not simple enough, clearly.

"Darius!" I bellow, watching his tailfin, that of a great white shark, twitch in the distance. Saturnus does not move from in front of me, so I move instead, rising above him as though he's no more than a ghost.

"Yes Sir?" I watch Darius part from the innocuous mass of my army, moving through the water toward me, not as cautious as I'd like him to be, but I find myself once again at the apex of paradox. I want my army strong, but I also want them to fear me. Why is it then they can't see that I'm more worthy of their fear than anything else under the ocean's surface? I hear a roar from the distance, bringing me back to myself as the crowd remove their eyes from me, and turn, looking toward the site that holds the Necrimad. I feel my eyes narrow, irritated.

Don't these insects understand that it's my power that made that beast? I wonder, gritting my sharp teeth and grinding bone against bone.

"The prisoners have escaped! What do you have to say for yourself?" I tighten my grasp around Azure's whip as Darius' gaze returns to my face, from where he had turned to look upon my power made flesh.

"I don't know. I left them with Caedes." My eyes widen at his careless attitude, shocked.

"But you were guarding the door. What exactly does that meagre intellect of yours think that means?"

"I wanted to help with the harvest." Darius rubs the back of his head, eyes dropping. I had asked for the Psirens to come out in force for the attack on The Zenith it is true, but I hadn't expected Darius to be stupid enough to abandon his assigned post. I look over his shoulder to the crowd behind him. They might seem still from this distance, but upon a closer inspection, as I let my eyes dilute black with displeasure and rage, I notice that some of them are whispering, smiling even.

This. Has. To. End. I think these words as my hand snaps forward, grabbing Darius by the throat. The crowd silences.

"I will show you all what disobeying me means. If it is the last thing I do." I raise my voice so they can all hear me. Saturnus puts a hand on my shoulder and I round on him, Darius still in one palm, my teeth bared like a feral and baited predator. Saturnus takes a stroke away from me, smiling. This only causes my rage to fly even further into unpredictable torrent. I project my next words, not even turning from my brother so he can see the conviction in my stare.

"One fifth of you, GO! Find the escaped prisoners and don't come back until you have them, or they're sand! Understand me?" The group of Psirens to which I stare depart with haste, moving away from the rest of the group. Darius tries to go with them, squirming in my grasp. I look up at him, slightly amused by his naive stupidity. I stare directly at him, his blue eyes widen, all traces of the darkness within them gone.

"Oh no. You're not going anywhere. The rest of you, TO THE SEAL!"

15
Healer
AZURE

"Get the hell off me!" I scream, writhing within the grasps of Kaiya and Rourke. Rourke is immovable and holds my elbows, while Kaiya puts her hands, dirty with camouflage, all over my flawless charcoaled tailfin. I feel my hair get yanked from behind as they carry me down the narrow streets. "OW!" I yell out.

I watch, squirming even still, as they move silently past Maneli that appear from the shadows of their huts. "Get. OFF!" I yell out, bending my tailfin in the middle and pushing back, Kaiya loses her grip momentarily and falls backward, waving her hands back in hopeless flailing half circles. Her eyes narrow and she bares her sharp teeth, regaining her balance.

"You!" She exclaims, monosyllabic and deep in her tone. Rourke stills, watching the action unfold, as I bring my tailfin up and smack her underneath the chin with it. Her head snaps back, but only momentarily. In a surprisingly quick motion that I don't expect, my captor brings her hands underneath my tailfin, where it is still raised from my assault, and wraps the lengths of her long fingers around the end of my fluke's muscle. She smiles at me slightly, taunting me, but neither she nor Rourke say anything as they continue to restrain me against my will.

Familiar but foreign tones dance within my psyche as though the words themselves are on fire with the ferocity of my baited inner darkness.

186

Freaking religious fanatics.

The tinkling of sea shells greets my ears as we turn the corner and coarse black sand is lifted from the ground by the strokes of the long tails of my captors, who I have no doubt I will soon end in the ugliest way possible. I snarl as the darkness falls over me, but secretly I am glad. My eyes are still diluted, so the shadow is no problem for me.

But it might be a problem for them. I wonder internally.

Before this thought has a chance to manifest into the spectres of momentum, I'm bathed in an acute white light. Looking up at the ceiling of one of the huts in this pitiful excuse for a city, I find myself in a tiny room where the innards of the space are so well lit every inch of the place is only too visible. There's nowhere to hide. Nowhere to skulk.

"Callista. From Akachi." Rourke announces us before he and Kaiya drop me into the dirty sand. I'm not quick enough in such a confined space to make a dash for the door and the two warriors block the exit with their sand clad backs. My black hair falls across my face as I push up from the ground, my shoulder blades rising in twin peaks of predation, like that of a panther. My eyelids flutter and the blacks of my eyes shrink, the light burning away my Psiren defences.

"Well, what have we here, a child?" The voice is kind, and not what I'm expecting. Still, I bare my teeth, my pallor haunting as I catch my reflection in a cracked mirror propped against the inside of the hut.

"I'm not a child... witch." The word slips from my lips before I know what I'm saying, but the sight that greets me, silhouetted from the crudely wired lighting from above, leaves me taken back. Her tailfin is zebra striped, her hair pressed into cornrows against her skull and strung through with seashells, as I realise the tinkling I had heard before was her head turning to look upon my horrific face.

"I'm no witch." She crosses her arms, pulling them to rest under the black and white scales that climb around her torso and down her arms in spirals. Her large white eyes stare down at me as I erect myself in one fluid wave of my

187

fluke, crossing my own arms and eyeing the door. Rourke and Kaiya stand there. Immovable.

"Well, apparently, I'm here for '*purification*'." I mutter, unsure of how to reply. I'm tiring of the conversation already, and I wish I could just be somewhere else, alone.

"Purification?" The woman's eyes widen slightly and mine narrow in response. We hang, innocuous in the moment. She reaches out to a table made of rotting wood in the corner, seeking something which I don't give her the chance to grasp.

Moving forward I place both hands around her throat, pushing her against the wall of the metal hut with a vibrational crash. I know Rourke and Kaiya will have heard me but, in this moment, I lack the ability to care. I just want out of this charade. Out of this life. I'm so done.

I hold her up so she nears the part of the wall where the glare is brightest and my eyes dilute as much as they can, the light fighting me. I expect her to flail, or panic, but she doesn't. She just hangs there, looking down at me with a calm gaze and a slightly eerie smile on her face. Her eyes turn fully white in a split second and she exhales, shocking me.

I drop her like a hot coal and she slumps to the floor.

"You are a dark one." She announces in a whisper.

Yeah, no shit lady.

What is it with people and stating the obvious?

Yes, I'm dark.

Yes, I'm evil.

No I will not take your crap.

It's like they feel the need to remind me; the one person who can never forget the darkness within myself. I need not be reminded. Every breath I take is a stale and painful reminder of that fact.

"Whatever, I'm so done here. Let me out." I know I've probably just been witness to something vessel-like, but I refuse to be involved any further. Especially seeing as Orion and Callie rushed so desperately to my aid. Not.

"Wait. We are not done here. I am Callista. Let me help you Azure." She says my name, pulling it from the vision she probably just absorbed. Again, this is me not caring.

"I don't need your help." I say the last word in disbelief. No preaching religious nut is going to 'help' me.

"Don't lie to me, Azure. I know you miss her. I know why you're here." The word *her* implies she really does know why I'm here. I falter in my stroke as I swim toward the ridiculous shell strung curtain that she uses as a door.

"What do you know about her?" I turn, unable to help myself, desperate.

"I saw her, through your eyes." She admonishes the fact I had already known.

What, does she expect some big look of shock? Maybe a parade?

"Yeah, so?" I cross my arms again, and my defences rise against this odd, zebra striped woman.

"I'm a spiritual healer. Let me help you." She reaches for me in the open water.

"I don't need your help. How many times do I have to tell you!" I yell at her, eyes trying to dilate in the light as I get in her face. She doesn't blanche, she doesn't even look scared. What the hell is wrong with this chick?

"You don't scare me Azure." She speaks again, her Afrikaans accent twisting around the words and making my mind come over slightly foggy.

"Good for you." I snarl back, my shoulders coming up as I hunch over. Bored.

"Starlet is gone." She says the words and I feel like launching myself at her. I almost do. However, what she does as she speaks these words alarms me. She widens her arms, opening herself up to attack.

"What are you doing?" I raise an eyebrow, surveying the room further, trying to seem interested in anything other than the woman in front of me. The space is odd, decorated with seaweed and fishing net strung dream catchers, crystals and seashells. There aren't any weapons, nothing even remotely offensive except for the ugly hollow gourd sat in the corner.

"If you wish to attack me please, get it over with. I have prayer in an hour." She smiles, her kindness a poison in the water between us.

189

"What the hell is that? You think you can smile your way into my deepest hopes and fears? If you knew anything about me, you'd know that's not how to play me."

"I'm not trying to play you. I'm trying to help. You are blessed child." Those words hit me and my only reaction comes as something entirely unexpected. I laugh, a wave of hysteria overcoming me as the words sink in.

What the hell! Has this chick been smoking something? I eye a wooden bowl of dried seaweed. *Yeah, that's probably it... What a crackpot.*

"Look..." I begin, feeling tears coming to my eyes from the uncontrollable laughs still spluttering from my lips. "It's real nice of you to say that, but what the hell are you talking about? Look at me! I'm the furthest from blessed you're ever going to lay eyes on. This..." I gesticulate to myself, "Isn't a blessing. This, lady, is damnation. Kay?" My eyes widen at the word. The word I've been avoiding as horror floods my subconscious.

"So that's it. You're trying to earn back approval. Trying to bargain your way back to her." Callista sits in the dark, coarse sand beneath her and picks up a palm full, letting it fall through her fingers.

"What are you talking about?" I look to her, unable to relax as my heart becomes stone in my chest.

"Please, sit." She gestures for me to join her and for some reason, whether it be because I'm feeling lower than a sea slug or because I want to leave as soon as possible, I sit. She breathes in, tossing her shell braided cornrows over one shoulder under the stark light. "I saw where you've come from. I saw it all. Flashes in my head. A gift from Ava. I'm supposed to help you."

"Those visions aren't from Ava. Trust me." I roll my eyes, *stupid Ava.*

"They are divine, regardless." She waves a hand, brushing sand between us in wavy lines.

"Whatever."

"So you think that saving the world will bring her back? You know that's not how things work. There is no eternal balance of fairness. We are pawns of the Gods. I have seen you already know this. So why would you think that saving mankind can bring her back to you?" She asks these questions,

190

unblinking and unfeeling. I feel their effect on me almost instantly. The rage mounts. "Don't get angry Azure. That won't bring her back either."

"I'll feel how I want." I retort, the spirit in my voice losing its hateful edge. Fatigue begins to sink in.

"How do you feel?" She asks me. I turn, looking toward the still spines of the two guards keeping me trapped.

"My sister died. How do you think?" I sigh, tired as I turn back to the scrutiny of her gaze.

"You just said you feel how you want to, so I don't know. I'm not you." Callista's full lips shape the words, but their meaning is lost on me.

"I feel..." For the first time in a long time, words fail me. I don't want to talk about it; I don't want to rip out the stitches on a wound that I have found so hard to close, beating Orion to a pulp in the process.

"Empty?" Callista pulls the word from thin air and my lips pucker, moving to the left side of my mouth in an irritated grimace.

"Yeah, alright." I answer, knowing it's what she wants to hear. What will get me out of here faster.

"You have no purpose..."

"I'm on this wild goose chase, aren't I? I'd say that's purpose."

"No, it isn't. You're just afraid of being alone. Afraid of not getting her back. That's why you're self-sabotaging. You want to help them, the others, and yet you can't stand the fear of not knowing whether it will redeem you." She speaks the words once more, the truth. It hurts me, but I'm too tired of life to bother retorting anymore.

"Yeah. That's right. I deserve to have her back. I'm good now. I'm doing good." I don't know if this is the truth, or if it's more lies I've concocted to protect myself.

"Deserve doesn't matter. If it did, she never would have died in the first place." Callista shuffles slightly where she's sitting.

"So what? I have to save the world... for what?" I ask her, feeling short-changed. The Gods and Goddesses owe me; Starlet's resurrection is the least I deserve.

"For the people of the world. It's what you were put here for Azure. Don't forget, we are given eternal life to protect and serve. Nothing is free. You've lived a long time." She smiles and I can tell she's seen pretty much everything from my past, her stupid vessel powers are greater than those I've experienced before. Perhaps it's because of her devoutness to Ava.

"I wish I hadn't." I admit, biting my bottom lip and letting my hair fall around me.

"It is a gift and a curse. That's why faith is so important."

"Faith to Gods and Goddesses who treat me like dirt? I don't think so. I've been used by them my whole life. Where has it gotten me? My daughter was ripped from me, my family perished before my eyes. So, I'm supposed to thank them for that? Worship at their feet like the maggot they think I am?" I start off asking the questions as a witty retort, but by the time the last word falls from my lips I'm actually curious.

"I sense that's not really your style." She cocks an eyebrow, surprising me with her response.

"Actually no." I admonish, leaning back on my palms, which I bury in the dirt, allowing sand to lodge beneath my claw like fingernails.

"Well, faith is a choice. Just like this quest you're on. You need to start focusing on yourself. When was the last time you were happy?" She asks me and I immediately can't help but raise my gaze to hers.

"When I was with Titus." I admit the truth despite my hatred for the fact that the information is falling from me like water.

"A man?" She looks to me, surprised.

"Yes, I don't think it was him that made me happy. But I knew who I was. I didn't feel this... this hideous weight inside."

"Guilt." Callista announces the feeling, naming it and giving it yet more power than it originally held.

"Yes. It's unbearable. I just want it to stop."

"And yet, you are still here. What does that tell you?" She asks me, reaching forward and putting my hand in her palm. Dark skin on pale, her hand is warm against mine as I pull away.

"I'm a masochist?" I laugh, trying to cover my discomfort.

192

"No, you're not evil. If you were, you wouldn't feel guilty." Her words shatter me as my heart constricts and I feel my curiosity get the better of me.

"I'm not?"

"No, of course not. You're not all sunshine, but you're strong. I've seen it. Through Ava. You're selfish, sometimes misguided and entitled, but evil you are not. I've seen evil." Callista lets my hand drop and sits back, assessing me in the light that never falters. It's inescapable.

"Starlet didn't think so. She said darkness is who I am." I admit, remembering my sister's words as she was sliced seven ways from Sunday atop the Necrimad's seal.

"Darkness and evil do not always go hand in hand. It is true, your magic, your body and strength come from the dark, the same place from which demons are born, but you can choose to use that power whichever way you desire. For good, or evil." The response once more surprises me. That was true. I hadn't killed anyone in a while. I haven't even thought about ending the mermaids recently, only throttling them into temporary silence.

"So you're saying that darkness can be used for good?" I articulate the concept once more, for myself. Trying to wrap my head around what she's saying.

"Of course. You already are. Even if for the wrong reasons, to get your sister back, you're still doing good. As you said." Callista replies.

"Huh." I scratch my stomach with my long nails, letting granules of sand fall into my navel.

"It might not be as inevitable for you to do good Azure, but you are, nonetheless, proving it is possible."

"It's still not fair. It's not fair." I repeat the words, knowing they make me feel like a small child, but unable to stop them.

"Life isn't fair. That's just how it is." Callista speaks, her gaze making me angry again. I clench my fists.

"But why? Why is it like this? Why are we being played and tortured this way? Why don't the Circle of Eight do something instead of us just letting their creations suffer?" I ask the questions that sit deep down inside my darkness.

"Because we have a choice. Don't you see?" The scary faith healer leans forward, imploring me as her pupils dilate slightly in the bright innards of the hut.

"Choice? What about this is choice? I didn't choose to live forever. I didn't choose to have my sister taken from me. I didn't choose to have my soul split in two." I remind her of these things, totally ignoring the fact that she is pretty much a complete stranger, she doesn't know me. She doesn't know anything.

"All of those things were out of your hands. But you do have a choice. You have the most important choice of all. You can choose to leave this place better than you found it, or worse. You've done bad things before; you've chosen the wrong side. That doesn't mean you can't do something different now. Making the right choice isn't right because it's easy, Azure, it's right because you have to choose it over and over again, in spite of your personal losses or gains. You have to sacrifice, every day." The last words fall from her lips and I look into her eyes. She's right, but I know I'm not strong enough to choose what's best for the whole over and over. I have had a hard enough time choosing it once.

"Yeah well, that's not me. So, you'll have to get over it." I snap, flicking my hair back over one shoulder.

"Doing the right thing, or even the wrong thing won't make your grief any better or worse. Grief isn't something that happens to you, where you can cry once and it is over. Grief is domesticated, Azure. It lives within you. Always. It will get better. But it will never be over. You will always grieve your sister. Forever." Callista doesn't even look like she knows what she's saying at this point. Her gaze is clouded over and her lips are parted slightly, like she's gone to another realm or something equally as cliché.

"Well, that's great, lady, I think I'm just going to go and kill myself now. But thanks for the pep talk. Real inspirational." I cock an eyebrow and cross my arms, rising from the sand below. I've had enough, I just want to get back to my wild goose chase and good for nothing brother.

"I can see you're hurting, but remember that you are more than your relationship with your sister. You are not only a twin, but an individual. Starlet is gone, but you're still here." Callista lowers her alarming white eyes, like she's finished giving me her crappy attempt at an inspirational speech. I roll my eyes. Yeah I'm still here, which is wrong on so many levels.

"Well, you're the vessel. I found you. I better take you back to my brother and his stupid soulmate. They'll be thrilled. We've travelled searching for you like some cliché Arthurian legend or something. So, aren't you special?" I reach out, offering her a hand and she rises but does not take it.

"I'm the vessel for Ava..." She breathes out.

"Yeah yeah..." I wave a hand but her eyes widen as her striped monochrome tail undulates from her waist.

"Those things... the things in my head like you, they're real aren't they?" She asks me. I roll my eyes again, unable to stop myself.

"Yep, but they don't all got my Little Miss Sunshine attitude. Trust me." She inhales, looking nervous for a moment.

"So the day has come again." She whispers.

"What's that, my little fortune cookie?" I ask her, trying to cover up her unnerving way of seeing right through my defences. She doesn't know me, but she's seen into my head, which I find more than a little creepy.

"The day where I must choose to sacrifice myself once more for Ava." Her words make my heart falter in its arrogant rhythm.

"What do you mean, sacrifice? Do you know something about The Conduit?" I ask her, moving across her body and taking her shoulders in my hands. I shake her without restraint.

"All will be known. One day soon." She's cryptic again.

Oh my god. Can we cut the fortune cookie bullshit please? I snarl internally.

"If you know something just tell me!" I find myself getting angry, more than I intend, but the stark light in the room makes it impossible for my pupils to dilate. I stare at her face, the infuriating calm, the beyond irritating half smile on her lips, and suddenly I'm reminded me of how I've withheld my visions from Orion and Callie. I narrow my eyes.

I won't be played at my own game.

195

As I move to threaten her, I feel my stomach begin to churn. I know it's coming, another vision. I can't stop it.

The last thing I remember before I collapse onto the sandy floor, are Callista's white eyes widening, and her lips parting to say something, which, I'm sure, will be just as annoying as the half-assed prophecies laid down by the Gods.

Everything hurts. My body is on fire.

He looks down at himself, tentacles squirm from my waist, pulsating and allowing my body to continue moving through the water. What the hell is going on?

Why am I here? Looking through the eyes of the tentacled loser who stole my sister's first kiss? Ugh. As if this day couldn't get any worse.

"Come on! Move or we're bloody dead alright!?" I hear Vex's voice call out to a body, crumpled and bloodstained on the sea floor. The sand sticks to his wounds, which are scattered holes that run right through his insides making him look like a bleeding piece of gouda.

No doubt the work of Solustus. I muse, recognising the blade work immediately.

"BLOODY WELL GET UP!" Vex roars, his tentacles wrapping around the metal master's limp form and dragging him along the sea floor through the sand, leaving an obvious trail behind them.

Amateurs. I snarl.

"I can't... I can't." Oscar's face looks up and into Vex's gaze.

"Well then just stay here and die then. Not like I bloody care." Vex turns from him, dropping him back down into the sand, uncaring about his fate.

"Tell Sophia..." I hear the whisper travel toward Vex through the water and suddenly he's turning on Oscar, arms up in outrage.

"I'm not telling your bird anything. You wanna tell her something? You get off up the bloody floor and stop acting like such a bloody nancy!" He bites out this retort and I watch as Oscar returns with a look practically feral. "Yeah that's right mate, get angry. It'll keep you..." He begins but trails off, something far off in the shadow of the distance catching his eye.

"GO, GO!" He hisses in a low whisper, desperate. Oscar turns, his face still angry as his eyes settle on the Psirens in the distance that have been sent to find them. Grabbing Oscar's elbow in one fluid pulsation of movement through the water, Vex turns on a sharp axis and they begin to flee, each moment bringing more pain to them both as they draw breath after breath.

Move faster dammit! I cuss, wondering shortly after why I care so much. It's not like I would care if Vex died. After all, he has been nothing but useless. He had watched my sister perish, and slept with the Crowned Ruler's soulmate. His popularity ratings with everyone close to me are practically zero, and yet a sharp thrill clutches at my chest at the thought of the pursuit. Then I remember my prior vision, when I had told Poseidon where to shove it and been cosmically spanked in return. Vex is a vessel, if he dies now we'll never be able to create the conduit. I'll never be redeemed.

As I watch the ocean rush past the two escaped prisoners, I wonder if Callista was right when she had said I was sabotaging myself. I wanted redemption, I wanted to ask Atargatis to bring Starlet back, to start fresh, but I also didn't want The Conduit to see the light of day, because if after everything was said and done I'm still irredeemable... well, the thought is just too much to bear. Starlet can't be gone. She just can't be. This thought makes me realise what a fool I've been. I've been sabotaging the one thing that might get me my sister back. Even if it's a shot in hell, it's not worth risking it because I'm afraid. I am a Psiren, and the word fear ceases to be in my vocabulary.

"Blood hell, faster!" I hear Vex's worried tones break through my reverie as the pair approach a drop off into even deeper water.

"Wait!" Oscar exclaims as Vex turns on him, furious.

"What now?" He exclaims.

"We'll never outswim them, we're too badly beaten. Let's dive deeper and try to find a cave to hide in until they're gone." His eyes are wide, imploring Vex to do as he commands.

"Oh bloody Nora. Fine!" He lifts his hands up again in exasperation.

The two of them dive deep off the edge of the drop off, sticking close to the cliff and searching with hands and tentacles, feeling around for a hidden cave. They come up with nothing.

Shame they haven't got camouflage like these nutcases. I think, remembering the attack which even I hadn't seen coming.

"I have an idea!" Vex grabs Oscar's elbow, pulling him deep to the bottom of the ocean. There, he grabs fists full of sand and debris, piling it on top of himself.

Can he hear me? I wonder, feeling my heart accelerate at the idea of him being able to hear my thoughts.

"We're just going to hope they don't see us?" Oscar asks, looking unsure.

"Yes, it's our best shot. Dig yourself a small hole and then cover yourself. Just keep bloody quiet while you're doing it, alright blabbermouth?" Vex snarls at him, impatient and not in the mood to justify his plan. I get it; he's focused on the task at hand, not placating the anxieties of a cry-baby merman with no balls.

After a few minutes the pair are completely covered, no thanks to me might I add, in sand and debris from the ocean floor. I lie in the sand there with them, watching the ocean surface from the wrong side as its silver light falls, threatening to expose them.

They wait in the silence, until long after the moon is risen. Then, without a word, they set out into the endless dark azure.

16
Faith
ORION

I am trapped once more between love and duty, as I feel Akachi's crocodile stare on the back of my neck. I bow and my own gaze falls on the spluttering body of Cole, my best friend and the best Knight any King could ask for, as the lines of poison that flow within him creep, like the long fingers of death, up his torso and ever closer to his heart.

"I am sorry for my sister, Akachi, she is… troubled, she just lost her twin." I breathe out the words, hoping they will placate his ragged temper. Among all this emotion I cannot seem to muster any worry about Azure. She has made her bed for the last time, and now she must lie in it.

Callie is by my side, her face solemn, though a twinkle of amusement dances beneath her eyes as I examine her face, no doubt finding the fact that Azure has been taken away funny to say the least. I can't blame her, Azure got what she deserved.

"Grief makes us do terrible things." Is his only reply as I look up to him, feeling the weight of his blessings heavy upon my shoulders. Yet again I am in the position of one who must ask so much, and of someone who owes me nothing.

"Please, by the kindness of your Goddess, Ava. Save my friend." I feel my heart palpitate in my chest, the thought of losing Cole too much to bear. I have already lost too many people I cherish.

"Akachi, a demon!" A familiar voice calls out from the distance and the Chief's eyes widen. Then, a smile moves, fleeting, across his face.

"Ava has spoken." His voice is thick with malicious intent and I worry of his motives, blanching slightly as Kaiya moves back toward the circle of warriors. It was she who spoke.

"I have word from the scouts, a demon has been seen about ten miles away from the bay." Her words are heavy with urgency as she halts, Rourke no longer by her side.

"Very well. Ava has spoken on these matters. The demon is a sign. I shall heal your warrior." Akachi begins and I breathe a sigh of relief, but then he carries on speaking. "If... your women can go and kill the demon. They look meek. Their survival will prove the Goddess lends you her protection." The sentence falls into silence and Callie's eyes grow wide beside me.

I rise from my bow, offended by the insinuation that we are not divine. I mean, we have tails, shouldn't that be enough proof?

"Our maidens are untrained, untested in battle. They will die. Do you want their blood on your hands?" I ask him, narrowing my eyes as sand plumes up from my tailfin which shakes with resentment for the man before me. His religion may be the most important thing to him, but I refuse to allow him to threaten me, or put my people in danger to prove that another Goddess values us.

"Fine. Kaiya, take the girls and give them some instruction. Teach them to camouflage. Then they will go up against the demons. If you are who you say you are, blessed by another Goddess, then you shouldn't be worried." He turns away, moving to sit back in his throne. I float, unsure of what to do and caught in between one man's ignorance and another man's life that hangs in the balance because of me.

"Deal." The word doesn't come from me. It comes from Callie.

I turn to her, my mouth open, but her stare is firm.

"I will look after them." She says, stubborn as always. Akachi rises, clapping his large hands together, making the crocodile atop his staff startle.

"Amara, come forth, take the warrior and save his life." With that single command Amara glides forward, her black velvety tailfin flaring out behind her and giving her a feline grace with a predatory edge. Her eyes are yellow and bright, and they catch my gaze as she clicks her long, claw-like nails together.

Two warriors who are still obscured by sand camouflage move forward, picking up Cole's body and moving him after her. I turn, seeking out Ghazi in the crowd as he moves past the mermaids, who look like they might throw up or pass out at the announcement of their upcoming demon encounter, and toward me with a stoic expression.

"Ghazi, go with Cole. Make sure they don't try anything untoward." I whisper and he nods, taking off after them. Akachi watches him before turning back to me.

"There is no need to send a guard to watch over the boy. Amara is the best healer in the world. We have not lost a single warrior in our history. Not one." The words reach me through the water and I inhale sharply. Not a single warrior lost? Not *ever*?

"Wait, you're wanting me to believe that you've never lost a single Maneli fighter?" I say, scrutinising him with narrow eyes. I cross my arms in disbelief, but he nods, sitting back in his chair and cocking his tailfin to the left. The small crocodile on his staff moves onto the bone of his throne where it perches, watching for any more surprise Azure attacks.

"That is the truth. I swear it by Ava." The words are simple and I gape. *Never lost a fighter?*

"How many years have you been fighting demons?" I ask him as his lips twist into something like a smile, sensing that I'm impressed.

"Too many to count, young one." He calls me young and I can't help but laugh.

"You know I'm almost half a millennium old?" I cock an eyebrow as the crowd of warriors from behind us depart, sensing the terms of Cole's fate have been decided. Akachi looks shocked, an unnerving expression to say the least, as his sharp teeth and amphibian eyes come alive in his face.

"You're looking better than I." He chuckles in a deep voice.

"If only I could say the same for my pod. Look at how few we are now, Sir." I gesture back to them and Akachi frowns.

201

"Demons I assume?" He guesses, only too accurate in his assumption, and I nod.

"Just one, but it's filled with the power of a God." Akachi's eyes widen at this and then his mouth goes slack.

"Nonsense, the only power over the oceans is that of Ava." He shakes his head and I sigh. This man isn't going to believe anything I say if it's to do with other Gods. He is devout to Ava, which is probably going to be quite the obstacle when asking him to fight for us.

"I apologise. Your Goddess' power clearly knows no bounds. Your record with fatalities is beyond impressive." Callie says, apologising for me yet again. I feel myself getting angry, how can she bend so easily to the beliefs of another when that individual won't even consider opening themselves to Atargatis? It's infuriating. The lights in the square flicker and Akachi grumbles.

"The electricity you have here is amazing. Hydroelectric power?" Callie continues and Akachi nods slowly, observing her.

"It's a great gift from the Goddess, such light, but it is less than reliable at times." He complains and I cannot help but find him slightly spoiled in this respect. He should try rummaging around in the dark like the Selkies, or living in the deep like the Psirens. The Maneli didn't have it that bad really, they are crammed into a small space by the looks of things, but electricity was a luxury not even the mer had mastered after so many centuries.

"Perhaps Orion, our Crowned Ruler, could see about boosting the power?" Callie replies, smiling. I turn my head to look at her with a confused glare. Boost the electrics? With what? My divine faith in Atargatis? I'm sure that Akachi wasn't going to hear of it. Regardless, he sits up in the throne, looking intrigued.

"You have magic, boy?" He asks me. I scowl at Callie. I don't like letting strangers know about my power over air. It doesn't exactly give me the upper hand if I put all my cards on the table at a first meeting.

"Yes, I have the gift of Aeromancy." I reply, knowing that now Callie has spoken I don't have a choice but to come clean.

202

"Show him, Orion." Callie nudges me forward and I look back at her again, glaring. I need to have a chat with her about thinking before just volunteering information like that.

I move forward, stretching the cramped muscles of my midnight blue tailfin that have been stationary for longer than they should be. I move out into the space where Cole's body had lain, his silhouette still visible in the dark sand, as I push my hands out from my body, letting my mind clear of worry and doubt. It's as I do this that I realise the insane tumult of emotion and worry that's been plaguing me every day since we left the Gelida Silentium. I needed time alone with Callie, I needed to talk to her and be close with her, and yet doing that in hostile waters was practically impossible. I think back to the early days, the days when I had taken her to my favourite places, for dinner and dancing. I miss those simple nights now, even though at the time they had seemed anything but.

I come out of my internal reverie as I note Akachi's expression turning bored, before I summon my strength. Shoving my hands out in front of me, I blast a gush of air out into the water, which displaces and pushes the bone throne of the divine ruler back, causing the Crocodile to flee to the safety of its master's staff once more. The front two legs of the throne move back through the water and hit the floor with a dull thud as Akachi's expression turns to that of interest.

"Well, you are a blessed one indeed." Is his only remark. He strokes his chin with a long finger before continuing. "Come. I will show you to the plant." I raise my eyebrows in surprise of his acceptance, then again, he is gaining something from my power, so perhaps that's why he's willing to overlook where it came from.

"Kaiya, take the mermaids to prepare for battle with the demons. I will bring the boy to watch them fight when we are done." I turn to look at Callie as Kaiya swims to her and they begin to chat. Akachi looks to me as I watch her, a forlorn expression crossing my face.

"Come." He commands, leaving me with no choice but to follow in his blessed wake.

We reach the power plant quickly, as I find Akachi's Crocodile tailfin moves unlike anything I've ever seen. It stems from his waist, moving from left to right in a snake like and horizontal slither as I follow him, swimming over the shanty town and high into the centre of the peak in which the town lies. We approach the hydroelectric power generator and its inner workings mystify me momentarily as I observe its function.

The whole thing glows in its centre, from where I assume the power is stored and distributed. Around the outside of the transparent contraption, water is lifted by planks that look like they could belong to an old-fashioned windmill. They rise on one side, pushing the water up the confined space, which is encased on all sides by a transparent but sturdy looking glass or plastic material, before the liquid rushes down the other side in a manmade waterfall, turning the turbines at the bottom of the machine. I look around the walls that surround the city, where waterfalls also trickle in. Each one of the falls also has turbines at the bottom, turning the momentum of the water into power and electricity, which lights the city. It's genius.

"This is incredible." I exclaim as Akachi hangs in the water beside me, looking upon the creation with a satisfied half smile.

"Yes, Gabriel is quite the engineer." He boasts.

"Gabriel?" I query him, my eyebrow rising at the use of such a biblical name.

"Yes, he's responsible for most of the engineering for the city, and our weaponry. He allowed us to heat rods so we can solder metal together. He also makes a lot of our long-range weapons; catapults, crossbows, traps for demons... you name it and he is working on it or has already created it. Ava gifted that boy indeed." His face is beaming with pride.

"I must say, Sir; I hope I have not offended you. I am in awe of your generosity, and your people." I nod my head, bowing and trying to appear humble.

"You know, I remember someone like you coming here once. I would not see him, for he spoke of other Gods, other Goddesses. I wonder now if that was a mistake. For all your faults, boy, for all your beliefs in that which

204

cannot be, your people are none the less impressive. Your Queen, she has spirit." His words have an impact on me he doesn't expect as my expression turns shocked.

"The name of the person came here before, was it Atlas?" I ask him, feeling my heartbeat start to race.

"Yes. He had a woman with him also."

"Shaniqua." I say the name, missing her almost instantly as a picture of her face floats through my mind like it's riding a lazy current. I wonder what has become of her, whether Saturnus has sent for her. I shudder at that thought.

"My father, Atlas, is the reason I'm here. We're looking for a vessel, someone to help us defeat the demon I told you about. My people, we lost everything." I hear how harrowing the words sound as they leave me.

"I understand, but I cannot help you. If we were supposed to be involved in your war, Ava would have sent a sign by now. As it is, I have sensed nothing of the sort. Our job is here, protecting the bay and the people of South Africa." He doesn't look apologetic, or sorry, just impassive and definitive in his reply and so I nod, not wanting to push the issue further.

"So, let's see if I can boost the power with this a little, shall we?" I say, smiling and trying to remain enthused, despite the sinking feeling that I'll be leaving this city empty handed and with potentially less people than I came.

"Yes." Akachi admonishes, plunging deeper into the water filling the inside of Cape Point. It's amazing that this kind of natural phenomenon exists, and I wonder what the chances are of finding other peaks like it in other locations around the world. We move close to the plant and I level out close to its base.

"I should be able to manipulate the water from here." I reassure him as he stills close to the muddy sand, placing his staff down into it and hovering, watching me intensely. I pivot to face the plant, place my hands out in front of me and move them gradually upwards, manipulating the oxygen within each water molecule. I drive the water upward faster, leaving it to plummet down into the turbines at an increased speed. I hear the whirring of the machine grow louder and Akachi laughing as he turns and the city's lights grow brighter instantaneously.

"By Ava. What a beautiful sight it is." He sighs, in love with his city, with his Goddess.

I float nearby, looking out whilst maintaining the increase in speed within the generator, wondering where the most beautiful of sights lies within the streets. Wondering where she is right now.

CALLIE

"So you're going to teach us how to fight demons?" I hear Rose's horrified tones move past me to Kaiya. She rubs the final layers of camouflage from her face, arms and torso as she rolls her eyes, looking exasperated and revealing her form beneath.

"Yes, that's what Akachi asked me to do. So, I do it. He speaks for Ava." She replies, her tone bored and monotone, in deep contrast to her eyes that blaze multi-tonal, the light changing which colour they exude. She's quite the unusual looking creature and her tail isn't flared at the end like the other Maneli, but rather curls around like that of the chameleon from which she steals her ability to camouflage to match her surroundings. Her dark skin is mapped with these scales as they climb around her torso and up her neck, elongating it. Her hair is so short she's practically bald, and her lips and nose are broad set, making her look even more fierce than I'd originally noticed when she'd been camouflaged. I glide forward to her, feeling the need to clear the air.

"I'm sorry about before, when I picked you up by the throat. I was scared. I love my people." I look around at them, their eyes full of concern for only themselves.

"Do not worry about it. I would have done the same to you if you hadn't have caught me off guard." She doesn't crack a smile, not even slightly, she just looks at me in silence, unfeeling and focused.

"Shall we go then?" I ask her and she nods silently, moving us away from the central square where we have addressed their leader.

I look after Orion, sensing he is angry at me for accepting their challenge. However, I can't quite bring myself to feel sorry about it. These women need to learn to fight at some point if they're going into battle with us against the Psirens, and what better opportunity than now? If we don't take the risk of putting them in harm's way now and letting them practice, it'll be more certainly lethal putting them up against the Psirens.

Kaiya begins to move away without so much as a gesture for us to follow and as she takes a lead on us, we tail her, keeping close but not close enough that the mermaids don't immediately burst out into worried babble.

"Callie, we can't fight a demon!" Alannah exclaims.

"We're going to die! We're all going to die!" Skye begins to cry.

"I don't even know what a demon looks like..." Emma whispers, almost lost in the loud and scared voices of the others.

"Well, I think that Akachi fellow was highly unreasonable. Did you see his eyes?" Marina asks me.

"I am NOT going out there." Rose crosses her arms as she swims forward and Fahima stays silent as always beside her, looking after where Ghazi had left with Cole. Sophia touches my arm and I turn to her.

"I'm scared." She says. It's a simple statement, but it's the most honest and sensible thing that's been said of any of the mermaids so far. So, I run with it.

"Okay, slow down. It'll be alright. I know we're all scared, but this time had to come eventually. I'd rather we had a practice run with a demon than set you loose on your first battle with the Psirens, okay?" I say this in a calm and even tone, silencing them immediately. I am so much younger than them all, and yet I'm the one they're all looking to for answers. The weight of this responsibility lies heavily on me once more, and I wish I had Orion here to help.

"You didn't even ask us if we wanted to fight. You just volunteered us! That's not fair!" Rose blurts. Suddenly the mermaids' eyes narrow in on me.

Oh, crapsicle.

"You would have said no. Cole could have died…" I remind them, my voice stern. My brow is creased and my blonde hair tickles the base of my spine as we move slowly together, keeping Kaiya in my sight, though now she is far ahead of us.

"Now we could die!" Skye squeaks, her face red and unattractive as she continues to cry.

"We're not going to die." I assure them all, getting slightly irritated at the drama they're creating for no reason.

"How do you know? You don't even believe in Atargatis!" Rose retorts.

The statement surprises me and I halt, falling silent as I hang for a moment in the water before deciding I've had enough. I exert myself, swimming past them and after Kaiya, no longer wanting to hear what they have to say. I've heard Rose run her mouth off before, heard her accuse me of being a bad Queen, but this is different.

Maybe, I ponder, *it's because I'm not sure she's wrong.*

Within the hollow peak of Cape Point, the Maneli thrive. I float through the streets at Kaiya's side, uncaring of whether the mermaids are in tow. I can't quite bring myself to face them. They're being ridiculous about fighting a demon, and I remember that we had given them an out back on the beach in Naples. If they didn't want to fight, they should have had the courage to walk away then. As for Rose's little quip about Atargatis, it's bothering me more than I'd like to admit.

I wonder if I'm that transparent. If it's that obvious, despite everything I've seen and done over the past year, that there's still a voice in the back of my head telling me that this is all some twist of biology, that there must be a scientific explanation, that Gods and Goddesses cannot be real, because they cannot be quantified in a lab, or tested via sensory experience. They are like ghosts, fleeting and ethereal and I wonder how the other mer believe so readily, wonder if they'd ever doubted. I mean, I have a tail, I'm a mermaid, two extremely unexplainable phenomena, but was I about to risk my life with the faith that Atargatis would make all things right again? No, I just can't.

As we pass through the packed shanty streets that hold stalls of people working with hot irons, heated from the electric power the city possesses, I can't help but think back to that night. The night I had died for a second time. I had been ready to die, ready to go and the thing that was in fact more surprising was that it hadn't felt real, it hadn't felt final to me even before. And yet... I hadn't expected to come back. Out of the whole experience, that had been the thing that shocked me the most. The fact that some power beyond my cognition or belief had brought me back to life.

Sometimes, I admit to myself, ashamed, *I guess I think it was just luck.*

I think about Orion as well as I see the Hydro Electric Power Plant in the distance, moving water up one side of its towering height before it falls down the other, spinning turbines and creating kinetic energy from that of gravitational potential. I had felt that same gravity when I had met Orion, and that same energy had transformed itself into kinetics, into his arms holding me close, his lips wrapping around mine, his unwavering gaze. It was all explainable, his love for me, it was all so ordinary if you take away the mer side of things. That was what the girls had meant back in Italy wasn't it? Things were intense right now, because it was new, it was exciting. But surely that was all subject to change after years had passed, Soulmates made by divine Gods didn't ever lose their fire, didn't ever settle into domesticity. So, I wonder now if all this talk of destined soulmates was just a story told by the mer to make eternity seem less daunting, just the way I had seen humans use religion to placate their fears about death and what lies after. Once upon a time people had thought the world was flat, so is it in fact possible that mermaids, magic and demons were something that science had not yet managed to explain, but one day in the future, would be dissected and made domestic like everything else?

We reach a large hut, with roofs and walls made of corrugated iron. In the doorway hang green vines spiked through with barbs from manta rays.

Kaiya brushes them aside as she moves into the building and I follow her, examining the makeshift doorway as I pass.

"This is lovely." I compliment, and Kaiya shrugs. I look around once inside, finding paintings on the walls that look flat despite the crenulations of the iron. There are a few wooden tables strewn about on the floor, low to the ground, which hold pots of paint and jars full of various substances. A pestle and mortar lies beside them with beetles crushed into purple mush within and as I look to them, I feel a slight disgust churn in my stomach. Weapons are standing against the very far wall, spears and crossbows, impressively constructed from raw materials and as I'm staring at them I hear movement behind me and the mermaids decide to join us. Sophia looks at me, apologetic in her stare. I shake my head and shrug in a way that only she will notice, I'm not mad at her, she's always been nothing but kind. Rose on the other hand, is another story.

"I will show you how to camouflage now. Come, sit." Kaiya instructs us. I turn away from the women who rely on me so heavily, who need to find their own voices and strength, vowing that now is the time for tough love. They need to learn to stand on their own and it's now or never.

"Oh my Goddess, you look ridiculous!" Rose chortles at Skye who is covered from head to fin in a deep green paint, matted with sand and other debris from the ocean floor. I'm sat against the back wall, far away from the group with Kaiya, watching them as they camouflage one another to match the right-hand wall of the hut, which is painted so they can practice different biomes.

"I am never getting this out of my hair!" Alannah complains and Sophia rolls her eyes.

"I'm sure it won't matter if you turn to sand, sand doesn't have to worry about paint in its hair." She says the words and the girls fall silent as she looks back to me and frowns. Kaiya turns to me.

"You don't want to try it?" She asks me, her eyebrows raised. Her mouth doesn't give away anything that she's feeling, not a whisper.

"Nah, I've fought before. I killed a Psiren once. It had tentacles. Talk about needing more arms." I say, trying to be humorous. "In a few minutes perhaps." I add. Kaiya doesn't get it. Instead she decides to be intrusive.

"You do not believe." She says it simply, her words surprising me.

"You heard that?"

"Ah yes, I have very good hearing. You'd be amazed what you learn about someone through not saying every little thing that pops into your head." She smirks, looking over to the mermaids and I smile. It's not that funny, but I think it's about as close to joke as I'm going to get out of her.

"I'm new to all this. I just can't go off blind faith. It's not me." I reply. She frowns slightly, cocking her head.

"I understand." Her response surprises me as I flick my tail up, disturbing the dirt mixed in with sand.

"You do?" I ask her, examining her face, but her stare doesn't reveal her as her eyes sit, dead and shimmering, in the white light from the flickering bulb above. Crude wires dangle down lower than they should, making the primitiveness of the wiring system obvious and yet taking nothing away from the marvel that is electricity underwater.

"I believe in Ava. But that does not mean I won't take spear out with me, or put on my camouflage. I'll get slaughtered. Yes?" She laughs slightly, and I put on a fake smile, not finding it at all funny. Instead I find it comforting.

"Yes. That is what I mean. If I could believe in a Goddess, it wouldn't make me act any differently." I say, looking to Marina, who is by far the best at camouflage. She's showing Sophia how to make her Kelp camouflage look more convincing, interspersing the green with black and brown.

"Then perhaps the Goddess does not need you to believe in her. Only yourself." Kaiya moves from the wall, over to the paints that sit, stodgy and immovable in the bottom of jars and pots. I have discovered they mix the dye with clay that is immovable in the water and I watch as she comes over, beginning to apply a thick layer to the base of my tailfin.

211

"Perhaps you're right. Thank you." I say and she nods, continuing her work.

"After all, if you are her creation, you will do what's right by her. It's who you are." She finishes the statement, making me wonder about the nature of free will. I had been chosen, supposedly, by the Goddess, I had instincts about people, instincts about situations that hadn't failed me so far. I had picked Conan as the vessel for Lir, despite his unlikeliness as a candidate. I had known there was something off about Saturnus, even if I hadn't seen what the instinct was trying to tell me until it was too late. I had known when I needed to leave Orion, and I had known when I was in too deep with the darkness, even if it had taken a giant mistake to make me realise. As I sit, watching the mermaids and Kaiya, I realise I do have faith. I have it in myself.

I rise from the sand, almost knocking my head on the lightbulb that hangs in the centre of the room. As I get close to it, I realise it's attracting all kinds of small fish and vertebrae towards its glow. They twitch upon and around its surface, unable to look away from the light.

"Okay, Kaiya, I think it's time we teach these mermaids to fight." I announce. The maidens look up at me.

"We're not ready." Rose scowls at me and I glare

"Yes you are, I know you are." I retort, feeling my heart swell with stubborn pride.

"And how, Your Highness, do you know that?" Skye asks, her face green but unmistakable in its rage.

"Because…" I say simply. "I have faith."

17
Camouflage
CALLIE

I lie flat against the wall, pressing my spine against the metal as I suck in breath, invisible as the camouflage of my skin melds into the surface behind me. I enjoy the lack of eyes on me, a moment to breathe without being judged, without being criticised. As I float here, hidden from prying eyes, I realise just how much I've been watching myself recently, making sure my position in the water isn't offensive in some way, making sure I don't look flustered.

I long for Orion's unbridled touch on my skin, his wild lips gliding across the flesh of my neck. My eyes close, imagining being alone with him as I disappear into nothingness, all pressure and urgency gone from me, lifting as though it were no more than smoke.

"Callie?" Orion's voice breaks through my calm moment of reprieve, making me both desperate for him and yet reluctant to move. I see his broad back turn so it's facing me and I admire the thick musculature that wraps around his torso. I'm a lucky woman. That's for sure.

I take a few moments longer, not wanting to swim forward into the spotlight, under the scrutiny of those who expect so much. Then I strike.

"Boo!" I yell and Orion turns as I dive toward him. He grabs my arms without a moment's hesitation, assaulting me and taking a few moments to realise what he's seeing. He slams me back against the iron of the wall, pushing my arms above my head. "Hey, hey! It's me!" I exclaim, squirming in his grasp. His mouth pops open slightly.

213

"Callie?" He cocks an eyebrow and I grin, the white of my teeth revealing me against the paint that's covering my body.

"Who else would be jumping you from the shadows? Something I should know about?" I ask him, a faux affronted expression plastered on my lime face.

"Oh don't worry, you're the only person I'd let live after jumping me like that." He purrs leaning forward. I wrap my arms around his neck, smearing paint around his shoulders and into his hair.

"Kiss me." I demand, winking. He pulls back with a slightly disgusted look at my face, which is covered in green clay camouflage. "What's wrong, don't you want a kiss from your Queen?" I tease him as he struggles inside my embrace. Before he can escape I strike once more, slamming my lips down around his, making sure to smear as much of the paint from my face onto his as possible. As he pulls away, he looks as though he's been smooching the incredible hulk and I can't help but laugh as he wipes it from left to right, trying to remove the paint, but only making it worse.

"Geez what is this stuff made of, sea slug mucus?" He complains as I laugh at him. Kaiya enters the hut behind us silently, but Orion quickly turns to her, recognising that we are no longer alone and with his face still covered in green clay. Kaiya smirks, the most amused I've seen her as her eyes twinkle in the bright light of the space.

"You have a little… something…" She chuckles, throwing her head back and spreading her thick lips wide, pulling them back over her extraordinarily bright teeth.

"Oh uh, thanks." Orion looks like he might blush. Totally professional rulers, that's most definitely what we are right now. No doubt about it.

"I came to tell you that the mermaids… they're…"

"Who got hurt?!" I ask immediately, wondering whether Rose has managed to piss someone off enough for them to finally skewer her to death.

"No one. They're a lot more equipped than I guessed." She says the words, her eyebrows bunching together in the centre of her forehead.

"You mean to tell me that they're actually good at fighting?" I ask her and she breathes out.

214

"Come, watch this." She demands, ushering me forward. She backs out of the barbed curtain and Orion and I follow her. Orion's stare lingers curiously on me, as though I know what's going on, but I merely shake my head back, just as bewildered as he.

Outside in the street we take a left turn, swimming to the end of this section of city. The cliff face rises in steep horizontal force at the end of the dirty coloured road, and as we near it I see the mermaids on a patch of earth, squabbling as usual.

"I'm just saying, how is this fair?" I hear Rose complaining first, which I find hardly surprising.

"What's going on?" I ask them, moving forward.

"Emma is blessed." Rose snaps, turning on me with a disgusted look on her far too pretty face.

"What?" I say, blinking quickly.

"You heard me! Show her!" Rose demands. The group turns to Emma who shrinks back toward the rocky cliff behind them. It's momentary, but suddenly she flickers out of existence.

"Huh?" Orion looks to me and I shrug. We move forward as I reach out to touch her.

"I won't hurt you, okay?" I promise her as she shrinks back from me, her baby blue tailfin shimmering like the most pure and fragile thing you've ever seen. I reach out to her, taking her hand. I'm stark green against the surrounding cliff, no longer camouflaged at all, but suddenly something shifts as I feel Emma's newly discovered power move into me. I turn invisible instantaneously.

"Callie?" Orion calls to me.

"Yeah, I'm still here!" I drop Emma's hand and we both reappear, becoming silhouetted against the darkness of the rising peak once more. I turn to her.

"You can turn invisible. That's awesome!" I compliment, looking deeply into her face. Her long blonde hair cascades down and shrouds her fragile and pale body in a white and gold glow. Her baby blue eyes look like they might start shedding diamonds at any moment. "Did you know about this?" I ask her and she shakes her head, unable to speak.

Orion moves forward, looking at me with curiosity as my gaze falls on the girls who are opposite me. They become silent as my mouth opens silently, unsure if what I'm about to say has any merit.

"Orion... I think... I think it might not just be Emma that's blessed. I mean, were any of them even ever tested for magic?!" I look to him and he shakes his head.

"No of course not, why would they have been? The only other mermaids with powers are my sisters, and Marina of course, but she's always known of her powers. The mermaids have had no reason to possess magic. They don't even fight." He looks at me like the idea is insane.

"Maybe they are blessed, but maybe they've never been in a situation that's brought it out?" I press the issue and he shrugs before turning back to the girls.

"Have you guys ever had anything weird happen? Like anything you didn't mention?" I ask, looking to them, suspicious, my mind racing at a mile a minute.

"We would have noticed..." Orion begins, but I cut him off.

"Not necessarily, if it weren't for those tests Ghazi put me through, we never would have known I was a vessel." I cock an eyebrow at him as Kaiya comes forward.

"That's not all, I noticed something else. Her." She points to Sophia.

"Don't look at me." She protests, crossing her arms.

"What did you see?" I ask Kaiya as she purses her lips.

"I don't know. Something." She shrugs, narrowing her eyes.

I move over to Sophia, brushing up some of the dark sand with my tailfin and feeling my heart race at the prospect of the mer having more power that we'd first thought.

"Sophia, take my hand. Don't be scared." I encourage her and she looks hesitantly toward my outstretched fingertips. Her dark brown eyes remind me so much of Kayla and I don't want to push her, but I need to know. She takes a moment's pause, before eventually reaching out and touching my hand. I grip her hard, summoning my ability to absorb her magic as I close my eyes.

There must be something there, there just must be. I think to myself as I focus, my hand the sole focal point of my energies.

Then it happens. I feel something flow through me and as I open my eyes, I see an orb of lilac, just like Sophia's tail and facial scales, expanding out around me. I move my right hand, which is free, and command the sphere out from me. The orb expands and Orion's eyes widen through the lilac hue as he swims forward. He goes to touch the orb which encases us, but moves back quickly as I exhale, letting the orb drop.

"What was that?" I ask him as he sucks on his index finger.

"Static shocks!" He exclaims, looking irritated as his hair stands on end, poker straight. I turn to Sophia.

"You can project some kind of shield, or barrier." I say to Sophia as her eyes widen and she looks suddenly shy, her cheeks flooding with colour. Rose glides forward, graceful as always.

"Me next." She demands.

An hour later we lie back in the dirty sand, I'm exhausted, the absorption of so much magic taking its toll on me. The mermaids all had magic of some kind, which is hardly surprising now I think about it. If destiny is real, these mermaids were supposed to survive the Psiren attack on the Occulta Mirum, in part because they're involved in the plan to help us stop them. It would only make sense the Goddess would give them a little magical assistance.

I look to Rose, who not an hour ago had blasted my soulmate against the cliff with a scream that had erupted from her like nothing I'd ever heard. Orion said it was like the Psiren screams he had heard from Azure in the old days. It fit her down to the ground when you think about it, because Rose clearly had a lot of pent up rage. Why not give her a power where she can scream herself hoarse?

Alannah's power stemmed from her love of music, and the spirit of her song had flowed through me, knocking Kaiya unconscious in a matter of

217

seconds. She has sung for years, and yet never been in enough danger during a song to unlock the potential of her voice.

Finally, Skye had the ability of astral projection and by absorbing her magic I had managed to transport my soul outside the walls of Cape Point, resting my eyes, if only momentarily, on the demon we are to face. Reptilian in its features, I stared upon it, knowing now that these women are destined for so much more than they ever realised. Fahima was telepathic with her soulmate as I already knew, and Marina's empathic abilities meant that every single mermaid in our pod had magic at her disposal.

As I lie back, I feel less alone than I have in a while. Then, my daydream of sorority and female power is shattered as Rose sits up.

"You know we really should go and kick some demon ass." She's cocky now, knowing that her voice has more power than she's ever known before.

"Just be careful, just because you have magic now doesn't mean you're invulnerable to harm." I remind them and Rose cocks her eyebrow me.

"Ooh, Little Miss Special not feeling so special?" She challenges me.

"No, actually I was just thinking how nice it is not to have to babysit you anymore." I stick my tongue out at her. "No more hiding behind my tailfin." Sophia looks to me, fear evident in her eyes.

"Callie, I don't know. Like you said, magic doesn't guarantee anything." I nod to her, knowing I need to balance out the responsibility I'm bestowing on them with a silver lining.

"No, but it does prove something. You were meant to be here. All of you. You surviving the attack on the city was no accident. You all have destinies that intertwine with this quest, with The Conduit. So, it's time you all step up to that. The Goddess has big plans for you if she's bestowed this kind of power." They look between themselves, their bright jewel coloured eyes connecting with the weight of the feeling of being chosen and of being special, settling on their shoulders. I have to admit, they're doing it with much more grace than I did, like they do everything.

Orion, who has been talking with Kaiya back in her hut about strategy for taking on the demon I've seen, returns as we sit, staring at one another and feeling the connection between us that is now more evident than ever.

218

"Kaiya is going to take us to Gabriel now. We're going to have our pick of the melee weapons and armour. The mermaids… they can't keep wearing that." He looks up to them, and I notice it again with a cringe. Their gaudy, badly decorated armour that is just a little too much. Encrusted with diamonds, shells and anything else they could steal from the aurora sanctum, they've really managed to mess up a seriously badass set of armour between them.

"You're right. They look like they've just come straight off an episode of extreme makeover, but it's gone very, very wrong." I quip. Orion looks confused and I shake my head laughing. I kiss his cheek, smearing yet more paint across his face. "Pop culture thing." I explain in a whisper.

"Ah. One day I'm sure I'll catch up." He runs his hand through his hair, tousling the strands that are floating out of place from Sophia's static attack.

"One day when this is over we'll binge watch bad television for like a week."

"You're forgetting about the fact the full moon dictates our time… but that sounds lovely." He sighs, shaking his head.

"Moonstones, remember?" I turn on him and he suddenly smiles, happier than I've seen him since we left the library in Castella Aragon.

"Right!" The satchel still hangs across his torso, and I can't help but wonder how he hasn't gotten tired yet, I mean Sedna's codex isn't exactly what I'd call light reading. He looks practically ecstatic; like he'd forgotten after this everything will be different. Our whole lives, in a matter of days, have altered forever. That is, if we're still around to see what different looks like.

Gabriel is an odd-looking man to say the least, among the high piles of metal debris from sunken ships and other litter that's been carelessly discarded in the ocean, he's managed to make what can only be described as masterpieces. His head is covered by a welding visor as I enter the large metal workshop and he's surrounding by debris and spare parts littered across the sandy floor. He is working at a massive bench, using a soldering iron that's heating the water around it, causing bubbles to escape as he melts the metal before him. It floats like mercury, the only liquid metal I can recall seeing, as he manipulates it into a mould before it can cool. I hear Sophia exhale behind me.

"Oscar would love this place!" She exclaims, looking to me with a hopeful gaze. I frown, hoping more than anything Oscar is alive, but it seems unlikely unless the Psiren's haven't already used him for all he's worth to them. I turn away from her, my blonde hair flaring out around me.

"Gabriel!" Orion calls out. He's been here before, with Akachi, who is nowhere to be seen now. I look around for him tentatively but cannot find his reptilian gaze.

"Orion!" The voice is coarse as the man at the workbench puts down the soldering iron in his hand. He lifts his facial mask revealing a large set of puppy-like brown eyes. He floats from the shadows at the back of his workspace, swimming into the centre of the room. "Is this her?" He asks, looking down at me. I examine him for a moment, his skin is dark and covered in black patches from the metals he's been handling. He holds a hand out to me and I take it, feeling the roughness of many calluses pushing against the soft pale flesh of my own hand. I move back, letting his grasp drop as I take in his tailfin, which is grey with black spots and not dissimilar to the soft skin of a seal.

"Have you been talking about me?" I turn to Orion, smiling kindly.

"Of course." He nods, taking my hand. It's a tiny gesture but my heart flutters in my chest as I catch his gaze and hold it as long as I can, before turning back to Gabriel.

"I hear you're quite the genius with engineering!" I compliment him and he smiles slightly.

"You're not the only one Orion has been bragging about then." He snorts, picking up a rag that hangs from a thick leather belt around his waist before he wipes away grease from his hands that refuses to be washed away by the water. His tail moves, restless and mirroring the fast pace of his thought train.

"The hydroelectric power plant is amazing." I compliment him myself now, feeling inspired by his presence. He's really doing the impossible, not letting the situation of life underwater change things for him and I can't help but be fond of him after so little time.

220

"Yes, when it works!" He rubs his hand across his forehead, transferring grease onto his dark skin just below where the thick braids begin at the front of his hairline.

"Can we stop with the pleasantries? We have a demon to kill in case you've forgotten? You can kiss Maneli butt later." Rose snaps, snarky. I turn to her, giving her a glare intense enough to shatter glass.

"Apologies about her, but we are in a bit of a time jam." I sigh and he looks past me to her.

"It's alright, I'm used to feisty women. I'm sure you've met Kaiya and Amara by now." He chuckles, his lips broadening into a wide smile. "Let's get you girls kitted out, and out of that uh… armour." He looks the mermaids up and down, confused as to their over glamorous attire. I sigh, feeling my cheeks flush red.

"You know they're not really used to armour…that look, it's not normal for us…" I feel like I'm stuttering and he laughs at me.

"Don't worry about it, girl. We'll get you guys looking like warriors of Ava in no time."

Gabriel doesn't just deliver new armour, but constructed pieces that fit the mermaids as individuals. I sit and watch them each be measured, making sure to confiscate the overly glittering pieces they discard. Each one of them is beautiful in their own right, and I wonder why they feel the need to add so much excess. If I looked like them I certainly wouldn't.

"Oh my gosh this is so much more comfortable." Alannah gushes as Gabriel fastens the last disk of her breastplate together.

"I took the inspiration for these pieces from crustaceans, like lobsters and crabs. Their shells work together to allow free movement, so that's what I try to achieve." As he speaks I notice that he's got the designs spot on. Curved plates cover their multi-coloured tails, but they manoeuvre seamlessly, allowing the wearer to swim without constraint.

221

"You and our metal master need to get together. He's amazing with armour too." I blurt, not thinking about Sophia, who is showing off her own armour to Emma who is looking up at her like she's the next Miss Teen USA.

"Yes! You do!" She says, hope filling her expression. I cringe, praying once more for Oscar's longevity.

"That's the last of you done. Let's go." Orion says as Alannah gets given a fascinator with fine, carbon steel netting to protect her eyes from potential projectiles.

"This is beyond cool." She says, placing it into her inky black locks.

"I can't believe we're going to fight a demon…" Emma sighs, looking terrified.

"You can all do it. Besides, I'm going to be right beside you. I can take hold of any one of you and project your power if you need it." I reassure them as Orion comes up behind me.

"We're not all done here. I want you to get a new set of armour too. They're your warriors. You should match." He looks to the engineer who smiles knowingly. Of all the people I've met so far Gabriel is definitely one of my favourites, he's so warm and his eyes are so kind. I kind of want to hug him for everything he's doing, no questions asked, let alone expectation of payment.

I glide over to him, turning and looking back to Orion, appreciation glowing from within.

"Okay Genius, show me what you got."

My armour is awesome. I stare down at myself as I move through the water toward the exit of Cape Point to see my body is protected by lightweight metal, something Gabriel had saved for just such an occasion, retrieved from some heiress' yacht that had fallen victim to a particularly nasty storm a few months back.

My mermaid troops are all in copper and gold, but not me. I'm in brilliant silver and aqua, just my colours. The pieces are fashioned to cover me almost completely as the metal is carved into smaller circles which slide past each other seamlessly once connected together, but I barely notice that I'm wearing it, giving me more free movement than I've had in a while. My hair has been braided by the other maidens and piled up on my head, where an ornate crown of metal has been fashioned for war. It doesn't rise into a small peak like the symbol of status I had received at the coronation, but instead falls downward across my forehead, creating two arches above my eyebrows before two transparent visors made of some kind of aqua plastic fall across my eyes. My arms are wrapped in Kevlar mesh and my hands are left exposed so I can use my ability as the vessel. My tailfin has been wrapped in more Kevlar netting which covers my precious scales until it reaches the bottom of my form, where a blade has been attached to the end of my fluke. I'm still getting used to the weight of the weapon, but I know without a doubt that it'll be lethal in action, giving me comfort.

As I look back, I see the other maidens clad in copper, noting that though my armour is similar, it definitely singles me out as the leader and gives me a sense of burden I haven't felt before. I have always loved Oscar's armour, but this was something special, not just because of Gabriel's understanding of materials, but because of his love of knowing the ins and outs of how everything works. His engineering knowledge paired with skills handling the raw materials made for a seriously unique look.

"You look…" Orion whispers as my head turns, aqua eyes flashing beneath the tiara visor. "Like a warrior."

"I didn't before?" I ask him, cocking my head.

"This armour… it's yours. It's you." He nods, and I wonder if he might well up.

"Hey, you okay?" I say, glancing back at my trailing troupe of mermaids who are still examining themselves in every single reflective surface they pass.

"This isn't something I ever wanted for my soulmate." He whispers, running his hand through his hair in a strained exhalation.

"This isn't something I ever thought I'd be doing either." I admit and he laughs.

"It looks good on you. Warrior-hood." He compliments me, though in a way I know he's sad, sad he can't wait on me hand and foot, sad he can't protect me from every danger the ocean holds, but that simply wasn't what life had in store for him. I'm just not that type of girl.

We exit into the clear waters of the South African coast, the brightness nothing compared to the electrics of the city, and yet I shield my eyes under the glare from the high sun. Seals play in a gleeful abandon of the civilised world, teeming just miles away in Cape Town, fading slowly into the distance as they become mere specks. I also catch a glance of Philippe, chasing some fish before stopping to graze at a small seagrass patch.

I'm caught up in watching him, transfixed by his equine beauty, when a voice breaks the silence, and I know we are not alone any longer.

"Come. We must go, find the demon before it reaches the shore." Akachi has joined us, and as I move to face him, I notice that his appearance gets no less startling in the light of day. I clutch my spear as he takes off into the deep blue hue of the sea, hovering over small reefs as angel-fish twitch below, not even acknowledging his silent and stealthy presence.

"Come on, let's go." I order the girls behind me to fall in line. They clutch their weapons to them, clearly afraid, except for Rose who looks ready for a tussle. Funnily enough she's the one I'm most concerned about, and I wouldn't put it past her to pull something stupid.

I turn the long spear in my hand as I swim realising it's heavy but feels wrong somehow. It doesn't feel like mine. I know the weapon which I'd much rather be holding but I'd thrown it away, telling Solustus that it wasn't the life I wanted for myself any longer. I had been stupid and now he and Saturnus have my scythe.

"There!" Akachi's voice rumbles from him like an earthquake in the endless ocean surroundings. He is not wearing armour, and his staff still holds the small crocodile upon it, golden orb in its jaws and un-fazed by the whole endeavour. I look to where the chieftain is pointing, and I see it, the demon that looks like a huge lizard. It's eyes blaze neon yellow, glowing despite the bright light source overhead.

As we approach, it's scales are revealed as a deep mossy green and its jaws are strong looking, with jagged teeth that are probably longer than my entire body. With the size of such a creature, it makes me wonder how demons go unnoticed in a bay such as this. Then again, the Maneli seem more than capable of taking these kinds of demons down with as little fuss as possible.

"Go. Your leader will stay here with me." Akachi points to the demon and I gulp, feeling another presence suddenly at my spine. I pivot quickly, anticipating another demon that I had not seen via Skye's astral projection powers.

"Watch it." Kaiya's voice catches me off guard as she grabs my arm in mid-rise. I startle at her sudden appearance.

"Hey, what are you doing here?" I ask her, surprised.

"You didn't think I'd miss this? A load of Princesses in armour?" She smirks at me and I roll my eyes before facing Orion once more.

"Okay, you stay here. No interfering. No matter what." I scold him and Akachi smiles, looking to Orion with an unwavering gaze that screams intensity.

"Fine, fine, but if someone gets killed then it's on your head." He warns me back and I frown. He isn't joking.

We could really die. I'm taking the mermaids... into battle with a demon. The mermaids... into battle... with a demon." I repeat this internal mantra to myself, eyes widening.

Oh crap.

"Okay, here we go." I say, trying to not show my fear at the prospect of fighting alongside the women who had told me I should moisturise more.

"Good luck." Akachi nods to me as his crocodile companion blinks slowly.

I turn away from them as they hang in the sea, watching. The mermaids are waiting for me a little far off, inching as close to the demon as they dare without me.

"Okay, let's go." I say, not waiting for a response as I pass them.

"So what's the plan?" Rose asks me, swimming to catch up and matching me with her rose-pink tailfin, stroke for stroke.

225

"Plan?" I raise an eyebrow, like she expects me to do all the work?

"Yeah, from the last time you took on a demon?" Skye rises on my other side, the girls sandwiching me between them so I can't escape.

"Uh…" I say, thinking back. *I've fought a demon right? Didn't I?* Suddenly it occurs to me that I've never actually fought a demon. I've fought Psirens, and I killed Alyssa. *That counts? Doesn't it?*

"Please, don't tell me you've offered us up to the slaughter with no experience?!" Alannah rises, swimming beside Rose, her eyes blazing and angry beneath her fascinator.

"I saw a demon once, and I watched Atlas and Orion kill one…" I begin but Rose cuts me off.

"You WATCHED????" She looks at me with wide eyes and a horrified look on her face.

"Yes, but…"

"Oh my god, we're going to die, we're all going to die!" Emma blurts behind me. Fahima looks to me from beneath my undulating form, her armour complimenting the caramel of her complexion beautifully. I right myself in the water, not taking my eyes off the demon in the distance for a single moment.

"Okay, yes, I've never done this before. But it's going to be fine." I assure them. They look uncertain. Marina puts her hand on my arm as she catches up with us, stopping me from turning away and continuing forward.

"You'd best not try lying to an empath, Callie. You're scared too." She looks slightly annoyed and I wonder momentarily if this was a giant mistake, but an instinct inside of me cries out that it's not. It can't be. These women are blessed and there's a reason for that.

"Fear means nothing, Marina. I might feel it, but it's not going to stop me going in there." I raise an eyebrow, tearing my arm away from her. I take off, clutching my weapon to me and allowing them to either hang there or follow. I can't keep pushing them into this; the choice must be theirs and theirs alone.

I reach the demon, and immediately rush forward. I'm not wasting any more time and so I use my rage at the mermaids' lack of courage to launch myself onto the creature's spine. I lodge my spear in the reptilian demon's hide, which is ridiculously thick. The beast roars, turning on me, it's weight moving

226

the water and throwing me from its back. It opens its jaws wide, exhaling a breath bad enough to send a pirate running for the hills. The stench of rot and decay washes over me and I cringe, looking down the jaws of evil in physical form.

"Callie!" Skye yells, from behind me. I stand there, unable to move, wanting to force them into action. I don't know if I'd come into this wanting to put myself at risk to force them to fight, but that's certainly how it has turned out.

Suddenly, I see something shimmer to my left and so rotate just in time to see Skye's astral self, hovering in the water by the creature's left eye. She distracts it, luring it from me as I hang there, amazed at her quick thinking.

Still clutching my spear, I look to the beast; it's about a hundred metres long, with spines on the top of its crocodile-like head. Its eyes glow yellow like the highlighters I had used in high school, giving me an idea.

"Its eyes! We need to blind it!" I say, raising my spear in the water to grab the other maidens' attention. They nod, or so it looks from this distance, as the beast becomes tired of chasing after what it soon discovers is a ghost. It thrashes, turning instantly on the rest of the women and I watch as Rose swims forward, pushing Emma behind her as she tries to move, before taking a large stroke and singling herself out against the others. She opens her mouth and screams, deafening me and everyone around her. However, the beast seems to not mind the sound for rather than moving away to flee, it only backs up slightly. I wonder why, but then I realise.

Swimming as fast as I can I pound my tail against the current and pick up a quick rhythm, launching myself across the path of the demon's lunging bite and spinning, throwing Rose to my left and slashing across the demon's snout with the blade on the end of my tail.

"Dammit, Rose!" I cuss under my breath, looking to her just for a moment and catching her angry gaze as she rights herself in the water. I look between the maidens, counting them as they hang, startled by the demon's colossal size, but I can't locate Emma.

"Emma!" I cry out, looking around, worried the beast has swallowed her whole. My heart hammers and Rose suddenly looks worried. I turn, looking

227

above me for any trace of her, and that's when I glimpse it. Emma has used her invisibility to swim close to the creature's eye and I watch her, just behind the limits of the demon's eyesight, too close to its eyeball to be visible as she looks to me and I raise my eyebrows, impressed. I nod to her and she strikes, ramming her spear into the demon's eye.

One down. One to go. I think to myself as Sophia catches my hand.

"I have an idea." She announces hurriedly, her tail undulating a frantic pace.

"What is it?" I ask her as she turns around and reaches out to Alannah.

"I'm getting her close enough to sing to that thing. Once I've got it sleepy, the rest of you should go about hitting it wherever you can. Okay?" She looks to me for permission.

"You don't need my permission." I say to her with a smile and she returns the expression, the smile flitting across her face as the creature lets out another enormous roar. Emma is hit as the demon's head swerves her way, caught off guard by its sudden blindness in one eye. She flies through the water, it's skull hitting her full force. Suddenly I'm being shoved out of the way by Fahima, who lurches past me in a flurry of bubbles and catches Emma in her arms like she is no more than a baby.

I pivot, knowing that Emma is safe and move to Rose and Marina as Alannah and Sophia move high above us in a violet orb of static energy.

"We are going to hit that thing once Sophia and Alannah have it down? Got it?!" I say, looking between them.

"I didn't... if Emma..." Rose splutters, looking heartbroken.

"Don't do that, just do this with me, okay?" I brush her guilt away and she nods, eyes glistening.

"I didn't know this was so scary... I've felt the fear from Christian when he was called away but..." Marina starts.

"Not now! After this thing is dead. Let's do this, together." I say and they both close their mouths. They nod back to me, their gazes turning fierce.

I somersault back on myself, looking up at the enormous jaws of the half blind demon which is now squirming. Sophia gets in close, her shield protecting her against the demon as it backs away from the violet orb, clearly wary of the static.

"Sophia now!" I yell and the sphere drops. Alannah's voice reaches out from her, wrapping around us all like a thick mystical blanket of warmth and comfort. I start to feel sleepy.

"No, stay awake!" Rose yells, shaking me. "Cover your ears!" Marina bellows, too loud because she can't gauge her own volume.

I slam my hands over my ears, noticing that I'm not the only one having this problem. Fahima looks like she's dropping off too, but Emma slaps her sharply across the face. I almost laugh because it's so out of character for the fragile, blonde angel that Emma appears to be, but then I remember I have a job to do.

"Get back!" I yell, feeling my heart thud within my ribcage. The reptilian demon sways, once, then twice, before crashing jaws first into the dirt. The mermaids and I cover our heads, the sand exploding up in plumes not unlike explosions. As the sand falls and clears, I see Alannah, crushed beneath one of the creature's jaws.

"Alannah!" Rose screams, lurching forward as I look to the other women.

"Rose, you get her, the rest of you, disassemble this thing!" I sweep in from the left, letting the water fly across my skin as I soar, throwing my spear into the creature's closed eyelid. It punctures the flesh, blinding the creature completely.

I dive in, banking past Rose who is pulling Alannah from beneath the demon with all her strength. Sand is in her hair, and as Emma sweeps past me in a rush of water with no visible source, I watch as she takes her spear and embeds it in the side of the beast's underbelly. The creature twitches, barely appearing to be uncomfortable, as I continue to swim, moving across its spine in one magnificently inspired moment of clarity.

I rise through the water, spiralling in my ascent, breaking the surface and flying high up to the sun, my visor stopping the glare from blinding me. I pick up my momentum as the sun dries my skin dangerously before gravity does the rest for me. I hit the surface of the water, using all my weight and tensing every strand of sinuous muscle in my tailfin to drive me down. I hit the fastest my body will move just before I collide with the tail of the creature and spin my body drastically, slicing clean through its skin and bone with the blade attached to my tailfin.

I gasp as the muscle and bone comes free, matching the demon's scream in my surprise, unable to believe that my tiny body did so much damage. Blood plumes like a mushroom cloud of destruction over me as my blue tinted world turns a bloody aubergine. The demon exhales a final breath as the other mermaids shoot collectively for its carotid with deathly and unpractised accuracy, ending its life, and with it, their innocence.

18

Ava

ORION

They've done it. Despite the fact that the women backing Callie don't know the hilt of a sword from the blade, they've done it. Against all the odds. Callie was right, Atargatis must have a plan for them, and they have become much more than they appear. Shame swells inside me, I underestimated them, just like I had done with my soulmate.

"That is impressive." Akachi compliments, sighing. He looks surprised.

"Thank you. They're far more capable than they appear." I reiterate the point, having been fooled once more by valuing the physical over the spiritual. I really need to trust those around me more, have faith in their abilities. After all, they're all we've got left.

"Kaiya, go and get a few of the others and strip the carcass for raw materials." Akachi orders and Kaiya bows quickly to him before vanishing from his side and back toward Cape Point.

"So, about the vessel…" I begin but Akachi turns to me, raising a palm mapped with crossing lines, a sign of his age.

"I told you, boy. No such thing exists here. I would have known of it by now if so. You've proved you are in the Goddess' favour, so I will heal your friend and return him to you. Afterwards, I expect you will be on your way. That is, after the cleansing ritual this evening." His gaze is unwavering as always, he is a very intense man, dealing only in the absolutes of his faith.

"Cleansing ritual?" I raise one eyebrow, curious as to what exactly needs to be cleansed. My thoughts linger on the face of my sister momentarily, before Akachi's gaze falls from mine, moving to the maidens who are returning from their victory. Skye and Rose are carrying Alannah between them; she looks hurt.

"Yes, these women have been close to a demon at the moment of its death. We don't want any of the darkness within it clinging on to life through them." He nods and I frown. I'd fought hundreds of demons in my time, and yet not once had I thought about what happened to them after death. Disposal of their colossal remains was as far as the thought had ever occurred to me.

I look at Callie, her tailfin spattered with demon blood and my head cocks slightly. She had absorbed Titus' darkness hadn't she? So, what was to say a demon couldn't latch onto her in the same way? The thought fills me with dread. Perhaps it is something about her role as the vessel for the mer, something about how she absorbed the magic of her friends with little care for the consequences, but suddenly I'm worried that she's susceptible.

"That makes perfect sense." I agree, the thought of Callie being infected with any part of a demon driving me to agree with his belief in cleansing after slaughter.

"Did you see us?" Rose asks me, straightening her body upon approach.

"I did! You did a great job. Very good team work." I compliment them and Rose beams, Alannah rolls her eyes.

"It would have been team work, if one member of the team hadn't almost gotten another member of the team eaten." She attacks Rose over her carelessness, her cockiness at the prospect of her new-found blessing.

"Hey!" Rose screws up her face, blushing slightly.

"It's okay, when I first discovered my powers over air I used to torment Ghazi all the time." I admit, remembering those days.

"Why Ghazi?" Callie asks me, her lips curving into a smile.

"He was a challenge. He's got hearing that's hard to beat." I laugh and she giggles slightly, more relaxed than I've seen her since we arrived in this place.

232

"Come, my warriors will strip the carcass clean, we must get your armour cleaned as well." Akachi orders and I agree, bowing slightly.

"Thank you for inviting us to the cleansing ritual." I say, trying to stay respectful despite the fact he's still refusing to help us. Akachi turns, not saying a word and launches back toward his city.

"What's that about a cleansing ritual?" Callie moves forward, placing a hand around my waist.

"You're shaking, are you okay?" I enquire, concerned.

"Yes, just adrenaline fuelled." She breathes out, exhaling bubbles. "So what's this about a ritual? You know how much I love those." She jokes, insensitive as she reminds me of the night where I had watched her fall through the water above the Occulta Mirum, porcelain and cold.

"I'll tell you on the way. Come on."

Within Cape Point, as I'm telling Callie about the fact that a vessel is still nowhere to be found, I start wondering whether Azure is okay. I wonder if she can take care of herself the way she makes out. She had survived among the Psirens for centuries, but she was one of them, and I worry about whether we'll see her return before we need to move on. As it is, we have no vessel and no army of Maneli fighters for our cause, so I suppose there is still time.

The sharp peak of the mountain rises around me as I watch time pass from a distance. Alannah is taken by one of the younger healers to get her tail looked at, and the other mermaids vanish with Callie to store their armour for the ritual later in the evening.

I let the city move around me, hustling, bustling with Maneli who watch me from within their huts. I observe prayer, watch as vials of what look like medicines are bottled and look on as the Hydro Electric Power Plant continues to run, unending in its fluid rhythm. I perch on the roof of one of the shanty huts, flicking my tail beneath me and taking a moment to be alone. I was alone for such a long time, seeking out someone to complete me, and it's only now that I realise what being alone for so long has done to me. It's closed my mind; it's left me stubborn and unfit to rule. I think back to all the times father had offered to teach me how to fill his throne, and once again I find myself wishing I'd listened.

As I sit back, listening to the rush of multiple waterfalls trickling down the rock of the peak, I wish he were alive more than ever. I wish Starlet were alive more than ever. They would know what to do, what to say to Akachi, how to find the vessels.

Instead, I'm floundering around, no better equipped than Callie, who is centuries younger than me, to rule. In a way, I wish I were a better King, maybe that way I could be of some comfort to her as she learns how to be Queen. Then again, as I sit here and lay eyes on her form as she emerges from Kaiya's hut in the distance, I realise she's already a far better ruler than I'll ever be. She has an open mind and an open heart, she's brave enough to take risks and clever enough to know which risks to take. I have none of these skills. The only thing I have is a sword and the ability to know which part of a demon to shove it in. Ruling a city however, requires a little more finesse, that which I do not have. Once I'm out of this fight, out of this war, perhaps then I'll be able to do what I need to, but maybe, just maybe, it's not my destiny to rule the people of the Occulta Mirum. Perhaps that destiny lies with a much more unlikely candidate.

"Orion!" My name is called from below and I sigh.

No rest for the Crowned Ruler.

"Yes?" I exhale, tired of all the attention.

"Well if you're going to be like that then I'll go and take the vessel for Ava back to where I found her." Suddenly, I realise the voice belongs to Azure and my head snaps downward, eyes widening as they move to where my sister floats in the street below, accompanied by a woman with the most startling eyes I've ever seen.

"You found the vessel?" I gape at her and she smiles, crossing her arms and cocking an eyebrow.

"Your faith in me truly is astounding, big brother." She snorts as I descend through the water, pushing off from the metal roof and sinking so I can greet the woman with the Zebra striped tailfin.

"It's a pleasure to meet you…" I begin, holding out a hand.

234

"Callista." She finishes my sentence for me and takes my hand. Looking sideways to Azure.

"I can see what you mean about him. He does need to relax." She says, abrupt in her statement as she looks back to me, unapologetic but with a half dreamy smile gracing her thick lips.

"I know, right?" Azure agrees, her eyes narrow as she assesses me.

"So you're okay?" I ask her and she nods.

"Turns out spiritual healers are actually kind of like therapists." She shrugs, tossing her black hair behind one shoulder.

"You gave my sister therapy?" I look to Callista, my eyes still wide as she nods, laughing, melodic and jovial in spirit.

"Well, I can see why Ava chose you as her vessel. You're a brave woman." I compliment her and she bows slightly, the shells in her hair clinking together.

"Crocodile dude said he wants her to do some cleansing ritual. You let the sparkle squad go and fight a demon apparently?" Azure crosses her arms with a crazed expression. I raise my shoulders, shrugging. "I'm sure they killed it with their skin care speech. Poor thing probably died of boredom." Azure quips and I laugh.

"They were actually amazing. Also, you might not want to tease them so much, you know they've all got powers we never knew about?" I explain and now it's her turn to shrug.

"You know, I'm not surprised. The Lunar Sanctum Spa isn't exactly the kind of environment where one feels under threat. Unless you're me and you hate all that breathe and relax crap." Azure seems more relaxed than I've ever seen her now I think about it.

"Callista... what did you do to Azure, like you're sure you didn't do some kind of body swap voodoo?" I tease her and Callista's expression stays deadpan.

"You'd be best advised not to joke about the powers of Ava young man, lest you want to end up cursed." She threatens and I exhale. Once again I've made a political faux pas.

Well done Orion. You're a genius. I condemn myself.

235

"I apologise. I've just never seen Azure so happy." I admit and Azure laughs.

"Yeah, amazing what a few hours away from you can do isn't it? Oh, and by the way, you're welcome, I just totally saved the day and all, but it's cool." She jerks her head sideways to Callista.

"Oh yes, well done, Azure. How did you uh, make this little discovery?" I query her, curious.

"I attacked her and she absorbed my visions, plus extras." She explains.

"Extras?"

"Yeah, she saw everything. My whole past. If I've seen it, so has she." She reveals this and I relax. This is good. I can use this.

"So you've seen the Psirens?" I enquire and she nods, waving her Zebra scaled tail from side to side in a rhythm that calms me.

"Yes. I've seen why you're here. I will talk to Akachi." She blinks a few times, but her expression remains unreadable. The bustle around us has been drowned out while we've been talking, but as I lean back in the water, letting my tailfin bend slightly under me in relief, I feel her gaze on me.

I turn, seeking her and finding her instantaneously.

"Callie!" I call out as she sees me too, our eyes locking as she passes the middle of the street in which we're floating.

"Hey you!" She moves through the water toward me, surprisingly upbeat considering the trouble we're having convincing the Maneli of our cause.

"Azure found the vessel!" I exclaim as Azure opens her mouth to speak.

"You really know how to steal a girl's thunder don't you?!" She snaps, looking annoyed.

"Oh, sorry." I apologise.

"I'm Callie, another vessel." Callie introduces herself to Callista with a small smile.

"I know who you are." Callista replies, sounding ominous. Callie shoots me a slightly worried expression before I spin, glimpsing Ghazi as he emerges at the end of the street.

"Azure will explain. I'll be right back." I exclaim, rushed in my tone, as I turn away from her and swim away, dazed by the sudden appearance of my

236

friend. I move past a few female Maneli who have been watching my conversation with Callista and their eyes follow me, examining me as I pass. I ignore them, swimming as quickly as I can.

"Ghazi!" I call, desperate in trying to reach him. He turns, seeing me and as he does he reveals Amara at his back. I try to read his expression from here, but he is, as always, stoic.

We have not lost a single warrior in our history. Not one. Akachi's voice echoes through my mind, and I only hope that I have not shattered their impeccable record.

"How's Cole?" I blurt, unable to stop myself. Amara moves around Ghazi, who smiles, and I can't help but feel relief clutch at me, if only slightly. I want to hear it from Amara before I get my hopes up too high.

She swirls around Ghazi, her body perfectly feline in the water. Her long lustrous hair and cat-like features continue to make her oddly attractive.

"He is resting, but he will be fine." She reveals and I reach forward, putting my arms around her. She stills in the water, unsure of what to do. I release her after a moment.

"Uh, sorry." I stammer, I had forgotten myself in my relief and so I turn, hoping Callie hasn't seen. She floats a way off, still talking with Azure and Callista.

"Would you like to see him?" She asks me as Ghazi floats between us, no use as he can't talk. I rotate to face them both fully and as I observe Ghazi a moment I realise that he appears exhausted and weary in the face. I wonder how close Cole came to turning to sand.

On second thought, I realise as I watch him turn to me, expecting me to reply to Amara's question, *I'd rather not know.*

"Yes. Can you take me?" I ask Amara as her expression remains flat and unchanged. I have noticed that most of the Maneli, except Gabriel, seem like they almost have a sense of humour, until they snap, returning to unfeeling and serious expressions almost instantly. When I'm talking with them I feel nervous, afraid that at any moment I may tread on some landmine of political incorrectness, blowing myself to smithereens in the process.

"Yes, this way." Amara replies, looking bored. Her bangles clank together as they fall down her long tan limbs which are covered in golden tattoos.

I follow her, looking back to Callie over my shoulder one last time. Now she's talking with Rourke, the large Maneli who it appears has a tailfin sporting cheetah spots upon golden scales now his camouflage has been removed. I swim, flexing my midnight blue tailfin and look forward now, trying to catch up with Amara in a few strokes despite her quick speed.

"Thank you for this. For saving my friend." I stare into her yellowish-green eyes as her head turns to me, black hair falling from her head in a waterfall of poker straight locks.

"It's my job." She shrugs, unfeeling.

"I don't care. You did me a great service." I push my gratitude on her, feeling suddenly irritated by the unfeeling approach this woman has towards me.

"It was Ava's will that he survive. I am just her implement." She says, eyes blazing with stubborn fire, ignited by her faith.

"None the less. You will always have friends among my people. I owe you and Ava a great debt." I think I finally get the point across and she gives the beginnings of a smile.

We arrive outside her dwellings, the atmosphere between us awkward as we dive deep, entering the large metal hut. The light inside surprises me. It isn't stark like the other huts I've been inside; instead it's green. The bulbs in the lights that hang crudely from between the metal slats of the roof are parakeet green, giving an eerie and supernatural feel to the space.

Cole lies out on a wooden bench in the centre of the room, his body coated in seaweed and other plant life I've never seen. His wound is smeared with green gunk that looks poisonous in itself and, as I move to his side, I notice that his face looks incredibly pale and off colour in the green glow of the room.

"Cole?" I call his name out, placing my hand on his arm. His black hair falls back from his forehead as his head turns to me.

"Hey… Your Highness…" He says, looking up to me through cracked eyelids.

"Oh for Goddess' sake if you don't call me Orion after this I'll kill you myself." I bark, feeling irritated. The man saves my life and somehow I'm still referred to as better than he. I owe him everything.

"Okay, whatever you say, Your Highness." Cole coughs slightly, sitting up and cringing.

"No! Sit back!" Amara, flusters over to him in one giant exertion of her panther-like tailfin, slamming him back down to the table with one hand. He winces.

"See, this is why I don't prefer the company of women. They're so damn pushy." He jokes and I laugh.

"Ah, don't I know that to be true." I wink at him. "Please though, Cole, in all seriousness, call me Orion. If you're going to be throwing yourself on poisoned spears for me I think we should at least be on a mutual first name basis. Don't you?" I cock an eyebrow, looking down at him as Ghazi enters the room behind me. I turn to him.

"Okay, Your... Orion." He sighs, breathing out and relaxing on the table.

"I have to go to a cleansing ritual. The mermaids took on a demon you know. And won." I say to him. He laughs, but then winces and ceases the sound.

"I'll have to be careful. They'll be giving you and I a run for our money." He jokes.

"Well, you're going to be training them, so rest up. You and I both know you're going to need it." He rolls his eyes.

"I throw myself on a spear for you and this is what I get. An aching gut and the mermaids..." He tuts slightly, looking as though the words are taking a tiny amount of his energy each time one spills out into the water. I laugh, smiling down at him. Glad he's still alive.

"I shall let you rest. I'll send for you when we're ready to leave." I inform him and Amara nods to me.

"He'll be ready in a few hours. That antidote works fairly quickly." She imparts this information and I nod. I swirl to leave, twisting in the water and looking to Ghazi.

"Stay with him. Don't leave his side." I demand this of him, but Ghazi looks to me communicating so clearly in this one look that I know exactly what he's thinking.

Never.

The thunder breaks high above the peak of Cape Point. I'm immersed in water and I'm inside a mountain, but I still can't escape its rumble. The liquid splash of the falls is also coming in faster and louder now, raising the level of the water that holds the city and alerting me to rain outside.

I make my way back to where we had first knelt before Akachi, placing Cole at his mercy, and as I sweep in from above, diving toward where I can see Callie hovering in the water below, I notice that a stack of bones and a large skull have been stacked in the centre of the circular patch of earth.

"Is that from the demon?" I ask, coming up behind Callie and Azure, who hover together, not fighting. Unusual, to say the least.

"Yes, amazing how they've stripped it down for parts so quickly, don't you think?" Callie turns to me while Azure continues to stare across the courtyard.

"Quite. What are you two talking about?" I ask her and she twists her mouth.

"Vex, and Oscar. Azure had a vision. They've escaped the ruins of the city. They're on the run right now. I don't know whether to tell Sophia." She looks torn and Azure turns.

"As far as I'm aware Oscar is still alive. However, my visions aren't definitive. Might not be a good idea to tell her until we're sure." She suggests and Callie nods.

"Well look at you two getting along." I say, putting one arm around each of them.

"Yeah, yeah, don't get used to it. I wanna get out of this place. Akachi is talking with Callista right now." Azure points to him, sitting in his throne, crocodile staff in hand.

"I…" I begin to speak but then watch Akachi rise from his throne, throwing his left arm to one side, disgust plastered across his face.

"Oh crap." Callie says and Azure looks to her.

"Excellent. I love old religious crackpots. They're so open-minded and helpful." She's seething with sarcasm, so much in fact I wonder momentarily if I shouldn't name her Azure 'Sarcasm' Fischer.

"He doesn't look happy." I admit, breathing out. I had thought Callista would be able to change his mind, but, apparently, I was wrong.

"You!" He points to me from across the square, moving up and over the pile of demon bones.

"Yes?" I say, feeling my hands ball into fists. I push Callie and Azure behind me slightly as I back up.

"After this ritual I want you gone. Hear me? I've had enough of you and your blasphemy! If I weren't so devout to Ava and it weren't necessary to cleanse your women you'd be on your way right now." He bares his teeth to me, but this time I don't flinch, I don't bow. I straighten.

"Fine." I say, unable to think of another way to convince him. He doesn't want to hear it and I'm done with arguing. Callista waits until he has vanished around the corner, clearly angry.

"He might not believe me. But I've seen the Necrimad. I believe Ava wants me to help you." She reassures me, looking straight through me with her ghostly alabaster gaze.

"You'll come with us?" Callie asks, sounding so hopeful I almost cringe.

"Yes." She replies simply.

"Thank you." I breathe out, half relieved, half disappointed. I need these Maneli, Gabriel in particular. I need them to fight for me. They're too valuable as warriors to ignore.

"Don't thank me. It's Ava's will." She reminds me and I almost sigh. I stop myself; not wanting to be rude, though I am getting quickly tired of these Maneli and their single mindedness surrounding the state of things on the higher plains.

"The ritual will begin in a few minutes. The rest of the city will be here soon, so I suggest you sit on the inner ring with me." She pulls my hand from my side, tugging me through the water so I'm close to the pile of demon bones. "Those who need cleansing will need to be in the inner most ring for this, so anyone near the demon at time of death." She explains.

As we hover in the middle of the square, drums made of sealskin and the wood of old baobab trees are beaten, struck at a primal rhythm to summon the Maneli to the ritual. They flock from the city, rising from their huts and shacks and descending upon the centre of the space, forming rings that expand outward from the epicentre where I hover, holding Callie's hand. Azure takes Callie's other hand, looking less than pleased.

Time passes and the circles grow outward concentrically. Soon we are all so close to each other we're practically back to front with the rest of the city's population. That's when I realise that they're greater in number than any of the pods we've seen before; even greater than the Adaro.

As I'm about to lean over to Callie to ask her if she has any ideas about how to convince Akachi to fight for us, he appears from around the corner. Faces gaze up to receive him, their smiles chasing his shadow as it blankets them one by one. He dips through the water seamlessly, his staff striking the sandy floor before he reaches us, falling into place next to the inner ring that now holds all the mermaids. Kaiya is here too after assisting Alannah, whose tail is still healing.

The drums desist in their rhythm for a few moments and the water falls silent as we float, waiting for something. Then the drums start again and I wonder what will happen next, feeling completely out of place as I look to Callie, whose eyes are wide. The drumbeat is different this time, haunting, deep and repetitive, inescapable from anywhere inside the peak.

Akachi, Kaiya and Callista look to one another, before Callista pulls my hand and our circle contracts, moving in on one beat and out on other. The five or six outer rings, each holding hundreds of Maneli push inward too, a stranger pressing against my spine and pushing the trident into the back of my skull. I've barely noticed I'm wearing it most of the time, but right now it's only too evident as I quickly become claustrophobic.

The circle expands again as we move back on the next loud drum beat before moving in again fast. After a few moments, the water begins pulsating,

242

and we're the cause, moving like the muscles of a heart and pumping the water over the bones that lie in the centre. We thrum in the water, stroking our tailfins to the primal rhythm of the drums over and over.

The Maneli begin to sing in Afrikaans and it's beautiful, but I can't understand it. Akachi rises as they do so, leaving the inner ring and moving up into where the force of our collective tails is pushing the water. He hovers in the centre of us all, rising and falling with the fluid heartbeat, lifeblood of the seas, raising his staff in the water as the orb begins to glow and he gazes upward to it, confused. The crocodile, holding the orb within its jaws, suddenly launches from his staff, clearly unexpectedly, for Akachi's expression is one of shock. I feel my heart rate escalate as the pulsations cease, Maneli inhaling sharply around me in a mutual gasp. The orb falls from the crocodile's jaws, descending into the centre of the circular collaboration of mer and Maneli. Callista reaches out, grasping it in her palms, instinctual in her response as the rest of the Maneli watch on, fascinated.

Suddenly, the orb's glow moves out, projecting itself on the surface of the water above, like a rippling television screen. On it are pictures of our city being destroyed, images of the Psirens, Titus, Solustus… Starlet… My heart breaks. This is Azure's memory and somehow Callista is projecting it. The images flash on a few moments more, showing the death, the destruction that had passed. Mer I had once known turning to sand before my eyes, Callie falling once more from the height of a city that once was, Callie dark, Saturnus' dark and true self. The images flash past in a whirlwind, the tragedy of what had occurred visible for all to see. The last image that plays is the swarm of Psirens before they had descended on the city, showing their colossal size before finally disappearing as Callista drops the orb like it's hot.

"What was that?" Callie asks me, looking confused.

"I'd say that was my greatest hits." Azure replies, looking annoyed. Akachi falls through the water, looking shocked as his face contorts in horror.

"Do you see now Akachi? We have to help these people." Callista gushes and the city watch on in silence.

"Callista, hush." He puts a hand up, moving to me. I drop the hands of those who float beside me, swimming forward into the centre of the circle and ready to fight if I need to.

"I have been blind to the will of Ava. Ava's eye only projects the desires of our Goddess. Her will is for us to help you." He bows his head. "I am sorry. Please forgive me." I exhale at his apology.

"It's okay. No apology necessary." I look to the crocodile as it picks up the eye of Ava in its jaws once more before returning to Akachi's staff.

"You will have the power of Ava behind you. I swear it. In her name." He makes a cross over his heart like some kind of religious promise I don't understand and I nod. "We have much to discuss. Come, all of you." He looks to the rest of my pod, his eyes intense and unwavering in their scrutiny as always.

With that, the ritual is over, and the people of the city erupt into chatter, talking in thick accents I don't recognise and exclaiming disbelief at what they had seen.

We follow Akachi to Gabriel's workshop, which he enters before saying a few words to the young engineer as they both turn to us.

"We must begin to make preparations for this war if we are to win. I want more information." Akachi commands.

I am stone still, my expression serious and mind racing as I try to keep up with this incredible change in attitude. Gabriel smiles to me and rubs his hands together, I can tell his mind is already whirring with the possibilities of a new challenge. I return his gaze, taking a seat on a nearby metal stool as the maidens sit down on the floor, looking up to me like I'm a God. I draw breath, looking to Callie and thinking back to where everything started to go wrong with the Psirens.

"I'll start at the beginning."

A day later and everything has been organised. We float once more before the unstoppable torrent of the whirlpool, which suddenly appeared after the passing of last night's epic storm. New debris scatters the ocean floor, and Maneli

244

scouts collect it, never faltering in their duty to better the community in which they live.

"We will see you soon." I bow my head to Amara and Akachi, Cole by my side and still bandaged with thick seaweed, but none the less functioning pretty much as he had before. The mermaids are kitted in their new armour, looking much more sensible than they had on arrival I might add, and Callie holds my hand, looking up at me. Pride shines from her like she's the sun, bathing me in her rays as I warm to her gaze and we share a moment to take in our success, longing to be alone, but not having access to such a luxury.

"Yes, thank you for everything, and don't forget…" I begin, looking to Callista.

"Yes, I know. The Pieces of Eight." She looks dreamy once more, like she isn't really there. Perhaps that's why I'm repeating myself, because I find it hard to believe someone who looks so distant has listened to what I've said.

"Yes. Thank you." I say it again, unable to express how grateful I am to them. They had been by far the most difficult to convince so far, but somehow we had managed it. I can only hope wherever we end up next isn't such a challenge.

Azure shifts in the water beside me, perching atop Philippe who has returned to us after his few days grazing and frolicking with foreign fauna. I had missed him, only too happy to see him return to us unharmed.

"Goodbye!" Callie says, waving beside me. The mermaids look to Kaiya with fondness and Ghazi moves over to Amara, despite harsh stares from Fahima, and wraps her in a bone-crushing hug. I laugh as she stiffens, uncomfortable, before he releases her and she flattens her hair, looking nothing if not ruffled at Ghazi's silent affections.

"May Ava guide you. Always." Akachi bows, closing his eyes and wishing us well.

I turn, pulling Callie behind me into the torrent of the whirlpool's thrashing waters, leaving the Maneli, and Ava, behind.

19
Duty
CALLIE

The water is calm around me as I exit the whirling portal, feeling my heart race at the sudden and expected exhilaration that had once terrified me. Cole exits next to me, looking pained as he reaches down to the place where his wound is still healing.

I pivot, looking around at my surroundings this time, not sure of where I am, but not wanting to leave myself open to attack as I had done with the Maneli.

"Stick close together!" I call out to the mermaids, who make their departure from the portal behind me, tumbling outward in fits of giggles, no longer afraid and scared as they had been the first time, but bolder, braver and even happier than I had ever seen them.

I gaze up to the rippling surface of the water, noticing pink petals floating upon it's transparency as I gaze out into the distance, noticing something I hadn't seen for a long time.

Boats.

"Orion!" I call out behind me, seeking his comfort.

"Yes, what is it?" He comes forward, placing a hand on the base of my spine, just below where my breastplate ceases.

247

"Look." I point forward, feeling my heart sink at the presence of humans so close. I don't feel equipped to cope with their proximity. Strange, when not a year ago I had been one of them.

"Okay, let's not panic, just keep together everyone and stay discreet. That means you Azure. No funny business." He turns around, glaring at Azure who halts at his side.

"I don't know what you're insinuating, brother. I am always on my best behaviour." She says, face deadpan and bored as she brushes her black hair behind one shoulder. In this one motion, she reminds me so much of her sister I almost make comment. It's often so easy to forget they were twins, despite the fact they had looked so much alike. I drop my gaze from Azure quickly, deciding not to open the wound Starlet had so clearly left behind.

"Let's keep low down to the sea floor." I suggest and Cole nods, immediately lowering himself without so much as a word. I can tell he's still weary, barely recovered from the toll the poison had taken on his body.

"Do you have any idea where we are?" I ask Orion, turning to him as he gestures to the rest of the pod to dive. He shakes his head.

"No, I have no clue. It just looks like a lot of sea right now." He shrugs and I pucker my lips to one side. Feeling paranoid, I glimpse over my shoulder as the hairs on the back of my neck rise, but I can't work out if it's just because we suffered so badly last time with the Maneli. Cole could have died, and as I turn back to see the whirlpool disappear, trapping us in our current mystery location, I exhale, running my hand through my hair and dislodging my visor slightly as I'm overcome with nerves.

"You alright?" Orion asks me, shooting me a concerned stare as we reach the bottom of the ocean.

"I'm just..." I pull my visor straight, exhaling heavily.

"Paranoid?" He finishes my sentence for me, grabbing my hand in his as we undulate side by side.

"Yes, is it that obvious?" I ask him, wondering if the anxiety I'm feeling is written all over my face.

"I feel it too. We should have been on better guard, last time we just appeared in the middle of nowhere. Just because these pods are linked to the

248

Circle of Eight doesn't mean they're all going to be friendly. After all, look at what Poseidon's pod turned out like." Orion replies as we swim forward and the rest of the pod suddenly hushes, clearly listening in to what we're saying, curious.

"I suppose that's true. It makes you wonder doesn't it, about Poseidon?" My brain starts to whir into motion, thoughts of what the higher plains must be like. I could have known. I could have been walking among them right now.

"Well, I'd say he's not the brightest spark in the box. After all, he chose Vex as a vessel." Orion rolls his eyes, trying to turn the conversation casual as the weight of the pod's silence makes us wary of saying too much. I have questions, fears about The Conduit, but if I voice them publicly I know only panic can ensue.

"I guess…" I wonder then what Atargatis must have been thinking when she chose me. What was it about the vessels that made us special? Why had I been chosen? I always carry the weight of the fact I may well die in the upcoming war with me, but I had never asked exactly why it is I've been put in this situation. Atargatis had hundreds of years to choose someone, so why me?

"ICK!" I hear the exclamation come from in front of me, of course it's one of the mermaids, though which one I can't tell from the back, as they're all in matching armour. As I move closer I discover the mermaid in question is Marina.

"What's wrong?" I ask her, concerned.

"That *thing* just popped right out of the sand in front of me. Frightened me half to death!" She shudders, her dark pupils retracting with disgust. I move around her, twisting my tailfin and turning to get a better angle on what she's looking at.

"Is that a…" I begin, turning to Sophia, who's arms are partially raised, as though she's anticipating expanding a shield.

"A what?" She asks me, cheeks flushing.

"I keep forgetting none of you have ever seen the discovery channel. I think that's a Japanese Spider Crab." I explain, looking down at the creature with a brown mottled shell and long spider like legs. It's not a beautiful creature, but I'd seen much worse in the deep.

249

"You lot are such babies." Azure snorts, looking at us all staring down at the spider crab as it begins to walk away toward its next destination.

"Do you think we're in Japan?" Orion asks me, looking hopeful.

"Maybe, I don't know. There were pink petals on the surface when I first arrived. Could be cherry blossoms. They have a lot of those here, right?" I think aloud, pondering the possibility.

"How should we know? We aren't geographers." Rose reminds me, I sigh. *After this I'm definitely making them watch the discovery channel.*

A mermaid had been frightened by a crab, I mean, we're supposed to be all zen with the sea and here Marina is having a mini heart attack. The reality of being a mermaid really isn't anything like the fairy-tales; those writers deserve to be shot.

"How do we even know we're going the right way?" Skye asks me with a worried look. I shrug.

"I have no idea. You know about as much as I do." I remind them. They look confused.

"What about Sedna's codex?" Cole asks Orion, looking tired.

"I've flicked through it a few times, nothing about any other locations. Just a lot about ice." He replies. His expression is one of fatigue also. This journey is taking forever.

"Why are we carrying it around then?" Azure asks him, sounding incredulous.

"Because, Azure, I didn't want to get half way around the world and then need it. Unless you'd have been the one volunteering to go back to the Arctic for it?" He snaps. She looks affronted but doesn't say anything.

"Come on, let's not float here bickering. Let's keep moving." I suggest and Orion crosses his arms before taking off into the distance. We follow in his wake as Azure looks to me with her usual irritated expression.

"What's got his tail in a knot?" She asks me.

"This is hard for everyone, Azure. He feels responsible for everyone and it's only becoming more apparent what a big responsibility that is. Look at what happened to Cole." I remind her. She shakes her head.

"He shouldn't worry so much. If you're gonna die you're gonna die." Her lips are moving but I wonder if she knows what she's saying.

"Look, put yourself in his place. He was alone for hundreds of years, not by his choice. He found me, and within the blink of an eye his whole world is falling apart. He's lost a sister too, and a father. Not everything is about you." I retort, looking deeply into her eyes as I feel my temper wearing thin. At one time, I would have been afraid to speak up to Azure, but right now she's whining all the time and sometimes I wonder why she's still here. I expect her to retort with anger, rage maybe, but instead she straightens her spine atop Philippe as her expression turns slack.

"You're right." She admonishes and I halt for a moment.

"What?" I ask her, not sure I heard her right.

"You're right. The world isn't just shit creek for me. We're all swimming in it." She lowers her eyes.

"Yes. We are." I sigh out, feeling the weight of everything pushing down on me too. If I'd thought I was bone tired in Italy, then this is something else. We just seem to have been lucky with all the pods so far, and I worry about how long a lucky streak like this can continue.

"You're not doing a terrible job." Azure attempts a compliment and I look up to her, eyes wide.

"Um… thanks."

"That's as close as I get to a compliment, so I'd just swim with it." She laughs as I debate whether to smile, laugh or act like I don't care. Azure is a bear trap, and I'm anticipating her snapping and taking my hand off any second.

I nod at her in return, unsure of what to say next.

"I better go and…" I begin, but suddenly another sound distracts me. It's Orion, calling out to me.

"Go on… go play hero, you know you want to." She raises her eyebrows and makes a shooing motion with her long fingers, letting Philippe's reigns fall slack in the water. Without another word, I swim forward, where I can see why Orion has called back to me. A giant pyramid like structure stands before us and, finally, I know where we are for sure.

"That's the Yonaguni Pyramid!" I exclaim and Orion laughs.

251

"Oh, I'm glad you know what it is, I was stumped there for a moment!" He admits, reaching out and pulling me through the water. My body floats, flush against his.

"Carl always used to have these random Conspiracy documentaries on the TV. I saw it on a show once, something about Aliens putting it there or something…" I explain, a smile creeping across my lips. I look up into his icy blue eyes and I'm home as I breathe out for a second, letting the relief wash over me. I reach up, placing a hand on his cheek.

"I wish…" I begin, searching for the words to express how I feel.

"Come on you two! Let's get a closer look!" Rose demands our attention and I huff out, blowing bubble rings.

"Duty calls…" He exhales too, dropping his gaze and moving away from my body with a wistful stare. I follow him, flexing my aqua tailfin and swimming close toward the building that looms in the centre of what look to be old ruins.

"Do you think they're inside?" Cole asks me as his black tailfin moves quickly, eager to reach somewhere more secluded.

"I don't see how they can be, these ruins have been explored a lot in recent years." I explain, remembering back to the days when I had been annoyed by something so simple as Carl not allowing me to change the channel.

Ah those simple days.

"So this isn't what we're looking for?" Sophia looks like she might cry.

"Okay, that's it." I round on the pod, whose forms have sagged at the thought we're in the wrong place. "Everyone take a seat on the pyramid." I point to the monument behind me, its steps even and perfect in their construction. Now I think about it, from the looks of this architecture and when the pyramid was supposedly built, it wouldn't surprise me if aliens *had* built it. That makes just about as much sense as anything around here does.

The mermaids, Orion, Cole, Ghazi and Azure plop onto the steps, looking like they've been fish slapped. Even Orion, who has dealt with more hardship than most of them, looks like he's about ready to give up. I float before them, swimming lengths over a small patch of sand as Philippe trots from foot to foot, looking to Azure. He clearly wants to move on, but I'm not letting that happen until I've spoken with everyone. Their resolve is clearly waning.

"Look, I know we're all tired. I'm tired too." I look to the love of my life, his gaze enough to melt my heart because he's so clearly proud of me and the mermaid I've become. I gulp, worrying I'll tear up at what I have to say next. "After this is over we can all sleep, dance, make love…"

"Uh not with you, thanks." Azure cracks the joke and I laugh, not even her sarcasm is enough to stop me as I realise what's been bothering me so much.

"My point is, we can all live once this is over, but if we don't make it, we don't succeed, there will be nothing left to live for. The Psirens will murder us. Take away the people we love. I know we're all tired, I know this is hard and it's taking forever. I know some of you have been injured, I know some of you are still grieving, but this, what we're doing here…it's worth it. The world is worth it, and so are we." I sigh, relieved as the words leave me. I realise that despite that I'm scared of the answer, I think I know why I've been chosen as the vessel. What if when I had died that was just a warm up? Preparing me for dying for real. What if I had been chosen because I was willing to sacrifice myself for the greater good… what if I had been chosen because they knew I'd lose in battle? I breathe in, feeling the horror of my beliefs sink slowly into my consciousness before understanding follows.

"Callie's right." Sophia says, looking to me. She turns to the mermaids who are sitting, scattered around her. "If we don't succeed, it won't matter how much we want to rest, want to be with our loved ones. None of it will matter. If this fails, then our lives are over. That's what is at stake here." She turns back toward me, a smile on her lips. The other maidens nod between themselves as Orion looks to Azure and she pokes her tongue out at him as Ghazi kisses Fahima on the temple and pulls her close.

"That's all well and good…" Rose begins, rising from the step she's been sitting on at the very highest point of the monument. She takes a tailfin's stroke backward and I can sense her negativity before she has even opened her mouth to speak again.

As though some power greater than me senses I really don't want to hear what she has to say, she trips backward as the bottom of her tailfin catches on

253

the edge of the next step up. She tumbles back, slamming her scaly behind into the flat of the topmost surface of the Pyramid. As she falls, she thrusts her arms out beside her to catch her fall. In the process, she pushes something and the wall behind her begins to shift. I look around at the rest of the pod as Azure's eyebrows rise in surprise.

"Oh my god! Rose! You did it! You found a use for your ass rather than being a pain in everyone else's!" Azure can't stop laughing as Rose flushes scarlet and scowls, rising once more.

"Hey, don't think I'm afraid of you!" She puffs out her chest, taking a large deep breath. I zoom upward and slam my hand over her mouth.

"Don't even think about it screamy. There's humans just over there." I point a few metres away, where boats are lazily floating on the surface. Her eyes travel, following my gaze.

"Oh… sorry." She bites her bottom lip, looking up to me as she sinks back down to join her friends.

"Good job for finding this though." I nod to her, giving credit where it is due.

"It was an accident." She admits, shrugging off my compliment in a half-baked attempt at modesty.

"Let's go." I say, looking to Orion. He's still sitting on the step of the Pyramid where he had been while listening to my spiel.

"Are you sure you want to go in there? It looks awfully dark. There could be traps." He looks concerned again, shooting a sideways glance at Cole's wound.

"I'd say it's our best bet to find the next pod." I reply, moving down to him and placing a hand on his shoulder. He looks up at my soft touch, searching my expression for something.

"I trust you." He smiles, his eyes gentle as they look upon me. He rises slowly from the step, as though the weight of the world is physically weighing on his shoulders, before swimming over to face me and gesturing onward. "Lead the way."

254

I'm surprised as I enter the doorway that has appeared in the peak block of the rock pyramid. I look into the darkness before I leap, putting my hands out in front of me and touching the opposing wall of the pyramid's supposedly solid peak.

So, there's no magically long corridor... I think to myself, sticking my head further into the darkness of the cuboidal space within what had once appeared to be solid rock. I look downward, where there doesn't seem to be a fourth side to the stone, just a long steep drop into the dark.

"It looks like we're going down." I mutter, feeling the pod at my back, waiting for our next move. I could turn around, have a discussion with them about the pros and cons of falling into the dark with no idea where the tunnel leads, but instead I figure throwing myself into the unknown so they have no choice but to follow me is the best option. I turn, winking to them as I stroke backward in the water, passing through the doorway where the rock has slid sideways, revealing the hole. Orion reaches forward.

"Callie!" I hear my name being called by him as I disappear, letting my weight pull me down into the dark of the steep drop. I keep my arms crossed over my chest so my palms rest over my collarbones on either side of my neck, careful not to scrape my arms on the walls.

As I fall, I wonder if I'm doing the right thing as I look above me through the water to what is now a speck of light above. Finally, my tailfin touches something resembling a sandy floor and so I feel my way around, seeking the wall and tracing it with my fingers as I swim, keeping close to it so I don't lose my direction. Suddenly, out of nowhere, I feel something sharp slide in beneath my chin.

Oh, poop. I think, knowing immediately that what I'm feeling is sharp enough to most certainly be a sword.

"Jibun jishin o tokutei shimasu!" I hear the words but I understand nothing. My heartbeat accelerates as the blade presses against my carotid, which is pulsating rapidly.

"I don't understand. I don't speak Japanese!" I gasp, feeling my gills pushing against the sharp edge of the sword each time I suck in water for breath.

"Identify yourself!" The man's voice comes out jerky and stilted, showing me that English is not his first language.

"I'm Queen Callie…" I stutter, hoping my title will save me.

"You're… woman?" The voice comes back, suddenly unsure.

"Yes, if you'd just turn on the light you'd see that." I say, speaking slowly in case he's having trouble understanding me. Suddenly, the space is illuminated, eels sparking into life as a surface slides away, the sound of stone scraping against stone alerting me to the motion of the wall behind me. I cover my eyes as even my visor isn't able to shield them from the sudden and blinding white of the eels in jars sparking, filling the tight space with stark light.

"Thank you." I say, though when I turn back I see that the man is still holding a short samurai sword toward me, chainmail hanging below his eyes, leaving them as the only feature of his face that is uncovered. His body is encased in gold armour, but his tail is bare, showing off a tailfin which looks like that of a black koi carp.

"Who are you?" He asks me, shoving the sword toward my throat once more.

Before I can open my lips to answer I see Ghazi descending into the small chamber, which consists only of bare brick walls and sand. He looks between me and my assailant, his face immediately becoming angry.

"Ghazi, no, wait!" I cry, holding out a palm and stopping him as he rushes forward. "Wait!" I command the man in front of me as he readies himself for attack too, forgetting that he isn't even one of my pod.

"I do not answer to you." He says simply, his words laced with his Japanese accent. His eyes narrow above his chain mail facial armour, and even though I can't see the rest of his face I can tell he's not a match for Ghazi physically.

I mean, he's barely taller than me. I think as he catches me looking him up and down.

"I may not look strong. But I'm more than deadly with a tanto." He jabs the sword forward again, his English becoming increasingly fluid the more he speaks it.

256

"Nobody is going to fight here. I can explain. I have more of my people on their way. We are here on an ancient quest from the Gods. A quest to save the world from falling into chaos." I gulp, watching him as his features relax and his eyebrows slacken. I take a second to look at him, his face is completely unremarkable, quite to the point where he could disappear and nobody would notice. His tail plays with the shadows cast by the high walls of the room and I find myself realising he could easily disappear into the corners with no one any the wiser. I was probably lucky to be alive.

"Callie?" I hear Orion calling my name as the man opens his mouth to speak. I ignore the call of my soulmate, knowing he will find me soon enough.

"Mizuchi?" I hear the man's voice lighten with curiosity.

"No, Atargatis, but Mizuchi... is involved too." I say, choosing my words carefully. I feel a hand on my spine and I turn to introduce Orion.

"This is Orion, the Crowned Ruler of our people." I explain as Orion holds out a hand. The man doesn't take it; he simply stares between us all like we're mad.

"Come with me." Is all he says as I turn, waiting for the rest of the mer to descend.   .

"Are the others coming?" I look to Orion who looks at me, half relieved and half annoyed.

"No, I thought it best not to have them fall into the big hole with no protection and no clue what lies at the bottom. Especially seeing as they're the last of our race and all." He cocks his head to the left and I smile sheepishly, putting a hand on the back of my neck.

"Sorry..." I begin but he sighs.

"Let's not pretend you're actually sorry about risking your life, I think we both know that personal safety has never been one of your highest priorities." He's whispering now as we follow the Koi tailed assassin into a dark corridor behind the wall that has moved to lighten the space. There is nothing to lend any idea about whom we might find within the pyramid as we swim through the murky water together and I observe my surroundings for even the tiniest hint of what they might be like. Looking around, the walls on every side are bare, and the only thing on the floor is sand and the odd crustacean. Everything is minimal but functional, giving nothing away.

After a few minutes of silence, I watch the assassin press in a rock that's loose on his left. A door slides to the right, flooding the shadowy passage with a stark light once more.

"Kira, I won't tell you again! You're not leaving this Pyramid and that's final!" I hear the words before I see the speaker, surprised this time it is in English and not Japanese. I swim forward, taking Orion by the hand and letting Ghazi trail after us.

"Fumio, what are you doing here?" I hear a high pitched and melodic voice ask. As I enter the space, I see it belongs to a young woman, her tail a gorgeous orange, black and white, taking on the style of a Koi carp yet again. She's floating high above the floor of the high-ceilinged room, which is clearly far underground.

"Ten'nō, shin'nyū-sha." He moves sideways in one small movement of his tailfin, revealing us.

I stare out into the room; two thrones are elevated on large bronze ornamental stands. They're wrapped in sculptures of bonsai trees that twist around the base of the chairs, supporting them on their collective flat tops. I want to understand what Fumio is saying, but I'm at a loss.

The young woman who was arguing with the man beside her looks down to us, her eyes growing wide with a childlike excitement. Her caramel hair is twisted into an elegant knot while two chopsticks hold it in place, suspending sea shells from their tips on fine strings. Her torso is covered in a half kimono, which comes to just above her tailfin in orange blossom and baby pink silk. The man beside her sinks through the water, descending to our level.

"You should bow before an Emperor, you know." He says, cocking a dark eyebrow. His tailfin is that of a golden koi carp, and his hair is longer than any man's I've ever seen bar Solustus. It falls in a sharp onyx sheet far past his shoulder and down to his scaled behind. His eyes shine golden from his pale face, not unlike those of a hawk and his pointed nose turns up at us as he speaks.

258

"We're sorry…Emperor." I say, bowing my head in respect. Orion is floating beside me and nods also, but the Emperor merely rotates stiffly in the water, on the axis of a pinhead, before ascending once more.

"Kira! Go back to your older sister, you are a Maiko now, you have chores." He barks, shooting her a disapproving stare. He waves a hand, dismissing her as she flees into the darkness of a corridor, placed high in the wall on the left-hand side of the room, between two ragged yet ornate tapestries.

"I found them in the pit of shadows." Fumio looks to us, ushering Orion and me forward, so we float far below the height of the throne on which the hawk-eyed Emperor is perched, looking down on us.

"Did you now?" He says, stroking his chin between long fingers. He narrows his eyes, his pallor striking in contrast to his dark hair.

"We have come on a quest. We are to go to war…." I begin. Suddenly the Emperor shuts his eyes and shakes his head.

"Sorera o sakujo" He says, the words no more than a whisper as his head turns toward Fumio.

"What did you say?" I ask, as Fumio moves toward us, binding my elbows behind my back and holding his sword up to my throat once more.

"Get. Out." He says, leaning down to stare at us as though we are no more than dirt under the ridges of his scales.

"What? WAIT!" Orion yells, rising. The Emperor looks to Fumio and nods, I feel the blade biting into my neck harder, almost drawing blood. I want to move, but I'm scared if I do it'll be the last thing I do.

"Leave this place. NOW. Or I'll have her served up like sushi!" The face of the Emperor turns feral as he bares his teeth, veins pulsating within his neck wildly. Orion looks between us, backing away.

"Okay, okay! We're going!" He exclaims, throwing up his arms in frustration and terror. He dives, grabbing me from Fumio in one quick and well timed swoop through the water, just as Fumio goes to lower his sword.

"Don't worry about us, we'll show ourselves out!" I call back, knowing I shouldn't bait the warrior with lightning fast hands, but unable to help myself.

As we turn back through dark passages, I am lucky Ghazi has such good eyesight and pays as much attention as he does, because each time we reach a blank wall, he knows where to find the release switch to open it.

Finally, we make our ascent up to the light high above, where Cole and the others are waiting for us. As Orion sets me back down on the steps of the pyramid, and the sun begins its slow descent to the horizon, the pod turns to us, eyes wide and eager for information. I stroke my neck gingerly, feeling the bite of Fumio's blade long after it's left my skin as Rose asks the question I don't want to answer.

"So, how did it go?"

20

Honour

CALLIE

"So you basically failed then?" Rose snorts, cocking her head to the side. Her long hair falls over her shoulder from beneath her copper armour, which shimmers gold in the sunlight. I've finished my story about what happened inside the pyramid, not that it amounts to much of anything, and they're all hovering with a look of dissatisfaction plastered on their faces. The sun is lowering across the unknown sky above, making the light filtering through from the surface dim with each passing second and casting shadows across our faces, only darkening everyone's mood further.

"Well… no. We know they're in there." I say, trying to lessen the degree to which I've so obviously failed. I think back, trying to recall a moment where I could have acted differently. For the entire two minutes we were talking with the Emperor I can think of nothing.

"Well that's a relief then. We know they're deep down in the ancient construct of a pyramid, and that they want exactly nothing to do with us!" Rose waves her hands in irritation and I scowl. Sophia interjects, her nose twitching.

"Callie and Orion are doing the best they can, Rose. These foreign pods, each one is different, they all require a different approach. With the Selkies it was strength, with the Water Nymphs it was bargaining and with the Maneli it was divine substance. We just have to figure out what this pod needs from us."

She makes the situation sound so incredibly simple, but I know it is anything but.

"Sophia is correct." I say, not wanting to fall apart on the one person who still believes Orion and I can do this. "We just need to find out more about them. Besides, it's not like we can leave, the portal is closed. So we're stuck here." I look out into the blue of the Japanese waters and even further into the distance where the whirlpool had dumped us. I wonder why they always close so soon after our arrival. Maybe it's because the Circle knows we need to be forced into staying put.

I sit on the step of the pyramid, feeling defeat run heavy within me like a stone, making my spirit sink. My eyes lower and Azure finally speaks up, having listened to the conversation with a half interested gaze.

"That Emperor has lost a child." She says, absent minded as her eyes glaze over.

"How do you know that? Did you have a vision?" I ask her, tilting my chin upward and giving her a suspicious stare.

"No, it's just a feeling I have." She shrugs, her eyes widening in something I haven't often observed on her face. I think it's fear, though with Azure I'm always unsure.

"Based off?" Orion cocks an eyebrow at her and rolls his hands in the water, gesturing forward motion.

"The way he reacted, and how he spoke to that girl. Over protectiveness of another young member of his pod, plus his anger at the moment you bring up war. I'd say he's lost someone close to him. I added in the over protectiveness and I got a kid. This is all based of what you've said of course. So it's probably as wrong as you are dishonest."

"Right…" I say, wondering how she jumped to such a conclusion on so little information. I'm not sure she's right, but I muse the possibility as we hang there, unsure of what to do next.

As I sit upon the sandstone step, wondering if the Emperor has felt the loss of one of his children, I hear the sliding of stone against seabed. My ears perk up as I wonder who could possibly be exiting the pyramid. Maybe the Emperor had second thoughts and has sent someone to find us.

"Shhh." I hush the chatter which has picked up between the other members of the group, raising a hand and then pressing my finger to my lips as I rise silently. I curve around the top of the structure, twisting my body around its peak to view one of the other sides. As the sliding of the door begins again I source the sound, I switch direction quickly, pushing back half a metre before rotating. My eyes lock on the cause of the noise, but it's not who I expect. Kira, the seemingly young girl I had seen being scolded by the Emperor is fleeing the pyramid, swimming off into the distance as fast as her tail will carry her. I watch as the shadows on the surface sit, silent and ominous in representation of the people I know sit just inches above. I wonder how exactly they would feel if they managed to capture someone like me, how high a price they'd put on me, or whether they'd just send me off to some secret government lab and slice me up for research. I shudder, the thought of the scientific methods I had always clung to in life sending a horrendous shiver down my spine. Then an idea hits me.

"Orion!" I call back, raising my voice. Orion is by my side in an instant, having been watching me ever since I put distance between us, protective as always.

"What is it?" He asks as I turn to him, a thoughtful expression plastered on my face as I bite my lip, feeling the beginning seeds of worry start to implant themselves in my gut.

"Kira... that girl, she's just taken off into where that fleet of boats is sitting. I don't know, but I'm not sure that's what the Emperor meant when he told her to go and do chores." I explain, looking to him as his lips slam together, pursing in thought.

"You don't know that, maybe she's going to collect something, or maybe they have a relationship with the fishermen?" He suggests, looking unsure. I look after her, her shadow now a pale orange blur in the distance.

"I don't know..." I begin, realising that what's clutching at me isn't so much fear as it is desire, an instinct in fact. I *need* to follow her.

"What is it?" Orion urges me to talk to him as I float, hair swirling in the clear water as I set my expression into one of sureness.

"We need to follow her." I state, looking at him and widening my eyes. He smiles slightly to himself, catching me off guard.

"What?" I ask him as he laughs for a few moments before raising his gaze to me.

"I knew it was an instinct in you. I just needed you to know it." He kisses me on the temple, looking at me with great pride and admiration and my heart swells. In this moment, I am beautiful and I am strong, because that's how he sees me.

"Let's go." I say, gritting my teeth and readying myself for the chase.

I rush through the sea, careful to lay low to the ground as my gills fasten in their usual open and close rhythm. I'm hoping that the depth will obscure me from the boats that cast shadows across my spine as the sun begins to set above the surface and I cannot help but grow anxious. This is not helped by the fact that I can see now that they're also not merely tourist vessels for leisure, but are functional fishing boats, with nets that are cast, hanging down into the water like flypaper for fish. It isn't long before I wonder if I'm mistaken in assuming Kira was headed here, after all, she could have turned in another direction, or even gone past the boats unharmed and undetected. I begin to doubt myself, my instincts. I begin to wonder whether I'm putting too much faith in myself.

Just as I'm contemplating turning back, I see her in front of us, a net rising from where it has lain slack on the ocean floor. Kira is writhing and struggling as I watch her, caught within its grasp, her kimono shirt stuck on one of the chain rungs as it climbs from beneath her, sweeping her up toward the surface. She squirms in the water, her orange, white and black spattered scales slashing left to right in sudden jerks and panicked pulls, trying to get free. The motion of the net clearly gets the attention of the boat above, as suddenly it begins to fold in on itself, trapping her completely within its heavy folds.

That's bad! That's very bad! I cuss internally, wondering how she got so careless as to be in this situation in the first place.

I look back to Orion who is following me closely, only to find that he's gazing up at her too, transfixed by the fact she's about to expose everything we

264

of the eastern Pacific work so carefully to keep hidden. Her wide eyes turn to look at me as she thrashes inside the net, trying to get free, but I remain still, unable to act as I'm caught between horror and shock at what I'm seeing. I watch her struggle in vain, the netting too thick and too heavy duty to be broken by her hands alone.

"We have to help her come on!" I call back to the pod, finally snapping out of my horror induced daze. I ascend, risking discovery, capture and everything else that comes along with it to help a girl I barely know. It's probably insane, but I don't know if I'll be able to live with myself if I don't at least attempt to save her. After all, her discovery could cause even greater problems than already exist for all of us.

"Callie what are we doing? We could expose ourselves!" Orion says in a worried rush as his long tailfin flexes quickly, bringing him to my side as I reach the underside of the net.

"Orion! We can't just leave her here! Come on!" I say, slapping his arm, startled at his lack of selflessness. I look down to the rest of the pod who are swimming to help us, their eyes wide with fear for their own self-preservation, the mermaids observing me as though I should be ordering them around. I glance between them, thinking about their newfound skills.

"Alannah, go sing the fishermen to sleep above. Keep your lower half submerged. Emma, you come with me, we'll unhook that net from the top." I bark orders, and Cole and Ghazi look to me like they're slightly surprised at the authority I'm suddenly taking. I turn to Orion.

"Go and keep her calm." I say to him. He looks unsure and I dive down to him, placing my hands on both sides of his face.

"Just talk to her. Give her something to focus on so she doesn't draw more attention to herself than she already has." I drag my fingertips along his cheekbones as I corkscrew away from him, quick but wistful in my motion as Emma and Alannah swim to my side.

"Callie, what if my voice doesn't work on humans?" Alannah is panicking, her expression frightened as I turn, looking back to Kira who looks as though she might cry.

"We don't have time to wonder. Just go Alannah, I know you can do this."
I try be reassuring, but don't know if I'm succeeding as I add, "If they don't
fall asleep, you swim as far away from these boats and as deep as you can, got
it?" I comfort her by placing my hands on her bronze shoulder plates.

"Okay. I got it." She says, narrowing her eyes as I smile to her. I turn next
to face Emma.

"Come on Emma, don't let go of my hand okay?" I question her as her
blonde hair forms an angelic halo around her petite blue features that shine with
fresh terror. She nods and I waste no more time, grabbing her hand and letting
the magic from her tiny body flow up my arm, turning her and then me invisible
in turn.

"Let's go." I whisper, ascending with her in tow. I rise to the surface, not
breaking it as I move in beside Alannah, who has surfaced, just missing the
sun's rays by seconds as a blanket of periwinkle twilight covers the world
above. Her hair is slick to her head as she begins to sing a sweet lullaby and I
watch as curious faces bend toward her, leaning over the edge of the boat. She
sings, lulling them into silence and edging backwards as they near her. Her song
works its magic after a few moments and the two bodies slump over the edge
of the boat, their hands hanging down into the water. I break the surface,
knowing they're asleep.

"Thank god for that. Good job!" I whisper, looking to them. Alannah
slinks back below the surface as Emma and I glide toward the boat, invisible
under the new birth of stars which glitter above.

"Come on, let's unhook this net." I whisper to Emma, her palm still solid
in mine, despite her invisibility. I swim, flex my tail to the left as I reach the
bow of the small wooden fishing vessel. I extend my hand, reaching out toward
the top of the net and take a few moments to examine it before finding the hook
that's folding it in half, trapping Kira inside. I push my fingers upward,
removing the right hook and slitting my finger open in the process.

"Ow!" I yell out, suddenly slapping my cut hand across my lips. I spin,
scared I've alerted one of the other boats which floats in close proximity as I
rise higher into the new night air and look out across them, making sure not to

let go of Emma's palm. I exhale, seeing that every single one of the men who had been waiting for their next catch lie fast asleep.

Jeez, and Alannah had been worried it wouldn't work on humans? I shrug, looking around as I feel a tug on my palm. Emma has unhooked the other part of the net. Time to go.

My gills take in water, the rich oxygen flooding my gullet once more as I look down where the net has slackened, falling to the floor as the chains that had hoisted it upward have been set loose. I dive, letting go of Emma's hand and watching my body reappear above me as I swim deeper, my hair being pushed back against my spine as I reach the ocean floor where Orion is helping Kira turn upright. Her eyes are wide, like a teenager looking at her favourite tween boy band.

"Thank you." I hear her say, placing a delicate hand across her face. Her body is curvy and her caramel hair falls down her back, dislodged from its bun in the panic of her almost capture.

"You need to be more careful! What were you thinking?" I exclaim, looking to her with an expression angrier than I intend.

"I… I…" She looks like she might cry and I go slack, feeling the weight of what's just happened sinking in my stomach.

"Hey, don't worry. It's okay. Accidents happen." Orion hushes her, trying to be kind. He shoots me an annoyed look and Cole and Ghazi look to me and then up once more, always on guard.

"We need to get out of here." Cole reminds us of the boats which hover above.

"I don't want to go back home!" Kira sniffles, beginning to cry under the night sky.

"Well we can't stay here. Those fishermen could wake up any second." I cross my arms over my breast scales and look to Azure who's sitting, examining her nails, with an expression of extreme boredom.

"I know a place…" Kira begins, her voice a tiny whisper. She looks scared of me.

267

Oh crap, have I been too harsh with her? I ask myself, second guessing my anger toward her. Seriously though, doesn't she realise how dangerous that was?

"Okay, well why don't you take us? As long as it's safe." Orion looks to her, placing an arm on her shoulder with an overly sympathetic glance.

"Let's go." Cole ushers us forward, looking better now a little adrenaline has hit his system. Kira's eyes light up her round and childish face as they continue to sparkle in the encroaching darkness.

We swim in silence, keeping our eyes to the ground and checking for more nets as we make sure to keep close together. Soon we have left the boats behind us and we surge through the cool open water, passing goblin sharks, sea snakes which make curving lines in the sand beneath, and turtles that paddle with slow grace under the moonlight.

The clear night air above inspires me as I bound above the water's surface without fear of further discovery. As I race among the still waters, my anger at Kira's carelessness and worries about finding the vessel dissolve and my scales bathe in the low moon's glow. I smile, taking a calm moment to allow everything to fall away, my heart slowing after the panic of Kira's capture.

After a few minutes, I fall fully beneath the ocean's surface once more, hearing Orion's voice call my name.

"What is it?" I ask him, my head clearer now I've swum out my angst.

"Kira says we're not far away now. You okay?" He asks me, his voice barely above a whisper as he places a hand above the tattoo on my spine.

"Yes, I'm just struggling not to feel angry at her, I mean, she's careless." I breathe out, feeling my chest constrict as he smiles, letting out a low and rumbling laugh. "What's so funny?" I scowl, wondering if he thinks I'm being silly.

"Nothing, I just find it funny coming from you that you're angry at her carelessness. You used to be exactly like this." He admits, looking to me with a semi guilty, semi amused expression.

"What's that supposed to mean?" I say, affronted as I turn to him, stopping in the water.

268

"Nothing, it's just when you first became a mermaid you were just as careless. She's clearly young, or inexperienced. Cut her a little slack." He doesn't look angry, doesn't look upset, he just looks amused, infuriating me.

"Hmph." I exhale, swimming away from him and following Kira.

There was no way I'd been that careless... was there? I wonder to myself as I think back. I had fled the Occulta Mirum, got close to demons with no idea what I was doing, that was true... but....but...

Dammit! I cuss. Maybe Orion was right. I had been like her once.

"Hey, Kira!" I call out, flexing my tail and speeding through the water so I'm right behind her, she stops, spinning in the water to face me with a worried expression on her face.

"What, what did I do?" She says, panicking and making me feel even worse than I already do.

"I just, I'm sorry about before. I shouldn't have been so hard on you." I say, lowering my gaze in apology.

"Oh, that's okay. I was pretty silly..." She admits, biting her bottom lip with a nervous and high pitched giggle.

"No hard feelings?" I ask her, making an effort to smile.

"No! Of course not! Come on, I've got something to show you!" She is too over excitable, to the point where it's wearing me out just being in her presence. When had I aged so much? When had I lost the energy for fun?

It was probably somewhere between being sacrificed by some dark psychopath and waking up alone after sleeping with Vex. I muse, sighing at my own sudden maturity.

"We're here!" Kira's practically screaming with excitement. The mermaids look to me and the air turns awkward because there's nothing that can be seen in any direction as we look about in the dark, confused. She watches us before sighing, pretending to be exasperated. "No, not here! Up there!" She points to the surface as she begins to ascend with an unpractised shake of her scaly hips. We follow her, passing a lazy shoal of parrotfish; a fish familiar to the Pacific, reminding me how much closer we've suddenly travelled to where we began this journey.

As we break the surface, I look to where Kira is now pointing as water drips from her palm. Orion slides in at my side and wraps his hand around mine.

"I'm sorry." He whispers, or at least I think he does. I'm too distracted, gawping at where we've arrived.

Before us are a series of interconnected islands, tiny in their individual size but collectively they create a macrocosm of green in the middle of the open ocean. The tiny bonsai trees, placed at the highest parts of the rocky surfaces to prevent them from getting soaked in sea water, are strung with fairy lights and tiny bridges, that look like they're only strong enough to hold the odd garden gnome, connect the islands together. It's a floating Japanese garden, with every inch of it pruned to perfection. In the centre of the entire system of islands and bridges, lies a giant cherry blossom tree, towering high above its bonsai neighbours. Everything else below it in miniature is coated in the pink petals of the tree, which is also strung through with fairy lights. I stare at it, a tiny haven of Japanese beauty in the middle of the ocean.

"Wow." I say, looking to Kira.

"Do you like it? I love gardening." She explains, looking to me with wide and excited eyes.

"It's beautiful." I gaze upon it.

"I wanted to make it underwater, but the bonsai, they hate salt water." She sighs before diving back beneath the surface, popping up a few metres away almost instantly.

"Come on!" She exclaims, gesturing for us all to follow. Orion, still holding my hand, pulls me beneath the water where the rest of the pod is already moving after Kira toward her garden atop the waves.

"I said I was sorry." He says, looking to me with an apologetic stare.

"I know. You were right though. I was too hard on her." I say, sighing outward as I shake my head, pained as I look back on the events of my early days with the mer. Knowing what I know now of the Psirens, I would have done lots differently, starting with not putting myself at risk so much. I was clearly important in stopping them, and I wonder now what would have happened to the world if I'd have been caught and killed before I was ever given the chance to form The Conduit.

270

"Come, take a seat!" Kira offers us rocks which protrude just below the surface of the garden to sit on, overlooking the garden which spreads out like a plush and mossy table across the shimmering ocean surface. The moonlight lightens her excited expression, making her skin milky as I take a seat next to Orion who has perched on a rock which is connected to the central island, on which the cherry blossom tree is perched. Its flowers stir in the light night breeze, showering us in pink petals that are softer than a manta ray's velvety back.

"Why were you running away?" I ask, watching the rest of the pod as they take seats around the central cherry blossom tree. It's surreal, this beautiful and natural sit down in the middle of the ocean, with only blinking lights of a nearby Japanese island in the distance reminding me we are not in a completely desolate and surreal oriental dream. I let my fingers play with the light and fluffy moss that coats the organic table top as I look at Kira side on, her tail is properly tucked beneath her, as though she's been trained to sit in a particular way. She sighs as she catches me looking at her, her eyes wide as everyone finally settles around the tree. We look to her and she blushes.

"I... my father..." She begins.

"Wait, your father is..." I begin, but she interrupts.

"Emperor Hironori. Yes. That's him." She nods, her face stern in its displeasure. "He and mother, the Empress, they want me to be a Geisha one day. Just like mother was when she lived in Kyoto all those years ago..." She smiles.

"Wait, how old are you?" Orion asks her, intrigued. I must admit, I am interested myself. I've always assumed the pods were a similar age to us, and I'd never had a reason to ask until now.

"I'm a little over two hundred." She smiles, and I must look shocked, because she rolls her eyes. "I get that a lot. You wouldn't think I'm two hundred would you? Mother and Father never let me leave the pyramid. This is the first time I've managed to sneak out in months." She explains, looking around the garden. "In fact, I'm glad the garden is still here. I was worried it would get washed away or something. I've had to fix it up a couple of times after

271

storms…" She starts to get off topic and Cole interrupts her, sensing her wandering mind is beginning to veer away from the valuable information we need to know.

"So you don't want to be a geisha?" He asks her. She shakes her head.

"Oh no, I hate being a Maiko, that's a trainee Geisha. I want adventure, romance, like in all the stories. I want to see the world. Not just the inside of a stupid pyramid." She wrinkles her nose in distaste, sighing.

"So why won't your father let you?" I ask her, and she shakes her head.

"It's a long story, but basically, me and my sister, Chiyoko, we were adopted. My brother was adopted too, Daichi, and he was amazing! He was the best at Kenjutsu, he loved swords, even when he was a new Kappa."

"Kappa?" Rose latches on to the new term.

"Yes, that's what we are." Kira replies, scowling like it's a stupid question. "Wait, I should ask you, who are you?" She looks suddenly frightened, as though she's forgotten we're total strangers in her haste to find adventure and freedom.

"We're mer, from the Pacific. Our Goddess sent us here, to find the vessel for your God or Goddess." Orion explains as I rub my fingers through the moss again, letting it suck the water from my skin.

"Mizuchi." Kira nods, her eyes closing as though she's saying a prayer and her body relaxes once more.

"Yes, Mizuchi." I nod as Kira turns to face me.

"You have to take me with you! To your home!" She exhales in a rush of emotion, placing her hands atop mine in the moss.

Yeah, that's so not going to happen. I really can't afford to have the entire Kappa army coming after me. I muse.

"I don't think your father would like that." Orion voices my thought and Kira scowls even more, pouting like a teenage brat.

"I don't care! Hironori doesn't care about me, he's not even my real father! All he cares about is his stupid legacy." She bangs her fists down on the table. I'm about to ask her what she means when she says that Hironori isn't her real father, when a voice calls to her that I'm not familiar with.

"Kira!" I hear it, harsh and distinctly Japanese.

272

"Chiyoko! What are you doing here? Go away! I'm not going back!" She cries out, dramatic in the way she pivots on her stone seat so quickly. I startle, turning to look to who has spoken.

The girl, or I think she's a girl, has poked her head out of the water. She pushes forward, swimming quickly toward us. She approaches the centre of the gardens within moments and pulls herself up onto the rocky ledge of one of the adjourning miniature islands that is little more than a single rock, her face angry. I get a better look at her as she rises from the sea, her tailfin a scarlet, black and white koi carp design like the other Kappa and she's carrying a long sword strapped to her spine, reminding me of Solustus only too easily. Her black hair is spiked, making her look like some sort of anime character and her eyes are dull and brown with short lashes. I'm examining her as I hear whispers, one from Azure comes to me a little too loud.

"Is that a girl or a boy?" She asks, completely lacking tact, as I glare back at her mortified and not wanting to offend.

"It doesn't matter." I snap, before I rotate back around to face Chiyoko. Her chest is covered in a spattering of scarlet, black and white scales, indicating I'm looking at a she.

"These must be the strange foreigners; I should have known I'd find you mixed up with the likes of them." Her voice sounds oddly harsh as she tries to wrap her tongue around the English words, indicating she prefers to speak in Japanese but is wanting to make us feel uncomfortable.

"Chiyoko, sister, they saved me. Please, I was caught in a fisherman's net. They saved me!" She leans back, looking to us with grateful and dreamy brown eyes. I smile at her, grateful for her defence of our actions.

"You were caught in a fishing net? Kira!!" She exclaims, pushing off the rock ledge and rushing to her sister. "Are you alright? They didn't see you!?" She asks these questions and a million more as we watch her examining every inch of Kira's tailfin, checking for any single scratch or nick.

"Kira is okay. Luckily, we managed to subdue the sailors and free her before they discovered anything they shouldn't have." I smile to Chiyoko, whose face melts at my words. She bows her head.

"I am sorry. I disrespected you. You have done me a great service. All of you. Thank you." The sentences are clipped as she lowers her head.

"It's alright, we're happy to help." Orion nods, making me frown slightly, wasn't he the one telling me to flee and save our pod instead?

"If there is anything I can do, please, tell me. I owe you a great debt. On my honour." She kneels slightly, bowing her head even further as she pulling her sword from behind her back, placing the long blade in her hands and offering it out to Orion. He leans back, startled, as Kira nods to him with a smile.

"What do you want, in exchange for your service in saving my life?" She whispers to him, nudging me and winking. Maybe this could be our ticket in.

"I want your father's help. Our people are in great danger. A demon with the power of a God is threatening to destroy this world as we know it. We need to find the vessel among you and we need your people to fight for us. With us." Chiyoko's gaze rises in surprise at the request.

"That's a lot to ask." She cocks an eyebrow and sighs.

"What?" I ask as her expression turns thoughtful.

"I can't grant you that. It must be the Emperor. I can take you and talk to him with you? I'm his daughter after all." She offers and Orion nods, accepting her offer.

"That would be wonderful."

"I advise you though, it must be your male ruler and he alone at the audience. My father doesn't respond well to women asking things of him." She admits, making my eyebrows rise in surprise.

"Wait, but you're a woman?" I exclaim, confused. If her father doesn't respect the word of women, why should he listen to her?

"Ah," She sighs, "That, is a long story... One which I will tell you on the way."

274

21

Legacy

CALLIE

"So what happened with your father?" I ask Chiyoko as we begin our journey back to the Yonaguni pyramids. She places her sword back into its sheath, which lies diagonal across her back, undulating quickly to keep up with me despite her shorter stature.

"My brother, Daichi. I don't know if Kira told you but he died. He was killed by a demon." She announces, her eyes distant as though she closed her heart to the event long ago. A shoal of clown fish pass by my left ear as we continue to travel and I look across to her as a few moments pass, awkwardly, between us.

"I'm sorry." I say, feeling the rest of the pod listening in around us. Orion is on the opposite side of Chiyoko, slowing his stroke to match hers and Kira watches us all as she lays on her back, swimming in front of us and not bothering to watch where she's going. She abandons all worry and concern of the world around her in a way I can't help but envy as she listens to the story she clearly knows so well.

"It was a long time ago. The thing you need to understand about my father is that he's obsessed with one thing. That thing is his legacy, his children... or the children he chose." She looks to Kira and smiles, though her eyes betray sadness curbed with irritation.

"So you're not his..."

"Biological daughters? Oh no." She shakes her head. "In Japanese culture it is perfectly acceptable to adopt an adult, especially if you think they can continue to carry on your legacy, be that a business, or in this case…" She trails off and Kira picks up where she leaves off.

"A monarchy." She looks sad even still.

"So the Emperor, he chose you to take over if anything happens to him?" I ask them, raising my eyebrows in surprise.

"Yes. Well, first he chose Daichi, and then he chose Kira and myself to balance out the masculine power required to rule. It would be our jobs as Geishas to keep the warriors happy. To serve Mizuchi and the men in her service, keep them relaxed and entertained so they can do their job." Orion's eyes widen as he listens, clearly surprised that such antiquated practices still exist. Where he is surprised, I am merely disappointed that the women here are marginalised to the role of entertainer. Then again, Chiyoko didn't look like much of an entertainer with that sword she was toting so I continue to listen, hoping for the best.

"After Daichi died, I picked up my first katana, it was one of his. I was angry for a really long time. So, I decided to avenge his death and kill the demon that had destroyed him." Chiyoko's eyes cloud over and I can tell she's lost deep in memory of the events she is describing.

"She's amazing with a katana. You should see her. I want to be just like her someday!" Kira exclaims, looking to her sister with pride and envy all at once.

"Yes well, I didn't get that way overnight. It took forever and I was exhausted. I was still training to be a Geisha, ashamed of my true self, so I trained in secret, escaping to practice whenever I could. Eventually, I decided to go and find the demon who had killed my brother. I found it, killed it and brought back the head to my father. After that he could no longer refuse that I belonged with the warriors, so I cut off all my hair and became what I am today." She grins, ruffling her spiky hair, as fondness at the final part of the story overcomes her expression.

277

"How amazing is that story?! Right?" Kira exclaims, too excitable. This time though I can't deny it is amazing. Chiyoko had fought her culture, which had formed over thousands of years, and her androgyny had won.

"It is amazing." Azure nods, looking to Chiyoko with interest. I watch her as she studies the Japanese warrior at my side, more intrigued by the fact she's so mellow than the story. The mermaids move forward, coming at Chiyoko and Kira in a rush as Orion and I fall silent, questions about the culture of Geisha and fighting techniques with a sword pouring from them in a flurry of angst and curiosity. I let myself fall back. Letting them have a chance to speak to another female warrior other than myself. They need to learn for themselves, and this is the perfect opportunity. Ghazi and Cole stay close to the back of the pod, sensing Orion's and my need for a little privacy.

"Well, this is going better than I expected" I say. "Except for the Emperor, this guy sounds like a misogynistic jackass." I feel anger flare in my gut, the repression of women still able to make me fume within a few seconds.

"He certainly has Kira under lock and key from what it sounds like." Orion nods, looking after her with a sad glance.

"If I ever have a daughter I'm never treating her like that." I vow, remembering being trapped by my own parent and feeling helpless.

"Callie..." Orion turns to me, his brows knitted together and his eyes amused.

"What?" I say, wondering what on earth has inspired such a look during such a serious conversation.

"Callie, you can't have children, you know that, right? Mermaids are infertile." He cocks his head to the side and widens his eyes as my expression goes slack.

"What..." I inhale, my heart falling through my chest like a stone.

It is ridiculous. Why haven't I thought about it before? None of the other mer have children, and just because my mother had gotten pregnant from a merman doesn't mean that I could automatically assume I can still become a mom. Why haven't I looked around and noticed the lack of little mer swimming about?

278

How have I been so stupid as to believe I could still have a baby one day? I don't even have the equipment for the job except for three nights a month!

I consider Orion's expression, which is turning from amused to concerned the longer I float, staring at him, my mind racing.

"Callie? Are you alright?" He asks me, putting a hand around my waist. I push my hands against his chest, curling up to him as he stills in the water and we let the pod leave us behind. We hang in the middle of the ocean as I begin to cry for a reason I can't quite fully put into words.

"This is so stupid!" I mumble, wiping tears from beneath my eyes. Having held me for a few moments, Orion looks down into my face, a look of desperate angst rooted in the back of his icy blue gaze.

"What?" He asks me, clearly not sure of what I'll do next. I don't blame him; I'm being completely irrational.

"I just… I didn't know…" I stutter, crying without a single explanation as to why I can't stop the tears falling down my cheeks. It hurts, but I know it shouldn't.

"Callie, Princess, please, talk to me." He sinks with me through the water, sitting me down on a lone rock on the sea floor.

"This is so stupid." I say, sniffling and brushing a lock of pale hair behind my ear.

"Nothing that makes you this upset is stupid. What is it? Do you want a baby? Is that what this is about?" He asks me, the look in his eyes more understanding than I'd thought he'd be in this situation. Weren't men supposed to run and hide at the mere inkling of this type of conversation?

"No. I… I don't know. I'd never thought about it." I say, my shoulders slumping, suddenly feeling like the weight of the water is bearing down upon me.

"I thought you knew you couldn't have a baby? I sort of thought it was obvious. This is my fault. I should have spoken to you about this…" He apologises and I laugh.

"This isn't your fault. I'm the stupid one for not putting two and two together. Of course, I can't have a baby. I'm a mermaid! I mean, I have a tail!"

I laugh, crying still and unable to stop the tears from falling down my cheeks. Orion pulls me to his body, crushing me against him.

"I… I'm going to be honest." He says, breathing out as I push him back again, nodding and wiping my oily tears from beneath my visor.

"Please do, I mean. Go ahead." I sputter, still feeling hysterical.

"If we were together and things were different, I'd want a child with you. I'd want that. A family. Any child would be lucky to have you as a mother. As things are, I wouldn't want to risk bringing a baby into all this. Even if we could. Even if it was possible. I just hope…" He rubs his hand through his hair, ruffling his tousles and placing his hand back on the aqua of my tailfin. "I hope you don't hate me." He looks up into my eyes, kissing me on the cheek.

"Orion, this isn't your fault. I love you…" I exclaim, worried he doesn't understand how I feel.

"I know you do. But I had a choice… and I'm afraid I chose wrong, seeing you like this." He breathes out heavily, ignoring a shoal of cherry salmon as they pass like a shimmering shadow, silent in the night.

"What do you mean?" I question him, sniffing again.

"I could have tried to save you, or waited until you had lived out a human life to introduce myself, you know, kept my distance. I could have let you have a baby, have a family… I could have waited for you. But I did the selfish thing. I found you before you had a chance at any of that. I took that from you. I just hope you can live with that. I don't want you to hate me." His words hit me like cold water and I feel myself worried that he thinks all of this is his fault. If he hadn't found me, the Psirens would have first. He forgets I am not just his soulmate. I am the vessel, and destiny, as always had swept me up like a riptide that neither of us could escape. I reach down, placing my fingers on his chin and taking a deep breath.

"Hey, no. I'm not going to let you feel bad for giving me something as wonderful as this life. You're right. It is no place for a child, and maybe that's okay. Maybe what we have together is enough." I look him deeply in the eye and lean in, giving him a tender kiss that makes the ice in my chest obliterate, thaw and melt away, leaving my heart fluttering lightly beneath my ribs.

"I love you." He whispers, sincere as he kisses me on the forehead.

Afterward, he doesn't say anything else and neither do I.

Instead, we move from the place where I have wept and off into the distance, swimming once more toward the duty which, as ever, weighs heavy on us both.

We don't catch up to the rest of the pod until they're almost at the Yonaguni pyramid. Things aren't awkward between Orion and me, and yet we don't speak because what's passed between us is too delicate to touch on again for now, not until I work out how I feel about it for sure. Then again, I guess I don't have much of a choice but to accept it. I'm infertile, and nothing can change that now.

"What held you two up? Everything okay?" Cole asks, looking to me and spotting my red eyes. His face grows concerned.

"We're okay. We were just talking about what I should say to the Emperor, you know, like how to word things. She's better at that than me." Orion speaks, giving me the grace of silence as he squeezes my hand in his, reassuring me that his presence will never falter. I love him so much in this moment I think I might puke, especially with the amount of emotions running rampant through me already.

"Okay, well Chiyoko says she's going in soon. So, you might want to go regroup with her? Callie, we're going to wait outside." He smiles at me and I flush, wondering if it's obvious I've just completely freaked out.

"Okay, good luck!" I turn to Orion and place my arms around his neck, clinging onto him and breathing in his sweet yet salty caramel scent. I kiss him on the cheek as he pulls back from me. He doesn't say anything, but our eyes connect and I can tell he's still concerned.

I don't know what to do; I could tell him I'm fine, that it doesn't matter to me, but is that true? I don't know if I ever would've had a child, but being told you can't have one is different than not wanting one. It's just not the same.

I feel numb inside, looking to the mermaids who are happily chatting together and unable to stop myself wondering if any of them had been mothers before they died. Azure is off to the left, separated from them and talking to

281

Philippe as he remains by the corner of the pyramid, having waited patiently for our return. I watch her, observing that her expression set firm, and so dive, deciding she's less likely to bother me with questions I don't know if I have answers to. I glide over to her through the water, hoping the others won't bother me for at least ten minutes. I definitely need to collect myself.

I sit down on one of the sandstone steps of the pyramid, leaning back and exhaling in a deep sigh.

"I would ask what's up, but I'm getting the sense you want to be left alone." Azure guesses without turning around.

"Wow, you really must be a seer." I say, coming off far more sarcastic than I intend.

"Or I notice the red rimmed eyes and the look on your face. You know I do care… sometimes." She sneers and I wonder if I've somehow managed to hurt the feelings she keeps hidden behind the million layers of sarcastic and spiteful armour.

"I'm sorry…" I start but she rolls her eyes, shaking her head and causing her long hair to swirl around her.

"Don't apologise, I think we both know I don't like listening to lies." She sighs, leaning back on the pyramid as she moves away from Philippe, his coat glistening under the moon's divine shine. "You know I don't really like you." She begins, but I cut her off.

"Yeah well you're not really my favourite person either." I swing my head toward her, feeling good now I'm distracted from my own pain. This must be why Azure takes out her sorrow on everyone else. It might not be pleasant, but I can't deny that, from what I can tell, it's effective.

"But…" She says, glaring at me. I sigh, wondering if I should just keep my mouth shut from now on. "You can talk to me if you need it. I did it with that Faith Healer. I have discovered after my entirely too long life that talking does actually help."

"Wow, that is shocking information. How long did it take you to find that out exactly?" I smile at her, joking and she flicks her tailfin.

"So what's up, buttercup?" She finishes, looking down at herself and then back at me, cocking her head so that I could swear she's actually interested.

282

"It's stupid." I shake my head, still feeling idiotic about the fact I hadn't realised I couldn't have a baby.

"I've seen you freak out over stupid stuff. Like ALOT. This doesn't seem stupid." She says, tapping her head. "Seer, remember?"

"You can't laugh." I say to her, leaning over and breaking eye contact. I don't know if I can bear to look her in the face when I say it.

"Psiren's honour... or whatever." She tweaks two fingers in the air and I roll my eyes. She's so unpredictable.

"I didn't realise... I couldn't have a kid. Like I didn't realise mermaids were infertile." Her breath hitches and I turn to her. "I know it's totally stupid. I don't even think it's something I would have wanted... I just didn't realise it was definitely not an option for me." I confess before realising that I'm being entirely stupid in telling Azure this. I mean, come on its *Azure.* What the hell was I thinking? I brace myself for her laughter, but it never comes, and as I stare back over my shoulder she drops her gaze.

"Do you want me to tell you something?" She asks me and my expression turns surprised.

"Sure." I reply, curious but half expecting her venom.

"Nobody knows this... Starlet, she didn't even know." She blinks quickly, swallowing hard as the name of her lost twin passes from her lips.

"I promise I won't tell. What is it?" I frown, unsure as to what she would have kept from the one person in this world she treasured more than anything.

"I... I'm a mom. Or I was..." She says the words and my heart falters into shocked standstill for a moment.

"You... You are?" I ask her and she looks like she might cry saying the words.

"Yes. I had a baby. When I was human. Arabella. She was going to be my everything. My husband, he took her from me... You know, because of my visions. I never saw her after that. I died because of the birth. I don't even know if he kept the name I gave her."

Suddenly, as I watch a tear fall from her eye, I realise the woman I'm staring at has had more pain in her life than anyone has ever known about. I wonder how she has kept the fact she has a daughter a secret for so long.

It's a wonder she hasn't gone crazy... I muse, but then I realise. She had. She had let the darkness consume her. But when you had nothing to live for, because the one thing you'd give your life for was taken from you, ripped away, maybe the darkness was a lot more appealing. At least as a hardened dark killing machine no one could hurt you. No one could take any more from you.

"I'm sorry, Azure. I had no idea." I lean over and give her a hug as I feel her stiffen in the water. After a few moments, she relaxes.

"It's okay, it happened a long time ago. I'm going to try and find out what happened to her one day. I think I need to know. Just, I told you because I want you to know, that there's one thing worse than not being able to have a child. That's being able to have a child, meeting her, loving her, and then losing her. Don't forget Callie, this world, the world of demons and of darkness, it's dangerous. A child has no place in it." She holds on to my shoulders as she says this, more conviction in her stare than I've ever seen.

In that look, in those words, I no longer feel sad. I feel grateful this had happened to me before I had to leave a child behind. Azure, unknowingly, puts the issue to rest. I am where I belong, and Orion, as well as the life I have here, are enough for me. They have to be.

ORION

"Hold eye contact at all times okay? Make sure you bow low, too. Like I showed you!" Kira is babbling as we swim, unsure of herself and obviously, me as well. I smile at her, feeling my heartbeat slow despite the tense situation.

The conversation with Callie had been intense, making my guilt tumble out of control and leaving me wondering if I should have let her live out her human life without me. The thought depresses me so I ignore it, pushing it out of the way and forcing myself to focus on the task ahead.

Chiyoko is silent as Kira continues to babble. I find her refreshing, just like I had found Callie, but I wonder how she's maintained such exuberance after two hundred years of life. I had found deep depression after turning one hundred and fifty, sinking deeper with each century that passed. She was alone too, without a mentioned companion or even a friend other than her sister, so I wonder how she does it. One day I hope to ask her.

"Okay, are you ready Orion?" Chiyoko asks me as we come to the entrance of the throne room, the passage we float in lit only with sparse jars of eels that spark and rage within their confines.

"Yes, let's proceed." I say, keeping my response simple. I must admit, I'm impressed with the English of these two young Kappa, but my experience with the older men and the warrior I had encountered had been to keep my answers short and to the point so that they could understand me with as little misinterpretation as possible.

As my words fall into silence, Chiyoko presses the stone on the left of the door, making the sandstone slab slide right, some sort of mechanism which I cannot see making the movement appear mystical and intimidating to outsiders, though I'm sure now that's the intention.

"Father!" Chiyoko says, clipping her words short and keeping them in English. It seems she only does this for my benefit, as I've heard both she and Kira speaking in fluent Japanese on the way down here when they didn't want me to understand what they were saying.

"Chiyoko!" The Emperors voice booms out, reverberating off the tapestry-clad walls of the throne room. I spot now that different types of swords hang on the walls with plaques under them, stamped with characters I can't read. "Kira! What are you doing here?! You're supposed to be in Shamisan Practice?" He looks angry, his face turning slightly red and his hawk like eyes narrowing upon her as she shrinks from me, revealing me floating in the doorway.

"Father, I shall explain. Please sit." The Emperor moves from his throne, eyes never leaving my face as he scrutinises me. I straighten, knowing I need to appear as though I'm hiding nothing to gain his respect.

"What is he doing here? What is the meaning of this?" The golden Koi carp tail of Hironori twitches, slashing from left to right in aggravated rhythm.

"Father, he saved Kira. She was caught in a fishing net. Almost captured by humans. He and his pod saved her." Her words reach her father and he stops,

285

dead still in the water as the words sink in. Kira shrinks further, knowing she will be in trouble for her insolence.

"Kira? Are you alright?" He moves forward to his daughter, capturing her hands in his and looking down into her terrified expression.

"Yes, I am fine, but only because of the mer." She turns to me, looking into my face with a slight crush. I'm not blind to it, but my heart belongs to another so completely I cannot help but ignore her affection, harmless or not. The Emperor glides forward to me, rising in the water and eclipsing me in his shadow. I prepare for him to grab at the sword on his back, dismembering me on the spot as I breathe in, wondering why I'm still floating here in a placid stance while he is readying to take off my head for going near his daughter. I wait, nervous and holding my breath, but the blow never comes.

"I… owe you a great debt young man." He nods to me, bowing.

"My name is Orion. Crowned Ruler of the mer." I say, exhaling slightly in relief and taking the opportunity to let my title be known.

"You're a King?" He says, looking to me with an odd glance as I nod, unafraid of what this might do to our relationship. I'm hoping the fact I've saved his daughter will be enough to at least grant me immunity to death, if not more.

"Yes. Indeed, I am." I say, bowing back to him as I show that I respect his authority here.

"I threw you out before. How hostile I must seem. I am sorry. You see, my daughter here is a careless young thing. She inflames the rage in me." He looks to Kira, narrowing his eyes. "I have not forgotten the fact you were out of the pyramid, ALONE. Go to your lessons. Now." He barks at her. She flees the room, before he turns to me with a smile. "Again, my apologies. Come, sit." He gestures out with a willowy and pale limb for me to take a seat in the throne next to him. Chiyoko ascends with us.

"I don't know, Your Grace. I am not King in this land, I do not think I can sit in your throne." I explain, still wary about the fact he has been so hostile in the past.

"This is not mine; this is my wife Samara's. Please, sit. It's the least I can do. I should be a gracious host in the very least." He nods to me so I sit in the high chair, lifted by statues of bonsai trees, leaning to my left so I can continue to talk to the Emperor.

"Father, Orion here has a big problem with demons. A demon with the powers of a God trapped inside and a swarm of Psirens. Poseidon's children gone bad." She explains and her father's eyes widen.

"I do not know much of Poseidon, but I do know of his temper. He and Mizuchi had… uh… many disagreements over the years. She with the power of a God in the body of a Goddess… it is known they do not get along." He explains this to me, his English far more fluent now he is relaxed.

"Yes, Poseidon does seem that way. It's known he and his other half Atargatis, our Goddess, do not have the easiest relationship either and they share a soul." I admonish.

"Then again, if any of the Goddess' are as stubborn as my daughter Kira, I can see why he might lose his temper." He looks to the corridor down which she's just swam, his face angry.

"Kira tells me she and Chiyoko are your adopted daughters? Is that right?" I ask him; curious suddenly about what he will have to say about that with which he is supposedly obsessed.

"It is how we raise our children, not how they come to be our children, that matters, Orion. I want to know that after I have passed from this place, my morals and the traditions that I think are vital to our survival remain intact. I do this by teaching my children how to rule. It is very important that they are not left in the dark. They need cornerstones to lean on, discipline, tradition, passion and ambition." He nods to me and I cock my head, surprised that I agree with him. I had thought Kira was being repressed, but I wonder now how much better off I'd be if I'd listened to my father. After all, when do young people ever know what's good for them?

"I completely agree. My father, he passed recently and I wish I'd learned more from him. I was stubborn." I admit, feeling his loss tug at the shattered part of my heart where he used to reside.

"You hear that Chiyoko? It's not just me and my crazy old man ways. This young man agrees with me." He beams, proud that someone else sees his views.

287

"I hear father. I hear." She nods, looking pleased that we are getting along before continuing. "They need our help father. We owe them a lot. They saved Kira." The Emperor pauses a moment, tugging on one of his long side burns and frowning at me.

"How dire exactly is the situation?" He asks me as I sit in the chair completely upright, staring into his golden pupils and wondering whether to lie or be honest. He seems to appreciate the truth, so I decide to be honest in the most brutal way I can be.

"I won't lie. The darkness multiplies by the day. The demon threatens humanity with extinction, if not worse. The men responsible for its existence are more than dangerous too. I'm fearful if they succeed in unleashing the beast that all will be lost on a global scale." I say, watching his expression turn glazed.

"Then, it seems I have no choice." He nods his head, blinking and appearing morose. I wonder what he's thinking, and whether I've completely ruined my chances. He looks up to me and gazes into my eyes, his stare intense. "You come here to me, having saved my child and my legacy along with it. Now it is time for me to help yours. For there is no better death than one for an honourable cause. I will help you. My entire army will be at your disposal." He says the words and I feel my heart almost stop.

"You're serious?" I ask him and he nods though his face is still sullen. Chiyoko smiles at his side, her face lighting up at our success. Emperor Hironori speaks once more as a zen-like calm passes across his face.

"Of course, Orion. Do not look so shocked. After all, a legacy left to a broken world isn't much of a legacy at all, is it?"

22
Kenjutsu
AZURE

I sit on the step of the pyramid in the still of the night; long after Little Miss Sunshine and Light has gone back to her real friends I'm still thinking about my baby. It's as if speaking her name aloud has broken a curse, which has had a hold on me for so long. I said her name, and now she really exists to me, she was my child, my baby, my daughter, and now she's long dead and buried, just like everyone else. I missed it all, her whole life, gone in the blink of a dark and dilated eye.

"Azure, Orion did it! We're going in now, you coming?" Callie asks me, moving up behind me and placing a gentle hand on my shoulder. She's never touched me before in a such a casual way, so I have to wonder when the hell she had suddenly decided she has touching rights on my person. I shrug away, feeling uncomfortable at human contact.

"Yeah, whatever." I sigh, not bothering to look at her. I don't want to see the pity in her stare. Perhaps telling her about everything was a giant mistake, perhaps now I'm going to be looking into that stupid pity plastered mug forever.

Oh, God. Why did I have to open my big mouth?

I had been so much more powerful when I hadn't spilled out my emotions like guts all over the floor. I had Callista to blame for all this. I think back to the moments after my vision in her hut, how kind her eyes had been and it makes my stomach curdle like sour milk. The next time I see her I'm going to make her pay, this was so much more painful than being angry, sarcastic and

289

violent. It is so much worse and it isn't going away, instead it's just bleeding me dry of all my energy, leaving a sour taste in my mouth and a foggy fatigue settling across my mind. Everything had been so clear before, before all this emotional crap. Everything had been simple. I was evil, and causing pain and suffering without caring who I hurt was easy. It makes me hurt, irritatingly enough, to admit it, but I envy myself as I had been then. I wish I could go back. People think that choosing good is easy, but after everything I've been through, I know now that evil is the easy choice. If only it was the right one.

I push up from the steps of the pyramid, stretching out my gracefully long limbs and swishing my tail from side to side for good measure. It's important to stay limber in these situations because you never know which pod might just turn out to be psychotic killers and I really can't cope with being left in charge of the mermaids. Callie is definitely better at dealing with their incessant whining than me. So, if nothing else, it's important to preserve her life just for the fact she's become Chief of whiner watch.

I slice through the water fast, barging Mr. Silent out of the way. I look back to him as he rolls his eyes and stick out my tongue, trying to curb the wicked wave of emotion which is threatening to drown me in its depths, leaving me drenched and shivering.

"Okay, let's go." I hear Chiyoko's Japanese accent coming from within the darkness of the pyramid's steep vertical drop that Callie had only too stupidly thrown herself into the last time we attempted to break bread with these people. I feel my Psiren senses prickle as I move past the group and down into the darkness after Callie, my eyes dilating and allowing me to see perfectly in the dark.

It's odd, the inside walls of the tunnel are covered in ornate Japanese paintings, ones you would never see unless you had my eyesight. They show a vast army of Kappa, fighting off various demons and in some of the paintings protecting whales and dolphins from fishermen. It's interesting, but I don't have time for a history lesson and, as my weight pulls me down through the water with increasing speed, I ignore the rest of the decoration, finding myself bored once more.

290

As I reach the bottom of the vertical descent, I come out into a smallish chamber lit by eels sparking off in jars. It reminds me of Cryptopolis, and before I can stop myself I'm wishing this pod had electricity, just like the Maneli. It was odd, the things you took for granted when everything annoys you all the time.

"Azure, move!" I hear one of the mermaids cursing, close to my spine, as I've stopped in the exit of the tunnel leaving them backed up behind me.

"I don't know, what do I get?" I ask, feeling malicious as I hear them start to land on top of one another in the water.

"Oh my god would you just move!!" I hear Rose gripe, shoving into my backside and pushing me forward. I fall out of the tunnel's end, spinning around as I quickly pivot, annoyed as Rose moves through the tunnel exit, her face angry.

"Don't you know not to piss off a Psiren?" I snarl, baring my teeth, as Chiyoko turns to me and I quickly retract my eyes, causing them to return to their usual icy blue. I don't want her knowing I'm what we're asking them to fight, we've had enough trouble getting into their oh so precious good graces as it is. I'm not sabotaging my chance at getting Starlet back anymore; I'm leaning into my fear, just like a Psiren should do.

"Hey you two, stop bickering!" Callie barks, an annoyed look crossing her stupidly perfect face. It's not my fault the mermaids are a bunch of impatient Princesses with egos the size of the Pacific. Rose blanches, but doesn't drop her scowl as the rest of the pod file in behind her.

Chiyoko opens the next passageway and leads us through, the pyramid unfolding before my eyes like the most over the top and pointless piece of origami you've ever seen.

"We're nearly at the throne room." Callie informs me, looking back over her shoulder, the light and shadows that play across her face. "Don't say anything stupid. I mean it Azure. It's a miracle we're even getting a second chance, alright?" She says this like I don't already know how difficult this has all been. I've been the one bored stiff waiting outside this damn pyramid for almost an entire day. I don't need her reminding me of how not to mess up.

291

"I'm not an idiot." I say, defensive and spiky like a sea urchin after our earlier heart to heart, if you can even call the shrivelled-up mass in my chest a heart after all these years.

"Whatever." She rolls her eyes as we reach the end of the corridor, the walls barren of any decoration as Chiyoko presses the stone in the wall to her left. I watch, still bored, as the stone slab covering the end of the corridor slides away to the right, flooding the passage with light.

We emerge and I shield my eyes from the glare before examining the bonsai tree sculptures that raise the thrones from the floor, high into the water.

Geez, this emperor has a serious superiority complex. I note. *What a surprise.*

I remember back to when Titus had ruled the Psirens, how he had thought himself so high above the rest of us we were practically different species. These notions of grandeur are, in my experience, almost totally delusional. A crown and a pretty chair didn't make you any better than anyone else, it just makes you luckier and, from what I'd seen of Callie and Orion's time as rulers, a lot more stressed out.

Speaking of my brother, my eyes rise to settle on the focus of all this unnecessary window dressing on what is basically a place to park your ass. I watch him, sitting high above us all, chummy with His Ugliness the Emperor.

Oh, for the love of all that is evil. I think, looking at him, perched like a child in a big man's seat as I roll my eyes. His tailfin might be gold, making him appear more regal, but his face looks wrong with such pale eyes against his even paler skin. His limbs are willowy, skeletal even, reminding me a little too much of Solustus. Immediately, I'm wondering why this pipsqueak has been causing us so much trouble, but I bite my tongue, almost laughing at the absurdity of it all as Chiyoko swims forward.

"I have brought the rest of their pod father." She announces, moving to his side and revealing the rest of the pod who are now advancing into the bottom of the throne room. I rise slowly in the water, as does Callie, approaching a height that is slightly lower than that on which Orion and His Ugliness sit.

"Thank you Chiyoko." Orion bows to her slightly, my self-respect for him plummeting by the second. He shouldn't be bowing to anyone; he's supposed to be the damned Crowned Ruler, isn't he?

"The Emperor and I have been discussing a few things and he has invited us to take part in some of the Kenjustsu training and drills with the rest of the Kappa. I don't think learning a little about handling swords would be bad. Especially seeing as how we know Solustus specialises in sword work." Orion informs the rest of the group of what he has decided for us. Of course, now it's *The Emperor and I,* like they're some sort of lame tag team. Hironori clears his throat to speak.

"The training is about to begin down in the base of the pyramid. So, if we can all adjourn that way. I'd also ask that you all bow before entering the dojo space, and bow once again before leaving." He issues the instruction and I feel like snorting, but restrain myself. Bow before entering and exiting a room? What the heck kind of weird mojo is that? Not to mention time consuming.

"Come on!" Callie beckons the rest of the pod, who are startled by the looks of their ridiculously idiotic expressions. I wonder if they're surprised at how easy going the Emperor seems. I mean, from what Callie and Orion had both said about their first meeting with him, he was a total tyrant.

I *knew* that they were making a big deal out of nothing. Load of Drama Queens, I'm telling you.

The journey into the heart of the pyramid doesn't take long. From how tightly packed everything is I'm beginning to wonder if there actually is an army down here, or if it's just some guy playing dress up in a chair with a few supporting actors. It wouldn't surprise me if this whole thing was a load of crap, especially because most things these days seem to turn out that way.

I bow as I've been asked to as I enter the dojo behind Orion, Hironori and Callie, with Chiyoko at my spine. I play along, doing what I've been told, like a dog or a wild horse that's been broken in by a rider called life.

I'm so happy. I sigh, sarcasm coursing through me in an attempt to cover my pain. I just want all this to be over, want to curl up in the corner and never deal with the likes of the cruel mistress called reality ever again.

As I swim forward, the corridor ends and opens into an enormous dojo. The walls are inlaid with wooden bunk beds, stacked end to end and top to bottom in each of the mile-long walls. The Kappa lie in wait, four men to a stack and silent as the darkness of the room slowly disappears. The Emperor watches as Chiyoko moves around in the pitch black, pulling out lamps filled with eels and hanging them one to a bunk. The light slowly forms a macrocosm, exposing the dojo to those of the pod without Psiren sight. So basically, everyone but me.

As I look around the huge room, which must cover the entire underneath of the Pyramid's base plus several miles outside, I'm startled by the amount of Kappa who are lying dormant, meditating in the walls of the room. There must be hundreds of men, if not more, stacked on top of one another and disciplined to the point where I wonder if they're not in fact dead because they're laying so still they could be corpses.

"Holy crap." I say, emitting the sound against my better judgement. Callie turns to me, placing a finger to her lips and telling me to cease all sound. I scowl at her, wondering when she got so damn bossy.

Oh, yeah, I humour myself, *that would be the day she was born.*

"Jōshō!" The Emperor barks, his voice piercing the silence like one of the fancy blades he's toting. Within approximately ten seconds, every single soldier has dismounted from their bunk and is floating, fully dressed and with sword at his side. My eyes widen.

Damn. Even I can't deny I'm impressed with that. I think to myself, looking at the identically dressed Kappa warriors. Now they're presenting themselves, surrounding the vast empty space of the dojo, I can estimate they must be at least nine hundred strong.

I watch as Hironori leans back, clearly proud of his men.

"Kamae To!" Chiyoko barks, her voice vibrating off the stone walls. I observe the warriors lazily as they fold inward from where they were previously floating and into the empty space, pivoting precisely so that the lines of men

294

rotate like the spokes of a wheel, each one moving at the same speed as the one next to it. They are now in identical rows, sixteen men in each and countless men in each column of the grid.

"Come, take a place at the front. Chiyoko will give you some practice swords, made of the finest Bamboo." Hironori gestures toward the dojo, in front of where he will stand, giving direction to his army as Chiyoko darts off to into one of the empty bunks, returning in a flash with swords for everyone. As I take the sword in my palm I realise I have missed the weight of a weapon. It may be made of wood, but I'm pretty sure I can at least maim with it. I smile to myself, the thought of violence familiar and safe, soothing the pain within, if only for a moment.

The training has been vigorous; well at least for some of us. I watch as the mermaids get their asses whooped, laughing. I'm getting scowls from lots of faces, but I'm sorry, I just can't help it. I'm kind of sad I missed them fighting that demon now I've seen this. It could have been the cherry on my cake of a week.

"Well, if you think you can do better why don't you step up and try! They're really fast!" Skye scowls, throwing her sword through the water at me.

"I don't think I'll be judging the level of difficulty based off your opinion Skye. After all, I have been around Solustus for longer than most of you have been alive." I remind her, my teeth spreading wide with repressed hysterics as I grab the sword she's just thrown, catching it and twiddling it between my finger and thumb. To the left of the stone space where we're now fighting one another (or at least some us are fighting, the rest of us are getting whooped) Kira and the Empress sit, Kimono shirts slack over their shoulders as they watch, fluttering fans just below their eyes.

"Pride is the winner's poison." Fumio says, bowing to me as I rise from where I'm kneeling, my tail twisted beneath me in the pose we've all been told to sit.

"Yeah, yeah Mr. Fortune Cookie, remind me to introduce you to a faith healer I know." I roll my eyes at him as Chiyoko rises from the opposite side

295

of the space where she sits with her fellow Kappa warriors. I look at them, each one having had a variation of the Koi carp tail I've noticed on the Emperor and his daughters. Chiyoko comes forward, her eyebrow cocked.

"If you think you're so great you won't mind me using my katana?" She says, challenging me. I can tell she finds me rude, or obnoxious, or both. She's not wrong, but I don't care, relishing the idea of a challenge. After all, it's been a while since I had a good scrap.

"Sure, don't use 'the finest Bamboo' on my account." I say, mocking her father. Her eyes narrow and Fumio looks between the two of us as Chiyoko takes her sword from its sheath, the long length of the katana supposedly intimidating. I snort. It's not only the word fear that's not in the vocabulary of a Psiren.

"Hajime!" Fumio calls, signalling for us to start. Chiyoko bends forward, assuming the traditional stance with her upper body where her lower body cannot. The boy cut of her hair is messy and loose strands of thick black fall across her eyes as I take the cue to ready my stance too, taking a stroke back and clutching the Bamboo sword in both hands. I twist, sensing her movement before she makes it and her sword slices through the water, missing my stomach by mere inches.

"Ha!" I yell out, victorious as the blade comes for me again. This time I duck, out of breath from my exclamation of non-victory as I dart beneath her tail. I move up behind her, hitting her around the back of the head with my wooden sword. It's a joke of a weapon, with no edge or blade and the best I can hope for is blunt force trauma. I lick my lips, my heart beginning to race in that familiar way which makes my dark spirit soar. It's the first time I've ever realised it, but perhaps it's not the darkness that I love so much, perhaps it's the fight.

"You were lucky." She says, her voice barely a whisper on her breath as we circle each other, waiting to move and put the other on the defensive. I let my tail movement become steady, my heartbeat pushing blood around my body in a pulsation that I hear like a drum, allowing me to act to the beat of its rhythm. I close my eyes, letting my Psiren senses work their magic as I feel her shift in the water before I even see her, spinning to the left and out of her way. In one

296

quick motion, I take the wooden sword and smash it up under her chin, knocking her off balance and onto the floor. Her hand falls from the hilt of her sword, which I quickly pick up from the floor, pinning her to the stone with its blade.

"You were saying about luck, Buttercup?" I cock my head as her eyes widen and fear roots itself deep behind her dark irises. I realise then that she's afraid... and when people usually look like that around me there's only one reason. My pupils have dilated, letting the dark overcome them in my battle fever.

Oh, crap. I let my pupils retract, irises returning to their familial ice blue.

"You're a..." She begins, out of breath slightly as I reach down and hold out a hand. She is so dumbstruck she takes it, a fearful animal in a trap who will take whatever help she is given, even if it comes in the form of the thing she's scared of. Her skin touches mine and she goes pale and ghostly as her eyes turn the colour of bone.

"Oh crap." I repeat, this time aloud, as I feel my visions pulled from me. *This memory lobotomy is brought to you by the Circle of Eight.* I groan internally, feeling irritated as the visions begin again.

Those bastards.

Every time I have an encounter with one of these damn vessels shit goes very badly wrong for me. It's a wonder I've gotten this far without killing one of them accidentally on purpose, especially with how they keep making me re-live the same boring ass stupid visions. It's bad enough I have to suffer through the mystically sponsored commercials in my head once, let alone three even four times.

As, I open my eyes, I find myself clutching on to Chiyoko who is slumped in my grasp, her body unconscious from the weight of my visions.

What a wimp, at least Casmire had been conscious after. I sneer.

I pivot now, suddenly realising that there's something I've been missing, something like the hundreds of long bladed swords now pointed at me from every single angle in a circle surrounding us.

"Demon!" Fumio snarls, pushing the sword into my spine.

"Hey, watch it! I can explain!" I complain, turning around and showing them I mean no harm. Before I explain however, I have the problem of the ninja wimp to worry about. Callie and Orion have risen slightly and are looking at me from outside the ring of warriors, totally helpless, or should I say, useless.

"Okay, now I don't want you to freak out, guys. I'm going to slap this chick awake. So, no freaking out, that means keeping your stabby sticks to yourselves okay?" I say, staring at them with wide eyes. "So we cool? No freaking out. I'm waking her up." I raise my eyebrows as I raise a palm. Instantly, I find myself with several katanas jabbed under my jaw. "Look, I said no stabby sticks! Do you not understand English?" I sigh, exasperated at the lack of co-operation from my captors. Idiots. Oh, well, I guess I'll just have to slap this chick and hope I can survive being skewered like a kebab. I raise my palm, bringing it down onto the side of Chiyoko's face in a sudden smack. She wakes with a start. "Thanks for joining us sleeping beauty. So now you've seen the movie, can you tell these guys to maybe not stab me?" I say, knowing now she has seen the visions, she knows what I am. It takes her a second to place herself, but as she does, she's upright in an instant.

"I will do no such thing. You are demon. You are dark." She says, pushing herself back from my grasp with wide eyes.

"Can you give me a chance to explain?" I ask her, placing my hands up as the warriors dart inwards and toward my body.

"What is there to explain?" She says, her eyebrow cocked. "You have darkness in you." She condemns me and I crinkle my forehead. It is most definitely time for an inspirational speech.

"Look, yes. I have power which comes from the dark. But I'm not bad. Well, not really. This faith healer told me that it's not where our power comes from that matters. It's how we use it. Now, I could have just skewered you where you lay, but I didn't, did I?" I ask her and she frowns, her eyes narrowing as she analyses my expression.

"No... you didn't." She replies, not listening or too dense to understand me as she nods to the men around me, signalling for them to make me into sushi. I flip her sword in my hand, thinking fast and holding on to the blade.

"Here, take it." I swallow, painfully aware of the proximity of blades that surround me in a tornado of edges.

"So you're one of them? One of the... Psirens?" She speaks the word aloud like it's made up, so I decide to embellish a little on my history.

"I was, but I worked with the mer. I found out information. I'm a seer. You just tapped into my visions, because you are a vessel." I nod to her, watching her expression turn surprised. "Mizuchi chose you. You're her vessel. You're why we're here." I explain further and the warriors swim away from me as she waves for them to back off. As they return to resting stances and sheath their blades, Hironori glides forward, his expression both curious and surprised. He looks upon his daughter, totally ignoring the fact I'm even here.

"You... I knew it would be you." He smiles, his eyes full of joy at the idea that his Little Ninja Princess has been chosen.

Well, isn't that sweet?

The hypnotic twirl of Salome's fans is enticing, soothing my nerves as I watch her from the ornate, low cushion on which I'm sitting. The table before me is low too, covered in old scrolls and other types of extremely dry and boring historical artefacts. Orion is pretending to look intrigued as Hironori explains the Kappa's history, but I can tell he's just as bored as I am.

Still, the Emperor and Empress insisted we stay for a little Japanese hospitality, even if that does involve sitting on the floor, which isn't as comfortable as it sounds. I watch across the table, to where Chiyoko is sitting, her eyes fixed on the Geisha Salome. Her gaze is one of love and I feel like laughing at the observation. I'm pretty sure she won't be daddy's Little Ninja Princess after that falls out of a closet with wooden sliding doors.

"So you're... part demon?" Samara, the Empress, turns to me as she watches her daughter Kira drop her fan for the fourth time and cringes, before trying to divert from the error by drawing my attention elsewhere. She's wearing blue, azure to be exact and I can't help but smile as I see her unusual baby blue, black and white koi carp tail tucked underneath her neatly. A black sea urchin is stuck on the side of her head, where her dark hair is swept up in a

299

tight bun and I watch it, fascinated, as I wonder how she's not getting stabbed. "Well?" She presses me for an answer, and I sense, as one usually can, that she's been waiting to ask me this question for a while.

"Uh, kind of... well actually no. I've been infected with dark magic, that comes from the same source as where demons get their power." I rush my answer, not really caring, before I continue, knowing I should try not to be rude, especially with the amount of skewering that almost just happened in the dojo. "I'm sorry, I just... I can't understand why that urchin is in your hair. Doesn't that hurt?" I ask her, watching the creature retract some of its spines as her head moves.

"Pain is beauty." She smiles to me.

That's it, this chick has cracked.

"Right..." I put the most calculated smile on my face I can muster, the sound of the two-stringed guitar being plucked grinding on my last nerve. I search the room's barren walls for a clock, anything so I can politely say, 'is that the time, huh it's late!' to give the inclination that I'd like to leave. After all, we've done what we came for.

As the music finally stops and Kira and her tutor take a rushed bow, she flusters over to her mother, who corrects her bun which is split from the bottom with some kind of red fabric before tightening her Obi quickly. I watch the two of them, her mother's tender embrace, the pride on her face, the way in which she is so careful and so attentive to each and every inch of her daughter's complexion as she looks upon her. It makes me wonder whether I would have been any good at that. Being a mother. I sit and ponder on this, before coming to the conclusion that I would have been a terrible mother. I barely know how to look after myself, let alone a helpless child. Arabella was lucky to have been taken away from me, so perhaps I had done her a favour by staying gone. At least I didn't have the chance to screw her up. Kira turns to me, eyes wide.

"So, you're part demon? How exciting!" I sigh, feeling the sudden urge to grab the urchin off her mother's head and stuff it in her mouth. That would shut her up, not to mention stop her asking any more stupid questions in the future. As I'm contemplating the realities of how to get the urchin down her throat, I hear something stir in the water behind me. The mermaids and the rest of our pod are at the door, having remained behind for further training on how not to skewer themselves with their own weapons.

"The whirlpool has opened. We need to go." Cole reports as Hironori looks to Orion, who bows his head, appearing sad to be leaving. I can't work out if he's being diplomatic or not.

"We must go. Come with us to the whirlpool. We will explain everything you need to know on the way."

The whirlpool is rushing again, not that impressive all things considered. I'm surprised the Gods haven't made us swim the journey, some sort of penance for something else we've got to make up for. The Kappa haven't come out in force, just the Emperor and his daughter Chiyoko. I look to her and she stares back at me, interest plastered on her face as I look away and down to Philippe who I've been riding since we left the pyramid. I look down on them, roles reversed as they look back up at me, concern passing behind their eyes. I continue to observe them as Orion and Callie give the most boring and repetitive instructions of all time. Pieces of Eight…Whirlpool… Be Ready… Yada, yada, yada. We really need to include a musical number or something, which I'm sure that would make things far more interesting. Or we could just tattoo it onto each of the vessel's foreheads in case they forget.

As I sit above the pair of Kappa who are still yammering on about something probably unimportant, I look out to the sky above and wonder if Arabella had ever travelled, I wonder if she had ever seen Japan. I wonder if I'd ever been close to her after I'd turned and not known it. I watch the Emperor, looking down at his daughter before we turn and enter the turbulent clutches of the portal, pondering if I'll ever stop wondering about her. About my Arabella.

23
Lash
SOLUSTUS

"Bring me that bollard!" I command my fodder, scowling as they swim too slowly, as though obeying me is a chore. "Now! Unless you want your throats slit before you can blink!" I bark, feeling my rage morphing into something new, something uncontrollable. They're too lazy, they're too young, they completely lack direction and they're useless. All these things I should have foreseen, but then again, if I'd been wise I'd have picked more of the recruits myself.

I look to Darius, his throat still crushed in my grasp as I dive down deep to the Necrimad's seal. I want him humiliated. I was the one who made him, so I will be the one to break him. I feel the whip in my hand, its leather tempting me to act before all are assembled. They will stand to witness my wrath. They will observe my fury. I. Will. Not. Be. Ignored.

The Psirens, at my word, have retrieved a large rotting wooden bollard. They slam it into the sand at the edge of the seal, still jagged with broken glass from the night I had reigned terror and bloodshed down upon the mer. I swoop, my infantile creation still hanging from my wrist, struggling now for breath. He writhes but is unable to match my strength, which is enhanced now that fury runs cold through my blood and causes my eyes to unusually dilate while my heart thuds in protest of his insolence.

"Regus! Chains!" I click my fingers and Regus moves from the crowd, diving with his bald head and stupid expression before pulling the chains from

303

the seal's surface where I had bled my sacrifice dry. "Give them to me." I demand, shoving the boy into his grasp. "And hold him, don't let him move so much as an inch." Darius squirms, trying to move from the strong man's grasp, hammerhead and great white tails slashing violently against each other. He is no match for Regus, who quickly subdues him with one swift punch to the gut. Darius slumps, weak.

Lassoing the chains around my head with my free hand, I wrap them around the bollard one by one, letting go and allowing the restraints to smash into the wood, leaving splinters flying out in all direction.

"BIND HIM!" I command, bellowing as I look to the Psiren army. They're so damn insolent. Well, this will show them exactly where that will get them.

Regus lurches forward, binding Darius' tailfin to the bottom of the bollard, and his arms around its broad width with the remaining two restraints. "See me." I say, lowering my voice. I gesture out, raising an arm that my army looks upon with curiosity. I curl my long index fingers, motioning for them to come closer.

"Come closer." I demand, watching them inch forward. Before they get to the edge of the seal, encircling me too closely, I smash the pearl strung whip into the metal of the seal, it's resonating sound causing my men to jump, proving just how much they are failing at Psiren life.

"Now. You have been raised for one purpose, and one purpose only. That is to destroy the mer, and help me gain access to the power of the Necrimad. This power was mine. It was stolen from me. I feel like you have somehow gotten the wrong impression, though it's hardly surprising when it comes to how stupid most of you are. That beast over there..." I point to the Necrimad, its shadow towering above the ruin of the Occulta Mirum and dwarfing it entirely. "Is my power, in demon form. Are we clear? If you think you're afraid of that beast, you must remember that it will only be a hundred times more terrifying when its power is in my body. As things stand, this boy, my own creation thinks you're here for a party, thinks you're here to follow your own desires. I will show you, all of you, what exactly that means for him now." I turn, raising the pearl strung whip above my head, bringing it down and letting

304

it kiss the back of Darius' tailfin. He screams out, his voice mangled with the sound of his own agony. I smile, feeling my heart begin to race, loving the feeling of power within my grasp.

I glide over to him, breathing down his spine in an instantaneous and powerful flick of my tailfin.

"Count with me Darius." I bait him, looking around the many faces, none of whom sport dilated eyes. I wonder if I'm shocking them as I spin, smashing the whip into Darius' spine and leaving a scarlet rip in his flesh. It begins to heal far too quickly, I strike again. "COUNT!" I roar, the only sound emitting from my victim being that of pain and fear. "COUNT! OR I'LL WHIP YOU UNTIL YOU CAN'T BLEED ANYMORE!" I spit, rotating and taking space to gain momentum this time. I skim the outside of the crowd, smiling as I corkscrew through the water, flicking the whip and slowing to a sudden stop. The pearl studded leather tongue of my personal demon extends, licking the scales of my victim and causing him to cry out with only one answer.

"ONE!" He screams, his head smashing into the bollard, trying to distract from the pain.

"That's right, One. Right on the bottom rung of the ladder of torment for your insolence. There will be a hundred where that came from. Now tell me, because I am so generous, do you want them fast or slow... son?" I say the last word, wondering whether I should add it for dramatic flair. Darius doesn't reply, his open flesh wounds closing before my eyes once more as it weeps bloody tears. His tailfin however does not heal so quickly and so I look to him, his body slumped against the bollard, relaxed. It isn't enough... it isn't harsh enough. If he's counting, if he's not only screaming, it isn't enough. I scowl, wondering what I can do to make it worse. Then, it comes to me in a delectable wave of evil.

"Regus!" I bark, feeling Saturnus' eyes on my spine. "Make me a hangman's noose."

The crude wooden poles form a right angle, high in the water above the jutting glass of the sea floor. I pull the chains over the top of the simple bollard,

305

releasing Darius' hands. His eyes are wide, diluted, like his darkness is only being further awakened by his torment. I pull the thick wooden length sideways from the sand where it is lodged, discarding my simple attempt at a whipping and adding my own flare and searching for riper fruit on which to suck so to speak. Here the bottom chain which is attached to Darius' tailfin still resides, it's end now untangled, meaning the restraint is free to be attached a different way. I grab the chain, yanking and pulling Darius down into the sand beneath him, causing his jaw to smash into the floor. He sags behind me, pulled tail first among broken glass and the sandy remains of those we've slaughtered. I hold out the restraints to some of his Psiren brethren.

"You will hang him by his tail." I say, my gaze unwavering as I stare upon their fear filled expressions. It looks so wrong on creatures of darkness. Fear. They should be ashamed.

Reluctantly one of them takes the chains from me, rising in the water and pulling Darius behind him, looping the chain restraints holding his tail around the metal ring of the noose which hangs down from the wooden pole, attached to a taller bollard than the first. He ties it off, and as the other Psirens move to watch this new spectacle, I breathe in, feeling myself excited at the idea of whipping someone in this position and presenting them like a human presents their latest catch. How marvellously iconic.

My 'son' hangs, upside down, blood rushing to his skull and hair flaring out beneath him, totally exposed for my pleasure. I pull the whip back again, my swordfish-esque tailfin slashing from left to right as I bring the whip forward, extending it in the water so it strikes him across the face, making one of his lips bleed and catching him just above the eye before it recoils. He cries out in pain, struggling to get free. I laugh.

"I don't hear you counting Darius." I taunt him, a smirk crossing my face at his helpless motion.

"You prick!" He cries out, unable to escape me.

I raise the whip once more and strike down again, hitting him, not once, but five individual times.

"I SAID COUNT!" I snap, moving to where his hand hangs upside down and digging my sharp nails into his skull. I yank his hair, pulling him forward.

"Count with me or I'll kill you." I grunt, unable to cope with the unsatisfactory foreplay any longer. If he doesn't count, I don't feel the same rush.

I raise my whip over my head again with fury, ready to strike down again when the voices of my recovery team come in behind me.

"Solustus! Sir!" I hear one of them, Tiberius I think, address me. I turn, unamused.

"I'm a little busy right now." I narrow my eyes, gesturing to their fellow scum-sucker.

"We just wanted to inform you that the escaped prisoners... they got away." His words penetrate me deeply, making the hairs on the back of my neck prickle in a wave of untamed rage.

"You've lost my metal master and the Psiren with a connection to the Gods we are so very much trying to undermine... Is that what you're telling me boys?" I raise my whip in the water, readying to strike them as their eyes dart between me and my prior target.

"Y...Yes." The children I feel so very disappointed in float before me, looking guilty and shame faced. Not exactly very convincing as harbingers of darkness.

"Well then, I'd say you have a great task on your hands. You're now responsible for making weapons. If I don't have at least 10,000 units by the blood moon, it won't matter whether or not we succeed, I will personally make sure you never see the sun rise or set on this earth again. Oh, and what do you know... You only have a few days left until moonrise." They gaze upon me, terrified and unsure of what to do next. "GO!" I scream, feeling control slip from me. I can't whip them all; I can't make an example of them all. They are, after all, too many.

I look around to the crowd of Psirens watching me under the stark sun above, before taking in the view of Darius who is hanging, probably unconscious with his weak tolerance for suffering. I gaze back to Saturnus who is staring directly at me, smirking as though he knows something I do not. Finally, I look within, ignoring them all, ignoring all outside influences and obstacles. I think of one thing and one thing only. That is that I cannot let them get away with thinking they can be insolent, they cannot think there will not be

307

consequences for disrespecting me. I gaze upon the opalescent extension of my furious will, it's dripping in blood which clumps thick in the water.

With that, I take off, slashing from side to side as I notice the Psirens begin to stray from my influence once more, glancing nervously between themselves and whispering like I am no more than a strict school teacher. I dive now, raising my left hand and bringing the whip down on Darius' torso again, startling him into consciousness.

"TWO!" He screams, agony tearing across his expression. I grin, looking back over my shoulder to Saturnus who is swimming away toward his office, black tail trailing behind him like smoke in its effortless motion. It would seem I can achieve respect and loyalty through violence after all.

24

Hue

CALLIE

I feel myself spinning from the whirlpool under a harsh and stark light as I exit the portal upside down and take a few bewildered moments before I realise the world is the wrong way up.

"Whoops!" I giggle, feeling glad that this journey is nearly over. I have no idea where we are, but I'm definitely feeling better after the Kappa have joined our cause. Not only because the vessel has been found, but because the army they have is incredibly well trained. It leaves me confident and satisfied, if only for a few moments before I'm thrust head first into more politics and mind games, if they are in fact not one and the same thing.

I spin in the water, adjusting my visor which has slipped up my face in my oh so graceful dismount, before noticing that I'm not alone. The rest of the pod exits at my back and Orion slams into me, knocking me forward and into the arms of a stranger who is smiling down at me with kind yet eerie alabaster eyes.

"Hello Children of Atargatis, welcome to Hawaii."

"Who... who are you?" I gape. My first instinct is to recoil, but the milky whites of the eyes staring down upon me make it impossible for me to tear my gaze from her.

"I am Aulani, Callie, fear not." Her face is tanned, flawlessly smooth, and spattered with dark freckles. I examine her carefully, noticing her hair is white, flowing down in ombre to a baby blue. Her tailfin is exquisite; being a pale blue on its edges, with smaller fins fanning out on her hips in deeper royal blue. Her tailfin is long, crisscrossed with deep navy lines and reminds me of a tiger shark. I look around, suddenly realising she is not alone either. Other mermaids float next to her, examining me in the bright light of the sun above the surface with curiosity. I push back.

"I'm so sorry! How do you know my name?" I ask them, a frown crossing my lips in a reluctance to believe this supposed good fortune.

"We have been waiting, child." The woman with the tiger shark tailfin smiles calmly to me, flexing her hips and tossing her hair over one shoulder. She's wearing a moonstone around her neck on a leather weave, drawing my attention to her chest, which is spattered with royal blue and cream scales.

"I'm sorry, I don't understand. Who are you?" I ask her once more, as I feel Orion press his hand against my spine, nervous in his lingering touch.

"I am Aulani. We are Sirena, Kindred of Kanaloa." She bows her head, smiling, and her face transforms into the most beautiful thing I've ever seen. She is magnificent. I look to the women behind her, finding them curvaceous and full in figure as they glow, each one utterly unique.

"I am…" I begin.

"We know who you are. We knew Atlas very well. You must be his son. Orion." Aulani takes a stroke forward, holding out a hand toward Orion who swims to meet her. He takes her hand and she pulls him into her body for an embrace, I watch him as he becomes surprisingly relaxed. I observe the moonstone around her neck once more, feeling my heart palpitate at the sight of it. This was where Atlas had come across them, it had to be.

I look to the other Sirena who are accompanying Aulani and decide to swim over to them, wanting to greet each one just so I have a chance to stare.

"Kala." The first introduces herself to me. Her hair a luscious aqua and lilac, which is pushed back into a thick French braid and strung through with white pearls. Her chest is voluptuous and spattered with opal scales and her eyes are opalescent in their shine, as are the individual strands of her colourful

310

hair. Her tailfin looks like it's captured the beams of the moon within the gait of her wide hips, holds them prisoner and reflects them right back out, reminding me of how I thought Sophia's skin had looked the first time we'd met. It is one of the most beautiful tailfins I've ever seen, fading from opalescent white through to dark lilac and pale lavender. It puts my own to shame and I flush, feeling so very plain. I move over to the next woman to my left, the water so very clear and refreshing after such a long journey that it almost tastes like home, leaving relief falling over me like a wave. These people seem lovely, hospitable to say the least; perhaps the last part of this quest would be easy.

"Luana." The next mermaid pulls me to her, her tail fuchsia and spattered across with violet like someone has spilt paint on her. As I follow the length of her tailfin I notice it splits into four parts at the bottom, where most I have seen split into two, making me stare, unable to help myself. Her eyes glow purple and as she embraces me I stare down her spine Her hair is hot pink, falling over one shoulder in a lazy braid, which I observe is interspersed with sand dollars and starfish. I notice her tailfin has a dorsal fin, which I have only ever seen on Psiren's tails before. I push back from her, smiling as she greets me with a glowing expression. I glide sideways to the final figure who is hanging like a decorative bauble in the blue.

"Calypso." She blushes, gentle in her motions like a lazy wave. Her hair is a rainbow mixture of pastels, interwoven with opalescent cream sheen. Her tailfin is a mixture of pale baby blues, pinks, apple greens, lilacs and lemons, each scale completely unique in colour and shine. She is a macrocosm of hue, a work of art in her own right, as is each woman I've met so far. I stare into her apple green eyes, transfixed by the beauty of The Sirena, Kindred of Kanaloa, whatever that means.

"You knew my father?" I hear Orion ask as I turn back to him and the rest of our pod. Their faces are stunned, especially the mermen.

"Oh yes, very well. We crossed paths often." Aulani says it like it's nothing.

"How did I never know?" He asks them, his eyebrows rising in surprise on his beautifully statuesque face.

311

"We are nomadic child. Never in one place for too long, we move to where we are needed, where the current takes us." She explains this and Orion still looks confused so she sighs, patiently continuing with a calm expression, serene like the surrounding water. "We travel over thousands of miles a year. It was not hard to run into your father on his travels. We became very good friends. How is he?" She enquires, glancing over Orion's shoulder to the pod behind him. Her eyes scan Orion's drooping expression at the sentiment and she places a hand on his shoulder. "Say no more." She bows her head to him so her milky blue locks fall around her face before she brings him in for a quick embrace. I almost want to laugh because this time he looks extremely uncomfortable, but at the same time I'm falling a little bit in love with Aulani already.

"Mother, we must go, if we are to be at the isle by sundown."

"Mother?" Azure cocks an eyebrow as she looks between the maidens, trying to ascertain some kind of resemblance.

"A title of respect dark one, not that I need it. We're all equal here." Aulani responds, looking at Azure with authority and a lack of fear in her stare.

"You know with everyone calling me dark one around here it's a surprise I haven't started skulking again." Her pupils glide in an irritated arc and Luana snorts behind me as Kala flips her hair back, looking at us all with complete disinterest.

"We have something of yours. Come, follow us to Isle Meahuna." Aulani gestures out to the open ocean before us, in all its sparkling aqua glory. I move to Orion, taking his hand and wanting to experience the waters of Hawaii by his side.

"What's Isle Meahuna? I've never even heard of it." Orion says, scratching his head as he adjusts the satchel on his shoulder.

"It is an island under the protection of Kanaloa. Only those who know where it is can find it." She says, reminding me of the training complex which had lain on the outskirts of the Occulta Mirum, it had been covered in runes, meaning only those who had been there before could find it again.

"So you fight demons?" Cole asks, intrigued.

"Oh no. We are non-violent of course. We are here solely for the protection of the ocean and the life within it. We are the caretakers of the waters
312

of this world. I'm sure you've seen what a divine mess the humans are making of the planet they've been gifted. It's our job to protect the oceans as much as we can." Aulani speaks, enlightening us as the other Sirena remain silent, undulating through the warmth of the water. I am enjoying being in such proximity to home, I must admit, and as I think now about what Aulani has said my heart leaps in my chest at the idea of this type of noble cause, rather than one of demons and darkness. The idea of saving the world's ocean life from harm and conserving the environment plucks at something deep within me. A dream I had thought was long lost.

"But you know why we're here?" Rose asks, speaking up as she eyes the Sirena tails with envy.

"Oh of course, the Psirens have been causing us problems for years. They are less than discreet with murder and mayhem of the world's marine life than they think they are, I assure you." Luana speaks up finally, her voice melodic in its irritation. I look across to her, hot pink hair falling down her back in vibrant waves as she moves with divine grace.

"That's true." Azure replies, allowing her eyes to dilate as she smiles, looking only too creepy in the stark light of the now setting sun.

"You do not scare me. I have seen far greater horrors than a little black magic. The true horrors are that which require no magic at all. Like the way humans are willingly blind to the world around them, or just too lazy to care for it." Aulani bites back, making Azure recoil slightly as I feel her get metaphorically slapped. I've said it before and I'll say it again, I am falling in love with this Aulani chick and her pod already.

"How big is your pod?" I ask her, wondering if they might have room for one more. I know I should probably be more loyal, but the thought of hanging out in Hawaii saving the ocean's marine life is tugging at my soul, reminding me of the dream I had harboured what feels like too long ago. I had wanted to become a marine biologist, make a difference with marine conservation. Instead I had become a mermaid, and a Queen no less.

"We are many, but we are scattered. Groups of us break off and attend to various incidents, oil spills for example." Calypso explains, undulating as her tailfin shimmers a rainbow of pastel colour against the azure of the open ocean.

A whale shark swims into view, it's giant body attracting smaller fish alongside and as I watch it, I feel the tug of my love for marine life inflate my heart, bringing a smile to my face which I feel has been stern and concerned far too often lately.

"That's amazing." I reply, my eyes wide. I glimpse Orion watching me from the corner of my eye, as I turn to him and see he's looking at me as if I am sun and stars rolled into one. I kiss him on the cheek as we move through the water and into the dying light of the setting sun, swimming ever forward.

Isle Meahuna peaks over the horizon as we approach, lying in wait for us in lush, green, tropical glory. If you didn't know it was here, you'd never have found it, being merely a long spit of land with a green lush centre of about fifteen square miles. It peters out into soft white sand, sloping gracefully into the sea in a chilled decline.

The sun is just about to set behind the horizon as we finally arrive, breaking the surface and taking in large gulps of the cool twilight air.

"What are you taking us to? You said something of ours? Is it something my father gave you?" Orion asks, blowing water out his nose as droplets fall from his long eyelashes.

"No, child. It is something far more precious. Come." Aulani dives deep again, making the last leg of the journey in mere seconds as her hip fins moving in tandem with her fluke, making her motion effortless. Her white hair flows out behind her as she swims, falling well past the line where her tail begins and her body ends. I move through a shoal of clown fish, watching them swim playfully and glow even more vibrantly orange in the last dying embers of daylight than normal. Orion turns to me, his face suddenly sullen.

"Callie, I don't know if this is such a good idea." He whispers, placing a hand on my shoulder and squeezing, halting me in the water.

"What do you mean?" I question him, feeling my stomach drop.

"What if these Sirena are actually luring us into a trap? I mean how do we actually know they have anything of ours at all?" He asks me, looking to the

314

rest of our pod as they follow the Sirena, none the wiser to our conversation or Orion's doubts.

"Orion, they have moonstones around their necks and they knew your father." I say, rationalising his doubts away.

"Yes, but how do we know that? They *say* they knew my father, but we don't know that. Don't you think he'd have...I don't know mentioned something... anything about them?" I laugh at this exclamation.

"Orion! Atlas didn't tell us about any of the other pods either and we know he met the Water Nymphs, and he tried to meet the Maneli too. I don't think sharing information was his intent." I remind him, not wanting to linger behind the others for too long.

"I don't know... something just doesn't feel right." He admonishes and I frown, running my fingers through my stiff mermaid locks.

"Do you think maybe we're just used to everything going wrong?" I ask him, looking seriously into his icy blue eyes which capture the light of the Hawaiian sunset, reflecting it back to me in a scorching chill which causes the hairs on the back of my neck to rise.

"Maybe... I don't know. I don't want to split up." He admits.

"Okay, so we don't split up." I shrug, flitting away from him with a single flick of my tailfin, eager to get going before darkness falls. I really can't stand the thought of missing something right now, but Orion follows me closely as I go to catch up, grabbing my wrist before I can get away.

"Promise?" He caresses the side of my face as we ascend close to the surface, crisscrossing on our sides as I'm mid turn and making artful half leaps between the foam of frothing waves.

"I promise." I smile, kissing him quickly on the lips as I enter the water, allowing my doubts from his confession to dissipate once more. I don't know why, but I can't help but feel at home in these waters, whether that's because I'm relatively close to the place I had first awoken a mer, or whether it be something else about The Sirena and their magic, I'm grateful.

We catch up to the others, who are waiting for us a short way from the beach's edge.

"Sorry about that. How many people know about this place?" I apologise to Kala who looks seriously unimpressed at my lateness.

"We have staff on hand here, plus many Sirena who choose to reside temporarily here when they wish to rest and rejuvenate in the surrounding overwater bungalows. We also had a fallen angel land here once..." Luana is babbling, her eyes wide and excitable at our presence. She keeps looking to Orion, almost like she's never seen a merman before.

"How many male Sirena are here?" I ask her, suddenly intrigued as to why none have greeted us. Surely these women needed muscle and protection against demons. I mean, after all, they travel the world. They must at least run into them at some point.

"No men, only women here. We are the nurturers. Kanaloa felt it best to keep men and their competitive spirit away from such conservative efforts." Aulani replies. As Azure opens her mouth to speak I automatically inhale, worried about what's going to come out of her mouth as per usual.

"Okay, am I the only one who is kind of confused about the fact this woman just said they had a *Fallen Angel* here?" She looks at us like we're all totally stupid and I realise she's right. What the heck is that about?

"Yes, a small child fell to earth from above, her memory wiped. We named her, raised her for a while and sent her on her way. Simple really." Aulani shrugs, like what she's just said is totally blasé. I could press the matter further, but I figure I'll have time to ask her about it later; besides, we do have more pressing problems.

"So you said you have something of ours?" I press the issue and Kala nudges Aulani.

"Just tell her, I want to go and bathe by the Moonfalls before I die of old age." She rolls her eyes, impatient and seemingly less serene than her fellow Sirena.

"The place you must go to is situated inland, but only two of you are allowed to visit." Her eyebrows rise and Orion's words echo in the back of my mind. I had promised him we wouldn't split up.

316

"Can't we all go?" I ask her, tilting my head up to stare at her as we surface together. The shore is only a few metres away and palm trees sway in the breeze, comforting me. I had always loved palm trees, and now I'm here, they remind me of home.

"No, it can only be two. Lolana's rules, not mine." She shrugs.

"Lolana?" I question her, cocking one eyebrow as the water swills around my shoulders and the surface shifts.

"It really is easier if you see for yourself, child. Where's your curiosity? Your sense of adventure?" She asks me, chuckling slightly. I turn to Orion, not answering her as he surfaces next to me.

"She says only two of us can go." I tell him and he frowns, looking unsure of both himself and the situation. I blurt my next sentiment before I can stop myself, proving that my curiosity and sense of adventure are still very much intact despite everything I've been through. "I want to go!" I say, placing my hands together in a pleading type pose. I flutter my lashes.

"This is the other reason we do not have men. They are too easily swayed by a pretty face." Calypso snorts, laughing at me.

"Look, if you're going, I'm coming with you." He replies, crossing his arms across his breast plate.

"I don't think we should leave the others without any form of protection. What about if I take Azure?" I ask him and his expression turns surprised as water droplets trickle down his nose.

"Okay." He nods, liking the plan more now that I've added in a little dark power.

"Right, that's settled! Head up the beach, our men will clothe you before you proceed up to Lolana's place. Go on!" Aulani shoos us and I reach forward, grabbing a moonstone from the satchel hanging off Orion's hip.

"I'll be back." I promise, giving him a wet kiss on the cheek as we bob above the surface. I take off my armour, disconnecting the plates around my torso and waist, before removing my visor and revealing my aqua facial scales beneath.

"Luana will take those for you, we will store them in one of the overwater bungalows over there. You can pick them up later." Aulani declares, glowing

317

softly as I hand over my custom armour, worrying momentarily that I'll never see it again. The moon is almost full as I stare up, but not quite full enough and that's when I realise we don't have too many more nights before the blood moon will most likely rise. Azure is offered a stone by Orion but she shakes her head, black hair heavy with water.

"I won't need no stupid stone, will I?" She reminds him of her ability to phase and he sighs, exasperated but not surprised by her characteristic rudeness as he sinks back beneath the waves and the rest of the pod disappears beneath the moon's wavering reflection. Aulani remains, watching us for just a few moments more as I hold my stone up to the moonlight that pours from the clear sky, and Azure and I transform into what we once were. She slinks beneath the surface, soundless, as we climb up onto the wet sand of the island.

Stark nude, I clutch the glowing moonstone in my palm tightly, reminding myself not to let go of it.

"You know if I was going to be super inappropriate right now I'd make a comment about how you have kind of a nice ass." Azure quips, trying to make me uncomfortable.

"Yeah well, I've always fancied your boobs so..." I retort, poking my tongue out. She laughs, covering herself as we scamper, freezing, up to where slabs of smooth stone form a path into what seems to be a small jungle.

"Not bad, Pierce, you're getting better at banter." She smiles to me, her eyes dilating as to increase her ability to see in the dark, demonstrating one of the few Psiren traits I miss. "So what's next on the magical mystery tour you think?" She asks me, cocking her head as we move a few metres forward into the jungle, our path suddenly lit by tiki torches.

"I'd say..." I begin as we turn a corner and my expression slackens, shocked by what I'm seeing. "Two men with fluffy robes and... COCKTAILS." I breathe, the smell of fresh pineapple slices hitting me full on in my ravenous face. I rush forward as the two men step toward us in sync, almost like they're hypnotised, and one of them passes us both robes while the other passes us alcohol. Hawaii is definitely my favourite place in the world right now.

318

"Wow, not too shabby." Azure nods, her mouth forming an impressed pucker as she sips on her straw. "You know Psirens would be a lot less pissy if you just gave them more alcohol." I watch her as she relaxes, shaking her hair out and sighing slightly. It's the first time I've ever seen her look, well, almost completely human. "Don't stare at me Pierce, I'm having a moment." She warns me in a harsh bite, her eyes still closed.

After a few more seconds, she opens them. "Okay, back to crappy reality. Where to next?" She looks to the two men who gesture, moving out of the way of the continuing path, tiki torches burning bright among the thick, lush forest on either side. I consciously slip the moonstone into the pocket of my robe, praying I remember to take it with me when I return to the sea. "Call me crazy, but who thought it was a good idea to put all these tiki torches near so much wood and crap. I mean, it's an accident waiting to happen." Azure tuts, taking another sip of her drink. She calls my attention back to my own cocktail as I roll my eyes, feeling suddenly stupid I was so nervous before. I look down into the dark liquid in my round glass, about to take a sip, before I stop.

"Azure..." I say, feeling something click into place.

"Uhuh?" She asks, pinging the straw out of her glass and hitting me in the eye with fruit juice. I wince at its sting.

"What about if these drinks are poisoned or something?" I say to her, pursing my lips. She narrows her eyes.

"I love how you let me take a freaking massive sip before saying something. Nice." She tips the rest of her drink out into the mud on the side of the path, sighing.

"They're probably fine..." I say, thinking twice about my paranoia. It was probably Orion's negativity settling over me again. Azure rolls her eyes almost immediately, snatching my drink out of my hand.

"My Mai Tai." She pouts, making me laugh. "Ah well, if it is poisoned it's not like I've got much to live for anyway."

We proceed up the path as she glugs the remainder of the drink, not caring for the consequences and I watch her as we walk, examining her face under the flickering flames. I wonder if she means it when she says she has nothing to live for.

319

Suddenly, as we walk deeper into the jungle, an exclamation so chilling and familiar breaks the silence of the night, causing Azure to drop the glass she's holding. It smashes into a million pieces. The exclamation reverberates around us. Causing us to stop, stone still, in our tracks, stunned. It comes again, proving that in fact it was not a dream, or some kind of trick played by a poisoned Mai Tai.

"Oh, Bloody Hell!!!!"

"You don't think?" I exclaim, shocked as I stand among the chirping of crickets, listening for any further evidence that I'm not losing my mind. Azure is staring, transfixed at the thought of finding Vexus. It's hard to read the emotions running across her face, because they're evolving so quickly it's like one of those fast forward videos of a flower opening or something. I mean, it couldn't be Vex, could it? What the hell would he even be doing here?

I take a step forward, pulling Azure behind me and around the broken glass on the path. We approach a corner, the view behind it obscured by lush bushes with fuchsia hyacinths spreading their petals, which release a sweet fragrance into the air. On the other side of the turn, in the middle of the thick green jungle, lies a hut with screens for walls to block out the sun and a straw roof. Under the high canopy are beds, medical supplies and one very stressed out woman trying to restrain a very pissed off Octoman minus eight of his arguably more lethal appendages. As I watch them struggle through the almost opaque screens, I continue to step forward, laughing at Vex until he's fully restrained and the woman beside scurries off to something new which demands her attention.

"Vex!" I call out, rushing over to his side as I bound through the open door. It lets a gentle night breeze roam through the space, cooling it and creating a healing atmosphere as I breathe in its tropical fragrance. I look down to Vex, a moonstone hung around his scarred neck which bulges thick with veins. He's bruised, like a cruel masterpiece of pain and I wince looking down at him, knowing Psirens don't bruise so easily. Azure moves past me, resting eyes on him which widen as her expression goes slack. I wonder if she's in shock.

"Azure, are you okay?" I ask her, waving a hand in front of her face. She looks to me, dazed, like she's forgotten I am standing here all together.

"I don't know whether to kill him, or just hit him really hard." She exclaims, no conviction in her sentence. Then I realise, she had told Vex to protect her sister, a task in which he had spectacularly failed. I stare down at him, noticing the fact he's had holes poked into him at almost every intercostal space. I know Psirens and mer have accelerated healing, so it must have taken weeks, if not more, of intense torture to cause these types of injuries.

As we stand there, robe clad and sticking out like sore thumbs against the natural décor, a woman with midnight blue hair and gold highlights, the same woman who had been restraining Vex, returns and addresses us with a stern tone.

"What are you doing near this patient?" She demands, pulling a white clipboard off the end of the gurney to which Vex is strapped. Struggling to get free.

"We're friends." I say, looking to her. "Are you Lolana? Aulani sent us." I add in quickly, not wanting to come across as a complete stranger.

"Oh! Right! You're from the uh… Oh, Atargatis' Kindred, right?" She asks, flustered. I feel the word Kindred resonate through me. I have no idea what it means, but I'm beginning to think I should.

"I guess…" I say, staring at her with intensity before turning on the spot to take in the space. That's when I lay eyes on someone else I recognise. "Oscar!" I exclaim, rushing across the slick floor and toward his gurney. He's not in as bad a shape as Vex, but he's not looking much better either. I move over to him, placing a palm on his forehead in the muggy Hawaiian heat. He smiles, his lips parting, though his eyes remain closed.

"Sophia…" He murmurs, the moonstone pendant around his neck slipping to one side. I almost kick myself, she should have been in my place, she should have been seeing him first. If only I'd known that what they had of ours was he and Vex. I lean in.

"No it's not Sophia, it's Callie, but I'll go and get her." I turn on my heel, ready to make my exit, desperate that my friend knows her soulmate is alive, if not all that well.

321

"Where are you going?!" Lolana calls after me, her eyes wide and face annoyed. She's a beautiful woman, but right now I don't care. If she stops me getting my friend, then I'm taking her down and I don't care if I have to turn Azure psycho to do it.

"My friend, she's his soulmate. He needs her." I state, stepping away from her to leave without further explanation.

"What he needs is medical attention. I'm no doctor. I'm a marine veterinary specialist. I can't make any guarantees, so I'd rather you didn't deliver her false hope. He's in a bad state. So is the other unconscious one. I can't work out why their natural healing processes aren't working as fast as they should be." She says, her expression exasperated like I'm the one being irrational. She can't just expect me to send for the people closest to those who are injured. Though I wonder now I've heard she's not really a doctor if telling Sophia would just be cruel. What if Oscar dies? What if Oscar dies and she's not here to say goodbye? Then something else strikes me. The other *unconscious* one? Vex wasn't unconscious. Or at least he hadn't sounded very unconscious when I'd heard him cussing.

I walk back into the hut and spot another gurney next to Oscar's that I hadn't even glanced at before. I slowly step over to it and encounter the face of someone I don't know.

"Who is this?" I ask her, looking at the man's face and trying to recall if I've ever seen him before. He has red hair and green eyes and his face is slightly round. He's also got a huge gash between his ribs.

"He found the other two and dragged them here all on his own. He's a warrior. I thought he was with you?" Lolana says, looking confused.

"Did he say his name?" I ask her as she frowns slightly, her blue eyebrows dipping low in thought.

"I think he said Jack, but I could be wrong. I was more concerned with getting them help." She turns on a heel and rushes back to Vex, who sounds like he is fighting his restraints again. I'm guessing it's probably because Azure's mocking him, though with those two I can never be sure of anything.

I look back to Jack, realising now who it is I'm looking at.

The man who had saved us all by saving Poseidon's vessel, let alone Sophia's soulmate. We owed him everything. Cole's soulmate, the man who he loved, the man he was made for and who he had known was still alive, even after everything that had happened, lies on the bed before me. I reach over to his hand, which lies still atop deep green sheets and observe he's also sporting a moonstone pendant, which lies on the rising and falling muscles of his bare chest.

"Thank you." I say, kissing his forehead.

"You're welcome… Your Highness." I hear his reply and I stare into his face. The man who had saved the world, all by himself, is staring at me, and in that one look, though I can't explain why, I know he's made for Cole.

25
Moonfalls
ORION

As we round a corner and I flex my tailfin, curving the arc of my path through the ocean, my eyes land on what they call 'Moonfalls'. I can see why immediately, as the entire bottom of the pool of water, which the numerous trickling waterfalls empty out into, is completely filled with the mystical sheen of moonstones that are radiant at even this distance.

Aulani moves into the narrow river, heading inland toward the falls as she swims through its clear and shallow rushing current. She hoists her body up onto a rock as she reaches her destination far quicker than the rest of us and looks back into the dark, searching for us. Rising her arms, hundreds of fireflies rise from the surrounding trees, lighting our path to the rushing waters of the island at her command. I stare up and around at them all, in awe of this one of a kind natural phenomenon.

"Take a load off." She yells down the river, gesturing to the numerous rocks which poke atop the froth of the falls as I swim, pushing off against boulders to keep my forward momentum against the current of the river which empties the water of the falls back out into the oceans. Hyacinth bushes line the riverbanks and as the fireflies settle once more I'm alerted to the bright pinks and stark whites of the surrounding flowers.

Finally, reaching the small pool filled with moon sheen, I pull myself up onto one of the rocks next to the woman with a tiger shark-esque tailfin. Her white eyes are unsettling and I can't help but want to ask if she's a seer too, just like Azure. I think about my sister then, about my soulmate who is with her right now. I hope my instincts are wrong about this place. I hope they are alright.

I exhale and Aulani reaches over, patting my tailfin with her smooth, tan skinned palm.

"You are too stressed out. This is Hawaii Orion, you got to chill, ya know?" She sounds so casual, so young in her words, and yet her face, despite the smoothness of her skin, betrays many years that have passed. I wonder exactly how old she is. She looks down to my satchel, reaching and grabbing it from me, pulling it up and over my head with such quick motion I almost fall from the smooth rock and into the water below. I pull the bag back toward me, scowling at her forwardness.

"I just want to relieve you. This looks heavy." She scowls back while somehow maintaining her calm and opening the leather bag before looking within after snatching it back and slapping my hand in the process. She takes out fistfuls of the moonstones that lie at the bottom, beneath Sedna's codex, and throws them, one by one, to her fellow Sirena.

The rest of my pod watches, pulling themselves onto other rocks and resting, leaning over to watch the strange curvaceous women examining the stones that shine like blue-ish opals. They hold them up to the moonlight, staring to them with wide and brightly coloured eyes.

"They are from these falls." A Sirena who I have never seen before, who I have only just noticed, is sat on a rock at the far end of the pool of the cove in which we're sat. Her hair is a stark orange, yellow and pink ombre, matching her tailfin which is tucked beneath her and her hair is covered in pearls which hang low down on her forehead before swooping up and burying into braids of tangerine, fuchsia and lemon.

"Thank you Kanula. That is what I thought." Aulani bows as I wave to Kanula, who ignores me, closing her eyes as she reaches out to her side for something. She pulls back a wicker basket from the bushes, or what appears to be a basket from this distance, before placing it in the water and letting it float over to the next woman beside her. I observe, quiet as the basket makes it around the group, never once veering between the Sirena as slowly, one by one,

325

they pull out leather strands that they begin to braid, making them into strong plaits of leather. I sit, the rest of the pod silent too, watching them as they work and slightly transfixed by their quick and able hands. They really are extremely beautiful, and more relaxed than any pod we've come across so far, but I take a deep breath, knowing that it's time to get down to business once again. I can't believe I'm saying it, but right now my priority must be political despite the fact I'd quite like to sit and enjoy this place and its serene removal from the civilised world.

"So, you know why we're here. Do you know of the vessel amongst you?" I ask them collectively as they work and my own pod startles, jumping as my voice breaks the silence, transfixed by the quick handiwork of the Sirena as well. Kala looks to me, examining my face with curiosity as she catches me staring and flips her hair back over her shoulder, before delicately placing her hand back in her brightly scaled lap.

"We have no way to test for such a thing." Aulani replies. She looks down to the water before her, taking three leather pieces from the basket that hovers over her reflection as it finally reaches her. She holds them up to me as she measures them, but doesn't actually look at me.

"Why is that? I mean, I've been wondering, why is it our pod have magic and none of the others we've come across do?" I ask her and she laughs slightly.

"You tell me. You've heard the origin story of your race I assume?" She smiles, raising her eyebrows. I inhale a little, thinking back to the tale. I continue to wonder even now why Gods and Goddesses can seem so incredibly human in their flaws, and yet they're deemed capable of ruling over our entire existence.

I shrug, "Yes, what does that have to do with anything?" She laughs again, as though I'm so stupid. Though I suppose in a lot of ways I am.

"The reason you mer are so powerful compared to the rest of us is simple. Atargatis has a weak spot for mortals. You have magic because it's her way of protecting you. A way in which the other Gods and Goddesses don't see as necessary for their Kindred." She explains, clapping her hands so fireflies rise, swarming around her in a gentle buzz and lighting the area in which she works, quickly braiding the leather intricately.

326

"It hasn't done us much good. There's hardly any of us left." I gesture to the women who are looking around and admiring the tails of The Sirena, though some of them look slightly jealous.

"Ah, the tides are turning though, child. Anyone can feel it. Do not fret. You are the Kindred of Atargatis, you will always be taken care of. Perhaps even more so than the rest of us." She nods to herself, like she's got the soul of an old wise woman trapped in the body of someone young and attractive.

"Kindred? What is that?" I ask her, frowning as I continue to feel rather stupid. I should know all this, though truth be told I'd never studied the literature like I probably should have. Now it was all gone, lost in the collapse of the Alcazar Oceania.

"It is the name for those of us given immortal life in service of the Gods and Goddesses." She explains, not looking at me as she licks her bottom lip, concentrating.

"So even though we're different races, we're all Kindred?" I query as the fireflies settle on her shoulders and down her arms, illuminating the blue and white of her hair to a level of supernatural glow.

"That would be correct." She smiles, tying off the knot she's working on. I notice now she's braided the leather around the moonstone she's holding, making it into a necklace. She holds it out to me as I open my palm, dropping it down in the centre.

"You have earned this." She praises me, as I close my palm around it. Her words irk me.

"What do you mean?"

"Well, your father kept these a secret for a long time. I believe he said he didn't want you gallivanting from your calling after a certain soulmate?" She laughs at me again, eerie in the alabaster of her eyes that lack any pupil, making me wonder how well she can actually see me.

"That sounds like him." I say, wrapping the cord around my neck and letting the moonlight shine down on the stone.

"He was a wise man. I am so sorry he is no longer here to guide you Orion." Aulani places a hand on my tailfin again, where would be my knee. She's acting like my mother once had and it makes me nostalgic.

327

"Me too." I admonish, looking to the mermaids as they're each handed their own pendant. They smile, relaxing together and giggling amongst themselves as Fahima sits on Ghazi's lap and he kisses her on the cheek. The look he gives her makes me miss Callie even more as a rustle sounds behind me.

As I turn, anxious to see my soulmate, Kala, the girl who is snarky to say the least, exhales.

"Finally!" She sighs, stroppy as she watches five men in white tailored shorts, tennis shoes and polo shirts emerge from the bushes, holding wooden trays with hot towels on top. They come to the water's edge, close to where we're sitting, with glazed eyes as they pass out the towels in perfectly synchronised motion. I blink, confused as to what I'm seeing.

"This is the staff you mentioned?" I ask Luana, as one of the men hands her a towel. She presses it to her shoulders and the back of her neck, sighing slightly as her mouth forms an 'o' of pleasure.

"Yes." She replies, scrunching up her forehead. "Swimming can give you such a bad neck ache!" She complains as she continues to move the steaming towel down her arm, sighing as she goes. I'm offered one in turn, but refuse it, rather keen on keeping my guard up. The servants look most certainly drugged, or like they've been charmed in some way.

"What did you do to them?" I ask Aulani, gaze suspicious as my eyes narrow and my lips press together into a hard line. I twist my torso back round to face her, demanding an answer.

"Nothing they don't innately desire, I promise you." She grins, her face serene as I turn to Kala, scowling further.

"What did you do to those men?!" I demand of her, appalled.

"Oh what, not liking men as objects created to serve women? Really? Finding that a little demeaning to such a fair sex are we?" She raises an eyebrow and crosses her arms across her chest.

What is their problem?

"These men are under the influence of something untoward! What is it?" I turn back to Aulani, only to find her expression is becoming bored, irritated even.

328

"I can assure you our staff is perfectly happy here Orion. In fact, they're probably happier than the majority of the human race. They serve us, and in turn we grant their deepest desires. They are perfectly contented, and any of them will attest to such." She examines her long white nails and smiles to me, righting the unhappy expression on her face. I look back to the men as they disappear, wanting to glare harshly at the maidens who are now pressing hot towels to their bare skin, but not wanting to ruin their fun. I know this journey has been anything but.

"Fine, as long as they're happy." I sigh, looking after them with curiosity. I exhale dry breath, looking to Aulani once more as she begins to braid another pendant.

"Ah, here come the next batch." She raises her eyebrows as more men dressed in white appear through the thick trees that surround us. These ones are only too happy to begin rubbing the Sirena's shoulders, looking them up and down with hungry eyes as desire filled expressions spread across their faces.

We grant their deepest desires. I recall Aulani's words.

Yeah, I bet they do. I think to myself, rolling my eyes at the heavy petting Kala is now receiving from a blonde man with flawless tan skin.

"Did you have a question for me Orion?" I hear the query come from Aulani as I watch Rose taking a massage in her stride, leaning back into the welcoming touch of yet another man slave.

"How quickly will you be able to assemble your entire pod for war?" I blurt the words, knowing I must sound forward but not wanting to waste any more time. I look up to the moon, which is becoming fuller and fuller with each passing night as worry fills me like volcanic sand, weighing me down.

"I think you misunderstand. I will happily find the vessel with you, but fighting? I already told you. We are pacifists. Non-violent. Of course, we will not be fighting alongside you." She gazes at me, her face deadly serious and lacking some of her beauty.

"Wait..." I try to stall, as she cuts across me again.

"I will not discuss it. It is not Kanaloa's way. Not only that, but who do you expect is going to look after the world's oceans after you and the rest of the Kindred have gotten each other hacked to pieces? Somebody has to stay

329

behind." Her expression softens, but mine doesn't. This is the last pod I need to convince to come into battle with me and I'm not giving up so easily this time.

"Look, I know it's a lot to ask..." I begin, raising my hands in a kind of surrender as a sudden rustling behind me catches me off guard and I twist, wondering what kind of services the men in white shorts will be offering this time. Instead, I'm greeted by a familiar, if not slightly bruised face.

"Jack?" The word leaves my mouth and I watch as Cole, who's facing out to sea, turns, snapping his head sideways at the single word.

"Jack!" He exclaims, his soulmate limping out into the water. They meet a little way from the rocky incline that extends out into the jungle, their hands finding each other's hair and pulling each other close before starting to kiss in a fevered passion under the pale moonlight. The water sloshes around them as they move and a few seconds later, my own soulmate clambers out from behind the thick tangle of trees.

"Callie!" I call out to her, waving desperately so as to draw her gaze. Her head turns, blonde ringlets bouncing around her face as she darts over to me, a robe in her arms.

"I can't stay long. I'm here for Sophia." She whispers, her eyes shooting from me to her friend who sits amongst the other maidens, looking to the pair of mermen kissing passionately with adoration and envy wrapped into the collective stare of sparkling eyes.

"Wait, what?" I grab her arm as she tries to pull away. She looks back to me, eyes flashing in warning that what she has to say is not for the entire pod to hear.

"I'll be back." She grimaces an apology as she leans in and kisses me on the forehead before dashing over to Sophia, whose long auburn hair is trailing down her back in a wet dark tangle. Callie tugs at her arm, whispering something in her ear and her face lights up suddenly. She holds the newly woven pendant up to the light of the moon above as she transforms, her scales rippling out of existence and being replaced with flesh. Sophia then scrambles up onto her feet as Callie wraps her in the robe she's brought quickly, the two

330

of them so urgent in their movements that I can't help but worry something bad has happened.

What was so important that it wasn't for the ears of the Crowned Ruler?

I continue to wonder, anxious, as I watch them flurrying about in a tornado of robes, legs and hair as they scramble from the shallows in which they're stood, sloshing. The two of them spin on bare feet as Callie looks back over her shoulder at me, worry in her eyes before she vanishes once more into the dark, sticky heat of the jungle.

CALLIE

"Is he alright? What did he say? Callie!!" Sophia pulls on my arm, finally halting my stride as I storm through the jungle. I turn, looking her deeply in the eyes. I'm scared now I've told her I'm doing the wrong thing, after all, Lolana said there were no guarantees.

"Sophia, I'd really rather not discuss this until you've seen him. I don't want to mess it up…" I say, anxious that I'm going to give her false hope. The crickets and creatures that inhabit the surrounding greenery chirp and thrum in the humid moisture of the air and a bead of sweat clings to the back of my neck, trickling down my spine.

"Is it really that bad?" She asks me, her eyebrows pinching together, eyes widening. Her chocolate brown irises pull at me, reminding me once again of my baby sister.

"Don't cry… please. Oscar won't want to see you that way, Sophia. It'll be alright." I pull her into my robed arms, cuddling her close to me. I know she must be terrified, but as we stand around in the middle of the jungle, the only sounds the song of nature and the overlaying crackle of lit tiki torches, I know the only thing that can really comfort her isn't here at all. "Come on. Let's go and get you to him. I'm sure he'll feel much better knowing you're there." I promise her, holding her tightly as she sniffles against my robe. I look into her eyes once more, wishing I could take her pain away because I know if it was Orion I'd be going mad with worry too.

"Okay. You're right. I don't want to look a mess when I see him." She sniffles and rubs her eyes on the sleeve of her robe before shaking her hair out.

"Better?" She asks me, putting on a fake smile.

"Much." I take her hand, pulling her down the path behind me at a quick pace until we reach the clearing with the medical hut. She moves toward the muted florescent light of the space, which leaks through the almost opaque screens, and I can sense she's suddenly scared of what she might see. I hold her hand, wrapping my fingers through hers as we move through the doors and past Vex, who is now bickering with Azure about who's seen worse injuries.

"Well one time I almost lost my entire arm." She boasts, cocking an eyebrow. "So really you got off easy." I hear him snort.

"You are bloody crackers, Love. Have you lost it? Torture is blatantly worse than getting cut up in some sick session with your ex boy toy or whatever the hell his name was," He sucks in air, hollowing his cheek bones as his lilac irises lock onto my form. Azure catches him staring at me, and then at Sophia. She smacks him on the arm.

"OW! What the bloody hell was that for?" He snaps at her. I laugh to myself quietly as we pass, but soon force my expression sombre as we approach Oscar's bed. Sophia squeezes my hand as she looks upon him.

"Oh, Oscar..." She breathes, rushing forward and caressing his cheek as he lies on the bed, eyes closed.

"Sophia?" He replies, his eyes opening a crack as he lets out a cough, wincing.

"Yes! It's me! I'm here!" She cries, kissing him all over. He winces but takes the affection, pulling her into him with a bruised arm. As he raises his head from his pillow to embrace her, he mouths his thanks to me, but I wave him away, not needing thanks at all. I notice immediate improvement at Sophia's presence as Oscar kisses her slowly. I turn away, averting my eyes and giving them privacy. Vex catches me turning from across the room and he smirks.

332

"Oh look at you, all prim and proper. How bloody convenient." He rolls his eyes and Azure smacks him again. "OW!" He moves against his restraints, trying to hit her back.

"You know, I kinda like him in restraints. Think that blue haired chick would let me take a pair for the journey?" Azure asks me with a wicked glint in her eye. I shrug.

"Whatever floats your boat." I poke my tongue out at Vex, turning from him and back to Sophia, who is now on her knees by the low gurney, talking to Oscar.

"There is so many of them. They've grown so much. They made me make chains for that.... thing. The Necrimad." He coughs after this statement, going slack on the bed for a few seconds, catching his breath. I frown.

"They've chained it up?" I feel something within me prickle, my instincts reacting as I realise that Oscar getting out alive isn't just good for Sophia. He might have information we can use.

"Oscar, I know you're tired, I know you're hurting, but please, what can you tell me about the Necrimad? Why have they tied it up? I thought they wanted to use it to kill people?" Azure is suddenly at my side, interested by the conversation. I hear Vex behind us mumble,

"Well don't bloody include me in the conversation. It's not like I was in on their meetings or anything before these stupid bloody visions." We all pivot to him, surprised.

"What do you know?" I ask him, feeling my patience wearing thin as I stare upon his bruising, which is beginning to fade slightly across the open-plan space.

"They want to absorb the power of that thing." He shrugs, no longer fighting the restraints that pin his hands to the bed.

"So the Necrimad is like a mule for the power? They didn't want to use it to just kill people?" I ask him, narrowing my eyes. I wonder now why I hadn't thought of asking Vex first, but then I remember it's because he's awkward as hell.

"Ding, ding, ding. We have a bloody winner." He rolls his eyes.

"I saw some of the books Saturnus had left out when he and Solustus were preparing for the ritual." He gulps slightly, eyes shifting to Azure in a subtle and sudden glance that's filled with guilt. They move back to me within an instant, but I know he's still thinking about Starlet. "That Necrimad has two powers which can be used once they're released, the power the demon can access, and the power it can't. The power it can use is the ability to boil the water around it, super strength, all that bloody Godly type mojo. The other stuff is a little more... well, bad. That dark magic stuff can raise the dead from the bottom of the ocean. They want to split it between them. Saturnus was obviously trying to find out how. Regardless... they need to cause the scales to tip before that even happens." He finishes his little information bomb and we stand under the fluorescents, wide eyed and staring at him.

"You can read?" Azure says, deadpan in her question.

"Oi!" He exclaims, snarling at her. I watch the two of them, amused.

"So what the hell are these scales?" I ask him, crossing my arms and ignoring their bickering.

"The Kindred Scales. The scales of good and evil, I guess. The books weren't exactly written for beginners. Either way, they need to get rid of all the mer, or enough of you to tip them. Something about destroying the light magic it took to make you, or something equally as bloody cliché. That's all I know, alright?" I bite my bottom lip, looking at Vex with a shocked expression. He's a lot less dumb than he looks, which I guess is lucky for us. If they needed to get rid of all the mer, then they must know we are returning for a fight or they'd be out looking for us already.

"Vex, do they know about the other pods?" I ask him, worrying about the surprise of our numbers being less than a total shocker.

"I don't think so. Wait, what other pods?" He asks me, looking confused. I turn to Oscar, not bothering to catch him up.

"Do you have anything else to add, anything we can use?" I ask him and Sophia turns to him, eyes still full of concern as we stand in the middle of the medical hut, questioning the two men who had barely escaped with their lives.

"This fight you're headed into. It was foretold. They know the blood moon is important. They will be prepared. So must you be." Oscar says, wheezing as his breathing becomes slightly pained, yet stronger. I look between him and Sophia, and something within me is desperate to preserve what they have between them. I know they've already been through so much with Oscar's capture, his time being tormented and tortured by humans. I can't bear the thought of more tragedy befalling them.

"I will always find you, my sunshine." I hear him whisper, kissing her cheek before laying back flat on the bed. Sophia lays her head on his chest lightly, not letting go of his hand for even one moment. A few moments pass before I hear the clicking of heels against the wooden boards of the floor.

"What are you all doing here? The patient needs rest! I said no more than two visitors!" Sophia is on her feet immediately, looking scared as her cheeks flush and yet she refuses to let go of her soulmate's hand. I stare between her and Oscar, noticing something odd about his torso.

"Hey, look at this..." I demand, noticing the patch where Sophia's wet hair has lain is lighter than the rest of the bruising on Oscar's body. I look between them, trying to work out what's caused the healing. Then I realise.

"They need salt water baths. That will speed up their natural healing." I turn to Lolana, her dark blue eyes wide at my words. I smirk, knowing I've just figured out what's taken her hours of researching, only to come up with nothing.

"Right, well in that case you all need to get out." She tries to shoo us, but I shake my head in protest, ringlets tickling my ears.

"I'm going, but this one stays. You've seen him, Sophia is making him better already." I gesture to them, talking and smiling, as Sophia stares at Lolana, an innocent yet cheesy grin plastered on her face.

"See, how can you say no to that?" I move around to Lolana, placing an arm around her narrow shoulders. She rolls her eyes, unable to stop herself as she shrugs me away.

"Fine, but she needs to get out of the way if I tell her to." She decrees, turning on her heel and moving back over to the bed where Jack had lain, remaking the sheets that he had left in a pile at the end of the bed. I turn away from her, grinning to Sophia before facing Azure.

"Are you coming?" I ask her, wondering if she'll stay or not. She puckers her lips, shrugging.

"I better stay, just in case he tries to kill himself, or more worryingly, someone else." The palm trees of the jungle stir outside as an inkling of a breeze begins but then dies, giving up in the intense heat.

"I heard that!" He yells out from the bed, craning his head to look at Azure.

She brushes her long black hair back from her shoulder before yelling back in a shrill tone, "I meant you to!"

I laugh, covering my mouth with one hand as I watch them, unable to stop myself thinking of how much they remind me of an old married couple.

"Good luck with that." I reply before taking off, putting one foot in front of the other atop the stone path and heading out into the night.

As I walk through the fragrant jungle, alone, to the Moonfalls where I had last seen my pod, I think about Sophia, about everything she had almost lost. As I tread carefully down the path, my heartbeat quickens in my chest, knowing that this journey is almost over. Knowing that what comes next could be the end of everything we've worked so hard to protect. Knowing it could be the end of Orion and me.

26
Kindred
ORION

The sun burns down, lethal in its warmth, from high above the sloshing surface of the Pacific. We are submerged fully once more and Callie is once again at my side, exactly where she should be. Her eyes are wide, taking in the tropical waters with an awe filled expression. I never tire of watching her experience the ocean; what has become so dull, she makes new and brilliant again, returning the magic of fresh eyes to me as well.

"I can't believe Oscar and Jack managed to escape, all those miles, and injured too." I hear Rose say, surprise fraught in her high-pitched tone. I gaze at her, and then shift my focus to Sophia who had returned to the ocean at the first light of dawn. She looks proud, her auburn hair falling in thick waves over her left shoulder and brown eyes sparkling as her skin glows a subtle floral white.

"Vex got them out. Apparently, it's harder to bind someone with tentacles." Callie puts in this little fact and I scowl, I've been trying to ignore the fact the tentacled ass escaped too, but it's getting no easier as she continues to bring him up every two or three hours at least. It's too much, and as the urge within me to kill rises uncharacteristically, I clench my palm, forgetting Callie still rests her hand in mine.

"Ow! Watch it." She exclaims, pulling her palm from mine. Azure snorts as we hang in the blue of the open ocean, relaxing before heading out with the Sirena to observe what they call early morning meditation.

"Look at that face. I think someone is a little less happy that Vex made it out alive." She teases, coming up close and pinching my cheek, I swat her away like the pest she is, accidentally hitting a passing blue tang as she darts from my side, quicker than a spinner dolphin in her motion.

"Hey careful! That poor fish doesn't know what just hit it, you bully!" Azure scowls, poking her tongue out at me. I'm glad that the Sirena aren't here, because I'm pretty sure that even accidentally hitting fish is frowned upon.

"Did he at least look badly maimed?" I whisper to Callie as she turns to me with narrowed eyes and an irritated look.

"Orion, stop! That's an awful thing to say! He saved Oscar! Not to mention the fact that we now have more information about the Necrimad because of him." She makes her case, her expression scornful.

"He treated you like garbage Callie. He's lucky he's still breathing." I retort, feeling hate fill me, turning my insides cold.

"I think you're being awfully over sensitive." Callie replies, her expression no longer annoyed but impassive as her blonde hair moves behind her shoulder. She spins slowly in the water, no longer clad in armour, toward the other mermaids, blocking me out of the conversation. I stare for a few moments at the tattoo along the base of her spine before turning to Cole, grouchy as I take a few strokes distance from her, trying to cool my temper.

"Women." I grunt, feeling the sting of the gender divide. How is it that Callie can be falling all over this guy *again?* He treated her like crap, I've seen it, and I can't work out why she can't see it too.

"They are a strange breed, for sure..." Cole replies, watching Ghazi and Fahima floating beside one another shyly. "Then again, if you're made for one another, they can also be the best thing ever to happen to you." He looks over to Jack who is resting on a rock a few metres away, still healing from the deep gash in his side.

I remember him telling us his story. How he had hidden under the rubble of the city for days before making his escape. How he had lain on jagged glass, shattered from the Alcazar, that had lodged in his side as he had dived into the debris against his better judgement to survive, meaning the wound was unable

338

to close. I wince at that thought, the feel of imaginary broken glass grating against the bare skin beneath my armour.

"You're a lucky man." I say to him, watching Jack's lime green tailfin move from side to side, absentminded in its relaxed stroke.

"Yes, I am." Cole smiles, brushing his black hair back from his eyes, his bracers glowing gold in the muted sunlight. We hang, suspended in silence for a few moments, hands on our hips as though they're stuffed in pockets, relaxed in the silence. Suddenly, I feel bold.

"Is it, you know... different being with a man?" I ask him, letting my curiosity about his sexuality escape me. I've always wondered, but I never asked because I always thought there would be another opportunity. If this trip has taught me anything, it's that there might not be any more tomorrows in which to ask these kinds of things.

"I don't think so... I wouldn't know. I've always loved men. It's what got me killed you know?" He shrugs, imparting this information that I had never known before. I had fought countless demons with this man, and yet there is still so much about him I don't know. "You know how I'll explain it? Think about the things you love about Callie, the way she smiles, how she talks. To me I love Jack for who he is inside; his gender is just a happy coincidence. Love is love, and I love him." He vows, staring deeply into my eyes as the conversation reaches its highest point of intensity. I grin, clapping him on the shoulder, understanding perfectly.

"Love is love." I repeat, smiling at him with a relaxed expression. He returns my happiness, his gaze wavering to his soulmate, the love there unmistakable.

As we continue to float, turning our conversation to the upcoming battle and the non-violent ways of our hosts, they appear, shadows becoming more vivid in the vast blue as they come into focus. Cole turns to face them and Callie returns to my side, swimming across the distance between us in moments and leaving the maidens to regroup. Ghazi and Fahima pivot, their faces lighting up at the return of the Sirena and in spite of their refusal to fight for us, I cannot deny they are some of the most hospitable Kindred we've come across.

339

Aulani appears, leading the group with quick and measured undulations of her tiger shark patterned tailfin, her face the picture of serenity as she glides forward, ethereal in her grace.

"Good morning Children of Atargatis. How are you feeling?" She enquires, her eyes not moving to any particular member of the group. Callie and I swim forward, taking large strokes with our tailfins in perfect time and moving easily through the weak and gentle current.

"We are well, thank you." I nod to her, keeping my tone polite and clipped.

"Very well, come with us, we are about to begin our morning meditation." She beckons, waving an arm as the rest of the brightly coloured women float behind her, watching us with gentle eyes.

"Thank you for including us." Callie is grateful in her response, looking to me with a carefree gaze that says her irritation at my reaction to Vex's return has dissolved.

"You are most welcome. Meditation is at the heart of what it means to be one with the sea. Everything about the sea is self-sustaining, self-healing, we in turn must learn to be the same." Kanula's voice is ghostly in its softness, and I wonder momentarily if she has something stuck in her throat. She waves a hand again, rising fast in the water before she completes the wave of her next undulation. Her tailfin flares out behind her, orange, pink and yellow in multi-coloured ombre and she has hips fins also, just like Aulani.

We move through the open ocean, past colourful reefs teeming with life and vibrant with an abundance of hue. Callie's eyes grow wide at the scene before us, her lack of experience becoming slightly more evident as I watch her fascination with it all. Sometimes it's easy for me to forget she is so new to all this, she takes everything in her stride, especially being Queen and helping me rule, so sometimes having a reminder isn't bad for me. I must remember to check how she's feeling more often. After all, this has been stressful to say the least and she's at the very heart of it all.

"You okay?" I press her for an answer, grabbing her hand through the water beside me.

"I'm better than I was before we got here. I feel... I don't know, different."
She shrugs it off, clearly still not coming to grips with her own emotions
surrounding everything that is happening and I frown, concerned.

"Is there anything I can do?" I ask her, bringing her hand up to my lips
and kissing her knuckles.

"No. Not right now. I just sort of wish things would slow down a little."
She admits, her expression softening at my offer of kindness.

"I understand. Meditating might help." She nods in agreement as the
sentiment falls from me, desperate to help her, to ease her worry about
everything that is looming over us.

We travel the rest of the way in silence, but she doesn't let go of my hand
and after around half an hour Aulani slows before a giant pattern in the mix of
dark volcanic and pale traditional sand that lies scattered across the sea floor.

"What is it?" Emma whispers, speaking up and causing us all to turn. She
flushes scarlet, her pale skin looking practically bruised at the attention of so
many surprised eyes. "See Skye, this is why I don't speak up!" She scowls,
turning invisible so we can't see her. Callie chuckles, muting the sound under
her breath as much as she can in an attempt to not hurt Emma's feelings.

"It's alright shy one, show yourself." Aulani comes forward, placing a
hand on Emma's wrist. I have no idea how she knows where she is, making me
wonder even more about her ability to see.

"Sorry... I" Emma stutters, still red in the face as she reappears.

"Do not apologise. Your spirit is bright. Do not diminish your own spark
before it has even had a chance to catch." She sounds like an oracle, like she
knows something we don't. I feel myself uneasy suddenly, not liking the way
she looks into people and reflects back their truths upon them. If she did that to
me, I know I would not like what she had to say. "This is a mandala we have
made this morning in the sand. Each day we choose where we feel calmest for
meditation, and we mark it like this. The symbol helps us align ourselves with
the natural world and its rhythm." She explains, speaking what sounds like
mumbo jumbo, but who am I to judge? "Join hands with us Kindred souls, in a
circle please." She gestures for us to move so we swim to surround the mandala.
Callie keeps hold of my hand, paddling to where she joins hands with the Sirena

341

on the left of Aulani, I think her name is Calypso. We hold hands and I watch Azure, who is opposite me, rolling her eyes. I can only imagine what kind of insults involving hippies are going through her head right now. On second thought, I don't want to.

"Close your eyes, picture yourself as being the ocean itself. Your waves beating against the sands of many different lands. Your body hosting the thrumming heartbeats of millions. Focus on the world around you. The song of nature." Aulani commands us and as the rest of the group closes their eyes, I can't help but close mine only for a moment, before peaking only to see Azure with both eyes open, trying to stop herself from laughing at the looks of serious concentration plastered on the faces of everyone else. My sister is such an ass.

"Azure!" I whisper, glaring at her to be polite and to not offend the hosts who have taken in our wounded. I had watched her make mockery of the Maneli's cleansing ritual, but with such a small group of us it is ceasing to be subtle or funny. She scowls at me before sighing and closing her eyes as her mouth twists into the inkling of a smile. I can't help but wonder if she's not completely wrong about the absurdity of the spectacle, but as she opens one eye and peaks around again I give her a warning glance, my eyes narrowing into a glare. Finally, she rolls her eyes once more before shutting them, relaxing and taking a large measured breath. I close my own eyes, surrendering to the sound of the ocean around me. I feel my eyes roll back into my skull after a little while, my heartbeat becoming louder and louder in my ears. My chest draws in breath from the water around me and my gills open and close at a steady pace, causing my blood pressure to fall. I'm getting light headed when I open my eyes, trying to fight the dizziness. That's when I notice what is going on around me and my eyes snap fully open in surprise.

Where before the ocean had been empty except for the odd straggling shoal of fish, making their way toward the next reef over from them, it is now chocked full of marine life. I watch as another whale shark, just like the one we'd observed yesterday, swoops over the circle, casting a large shadow over the faces of the group. Shoals of manta rays form balls, twisting and turning as they approach us and hovering over us like a flock of birds, bursting from the surface in less that graceful leaps. Spinner dolphins, a pod of about ten, move

342

from the shadows of the distance and toward us, breaking up the mantas as they dart through the water, spinning and singing in their playful folly. The sound alerts the rest of the pod, who open their eyes and inhale collectively, stunned, as I continue to gaze up at the spectacle. I've lived a long time, but I've never seen anything like it. Green turtles come after a few moments, joining the concoction of life that is circling the mandala, moving and jumping from the water and into the air above, energy filled and carefree with liveliness. Bandit angel-fish, blue tang, anemonefish, reef triggerfish and more colourful breeds of salt water shoals flutter past us like butterflies, fragile in their strokes through the water. A blue tang moves past my ear, potentially the same one I had bombarded earlier with my carelessness, and it pecks me on the ear, almost like it's kissing me. Callie laughs as she watches, her gaze upon me one which I wouldn't break for all the world. She is so in love in this moment, with me, with the world around her. It was exactly what I had wanted for her. What I still want for her.

All too quickly, something happens to end the moment.

Calypso, the girl holding Callie's hand, gasps, breaking the connection between them, raising her hand to her mouth in surprise.

"What is it?" Aulani asks her, breaking the connection between herself and the two women beside her too, observing Calypso as her apple green pupils dilate.

"I heard... I heard them." She says, her expression both confused and shocked. Callie turns to me, her expression happy as she says the words aloud, knowing that there is only one explanation for such a phenomenon.

"We found the final vessel, Orion! We did it!"

AZURE

It is unbelievable, Little Miss Sunshine and Light had even managed to win over the non-violent pacifists to our cause. I can't believe these suckers. I have sat through the bullshit kumbayayas and I am officially bored as I swim through the ocean, the day having been passed observing Little Miss Special and all her specialness. *Oh, joy.* The Sirena seem to think she's got gifts linking her with Kanaloa as well, or something to that effect, I don't know. I wasn't really paying attention. According to the young Sirena with sickly lime hair that looks like snot, that Lolana chick says her patients are all healed thanks to the salt baths that, surprise, surprise, Little Miss Sunshine had suggested too.

I stir, looking down at my nails as Calypso and Callie speak to yet more wildlife that none of us can hear. I mean, don't they realise how incredibly boring this is for those of us who aren't branded the picture of special buttercupness? Don't they realise that sometimes, there is a little thing known as showing off that you should really refrain from.

I mean come on, enough is enough, you're making the non-special, mere mortals among us feel bad. I quip internally.

"Azure?" I hear my voice being called so I turn off my sarcastic internal monologue and pretend to look vaguely interested as I raise my eyes from my nails slowly.

"Can I help you?" I say, droll in tone. I know it comes out rude, but watching someone speaking to a dolphin for over an hour tends to do that to a person.

"I just asked if you want to come with us? The Sirena are throwing a luau to celebrate Oscar and Vex finally healing." Orion looks to me, his eyebrows raised in irritation.

Yeah that's right brother, look at me like you actually get to have an opinion about how I act, see how well that ends for you.

I take a deep breath, trying to quell the surges of surliness that are causing me to snap like a bear trap.

"I guess…" I mumble, knowing that if I don't go then Orion will likely kill Vex before I have the chance to end him. I won't let that happen. I think about Vex as I float and the eyes of those looking to me finally turn away, no longer caring what I have to say. I wonder why I can't decide if he's dead meat or just lightly maim-able. Is it because Starlet had chosen that loser to give her visions to? Is it because she kissed him?

No, that can't be it. I conclude, realising I would never spare someone who I had vowed to kill for such ridiculously sentimental reasons. I know I can't kill him yet; I still need him because he's a vessel. I need him to help me get my redemption in the eyes of Atargatis, but after that, well, he's fair game I suppose.

I travel behind the rest of the too bright tailfins as the sun begins to set. Jeez, have we really been out that long? Wasn't it just a billion years ago we were out for early morning meditation? Callie Pierce has officially reached a new level of annoyance.

I shall dub thee, attention whore.

The sky is vast as flickering tongues of flame spark high in the air, snake like in their motion. The beach I'm sitting on isn't that big, and I park my ass far from the crowds of people who are laughing, singing, kissing near the bonfire of the Luau. Alone. I watch them from a distance, their shadows twirling as Polynesian songs rise high around the flames, washing over them all in a blanket of ignorant bliss, except for me who just finds them about the most annoying thing on the planet.

I push my feet out in the sand, wrapping my robe around me tighter as my black hair blows around me in the light breeze that's chilling, even though only hours before the sun scorched this place bare. I watch Orion and Callie as their arms wrap around each other and Callie rests her head on Orion's shoulder. He looks down at her, his gaze one of undying affection.

Bleugh.

"Azure! Come join us!" Orion gestures for me to come closer, but I shake my head, unable to move forward into the light with them. I look around me, where no shadow falls, because I myself am my own shadow that I absorbed long ago. The moon is high above, threatening us all with the heaviness of its full curve and I feel my eyes dilate as I stare up at the stars, praying beyond words that I can somehow become redeemable, but afraid more than anything that I am too far gone. I don't want to sit by the fire with the mer, I don't want to pretend everything is fine, because I know too much of the Psirens to ignore

345

the enormity of what it is to stand against them, especially now with how big they have become.

"Mind if I join you, Love?" The voice creeps across my shoulder like noxious gas. It's him. They've finally been let out by Lolana after having healed far too quickly for my liking.

"Yes, I do actually." I watch as Sophia and Oscar return to the rest of the pod from the jungle behind us. Callie and Orion rise to their feet and Orion claps Oscar on the shoulder as Sophia clings to him as though he might disappear if she lets go. I roll my eyes.

Stupid mer and their stupid Soulmates.

I ball my hands into fists at my side as I whip around to see that Vex has completely ignored me and is sitting down before leaning back onto his elbows.

"What did I *just* say?" I raise my eyebrows, letting my eyes dilate black.

"Woah, Love. Chill." He raises a hand and moves to touch a lock of my hair. I slap him away.

"Get the hell away from me." I snarl, not bothering to raise my voice. He smirks, his white teeth practically day-glow in the darkness just past where the light of the bonfire diminishes. Where I belong.

"What the bloody hell did I do?" He asks me, his eyes actually portraying hurt. I turn from him, focusing on the sloshing of the Hawaiian waters rushing up the beach in an unstoppable caress, washing everything clean, like the hand of a mother. The mother I never was.

"You remember we had a little deal? About you protecting my sister, Vex?" I ask him, wondering how dense you have to be to forget a death threat.

"Yes. I do." He lowers his eyes from mine, puckering his lips as he lets out a sigh and sits up, rubbing the cap of his skull with a broad palm. "I'm sorry. Azure." He apologises and my heart startles in my ribcage, my rage extinguished. I had expected him to be an ass about it, to act like it wasn't his fault. To act like he didn't care, and his promise had been empty, just like mine had been for so many years. I brush my hair back from my face with one hand, looking back to him over my shoulder as he slumps onto his elbows once more. I reach out slowly, like I'm going to caress his cheek, before quickly slapping him so hard my palm rings with the agony.

346

"Bloody hell! Ow!" He exclaims, surprised and scowling.

"That's for kissing my sister." I sigh, turning back and looking out to the ocean, my mood plummeting into depths I seldom explore. The outburst doesn't help me sort through anything. I should be furious with Vex, but I'm not. I'm not angry... it's something else, I just don't know what. I stare over to the others who are eating, laughing and chattering together, they all look so happy, so at peace with themselves.

"Why don't you join them?" Vex is suddenly next to my ear, whispering, among the black shadows my hair casts across my face on all sides.

"You know why not." I reply, feeling my heart rate accelerate once more as I find myself unable to move from his proximity, stuck in the place between the dark and light once more.

"Because we don't belong." He whispers again as my head snaps sideways and my gaze becomes caught looking deep into the bright lilac of his irises.

"No. We don't." I admonish, narrowing my eyes in the shadow. The breeze stirs once more and I hear the rustle of the jungle behind us. The flame of the bonfire flickers, standing strong against the wind but only barely. That's the thing about the light I suppose, it's weak, always wavering too easily. The darkness is much more definitive, stronger, all consuming in its ferocity and too strong to escape when you've had enough. The Sirena begin to dance, rising and casting their detached shadows in a circle around the flame. Callie and Orion watch them, transfixed and clearly impressed by the grace with which they move.

"Don't you ever worry?" He asks me, his gaze burning as I cock an eyebrow.

What is he blithering on about now?

"About what?" I ask him, unsure as I tilt my head to the left, uncertain that I want to be having this conversation with his stupid mug at all.

"That once they're done with the army, they'll turn on us. We don't belong, Love. You know it, we know it. What makes you think they don't know it too, what makes you think that once they're done with the Psiren army they won't move right on to us?" He speaks my worst fear aloud, so much so that I can't bring myself to address the issue. Then I wonder.

It's true though isn't it? What stops them from killing me?

Then, as I ponder this in the night air, I wonder if perhaps I haven't thought about the truth of this because I don't care. If after this is all over I get Starlet back, then perhaps I'd feel differently, but I've already told Little Miss Sunshine the truth of my thoughts about it all. I have nothing left to live for.

I watch their shadows, that of the eternally beautiful Sirena indistinguishable from that of the mer. The same. United in belief and cause.

"I wouldn't blame them. I've murdered Vex, you don't know what I've done." Vex looks to me, his eyes wide at my sudden confession of the true me, the darkness that had become synonymous with my name many centuries ago.

"It doesn't matter. You're still beautiful. You're still a hero today. Even if you have done all those things." He says it like he knows, like his meek experience with the dark, which has been diluted as it's passed from generation to generation of Psiren, equips him to know me. Equips him to make statements that are so clearly deluded in their thinking. I speak my next few words with resentment for my own existence coursing through my veins, fighting the dark poison lacing my blood. I speak that which I know to be true most of all as I stare into his face, wanting him to see that what I say next is with the most sincerity I can muster.

"Did you ever think that, perhaps, the world isn't built for people like us? Perhaps, Vex, it'd be better off if we were sand."

27
The Last Sanctuary
CALLIE

Long after the last flickering embers of the bonfire of the luau have died, we slink through the current toward the over-water bungalow that we have been so graciously given by the Sirena. The rest of the pod is moving to their accommodation as well, but luckily for Orion and I we've been given a bungalow to ourselves. I feel relieved at the thought of some alone time with him, especially because the idea of going through the final whirlpool and returning to the Occulta Mirum tomorrow has me on edge.

Azure and Vex are in the bungalow next to us, so I can only hope I won't be listening to them bicker all night as I watch them climb up a metal ladder and onto the deck of the small hut, which rises atop stilts from the sea. I watch as Azure slams the door in Vex's face before locking it, and he shakes it in its frame, attempting to get inside a few times before giving up and swearing harshly. He turns, leaning over the railing of the small deck that spreads out from the front door as I observe him from the water.

Orion and I swim, our bodies relaxed and in sync with our strokes as we approach the ladder that leads up to our own deck.

Waiting a few moments, Orion holds the moonstone pendant in his palm so it can absorb the beams of the almost full moon. I watch as his scales shimmer to flesh and his legs return before he climbs from the ocean and up onto the wooden platform. I follow him, taking a few moments to gather myself before exiting the water.

As I reach the top of the ladder, Orion helps me up before pushing my naked body behind him. I peer around his ripped torso, watching the two naked men staring at each other with feral competitiveness plastered across their faces. Vex watches with a smirk as Orion pushes me behind him.

"That's alright, mate, nothing I haven't seen before." He yells over to us and Orion growls in a low tone as he continues. "Don't stop the lady from looking either mate. If she wants to get a good old eyeful of this..." He gestures downward to his naked self. "Then let her. Don't be such a bloody spoilsport now! Or are you afraid she might see something she likes better and..." He continues to taunt Orion, and I can tell that it's working.

"I'm going to kill him. Dead. Callie, get inside!" He barks, turning his to peer at me over his shoulder while still shielding me from view with his own nakedness. The two men stand, full frontal and feral in the moonlight, examining one another in far too much detail as Orion holds up a steady hand and blasts a wave of air at his opponent.

I hear a splash followed by a... "You bloody cheater!" as I open the door to the bungalow and step in sideways, before yanking Orion into the over-water space behind me.

"Callie!" He yells in protest.

"Hey, if you're going to beat the crap out of him can you at least get freaking dressed first? I don't want anything getting ripped off! Capiche?" I scowl at him and he rolls his eyes as I continue, "However, I was thinking, how about we make tonight about us. Not about the tentacled Brit with the bad attitude?" I cock an eyebrow and he sighs, rubbing a hand through his hair which is still dripping wet.

"Fine. But if he so much as..." He begins but I shake my head, no longer content on listening.

As I pivot on the balls of my feet, turning away from him and his male pride, I take in the bungalow, if you can even call it that. It's more like a hut really, in the fact that it's tiny but functional. The inner space is completely made up of thick cypress wood with a thatched roof. The floor however isn't wood, but glass, giving a clear view down into the ocean below. I see fish swimming beneath my feet, drifting about their existence without expressing

350

so much as an inkling that they know I'm here. The decor of the room is simple as the only real furniture it holds is a king size, four-poster bed with white linen drapes and fine white linen sheets and two cypress wood bedside tables on either sides of the bed frame. Propped beside the left table is my armour, placed there by the Sirena who had taken it from me before I had gone to first visit Vex, Oscar and Jack.

I take a step toward the wall, looking to Orion as I grab yet more white robes from a hook on the back of the front door, throwing him one and placing the other over my shoulders.

I sidle closer to him as he dresses, tying the robe around his waist with a disgruntled expression as I stand on tiptoes on the glass pane. I step with light feet over the criss-crossing wooden beams that hold the floor together and look up to him with fluttering lashes as I smile, feeling relieved.

"Alone at last." I sigh, reaching up and placing my hands around his neck. I don't kiss him though, instead nuzzling my cheek into the warmth of his chest and seeking comfort over passion. Orion exhales, crushing my body to him and resting his chin on the top of my head where he plants a soft kiss. I pull away after a few moments, feeling the need to lie down.

"Hey, wait. I've been waiting for a hug like this for a long time. Just a few more moments." He complains as I roll my eyes, but secretly smile, loving the fact that he doesn't want the embrace to end. After a few more minutes, we part and I take a few quick steps across the glass floor, careful not to trip on the puddles of water that I've left behind me, before bounding onto the bed.

I close my eyes, looking up to the rotating wooden ceiling fan, noting that the hut holds no windows, except the glass in the floor, so we have all the privacy we could want. Suddenly, everything in my body goes limp and I find myself almost ready to cry.

"We did it." I say, breathless and emotional as I lie back into the mattress, which holds me like a cloud.

"We did, but we still don't have the Pieces of Eight." Orion reminds me, flopping back onto the mattress beside me. I turn my head, looking into his beautiful eyes and realising how much I have missed being alone with him.

351

"I know…" I say, tucking my knees up and nuzzling onto his chest again. He puts his arms around me as I lie in the nook of his arm, head against the place where his heart lies beneath, beating. We lay here in silence for a matter of moments, as the enormity of what is going to happen in what could be only hours settles over us both.

"Orion…" I breathe, feeling my eyes well with tears.

"Yes, Princess?" He replies, using the nickname that I haven't heard in so long. I miss those days, where everything was new, when years spread out before me and everything was certain. All that is gone now, and nothing is assured.

"I'm afraid." I whisper the words and my tears spill over, my body shaking as I sob silently and Orion cradles me, kissing the top of my head.

"Shhhh… Callie… Shhhh…" He says, holding me close. It's no use though, because his own voice is faltering. In this space, this tiny shack in the middle of the sea, there is nowhere left to hide from what is to come. There is nothing left to do but fear the future and to acknowledge that the death of those I love, those I cherish, is entirely possible and probably inevitable. I feel my gut tense at the abhorrence of loss, of Orion's heart faltering in its beat and I melt down, becoming a mess of emotion and pain in his arms.

"Callie… Shhh. Listen to me." Orion sits up, pushing me from his chest and placing a finger under my chin, he raises my eyes to his, wiping cloudy tears from my cheeks. "What is this about?" He looks concerned.

"We're going to war tomorrow Orion. I'm involved in this Conduit… we don't even know what it is. What if I die?" I ask him and he frowns.

"Why? What do you know? Why would you say something like that?" He looks terrified, just like me.

"I don't know anything. I swear, this isn't like before with Titus… but what if… what if that's why I've been chosen? Maybe I was chosen because Atargatis knew I was willing to die for the mer?" Speaking my fear makes it real, and Orion's forehead creases as his expression crumples beneath the weight of my words.

"Callie…" He is speechless, unable to speak words that comfort me because he doesn't know if what I'm saying is right or not. The only person who knows that is the Goddess.

"Orion, I don't want to die. I want to be with you. I chose you. I chose to come back here to be with you. This can't be it, can it?" I ask him, placing a hand on the side of his neck as I feel my heart rate refuse to slow.

"Callie… I…" He is still speechless as I stand from the bed, pacing across the glass of the floor.

"I mean, the Goddess wouldn't do that to me, right? I was given a choice… a choice to be with you or become a Goddess… Why would she just take me away like that after everything?" I ask him, my eyes still brimming with unshed tears.

"It doesn't work like that Callie. Life isn't fair. You know that." His expression is broken, torn at the thought of losing me again.

"Orion I'm afraid… I'm eighteen years old. I don't want to die." I feel my bottom lip shake as my eyes spill tears once more. The chilling realisation that I've brought on with my own words running rampant down my spine like ice water.

Orion strides to me, clamping his mouth down upon mine as he lifts me off my feet, kissing me so intensely that I know he's just as scared as I am. His hands reach for my robe, trying to undress me, but I refuse him, pushing away from him and opening my eyes, breaking the kiss abruptly.

"No… please Orion." I whisper, my face tear stained and frightened.

"Callie, please… I need you." He pulls me to him again, the two of us caught in a tango of pleasure and pain. Denial and acceptance of what is to come.

"Orion, if you make love to me now… it's like you're saying it's the last time. It's like you're saying I'm going to die. Like it's over. I can't do that. I need you to believe in me, believe that I can come through this in one piece, believe that we will have the future together that was promised. I just… I love you so much. I can't get lost in you. I can't." I exclaim, connecting with his gaze on a level I can only describe as soul deep in its ferocity.

353

"Why not?" He begs, pulling me closer still, his fingertips tracing down my spine in a wanton and delicate caress.

"Because if you take me now then I will never walk out of those doors again. I'll just stay here, lost in you." I explain, but he pulls me closer still, kissing me gently this time, tickling my lips with his as a smile graces his masculine features. I reach up, kissing him back this time, but gently and with caution.

"Alright." He breathes, exhaling as his breath tickles my face and the icy blue glow of his irises shines down over me. I stare up to him, doing what I had done the first time he had ever made love to me.

I take in his features, ingraining each one in exquisite detail into my memory. Never wanting to forget his face.

I look up into his eyes, my soul seeking its other half and knowing in this moment, when he doesn't push, that he is different.

Now, I think to myself, *that's the kind of man you marry.*

We lay together in our robes, holding one another and talking for hours, propped up on the fluffy pillows of the four-poster bed. The topic of conversation is not the kind of thing you'd expect us to be talking about on a night like this. You'd expect us to be talking about the war, the Psirens, the Pieces of Eight, the other members of the pod. Instead, we don't. We do what I have always wanted. We really get to know each other, at long last.

"So, you kissed Daryl before?" Orion asks me, his expression amused.

"Well, yeah, but Chloe spiked my drink!" I say, remembering how off kilter I had felt. Orion's face lights up at this new information.

"Oh you mean the notorious little flirt who thought she could get me in bed with her after just a few words of conversation at your party?" He smirks at me and I blink a few times.

"Yeah, she always acted like she could have had anyone she wanted. Guess she didn't count on the soulmates thing." I say, laughing at Chloe's long forgotten immaturity.

"No, she didn't, but regardless… I was thinking about what you said, about soulmates not being real…" Orion begins, making my laughter cease, intent on hearing what he has to say on the subject. "I was thinking, even if you weren't the other half of my soul. You're still the love of my very, very long life." He kisses me on the cheek and I blush. We're on our sides, like we had lain in the sand together on our beach in San Diego, so very long ago, propped up on one elbow and listening to one another intently.

"You know you never did show me how you died. I wasn't ready before… but I want to see now." I request this of him and he laughs, shaking his head and rolling his eyes.

"You're a glutton for punishment, but alright." He places his fingers on my temples and closes his eyelids slowly, taking me back.

Philippe whinnies, bounding from foot to foot, hooves slamming down against the dusty earth in a gallop. I am seated atop him and I can feel Orion's heart hammering harder than I ever thought possible. He holds up his sword as they race into the din of men praying that they will survive just this one more battle. They're coming, the enemy, crying out beneath the midday sun. A cry of both terror and warning. A cry of war. The spear comes from nowhere, slamming through Orion's back and into Philippe. Was it an enemy spear? Was it friendly fire? I suppose he never knew, so neither will I.

Philippe falls to the ground, a clatter of armour reaching my ears like the hollow sounds of a gong being struck, signalling that life is almost at an end. He lies there, a man and his horse, bleeding to death on the ruddy earth. Everything is pain and chaos as the battle continues around us and the tenuous traces of life that once was begin to fade.

I gasp, exiting the memory. This time though I don't cry. I had felt such sorrow the first time I had seen Orion's memory, exiting before I had to see him die back in our apartment before we were Crowned Rulers. I do not cry now, because I know it is the reality of the world we live in. War is the reality of life for everyone. Whether it's a war on ideology, that which is like fighting smoke, or war on those in far off lands, the world is covered in it. I had been naive

355

before, young and inexperienced, but it's now I know that war is a constant. For, now, we're heading into our own war, fighting to protect the people above the surface of the waters we inhabit. Those same people who do not care to look after the planet they have been gifted, and yet still I will fight for them.

"Are you alright?" Orion asks me, pulling me to his chest with haste.

"Yes, I'm fine. I can handle it. You were right though…" I begin as he raises his eyebrows and his gaze grows intense.

"I was?" He questions me as I exhale, feeling my heart palpitate.

"Yes, this is no place for children." I admit, contented by the words that leave my lips.

"Oh. Yes, I agree. We are built for it though. I can tell you that." He says these words as I roll from his embrace, feeling anxious as my feet jiggle a restless rhythm.

"I suppose I feel like I'm floundering so frequently it barely feels that way at all any more. It just feels normal to not know what the hell I'm doing." I snort slightly, finding my incapability hilarious in the scope of events happening around us. I had thought when it came to something like this, I would have grown, would be strong and immovable, a warrior. Instead I don't feel like much more than an eighteen-year-old playing dress up.

"Look at how you convinced the Sirena to fight with us today though…" Orion begins but I cut him off.

"Didn't you hear what they said? They'll fight, but they won't harm another living thing. That's not much use." I shrug off my success, doubting how much use people who won't cause harm on principle will be in a war zone.

"Yes, but I'm sure it'll work out." He kisses me on the forehead.

"You don't know that!" I say, gazing at him from across the cotton sheets as I feel my fear threatening to engulf everything once more.

"It's just what you say." Orion replies, his eyes full of concern.

"Well, don't. Just be honest with me. Please." I beg him and he sighs, puckering his full lips and scratching the stubble along his jawline.

"Fine. I don't know what's going to happen. I don't know if we'll survive, or if we're taking these people off to the slaughter. I have no idea." He confesses and amazingly, instead of worse, his acknowledgement of this harsh reality makes me feel better.

"Thank you." I kiss him on the cheek, holding his hand in mine and squeezing it as they lie atop on the sheets between us. "I've been thinking. About what ifs... what if this goes wrong... I had an idea, but it means cutting one of our most precious assets loose. I could send someone else, but a task like what I have in mind, it requires a large amount of trust." I explain as Orion frowns, concerned before I've even voiced my plan.

"What is it?" he asks me, his eyes curious and concerned all at once. Regardless, the caring in his gaze centres me for a moment, making my anxiety dissolve as I feel him right here in the moment with me. Letting me know I'm not alone.

"Well, I was thinking, if we fail, if we can't stop Solustus and Saturnus... the first place they're going to go is ashore. I've been worried about..." I begin but he cuts me off, placing a finger to my lips as his eyes widen.

"You don't even have to ask. Yes. I don't know why I didn't think of that before. We need to warn them." He strokes my robed shoulder, his fingers gentle and soothing in their caress. I smile, I knew he would understand. "So, speaking of our origins, you think we'll just come out near the Occulta Mirum tomorrow?" He asks me and I frown. I hadn't thought of that.

"I don't know... I hadn't really thought about it. I suppose so... I guess that's where the other pods will come out too."

"We'd better have a plan already in place for how to utilise each one of their armies then." Orion sighs, running his hand through his hair.

"I suppose so. Don't we need to talk about it first though?" I ask him. I'm unsure of how these types of battle plans work, but I am sure that communication is key.

"Yes, usually, but I don't really want to sit around talking while the Psirens start picking us off." He confesses.

"That's a good point." I nod, unsure of what to suggest. In the end, I let it go, too weary to think about everything that's resting on just us two and the choices we make.

"If we ever do a world trip, promise me it will involve less war talk and more alcohol?" I plead, raising an eyebrow and plastering a smile on my face, trying to lighten the mood.

"Oh definitely. A little more alcohol, little less stress…" Orion holds me close to him again, squeezing me against his body.

With that, we start to plan the trip we don't know if we'll ever take. We talk about the past, about the future, and what we want for it together. We dream, endlessly, and without caution, because in a few short days we could be gone.

AZURE

I swing the doors open toward me, revealing myself to the ocean in front of the hut that spreads out as far as the eye can see. Isle Meahuna is invisible in the dark, except for the odd flickering flame of a torch and the warm night air blows inward, moving the dark locks of hair, that are still damp, from my shoulders as I take it all in now.

Vex is sitting on the deck, stark naked, just where I left him, so I reach to my left, grabbing a robe and throwing it at him. I haven't got time for naked and entirely unimpressive men right now.

"Cheers, Love." He grabs the robe, which has landed on his shoulder, still slick with sea water.

"Yeah, yeah, can't have you blinding any wandering locals." I roll my eyes, feeling the predictability of his not-giving-a-crap attitude wearing thin.

"It's true the body of a God can be quite harmful to mere mortals…" He pulls the robe over his shoulders. "Better cover up, protect and bloody serve and all that jazz."

"I don't recall any Gods with tentacles, though my mythology might be a little off…I never was much of a student." I smirk, taking a few steps forward and sitting down on the deck beside him, bored of the entire ten square feet of

358

accommodation we've been provided already. I could have built a sea hut from scratch with more personality than this crap heap.

"Gods wish they had my tentacles... Goddesses wouldn't be off ogling humans if they had this many arms at their disposal." He wiggles his eyebrows and I almost laugh, though not quite.

"I don't know... Callie doesn't seem too keen. She's back with Orion now, so you can't be all that great in the bedroom." I know it's probably a low blow, but I don't care. He let my sister die and apology or no, I have decided that it is my job to make the rest of his existence as miserable as possible.

"Little Miss Priss? Not really my style, Love. If I'm honest, it was the darkness that attracted me, not her. Still... won't stop me using that night against Onion head at every bleedin' opportunity." He stares off into the distance to where flickering light boasts the lives of the pure... unable to look into my eyes as he mashes the English language. He swings his legs, clearly just as bored as I am. "Do you wanna play a game, Love?" He asks, his eyes hooded heavily by pale lids.

"Like what?" I demand, suspicious. This has to be some sort of dirty trick so he can get some before he goes into battle.

"I dunno. I- Spy?" He replies, shrugging and licking the front of his teeth.

"You're not serious?" I exclaim, surprise evident in my tone.

"You got a fag in that robe of yours?" He peers down into my visible cleavage and I slap him on the forehead.

"Back off! You know I don't!" I yell, my voice coming out louder than I intend, but in my usual style I struggle to find the energy to care.

"Well then it's I-Spy or I go and pick a fight with Onion head. Nicotine cravings are the worst in human form, bad enough that I'd risk even seeing him bollock stark nude again for a nice shot at a left hook to his pretty face." He looks to Callie and Orion's hut. No doubt they're doing it. Some stupid last night goodbye or something ridiculously over the top and sentimental. I shudder at their only too obvious affection for one another.

"Fine. I-Spy it is." I admonish. Anything to prevent seeing my brother in the midst of ploughing his soulmate. I've seen a lot of crap, but that shit takes the biscuit and afterwards I'll be needing a lot more than therapy.

359

"I-Spy with my little eye... something beginning with... S" Vex puckers his lips, crossing his bulging arms across his robed chest and sighing outward.

"Sea?" I guess, bored and entirely unamused by something that is supposed to be a game.

"Yeah, but that was easy." Vex sighs, amusement twinkling behind his irises.

"Well of course it's easy, there's only the sea for miles!" I retort, exasperated at his lack of imagination.

"Fine... I-Spy with my little eye, something beginning with S. Again." Vex says, eyes upward. I follow his gaze.

"Sky." I blurt, bored out of my skull at his inability to come up with a decent challenge. "I thought this was supposed to be fun and I'm about ready to go impale myself on a sea urchin just to end the suffering. You suck at games." I insult him without a second thought, scratching the underside of my neck with my long fingernails. Vex shuffles, turning to face me on the deck and making sure he holds my gaze with a salacious smile.

"Fine... here's a mystery for you. I-Spy with my little eye something beginning with...C" He doesn't turn away from me, instead staring at me intently with a dirty smirk plastered across his face. My expression falls, deadpan and still unimpressed.

"You're such an asshole." I cock my head, rolling my eyes and sighing. He is a huge burden on my time. I'm actually not far from building another hut just so I can put him in it and lock the door behind me.

"What!? I didn't bloody say anything!" He feigns innocence but he and I both known to which C word he was referring.

"Yeah, yeah, tell it to Poseidon. I'm sure he'll be glad to know his vessel is a potty mouth." I roll my eyes, slapping him on the arm.

"I think you need to stop bloody hitting me, alright? I am the vessel for Poseidon, as you just so nicely reminded me. No touching of the vessel please, Love." He gazes into my eyes with irises that blaze lilac and I scrunch up my face, unamused even still.

360

"I'll hit you if I want." I slap him again, this time across the face.

"Oi!" He says, grabbing my wrist as I raise my arm again to deliver yet another slap. He pulls me toward him, growling like a feral dog. I debate spitting in his face, but his gaze holds me in place, unable to move as I continue to stare at him, purposefully not making him aware of any emotion I might or might not be feeling.

"I-spy with my little eye, something beginning with A." I say, leaning forward and making sure he knows I'm looking at him and nowhere else. He lets go of my wrists and rolls his eyes.

"Arsehole." He says, though I can't work out whether or not he's saying it in response to my challenge, or in insult. I sit back, putting my hands on the damp decking and letting my hair fall back in a thick wave of dark tangles.

"Very good, Vex." I retort, smiling and satisfied at last.

We sit, watching the night pass as the stars revolve around the earth in too slow motion, silent.

"Why did you say yes when I asked you to protect Starlet?" I speak my thought aloud, though to begin with I don't really intend to. The silence makes a nice change from Callie's all too chipper motivational speeches, or the slur of foreign tongues mincing the English language.

Vex turns around, his eyes glassy as though wet from tears. I wonder if he's been thinking about the upcoming battle, fearing for his life. It's true there aren't many things to fear when you're a Psiren, and even less when you're young and a Psiren, so perhaps he's afraid at the thought of real battle, of death. He licks his bottom lip, the heavy moon casting shadows across his bony skull.

"I saw what the Psirens did to that city. It wasn't... I don't know. What they had promised. They acted like we belonged there. It wasn't until after I saw those ruins that I realised they didn't want to take the city for themselves; they just wanted to bloody destroy it. I don't know. I kind of like this planet, how it is. Fast food, fast women, cigarettes, alcohol. It's not all bad. I just figure it's better off without all the bollocks like mass murder. But what do I know?" He shrugs, not looking at me as he speaks. I am thoughtful at his words.

"You didn't see the world when I was alive. It was awful. Perhaps if you had you'd see why they want to end it now." I reveal, feeling myself open ever so slightly to him, it must be all that battle fever getting to me or something.

Oh, for God's sake. I cuss at the thought of such sentimentalism.

"Maybe so, but it's not so bad now. Not compared. I also don't want my family to get slaughtered." He looks up to the sky and suddenly I see him differently. He's not a just Psiren, he's a recently turned human, he has roots, an origin. A family.

"You have a family?" I say, surprised. He narrows his eyes at me, cocking his head to the left in confusion.

"Of course I bleeding do. What did you think I just sprung up out of the bloody deep?" He asks me the question and I shrug. Everyone I deal with is so old, I hadn't even thought about the fact that these new Psirens would have living family. It startles me, giving me tenuous connections to those who walk on land for the first time in centuries. Perhaps the Psirens and mer weren't as detached from humans as I had thought.

"Sorry, I just hadn't thought about it." I shrug, realising now that Vex has motivation to side with the mer, even more than I do.

"I don't know. Those two, Solustus and the other one, they just seem like bloody psychos to me. For whatever it's worth." He looks to me and I nod, agreeing with him on this one point at least.

"They are. They are working together which makes them strong, but Solustus can't be happy with that. The power within the Necrimad was his once, and I've never thought of him as the kind of man who would share." I swing my legs, thinking of the man with the silver hair and swordfish tail who I had studied, even confided in at times. How had he become so power hungry? Or perhaps he had always been that way and I was just too messed up to notice.

"You do for family I suppose. That nonce Saturnus is his brother after all. Maybe it's all that bloody romanticism with bonds between brothers and all that other twaddle." Vex wonders aloud; articulate in his response as always. I look away, my eyes resting on Orion and Callie's hut, frowning at the truth of Vex's words and wondering if the fact I am still here doesn't have anything to do with getting Starlet back at all. Perhaps my real motivation is just feet away,

362

snuggled up with Callie Pierce under a blanket of denial about what tomorrow will bring.

"You do for family." I agree as we still in our conversation yet again. Sitting side by side, soundless, we wait for the sun to bring dawn, and with it, war.

28
The Triangle
CALLIE

Before the first light of dawn breaks over the glistening horizon, Orion and I swim across the row of over-water bungalows, holding our robes above the water in a basket as we paddle in the dim light and seeking out those who we must now say goodbye to, even if it is for the best reasons. I climb the ladder, pulling myself up and feeling sober in the fact that the day I had never wanted to come is upon us.

As we stand on the deck, Orion and I place our robes back over our shoulders and tie them tightly at the waist, dumping the basket and becoming nervous about the conversation we're about to have. We glance at each other but do not know what to say.

Remaining silent, I take a few steps forward, holding up a hand before I knock on the door of the bungalow and after, exhaling with a heavy heart, Orion claims my hand in his, comforting me when I need it most.

I knock, the sun's rays threatening us with so little time in which to convey so many words, and the door swings forward, revealing Sophia who is wrapped in a robe and Oscar who's lying down, snoozing on the bed behind her.

"Callie! What are you doing here? Did something happen?" She speaks too quickly, the anxiety obvious in the straining of her voice as her face turns immediately worried. She's been through so much, as has Oscar, and I cannot help but know now, despite my disappointment that I may never see her again, that I am making the right choice.

"Let's take this inside." Orion asserts, ushering us through the door.

We stand upon the glass floor of the hut, which is designed identical to ours, as Sophia shakes Oscar awake. He is still recovering from the torment of Caedes and even if his body doesn't show it, I know it's taken its toll mentally too. He startles, grabbing Sophia by the hand as he sits bolt upright, cringing as his internal injuries spark hidden pain throughout his body. His blonde hair is messy and his green eyes sparkle with sleep as he catches us in his field of vision, frowning with confusion.

"Good morning Oscar." Orion bows his head, putting the man at ease with an awkward smile. I laugh, feeling my wet hair dripping down my spine.

"What is this about?" Oscar asks, curious, as Sophia sits down on the edge of the bed beside him, keeping his hand in hers and holding it tightly.

"We have been talking, and we need to speak with you about something of utmost importance." I swallow, feeling what I must ask them to do weighing like lead in my stomach. I know, as I enter the moment of asking, that it's not what I must ask them that is awful, but why I must put this measure in place which scares me so deeply.

"What is it? Callie, why do you look so..." Sophia begins but I raise a hand, looking deeply into the eyes of the couple. I have made the right choice; it could be nobody else.

"I have something to ask of you both. I know, for you in particular Oscar, it is a big ask. But I must ask you none the less, not only as a Queen, but as your friend." I begin, feeling my wet feet become slippery on the glass of the floor as I fidget, nervous.

"Whatever it is, we will oblige. You have done so much for me, Callie. You showed me I had power when I thought I had none." Sophia smiles at me.

"Okay, well, I need to tell you right now that you will not be coming with us through the final whirlpool. You won't be coming to war." I explain, smiling to them, happy I can at least deliver this piece of relief.

"What do you mean? Of course we're coming!" Oscar sits up straighter, cringing as I cock an eyebrow.

"No. You're not. You've both been through enough already. I have to be there, I'm a vessel. You on the other hand do not. Besides, I have a far more important job for the both of you." Orion looks to me, smiling and letting me take the lead. After all, it is because of me that we need their help.

"What, what is it that could be so important?" Sophia asks me, her eyes filled with fear. I stare upon her for a moment, loving her expression because she cares. She knows what it is to love and lose. She knows the value of what I must ask her now to protect.

"I need you to take a long route back to San Diego. I need you to go to my old house. Then I need you to get my mom and sister out of San Diego. I don't care where they go, just get them somewhere safe, somewhere inland. Here's the address." I say the words and Sophia purses her lips as I reach deep into the pocket of my robe. I pull out a half page I'd ripped from the phonebook in the nightstand, the only paper I could find in the bungalow, with my address scrawled upon it and feel myself letting go of my family as Sophia takes the paper from me. My heart shatters at the thought that I might never see them again.

"You think that's necessary?" She asks me, her expression deadly serious as she places the paper in her own pocket.

"I don't know, but what I do know is that I'm not risking my family if this thing goes wrong. Get them out of there. Stay with them. Stay out of the sunlight. But you can protect them. I believe that's why you've been gifted such protective magic." I look to her, trusting them with the most precious thing in my world. My family.

"Are you sure? I mean..." Sophia starts, looking to me and unable to believe that I think we may fail.

"Sophia, when I was born my parents kept my identity from the mer so that I wouldn't fall prey to Psirens. Now it's my turn to do the same for my mother and sister. I trust you and Oscar with this. Nobody else." I hold out my hand to her, a sign that I believe she can do it. I don't care if we win or lose, as long as I know they're safe. I know I can't fight with the pressure that they may fall victim to Saturnus, or worse, Solustus.

366

"Okay. We'll do it." She stands, taking my hand and pulling me into her for a long hug as I close my eyes, feeling her proximity like a stab in the gut.

"This might be the last time I see you. Tell my mom I love her. Tell Kayla that you'll take her to see a dolphin once she's old enough. On my orders… and I expect you to follow out that promise so long as the seas remain safe." I say, giving a faux stern expression. She smiles, a tear trickling down one cheek as she lets out a laugh.

"Okay. Swimming with dolphins. We can do that, right Oscar?" She turns to him and he nods at me, seeing the desperation for comfort in my stare.

"Of course. Anything for Callie." He winks at me and I smile back at him. Orion reaches out a hand as he leans forward on the bed to meet him.

"You stay safe Your Highness and if you need anything, don't be afraid to ask." He nods to Orion, his gaze sincere.

"We've got another metal master coming, Oscar, so we won't go without, but I'm sure he's nothing compared to you." He states, giving Oscar a sly smile, knowing full well how talented he is when it comes to armour and weapons.

"Oh and the Psirens…Give em hell from me." Oscar's expression turns dark.

"Oh don't worry about that. I'm sure with the Scots on our side they'll be nothing more than chowder after all is said and done." Orion laughs, his voice portraying the most false of optimistic tones I have ever heard come from him. With one last look to Sophia and Oscar we walk from the hut quickly, knowing only too well that we are racing the sun.

A few hours later and we're hovering, miles away from where we have left Sophia and Oscar and next to the whirling torrent of the portal to wherever our final destination will be. Azure and Vex look practically vibrant with the energy they're mustering, despite the fact that my own heart is heavy. I'm clad once more in the lightweight armour that had been on the floor of our bungalow and Orion is suited and booted in armour too, the trident flat against his spine. The Sirena hang in the water, smaller in number than we had hoped, and without a speck of protective clothing anywhere. I sigh, rolling my eyes, they really aren't thinking they're going to be getting attacked at all and I worry momentarily that we are leading them to the slaughter.

"Are you ready?" I turn to the pod, whose expressions are solemn.

"Wait, Oscar and Sophia aren't here yet!" Cole calls to me from the back of the gathering of mer.

"Oscar and Sophia won't be joining us. They are headed ashore to warn the coast guard and the sanctums, as well as Callie's family." Orion informs them and the maiden's faces drop.

"But Sophia's protective powers..." Rose calls out as I grimace. I had known there would be questions about my choice regarding my family.

"Sophia is best suited for this *because* she has protective powers. Those are better utilised saving human lives should it come to that. We need a second line of defence." I clarify, causing Rose's queries to fall into silence. I adjust my tiara visor against my forehead, feeling my heart palpitate. Soon we're going to run out of things to talk about and then what? War? It feels too soon. I don't feel ready.

"Everyone on your guard for exit from the portal please. We don't know how close to the city we will be coming out. So, it's important we're on guard." Cole calls out as Orion opens his mouth to speak. He turns to me upon seeing that Cole has us covered, as we float there in the soothing Hawaiian current, waiting to enter the battle which may very well end us all.

"Are you okay?" Orion asks me and I frown, knowing not to lie to him at a time like this.

"I'm nervous. I love you." I reach up and kiss him on the cheek, savouring his scent as it washes over me with his proximity.

With that we spin, the pods at our back, and move forward, letting the hurtling speed of the whirlpool encase us, whisking us off to the place from which we have come. The Occulta Mirum.

The whirlpool spits out my body into the waters that I have most feared ever since I left. My stomach churns with nerves, feeling unprepared in every sense

368

of the word for this moment. I take a second to centre myself, regaining my upright position in the water before opening my eyes. That's when I realise something. The light is dim here. Not what I expect. That's when I also notice that we aren't close to the Occulta Mirum. In fact, I have absolutely no idea where we are.

"Callie." My name is called by a familiar voice that chills my blood, but only because I am so shocked that it's here.

"Shaniqua?" I call out, feeling her presence even though it's been so long since we were last together.

"Yes, my dear girl. Oh, aren't you a sight!" She appears from behind the corner of a square rock and the hairs on the back of my neck rise as she nears me. Her thick black hair falls down her spine, caressing the dark skin of her shoulders with its soft flow as her lime green scales shimmer, a light in the darkest of moments. I gape, unsure of where I am or why she's here.

"Why are you here? What... I don't understand!" I burst, my voice a high-pitched muddle of sound. I feel Orion at my spine, his touch as familiar to me now as the ocean's caress. "Orion... look!" I exclaim, my mind racing as her face fills my vision. Orion grins.

"Yes, I see her too." He moves forward, taking her into his arms with a huge smile on his face. He twirls her around. "How glad I am to see you, Shaniqua." He breathes, holding her in the water for a good minute before she pushes back from him and he takes in her appearance. How welcome her friendly face is to us, just as we are on the cusp of war and headed toward an end unknown.

"Why are you here? Where is here?" I stutter, feeling the rest of the pod watching me, watching this reunion of parted souls, across many hundreds of miles, with awe.

"Oh, dear child. You have come so far, and yet you still know so very little. Surely you didn't think the Circle would leave you so ill prepared for a war they had caused?" She asks me with sadness in her eyes and I shrug.

"I don't know. I've been feeling pretty alone since this all started." I admit, unable to quite put what is happening into some kind of linear sense. Shaniqua watches me, knowingly, in every sense of the word.

"I have been sent by Atargatis. To wait for you here, in the most poignant location that shows why the power of a God, or in this case, a Goddess, has no place in this mortal realm. Welcome, all of you, to Atlantis."

"Atlantis?" I spit the word, unable to hold it in my mouth. Orion shifts his gaze, his eyes wider than I've ever seen them.

"Yes. We are currently in a pocket dimension created by the Circle of Eight. It holds the ruins of the lost city that one of their own, Atargatis, doomed. We are removed from time here by a small increment. Buying you time to come up with a plan. If you look around, you'll see that all whirlpools now lead to this location. I am sure we do not have long before the others arrive." She looks down to an invisible, non-existent watch on her wrist, cocking one eyebrow as I stare around, noticing that multiple whirlpools encase the circular space.

I examine the rocks that Shaniqua had appeared behind, realising that they aren't just rocks, but ruins. They sprawl, a mixture of dark greyish silver, light blue and gold stone, which rises in half collapsed and dome-like architecture, silent. The city vanishes beyond certain boundaries into nothing, where shadow encroaches this place on all sides and is distinguished only against the roaring whirlpools that encase us. The city has obviously been decimated, and yet the unique and strange cyclical shapes of buildings remain beautiful, if not a little eerie in their still emptiness. I try to get a closer look, seeking out more detail and trying to take in all I can, but I struggle to see beyond half collapsed turrets and spires which now fall into slopes of rubble, dust and the bones of those they have buried. The odd half-light of this place obscures much of it and as I stare into almost shadows and light, squinting to see, Azure perks up behind me, her expression entirely unimpressed as I turn to face her.

"So wait... let me get this straight, the Circle just removed a whole city from time and space?" She speaks up and Shaniqua's eyes rest on her, perched atop Philippe.

"Yes. People have marvelled over the Bermuda Triangle for years. This is what lies there, but it vibrates within our dimension ever so slightly out of frequency. Meaning you can't see it. Some people have crossed over, but

370

they're lost, unable to return to our world. It is only now, the first time in over half a millennium, that the dimension has been accessible. It's opened its doors, for you." She gestures back to the city.

"Figures. Entitled much?" Azure points out what we should all obviously be focusing on, *not.*

"You might think so. But these ruins are home to some of the most precious mystical items within the seven seas, they need to be protected. Hence why we have to hurry. Time is out of frequency, but only slightly, we have to move quickly if we are to return to the Pacific before the blood moon rises." She is so attuned to everything that's been going on I can't help but wonder if she's been spying on us. Then again, the Goddess clearly knew what was happening if she'd reached out to the one person she knew we couldn't help but trust.

"Hurry, for what?" I ask her, curious, as to what we can do without the other pods present.

"Come, Orion, Callie… and Calypso." She commands, squinting up through her lime pupils and singling out the vessel for Kanaloa.

"Wait, if it's vessels you're after, shouldn't Vex go too?" Azure asks this simple question, but Shaniqua frowns.

"No. Nobody with dark magic in their blood can set foot within the ruins of the Atlantian temples. The swarm will eat you alive." She explains. Vex's eyes widen, his face pale in the dim light which falls from no discernible source.

"I'm good here. Swarm sounds bad." He relinquishes and Azure rolls her eyes as Philippe beats his wings ever harder to maintain their height in the water.

"Cole, you stay with everyone else. If anything changes, send word." Orion orders and Cole nods.

We take a few minutes to swim further into the centre of the city before we sink to the sandy remains of a broken courtyard which lies at the centre of it all. As we travel, I continue to examine the remnants of what had once been a great city, now turned to nothing but bone and stone.

When we reach a lower depth, I notice cracked blue paving stones that look like they're made from lapis lazuli, shimmering dully in the too blue light.

The cracks that run through them haunt me, their broken facets cutting into my sense of belonging to the Goddess. This destruction, it had been caused by her anger at Poseidon. It makes my insides hurt, the sight of skulls lying discarded and worn smooth by the beating tides which had claimed the lives to which they had belonged.

I avert my eyes as I sigh, focusing instead on where Shaniqua is now leading us. A huge hall, the outline of which had been nothing but blocky shadow, stands. Its cyclical architecture is beautiful and unique in a way that I'd never thought possible from stone. We approach the crumbling entryway, which towers above us by a good ten feet and I wonder who would require such a large entryway. As though reading my mind, Shaniqua speaks.

"Entryways were made this large because the people of Atlantis wanted the Gods and Goddesses to know they were always welcome to enter." I nod, accepting her wisdom as fact, as I have always done. It is uncanny how she and Atlas had shared that ability to make you feel as though they knew everything. I just wish they'd shared a little of that wisdom with Orion and me.

"What now?" I enquire and she smiles at my question, turning to face the stone. Her voice rises, encasing me in a tropical wave and rushing through my grey matter like the most calming surf you can imagine. I feel the warmth on my skin, as though I'm really there with her, in the Bahamas from where she has come. The vibrations of her voice soothe me, taking me back to a time less complicated than this, where I was a passenger in the world of the mer, an observer who was new and young, not the driver of my and so many other destinies as I am now. The sound of her voice does something to the doors, just as it had rolled back the once protective glimmer of the Occulta Mirum, causing them to swing forward and reveal a path into nothing but blackness. The hallway is tall and I feel Calypso stir at my side, clearly uncomfortable at the prospect of moving into the unknown.

"It's okay. It's just the darkness. There's really nothing to be afraid of." I promise her, though I don't know if what I'm saying is true. Suddenly, from nowhere, the shadow within the corridor shifts, rushing forward and separating into thousands of individual, black, piranha-like creatures interspersed with a bloody glow, which emits from thousands of unblinking eyes.

372

"The swarm…" Shaniqua explains, though I still have no idea what they are, as she continues on, sensing my wordless desire for more information, "They are the guardians of Atlantis. They are designed to target anything infected with dark magic crossing this threshold. Almost impossible to kill, where you kill one, two are born from its remains." She lifts a hand, caressing the ugly red eyed face of one of the passing onyx fish, her mouth exhaling bubbles as though she's touching nothing more than smoke.

"Come…Follow." We move into the corridor, moving past walls that are tiled with the same blue material as the stones outside. I've never seen it before and wonder if it's unique to the city because where I had first thought it was lapis it seems too veiny. The ruins creak and groan around us, the water tasting like chalk from the lack of life that has passed through them. I have to say; I've noticed a distinct lack of wildlife, other than the swarm, since we've arrived. Everything is an eerie quiet, and yet a calmness settles over me as I swim through. This place feels not only lost as well as full of the voices of those who drowned within its passages so very long ago, but also blessed, like there is some kind of divine energy seeping throughout its barren hallways. The corridor is expansive and out of the gloom, which seems impenetrable, an eye appears.

"What the hell is that!?" I exclaim, observing the purple ugliness of a fish I have never seen before and don't recognise cast before me in unapologetic suddenness.

"It is a Coelacanth. They are the eyes of the Gods and Goddesses down here in the ruins. If the swarm fails in protecting such a place, not that it ever should, the Circle can watch potential intruders through the eyes of these ancient wonders. Fascinating, don't you think?" Shaniqua explains as the sheen of Calypso's opalescent hair comes into view next to me, making me startle. This darkness really is troubling, more evidence of this coming soon after I think it as Orion exclaims a large "Ow!"

"You okay?" I ask, feeling out in front of me. My fingertips brush the back of his breastplate and I back up.

"Yeah, I just swam face first into a wall, but I'm fine." He exclaims with no humour in his tone, backing up and encasing my hand in his. I can feel his pulse in my palm thrumming and fast from his veins and I know the ancient mystique of this place is affecting us both as we hang in the dark.

"There's a wall?" I query Shaniqua and she nods, taking my free hand and leading me forward through the water to the end of the passage where smooth stone shoots up vertically.

Upon its surface is a symbol, I think, barely distinguishable in the dark.

"Sing." She nudges me slightly, so my lips part and I let words flow out from me, not really thinking of any song in particular. Somehow I end up on 'amazing grace' but it suits the mood of us all, dwarfed by these towering ruins and feeling so utterly small in our existence.

As my voice hits a high note, stark blue light, like that I had experienced in the Temple of Atargatis floods the passageway, blinding me temporarily through my visor. The wall parts, sliding away in two halves and giving me only moments to recognise the now illuminated symbol on the doors as my sight returns covered in blotchy blue patterns. Four crescent moons, overlapping to form a circle. Within this mark is an infinity symbol turned sideways, or perhaps an eight, which I had never noticed before. As I catch a final glimpse of the mark before it disappears, something within me shudders and the lit passage behind comes into view, my heart racing as it tries to catch up with my mind.

That symbol, it had been on my scythe, it was on the Temple of Atargatis' walls too.

Is it possible these things are connected? Is it possible that everything I've experienced so far has been leading to this?

My pupils dilate, taking in the fully lit passageway ahead.

The walls are laden with slick blue stone, something unlike anything I've ever seen as it shimmers with threads of neon blue light lacing through it.

Oh my Goddess. Is all I can think as my mouth falls open.

Orion, who grabs my hand once more from where I had dropped his, pulls me forward and through the corridor, the blue light hitting us and turning our scales cold in the pale hue. Orion's eyes practically jump from his face as they refract the pale blue light back from their glacial surface, contrasting starkly with the dark mask of his facial scales.

374

"Come on, we don't have time to hang around." We watch as Shaniqua and Calypso overtake us together, their tails undulating and equally cold in the supernatural glow of the corridor's walls. I inhale, feeling the water, scented with a kind of musk like what you would expect when opening an old book, coat the inside of my gullet and quench my thirst for air. As we reach the end of the starkly lit space, we come to a crossroad. To the left there is a door with the four-crescent-moon symbol upon it's flawlessly smooth blue sheen and to the right, there is a door with a crack right down the middle. I hang, torn between which one I should choose. Letting curiosity get the better of me, I choose the right door, wondering why it has been so badly damaged.

"Callie, I'm pretty sure we need to follow that symbol…" Orion calls after me but I raise a hand, silencing him and following my gut.

As I approach the door, it groans open, sliding against the stone of the floor. I move across the threshold, and into the smallest room I've ever seen, it's practically cupboard size in fact, now I look around, seeing that there is nothing within except for a blue stone pedestal, holding a glass bell jar. I peer into its transparent surface, transfixed by what lies within.

"What's that?" I hear Orion ask, his tone concerned as I bend forward, wanting a closer peek at what lies inside.

"I don't know. I never even noticed that door was there before. It just looked like a dead end." Shaniqua's tones penetrate my dreamy and distant state, causing me to turn away.

"You didn't notice the giant crack in the door?" I ask her and she frowns, confused.

"What crack?" She asks me. I shrug, maybe I'm just imagining things. Regardless of how I came to find the room, I take a stroke back in the water, letting them gaze upon what I've been staring at.

"It's… a flame." Orion looks baffled.

"Yeah, it's weird huh? It's like on fire but there's no source. It's just sort of… alight in the water. It's pretty though, keeps changing colour…" I muse, feeling my eyes continually drawn to it, something about its unwavering burn instinctually pulling me toward it. I reach out to touch the glass, but Shaniqua coughs, breaking the hold of the flame once again.

"That, Callie, is not why we're here. We aren't supposed to take what isn't required. Come along. I'm sure this object has been housed in such strict security for a reason. Don't want to be destroying the world by accident now do we?" She pulls me back, resting her long fingers on my shoulders and withdrawing from the room as she drags me behind her. I turn and she looks at me, waving a hand in front of my eyes. "Callie! Concentrate!" She snaps and I start, suddenly aware of my surroundings and of the eerie silence yet again. It creeps into the empty corners of my mind, making me want to press on.

"Sorry." I mumble, picking up the innate rhythmic stroking of my tailfin and swimming past her.

Back across the corridor I float before the door with the symbol of four crescent moons, carved into the stone and alight with neon blue magic. The door slides open at my presence, revealing something amazing inside. The blue stone covers the floors, the walls, even the ceilings, and the cyan light continues to burn bright throughout, forming patterns which look like carvings across the chamber's various surfaces. This isn't what alarms me though, what alarms me is the round wheel shaped rock that's been placed in the centre of the space. The circle is divided into eight, and in each place a different colour crystal anvil stands, the likes of which I had seen only once, encasing what can only be described as the most unique weapons I've ever seen.

"The Pieces of Eight." I gasp, knowing now, without even taking a second to think about it, exactly what it is I'm looking at. I stare at the circle, all the weapons there, encased in their individual multi- hued stones. All of them, except two.

I glide into the space, letting the bright cyan cover me as it illuminates everything and exposes every detail of the space, leaving no corner hidden.

"This is what they are? Weapons?" Orion asks, his expression confused. I curve my body around the circular table, flexing my tailfin and curving my course through the water as I look to each one of the weapons in turn. A bow and arrow, a spear, a shield, a shark toothed club, a sword and a hammer. Here they are… the only problem is, there aren't eight. There are only six.

I swim further around the table, to the place where Poseidon's weapon should be. A symbol of a trident has been etched into the stone and is glowing

376

neon like the rest of them next to an empty black crystal anvil with three empty holes in its flat top. I look to Orion, to the trident hanging against his spine. We'd had it all this time....

"Callie, what is it?" He asks me as I move to the next segment, that of Atargatis. This time not only the weapon, but also the crystal in which it was set is gone too. The only remnant that there was ever a weapon here is a glowing symbol... my heart sinks.

"The scythe... The Scythe of Atargatis. My Piece of Eight... it's gone... It's with..." I begin but Orion's mouth falls open.

"Saturnus!" He finishes, cringing visibly.

"You have the other one right there..." I say, looking to the trident as its dark purple and black handle glistens, blue light caught in the faces of the handle's angular design. Calypso brushes past him, her tail fluid and ethereal in the ghostly light. She almost looks like she's entranced as she lowers her body so her spine is poker straight as she examines the shark toothed club, which lies embedded in pink crystal.

"It's a leiomano." She whispers in awe, breathless.

"Sing... Sing and it will come to you." I command her, my face alight with so many mixed emotions. She parts her lips, her voice hypnotic and entirely beautiful, though I expect nothing less. The leiomano slips from the stone easily, her hand fitting its grip like it was made for her, because it was. The club is opalescent in body, with sharp and jagged shark's teeth embedded into its head. Her eyes widen and I can tell that her mind is boggled by the kind of damage the weapon could inflict as she holds it in her palm and her eyes rise to mine. I gaze upon her, knowing the rush of power that the weapon will fill her with. I know because the scythe had done the same thing to me. Now though, it is gone.

I spin on the spot, looking to the wall behind me, upon it are many carvings, in writing I don't understand, but one image is clear. A circle with eight dot markers within its unending curve, each one accompanied by the symbol of a different Piece of Eight, which meet in the centre of the formation. Above the diagram is a filled in circle cut deep into the stone, which I assume to be the moon.

377

So this is the Conduit. I think as Orion comes to my side once more, his movement graceful and silent so as to not break my concentration.

I continue to stare at the diagram, scrutinising the dot with the scythe picture next to it.

That's me, I think, a shudder running through me at the finality of seeing my destiny carved into stone. This had all been decided before my birth, before maybe even Orion's birth. How I was going to live and die. Right here on the walls of Atlantis all this time. As I look upon the stone the message sinks in.

The vessels are The Conduit; I am a part of The Conduit...

If only the diagram told us what The Conduit's role is or what it does. What was to become of the vessels?

What was to become of me?

29
The Gathering
ORION

I stare at the weapons before me in the larimar coated chamber, blue veined through with white; it is eerie, and not just because of the deafening silence which has my gut twisting like it's straining to get out of a vice. Those weapons, the Pieces of Eight, confirm perhaps my worst fear. The Conduit will in fact involve Callie going head on with the Necrimad. I do not know for sure, but what else could you possibly need mystical weaponry like this for? Perhaps she will not be alone, but I find it odd at best that the weapon tying her to all this was placed in a separate venue to the others. How did it get there, and how did Poseidon's trident end up with the Psirens? Surely Vex wasn't around to remove it, so how had these things happened?

"Come on Callie, we should get back." I pull on her elbow as her blonde hair hangs around her, still and ghostly in its suspension.

"You're right. My Piece of Eight isn't here." She frowns, eyes falling upon my trident. I watch her gaze as she opens her mouth to speak, but then closes it. I wonder if she's thinking about asking me to hand it over to Vex.

Over my dead body.

"This thing… it's so powerful…." Calypso's words break the silence between us and we both spin to see that she's still passing the leiomano between her palms, her opalescent hair glowing cyan and making her skin appear darker than usual. Her irises rise to my face, where they find me watching her intently and wondering whether she will suffer the same fate as Callie. I'm beginning

379

to worry even more than I already have been; especially now we have the Pieces of Eight. I had hoped, silently, that without them we could beat the Psirens back by other means and then deal with the Necrimad later when I could fully protect her, but I guess the Circle has other plans.

Shaniqua coughs before floating past me in a lime flurry.

"I think it is wise that we go and meet the other pods, if memory serves me they're volatile on their own, so who knows what they'll be like together. We have a mixing pot of cultures, beliefs, temperaments and the rest." She muses and her eyes catch mine in their lime charms.

"How could you not tell me, Shaniqua? You knew all this, and you kept me in the dark all this time." I ask her the question, causing a sudden and brutal tension to develop in the already tense room.

"It was not my job to tell you Orion, it was your father's. He was hoping he would be around to tell you all this after the threat had passed. We could not possibly have anticipated..." She begins, but I'm uninterested. How dare she and my father put me through all this? They knew. They knew we weren't alone and they decided not to tell me, knowing full well I'd be most likely to rule in father's wake.

I swim, darting out of the door in a single powerful exertion of my tailfin.

"Orion!" I hear Callie's scolding exclamation, but I no longer care.

I make my way back through the temple and out into the courtyard scattered with skulls and cracked stone. Looking up, I avoid the interest of the mer and Sirena who rise in the water, ascending to hear what we have found, and stare toward the whirlpools that surround the city, or what is left of it. I watch them thunder cyclically and in close proximity to one another, yet another show of the Circle's unstoppable power.

"Orion!" I hear Callie's voice behind me as a hand touches me on the shoulder.

"What?" I bark, spinning, with fury in my gaze, to face her. Her eyes narrow and she backs away.

"Calm down. Jeez." She exclaims, scowling. "What's done is done. You can't blame Shaniqua for Atlas' choices. Aren't you grateful she's here?" She

380

asks me, tilting her head and causing me to falter under her intense stare as blonde hair tumbles down over her left shoulder.

"I suppose… I'm just frustrated. I thought we had found the final piece of the puzzle, and we're still missing the scythe." I lie, knowing full well that in a way I hadn't wanted to find the Pieces of Eight. I hadn't wanted any of this. All I had wanted was to meet my soulmate…

"Look, I know it's frustrating, we were prepared to end up in the middle of a war zone this morning, but remember, this gives us a better chance. It means we can prepare." Her logical reasoning makes me even more frustrated. How is she not falling apart?

"How you are still standing after everything, I'll never know." I whisper, leaning forward and touching my forehead to hers.

"It's an act Orion. I'm freaking out inside. Please remember that, but part of being a leader is appearing fearless… even when you aren't." She expresses, giving me a chaste kiss. She's right; I should know that, particularly seeing as I've started putting on an impassive expression in place of fear.

"Okay, I'm sorry." I apologise, seeing now, behind her irises, that fear really does lie within.

"It's not me you snapped at." She replies, looking back to Shaniqua and Calypso who are now catching up to us. Shaniqua's lime green eyes are concerned.

"You're right. I'm sorry." I say, tilting in the water to face Shaniqua as she nods her head, returning to her usual state of serenity.

"It is alright, Orion. I understand that this is difficult for everyone." She remains still as she speaks these words, her features calm as always and I cannot help but wonder what her secret is. Calypso moves in front of me, returning to her pod as she glides, gracefully slow, through the water and Cole pushes forward toward me in a single elongated stroke of his black fluke.

"What is it? What did you find?" He asks me, urgent in his tone, as I glance back over his shoulder as he lowers his voice.

"The Pieces of Eight." Callie replies, cutting across me before I get a chance to speak.

381

"Yes, we're now waiting for the other pods..." I begin, but as I move to continue my sentence one of the whirlpools lights up, as though it's being struck by lightning from the inside. Callie jumps beside me, startled.

We watch as the Kappa emerge from the portal, their mass distinguishable collectively by the way in which their armour makes them meld into one large shadow in the distance. At the front of the army, Hironori leads them, his long hair atop his head in a high ponytail which is slick and falls in long, inky-black tresses. His golden, black and white spattered tail fin shimmers, picking him out from the army that sticks close to him, bewildered and staring with stern faces into the half-light. Fumio and Chiyoko descend toward us behind the Emperor, carrying a large and ancient looking chest between them as I notice that several of the warriors who accompany them hold chests as well.

"Orion!" Hironori exclaims, this time bowing to me as he bends at the waist with hands pointing up like he's in prayer. It's startling really, especially when you consider the fact he'd almost had both me and Callie beheaded just a few days ago.

"Emperor. Very punctual! Your army is looking wonderfully large, it's hard to gauge scope without seeing them out in the open, so observing them now fills me with confidence." I glide forward, undulating quickly and holding out a hand, which he takes, shaking it twice. I look around, noting the absence of Kira, her mentor Salome, and his wife Samara.

"Indeed. We are at your service... the enemy?" He questions me, frowning as he looks around, golden eyes narrowing in his paranoia.

"This is the lost city of Atlantis. We've been brought here to prepare..." I begin and the Emperor stares at me, his eyes widening.

"Atlantis... Great Goddess Mizuchi..." He exclaims, turning back to me after a moment of taking in the ruins. I nod, forcing a smile.

"Indeed... Oh look, another pod!" I exclaim, catching the flash of lightning within a different whirlpool, it would be next to the one the Kappa had arrived through, if it hadn't dissipated right after the last warrior had fallen from its sodden clutch. I gesture for Hironori and his men to set up to my right. I guess the best way to do this is by separating them, that way once all have arrived I can summon the leaders forward and we can all begin to discuss plans

382

for battle. In this moment, as I float here with what can only be described as a mammoth task before me, I have never felt so inadequate.

The portal flickers with a lilac glow from the lightning within, expelling Akachi and Rourke, their animalistic tails appearing unnatural to me even now. The forces of Maneli fighters pour forth from the portal, their armour and weapons unmistakably the work of Gabriel, as I watch Akachi fall through the water, his crocodilian tail moving from left to right as he slows his descent.

"Akachi!" I exclaim, swimming over to him at speed. He glides forward, putting his arms around my shoulders and pulling me in for a masculine embrace. The crocodile on his staff shifts uncomfortably at the commotion, still clutching the eye of Ava in its jaws, as the small pod of my people watch me like hawks. They decide to shift positions, swimming forward so they are behind me, realising we're going to need all the spare space we can get as the enormous number of warriors dwarfs us quite considerable.

Kaiya shifts her gaze to me, moving through the water with hypnotic forward strokes of her chameleonic tailfin.

"Who are they?" She asks, gesturing to The Kappa. Her eyes shift a little too quickly, suspicious in their stare. I figure I should make introductions before they start trying to poison yet more good men.

"These are The Kappa, belonging to the...." I start, remembering how very wrong my attempts at talking about Atargatis had gone. Perhaps not mentioning their Goddess was a better tact. "Seas of Japan." I finish, thinking quickly as yet more lightning strikes up in another whirlpool. "Callie, can you go and greet the next pod?" I ask, shooting her a quick glance over my shoulder. I hadn't realised exactly what I was getting into recruiting so many. Have I bitten off more than I can chew?

"Chief Akachi, this is Emperor Hironori." I introduce the two men, beckoning the Emperor forward. He bows and Akachi licks his lips, his horizontal eyelids flickering across his vision as he takes in the man before him. The water between them becomes tense.

"Welcome to Atlantis." I say to them both, trying to prevent them from staring at each other for too long. I don't want either one offending the other. "Akachi, why don't you go and set up over there..." I suggest, pointing to the

383

space next to the Kappa, who are now sprawling out, setting up racks of katanas that hang, long and lethal, blade down.

"My healers will need space for their tables..." Akachi looks to me, raising a speculative eyebrow as his dark skin shimmers with a blue tinge from the Larimar beneath us.

"Healers? How wonderful!" Hironori compliments, genuine in his sentiment. Akachi pivots to face him, interested in a conversation all of a sudden.

"You know we've never lost a Maneli fighter..." I hear him begin and so leave them to their conversation, rotating in the water and heading over to Callie who is now welcoming Isabella and caught in a huge hug.

"Orion, darling! Come here!" Isabella pushes Callie away, pulling me in against her golden corset, crushing me and burying my face in her thick raven locks. I look to her as she embraces me, squeezing me in a way entirely inappropriate, but not at all unexpected, as I look to her armour-clad torso. What she's wearing is less ornate than what I'd seen in the Temple of Neptune, this corset being thicker and bolder, with no lavish jellyfish baubles or mesh, but purely solid gold for protection. Her tailfin is wrapped in a gold net dripping with rubies to match her scales as she flexes it out behind her, like a small and over excitable child.

"Isabella!" I exclaim, plastering a smile on my face once more as I push back from her willowy body, taking in the faces of Paolo, Enzo, Casmire and Claudia behind her. Their faces sparkle wildly with the different coloured stones, but as my eyes land on the deep Sapphires of Enzo's facial mask I can't help but notice a sullen look behind his irises which doesn't match the happy glow of the other Water Nymphs.

"Oh my goodness, darling! Atlantis? You know I'll be looking to add to my little collection of goodies..." She giggles and I frown, cutting her off.

"I don't think that's such a good idea. These are mystical objects... they have no market worth." I say, making this fact up on the spot. I have no idea the market worth of this kind of object, but I can't have her looting the city. I look into her brown eyes, subtly watching her ruby clad tailfin undulating to the left as she waves a hand.

384

"Oh no, darling! For my personal collection, of course!" She laughs, cackling in her happy Italian accent and causing the other pods to look over. She causes a wave of mumbling and disapproving glances from the other pods with her entirely over the top demeanour and so I glide over to Callie, leaning in close to her as I see another whirlpool with lightning forking in its epicentre. I gaze back to the opposite side of the large courtyard of the ruins, watching Azure as she makes her way over to Callista and brushes her hair behind one shoulder. I roll my eyes, feeling my gut constrict. She makes me nervous to say the least; I just hope she doesn't try to take on one of the Kappa warriors with a sword again.

"Don't let her touch anything..." I whisper in Callie's ear, addressing Isabella's sticky fingers quickly before she has a chance to cause any trouble, as I pass, making her giggle.

I swim to my left, reaching the far-left face of the enormous rectangular courtyard that is filling, only too quickly, with bodies.

"Bludy whirlpool! Guid God, th' Kelpies didne loch 'at!" I hear the rumbling thunder of Domnall's Scottish accent reach me and I can't help but smile. His accent creates an invigorating nostalgia within me, reminding me of how far we have come.

"Domnall!" I exclaim, greeting him before I see him. He swoops around the outskirts of the portal, having exited on the wrong side. He pulls on the reigns of Magnus, his Kelpie, who is equipped with two heavy saddlebags on either side of its scaled, mint green body. The Fist of Lir departs behind him, racing forward on their mounts, and I look back as the other pods cannot help but be drawn to the spectacle of these majestically insane, tattoo covered, ginger warriors. They watch, curious about them, whilst moving to touch the hilts of their weapons with tentative fingertips.

"Orion, me Lad!" Domnall jumps down from Magnus' spine, clapping me on the shoulder and causing me to dip in the water under the immense weight of his arm. He gazes around, taking in the eyes of all the other pods staring at him as their conversations fall into silence. Flannery chuckles behind Domnall's broad width and Conan peeks around the Chief also, watching the reactions of the other Kindred with amusement.

385

"Whit ye bludy lookin' at!" He roars, causing the water around us to tremor. The other pods jump, raising their weapons momentarily as Domnall bursts out into laughter. "Bludy numpties." He shakes his head, running his hand through his knotty hair and chuckling. "So where's th' war 'en?" He asks me, crossing his arms across his bulging pectorals and staring from left to right, looking unimpressed at the lack of enemy.

"This isn't the Pacific. We've made a slight detour to Atlantis, to prepare for battle." I explain. Domnall nods, glimpsing back to the men behind him, whose steeds are whinnying, exuding bubbles with impatient and fidgeting twitches of their tails. Domnall turns back to look at his men, clearly not fazed by the fact he's just entered a mystical lost city.

"An ye thooght the Burn Kildrummy was a jobby hole eh?" He laughs again, wiping an oily tear from his flushed cheek and clearly finding himself far more hilarious than I do. I smile, not entirely sure what a 'jobby hole' is, but utterly sure I don't want to find out.

"You can set up over there," I point to the far corner as I spin, knowing that stationing him between Isabella and the rest of the ruins is surely enough to prevent her from pillaging the sacred space.

I feel a flurry of bubbles against my spine and glimpse a flash of Aqua behind me as I turn. Callie is swimming to the one whirlpool that remains open and I know she must be anxious to see her father again.

I rotate back to face the enormous mass of people, noticing our pod, tiny by comparison and sitting uncomfortably in the centre of it all. Their gazes collectively rise as I pivot again, not quite able to keep up with how much there is to see, as I finally rest my eyes upon the mass pallor of the Adaro. Gideon is at the front of his army, pale hair tumbling down his chest in a long beard. His white and ice blue tailfin flexes, powering his body down as he dives, launching himself at Callie. She throws her arms around him, curling her tail backwards and letting him hold her for a few moments, like she's no more than a little girl.

"Who the bloody hell is that?" I hear Vex's question and turn, cocking an eyebrow with a smirk.

"That would be her father, big isn't he?" I call back to him and grin as I look over my shoulder and he scowls, his eyes flitting between my amused expression and the trident on my spine. I wonder if he knows it's rightfully his. Well, if he wants it then he can fight me for it. He might have tentacles, but compared to me he's an amoeba.

I swim backward, turning over in the water and readying myself to make nice with the father of the girl I would die to protect. I like Gideon; we have that desire to protect in common I suppose. Unfortunately for me, Callie only accepts this behaviour from one of us.

"Gideon!" I exclaim, watching as a pair of familiar and adoring eyes settle over me. Sirenia is watching me like a besotted hawk, so I place my arm around Callie's waist, sending the clear message that I'm not interested and watch as Gideon follows my gaze. He cocks an eyebrow and chuckles to himself, rolling his eyes.

"Orion! I see you've kept my girl safe! Thank you!" He claps me on the shoulder, reminding me so of my own father in this moment that I feel my heartstrings plucked a melancholy tune. He observes the crowd of Kindred, his eyes widening. "My, you have been busy. Look at all these other pods... Incredible. There must be at least... why three thousand here." I sigh, feeling my stomach churn at his address of our numbers. It's true, we're many, but I still don't think it's enough. I would have to ask Vex to be sure, but I'm sure that can wait until a later date. Preferably one where he is no longer such an enormous ass.

"Yes, there are many. But I'm not sure it's enough." I sigh, rubbing the back of my neck and feeling weary. I look back to the Adaro army. Being mounted on Narwhals they're garnering the attention of the others, particularly the Selkies who are far to my left, staring at Gideon with impressed faces and the odd whisper between themselves.

"Well, why don't you introduce me?" He suggests, his aqua eyes sparkling as he looks down to Callie. I move out of the way so that the army can pass, watching their vast numbers and feeling entirely too tanned in comparison. Sirenia flicks her hair over one shoulder and flutters her eyelashes as she brushes my abdominals with her fingernails in passing. I turn away, uninterested being the biggest of understatements.

I swim after Callie, wanting to be at her side and intent on getting a moment alone with Gideon, to ask his opinion on what he feels would be best strategy with the Psirens. Unlike any of the other leaders here, he actually has prior experience with them.

"That's the Kappa, they're from Japan, God or Goddess Mizuchi, we're not quite sure. Though I think Hironori referred to Mizuchi as a Goddess. Then next to them is the Maneli…" I hear Callie explaining this to her father and I watch as she reaches the Water Nymphs, where Isabella is nowhere to be found. I scan the area, worried she might have been lost, or worse. I had seen the swarm move past us, but it wasn't until her loud tones had gone quiet that I worry that they could be vicious if tempted.

I wouldn't put it past Isabella to try and skin one for a handbag or something, so I push through the water and over to Marina quickly, who's talking with Claudia near the Water Nymphs as the soldiers behind them begin to unpack their trunks full of gold and silver weaponry. I grab her elbow, feeling urgency clutch me.

"Have either of you seen Isabella?" I ask them, panic stricken at the absence of the woman I had quite often contemplated gagging due to her lack of volume control. Suddenly, I hear it. The sound you never want to hear in a delicate political situation.

That of an angry Scotsman.

"I say, move aside!" Isabella's voice rises, high pitched as she floats, entirely dwarfed by the enormity of Domnall's breadth.

"Ah wulnae! Ah dornt move an army oan th' demands ay a Lassie. E'en a body as braw as ye.." He crosses his arms in his usual stubborn pose, cocking his large, midnight blue tailfin like he's a male model. It's a feminine pose for a man of his stature, but somehow he makes it work.

"What did you just say to me? You great brute! Do you know who I am?" She bawls as Enzo moves up behind her and I watch the scene unfold with a terrified fascination.

"Ah dunnae kinn, a princess?" Flannery answers this time, his height even more daunting to Isabella and yet somehow she remains un-fazed, I cannot help but admire her a little for that. "Nae much ay a warriur ur ye? Whit waur ye thinkin' Orion, recruitin' lassies?" He turns to me this time, and at his words the Maneli and Adaro start to stir. Kaiya is the first to speak and break the tense silence that follows.

"Excuse me? What you say? That we women are not equipped to fight?" She asks, baring her teeth as she darts across the courtyard faster than I've ever seen her move. Nika shortly follows her, harpoon in fist.

"Yes, you ginger illiterate, what exactly was that you said about women not being fit to fight?" They circle him, like sharks trying to tackle a humpback whale, except this whale is ginger and has quite a temper. Callie looks to me as Gideon moves to call back Nika. I feel things getting out of control quickly.

"Please, warriors. This is not a time for violence. Why don't we all just calm down, take a few deep breaths and relax." I hear Aulani's serene tones flow through the water, reaching out in seductive tendrils of tranquil sound. Instead of this effect claiming all of us, Domnall makes the chief mistake of any man in this kind of situation, he just can't stop himself opening his big mouth.

"Ha! War? Nae a place fur violence? Thes is wa Lir wasnae sae stoopid as tae recruit lassies tae his cause. Soft as jobby, th' lot ay ye!" His voice reverberates out as he takes a stroke forward, swatting away Kaiya and Nika like they're no more than flies irritating a horse. Isabella on the other hand, follows him, undeterred by his gait. She puts a hand on his shoulder and he turns, striking her across the face by accident as he raises a palm in quick motion. I hear a collective gasp, as both the Kappa and the Water Nymphs intake breath and Isabella flushes scarlet in her complexion, turning all shades of wrath in turn.

"You dishonour yourself sir!" I hear emperor Hironori's harsh voice cut through the water like a razor. Unforgiving in every respect.

"Honoor, whoo said anythin' abit honoor? Thes is war!" Fergus calls, his rotten-toothed mouth delivering yet more fuel to the fire. With this sentiment, the Water Nymph's army draw their swords and the Kappa follow shortly

389

afterward. I watch as the Fist of Lir draw newly carved arrows in their bows. The Sirena and mer float in the centre of it all, watching as Isabella hangs, toxic in expression as she looks up at Domnall, who in all honesty, can't understand what he's doing that's so wrong. I watch as Azure turns in the water, as suddenly voices erupt from every corner of the courtyard and she takes in the scene, balling her fists at her side. Gideon swims over among the rabble as the armies start to spit venom at one another, attacking one another's beliefs, blaspheming foreign deities and baring their teeth.

I just float, not knowing what to do and unsure of how to possibly to communicate to all these people in a way each one understands and respects. I had struggled to deal with them all separately, and yet this is so much worse, because it is almost impossible to say anything without offending someone. The Water Nymph army begin to inch forward, ready to defend their violated Queen. Casmire is among them, his expression practically feral in concentration on Domnall's body as he assesses him for weaknesses. The Selkies lurch forward too, clearly having the advantage with their long-range weapons and massive bodies.

Oh my God, it's going to be a bloodbath. I think, watching the armies without any inkling of how to stop them. I have no power over them. It is the role of their Chiefs, Emperors, Queens and Kings to do that, not me.

The water suddenly gets eerily still as the armies get too close to one another for comfort, raising their weapons and looking at one another with suspicious glances, but neither moving even an inch.

The moment is tense, and seems to last forever.

Suddenly, an ear-splitting scream causes every single one of us to duck, covering our ears. It's deafening, something I've only heard a few times, and rarely from my sister.

Azure rises in the water, her hair trailing behind her in a black waterfall as her mouth hangs agape, the scream emitting from her ferocious to say the least. It cuts through everything, all the drama, the hatred and the egos. She silences after a few moments, looking to me with a stern expression and a cocked, expectant brow. I nod to her, knowing now what I have to do.

"Look!" I yell, rising through the water so I am high above them all.

390

This better be one hell of a speech.

"You're all forgetting who the real enemy is here. It's not the Selkies of Scotland, or the Water Nymphs of Italy. It isn't any of you. Our enemy isn't here. So that you understand the severity of this, which I'm not sure all of you do, I'm going to show you." I reach out, searching for Akachi's face. I find him looking weary, but as though it's not in his control the crocodile on his staff leaps, swimming for me and dropping the Eye of Ava into my palm.

Within moments it does what I will it, showing the decimation of the Occulta Mirum through flashes from my memory. It projects the images for all to see onto the surface of the water high above. I watch as the eyes below me widen and several of the expressions turned shocked, or even cringe at the kind of feral violence being presented by the rippling screen.

"See? Each one of you don't have to be friends, you don't have to like one another. But you *do* have to work together! If not, it won't matter what your beliefs are, where you come from, your gender, who you love, or the colour of your skin. You will perish. The Psirens won't discriminate in torturing and killing each one of us in the most gruesome way possible. So, we must not discriminate in our alliances and the way in which we come together to beat them back. Do you understand me?!" I say, out of breath from the exclamation as I give the orb back to the crocodile, which quickly returns to Akachi. He gazes upon me with approval as he raises his staff in the water.

"I'm with you." He says, unwavering in his gaze, respect now mutual between us. I look next to Hironori who bows, staring at me with an inspired expression. I rotate in the water, staring back to Gideon who gazes upon me with wise eyes, expressing satisfaction with his stance in the water. The Sirena are gazing up from directly beneath with wide, jewel coloured eyes and besotted expressions as I descend now, getting in between Isabella and Domnall.

"Now, you can float here all day, or you can apologise and move on. You're supposed to be rulers, examples to your people, so I expect you to think carefully about what you choose. Especially seeing as how I have the mer, Adaro, Kappa, Maneli and Sirena behind me. I don't care what race you are, you're not vicious or skilled enough to take us all." I cock an eyebrow and

391

Isabella lets out a sigh, as Domnall snorts like a pissed off bull. After a few moments, he holds out a reluctant palm, the size of a saucer, to Isabella.

"I'm uh, sorry I hit ye." He mumbles, lowering his eyes. Isabella refuses to meet his gaze, ignoring him before slouching and taking his palm. She looks up into his large face with a small smile, which I could swear looks almost timid.

"Well, I suppose it was an accident darling." She rolls her eyes and something passing between the two of them that I can't quite describe. I sigh, relieved. Callie is at my side before I can pivot to find her in the crowd.

"That. Was. Amazing." She breathes in staccato, kissing me on the cheek. I nod to her, knowing that with all this fighting we've wasted valuable time.

I cough, clearing my throat and drawing attention to myself once more. Multiple eyes examine me from every angle and I breathe, heavy hearted from the stress of it all.

"The vessels and leaders from each pod please come forward. We will take you into the temple. Your Pieces of Eight await inside." Vex opens his mouth to speak, but I hold up my palm. "Not you." I bite out, catching a whiff of his idea to follow us in his stupidly ugly face. Not content on giving him the chance to express it in his usual monosyllabic slur. Azure looks to the armies, rolling her eyes for the millionth time this trip.

As I turn, the vessels in tow as they ready themselves to make the journey into the Atlantian temples, I hear Azure's snide tones as I turn my back on the ring of Kindred.

"Sure, I actually stop the fighting by Psiren screaming myself hoarse, which I *never* do because it's freaking undignified, and *he* gets all the credit for the save! Bloody typical!"

30
The Fight
CALLIE

Within the Atlantian temple, the blue light of the corridor illuminates the faces of the pod leaders and their accompanying vessels. Their eyes are wide, taking in the surroundings with awe struck expressions and their lips slightly parted, allowing whispers of astonishment to fall into the eerie silence. As we reach the end of the corridor, I take a left, immersed in the chalky water and hanging before the door etched with the symbol of the Circle.

The door slides away, its stone grating against that beneath and revealing the five Pieces of Eight that remain.

Isabella pushes her way past me, scaly hips gyrating as she scans the room, presumably for anything she can pawn off to the highest bidder. Hironori enters next, as I swim to my left, clearing the doorway and allowing the rest of the group to pile in. Domnall is by far the tightest squeeze as he follows the other leaders, ducking his head so he doesn't hit the high ceiling. I observe the faces of Cage, Conan, Casmire, Callista and Chiyoko as they take in the chamber for the first time, each vessel's eyes immediately falling to one of the five remaining weapons, still stuck in multi-coloured crystal.

Calypso glides over to me, ethereal in her stroke and with Aulani in tow, as she clutches her opalescent leiomano to her chest, protecting it like it were a child. Conan moves to the bow and arrow, Cage the hammer, Casmire the

393

shield, Callista the spear, and Chiyoko the katana, each one awestruck at their proximity to the weapon that had been made with them in mind.

Conan is the first to reach out to take the weapon in front of him, his green eyes transfixed by the quiver of arrows and bow made from what looks like extremely thick oak. He heaves, unable to shift it from the stone as Domnall coughs behind him, trying to cover a laugh.

"Lit me help ye thaur, Lad." He says, pushing Conan's meek frame out of the way and taking a stroke forward as the shadows of his thick cheekbones cast darkness across his face and the tangle of his beard. He reaches out, his hands dwarfing the nimble size of the Piece as the other leaders watch, looking bored at his continual need to prove his strength.

He tugs at the bow, exerting himself as he realises he is unable to shift the weapon either. Flushing red in the face he coughs again, looking embarrassed as the Piece of Eight refuses to budge. I laugh, placing a hand across Orion's chest as he moves to speak, wanting to let the Selkie chief embarrass himself a little more before revealing the way to release each Piece.

Isabella's eyes shoot to me and she sniggers and I roll my eyes back as Domnall is now atop the blue stone table, making a true ass out of himself as he strains, taking deep breaths. He pulls on the wood once more, quite to the point where I worry it might snap in half.

Eventually, after around ten minutes, I cough, drawing attention to myself and trying hard not to show my pleasure at his struggle.

"You can't release it from the stone. Only Conan can do that. You have to sing." I nod to Conan, who has moved back into the shadows of the room, ashamed by his lack of muscle and even more so by Domnall's refusal of defeat at the hand of the bow's mystical seal.

"Sing?" He looks to me, his green eyes fearful.

"Sure, just a little tune. Anything." I shrug, smiling at him and willing him to hurry up.

He gulps, singing a few words of a Scottish song I've never heard before as he reaches out, grasping the bow and quiver in his palms. Blue light illuminates his freckled complexion as he lifts both weapons from the jade green crystal only too easily, gripping onto them as his expression turns to one of pure joy and his red hair is ruffled by an invisible and impossible wind. Domnall's expression is one of dumbstruck shock, his mouth hanging open as Conan lifts what he could not. His expression soon becomes slightly irritated as he crosses his arms across his chest, defensive.

I stare at my father next, whose aqua eyes sparkle from behind the equally aquamarine tresses of Cage's hair, his pallor frightening in contrast to the hue of the room. He hums a few bars of a song that sounds Inuk in origin, before releasing the large white marble hammer with a concrete handle from its icy blue stone. He smiles, his eyes glowing as he tests the weight of the weapon in his hands, handling it as though it were weightless.

I turn next to Casmire, who is staring at the shield in front of him with intensity. He begins to crow a ballad about the depths of his love, releasing the shield from the indigo crystal's clutches as he grins, satisfied with himself. Isabella peers over his shoulder to inspect the weapon and I can almost hear her guessing its value.

Callista's tones rise next, deep and soothing in their rhythm as Akachi watches her, pride filling his face. She yields the spear from the orange crystal's hold as though it weighs no more than a feather.

Finally, under the watchful eyes of all the other vessels, who now have the power of the Circle flowing through them for the first time, Chiyoko moves forward as Hironori gives her a small shove of encouragement. She begins to sing, clearly self-conscious about her voice, which does not match that of her sister Kira, who I notice is sadly, but not surprisingly, absent. Chiyoko pulls the sword, encased in a golden sheath wrapped with kelp vines, from the deep bloody red of the encasing stone. Her eyes sparkle, excited at the feel of the blade as she un-sheaths it, examining its length with a satisfied and energetic smile dancing on her thin lips.

"That's everyone. You feel it, don't you? The power…" I say, moving forward and pulling Calypso with me. They nod and we look between one another, knowing that we are connected too, and yet I cannot forget there is still one vessel missing. Not that I've been wanting to address it, mainly because I know Orion isn't going to be happy when I do.

"It's... I've never felt anything like it." Callista breathes, looking down at the black and white marble spear in her palms. It matches her tail and her white pupils glow in a surreal ghostly aura, as her lips part into a large smile. I point to the wall, between Hironori and Domnall, who part, revealing the diagram of The Conduit.

"That's us. Right there. That Circle, underneath the blood moon, weapons pointed into the centre." I explain, and watch them as they stare, not knowing what to make of it. I understand, for I still have no idea how to feel about it either.

"Yes, but what is it? This Conduit?" Isabella asks me, taking the words right out of Casmire's mouth, whose emerald encrusted facial masking is dancing a myriad of colour in the too bright cyan light.

"We don't know." I sigh, looking between all the leaders with a concerned expression.

"Wait, you still don't know what it does?" Casmire scowls, his expression outraged. I turn to Shaniqua who, after everything, is hanging in the doorway next to Orion, watching the seven of us with fascination as she speaks up.

"I don't know. The only thing I'll say is that if the Circle hasn't made its function known, there must be a good reason. They've invested a lot of time, not to mention magic, bringing you together. I'm sure they know what they're doing." She waves a hand, dismissing the fact we have no idea what The Conduit does like it's a trivial matter. I know it is anything but, and yet I know I don't want an argument over it either. We have too much to get done to waste time.

My father gives me an appeasing smile and my heart melts, glad for his proximity when I can hardly swallow down my fear at the coming war long enough to speak.

"Come. We need to make a plan for battle." I command, biting my lip nervously as the rest of the group, except for those of the Maneli pod, look to me with incredulous faces at my quick acceptance of Shaniqua's response.

Orion backs me up, gesturing for everyone to move out as I swim past him and he gives me a worried glance. Taking my hand, we leave together, Pieces of Eight and vessels in tow. Well, all except one.

Out in the courtyard we're bombarded by a very pissed off looking Vex. His expression is one of wrath, lilac irises ablaze with unchecked anger, and I wonder what the hell has happened in the mere thirty minutes we've been inside. The leaders and their vessels move back to their individual pods, the warriors of each one gathering to view the weapons that have been collected except, of course, for the Selkies who look irritated toward Conan, uninterested at best.

"What the bloody hell is going on? I'm a vessel, right?" Vex pulsates toward me, his tentacles twitching as individual entities from his body. I roll my eyes.

What is he on about now?

"Yes, that is correct." I reply with a sigh, crossing my arms, as Orion inches across the courtyard toward Gideon.

Ugh, and what's his problem? I wonder, also confused as to why he has not yet handed over the trident to Vex.

"Well then why am I being treated like I've got bloody cooties?" He asks me, cocking his slashed brow with a seductive glance down my body. I roll my eyes, not having time for his crappy suggestive stare.

"Look, you're a vessel, but you heard what Shaniqua said, you can't go into that temple, or the swarm will kill you." I say, shrugging as he narrows his eyes. I blink, and before I know it he's behind me, whispering in my ear.

"You know, I'm not as bloody thick as everyone thinks. All the other vessels got weapons. Where's *mine?* Come on, Blondie, where is it?" I spin back to face him, settling my eyes on his expression and sighing again. Suddenly my eyes flick, if only for a moment and without conscious effort, to Orion who is facing us with his back, putting the trident in full view. My gaze travels quickly back to Vex's face as he cocks his head to the left, rounding like

397

a male predator. He growls, feral like an animal as his eyes settle on the trident and I hear him mutter, "I bloody knew it."

I'm about to open my mouth to protest, falsely claim the trident isn't his, but he's already halfway to Orion before I can summon a single syllable of a lie.

I propel through the water, heart racing and anxiety reaching an all-time high, reaching Vex's spine just as he's tapping Orion on the shoulder. Orion pivots in slow motion, his whole body visibly tense.

"Can I help you?" He asks and Gideon watches the two of them with interest as I stare at him, warning him with my eyes that trouble is imminent.

"That's my trident you great git." He exclaims, gaze narrowing. "Give it to me." He demands, placing palm out as his tentacles flare upwards.

"Excuse me, Vex?" Orion smirks, turning around to Gideon as though looking for his support or something. "I don't know what you're referring to, Callie gave *me* this trident. Just like she chose *me*." His expression turns nastier than I've ever seen it. I don't know what it is about Vex that brings out the beast in him, but I give up trying to understand them, they can draw them out and measure for all I care.

"That's it!" I hear Vex's words and begin to lurch forward, but before I can intercept the fist being pulled back, Gideon has moved around the two men and pulled me to safety.

"Oh no you don't! Let them at it." He orders, as we swoop upward in the water.

I right myself, rolling my eyes as the two grown men, blessed and chosen, begin to fight.

Vex's fist cracks Orion's square jawline as Orion moves to grab one of the larger tentacles attached to Vex's waist. He pulls him through the water and smashes him into the blue bricks of the courtyard floor, hitting his head on a skull in the process.

"You bloody great git!" Vex roars, upright once more as the Selkie army cheer, rising through the water to watch the brawl with fascination. Vex launches himself at Orion as I look to my father, who is shaking his head, half amused, half disappointed at the entire fiasco. Orion moves back, sensing Vex's attack and grabs him by his skull, pulling him under his armpit while bringing the heavy muscle of his tailfin up to smash into Vex's abdominals.

"Is this fight over that trident? Really?" Gideon looks to me with narrow eyes and I look away.

"Uh… not exactly…" I think about explaining, but the thought pains me too much.

"That's my girl." He winks to me and I laugh, finding great relief in just laughing about the absurdity of it all. We watch as the two men continue to beat the crap out of each other, hanging and waiting for them to tire themselves out.

"Tentacled asshole!" A full half an hour later, we're still suspended a small way from the ground, watching the fight as Vex and Orion cuss and swear so much I'm surprised they're not both blue in the face from all the breath they're wasting. I hear Orion's grunts rise from below and when I look down, deciding to watch some more, I see them both on the floor, scrapping around as Orion arcs his spine, trying to get away from Vex and moving so that it's impossible for the octoman to reach the trident which is rightfully his. It started off as an epic battle of sorts, but now it's just descended into a schoolyard tussle no more impressive than a junior high wrestling meet, with tentacles of course.

"Onion headed Nancy!!" Vex grunts, finally crawling free of the scrap by wrapping his tentacles around Orion's neck and pushing away. He ascends in the water, twisting around as Orion rises to meet him, fury flashing like wildfire across his expression. It's kind of like all the anger, all the anxiety had been leading to this; two men in an epic battle of… bad insults and fish slapping?

"You want this trident! Fine, I'll show you where you can shove it!" Orion yells, pulling the trident from his spine.

Mistake. I think, watching as the two men circle one another.

Vex inhales, breathing and letting his tentacles flare out in tendrils that curl, flexing and asserting his masculine, brute strength. Next, he simply places his hand out in the water, knowing instinctively what to do and claiming what he knows, bone deep, belongs to him. The trident flies to him through the water, landing in his palm before he wraps his fingers around it, smug as smug can be. Orion is yanked through the water slightly before he reluctantly lets go and Vex smirks, his face contorting with victory.

Orion cocks an eyebrow, pushing his hands out and blasting a wall of air that slams into Vex, causing him to crash into the floor at the very far edge of the ruins.

Orion looks up to me, his eyes narrowing in on my face as he turns, stalking off to begin talking with the Azure, who looks highly amused at the entire spectacle. He's yelling now, gesticulating wildly and causing yet more of a scene so Gideon and I dive deeper, deciding it's time to intervene.

As I push through the water and over to Orion, I hear my father say, "Nothing to see here folks. Keep on sharpening your... weapons and whatnot." He waves a hand as the hustle and bustle of the toiling armies picks up again, though several of the Selkies have helped Vex to an upright position and are shaking his hand as he nods, letting them examine his tentacles with fascination.

"I'm not his mother Orion! And that trident is HIS." Azure is saying, looking extremely annoyed as I approach.

"I'm just saying, you need to keep your pet under better control, Azure. I'm the Crowned Ruler of the Occulta Mirum for Goddess' sake. I could have him executed for what he just pulled!" Orion throws his arms up, muscles bulging as he turns to me, sensing my presence.

"You! Why did you tell him about the trident?!" He rounds on me and I scowl.

"It's HIS! And you weren't exactly giving it up voluntarily." I retort, looking into his eyes and entirely sick of his childish vendetta against Vex.

"But..." He begins, but I cut him off.

"Unless you want me to make a huge scene right here, which you've already done a fine job of doing yourself, I suggest you go and make yourself busy. You're supposed to be Crowned Ruler, as you don't mind yelling to your poor sister over here, so why don't you try acting like it?" I give him my sternest glare, as he balls his hands into fists, veins popping with rage.

"But he…" He begins.

For Goddess' sake, he's so immature.

"Orion, it's over. Get a grip on yourself." I spit at him, turning and gliding to position myself next to Azure as we both cross our arms with unamused expressions fleeting across our faces. Orion turns his back on me, swimming over to where Gideon is now talking with Cain and Cage, examining what they've decreed to be Sedna's Hammer. Azure holds her hand up and I high five her.

"You tell him. Stupid Nancy." She scowls without turning to me and uses Vex's insult readily. We both look out over the other armies, not looking at each other, but a smile creeps over my face against my better judgement.

"That was pretty funny though, right?" Azure quips and I purse my lips, fighting a laugh and still refusing to look her in the eye, knowing that if I do we'll both burst into hysterics at the stupidity of both Orion and Vex.

"Yeah." I say, keeping my expression as straight as possible, "That was pretty funny."

A few hours later and Orion finally returns to me. He's been talking to the other pod leaders, being careful to keep out of my way, so I've spent my time watching the mermaids receive instruction on fighting from the joint efforts of Kaiya, Nika and Chiyoko. Surprisingly, they make a good team, and as the pressing feeling that I should be doing something more than just sitting begins to weigh on my mind, I feel Orion's touch on my shoulder.

I turn back from the cracked rock I'm perched on, looking over my shoulder and into his glacial gaze.

"I think it's time we gather the leaders together, we need to make a plan." His expression is unapologetic and stern, not that I should expect anything else. In his mind the violence between he and Vex is natural, after all, he tainted the idea that Orion was the only one to ever lay hands on me. I wonder if that makes Orion feel like our intimacy is less so, but I suppose this isn't the time to be thinking about that. This is the time for battle strategy.

"Yes. Great idea." I reply, swizzling atop my scales and bounding high off the rock, twisting as energy thrums through me. I've been stationary too long, and I feel less anxious when I'm moving, like I can trick myself into thinking I'm being productive or something.

Orion coughs loudly, silence falling slow over the crowds as people position themselves to hear what he has to say.

"Silence if you please. Can the leader of each pod please come forward? We're going to have a meeting about strategy. More importantly, to the armies that surround me right now, I want you to listen in. You'll need to know what we decide. I don't know how much longer we have here, so I think it'll just be faster if you listen. Alright?" He commands them, instantaneously back to the man with all the potential to lead running in his veins and yet little desire for the job. He is far removed now from the immature brawler I had watched pummel Vex, and I wonder if all men have this kind of Jekyll and Hyde dichotomy inside them.

Orion swims toward Ghazi as he hangs in the water watching Fahima, who is trying to master the use of a katana, which if you ask me, is a disaster waiting to happen. Orion speaks a few words to him and the strong man nods, shooting off in the shadows of the ruins as Orion pivots and returns to the centre of the courtyard. I watch as Ghazi returns, muscles vein clad and popping with a large cuboidal stone from the ruins. He releases it from his grasp, watching the mer beneath scatter as it falls into the centre of the courtyard where they were previously sitting, looking tired.

"Gather around!" Orion bellows, moving in around the makeshift stone table. I watch him as he holds something in his palm; it's a flint he's taken off one of the warriors in the Selkie pod. He uses it to scratch out a rectangle first, before dividing it into two smaller rectangles at each end and leaving one fatter rectangle in the middle of the crude and makeshift diagram.

The leaders gather with him and I sink to take my place among them, knowing I have more than earned it. Domnall, Isabella, Aulani, my father, Hironori and Akachi join us within moments, looking between each other and exhaling simultaneously. This is going to be a long night.

402

"So, I think we should talk numbers first, don't you agree, Cole? Cole... where are you?" Orion looks around, not able to find the man among us with probably the greatest military knowledge.

"Um, I'm here..." He replies, moving in from the crowd that is now encircling us, leaving little breathing room.

"Why aren't you up here? And where's Ghazi?" Orion demands an answer as Cole looks sheepish, pushing through the crowd and moving forward into the light which shines down brightest upon the centre of the gathering.

"You said leaders..." He begins and Orion laughs.

"You are a leader. You're the military leader of the people we have. I have other fish to fry. No pun intended." He quips as Ghazi also lowers himself from his position high above. Now I observe the people around me, noticing that it's as though we're in a great amphitheatre, as the further out in distance the crowd becomes from the leaders, the higher they rise to get a good view. I take a moment to take it in, so many eyes and all of them on me. I look to Orion next, suddenly realising what it is he's just said.

"Care to elaborate on that?" I ask him but he shakes his head.

"I'll get to that in a moment. Do we have all the vessels close by as well?" He calls out, watching as several figures begin to move closer as the other Kindred part to let them past. "Oh and lastly... where's Vex?" I hear him announce this and I raise my eyebrows in surprise. He's the last person I expect Orion to be asking for.

"Who wants to know?" I hear the British tone, surly in retort, grow closer from behind Azure who is opposite Akachi and directly across from me. Orion nods to him.

"I do. I need to ask you about the Psirens." Orion replies, his expression hard to read. The other leaders look as surprised as I am, and as Vex moves forward toward us, I can tell he's not happy about being called on.

"You want my help? You just tried to beat bloody ten bells of shit out of me! Are you completely crackers?" He asks, raising one eyebrow and letting his tentacles undulate freely.

"Look, I'm sorry. I should have given you the trident. But… you hurt the one thing in this world I will die to protect, Vexus. I won't apologise for avenging your foul treatment of her." Orion narrows his eyes and I wonder if he thinks this half apology will actually work. Vex puckers his mouth.

"Well I suppose that's fair." He mumbles, rolling his eyes. Orion reaches out a hand for him to shake and Vex takes a stroke back. "Not bloody likely mate. Let's just say we don't like each other and leave it at that, shall we?"

"Fine by me." Orion smirks and then continues with his business, the leaders appearing just as confused as I feel, making me feel relieved that the psychology of these two men is not only mystifying to me. "So, how many are we looking at?" He says, inhaling as though he doesn't really want to hear the answer.

"I'd say about seven, seven and a half thousand…" Vex muses and I spin on the spot, looking out across our forces. I doubt we have half that. Orion runs his hand through his hair, exhaling bubbles.

"Right, so that's a lot. Let's see, how many men do each of you bring?" He asks the leaders. Domnall starts.

"We're abit fife hunder." He replies, puffing out his chest with pride.

"Same." Isabella says, looking to Domnall as she speaks. There's definitely something odd between those two and I watch as Enzo twitches slightly in the crowd, his sapphire encrusted facial mask glimmering and singling him out against the others.

"Ava brings eight hundred warriors." Akachi says, bowing his head.

"About four hundred." Gideon adds next, looking back over his shoulder to the pale faces that watch him.

"Nine hundred." Hironori smiles, knowing his force is by far the biggest. It's amazing when you think about the fact they all live inside one pyramid and yet the smaller pods have entire cities at their disposal. Aulani speaks next, unapologetic in her reply.

"Seventy-five." She announces and the myriad of colourful tailfins behind her continue to float, innocuous and serene as Domnall looks like he might bust or lung, or worse, start talking about the mistake of recruiting 'lassies' again.

"And we have... well hardly none." Orion says, looking back to our feeble numbers. It's true, compared to the rest we've been all but wiped out, especially now we've lost Sophia and Oscar as well. "So, in total that's... Just shy of three and a half thousand. We've got less than half their numbers. This is going to be harder than I thought." Orion lowers his eyes to the makeshift table, marking the two ends of the battlefield he's drawn with the numbers. I feel the urge to speak and touch his arm as it recoils from the rock in the centre of our meeting and Shaniqua catches my gaze from across the assembly of bodies, smiling.

"Wait, so we have less than half their numbers... but we need to remember, a lot of the Psirens have been made recently. They're young. They might be savage, but let's be honest, the last time we were confronted by them we weren't prepared. Saturnus had an edge on us, but this time he doesn't. We know what he's capable of." I reason and the others cock their heads. "You guys need to know the main players here. Saturnus and Solustus, they're the two we're really concerned about. They are the two trying to take the power of the Necrimad for themselves. You've also got Regus and Caedes who are the next oldest and equally as dangerous, especially Caedes, because he's insane and completely unpredictable. Then the rest of their army are young in comparison. So... let's look at what skill sets we've got here." I suggest, leaning forward on the table. Orion watches me and I turn back, not wanting to undermine him but knowing that numbers aren't everything. "We need to come at this logically, but not dwell too much on the numbers. The fighters we've got here... they have years of experience. So, let's mount that up against a bunch of kids with a little strength and some weapons and see where our strengths lie."

"Well, I think the Adaro could serve as your cavalry." Gideon suggests. "We have Narwhal, they're weapons on their own in the right circumstances, and fast, plus harpoons can be shot from Narwhal back." He adds, proud as I agree with him. I look to Domnall next.

"Do you think you can join with the Adaro? Lead them? Gideon has a special way with the cold. I was thinking about the Necrimad..." I turn back to Vex.

"You said that thing can boil the water around it?" I ask him and he nods, eyes dark with experience of the horrors this has caused.

"Bloody right it can. I've never felt anything like it. It was like... like the water was on fire. You couldn't escape it. Mind you I was only around it a small while before they chained me up and started with the stabby, stabby, but... yeah, you don't forget that." I look back to the aquamarine eyes of my father.

"I want you to try and combat it. I can't have whole segments of our men taken out like that. Think you can manage it?" I ask him and he frowns.

"I can try. I've dealt with fire demons before, but nothing that can boil water... none the less, I'll give it my best shot. If that's where you think I'm best positioned." He agrees and I smile, glad for his support as well as his power.

"Isabella, what about the Water Nymphs?" I ask her, and she smiles.

"Darling, you put us wherever you see fit. However, me and Hironori, we think we might have come up with something... a little explosive. It's never been tested, but it could work." She muses, looking to the Emperor who bows his head in return.

"Explosives? Like what?" I ask her and Hironori smiles.

"We have some grenades, water tight, which we have brought with us. I've been saving them for the right occasion. They've never been tested." He explains and I nod, wondering exactly what will be left for salvaging after the city is cleared of Psirens. *If* the city is cleared of Psirens.

"Oh!" I exclaim, satisfied as Orion begins to look slightly more contented beside me. Hironori raises a long willowy finger, the long sleeves of his chain mail kimono shirt falling far below his arms.

"We have also spoken with the Maneli. Their camouflaging techniques mixed with our stealth... we can surely also utilise their long-range weapon technology as well..." He says as Akachi interjects.

"I think that the Maneli and the Kappa should stay back, or perhaps even come from a different direction. The element of surprise once the battle is underway might be crucial. Sometimes appearing weaker than you are can be advantageous." He blinks horizontally and the crocodile around his staff does the same as they gaze at me, seeking my approval.

Do they actually think I'm in charge? I wonder, looking to Orion for support. I have absolutely no battle experience; after all, high school level calculus just so doesn't count.

"Good plan. I think that's a very good idea. Now... onto weapons. What kind of weapons are we packing?" Orion asks, not wanting to waste any time.

The leaders speak in turn, showing that we have an accumulation of grenades, catapults, swords, flails, maces, katanas, harpoons, bows and arrows, polearms, daggers and of course the Pieces of Eight. As we stand, I find myself drawn to Aulani, who has remained silent through this entire ordeal.

"What about the Sirena?" I ask, looking her directly in her white eyes. Orion coughs, looking uncomfortable as the other leaders rotate toward her.

"We have a plan of our own. It involves meditation as healing and helpful energies will be summoned from all corners of the seas. We will aid you. Worry not." She nods, smiling like an ancient wise woman, though she is so young in appearance.

"Okay..." I nod, unsure of how to respond to that. The other pods expressions turn confused as they wonder what the hell we're doing including the peace keeping hippies who refuse to fight for the cause we're all prepared to die for.

"Next... The Conduit." Shaniqua comes forward from the shadows with wide eyes. "You need a plan to assemble them. It's going to be a warzone... not exactly perfect for a ritual, or whatever it is that will happen." She frowns, looking to me and clearly annoyed she has no idea what is going on either.

"Also, we have the problem of the fact that Saturnus has my Piece of Eight. The Scythe of Atargatis." I remind everyone. Orion coughs, putting a strong hand on my armoured shoulder.

"I'm going to be retrieving it, while you..." He pauses, looking uncomfortable, "wait with the other vessels away from the battlefield." My eyes narrow, watching him gauge my reaction.

Rage begins to build as I hang there and my fists ball at my sides.

Without warning, we break out into an argument so fierce the other leaders can do nothing but float and watch, transfixed.

31
The Fear
AZURE

I float, unamused, in the water as the domestic to end all domestics rages on. It's been an hour and Callie and Orion are still going at it. I roll my eyes as they start up once again, going over the same points time after time and getting nowhere.

"Orion, you're being *ridiculous!* I can call the scythe to me from a small distance away; I won't even have to fight Saturnus! You could be killed even attempting to get it away from him!" She shouts, my brother's expression getting more incredulous by the second.

"Wow, thanks for your believing in me! Besides, if you go out into that battlefield and die, then what? You won't be able to enact The Conduit anyway! God you're so stubborn! This isn't even about you being strong, or independent, or whatever the hell it is that is so important to you that you have this stupid death wish! This is about what's best for *everyone!* It's all very well you trying to be the hero and all, but even if we win the battle, if we can't enact The Conduit we're screwed!" Orion is out of breath and the leaders start to look beyond bored to the point where they might well fall asleep. Gideon watches the go between, torn between standing up for Little Miss Sunshine and condemning her to most certain death at the hands of a raving maniac. So, all in all, it's a complete hash.

"Okay!" I yell, swimming forward and swinging my hips with rightful authority, sick of the yelling. If I'd thought the visions were bad I was wrong, compared to this they're a swim through a kelp forest. "I think we've officially had enough of this domestic row. The rest of you, go back to preparing. If all you're going to do is fight, then there's damn well no point the rest of us hanging around. Your personal issues aren't a freaking spectator sport." I shoo everyone away and the leaders turn their backs, pivoting with unimpressed faces before they return to the outskirts of the courtyard, where the massive amounts of, probably pointless, crap they've brought with them is stashed. I roll my eyes as the Sirena sit down on the blue stones of the floor, central to it all, before holding hands and beginning to chant some useless mumbo jumbo. I propel forward to Orion and Callie, who are both red in the face and scowling.

"What? Don't you look at me like that! Go sort your crap out over there, and when you've finally figured out which one of you wants to play hero and which one wants to watch, then maybe we can all go finally get slaughtered. Alright? Good." I push them away, rolling my eyes for the millionth time and bored of their stupid love affair with drama. I turn around in the water, no longer wanting to lay eyes on the pitiful excuse the mer pod has for a royal family. That's when I come face to face with Vex.

"Thanks for that. I was getting rather sick of listening to them go round and round in bloody circles." He sighs, a bored expression falling across his face.

"Whatever. I'm sure they'll sort it out and we'll all be back to deciding exactly how it is we're going to swim to our deaths in no time." I frown, feeling tired of all the build-up. Can't we just get to the fighting already? I'm in the mood for a good tussle.

"I hope Onion head can talk some sense into her." He shrugs, turning away, and suddenly I'm irrationally angry, no change there, but now it's directed at Vex.

"What, you don't think she should be able to fight because she's a woman?" I challenge him, baring my teeth and watching him cock his slashed brow, irises ablaze.

"No, Love. I don't think she should be able to fight because if she dies, which, let's be honest, is bloody likely considering she's a complete twiglet, then all the other vessels are bloody useless aren't they? Oh, and by the way, don't bloody well snarl like that, it's making me tingly." He stares at me, his eyes sparkling, goading me. I wonder if he's waiting for some great reaction, like me slapping him, which I must admit I do rather enjoy, but instead I just hang there, annoyed at his logical response. As I think about what he's said, an unfamiliar feeling creeps into my stomach, making it unpleasantly heavy as my heart flutters, weak in constitution.

"What, no name calling? No violence? I'm hurt, Love." Vex teases as I look away, not wanting to hold his gaze any longer.

"Whatever." I mumble, knowing the name of the feeling within me but not wanting to admit that I've been infected with it. I take off into the shadows to skulk, longing for the security of the darkness.

"Azure?" I hear my name being called, the caller not someone I desire to be present, as I perch atop the ruined dome roof of one of the Atlantian buildings. I turn away, knowing the direction from which he is coming. "What the bloody hell you doing all the way over here, Love? They're back at it, talking about battle strategy again." Vex's words reach me as the deep and eerie blue ripple of the surface high above falls upon my face.

"I'm sure they'll survive without me." I snap, having absolutely no desire whatsoever to go back to talking about the fight.

"What's wrong?" Vex asks, faking concern for me, probably because he's bored or, more likely, nosey.

"Why do you care?" I snap, finally turning to face him as my long hair billows out around me.

"Because... I don't know. I just bloody do, alright?" I meet his gaze and my eyes widen as they bear into his, the weight of everything going on around us causing us to stop, caught in the clutches of a nameless emotion that flickers behind his eyes. Vex sighs, sitting down next to me on the domed ruin as we

411

look out over the city, or what remains of it anyway. My defences retreat as the sarcastic and vicious part of myself recedes, unwilling in all senses of the word.

"You're afraid." Vex states this as fact, his expression grave.

"Yes." I admit, my hair falling down around me as I lower my head and look upon the dull shine of my fluke.

"It's okay." He replies, turning from me as his irises flash, shining out into the shadow.

"It's not. I didn't think I'd feel this way." I admit, letting fear clutch at me in the darkness with him.

"Why? It's only natural." He says what he's supposed to, predictable and failing in surprising me. The swarm moves overhead, their red eyes staring out at all angles.

"I guess I don't understand why I'm afraid, because there's nothing keeping me here. I have nothing left to live for." I confess, bashful as I feel my heartbeat falter, weak as it may be, in the monochromatic rhythm of the eternal funeral march I have been waiting to cease.

"That's not true." Vex says, like he could possibly know what I'm feeling, what my life has been like.

Stupid child. I think, wondering why it is he's still here.

"You don't understand. You don't even seem all that evil if I'm honest." I say, looking to him with a serious expression, he laughs.

"Darkness isn't the first addictive substance I've dabbled with, Love. The night I was turned... well let's just say I wasn't on that beach shooting up with tea." He explains, turning his arm sideways. I look to his pale flesh, which is scattered with long closed injection sites.

"I see. So, it's like that..." I ask him, really curious now. The darkness shimmers around us as the swarm move like deathly fireflies.

"Like a drug? For me, yes. I've come off the hard stuff before. It's not so different. Granted drugs don't consume your thought processes like being a Psiren. That magic, or whatever the bloody hell it was she did to me, it's hard to know what's still me and what's *it.*" He explains and I nod, agreeing. I know only too well how addictive the rage within can become; it makes you strong,

412

makes you invulnerable, but at the same time is almost impossible to cleave from because you start to need it.

"Still doesn't explain why I'm scared. I have no reason to be. My soulmate is gone, I failed my daughter, everyone around me just gets hurt. When I lash out... I'm not making the world a better place. It would be better if I weren't in it. I wasn't even supposed to live this long. I've outstayed my welcome." I conclude, looking around at the ruins and wondering what will be next for me. The fires of hell perhaps?

Who knows.

"Maybe. Or maybe the people around you just aren't strong enough to handle who you are." Vex muses with a discreet smile and I realise it's the first time I've seen a genuine expression cross his face that's not laced with innuendo or disdain. I can't explain it, but with him I can't help but spill emotion from my seams. It's unusual to say the least, but this is the second little chat we've had in as many days, and I'm beginning to wonder why he's following me like a stray dog.

"Why do we keep ending up having these little heart to hearts you think?" I ask him, quelling my instinct to flee.

"We're the only two Psirens. Bloody figures, don't it?"

"Yeah, I guess." I shrug, realising I'm being completely irrational in making up feelings and fantasising connections where they don't belong. I must really be scared.

God, what's happening to me?

We sit there atop the ruins, looking out into the darkness where this place, whatever the hell it is, ends.

"I'm glad you're afraid, Love." Vex finally turns to me fully, his face acute in its bone structure and oddly beautiful in every wrong way he can be.

"Why?" I ask, not knowing if I want to hear his reasoning. He turns to me, placing a hand over mine hesitantly, almost like it's by accident but not quite as I flinch, my body tensing at the soft touch of another.

"Because if you're afraid it means, despite what you say, that you do still have something to lose. The fire behind your eyes isn't extinguished yet, Love, and you know, I personally can't wait to see what happens when you let it blaze."

We sit in the dark, silent, as I hear my name being called from afar once more, this time though it's by Callie and Orion, so I suppose I had better go and see what they want.

"Come on." I say to Vex, who is still beside me with his hand over mine like a limp dead thing that would frighten small children.

We pass over the deathly quiet of the ruins, moving toward the light of the courtyard that seems to come from no determined source. This dimension is certainly a strange place, almost lit, almost dark, almost within time, though not quite. A city almost gone but not quite enough to be forgotten. It is a place of in-betweens, a place of almost and not quite, as we cast our darkness upon it's half shadow, almost taking in each part of the sprawling piles of rock and crystal, but not quite caring enough to bother.

"Yes?" I ask, sounding tired, as I glide to the centre of the once more cyclical assembly of Kindred before staring down into Callie's wide and too sparkling eyes.

"We're assigning targets. Want in?" She asks, cocking an eyebrow and smiling, self- satisfied as my expression unwillingly lights up.

"Finally!" I gasp, glad that we're getting down to the nitty gritty at last. "Who do I get to kill?" I ask her, rubbing my hands together and barging in between Isabella and Domnall who are ridiculously close in proximity.

"We were thinking… it's a big ask."

"If it wasn't someone important I'd be offended. I want to gut someone who's at least a semi-threat to the world. I need them for my severed-skull shot glass collection." I joke, but Orion's expression turns worried and I roll my eyes, which I somehow can't stop doing as a natural reaction to almost everything lately. Maybe it's because all these righteous heroes make me want to hurl. "I'm joking! Jesus, a skull isn't a good shot-glass, stupid! It has holes in for a start!" I say, exasperated but for some reason my reply makes him look

414

even more concerned. "Oh for God's sake, who am I killing?" I ask him, bored of waiting. Callie breathes in and then out again.

"You're paired with Solustus." She names him, and I fist pump the water. "Yes!"

"Hey, don't get too excited, we're sending Ghazi with you." Orion scolds, spoiling my fun as per usual.

"Seriously? Why are you sending him if I'm going?" I whine, not understanding the bug up Orion's butt about women fighting alone.

"You've been paired with Solustus because you've known him a long time. Studied him. I'm dealing with Saturnus, but I can't stick around, once I've got the scythe I'm out of there to get it back to Callie. I need you to hold them off while I'm gone. Ghazi will be helping you deal with them both should it come to that." Orion announces as I look to Callie, realising that she must have lost their prior argument.

"Okay, so what about everyone else?" I ask them, feeling my heart racing at the thought of going fin to fin with Solustus. It's a lot of trust to put in me after everything that's happened, but then again, he did kill my sister and I owe him infinite amounts of death for that.

"Did you bring Vex with you?" Orion asks me and I feel like sulking. What am I? The tentacled jackass' sidekick?

"I'm here." He raises his short arm above his head, coming forth from the shadows with an unreadable expression.

"You're on Caedes watch. Figured crazy versus crazy fit." Orion jokes and Vex's face goes slack, deadpan and irritated.

"I get to babysit. Bloody brilliant." He complains, crossing his arms over his chest.

"Hey, you're lucky you're fighting at all. You're a vessel, so when the time comes and Rose gives the signal, you get to the formation, got it?" Orion says and Callie looks pissed, her face is super sulky, like someone has taken her favourite toy away.

"Wait there's a signal? That's a bit crap. Not exactly bloody stealthy." Vex retorts and the rest of the group slouch, clearly tired of this discussion.

"Yes, we've already been over this. The pros and cons of a signal, but missing the moment when the blood moon reaches the peak of its ascent in the sky is the biggest con out there. When it's time for The Conduit to be put into play, be there." Orion doesn't pause for effect; he just carries on dishing out orders. I stare behind me, finding the surrounding people immersed in the action and watching Orion as though transfixed.

"As for Regus, I have a bit of an odd request for this. Callie, I don't know what you think but seeing as how he's a brute, what do you say to pitting the remaining maidens, not involved in the signal, against him? They worked well as a team before." At these words Callie snorts, looking aggravated.

"Are you serious? I can't fight because I might get hurt, but you're putting the maidens against freaking Regus!? Really Orion!?" She starts, waving her hands up in the air and once again an eruption of sound explodes from around me. The maidens are behind Callie, their eyes fearful, but suddenly everyone except them has an opinion on how to tackle Regus. I hang there, stuck between a myriad of foreign tongues spitting at one another, all wanting to be heard, all wanting in on the action. I tune out, knowing that soon I will be facing off with Solustus.

As I'm thinking this, I feel something creep in beside me and wrap around my hand like a limp dead thing. At this simple touch and for just a moment, no matter how small, I am once more afraid.

SOLUSTUS

They toil, readying for war as I look out over the smashed debris of my city. Readying itself for not only the arrival of the mer, but what happens afterwards, when we move inland to slaughter, pillage, kill and rape. Whatever satiates my desire most at the time. More importantly, tonight is my re-ascension to the rank of God, or in this case, as close to God as one not naturally born on the higher plains will ever get.

My hands shake on the disgustingly bright sill as the sun begins to set above. I feel my heart hammer, unusually perky within my ribcage and I wonder why it is I'm breathless, why it is I'm trembling on the eve I have waited for so long. Fear is clutching me in its poisonous grasp, reminding me that I am treading a thin line between success and the punishment of infinite life. I can only hope the mer will return on this prophesised night, though I have no doubt that Azure will make sure of that. After all, those chosen to protect this world are unlikely to leave it completely unguarded for too long, even if they have been absent all this time.

As I muse their whereabouts, I watch the men below, lining the streets as the pitiful armour, that has been collected or created by the group of Psiren's I was punishing for losing my metal master, is handed out. A small hiccup, one can hope.

I turn away, bored by the spectacle of observing the insects from a great height quicker than usual.

As I turn to swim back into the study, I come face to face with my brother who has been watching me as he leans against the front of his desk. I jump, startled.

"You, jumping? Really Solustus, that's not like you at all. Feeling well, brother? I hope you won't have to sit out of battle. That would be no good at all." Saturnus smirks, reminding me that he too is in line for half my power, his face a collection of both glee and concern, though why he's concerned I can't tell. I shake my head, waving away my paranoia. Of course, he's concerned, we're family, brothers in blood.

"I am... nervous." I choose my words carefully, letting my shaking fingertips caress the handle of my rapier, trying to calm myself.

"That is to be expected, on an eve such as this." Saturnus begins, moving his black and white tailfin to sit behind the desk in the centre of the room. The cyclical height of the tower casts shadows across both our faces, streaking them both darkest black and blazing orange from the setting sun of twilight. "Don't fret, all will be well. The mer will come, meek in forces to be sure, and we will be rid of them in mere moments. The army is only precautionary, plus... it might weed out some of the weaklings. I doubt there's even a handful left. Even

417

if they do have Azure and Orion, their powers are limited by their numbers. It will be easy. Like taking candy from an army-less baby." Saturnus smiles, his face content.

"How can you be so sure they will come? How do you know they won't know we need them dead and stay clear of here?" I ask him, cocking my head to one side and knowing I am late in asking these questions. My silver hair is stiff in the water, spiky like the spines of a porcupine as I watch it turn my shadow jagged.

"They are… good. Good people don't do the smart thing brother; they do the right thing. Of course, they will come. They feel it's their duty to stop us." He reasons this with me and I feel less than convinced. "Any requests for the battle ahead? I personally want to kill the boy." Saturnus' eyes flash wicked in the light, turning ice blue for just a moment as though just the thought of Orion has made him appear as a glimmer. A mirage atop a man thirsting for blood.

"Why him?" I ask, feeling curious and allowing the conversation to divert from my nerves.

"He took my throne." Saturnus snarls, his eyes narrow and his face becomes animal in its feral cruelty.

"Very well, I have no preference. Death is death. Blood is blood." I take my sword from its sheath, looking at the length of it, still sticky with scarlet as I put it to my tongue, licking it clean and enjoying her rough bite. I want Scarlette looking pretty for company.

Saturnus spins from me in his chair and looks to The Scythe of Atargatis.

"This will be my weapon." He says, satisfaction in his tone. "It is only too perfect, the use of the scythe created by Poseidon to help Atargatis protect the seas, used in the act which will set about its destruction. It is perfect." He purrs.

"So what about the Necrimad? Exactly what are the details of the ritual, have you discovered how to split the power?" I ask him, narrowing my gaze and watching his face intently.

"No. However, I think if we both speak the incantations and keep in physical contact at the time when the Necrimad's power is ready to transfer, it should work effectively enough." He replies, his gaze deeply penetrating in its intensity as he speaks. I can tell he has thought long and hard about how to split

418

the magic that's been stolen, and I can only hope he is right. Regardless, if he isn't he won't have the power to stop me once it all belongs to me anyway.

"How will we know when enough blood has been shed?" I ask him, thinking aloud. "I don't understand why we have not already tipped the scales. After all, we have thousands of Psirens. They must be but a handful."

"Ah, but here's the thing, we are not making more dark magic, we are simply diluting it and spreading it through more bodies. Each one of the mer was created by the Goddess herself. They are worth much more in light per single entity than a Psiren." He explains and, though I nod, I'm still not sure how this can be correct.

"But how can almost seven thousand men not outweigh the power of a handful of mer?" I ask and Saturnus shrugs.

"I don't know. They must be more powerful than I thought. Callie is the vessel, so no doubt she's full of light energy. Then you've got Azure and Orion, both descendants of the original mer, Atlas." He spits the name like it's poisonous and I furrow my brow.

"But Azure, she's one of us. One of the very first." I recall, trying to catch him in a lie.

"In spite of Azure's pollution with the dark, she's now using it for other means, that makes her a positive force. Remember, brother, it is not only how much of what source of power is present, but also how said power is used which matters. It's a complicated equation to balance, but once the time comes we'll know. The Necrimad will show us the way." He explains, but I still don't understand what this means. I'm not one for book learning, never have been, I have always learnt through doing what is necessary for survival.

"I don't understand it." I admit, shrugging and Saturnus smiles.

"We are not supposed to. It is near impossible deciphering texts on the subject. One of the reasons, I'm sure you recall, I was so glad it took the mer centuries to discover my true face. I wasn't sure of even the vessel's true purpose being to bring down the energy from the higher plains to unlock the Necrimad's seal, which Poseidon created, by absorbing it and trapping it in the scythe, until recently." His eyebrows pinch together and I can sense the frustration which has plagued him for longer than he wants to admit. "These

419

texts have been my life's work and if I've learned anything, it is that the Gods and Goddesses, selfish in nature, not only want to lord power over us, but they want information kept to themselves too. It's pathetic when you think about it. It's all about them keeping everything sacred and good for themselves. Perhaps if the information was around in a more common tongue, someone would have already succeeded them." He rolls his eyes and I can tell he feels passionately about the issue. I can't deny he's right though. The Gods and Goddesses of the seas are selfish. They do nothing while we slave for them, squirming around in a puddle like insects. They keep us stupid and powerless because they like to watch us flail, it amuses them when they become bored of their own mightiness.

"You are very clever, brother. If it were not for you, we would not be here. No matter what happens here tonight, thank you." I find myself faltering in my ways, thanking my brother who I often want to kill. It is true; he has shown me the way of the rituals. I had craved the power, but he had carved the way back to it.

I watch him as he picks up the scythe, passing it in his hands and looking to me with fondness in his eyes; though for me or the appropriate irony of his choice of weapon I cannot tell.

"Come Solustus. It is time we ready for ascension."

32
The Approach
ORION

Gabriel fastens more armoured metal plates around my torso, linking them together to prevent injury in battle. His hands touch my flesh intermittently in the odd, eerie light of the Atlantian courtyard, as the rest of the army are swimming quickly between each other's pods, preparing for us to move on in only a short while. Callie is floating before me, a scowl on her beautiful face and fire in her eyes. She's not coping well with the idea of being left out of battle.

"I just… I don't see how you can possibly rationalise allowing Vex to fight, allowing the mermaids to fight, and yet not allowing *me* to fight. I'm the only one out of the lot of them who's actually killed a Psiren single-handedly!" She rages, her armour being checked over by Amara, who it seems is very good friends with Gabriel, a match I never could have foreseen.

"You're a vessel Callie!" I exclaim, going over this once more with feeling. Trying to get her to compromise, to see my side.

"Vex is a vessel." She retorts, crossing her Kevlar covered arms across her silver and aqua breast plate. She's pissed.

"Yes, but Vex is also…." I begin, but she cuts me off.

"He's also nothing. The only difference between him and me is that he's a man." She looks away, anger in her stare. I sigh out into the water, bubbles rising from me in a torrent of frustration.

"Look, I can't do this with you there. If I take on Saturnus to get the scythe back and you're there, he'll use you against me." Her gaze narrows, as though she knows for a fact she is right, but she isn't. It's not because she's a woman. It's because she's *my* woman. I can't fight Saturnus without holding back if I'm worried about protecting her.

"That is total and complete crap. He can only use me against you if I let him. I have no intention of doing that. I thought we had put this to rest." She scowls again as the final piece of her armour is detached and reattached, just to make sure it's fully functional.

"This is different. This isn't one demon, or even one Psiren. It's a war. We're swimming into a massacre, and you're a part of the greatest hope we have of stopping it before we lose too much. Please, Callie, do what you were put here for; fulfil your role as the vessel. Let me worry about Saturnus and your scythe." I beg her, seeing Cole swimming over from the Adaro, where he's just introduced Domnall to the rest of his cavalry.

"Orion! You wanted to see me?" He calls, gliding through the water toward me through the rushing about of bodies, the clatter of armour and the grunts of people practising with their weapons.

"Yes, now I know I said I wanted you to oversee things in a wider sense, but I actually have a more important job for you." I breathe, looking to Callie as I speak and wondering how she'll react to what I'm about to say. The only thing I can think is, *it's a good job I have armour on.* "I want you to protect the vessels. While we're waiting for the signal, they'll be vulnerable. It is vital that they remain safe." Callie's mouth pops open as I hold my breath.

"Oh nice, I get a babysitter now?!" She cries out, throwing her arms up into the water and taking a stroke away from Amara. Gabriel is now finished with my new armour also, so the two of them retreat away from the fiery temper of my soulmate, looking back over their shoulders and smirking.

"Callie, do you want to be the reason that The Conduit fails? Do you? Because that's the risk you're taking by going into battle. Also, you know we could have saved ourselves the trouble of almost being killed several times travelling the world looking for the other vessels if you'd told me this earlier." I scowl now, annoyed she won't see reason. I understand she feels the need to

422

be strong, independent and capable, and I no longer doubt that she is all of these things. However, she is too precious to the cause to risk losing, regardless of the fact she is also precious to me.

"Fine!" She blows bubbles out again and turns her back on me as Cole's eyes fall downward, his expression guilty. I know he likes Callie and I hate putting him in between us.

I reach out, grabbing her hand before she has a chance to storm off and pulling her toward me. I caress the side of her face, her expression remaining stormy as I do.

"Callie, please. Don't be angry with me. Soon we'll be in the thick of it, I don't want the last memories I have of us to be us fighting." I whisper, looking down into her fiery gaze as it extinguishes.

"That's a ridiculous thing to say and a crappy way to get me to forgive you." She mutters, ignoring the fact that I might well be right.

"Regardless, I love you. Please, don't hate me. I'm trying to do what's best for the whole. I know you're strong, I know you can kill Psirens, I know that. You don't have to prove anything. I just need you to look after the other vessels, make sure that part of the plan is taken care of. It's the most important part. I wouldn't entrust it to anyone else." I nod my head, to her trying to give reassurance, and she rolls her eyes, unable to stop herself smiling.

"God... How do you do that?" She asks, reaching up and touching the side of my face.

"What?" I ask her, feigning innocence.

"Act like you're not protecting me for utterly selfish reasons." She moves her head close to mine, the aqua plastic of her visor making her eyes sparkle even brighter than usual.

"Well, you get mad if I admit I don't want you to die." I laugh, hearing how absurd the sentence sounds.

"Well, I don't want you to die either. So, should I get you a babysitter too?" She asks me, cocking an eyebrow.

"If you wish." I say, looking to her with a relaxed expression. My nerves somewhat dissolve at her odd humour as it keeps me both grounded and distracted.

"Hmmm... who should I pick?" She runs her fingers through her long hair, dislodging her visor, as she taking in the crowds of people. Finally, her eyes rest on Cole and widen, the look she always gets when she's inspired.

"Cole, can you ask Jack to go with Orion? Just as a precaution, someone to watch his back? I think it's best if we don't have anyone fighting totally alone." She requests, her breath caught in her throat a second. Cole's eyes glint and his lips turn up in a smile.

"He'll be honoured you thought of him." She beams at his reply, turning back to me.

"There. Now we'll both have babysitters." She reaches up and gives me a slow and careful kiss, running her hands through my hair.

"Orion?" She says my name, her eyes fearful as she pulls away.

"What?" I ask her, my heart beating wild in my ribcage at her closeness. I wonder if it will be our last kiss.

"If you die, I'll kill you." She vows, expression serious. With that she turns away, but not before I catch a glimpse of her eyes, sparkling still, but this time with unshed tears.

The hour has moved slowly, and with every passing moment the water between each of the three thousand plus soldiers grows increasingly tense. It's gotten to the point now where everyone is silent, even the mermaids, even Azure and Vex. Not a word passes from any of them; afraid that if any one of them speaks that everyone will fall apart.

In books and films, from what I know of them anyway, battles are shown to be exciting, an adventure. In reality, they are not. In reality, they are terrifying. It is terrifying now, as it was all those many years ago that I am only minutes, perhaps an hour at most, from the cusp of what may be my final moments.

In these seconds, as I float, watching people moving, falling into formations and packing up the last of the supplies they will need, everything moves in slow motion.

I savour each breath, letting the water rush in through my gills and the air pulled from it diffuse throughout my body. I let the zing of the ocean's water sizzle on my tongue, and the sound of liquid moving, fluid and unstoppable, soothe my ears. I let myself hang in this calm, appreciating each of the senses that constitute, together, what it is to be alive. Finally, my eyes rest on her, taking in every inch of her form and feasting upon it like an eternally starving man.

I close my eyes, blinking slowly as the moment passes, before I turn, watching as the last of the soldiers fall into place. Domnall moves to my side and we look out over the warriors of our cause, each one ready now for the battle to begin.

The warriors roll back from me, where I am suspended in full armour by the front end of the courtyard, in their thousands. First in the assembly are my friends, my family, my pod. Oh and Vex. The maidens look up to me, holding their weapons and shields with shaking limbs. I know they must be terrified, perhaps more so than everyone else, but still, they've come a long way from where they were only months before, and I know they can do this. Simply because they have little other choice.

Behind the Children of Atargatis, the Selkies and Adaro float, merged together. Narwhals and Kelpies fidget in the water, bridled and ready to move onto the battlefield. Their riders, all pale, though to varying degrees, look solemn, as though they're too busy focusing on what is to come to notice what is going on right now and they clutch broad swords, bows and harpoons to their chests.

Beyond the Cavalry, the Water Nymphs are stationary, gleaming in gold and unmistakable in the unbridled shimmer of their tails. They hold an assortment of weapons in their palms and a look of complete focus on their faces. Isabella is at the front of this section of the deathly procession, her eyes sparkling and maniacally hungry for bloodshed.

Toward the rear, the Maneli and Kappa merge as one, with several fighters lifting large mechanical weapons like metal catapults, traps involving netting and other such devices between them. The remaining fighters, fully covered in camouflage and directed by the maidens in design to match the sea floors of the

425

pacific, do not even stir, so much so they could be statues. The only thing which will distinguish them from being a natural formation are the long samurai swords, katanas and tantos which are strapped to their spines.

Bringing up the rear, the Sirena float, ethereal and ghostly as ever in their permanent poise. They hold no armour, no weapons. Nothing to even indicate they will so much as raise a finger to defend us.

To my left, separate from the masses, Cole and the vessels, including my beloved, are waiting for us to move, each holding their sacred weapon to them as though it's the most precious thing they've ever owned. Gideon hovers beside his daughter, hand on her armoured shoulder and a serious look on his face as Jack moves from behind them, walking out an old friend toward me, fully saddled and ready to go.

Philippe whinnies as I rise in the water.

Perching myself atop his spine. I look out across the army, across the many men and women from many corners of the earth and smile. Regardless of whether we win or lose, it is incredible that they are all here, collected in one place for the very first time. Shaniqua ascends in the water before me, with a tranquil expression, holding a spear in both hands. She passes it to me and that's when I realise she's wearing armour too.

"You're coming with us?" I ask her, feeling silly I had never asked before.

"Of course. It was Atlas' biggest hope that one day the Psirens would be defeated. I wouldn't miss it." She admonishes, looking me up and down. "He would be so proud of you, Orion. More so than you'll ever know. You have become a far greater man than he could have ever anticipated." She moves forward, placing a kiss on my cheek before she retreats to float among the mer, her lime tailfin glittering wildly against the dark contrast of her borrowed Maneli armour. I look down to Azure who is wearing not a speck of armour and is, as usual, looking bored and inhale, ready to say something inspirational, something I know they're all expecting to hear.

As I go to speak, a lightning strike sparks behind me, illuminating the faces of everyone in the assembly. Domnall claps me on the shoulder from where he and Magnus float beside me as I look up to him, Philippe dwarfed by Magnus' size.

"Let's gang, lad." His expression is half feral, half joyous, the impending violence making him impatient and excited. I only wish I could feel the same as I look back over the gathering of pods and raise my spear in the air, turning Philippe a hundred and eighty degrees to face the new whirlpool which has just opened up before us.

I gulp, knowing that on the other side everything I've been relentlessly thinking about, worrying about and dreading these last few weeks will become reality. It could be the end of everything. It could be our extinction.

The whirlpool rattles Philippe, who cries out, the sound of his scared whinnies breaking the still darkness of the ocean where we are spat out onto the sand. Philippe's hooves touch down as, amazingly enough, the rest of the army departs from the portal in much the same order as they entered. I stare around, the darkness bloody from the orangey-red moon, which I can see has only just broken over the horizon. I curse internally, realising that I hadn't thought about the fact it would be dark, and wondering how much of a problem this will cause us. The Psirens have better night vision that we do and this gives them an immediate and unfortunate advantage.

I examine my surroundings further, finding only flat expanses of sand for miles, but I know where we are, and the place where the Occulta Mirum lies in ruin is not far. Still, we are far enough away for me to issue out orders to the army and make sure that the Maneli and Kappa make themselves scarce, waiting to come into the fight later as a second charge of sorts.

I pull on Philippe's reigns, turning in the water as to face the army as the last of the Kindred depart from the whirlpool. Shortly after, it dissipates into nothingness.

"Maneli and Kappa fighters, you will move off from this point to the left, but stay clear of the field of battle until the first charge has been made. Hironori, Akachi, I leave the judgement as to when you join the fight up to you. Watch, but keep your distance." I order them as Hironori and Akachi rise, wordless as they swim with measured speed forward through the water toward me, both men shaking my hand before they depart in complete silence. They take most

427

our fighters with them, almost half in fact, leaving the fin soldiers and cavalry with me.

Callie moves from my right, where she has been watching me issue out orders with wide eyes, as though she can't believe this is all really happening.

"I want to come with you to the battle field. We'll need to be nearby anyway, but I want to see you off." She pleads with me, her gaze only exuding the highest levels of affection mixed with terror. I smile to her, obliging her request, and glad to know she has made peace with the fact that she won't be following me into battle.

"Of course." I admonish, as she takes a stroke back from me before taking her place next to her father. I stare out over the remains of my army and then back over my shoulder to where I know, just over the top of the sandy horizon, the Occulta Mirum lies, decimated.

I breathe in, not sure whether I am quite ready to see the sight of my Kingdom in ruins, but knowing I have no other choice.

The Psirens had come in, uninvited and taken my home, smashing my father's legacy to pieces in the process. Now it is time for me to take it back. It is time for me to reclaim what rightfully belongs to me.

I raise my spear in the air, beckoning the horizon.

"Let's move out!"

SOLUSTUS

"It's time." Saturnus announces, his voice booming out over the city. The Psiren army is assembled in full force, the flames of their lit arrows casting deep shadows into the crevices of their bony skulls, making them appear demonic and feral.

I twist my lips into a smile, nervous but satisfied with the colossal mass of bodies which float, just below the edge of the sand bowl in which the Occulta Mirum once sat. They cover the bowl all the way around, leaving only the centre, where the ruins lay, free from bodies.

I watch them, eyes wide as they stare at me and my brother as the Necrimad sits back on its haunches to our left, breathing heavily, carefully, as though it knows something is about to happen.

"You are to kill. Leave no one alive. Understand?" I bark out to them. I could order them to turn, but I won't risk any of their so-called heroes turning vigilante like Azure. I would not repeat Titus' mistakes.

Darius twitches incrementally at the sound of my voice, still tender from where I had whipped him raw. I feel the power I have exerted over him, how I have broken him, and I grin to myself, ready to ascend. Ready to grasp the power that is rightfully mine. He is a reminder that I am worthy. After all, if I can break and ruin him with perhaps a quarter of the power that rightfully belongs to me still thrumming through my veins, I know that with the entirety of that power returning, Saturnus and I will be unstoppable.

We pivot, staring into the darkness of the battlefield ahead and I feel a sense of disappointment, there is nothing but shadow.

"Archers, release one round of arrows, aim for the centre of the battlefield." I command, wanting to do something to calm my nerves. I am nervous the mer will not come. I am nervous the blood moon will rise, only to fall once more with nothing but sand before me. No bloodshed, no death. Only calm.

I hear the sound of arrows loaded into bows and then the satisfying spring of them being let loose as the flaming arrowheads, set alight with the same magnesium flare we had used in the fall of this city which Saturnus had so cleverly preserved, fly through the water. They land in the centre of the field where they continue to burn a hot flame, illuminating the sand and casting red light throughout the space, creating ambience for death.

"You're one for dramatic flair." Saturnus laughs, his mouth too wide and his eyes bottomless black. He looks maniacal in his glee.

"I've been waiting for this for so long. I have high expectations. Least of all that the mer will actually turn up." I voice my doubt again and Saturnus turns as I examine his form. Neither of us wear any armour, not wanting to be weighed down and our pale skin and dark eyes look evil in the shadows cast by the night as we remain suspended, waiting.

"They will come." He exhales, tired of having to reassure me again. "You remember the incantations?" He asks me and I nod, bored of them already. It probably would have only taken me a few seconds to learn them, but Saturnus is fastidious, taking a whole hour of barking and reciting to ensure I know only three simple words.

"Revertere meis potestatem." I repeat, rolling my eyes at his lack of understanding that other creatures in fact possess brains too. The way he acts you'd think he thinks I'm an idiot.

"Good. Keep repeating that to yourself." He instructs me, tightening his grasp on the scythe in his palm. I look back once more, studying Regus who is at the head of our army, his expression stern and unyielding. Caedes is by his side and he stares at me, seeing right through me as though I were translucent.

Suddenly, as I'm pondering the depths of his madness, I feel Saturnus inhale and rise in the water beside me. I turn, my eyes greeted by a sight I had not expected. Over the horizon they come, more in number than I had ever anticipated. They are not as large as us, not even close, but they are not a handful. They hang there, a mass of shadow on the horizon, illuminated only slightly by the line of flame created by our archer's arrows, perhaps more in number than they had been before the city had been taken.

"Saturnus! How is this possible?" I ask him, my eyes wide as I take in their vastness. He snarls, his eyes narrowing in on them.

"I don't know. I just don't know. It doesn't make any sense!" He barks looking to me with madness flickering across his face.

How can he not know?

I feel my heartrate accelerate.

"You said it would be easy." I round on him, feeling everything that I've worked so hard for threatened in but a moment as they have appeared.

"I didn't know there was more of them! It's the only explanation. They've found more mer somehow..." He looks startled as I run my hand through my hair, my breath shaking in my chest, vulnerable.

"You SAID it was going to be EASY!" I bark, feeling my rage spilling from me in an uncontrollable torrent. His eyes widen at my reaction as he places out a hand to my chest, pushing me away.

430

"I cannot be expected to know everything. Clearly... Atlas, that old fool, had something to do with this. I always wondered if he knew of my true nature... what with his ability to read auras." He mutters to himself, making rationale for the army we are now facing. I have been preparing for a bloodbath; I have not been preparing for war. Saturnus looks to them, examining their numbers as they continue to file over the horizon in the distance.

"They are perhaps a quarter of our numbers. It will still be a massacre." He reassures me, clenching his fist at his side as he snarls, feral in his anger.

How could I have been so stupid as to trust what he thought he knew? I growl, turning back on my army to view them.

Now I look at them, I see that perhaps they are not the feral killers I have always thought them to be. Are they not just a large group of teenagers with clubs and shields? I wonder if I should have trained them better, spent more time preparing them.

No. They are but fodder. I remind myself, scowling that I had ever doubted my own judgement. I am about to become a God in flesh, my opinion is fact, my decisions law.

I speak next, placing the order and believing as firmly in my action as I do that I am the rightful owner of the Necrimad's dark magic.

"Let us get in formation for war." I shoot upward, a single flick of my acute tailfin enough to move me to the height I require.

"The mer return! We will end them! Build a wall!" I exclaim. Regus is below us, barking my orders only moments after they have left my lips as he makes sure they can be heard and understood by all.

The swarm of Psirens rise, swimming from the depths of the bowl holding the ruined Occulta Mirum and upward, laying themselves out in a vertical wall of bodies. Saturnus and I glide forward as my heartrate declines, feeling control return to me as I adjust my expectations of the night ahead as quickly as they had changed. Nearing the line of flames, which still burn hot, I scowl at the mass of mer in the distance, wondering how it is that so many of them have returned, and wishing I had answers as to how they've been kept hidden for so long.

431

The Psirens continue to move, the displacement of water loud in my ears as the darkness of their forms rise from the sea floor, casting its shadow across the entirety of the sandy plain in front of us. Saturnus shifts his gaze to me, looking back up at what we have done, what we have created.

"They are formidable." He whispers, awestruck by the show of their numbers and how much they have grown. I feel my heart jolt into a sprint as I look back at them and the Necrimad roars as they eclipse its body from view.

"It's still not enough." I say through gritted teeth. "It will never be enough."

33
The Charge
CALLIE

Orion is atop Philippe beside me and the flickering light from flaming arrows is casting dark shadows across all our faces, bringing out the grave nature of what is about to begin as we float here, united in cause and yet so different in origin.

We hang, gazing upon the once great city I had come to love in but a matter of moments.

I look up to Orion, wondering how he will take it when I totally disregard his advice and go after Saturnus against his wishes. I don't know what else he expects me to do. Surely he knows me better by now than to think I'll be sitting on the side-lines after everything Saturnus has taken from me. It was because of him my father had to flee, that I had waited so long to know him. It was because of him that Atlas, one of the wisest men I'd ever known, was dead. It was because of him Orion and I had almost lost one another to the darkness of Titus. He deserves to suffer, to pay for his crimes against the mer. I cannot allow Orion to take him on alone. I just can't.

"Look at that." My father breathes, the white of his hair ashen in the dark orange light of the sandy plains before us.

"I know." I reply, looking past the line of fire separating us from the enemy. They're mighty in number, even greater than I remember as they stack up against us slowly, mounting in a mighty vertical wall of bodies. I shift my gaze back to him and he glowers at me.

433

"Callie Pierce, you have the same look your mother gets when she's planning something." He narrows his eyes and I shake my head.

"I don't know what you're talking about." I deny my secret plans to fight, annoyed that a man who has known me for so little time can peg me so utterly to the post.

"Stay safe." He orders me and I glow a little at the fear behind his eyes. I'm precious to him, just like I'm precious to Orion.

That won't stop me from doing what I have to in order to retrieve my scythe though.

"I promise." I rise and kiss him on the cheek, glowing at his affection as I feel fear clutch at me, reminding me not to be too happy as we float here, waiting for the bloodshed to begin.

As we wait, I see the beast I had been afraid of for so long. The Necrimad, obscured by many bodies, is gargantuan in size, the fire blazing from beneath its scales obvious to me even from this distance. I shudder, hearing it roar from afar as Philippe shuffles next to me with nerves.

Domnall is beside him, his eyes wide.

"Och aye. Yoo're gonnae need a bigger hoorse, laddie." He teases Orion, looking down on him from the height at which he sits upon Magnus. Orion shifts, looking uncomfortable as he dismounts Philippe, making a decision and pressing his lips into a hard line. Taking the reins, he pulls Philippe past me, handing him to Conan who looks to him with surprise.

"Fer me?" He asks and Orion nods.

"He will keep you safe." He says, handing him the reigns. Conan looks like he might cry, his body tiny in its traditional Selkie armour which is minimalistic at best. I feel my lips curve as Orion turns from his horse, cocking an eyebrow with a curious expression on my face.

"Not taking Philippe?" I ask him, and he shakes his head.

"I'm not part of the Cavalry, and he's not exactly discreet." He shrugs, swimming past me in a flurry of bubbles. He rises in the water, moving over everyone as the Psiren wall of bodies nears completion. Azure and Vex are beside me and I look back to them as they raise their heads. Dark eyes diluted

434

in the dim light, they have no problem with sight at all as they float without a speck of armour covering their too pale skin.

The smell of burning is rancid in the water, coating the back of my throat like ash and charcoal is tainting the water I'm breathing. My stomach acid curdles in anticipation of the coming fight, staring at Orion, who hangs above us all, a ruler, a warrior. The man who had, for me, started it all.

"I know they look many. I know we might be few, but we are stronger. We are chosen. They are not." He looks down to me, to Azure, to Gideon. His eyes full of grit and a determined certainty that is evident also in the way he holds himself, telling every one of us here that he will fight like the warrior I know he is. "You know what to do. Rose, Fahima, Marina. The signal- you will alert us when the blood moon is in position. Vessels, you will wait back here. Only enter the battlefield once you have received the signal to assemble. Cavalry, you're leading the way. Vex, find Caedes. Kill him. Azure, Ghazi, keep Solustus busy. He can't absorb the power of a God if he's too busy fighting you off. Emma, Skye, Alannah… you're after Regus, use your instincts and your intellect, he's dumber than a fish with memory loss. Gideon, the Necrimad. Jack, you're with me… and I'm going for Saturnus." He lists off the duties, running through it in his head one more time, clearly wondering if he's missed anything. His eyebrows hop up on his brow in surprise. Remembering something, he pivots to his left.

"Sirena, stick out of the line of fire. Do whatever Kanaloa wills of you, but be careful. You might not be violent, but the Psirens are. They won't hesitate to kill you." He concludes, finally turning to face the battlefield ahead. The Selkies stir behind him and, in the distance, I spot the two leaders we've been dreading, moving slow and concise through the water, rising to address their own army.

The seconds tick away, leaving me short of breath. I see it from this distance, though it's but a speck. My scythe, clutched in the hands of the man who had betrayed an entire city. I clench my own hands into fists and Cole looks to me, sensing my anger.

435

"Callie, it's alright." He whispers, but I ignore him. It freaking well isn't alright. It's wrong. All of this wrong. Good people are set to die because of the selfish actions of a pair of brothers.

I sit, seething in my anger and allowing the emotion to fill every part of me as I prepare to go against the wishes of the two men I love most.

After the last Kelpie stills and the last Narwhal exhales bubbles, a silence falls between the two sides. Orion and Solustus stare into one another's eyes from across the vast expanse of sand, faces both flickering with shadow and fury.

Orion looks to me one last time, before turning to face the enemy once more. The moment is eerie, and too short, as it passes and his spear pierces the water above him.

He bellows, using all his might to expel the command we've all been waiting for.

"CHARGE!!!"

The sound is nothing like anything I've ever heard. Through the darkness the roars of thousands of voices break the silence and the clattering of weaponry shortly follows. Saturnus and Solustus point forward and the wall moves, solid and never ending, as even more Psiren bodies pour from the bowl of sand which had once held the Occulta Mirum. I watch as my father takes off in the water and Cole clutches my hand in his, his eyes following Jack as Orion lurches forward too, their spears erected and ready for battle. The Selkies, mounted on steeds, and Adaro, riding Narwhals, race forward, brushing past me as Philippe whinnies next to Conan, frightened by the sudden jerking movement of the entire cavalry.

The blood moon rises ever higher above as I seek the knowledge of how far it has ascended, looking upward and through the rippling surface. As I lower my gaze, I come face to face with the Water Nymph's forces who have also begun to rise and disperse in different directions. They move wide to tackle the wall of savage fighters on all sides and I find myself unable to move or look away, transfixed by what has been put into motion and cannot be undone.

"Callie, come on!" Cole yells at me above the roar of water being displaced, moving to swim away as he pulls on my hand and I stare at him, blinking and unable to move for a moment as I make my choice.

The last of the fighters are long past me now, moving so much quicker than anything I've ever seen, splitting off to find targets and protect their fellow warriors in all directions. It's stunning and I am transfixed, unable to move as a line of arrows soars through the water, ablaze just like the line that illuminates the space between the two armies. They fall on our fighters and I hear the muted multiple Kelpie cries in the distance, the roar of our warriors being exposed to fire for perhaps the first time since they began life underwater.

"Cole... I can't." I breathe out, looking to him, scared.

"Don't do this, Callie." He warns me, grabbing onto my hand and refusing to let go.

"I have to." I whisper, terrified of my own actions. I pull away with a sudden jerk and take off, moving far away from him and the other vessels, before rising to the height of the ocean and looking down upon the battle as it begins.

How am I supposed to find anyone in this? I wonder, watching as the two sides meet, becoming a mash up of indistinguishable bodies. I guess I have no choice but to move first and ask questions later.

I see Cole moving to follow me below and so take one stroke, breaking the surface and then re-entering the ocean's waters a metre from where I've just been hanging, watching with morbid fascination as I hit the surface once more. I work my tail with more power than I've ever managed to muster before, my heart picking up pace within my chest and adrenaline hitting my system as the smell of fire overtakes my nostrils as I breathe in deep, feeling my lungs straining to keep up with my speed. I dive, twisting and turning through the water, not looking back to where I've come from.

I can see the Water Nymphs, still yet to reach the fighting of the front lines where the Selkies and Adaro are clashing with the Psirens as I corkscrew, darting in-between fighters and grabbing one of the swords from the back of a passing warrior.

"Thanks!" I call back over my shoulder as I dive, ducking close to the sea floor and using the light of the flaming line of Psiren arrows as my guide. I rise through the crowd, trying to get a fresh vantage point as I've manage to cover significant ground by keeping low beneath the numerous Kelpie and Narwhal bodies. I see Domnall beneath me, taking on five Psirens at once with his broad sword. He's lopping off tentacles and heads all over the place as I watch him dismembering them with a shocked expression. I've seen death before on a large scale, but nothing like this. Flannery is beside him too, swearing and crying out in discomfort as he's bitten and slashed with crude weaponry. The two of them are almost completely overcome with Psirens until they pull on the reins of their Kelpies, let out the most feral roar I've ever heard, and rising, in unison, out of the mass of bodies, only to start again on a new level of the thick wall of enemies.

I spin, knowing Orion must have somehow breached the wall if he's found Saturnus, who is no doubt on the other side. If I was he and Solustus I'd be keeping close to the Necrimad, so I better find a way around all this, and fast.

I ascend, figuring keeping close to the surface must be the best way to reach them. I yield my sword as a Psiren lurches toward me, finally noticing I'm here after being distracted by the much larger and more terrifying army below. His eyes are dilated black and his lower half is that of a charred lobster.

I cringe, moving forward to strike him first as he twists, rotating in the water and smashing into my sword with his armoured bottom half with spindly legs, which make him look utterly ridiculous. I grit my teeth, feeling the sword's weight being used against me. I pull it back, dislodging it from the hard shell of the Psirens lower extremities and swing it once more, faster than he can handle, lopping his head off in one fell swoop. I watch as his body falls to the ground beneath, being lost in the din of clashing swords and cries of pain and terror. I take a tailfin stroke left, avoiding an arrow from Fergus. He winks to me from below, only distinguishable because of his rotten teeth, but I turn away, not bothering to acknowledge him in my desperation to keep moving as more arrows are released on both sides.

I look out to my right, seeing where the wall ends and decide to go around sideways. Undulating, I feel my heart race as the Cavalry and wall continue to

438

push against one another, stabbing, beheading, and maiming without any regard for how many men around them are being torn down or made victorious, blinkered to their targets alone.

Swooping through the water I wrap around the wall of men, finding it about three Psirens thick with more pouring from the city.

Damn they're huge in number. I cuss internally, my heart stopping in my chest as an only too familiar face suddenly rises from beneath me.

"Why whatever are you doing here?" Solustus smiles, his teeth too sharp. I clutch my sword as he lunges for my throat and take a long stroke backward. However, just before his long clawed nails can so much as scratch me, something white and large comes from my right, smashing into the side of his body and throwing him off course.

"Callie!" My father's voice expels my name as he railroads Solustus from the side, looking to me with a semi-horrified expression.

"Dad!" I call out as he thrusts his fist into Solustus' abdomen. The swordfish-esque Psiren squirms, breaking free from my father's grasp and drawing his sword from his side in the blink of an eye.

"Get out of here Callie. Go!" He looks angry, but I don't care. I'm here now and I want to help.

I pull out my sword, rushing to Solustus and deflecting his blade with mine. I twist in the water, vaulting over his body as our swords meet, but he deflects my blade and pushes me away with it as I spin out of control and he laughs.

"You really think you can beat me in a sword fight?" He cocks a pointed grey eyebrow and his eyes show me now that he is truly dead inside.

"I think someone needs to." I growl, my visor slipping down my face slightly. I move to adjust it and in the second I reach up to touch my face he's speeding closer again, closing the distance between us too quickly.

I raise my arms, aching from the weight of the sword, to catch his blade, the clash of metal on metal ringing in my ears. I pant, buckling under the momentum of his too-fast stroke and so dive, dropping from the confrontation and then driving myself up again, this time trying to skewer him from beneath. My heart is in my throat as my father looks on, drawing his spear from his back and moving in to help. Solustus has a spear pressed against his back too, but he

439

doesn't reach for it. Instead, he flicks his body up, somersaulting backwards and kicking me in the face with his tailfin, knocking me backward so that he can address Gideon.

"Hey! You found him!" I hear Azure's optimistic tones as I turn, my head still reeling from Solustus' assault of fin on face.

"Yeah, sure did." I retort, out of breath as the sound of battle continues, too loud, around me. I'm gasping to take in water as Ghazi moves in behind her, scowling at me.

"Hey, wait. You're not supposed to be here!" Azure accuses me, her eyes narrowing as I roll mine back at her.

"Yes, I know that." I sigh, looking to where Solustus is fighting my father.

Gideon's fighting style is raw and I watch as the two men fight dirty, grabbing each other by the hair and just narrowly missing skewering one another by mere inches. I feel myself wanting to jump in again as they twirl together in the water and I cringe, heart unable to slow down. I spin back to face Azure, reluctantly deciding to move on.

"I need to find Orion." I demand and she looks conflicted, her mouth puckering to the side as she very suddenly jerks her arm out to the left, grabbing one of the Psirens by the throat and tossing him to the ground as though he were no more than a chew toy.

"He's not going to be happy, Callie. You could get him killed!" She yells, punching out another Psiren who has lunged, diving to take me in his grasp. Azure wraps her fingers around yet another throat, using her momentum to throw her body upside down and toss the Psiren away into the shadows of the distance.

Turning back to me she rolls her eyes, giving me an exasperated but semi-supportive look as she grabs onto me by the shoulders, her nails digging in and her hands shaking with the adrenaline of everything that's going on around us. She pivots with me, pointing quickly up to where I see Orion, shooting through the outpouring of Psiren bodies and toward Saturnus.

"Thank you!" I call back to her as I take off once more, pounding through the water with my tailfin and undulating at a speed I've never reached in my life.

440

I see Orion, the royal blue of his tail unmistakable in the dim light and I spot Saturnus too, though now he's Psiren-esque and entirely black in scale, a far cry from the God-like persona he had once projected to us.

I race against the current being created by the many dark creatures still spewing from the sand bowl, speeding through the water to catch up to him so we can take back what belongs to me together.

"Come on then you bloody nutcase!" I hear Vex's tone, distinguishable above the battle noise because of his distinctly British accent and so turn my head, catching a flash of scarlet flying toward his tentacled form, which I assume to be Caedes' hair.

Continuing forward at high speed, I dart left and right, swimming as though each moment could be my last in-between streams of dark warriors, not one of which is focusing enough on their surroundings to notice me. They're all too focused on the colossal fighting occurring at the body wall.

Finally, as I rise high above the sea floor, I catch up to Orion and by default, to Saturnus as well.

"Ah, so nice of you to bring the entire royal family to this little face off, Orion." Saturnus laughs, his white skin and dark hair shocking. His eyes are yellow, feline, and glow in the darkness in a way entirely terrifying. Orion looks downward at this comment, catching me in his vision as his eyes focus in on me, anger flashing behind them.

"Callie! Get out of here!" He barks, furious.

"Yes that's right, little girl. Go home." Saturnus snarls, his eyes wide and his mouth spread in a smile. I ascend, moving in next to Orion.

"No. That's *mine.*" I growl, feeling my fist tighten around the sword in my grasp. I catch the scythe, now strapped to Saturnus' back, glinting in the corner of my field of vision and sigh out. I wish he were holding it, that way I could call it to me without a problem. As it is, I'm going to have to bait him into using it. Orion turns to me, glancing to Saturnus with fear behind his eyes as he shakes my shoulders.

"If you die, I'm going to kill you!" He looks angry, but something behind his irises is glad, glad I'm here with him. I place his hand in mine and we turn, facing Saturnus together.

"Oh, how sweet. Well, at least I can kill you together. Poetic, don't you think?" Saturnus continues to exude a wicked grin, so sure he's going to win, going to beat us. But why?

I turn back, feeling heat on my spine. The Necrimad is closer than I'd realised, it's eyes glowing orange and its scales lit from beneath with fire. I turn back to where Saturnus was. Or at least to where I think he was. Where he was floating, Orion now hangs as I pivot, confused, looking to Orion who is next to me.

"Nice party trick." I mutter, unimpressed. He might have Orion's face, but the gaze he's exuding from the icy blue of his eyes is all Saturnus. Orion could never look at me with such cold hatred, even when we fight.

"Glad you think so." Saturnus whispers, suddenly changing instantly to stare at me through my own eyes this time.

"I'm still not impressed." I say, wondering when exactly my hair had gotten so long. Orion snorts.

"Look, Saturnus. I haven't come to play games. This isn't about Callie. It's about you and me. So, what say you that we cut the cheap magic tricks and we fight like real men. You think you're stronger? Think you can beat me fair and square? Prove it. I won't use my powers over air either. In case you're wondering." He bargains and I hope for his sake he's lying as we turn in the water, the heat of the Necrimad's proximity prickling the skin of my back.

I look down for a split second, seeing the wall getting thinner. The Psirens are starting to disperse a little more now, moving into clusters where they fight individual Selkie and Adaro warriors, but the bottom part of the formation still stands strong and is now being handled by the Water Nymphs. Azure and Ghazi creep ever closer, keeping an eye on us too, as Azure twists her body around Solustus, squeezing him like she's a boa constrictor. I draw my attention back to Saturnus quickly. He's closer to us now.

"Very well, boy." Saturnus growls and suddenly, as I see the ferocity in his stare, I realise that he has a real hatred for Orion. I wonder where this has come from, was it about the throne, or was it something more? Orion holds his spear in one hand, raising it in the water and pushing me behind him as I raise my heavy sword once more.

442

The two men circle one another, their eyes narrowing as a war rages on around us and a demonic dragon looking thing stirs at our spines. Saturnus twitches his eyebrow, baring his teeth as he leans forward, ready to strike.

He says only two words before he and Orion launch up into the water, ready to fight to the death.

"Bring it."

34
The Horrors
CALLIE

The moon is rising ever higher through the night sky above the thrashing tension of the water's surface, disturbed by Psirens and mer, locked in epic battles, whirling and flying through the water and manoeuvring faster than I'd ever thought possible. The fire still burns below, illuminating the undersides of Saturnus and Orion's tailfins as they rise through the water, clashing in a meeting of scythe and sword. I clench my own sword, knowing now I have the opportunity to call the weapon to me.

I watch as the two men struggle, realising this will be more difficult than I'd anticipated as I worry I'll hit Orion. As they try to strike another over and over, I realise I'm all but being left out of the fight and so I kick my tail in high gear, letting the cords of muscle which I had once found so unnatural pull together, giving me natural ascension through the water at high speed. I bring my sword up, scraping the bottom scales of Saturnus' flared tailfin. He grunts and Orion takes the opportunity to swing his spear, jabbing it toward Saturnus' heart. He dodges as he arcs his body right, causing it to shape like the crescent moon which had once held his Adam's apple in its curve.

Saturnus looks down to me, his eyes diluted black and his lips parted in a snarl. He spits his words, like a snake, reminding me of his predecessor.

"I'm not wasting my time with a piece of slag like you. No woman could ever match my power!" He throws his head back, tensing his pectorals and spinning in the water, bending at the waist and bringing the end of his tailfin

444

around to hit Orion in the face. Orion falters as he's pushed backward, losing his hold in the water as he tilts. I watch as he rolls with the loss of balance, rotating backwards and diving slightly, tracing a steep curve and moving his spear toward Saturnus in an instant. He skewers the bottom of his tail, but it's merely a flesh wound.

I feel the displacement of something moving behind me so I spin on the spot, finding Azure and Solustus dancing with one another at a closer proximity than I had anticipated. Azure's black hair trails around her in inky ribbons, falling around her face as she moves, jagged and yet graceful in her too quick motion. She brings her fist around the back of Solustus head as she moves above him, smashing into the back of his neck and grabbing a fist full of hair in the process. Her charred tailfin is hypnotic, avoiding Solustus' jabs with only inches to spare.

Damn he's fast. I think to myself, watching as he slashes toward her abdomen with his rapier once more. That's when I see it, her eyes fixing on something at his side. Her whip, the one she was carrying the very first time I'd ever seen her. I blink, only taking moments to observe their fighting but knowing that it's too long.

I curve my body, intending to assault Saturnus as I round in the water and drive my body upward. However, just as I move to reach him he shifts, placing Orion in the way of my blade instead. I halt, my forward momentum causing me to topple into a passing Psiren warrior. That's when I see him; Jack is fighting off other Psirens, those coming to aid their masters, but he's only one man, and others are coming closer too. I see a Psiren ascending through the water, noticing that Saturnus and Solustus are both occupied. He's got dark skin and a piranha like tail. I've seen him before... when I was with Vex.

Regardless, he's swimming right below me, not even noticing I'm there, with a crude looking spear made from flint and coral clutched in his palms. I rotate, diving down and raising my sword over my head before I bring it crashing down on him. He's caught unaware and so cries out, falling slightly as I dive, driving him down whilst keeping half an eye of Saturnus.

"I knew you were no good." He snarls, his lip upturned. Now I see his flesh I'm horrified, it's half melting off his bones, no doubt a remnant of the

445

Necrimad's power. I want to look away from the monstrosity he has become, his eyes black with red lightning forks in their depths, but instead I choose to fight as I plunge forward, smashing my sword against his spear and breaking it in two.

I grit my teeth, turning back on myself and going in for another strike. This time I crack the flat of the blade against the back of his skull as he's about to pivot to face me, but he can't make the turn fast enough.

Instead he's thrown forward as I pull back my blade, thrusting it forward and down into the back of his spine. I cry out, the weight of his flesh surrounding my weapon almost too much to bear. I hang there, allowing myself to strain, as have no choice but to pull my blade from his body, my strength not enough.

I breathe in, taking a moment before I swing the blood covered blade, slashing across his throat and beheading him. I feel the crack of bone as his skull comes away from his body, brain matter and blood pluming outward in a horrendous display of the realities of this thing called war.

After, I look down to the wall of Psirens as I watch him fall, where I can just see Flannery is covered in cuts, his skin practically half ripped from his torso. Despite this, he keeps on fighting, but I wonder how much longer he can hold out against the group of six Psirens who are focused on him alone.

I move to look up now, finding Jack who is just above me and then, far above even him, I see Saturnus and Orion, still locked in a stale mate of a fight, matching each other strike for strike and blow for blow against the pale red light of the rising moon. My heart hammers against my ribs, watching as Orion narrowly misses the too-sharp blade of the scythe that rightfully belongs to me.

I stir, narrowing my eyes and feeling rage build within me, unstoppable.

That's my scythe. I growl again, focusing my anger on the two men.

Silencing out the din of the horrors of war, I focus, feeling the water around me and remembering those nights back in the depths with Vex. I needed to feel it, use that sense to predict what was going to happen next in the fight, that way I can get the scythe back without hurting Orion in the process.

I corkscrew, barrel rolling sideways and taking a wide look as I fly through the water, weightless and unobstructed in flight as I feel the Psiren's movements around me seconds before we would potentially collide. The noise is drowned out in this moment as my hair is pushed back against my skull at the speed I'm picking up in the water and I cannot help but smile, despite the death, despite the horrors, because I am flying, gliding through the ocean and as free as any mortal can proclaim to be.

I take the moment for what it is, before focusing back in on where I'm headed, to the two tailed men scrapping at the height of the ocean's depth.

I clutch my sword in my fist, watching as they contort, scrambling for any advantage over the other. Saturnus' body is rippling, his muscles straining and I can tell Orion is giving him a run for his money. His black hair is floating, feathered out like a lion's mane around him and causing his face to protrude in blatant and pale comparison. His features are angry, cruel. He's so furious it's a wonder he's not lost control yet.

That's it. I realise, knowing that if I can get Orion to cause him to over shoot a strike perhaps I have a chance of getting the scythe away from him. I continue to observe as Orion kicks Saturnus backwards, scrunching up his tailfin against his opponent's chest and then pushing hard. Saturnus is thrust from where he was previously floating, but only by a metre or so.

Orion pivots and I catch his gaze, taking a few strokes back in the water and trying to alert him as to my plan. He glides toward me and Saturnus, of course, follows him, bringing the scythe backward and up as he readies himself to hit Orion across the back of his skull, ending him. I nod to him, signalling that Saturnus is almost within striking distance and Orion drops, sinking through the water like a stone as Saturnus swings, missing him entirely.

I hold out my palm, moving to the right as to follow the path of his swing and the scythe flies from his grip, continuing with the momentum from his flailing attempt at beheading Orion. I smile, watching as the weapon shoots through the water before landing in my palm with a soft thud.

I drop my sword, feeling the power of the weapon that was made for me flow through my arm and into my chest, warming my heart and igniting my senses.

Lifting my gaze once more, I watch Saturnus' furious expression as Orion rises in front of me, raising a palm in almost slow motion and firing outward a

447

wave of air, causing the irritated Psiren to fly backwards through the water as he crashes into his brother and almost takes out Azure in the process.

Orion faces me now, eyes wide and concerned as I swim to him so my back is facing Saturnus and Solustus, who begin to disentangle themselves from one another below.

"Okay, you got the scythe. Now go! Go! I can't lose you!" Orion's face is mad with emotion, his gills opening and closing and his chest rising and falling in hurried and struggling rhythm that is far too fast. I stare into his eyes as his gaze catches something behind me. I look down, Saturnus and Solustus are gone from where they had fallen.

"Callie watch ou…" Orion begins to exclaim, but it's too late. He spins me in the water, taking my place as Saturnus lets go of the spear he's taken from his brother. It makes a straight shot through the water, lodging itself through the back of Orion's neck and protruding through the front of his Adam's apple, decimating him. His eyes widen in shock as blood plumes from him and he chokes, more blood spilling from his mouth as though he can't breathe.

"Orion! No…." I gasp, my heart cracking to pieces as it freezes in time. I can't breathe as his grip on me goes slack, the spear internally decapitating him.

His eyes roll back in his head, the icy blue of their depths disappearing forever as he falls through the water, down from the light of the surface and into the darkness of the war, which still rages on, beneath.

AZURE

Shit.

That's the extent of my reaction as I toss my body back, arching and missing yet another strike from the needle point of Solustus' rapier. I watch as Orion falls far to the ground beneath, his eyes watching me as he goes.

How is he still conscious? I wonder as I spin, pirouetting and exhaling in a grunt as I dodge yet again, only narrowly missing Solustus' blade, which was aimed at my throat. I watch Orion as he falls, my heart sinking despite knowing better. I cannot focus on Orion right now. Instead, I must focus on the task he assigned to me.

I must take out this nimble and quick-finned bastard.

I glance up to Callie who is taking off, out of the way of Saturnus who looks like he may take off right after her.

She's dead. Ugh. Why do I have to do everything around here? I wonder, moving to Ghazi who is at my spine.

I'm holding a mace I'd been given by Isabella who insisted it went fabulously with my 'medieval look', whatever the hell that means.

"Silent man! GO! Protect her!" I order him as he moves, fleeing immediately from his current target as I whirl, a killer tornado, thrusting the mace into the skull of the Psiren he's just been fighting off with his thickset hammer, a gift from the Adaro. I feel my heart race as I twirl the mace over my head, bringing the tentacled Psiren with it and using it to hit Solustus full force.

As I let the mace go, I quickly grab a sword from the belt around my waist, knowing it's time for a fresh weapon. Solustus recovers from my Psiren projectile, too quick once again. His speed is frustratingly consistent and, as his eyes narrow, I hear the roar of the Necrimad.

He turns, stopping in the middle of our fight and looking to where behind us Gideon is freezing the head of the demon over and over as the beast melts his ice blasts in retort. I take the moment he's distracted to reach in, grabbing my whip, which is looped around the crude sealskin belt that holds his rapier's sheath.

My pretty. I think, victorious, as I unwind the length of its pearl strung leather and smile, watching as the pearls capture the light of the fire beneath and reflect it back from their dark shimmering surfaces.

"Ha!" I say, sticking my tongue out as Solustus snarls at me, making a full three-hundred-and-sixty-degree twist, still upright in the water, and striking out with his sword so it almost cuts me across the cheek.

Behind us, Ghazi is coaxing Saturnus down from the height he was fighting at before, presumably knowing if he can get him into a more confined space, filled with a greater number of bodies, then he can use his strength to greater effect. He might not speak, but the man knows his way around a fight.

I raise the sword in my right hand to the right side of my face, clanging against the edge of the feeble rapier, deflecting its master as I duck under the sword's breadth. Twisting, I thrust my left arm straight and extend the whip's tendril to smack Saturnus in the face, which is getting increasingly near with each deflection of Ghazi's mighty strength. The stout warrior's thick, vein-strung arms are moving in for another hit as I pirouette, recoiling the whip and laughing at Saturnus' shocked expression as I swing my body around an invisible axis, bringing the leather this time to assault Solustus' long tail and slashing the pearls against it, drawing blood.

Take that you great slimy ass. I laugh internally, sheathing my sword once more and straining my tail muscle with all those deliciously and rarely used muscles that have been lying dormant for this moment, waiting to kill.

Pouncing forward my eyes dilute black, free hand outstretched and reaching for Solustus' throat. I know I can't beat him in a sword fight; so perhaps playing dirty will work better. I cover his gills momentarily, feeling my stomach slit by the closeness of his own blade and scowl, gritting my teeth through the pain.

"You killed my sister!" I scream, knowing that this is the time to allow my rage to consume me. I let the grief roll out from me, controlling it in a miraculous and liberating flow of energy that prickles my skin from the tip of my tail to the end of my fingertips. I curl them around my whip tighter as I manipulate the long leather tendril to wrap around his throat as I swing it from my left. It does, bejewelling the neck of the grey and dull Psiren with the glisten of blood bathed pearls as I let out a feral roar, holding my head back, my dark hair extending out around me. I feel the shadow creep in across my skin like a spider web, mapping the anguish within across the white of my flesh.

I move in to bite him, to rip out the skin of his cheek but something hard hits the back of my head with a thud and I lose my hold. I float, bewildered, as I glance up.

450

A familiar face floats in front of my vision as I see a boy with a slingshot turn, his fin that of a great white shark and his back mapped with still healing scars. I narrow my eyes.

He will pay. I vow, turning around to see that Solustus has righted himself.

"Bitch." He spits and I roll my eyes.

"Oh, shut up." I cock my head, sick of his misogynistic slurs. I flick my wrist, allowing the tongue of the whip to extend from me again, smashing it into the right hand of Solustus and dislodging his sword. He dives for it, giving me mere moments to watch what is going on beyond the purview of our fight.

I see Ghazi, almost victorious. He has managed to heavily bruise Saturnus and has now raised his hammer and is ready to deliver the finishing blow. As Ghazi moves in for the kill, I hold my breath, wondering if this could be the end for the man who had betrayed my brother.

Go on silent man! Do it. I egg him on, as I rise slowly with the anticipation of watching Saturnus have the life knocked out of him. Ghazi wraps his hand around Saturnus' skull, burying it in his thick black hair and raising the hammer in the water. Suddenly, Saturnus shimmers, no longer looking like himself but the silent man's soulmate.

Oh crap. I cuss, watching as Ghazi falters, so shocked at seeing the face of his beloved that he can't help but pause. The moment is enough, as Saturnus reaches through the water and bites the side of Ghazi's thick veined neck.

As Solustus rises to meet me once more, his face sour at the fact I had disarmed him, Saturnus holds out a hand, still teeth deep in Ghazi's carotid. Solustus throws him his sword, which his brother then swiftly uses to decapitate the silent warrior. I watch as he turns to sand, speechless as ever.

Saturnus looks to me, then to his brother, his face turning odd as Ghazi's blood drips down across his chin, sticky in the water still. He moves forward too slowly, reaching out as though to hand the sword to Solustus, who extends a hand to take it. However, instead of relinquishing the weapon, Saturnus smiles salaciously, bringing the sword up and plunging it right into his brother's heart. A warning shot if you will.

Drawing the sword from him in one quick motion, Solustus looks beyond shocked, his mouth agape as Saturnus watches the pain he has caused.

451

"Sorry brother, but there can only be one."

So what am I? A freaking pre-show before the main event now? I roll my eyes. These guys are unbelievable.

SOLUSTUS

Blood dribbles from my chest as my heart finally shrivels into nothingness. I have trusted the wrong man. My own brother, but still, the wrong man. I look up to Saturnus as he pulls my sword from me.

"Sorry brother, but there can only be one." He says, no pity in his eyes, no sadness. He holds Scarlette in his grasp, my sword, my blade in his hands, plunged into my chest, and for what?

"You... this was what you wanted all along." I stutter, unable to come up with a witty retort. I'm not able to think, to move, to breathe. All I can do is float, flames flickering below and bodies being dismembered above.

"Of course, surely you didn't think I was going to... what... share ultimate power? That's sort of what makes it ultimate, the fact only one of us can absorb it." He smiles, laughing and finally showing me his true face, after all this time.

"I would have shared this with you." I state, weak in my response even still. I am heartbroken. I thought I had lost the ability to care long ago, but no. I suppose this is what you get.

"But why? Why all this preparation?" I ask him, so confused, so betrayed that I can barely think in linear fashion, all clarity lost.

"The incantations... simply you directing the energy to me. That is all." He smirks, eyes black in their abyssal emptiness.

"I thought we were family." I state, still in shock.

"We are family. That just doesn't mean what you think it does. You think it means sharing everything... I think it means taking one for the collective and letting me kill you so that one of us can move forward with all of the power the Necrimad has to offer. You forget, brother; this will be the legacy of our name.

I will be a God. Gods don't have family, or those they love. It makes them weak. Just look at Poseidon and Atargatis. They nearly ruined everything, destroyed the world over which they had complete and total power over... and for what? Love?" He chuckles as though I'm completely stupid, as though my dream to share my power had been delusional. I suppose, knowing what I know now, it had.

I watch him as he fingers my sword, Azure still hanging to my left and watching us with a scowl on her face.

"And the army? What of them? Aren't they weakness? They're only children after all. If you think you can contain them..." I begin and he throws back his head in a cackle.

"Contain? You really think I'm going to let them continue to have their way with the world? Making sad excuses for warriors with the diluting of dark magic? You are dense sometimes, Sol. You really are." He uses his childhood nickname for me; one I have not heard in so long I had forgotten it existed.

I stare down to my sealskin belt. I have no weapons. I glance around me. The Psirens are killing, but many are also strewn about in various dismembered parts across the sea floor. Their once proud forms have become nothing more than a flesh jigsaw puzzle that will never be put back together. Saturnus watches me, amused.

"You see, you have nothing. You're pretty good with a blade, but that's about it really, isn't it? Not smart enough to work out the rituals, not strong enough to control an army, not bold enough to even call out your own brother when you got suspicious, nor influential enough to gain place within the Occulta Mirum as I have. You're really just a speck of a man who just so happened to be in the wrong place, at the wrong time. I should have been the first Psiren. You know it, I know it and Poseidon knows it."

"I never wanted to be the first Psiren. I just wanted to die." I remember, feeling the hopelessness that had once engulfed me at the idea of so many years of mortal torment, stretching out before me like the world's largest prison cell. Saturnus raises Scarlette, his eyes glowing.

"I can at least grant you that wish brother." He says, gliding toward my body.

I hold out my arms, welcoming the strike, welcoming the end. I am ready for the scorching fire or blistering cold of whatever comes next, because in this world, in this place, nothing good survives. Not even the love between brothers.

The last thing I see before I am released from my torment is Scarlette, shimmering and majestic, reflected in the cold light of my brother's dead stare.

35
The Conduit
CALLIE

My heartbeat is the only thing I can hear as warriors fall around me like snowflakes, calm and slow in their devastating descents. I glance back over my shoulder, to where he fell, to where he's now nothing more than sand.

What did I do? I think, closing my eyes, blinking in slow motion as, from my right, the second charge comes from the shadows of the night. My heart inflates, watching the Maneli and Kappa fighters pouring forth onto the field, swimming in a large group as katanas remove heads from bodies, but before they can reach the middle of the field, they halt, waiting. But for what?

Suddenly, I know, realising all at once that I also have to move. I'm stationary, having just escaped the clutches of Saturnus and as I spin to make my getaway, I see it.

Saturnus ending Ghazi.

No. I feel like my world is disintegrating, like everything I've ever known, everything I had to fight for is lost. Orion is gone. Ghazi is gone.

Then I remember once more why I need to move and take off to the right, swimming far from the centre of the fighting and getting as much distance from the still disintegrating wall of Psiren bodies as possible.

I watch as I stare back over my shoulder, waiting, heart hammering in my chest at such speed that I'm sure that's the only reason it hasn't yet broken into a million pieces. Then, in the blink of an eye, it happens.

455

It's not loud. You'd expect an explosion to be loud, but this isn't, this is merely visually devastating. The grenades have come from nowhere, or so it seems. I look back into the shadows behind where the second charge float, watching as the sand before them is flung high toward the surface of the water. Catapults stand at their backs, tossing explosives into the middle of the fighting as I hear Kelpies whinny and Narwhals scatter, fleeing from the blast at all angles with mad, terror-filled expressions.

They soar, taking out Psirens which are hanging, transfixed and in their paths, skewering them clean through. It flashes across the back of my mind. Orion's face as the spear had come through his throat, ripping out everything he once was. I blink, willing the image to scatter, as for just a moment the battle ceases as the debris, which has been blown high in the water falls slowly back down to where it had come from.

As it clears, I squint downward, where it appears not all the fighting has been disrupted, for I see Vex still wrangling Caedes into submission and Alannah, Skye and Emma hitting Regus across his bald head as he lies, conked out and asleep on the ocean floor. I cannot help but smile at that, as I watch them triumph over what they had thought they could not. Orion is wrong about them, and I had always known it.

Wait. Had been wrong. I correct myself internally, wanting to fall down and weep, but knowing I must not for the sake of the world.

I look down to the scythe in my palm. I had brought this upon myself. I hadn't listened. I had put myself in the way. I had made him take the spear in my place, because of his love for me. Because he had always said he would die to protect me. I had never taken that seriously, never realised what those words really meant. I had never thought about the fact that in dying to protect me, I would be left behind, alive, and guilt ridden for the rest of my terrifyingly long life.

"Dammit, Callie. You complete idiot!" I curse at myself, wishing I could turn back the clock. Wishing I could change what had happened, that I could have stayed with the vessels, just like I was supposed to. I hang in the water, on the brink of giving up and letting myself be killed just to end the madness.

As I stare around at the pain on the faces of my people, at the dead, at the destruction, I find myself moved by the water around me as something I never expect to see barges me out of the way. In my darkest hour, in the moment where I cannot bring myself to move, and where I continue to risk everything by hanging in the middle of a war zone, they have come.

Help. The single word warms my heart, bringing me back to the moment as Blue and her baby race past me. This time though the cry of help wasn't a plea, it was a fact. They're not alone, as Orcas move in pods of ten to twenty, shooting past me and taking out Psirens on all sides. Shoals of tuna appear from nowhere, darting in and out of the battlefield and obstructing the vision of Psiren fighters while leaving those siding with the mer untouched.

What is this? I wonder, staring in all directions and unsure where to look first, bewildered. Then I realise as I look back to where I've come from, from where the battle started for the mer, exactly what this is.

The Sirena are hovering in a circle, high up in the water, chanting and meditating. They might be the pod among us with the greatest power, and yet, sadly, I had underestimated them.

Healing energies... I laugh aloud, wonderment filling me and causing my skin to prickle with the majesty of the sheer number of oceanic creatures that are joining in, targeting only Psirens as they shoot forward from behind me. They're coming from all angles, converging on this spot as Sharks, Dolphins, Whales, fish and crustaceans are flocking to us, feeling our hour of need as the warriors on the ground continue to dwindle.

They swoop in, Sharks using their mighty jaws to bite and devour the heads of Psiren fighters with fish creating diversions as they flurry, silver scaled and massive in number, twirling around the fight and causing great confusion as they distract those infected by the dark. Manta rays soar overhead like birds, diving deep and creating a sphere with their bodies, trapping warriors inside their flesh cage with barbed tails that flash deadly as they revolve. Jellyfish flock, giant squid pulsate and fish flurry all to help save their home.

As I continue to watch, Big Blue rushes the army, parting them through the middle with her calf alongside at all times. I turn, watching with an awestruck expression, before realising that I need to move on.

457

Orion might be dead, but that doesn't change anything. My people need me. The world needs me. So, I will fight.

As I rotate, I notice that Domnall has swum up beside me, with Magnus looking battered and bruised but holding out none the less.

"Get orn!" He demands, face covered in feral looking slashes and weeping blood as I nod, ignoring his injuries and swimming forward as I launch myself onto the back of his steed. We curve as Magnus lurches forward, sweeping down and over the heads of the warriors who fight below.

"What are you doing here?" I call out over the din as Domnall swings his sword low, making a clean sweep for a tentacled female Psiren who was trying to stab Isabella right in her pretty face.

She whirls high, swinging a nimble and ornate sword above her head as she waves to us with her free hand, before moving back to the fighting.

"Ye didnae thin' anyain actually booght 'at yoo'd be stayin' behin'. Reit?" He chuckles, bringing up his sword and twizzling it around his hand with a masculine flourish. I laugh to myself, am I really that predictable?

As we continue to fly through the battlefield, I see Kaiya to my right as she grits her teeth, shooting a crossbow and struggling to keep up with the five Psirens that surround her. I find Hironori and Fumio next in the crowd, back to back and fighting off a ring of Psirens, all with shark-like tails. I look above me as Big Blue sweeps overhead again, making her way around the back of the fighting to disrupt the path of the Psirens and causing them to leap sideways.

Manta Rays disperse, swimming in effortless flocks. As I'm watching them, I see Marcas high above, holding his own despite his lack of sanity, his expression both rage filled and dreamy as Domnall laughs, the sound rumbling from his chest as he watches him too.

We turn, making a full circle and soar high across the middle of the line of flaming arrows that lie now almost extinguished, below. Far to my left I see Saturnus and Azure fighting, doggedly, but where Solustus is I cannot make out, as Gideon continues his work with the Necrimad, shooting out ice in long streams from his palms. The beast roars, it's voice only just louder than the cries of those being cut to ribbons beneath us and, as our path curves once more, Domnall reaches out to cut the tailfins of a few Psirens fighting on a higher level. With a sudden jolt, I realise that I have somewhere to be.

I move to speak, deciding to ask Domnall to find the other vessels and take me to them so I can make sure we're ready, but that's when I hear it, an ear-piercing scream which I know is coming from Rose.

The signal! I gasp internally, my heart pounding a frantic tattoo. Is it time already? I'm so far from where I need to be and wonder how I'll possibly get there on time.

We race through the water and I see that Vex has gotten Caedes on the floor as he hovers over him with his trident, ready to end him while using his tentacles to restrain him. I grab onto Domnall's waist with my free arm, seeking greater stability as Magnus increases his speed through the water. Leaving nothing but a trail of bubbles behind us, we return to the edge of the battlefield from which the mer had charged.

Good. I think, glad that Vex has the upper hand as I lose sight of him. At least the world will have one less psychopathic killer in only a few moments.

Domnall pulls back on the reigns as a group of Psirens rise from the sea floor below, tentacled, tailed and intercepting our path.

"Nika!" He calls out, raising his spear as his abdominals tense beneath my fingertips. In an instant, a narwhal is in sight, racing beneath us and keeping our speed stroke for stroke. Without warning, Domnall pushes me from the atop the Kelpie, causing me to fall through the water haphazardly. The shove he gives me is so powerful I feel it like a blast of Orion's Aeromancer abilities as I flail, unable to stabilise myself and winded by the impact of the Scotsman's palm. As I fall, a hand wraps around my wrist, grasping me hard as I cry out.

"Get on!" Nika growls, yanking me upward so that my tail slides over the slick back of her Narwhal and my scaled behind finds hold. We swim faster than I've ever been before, faster than on Philippe or Kelpie back and I watch as the fighting continues. Maneli twisting and jabbing, shooting heavy arrows from crossbows and hitting Psiren opponents in the heart, side by side with Kappa who spin, sword in palm.

As we swoop in low, nearing the edge of the vast sand expanse which is furthest from the city, the Narwhal crashes into the sand with no warning.

"NO!" I hear Nika's exclamation as I look back over my shoulder, seeing that an arrow has found its way into the tail of the creature.

I feel its pain, its anguish as it flails. Nika acts quick, ending the creature's life and putting her fingers to her lips as she makes a loud whistle. From behind us, the last person I expect to see finds his way to me from the shadows.

"Come orn!" Conan calls from atop the familiar silhouette of the Equinox. He looks unsure, but his back is poker straight as he moves beneath the moonlight, a show that he is trying to appear confident. He's riding side-saddle, his tailfin strapped into the left side of Philippe's saddle which is especially designed for mer riders, as I ascend, vaulting over the spine of the aquatic creature. Conan pulls on the reigns and Philippe's scaled wings begin to beat frantically, picking up slow speed in the water. We retreat into the shadow, passing under the ever-constant voices of the Sirena who stick out above us, a rainbow of colour in the dark.

We ride out, away from the fighting and yet we are not alone. As Nika disappears behind us, becoming but a pale speck in the distance, the shadow of a Psiren with an eel like tail and a spear made from the bones of dead animals comes from nowhere, causing Philippe to rear up and almost tosses us to the floor. The Psiren descends, face wicked with bared teeth, blocking our path and lodging the spear in Philippe's skull with one fluid stroke, unapologetic and without pause in the brutality of the act.

We fall, and the Equinox, who had carried us with him across the seven seas, collapses dead as he exhales a final and brutal cry that pierces the night. We hit the sea floor, sand billowing up around us and I twist as the Psiren nears us, squirming to get away with heart in my throat. Conan pulls the bow from his spine without pause and draws an arrow against its string before shooting the Psiren in the eye merely seconds after we've come crashing down. He looks shocked as he hits his target, unable to believe what he's just done without even thinking.

He acts quicker than I ever could and I rise, squirming from under the dead weight of the Equinox and out, beheading the assailant quickly in one

460

sweeping swing of my scythe. I pivot as his body collapses, eyes bulging at the battle which rages behind us, before my gaze shifts to Conan who is pulling himself upright next to Philippe.

The creature who had never failed me is dead, strewn across the Ocean floor for only moments before his body turns to sand, just like his master had not moments ago.

"Philippe." I breathe, unable to believe that after so much, he's really gone. Conan puts a hand on my shoulder, squeezing.

"We hae tae gang. Noo!" He exclaims, pulling me with him as we swim, seeking out the rest of the vessels in the darkness. I feel something brush past me and I spin, tensing my arms to swing the scythe as I pivot in one fluid motion.

"Hey, hey! It's me alright? Bloody hell!" I hear a clunk as Vex's hand catches my blade in mid-air.

"You don't just sneak up on people like that Vex! Don't you know this is warzone?!" I scold him and he rolls his eyes, his bottom lip sticky with blood and his body covered in abrasions and gashes. I reach up to touch his face, my palm seeking his skin. He flinches away.

"Oh don't be such a baby." I complain, turning from him as he snorts.

"Babies don't get into fist fights with bloody psychopaths." He retorts and I turn to him.

"Is he dead?" I press him for an answer, needing to know for sure that at least one of the brothers didn't make it.

"As the proverbial dodo, Love." He caresses the words with his tongue, but I rotate, knowing if I stop I'll break down. About Orion, Ghazi, Philippe... everything.

"Vex, use your Psiren eyesight. We need to find the others." I command and he tuts.

"Alright bossy." He sneers, but I ignore him again, I don't have time for his crap. Well, I never have time for his crap, but if there was ever a time to not get into banter with him, this is it. "Over there!" He points to a shimmer, something I never would have seen without him indicating, in the distance. We

461

swim, bolting for the group of vessels who wait, Cole standing guard and looking worried as we emerge from the darkness.

"Callie! Vex! Conan!" Cole exclaims as the other vessels rise in the water, eyes wide.

"I'm sorry…" I start, but he hushes me.

"Not now. We have to get you in the middle of the battlefield. Right under the blood moon. Come on! The signal gives us around ten minutes, that was about 8 minutes ago!" He shoves past me as I look to Chiyoko, Cage, Casmire, Callista and Calypso, they don't look angry with me, but they do look terrified, each one clutching their Piece of Eight to them tightly. Calypso, who is closest to me, whispers to herself, a soft prayer to Kanaloa.

"Come on, it'll be alright." I promise, breathless as I exhale. I have no idea if any of this will be alright. The conduit could kill us.

Then again, in the words of Azure, I really have nothing left to lose.

My muscles ache as we hurry back into the battle, the now dying embers from the flaming line which has scorched through the middle of the battle field gives dim light, but it matters not for as we rise closer to the surface, the moon, full and bloody above provides light enough.

Glimpsing down now, it's harrowing to see the number of dead strewn through the water. They're all Psiren, but none the less, the Kindred fighters will have turned to sand just like the mer, and I know that there are many less of them than we first started with.

I close my eyes, not wanting to see it anymore, just wanting the death to stop as we move over the battlefield and in an instant I'm transfixed by the eyes I've been dreading seeing again.

Saturnus is watching us from afar, his face deadpan as he tosses Azure to his left with one hand as though she were no more than a rag doll.

Suddenly, as we move into the centre of the field, the Necrimad roars, more deafening than any of its prior beastly noises, this sound is different.

Saturnus spins, ascending in the water with both his arms stretched out to his sides. The beast's eyes glow orange, before changing colour to red. A few moments pass as we watch him writhe in the water, moving like he's possessed, until, finally, he relaxes a few moments, going slack with his back facing us. Eventually he turns, his body beginning to ripple and becoming mapped through with scarlet lines of power as his eyes glow scarlet, supernatural and crackling with dark energy. He gazes to us, his hand extending out as veins of red begin to pop from them, escaping his flesh like they cannot be contained.

His voice morphs into something terrifying, deeper and louder, as he simply points and commands his army,

"Get them."

ORION

Ow.

That's all I can think as I look up at the ocean's surface, rippling and in turmoil, as the masses of bodies flurry and struggle beneath its surface to maintain life. I feel Jack's hands caressing my forehead as I gaze up. He's bent the spear running me through upward at its base so I can lay my head against the hard coolness of the pole that will end my life. I can see Saturnus high above me, glowing scarlet now and pointing out at the vessels, silhouetted against the bloody hue of the moon. Callie is with them.

My beautiful girl. Beautiful and stubborn. I should have known it would get me killed, trying to stop her from fighting, but alas, I suppose I shouldn't have expected anything else.

I sigh, coughing blood as I feel the spear, which is rammed through my throat, shift. I exhale, the pain ebbing through me as I lie among scattered Psiren body parts, unable to move, unable to breathe, stuck in the in-between place between dying and living.

"Sir, I fear that if we remove the spear, it might internally decapitate you. Which would most definitely kill you. In fact, I'm not quite sure how you're not dead already, so well done." Jack is babbling, unsure of what to do or say, but none the less his freckle spattered nose and wide eyes are soothing to mine in the dark. I doubt anyone has noticed, but the water is tinting red, and I can hear the blood being spilled around me, even if I cannot turn my head to see it. I want to speak, to ask what's happening, but I cannot. Mainly because of the spear which is lodged in my throat.

I exhale irritated, my chest muscles constricting around my torso as pain continues to throb everywhere, starting in my neck and journeying down my spine in rapid jolts that make me cry out and my tailfin flail like that of a fish out of water.

In this moment, I cannot stand to close my eyes as the Psirens above converge on the vessels, using their full force to devour them. I feel Jack's gaze follow mine as his eyes move upward, presumably to rest on Cole. I can't see him from beneath, but I know he's watching him, simply because I cannot take my own eyes off my soulmate either. My pulse is weak in my veins and my head cloudy with the relief that comes only after your worst fear is realised. I start to wonder, about Callie, about me... about what could have been. Her walking down the aisle, her smiling beneath me as I made love to her, her laughing, smiling, talking... anything. What would our love have been like in a hundred years, a thousand?

The same. I think to myself, knowing the truth of my own answer.

Callie had always been consistent. It was me who was straggling behind her. She was like... the sun. I had found myself burned by her intensity, rather than enjoying the light she exuded. I had trapped her in, caged her up, because I loved her. I regret that now, as I lie here with nothing but my thoughts. I wish I had given more time to talking to her, knowing her inside and out. I think back to the night in Hawaii, her eyes, the intensity of her desire that I could not satiate on her orders. She was so beautiful. So young. So much fun. I could never be like that. I was just... stuck in my ways. She scares me, but I love her. Ever since I first heard her speak. I have loved her. And now, as promised, I will die for her.

"Sir, stay with me." I hear Jack's voice, strained and scared, as I float in and out of consciousness. I smile to myself. My father, my sister, my mother... they would all be waiting for me, on the other side. Then, one day, maybe she would be there too. I have waited for her to die once so I could love her, so I will wait once more so I can continue to do so. It really is very simple.

"Orion!" I hear her voice, distant and faint above me. I open my eyes now, straining to see anything as my vision becomes blurred, but she's not here, so maybe I'm imaging her for comfort.

"Cal..." I begin, but throbbing pain hits me in the head like a mallet, so I cease sound.

"No sir, don't speak. It'll be alright." I open my eyes, mouth still agape and in mid call.

Above me the Psirens are swarming, their mass of darkness, of polluted flesh swarming around the colourful specks above, outnumbering them twenty to one.

As I lie here, something else begins to happen. A hand breaks through the surface of the bedrock beside me, rotten and cold. Jack recoils, pulling my body with him as I grunt, agony flaring outward like a new and excruciating flame as the spear moves.

I continue to stare to the surface, not having a choice but to look away from the un-dead horrors being birthed from the bottom of the sea. The body parts scattering the sea floor begin to move too, and I look to Saturnus who is glowing scarlet, laughing as his eyes burn such a bright yet empty chasm of scarlet light that I can see them even from the ground. I feel the earth rumble beneath me, feel the trembling hands of Jack turn my head back to him.

"Orion. You have to help them." He says to me, helpless in himself. I swallow, cringing as the spear moves once more. I have so little energy left and I have to wonder if I even can be any more help. As I close my eyes, picturing the full lips, round eyes and long blonde hair of my beloved, I know I have to try. I grit my teeth, balling my left hand into a fist beside me as I raise one hand above me, shooting it straight for the sky.

I believe in you. My girl.

I take the last of my energy, the last of my love for her and I transform it, creating something from nothing and allowing myself to protect her one last time. From my hand I blast a single, epic wave of air so big it takes my life force with it and blows back the Psiren forces from their target.

465

The vessels form the Conduit merely seconds after, and their Pieces of Eight cast shadows across my body as a bright white light, so bright it blinds me, suddenly falls down from the sky above when the weapons connect, shattering the ocean's surface tension.

That's the last thing I see, before one last breath leaves my body and my final thought of Callie disintegrates as though it were no more than a sandcastle being destroyed by the inevitable, constant, tides of time.

36
The Tidal Kiss
CALLIE

Everything that I know shifts within a few seconds.

I blink.

The Psiren army is closing in.

I blink again.

The water is rushing past me as I swim against it, the surge of air coming from nowhere I can see. Could it be Orion? I look around frantically. He is nowhere in sight.

I blink once more.

Turning and forming a ring with my fellow vessels, I hold out the scythe so its tip connects with the other Pieces of Eight, as I breathe in, terrified.

I shield my eyes as a beam of light bigger and brighter than anything I've ever known shatters the surface tension of the ocean, a wave of energy rippling outwards with such force that the Psiren army have no choice but to remain where they are immersed, helpless to the blinding and technicolour beam which has shattered everything in my world so completely.

I blink a final time.

The white beam splits into eight, travelling down the length of the scythe and into me. It takes hold of my body, transforming me into what I know not. I feel my heartbeat flutter in my chest and my eyes widen, as my pupils dilute and everything which makes me up inside is set alight with a power I've never known was possible.

467

The transformative power of the beam of energy changes me at a molecular level. Everything about me is glowing, thrumming, shimmering and technicolour. I realise now that being a vessel is exactly that. It's being empty, being a container for something greater, and I know, instinctively, what the magical white light was. I know it wasn't a light at all. It was transport.

A few moments after the immense charge of magic has been delivered beneath my flesh, and my heartbeat turns rapid like that of a hummingbird, I stretch out my arms in a weightless motion, my skin feeling fragile and tight. My scales are multicolour, rippling and my hair around me flows lilac and boundless like frothing rabid waves.

I am Atargatis and she is me. We are one.

I stare up and around as the blinding light ceases in the water, the transformation complete. I feel her everywhere, and I know… *everything.* Solustus' death, the fact Orion is but moments from turning to sand, living longer than I had ever expected with such a wound, and that Atlas is watching us all with baited breath. I know the Gods and Goddesses around me intimately; I know where the seas began and where they are headed. I know how the mer came to be, how the first Psiren was made. I can see it, feel it in my heart and mind.

Hello, my daughter. She's in my head. Speaking with me.

Oh. My. Goddess.

I feel her flowing through me, her magic, her power, her omniscience coursing through my brain as I let her take me over, like I'm on autopilot.

As I stare at the other vessels, I see that they're much the same. Vex's tentacles are rippling a magnitude of different blues, making him look like the Ocean itself as his eyes spark, ferocious with white lightning.

Just like Poseidon. Atargatis' words force their way in and consume my mind's space, like having two souls in one body isn't intrusive enough already.

"Come, my fellow Gods and Goddesses. We have much to attend." The words fall from my lips, but they are not my own. It's almost as though I'm a passenger in my body, simply watching as Atargatis takes me over, using my form to project her power, to save us all.

Mizuchi, Lir, Sedna, Poseidon, Kanaloa, Neptune and Ava are here. Having taken control of the bodies of the other vessels I see them in the eyes of each one of my fellow Kindred, ready and all powerful, knowing what needs to be done. I rotate in the water, the scythe still clad firmly in my palm. My eyes settle upon Saturnus who is menacing and mighty in the sea before the Circle.

My body, technicolour and weightless, now glides effortlessly to him as though this whole time my body has been wading through treacle. I have never known this ease of motion, this speed. I have never felt this strength that now trickles through my muscles, causing them to clench and tighten where needs be with no human thought or mortal pause.

"Saturnus." My voice reaches out, not my own but a combination of a gentle Hawaiian surf and a stormy night's thunder.

"What is the meaning of this?" His low, maniacal voice demands, confused as to my sudden change in attitude and, more specifically, my lack of fear.

"The Circle of Eight have assembled here. To end you." Atargatis' voice pours from me with such calm I have to replay back what it is I'm actually saying in my head. Saturnus, his eyes aglow, snaps as his head jerks to the side and his eyes fall on the battle beneath. My own eyes lower, seeing the fighting has stopped. Even the Psiren warriors are watching us with awe, having dropped their weapons as they float, next to those they have been trying to murder, staring up like they're seeing the sun for the very first time.

"What are you doing?! I didn't say you could stop fighting!" He bellows, clenching his fists as the undead begin to climb their way back from oblivion. They are the lost souls of the sea. Those who cannot be redeemed. Those who cannot move on to Mortaria because the Necrimad's power has trapped them here. The waves claimed them and so it is only the waves who must let them go. They have been waiting all this time to return, waiting for the day the power once given to Solustus in the very beginning would be thwarted.

"They do not listen to you. Not now their real creator is here." I retort in Atargatis' words, as they fall from my lips, bathed in disdain.

"You did this. All of you. You couldn't see me for what I was. I was never good enough for your divinity and now you will all suffer." Saturnus spits, looking down with a maniacal laugh as the dead begin to rise, clambering to their feet on bones which seem only to be held together by molluscs, whelks and crabs.

"Oh. I see you. I see you clear as day. A mortal wearing the mask of a God. Want to play with us? Step on up." I challenge him as my heart races in my chest. I'm afraid again.

Do not fear daughter. No harm shall befall either one of us. Her voice comforts me like a warm blanket, wrapping around my heart and calming it to a steady thud. Saturnus does not speak anymore, instead he growls, low and feral, his eyes blazing with the fury he's suppressed for so long. He pulls back his left arm, throwing dark energy toward me as I raise my left hand, waving it and turning the dark projectile into a shoal of silver fish that swim away. Saturnus throws another ball of magic, black crackling scarlet, and I toss the scythe into my left hand, waving my right hand in turn. This time the projectile of dark magic transforms into a manta ray, that continues to soar away free in flight as a smile graces my lips.

I have nothing to fear.

My heart soars as my arms come out to my sides and I twirl, rotating like a tornado in the water, laughing wildly. This man cannot hurt me anymore and I'll die before he hurts another.

As I rise, the other Gods and Goddesses stay at my back. This is my fight, just as this is Atargatis' choice. Saturnus had been chosen by her to serve, and he had failed miserably. Now, he will die at her hand.

I dive now, turning to face the rest of the Circle.

"Take care of the undead. Poseidon, you know what to do, my love." The words pass from lips before I can stop them. I know they're not mine, but it feels odd to say the least to refer to Vex, even if it is only his body, in such an intimate way. I watch as Poseidon moves, going to relieve my father who has, through all of this, managed to somehow to keep a check on the Necrimad. The beast no longer glows, having been stripped of its magic by Saturnus, but it is

470

still a demon, and a mighty one at that. Still, Poseidon will take care of it. After all, it's his creation.

As the others depart, I glide forward toward Saturnus, gazing across his scarlet veined body and face without fear. His eyes betray no goodness; his soul as black as coal. I don't know how I know this, but I do, and so reach out, caressing the side of his face. He flinches, transfixed by mine.

"You were so beautiful once." I say, my forehead creasing in pained thought. Atargatis had watched his life, and now I could see it too. Torment, a glimmer of love, then darkness.

"Bitch. I was never good enough for you." He spits the words in my face and I recoil, placing my hands on his arms. He is hot to touch but I don't flinch, instead the water around him moves, cooling my fingertips and it slithers to restrain him in unnatural lines.

"No. You were never enough for *you.*" I speak the words, definitive in my assessment and moving in as he struggles against the water's restraints. I know Atargatis' plans before she moves to carry them out. Saturnus' soul is too dark to ever be saved by what lies beyond in the underworld. So his soul will be destroyed instead. She leans in, my lips brushing against the forehead of the man I so want to kill. I kiss him, letting his soul shatter into a million pieces under the force of her Godly magic.

Callie. Would you mind doing the honours? Atargatis' voice reaches me and I smile.

My pleasure. I think, knowing she can hear me. Tightening my grip on the handle of the scythe as I spin on the spot, using my effortless momentum to bring down the blade into the top of Saturnus' skull with a satisfying 'clunk'. I drag the length of the blade through his flesh, as though it were no more than butter, my enhanced strength making light work of him as he splits in two. My motor function diminishes as Atargatis takes back control, waving a hand and setting a pack of sharks to devour his meat.

He will be returned to the ocean he tried to destroy as energy. Atargatis explains as we turn from the body, leaving him in my past.

Atargatis lowers my body through the water as we dive, slashing through several un-dead sailors who are crawling from fresh cracks in the earth. We

471

soar over the battle and the surrounding Kindred, Psiren or not, follow in my wake, transfixed by my body as I glide through the water with a Goddess' grace.

Suddenly, we stop and turn; darting quickly to the person I have been most wanting to see, to hold him before he passes on.

Beneath my rainbow scaled tailfin, Orion lies in Jack's arms. Dead.

I'm keeping him here. Atargatis' voice explains as I wonder how he can be dead but not gone. I remember back to when I had died, the second time, she had kept my body here too.

"This is no good at all. He is needed here." Atargatis' voice sounds out like the calm after the storm, taking Orion's limp form in my arms, from Jack whose eyes are the size of saucers.

"You're..." He begins and Atargatis smiles at him.

"Callie and I are connected. We are one. She is still here, but so am I. Worry not. It is confusing." She explains away the magic of our connection, the fact I'm her vessel simple to her. To me it is comfortable, as though I had always been destined for this.

That's because you have. Her reply comes, serene and silent to me through the murky waters of my mind.

"Why is he not dead?" I hear Jack ask, his eyes reflecting my own ethereal glow at me.

"Orion was always under the misconception that Callie was his gift for immortal life in my service. On the contrary, he is her gift. The only gift I could think adequate for her allowing me to take over her body. Contrary to Orion's opinions about himself, he is extraordinarily selfless, kind and a righteous hero. Plus... look at him. He is attractive for a mortal. Callie both needs and deserves all that." Atargatis speaks for me and I startle slightly at her response. Orion was my gift? For this?

As I'm pondering this, Atargatis looks down to Orion who is lying in my arms, the spear still running through his throat. She waves my hand, willing the metal to dematerialise and leaving it as no more than water. She waves her fingers again, the motion entirely natural to me after just a few moments and the wound is gone. Orion's eyelids begin to stir and my breath hitches. I have never wanted to see the icy blueness of their depths more desperately than I do now.

I turn, still holding him in my arms, seeking my fellow Gods and Goddesses as I look out around the battlefield, my eyesight perfect even though it is dark. Atargatis' senses are immense, her soul attuned to the fact that Poseidon is barely breaking a sweat as he dismembers the Necrimad as though he were no more than carving up an oversized thanksgiving turkey. The undead are flailing as Sedna's power freezes them, shattering their exposed bones to dust. Lir on the other hand requires no acute sense as Conan's meek form has been transformed into one twice the size of Flannery. The red headed Selkie watches as Conan shatters his opponents with a single fist slam to their foreheads. Neptune also has quite the fighting finesse, as Casmire throws his shield through the water, decapitating his opponents like he's no more than playing ultimate Frisbee on a college quad. Calypso is surrounded by fish and marine mammals, commanding them to consume those lost to us, cleansing this place of death, as Ava and Mizuchi fight back to back, both their weapons taking out several undead opponents in one tornado of sharp edges as they spin, mighty, in the water.

Around me the Psirens stir, scared as they watch the Circle in action, not knowing what is to become of them, and as I gaze upon the rest of the Circle demolishing the opposition, I well up inside. I could never have anticipated this. I thought I was going to die. I didn't think I was, instead, going to truly live for perhaps the first time.

Vex and the other vessels finish in their destruction as the Necrimad is devoured by a giant squid. It is summoned by Poseidon in a flurry of furious storm clouds, somehow materialising underwater and revealing the beast in their wake as lightning strikes follow, chargrilling what is left of the demon's meat. The Kindred regroup, forming a circle around me as every one of our people surround us, looking inward to where we are gathered. Azure is watching us with wide eyes, and I know we must be a sight if even she's shocked.

I realise I am still carrying Orion in my arms, though he weighs nothing to me. I examine his gorgeous face as he lies, draped like a delicate and beautiful ornament, in my arms. As he stirs, finally opening his eyes, the Goddess and myself inhale. His eyes shine out, taking in every inch of me, devoted, beautiful, and ferociously icy blue.

ORION

I awaken. Opening my eyes and expecting to see the face of Starlet, my mother or father. Instead, I inhale sharply. What greets my eyes isn't anything like what I expect. Instead, it's awe-inspiring.

Callie, or at least what looks sort of like Callie, is staring at me through familiar aqua eyes. That's where the similarities end though, as her hair is glowing lilac in waves that fall from her, weightless as though it's nothing more than purple light. Her scales shimmer multihued, her lips pinker and her skin glowing ever so slightly white like the moonlight.

"Callie?" Her name falls from me, instinctual and unstoppable. Then I realise. I can talk. I move my hand up to my throat, which has healed.

"I am Atargatis." Callie speaks, but it is not her in tone or sentiment. Something is very wrong.

"I don't... I don't understand." I stutter, moving from the arms of the odd Callie doppelganger.

Righting myself, I can see that the war is over and extending out from me what's left of the Kindred float, watching and amazed. Among them the Psiren also watch on, though their eyes are filled with horror.

"Orion, child. Callie is my vessel. We are one. The Conduit, it was our way of intervening. The Circle's way of fixing our mistakes. We have come here, to your plain of existence, risking the very structure of the universe to protect you." Callie speaks and then I see it. She *is* the Goddess. That's when I take a moment to look to the other vessels. Conan is covered in tattoos and three times the size he once was. Cage's hair has turned white from Aqua and his

474

scales look frostbitten. Vex's tentacles roll out from him like waves as a myriad of deep blues and whites as his eyes flash like an Ocean storm. Callista is covered in deep greens, blues, reds, pinks and purples, luscious and vibrant just like the jungle. Calypso is a rippling wave of periwinkle and aqua, her eyes glowing blue as Chiyoko's body is slashed through with red, like bloody cuts, and her eyes glow gold. Casmire is a crown jewel of crystals, dripping with diamonds, rubies, sapphires, emeralds and amethyst, each crystal clinging to his now golden tailfin as though he's been drenched in the entirety of the ocean's buried treasure. I pivot slowly, staring at them, their bodies straining with muscle, glowing with energy and vibrant with colour, as the hairs on the back of my neck rise at the proximity of so much power.

"You're all... here." I stutter, spinning again, this time in the opposite direction, as my mind struggles to catch up with what is happening.

"Yeah, we all got that part about a year ago. Did you get brain damage as well as a flesh wound?!" Azure snaps from behind me and I turn, rushing to hug her.

"You didn't die!" I exclaim, happy beyond belief to be alive. Azure, on the other hand, doesn't respond to my affections with the same joy.

"Oh my God, can you get off? If you want to hug someone go hug your soulmate." She snaps, shaking me off and looking extremely unhappy while doing it. Everyone is watching us as I spin in the water, turning yet again to face the Goddess as I feel my heart stop.

"Callie..." I begin, but don't know how to articulate what I want to say. I don't want to sound ungrateful that Atargatis is here.

"She's safe and sound. Glad you're alive." Atargatis nods to me, untouchable as I contemplate hugging her close to me and then reject the idea immediately.

"So Saturnus is..." I begin.

"Gone." She replies quickly, looking bored.

"The Necrimad is..." I start again.

"Dead." Vex speaks, though his voice isn't British anymore, instead it's brutish.

"The undead..." I begin and Atargatis swims forward, placing a hand on my shoulder. Her aqua eyes and lilac hair glow, bringing out Callie's natural beauty even further.

"Everything will be alright, Orion. You have done well, saved the world in fact." She smiles at me and it feels like I'm the only man in the world.

"I didn't save the world. We did." I look back to what's left of my pod. I can't see Ghazi anywhere, but Azure, Cole, Jack and a handful of mermaids remain, looking to me with shocked and smiling faces.

"Yes *we* did." Azure's cocky tones creep from behind me as she takes a few strokes forward with her dark tailfin.

"Azure. My dark flower. How very important you are." Atargatis breathes, beckoning Vex or Poseidon, or maybe both, forward.

"Yes. I am important. So, I have a request... I want..." Azure begins, but is silenced as Atargatis holds up a hand.

"I know. You want your sister back." She breathes, shaking her head. Azure inhales, puffing out her chest with hopeful eyes.

"It is not possible Azure, your sister died in an act of nobility. She sacrificed herself for the greater good. To undo such an act... well, it is against the laws of nature as well as her wishes. Also, in returning her to you, it would make your role in the saving of this planet one driven by selfish motive. I cannot do such a thing by the laws of the Kindred Scales." Azure scowls and Poseidon laughs.

"Don't look so disappointed. Listen to what my beloved has to say." He says, chuckling, his laugh like thunder.

"I do however... have another gift for you." She speaks calmly, unafraid of Azure, which I'm sure is a first for my sister, who is so often confronted by those who fear her.

"A gift?" Azure asks, suddenly looking more appeaseable as her expression relaxes. I roll my eyes. She's so easily bought.

"Yes, come here." Atargatis gestures for her to move closer and Azure glides toward her, her tailfin hypnotic as always. She kneels on the sand among body parts and bloody stains as the Goddess dives downward, her lips pressing lightly to Azure's forehead. She gasps, inhaling slightly and then jerking

476

backward as though something has been physically pushed against her skull with a sudden slap.

"Arabella...." Her lips form the word and I scowl because I don't know what that means. Azure's eyes fill with tears. I lean down to her. Worried.

"Who's Arabella?" I ask her, my heart palpitating.

"My daughter." She whispers, tears trickling down her cheeks and separating from the water, oily in constituent, but still not turning to diamond.

I feel my mind explode. Azure's a mother? I'm an Uncle? When did this happen? How had I not known?

I watch as her darkness recedes, falling back through her as the azure of her scales protrudes through, bright and beautiful as a wishing star in the great expanses of the night sky. "Thank you..." She breathes, falling to the sand in a bow before the Goddess. I've never seen her act like this, the darkness practically non-existent in her form.

"You are welcome. Poseidon and I have had some choices to make. You have been instrumental in those choices."

"Choices?" I ask, curious as the pair shift their eerily familiar gazes to me.

"We've had to decide what to do about my Kindred." The voice falls from the bony features of Vex, but it is distinctly more powerful. I narrow my eyes, turning full circle.

"The Psirens?" I ask him and he nods. Atargatis' lips purse.

"We have had so much trouble getting rid of them... and yet, those of them who were made recently, they are but children. Innocents who have been infected. They have been influenced by the likes of Solustus and Saturnus. We feel it is not fair to judge them based on those actions. Especially when those of you such as Azure and Vex have shown that the darkness can be used for light." Atargatis' voice falls across me and I scowl. Azure glimpses behind her to the rest of the Psirens.

"My darkness... it's who I am." She expresses, like she's finally understood why she's here.

"Yes, my child. It is. So, you will rule them." Atargatis speaks as she and Poseidon turn to her, the full scrutiny of their gazes falling upon her shocked and semi-affronted expression.

477

"You and Vex will rule them together." Poseidon wades in. "You must understand; I do not want to wipe my Kindred from this place, but I will if I have to. It is up to you to guide them, show them the power in their darkness, but also show them how to master it, manipulate it for the *right* reasons." He places a hand on Azure's shoulder. "If this goes wrong, I will hold you personally responsible." He vows as she nods, her eyes wide and icy blue as they bear into his.

"Azure... a Queen?" I ask them, incredulous, and they nod. I look to her and smile sheepishly as she sticks her tongue out.

"Yeah, that's right. Who's your Queenie?!" She cocks an eyebrow and we laugh as Atargatis turns to Poseidon.

"You see why I love them so?" She asks him and he actually appears as though he's wavering.

"I suppose. Though having an angry Englishman in my head isn't doing much for my temper." He rolls his eyes and I laugh at the thought of Vex's discomfort. Spinning on the spot, I move toward the other rulers, or what's left of them bobbing up and down.

"There are some people... I want you to meet." I gesture around to the circle, asking them to come forward. They do, ethereal in grace and lightning fast in speed.

Domnall looks worse for wear, but as Conan's immense height towers over him, he looks up and throws back his head in the mother of all guffawing laughs.

"Bludy hell, lad!" He can't stop laughing, as he takes in Conan's new body, holding out a hand as Lir moves to take it. "Ah uh, micht hae underestimated ye." He admits, winking as he examines the bottle green lightning strikes mapping Conan's morphed, pale, freckled skin.

Isabella comes forward next, looking to the jewel encrusted body of Casmire who is holding Neptune within flesh.

"My gracious. You are divine." She purrs, swimming to his left side as the other leaders rush past me to meet their deities made flesh. Gideon is the last to come forward, his too familiar eyes wide and his mouth slightly agape, as I search behind him for Akachi to only grim avail.

478

"Poseidon made mincemeat of the Necrimad... I've never seen anything like it." He addresses me as his eyes drift to Atargatis.

"She's incredible." I breathe, unable to express how in love I am with Callie, let alone the Goddess inhabiting her form because right now they are one and the same. Atargatis turns to me, pulling Sedna to her side. Cage's eyes flicker with recognition at Gideon's face.

"We need to tell him. It's only fair." Atargatis nudges the Arctic God, who breathes out causing the water around me to chill by several degrees.

"Oh, alright. I suppose we've done all the damage we're going to." He replies, crossing his arms across his broad chest, as I begin worry the water around me might freeze.

"Your soulmate... she still lives." Atargatis smiles, parting Callie's lips in an excited expression.

"Alyssa?" Gideon asks, urgency taking over his tone.

"No. Patience." Atargatis reveals that Callie's mother is too to become a Mer and Gideon's eyes light up, his expression no longer worn, but one of a young man in love.

"Thank you." He exhales in a rush of cold breath and Callie's eyes turn excited once more.

"That reminds me!" Atargatis claps her hands together, grabbing my hand and pulling me along with her.

"Mer, Kindred of mine, I have to tell you, I am not only here to end the darkness and murder which has reigned. I am also here to make a fresh start. A new beginning. I am here to enact something which has only ever occurred once before in history." The mermaids are transfixed before the Goddess as she speaks, and the other leaders and their vessels fall into silence. I continue to stare at her, caught in her presence like metal to a magnet.

"The Tidal Kiss... but why?" I ask her, and she cocks her head sideways.

"The mer were all but wiped out Orion. How can I hope Callie will lead with you by her side if you have no one to lead?" She asks me, curious as to my reply, as she cocks a lilac eyebrow.

"More mer?" I ask and she nods, lilac hair cascading around her.

479

She turns from me as Callie's skin begins to glow brighter, magic shining from every inch of her as Atargatis rises in the water.

Bringing her hands to her lips she kisses Callie's fingertips, blowing a kiss outward as a ripple of aqua light falls out from around us in the water, covering everything as it expands to cover the globe. It causes my hair to stir in the water as the chatter around us stills and everyone watches the immense aqua light of her magic as it diminishes, the light vanishing over the horizon as my heart expands with it. More mer. More modern mer like Callie.

"Mer are being chosen now as we speak, their souls split and new soulmates created in their hundreds. You must find them. Find them as you found Callie. Take them into the sea's embrace and have them serve me as you always have." She claps her hands calmly as the pulsation of her kiss vanishes completely and new mer awaken, chosen and blessed with this life.

"Now… do you have any questions for me before we begin?" She asks me this directly and my eyes widen as my mind explodes with the possibility. Questions? Only about a million. I go for an easy one first.

"Here's a question, becoming a mer isn't genetic, or whatever it is Callie says, so why are so many of us related?" I ask and she smiles, underwhelmed.

"Oh that's easy! How about I answer by asking you a question. Why is it my mer are so willing to serve, but the Psirens are not?" She asks me and I frown. I had never really thought about it.

"I honestly have no idea." I reply and she giggles.

"Of course not, you're practically mortal. I'll explain it like this; shortly after you became mer I gifted the mer soulmates, but it was even before then that I realised something else about humans, which Poseidon did not. In order to create great warriors, you must give them something to fight for. By creating mer from suitable relations, it gave you something to hold on to. Much as Poseidon is that for me. Immortality, you see, is both a curse and a blessing. It is a beautiful thing, if surrounded by those you love. If you are alone, it can be awful." She explains this and I understand. It is true that my father, my sisters, they gave me something to fight for before Callie even existed. As time has gone on, my family had become the mer community at large; Cole and Ghazi had become my brothers, Shaniqua my surrogate mother. I frantically squint into the crowd at this thought but I'm unable to pinpoint two of three anywhere.

"I have another question..." I say, unsure I want to know the answer, but knowing Callie will want to know.

"What would that be?" She enquires, staring at me as she reaches out a palm, distracted by dissolving Psiren body parts into sand.

"Why Callie... and in a wider sense, why the vessels? Why did you choose them? What makes them special?" I question her and her head snaps to the side.

"You ask this for Callie? She wondered why I chose her?" She asks me, stern as her full lips press into a firm line, and I nod, unable to speak as I shrink, worried about angering her.

"Yes." I reply, finally finding my courage. She looks troubled by this, but continues to answer anyway.

"Callie was chosen because she didn't want the power of a Goddess. She just wanted you. She was given that choice by me not so long ago. She chose love over power. If that isn't someone worthy of power I don't know who is. If you look at the other vessels, it's much the same story. Poseidon was the hardest to pair with someone." She admits, reaching out a palm and letting it hover over the sea floor as she heals the cracks in the earth.

"He chose Vex?" I ask her and she laughs melodically.

"Funnily enough, yes." She chuckles, looking to me with a cocked eyebrow.

"Wait..." I say, thinking back. Atargatis had asked if I had questions before we were to begin.

"You said... before, that we were going to begin? Begin what?" I ask her, feeling afraid that they will leave, or in exiting Callie's body Atargatis will leave her less than she was.

"Rebuilding the Occulta Mirum of course. You didn't think we were going to make the trip of an immortal lifetime, only to leave you with sand and bones, did you?"

481

"Of course not!" I exclaim, worried about offending her. The Circle have done so much already and I hardly know how to begin in thanking them.

"That's the other thing. The Circle and I have decided... we're bringing the Kindred into the future." She gets a knowing and satisfied look before she turns and I follow her gaze, watching as the rest of the animals who have aided our cause depart, swimming off and following the long gone aqua glow of the second Tidal Kiss.

"It is time. We must begin." She commands the other Gods and Goddesses, who turn from the leaders they are speaking with, eager and with sparkling eyes. The Circle swim toward the sand bowl of the city, bursting forward and parting the crowds of Kindred who are left trailing to keep up. By the time we catch up, the vessels float, surrounding the bowl in a circle at even intervals. They reach out, extending their hands and beginning the transformation of the place I had always called home.

After a few moments, the sand around us begins to move, flying up from the ocean floor and surging toward the centre of the ruined city, a sand storm unrivalled by any I've ever seen. I shield my eyes, feeling the weight of the debris dislodging water around me as I struggle to keep upright in the water. After a few moments, the sand clears and I right myself, eyes widening as they rest on something resembling the Occulta Mirum... well, almost.

If I'd thought Saturnus had done a good job with Regus' assistance building the city, then I'd been wrong. In comparison to the new metropolis, which now stands in its place, the Old Occulta Mirum looks like a wooden hut with a leaky roof, much like my childhood home, actually.

Eight shards rise, each in a different colour sea glass from the ground in Black, Aqua, Ice Blue, Jade Green, deep indigo, bloody scarlet, tangerine Orange and grapefruit Pink. They eventually form one multi-coloured spire as each building twists in with the rest over the centre of an enormous round courtyard. Beneath the meeting spires of the eight separate Alcazar are not one, but eight golden statues, which stand, surrounding a black and white stone mosaic of the symbol of the Circle of Eight. The city sprawls further than it

482

used to, the streets shimmering with new glass bottles interspersed throughout. Restored, the cyclical surface scrapers shimmer the colours of the rainbow too, each one sand stone and crystal in structure with swirling lines wrapping around the outside from multiple glass bottles set into their walls.

After I'm done gawping, I watch as the Gods and Goddesses turn, their eyes sparkling with triumph and the thrill of being held in mortal flesh. Atargatis and Poseidon open their mouths, speaking in unison.

"This is the Capital, the Occulta Mirum, hidden wonder of the Ocean. We wish you to live together. To join as a whole, as a family. A new type of rulership will be born, whereby you will not only rule your people, but govern the Kindred as one. The vessels and leaders are to form a new council. The Council of Eight. No longer will you be divided. You will stand strong and be as one as whirlpools are left open surrounding the city, giving you a global transportation network as well as providing you with protection from the human world above. You have proven yourselves more than worthy of this gift, blessed ones, and we thank you for your undying devotion to our causes, for your struggle, and above all, for showing us that your race, where you have come from, truly is worth saving."

The couple complete their speech, bowing to us all, as we hang, unsure of what to do.

After a few moments of silence, I hear Domnall begin to clap beside me. More people join in and soon the entire crowd is applauding the Circle, their faces glowing with an inability to keep up with what has happened, but enraptured by the fact that everything is finally changing for the better.

I watch as they turn back to look over the city they have created for a few moments and the Kindred stare out behind me, watching the sun rise over the horizon and casting fresh light on a new world. A world of co-operation, a world of global unity between the Kindred of the Circle.

I observe as Atargatis turns from the city and glides over to me, placing her hands in my palms. She winks at me before simply saying.

"She'll say yes. When she does, open this letter together." With that final sentiment, she shoves a wax sealed envelope into my palm and her eyes turn white. With that, the bright glow surrounding Atargatis diminishes and the

483

technicolour of her scales vanishes. I watch as the other vessels collapse into the sand beneath them, and I'm left with a sleeping Callie, who falls into my arms with a smile plastered on her perfect face.

37
The wreckage
CALLIE

I stir from unconsciousness, everything that has passed crystalline in my mind as I open my eyes.

"Hey beautiful." Orion's words reach me as I look up into icy blue eyes. I exhale, tears prickling my own eyes in a fast, emotional rush as I lurch up from the bed and wrap my arms around him, holding on for dear life.

"Orion!" I breathe, my heart shattering. I had been so proud, too proud. So desperate to prove I was strong enough to survive. It had never occurred to me that he who seemed so immovable in my world could be fragile, breakable too. I clutch him to me, sobs wracking my body. He had almost died and it was all my fault.

"Hey... don't cry." His voice soothes me as his fingers trace down my spine.

"You... you almost died." I sputter, still not letting him go as I weep down his back.

"Yeah, sucks, doesn't it?" He asks me, a cocky tone falling from him as I push away, staring at him with incredulous and tear filled eyes.

"Oh my god, you are such an ass!" I slap him across the arm, half laughing, half crying. I can't take in his face enough. I can't stop staring at him and, in an instant. everything becomes just too much because I fear that with every passing second I grow closer to losing him again.

485

I take a moment to place myself in my surroundings, staring at the room I'm in for the first time. The bed I've woken from is aqua crystal, forming the shape of a giant green sea turtle. Nestled on its back, where should be a shell, is a large circular mattress covered in chocolate coloured, crushed velvet sheets that I've been wrapped in.

"This isn't right…" I mutter, turning from Orion whilst making sure to keep one hand on his forearm. He laughs, amused at my reaction.

"Yeah, I'd say we've been upgraded… by like… a lot." He expresses as I turn back to him, looking past his features as I see the extent to which the royal suite spreads. The walls are made of the same highly polished sea glass they were before, but the room extends out, a large, multi-coloured chandelier hanging from the arching ceiling above which houses bubble-like glass baubles which are filled with glowing aqua algae. Dressing tables, cabinets and wardrobes are all fashioned from the same material, glistening in the light of a new day, as they seem to climb, almost seamlessly, out of the floor.

"How long was I out?" I ask him, concerned I've missed something important.

"Not long considering… I'd say about 5 hours." Orion replies, swimming through the water and toward me as his hand travels to my wrist. I feel him tug me to him and I let myself be pulled. "Are you alright?" He asks me, face concerned. I realise now he's worried about *me*.

"Orion I… I was her…" I smile, unable to keep the expression from my face. He exhales, a grin forming on his lips too. We float here basking in the glow of our success, of what we've achieved together.

"Everything is different." He kisses me on the cheek. "Because of you."

"I know. The Tidal Kiss." I remember, gasping, thinking now to the future of the mer, the fact that we have a future. It wasn't just the Tidal Kiss; it was the kiss that changed me. The act had meant so much to me personally, because I had seen the faces of each soul that had been picked, destined for a life immersed in the most fantastic place on earth. I had felt their collective strength, seen their potential. I know now that the mer have a bright and long future ahead. The Tidal Kiss had filled me with hope, given me a new lease on life. It had set me free.

486

"Not just that, Callie. Sit." Orion lowers me, pulling me through the water to the crushed velvet of our new bed. His eyes are wide as he takes my palms in his hands. "Not everyone made it." He explains, I remember Ghazi turning to sand. Philippe lying dead…

Who else had perished? I wonder.

"Who?" I ask him, my voice shaking with fear as he sighs.

"Ghazi. Marina. Fahima. Shaniqua. Akachi. Sirenia. Enzo. Paolo. Claudia. Cain. Fergus." Orion lists off the names, beginning with the members of our pod and moving through the rest of the Kindred. My heart falters as a heavy pang of grief settles over me. Marina… the Italian surrogate mother I had loved. Shaniqua, her wisdom and grace lost to this world. Fahima, her wordless kindness, disappeared from my life in a matter of hours.

"Orion… I'm sorry. I'm sorry she couldn't save them all. That I couldn't…" I whisper, guilty. I had the power of a Goddess, and yet I could not save them. I feel my heart shatter and my eyes well with tears, as everything inside me seems to break apart.

"Hey, it's not your fault." Orion reassures me, his eyes kind and his touch gentle as I sit atop the sea turtle frame of our bed. The room is still and silent for a few moments. "That's the other thing." Orion continues when he feels I am ready to hear what he has to say next, running his hand through his hair, clearly stressed.

"What?" I question him and he begins to look more worried with each second that passes. Like he's worried I might break.

"There's some disagreement about the Psirens. The other leaders, well, some don't agree that they should be left alive. Particularly the Water Nymphs and the Maneli, they've lost so much." He poses the problem to me.

"We need to have a meeting." I state, knowing that my work still isn't done despite everything that we've already been through.

"Yes. The Council of Eight, which the Circle decreed we assemble are ready. We've been waiting for you." As these words fall from his lips I'm upright.

"Come on. Let's get down to business." I feel a sudden energy spark through me, worried for my people, worried for the city. Orion catches my wrist as I move to dart to the exit, pulling me to his chest as he crushes my lips against his and kisses me as though I'm the only woman in the world.

A shiver runs down my spine as his fingers cradle my face and he holds me to him, the other half of his soul craving my proximity like an open flame seeking oxygen. We are necessary to one another, and I had never felt that more than I do now.

"Sorry." He says, breaking the kiss as we both become out of breath. "I just had to do that first."

With this, we turn and he leads me from the room, reluctant but unmistakable smiles plastered on both our faces.

The Alcazar is nothing like it once was, it is larger and has been filled with decadent furniture, libraries with once lost texts stacking their shelves, and most importantly, a new council chamber for us to meet with the other Kindred. As we descend through the extremely wide central column of the structure, Orion tugs at me.

"Come, there is something you need to see first. Or more importantly, something I need to ask you before we proceed." I raise my eyebrows, wondering what could be so urgent, as he pulls me to the left before we dive into the new throne room. It's much the same as the old one in many ways, the floor being made of stained glass designs, but this time instead of depicting Atargatis, they depict the battle we have just fought, showing The Conduit as it is activated. I know that I will never forget the events of that night, but I also know that this mural is there to give perspective to Orion whenever he takes his throne.

I swim over to the new construct, no longer made from the wood of Olive trees from Orion's homeland, this single seat is now crafted from Coral and Crystal, dripping with sparkle and precious stones, it is a chair fit only for a God.

"There's only one throne." I say, absent minded as I take in the newness of the Occulta Mirum through the panoramic window of the room. The Aqua

Alcazar is central to the others, looking out over the majority of the sparkling city head on.

"Yes. Come." Orion moves high, to the peak formed by the throne. From it, he lifts something.

"What is that?" I ask. He descends through the water so he's on eye level with me once more.

"This was here when we arrived. I believe the fact there's only one throne speaks to the desires of the Goddess in this case." He says, handing me what he's holding.

I look down at the object, my expression changing to one of surprise. An aqua and mint tiara made from triangular sea glass, rising in a high pyramid around an icy, teardrop shaped aquamarine in the centre of the headpiece, glistens in my grasp.

"A tiara?" I laugh at him. "That's not a great look for you." He stares back at me, not saying a word, his gaze excited yet serious as the manly line of his jaw clenches, waiting for me to grasp what it is he's saying. After a few moments, I gasp.

"You think. She wants *me* to rule?" It sounds ridiculous. It's one thing helping Orion rule, but I know nothing of this city in comparison to him. I'm only eighteen.

"Callie. It's always been you. I'm not cut out to rule. I'm a warrior. This is *your* destiny. I know it is." He takes a stroke forward in the water, caressing the side of my cheek with his thumb and staring down at me. I almost want to laugh; he's being absolutely insane.

"Orion... I... I'm not cut out for this." I stutter, rubbing the pads of my fingers against the sea glass of the tiara, nervous.

"Callie. There's no crown here. I think it's pretty obvious that you *are* cut out for this. Besides, I'm not disappearing. I will still be by your side. I just know I'm better suited for military life. For keeping everyone safe. I'll happily be your military adviser, your bodyguard and consort. But I think the Goddess is right. You are a natural with people and you *can* make the hard choices. You already have. You've gotten us this far. So please... take it. The throne. It's what you're meant to do. Queen is in your blood. It's who you are." I stare up at him, dumbfounded by his confession. He thinks I can be Queen? He thinks I can do this? Is it all just a way to keep me under lock and key?

"If I take this throne, will it mean I can't go out and fight?" I ask him, my mouth forming a hard line at the thought of him trying to cage me in again.

"Callie, I think we've both seen how well telling you 'no' ends. If you have this power, you can do whatever you like. You're in control. However, if you don't want the power, if you don't want the throne, I'll understand. It is a big commitment and you're so young. Just don't decline out of fear. You're the strongest woman I know. The Goddess chose you to house her soul here on earth. You are special and more than equipped for this. I won't have you thinking otherwise." He stares at me with such love in his eyes that I know he's not lying to me. He's passionate about seeing me succeed and I can't imagine he'd be saying these things if he thought I'd fail.

I look back down from his eyes to the tiara in my hands. It's heavy, as it should be; it represents a hell of a lot of responsibility. Exhaling heavily, I close my eyes, lifting it through the water and placing it on my head as the bands nestle against my skull. It fits perfectly and I smile at that, before I swim from Orion's side, sitting back in the new throne and allowing the seat to cup my back, cradling me.

I look down to Orion who has now taken a stroke sideways and is kneeling, his tailfin tucked beneath him as he bows down before me.

"How do I look? Queen-ish?" I ask Orion and he laughs, lifting his torso and rising.

"You look like you're where you're supposed to be. Oh… and beautiful, of course." He rushes to the throne and kisses me on the cheek as I flush.

"Now that little detail is taken care of, we better go. The council are waiting." He reminds me and I sigh. I can't stop for long enough to take in what's happening, and, as Orion pulls me from the throne room, I wonder what kind of dilemmas await me with the council.

The corridor extends out from me as I see Cole up ahead, bathed in aqua light and beaming at me as he opens the doors to the Council Chamber. The rest of the council members, including Vex and Azure, turn in their crystal seats, rotating on an invisible axis as they see us. All faces light up at the sight of me and they stand, rising in the water and clapping loudly like I'm some kind of award winner. I smile, the tiara still weighing heavily atop my head as everyone's eyes in the room rise to it. Azure is flying toward me, an angry look in her eyes, before I can so much as blink.

"I see you took the throne?" She asks and I nod, blushing as I feel like a child, admitting I have just become a monarch like it's something naughty.

"Well, that's a relief, because you know that *she* won't let us be slaughtered in our sleep." Azure spins to Isabella and sticks her tongue out as I roll my eyes.

"What does she mean?" I ask Orion, who is still beside me, his hand in mine.

"As mer ruler and vessel, you're the head of the council. We brought the pods together. So we're unbiased... or so that's how this *supposedly* works." Orion explains the concept and I feel my heart begin to pound. This is all too much. Head of the monarchy? Head of the Council? Goddess' vessel? My head is spinning with the amount of power I've amassed in such a short space of time. I have never wanted this kind of power, though I supposed I had never wanted to be a mermaid either, and that happened anyway.

I take stock of the members of the council, rising slightly in the water to see who is here. From the Adaro, Gideon and Cage are seated, the pride in my father's eyes so obvious it's almost embarrassing. On their right are Conan and Domnall who sit next to Isabella and Casmire. The Maneli pod, Kaiya is now standing in for Akachi, and Callista is looking bored as Aulani and Calypso lean back in serene poses. Beside them Hironori and Chiyoko sit, watching me closely and with intense gazes. Finally, Azure and Vex are seated near to where two empty seats stand, presumably for Orion and I.

I glide through the water, the doors closing behind us with a soft thud, as I undulate and the group watches me like I'm some sort of animal in a zoo. I flush red, feeling their eyes on me as I take my seat next to Gideon, and Orion sits next to his sister.

"Sorry I'm late." I breathe as the council turn to me, their gazes worried.

491

"We need to talk about the Psirens." Kaiya says, her chameleonic tail shimmering from deep red to orange in fury. Her eyes are narrow as she clutches the old staff of Akachi in her left arm and the crocodile, still clutching the eye of Ava in its jaws, blinks coldly with an unfeeling expression.

"I know. Give me a moment." I explain, not wanting to be bombarded as Isabella speaks almost immediately afterward.

"We cannot possibly let them live among us. They are monsters. The Water Nymphs have suffered many casualties. How can we possibly break bread with these... things?" She spits, and I sigh, this is going to be harder than I thought.

"Look, I'll be honest. I don't like the idea completely myself. But it isn't our choice. Poseidon and Atargatis have spoken on this matter. It is a trial run. You have fought alongside Azure and Vex, both of whom were instrumental in the destruction of Solustus, Saturnus, Caedes and Regus." I retort, remembering back to Poseidon and Atargatis' declaration that Azure is to be made Queen of the Psirens. I look at Azure now, her tailfin and scales electric blue instead of black. She looks more mer-like than I've ever seen her.

"Azure, what do you have to say on this matter?" I ask her, knowing I need to give her a chance to say her piece. She rises, clearing her throat.

"I'm not asking that we forget that the Psiren's power is rooted in darkness. Nor the high price of life, that we have all paid in the course of taking them down. What I *am* saying is that there is a difference between The Banished, which I was once a part of, consisting of Solustus, Saturnus, Caedes, Regus and Titus, and what the Psirens have become. The darkness within these new Psirens is diluted. They are able to be contained, to be harnessed as a power for good. Look at myself and Vex. If I'm darker than any of the new Psirens and I manage, so can they. Callista, I ask that you and I have classes, whereby the Psirens undergo spiritual meditation and counselling. I also think we need to put their energy into something productive. From what I've managed to observe in the last few hours the Psiren district of this new city has a gym. Mandatory exercise..." Azure begins but Casmire cuts her off.

"You're kidding? Counselling and exercise? That's what you've got for us?" He scowls, his thoughts tainted by grief.

"It works. I've seen it." I vouch for Azure, remembering how different she had seemed after just a small amount of time with Callista.

"I'm not saying it to hear myself speak, Mr. Sparkle. I'm serious. I know them better than any of you. So does Poseidon. He and Atargatis ruled they stay. SO, they stay." Azure slams her fist down on the crystal of the table, unwavering in her glare as she stares at everyone. I look around the table to each one, hedging my bets on who is for and against our new neighbours.

"Look, let's put it to a vote." I suggest, pulling on democracy when I have no other words that can possibly convince them that the people we have been fighting and killing are worth now saving. Orion covers my hand with his on my armrest and takes the conversation from me, for which I'm grateful.

"All of those in favour of following the Circle's wishes and keeping the Psirens as one of us, raise your hand." He asks the council with a stern expression. Around the table, all vote to take in the Psirens except Kaiya, Casmire, Isabella, Calypso and Aulani.

"That settles it. They stay." I decree and Isabella shakes her head.

"If they so much as touch a Water Nymph it's on your head darling." She scowls and I nod, accepting the responsibility.

"Fine. Azure, Vex. This isn't a game. I want you both to know that if I find out any Kindred have been harmed, or any humans so much as approached, the offending Psirens will be killed on site. Got it?" I look at them both with a scowl, knowing that I cannot take any risks with the lives of innocents.

"Yes. I also personally want to rule that no more Psirens be created." Azure vows and the other members of the table watch her with interest, their expressions turning surprised.

"I think that's wise." Orion nods, agreeing with his sister.

"I know it is. I thought of it. I can be wise you know!" She scolds him and he rolls his eyes. I interrupt them, ready to put the issue to rest. As far as I was concerned, the Circle had risked a lot in making their visit, so I wasn't ignoring anything that they had suggested. I can't claim to know better than a Goddess, and I wonder why anyone at this table would think they can either.

"We will revisit this in six months. Azure, Vex, it is your job to make this work. Don't let me down." I stare at them as they roll their eyes in sync.

"So... other than the Psirens, what else do we have to discuss?" I ask, looking around the table.

With that, the council chamber erupts into a hearty debate about everything that has changed. I settle back in my throne, tiara weighing heavy even still, but ready to get to work.

AZURE

"Well that went bloody swimmingly." Vex curses as we swim through the entrance of the Dark Alcazar. We've moved through the newly paved black and white Courtyard, and he can't keep his eyes off the statue of Poseidon.

"What did you expect? We're murderers." I mutter.

Vex closes his eyes as we pass through the halls of black crystal, blue luminescent algae illuminating the space and making it cold. We glide up through the central column of the shard, silent in our anguish and fury. I don't know why I had expected anything to change just because the Gods and Goddesses had given us a chance. Human nature was not so forgiving and we are still public enemy number one, even though I had risked everything to aid the mer in their quest. Everything I'd done still didn't matter, or at least to the foreign Kindred it meant nothing. Callie and Orion at least seemed reasonable.

I move to my right, taking long strokes into the throne room, the floor alight with red stained glass giving the room the effect it's on fire. The image it projects is one of flames, breaking through from a chasm in the bottom of the Ocean. It's a reminder of what awaits me should I fail. Poseidon's wrath.

I look out from the dark throne, a tiara of blackened, smoky quartz awaiting me atop it's rising crystal edge. I pick it up, remembering seeing Callie's atop her head.

Vex hangs in the doorway behind me, his tentacled form shrouded in shadow as I turn to him.

494

"I'm no queen." I admit, throwing the tiara to the floor and watching it shatter, skidding in a pile of broken, cracked stone across the fiery stained-glass of the floor.

I feel rage start to pulsate through me; yet again I have become a pawn in a God's game. I don't want to rule. I don't want to be responsible. I don't even know if I'm worth saving, let alone the rest of the Psirens.

Vex is suddenly before me, the rough skin of his palms grasping at the crevices of my elbows. His eyes blaze lilac, intense, as he inhales.

"Breathe, Love. You're showing me all those pretty colours." He growls as I feel my pupils dilate. The darkness is returning and all I'm left with is a tiara I don't want and shattered memories from the life of a daughter who is long since turned to ash.

"Get away from me." Raising both my arms I push him away, but his expression turns feral, his pupils dilate in the eerie blue light which bounds from the surfaces of the throne room, cold and azure.

"You know, Love. You really need someone to break down those walls you're building. Must be getting pretty lonely in there." He snarls, the lilac lightning flashing behind his irises from the storm within.

"Vex. Don't you get it? We're all alone. Psirens don't need anyone. I don't need you. Nobody needs you. You just won't go the hell away. Imagine how disappointed I was when The Conduit didn't leave you dead." I snarl, crossing my arms and narrowing my eyes.

I let all the anguish, all the hate that I'm feeling for Poseidon, project on to the man whose face Poseidon had worn. Vex tilts upright, his expression falling deadly serious as my heartbeat accelerates. He moves toward me through the water, backing me into the dark shadows of the corner of room, where I belong.

The blue light of algae shines down upon me as his shadow casts darkness across my face in turn. He gazes down at me, eyes black, offering me nothing I don't already possess in abundance as he grips my wrists, holding them above my head and he sliding his body against me.

"Don't you dare..." I snarl as he lurches forward, slamming his lips against mine. The skin of my body tremors at the touch of another, suddenly on

495

fire with the nearness of him and yet I struggle against him, kissing him back. I discover an inability to stop myself, but hold my form rigid in hatred for everything he has become. The kiss sends shivers up my spine as my eyes roll back in my head and I let it possess me for a moment, the ghost of affection, so close and yet that which can never be real.

I tire quickly, bored of his grunts of pleasure as I thrust my palm to the centre of his chest and knock him back through the water before he's aware of what's happening. He crashes into the floor as I catch my breath, fuming.

"Get the hell out of my throne room!" I scream, furious that he dares lay a finger on me. What the hell is he thinking? How could anyone ever lust after someone like him? He's the absolute sum total of everything I hate about the world.

As he climbs back to his usual height in the water he smirks.

"You're welcome, Love." He raises his slashed eyebrow, cocky as he licks his bottom lip, like he's savouring the taste of me.

"If you *ever* try touching me again I will kill you where you stand. I don't give a shit if you're Poseidon himself. Nobody touches me. Ever." I growl, getting ready to charge him.

"That good huh, Love?" He asks, turning to leave.

My heartbeat is rapid, my stomach fluttering with an unfamiliar level of rage I've never encountered and never wanting to feel again. He saunters through the water, tentacles undulating from left to right in cocky twitches that make me want to kill him all the more.

He turns, leaning against the arch of the entryway, his eyes on fire.

"You know where I'll be when you want that cork popping. After the amount I've shaken that sweet champagne of yours, I'm sure it'll be one hell of a party. Call me." He winks, pulsating out of the room and falling through the central spire.

I breathe as the last scent of him vanishes in the water, pissed. Narrowing my eyes, I curl my fingers into a fist but find myself unable to move after him, heart still pounding like it hasn't for... I don't know how long. Spinning, I'm frustrated that the darkness has found its way back to me as I think on the memories that I had been shown of my daughter. Glimpses of places, a whisper

496

of her expressions, her face, who she knew, how she died. But nothing concrete. Nothing Linear.

As I look to the throne, I notice that the tiara I had tossed aside is hanging once more atop the smoky quartz throne that stands, solitary and alone, in the middle of the room.

I guess destroying it once wasn't enough.

I pick it up, hurling it across the room and watching it shatter once more, before I spin, done with the whole idea of ruling, let alone over a band of murderous teenagers.

That's when I see it. The tiara, sitting once more atop the throne I hadn't wanted.

This time, I don't toss it away, smash it or try to end its existence, I just turn, swimming from the room and thinking back, however reluctantly, to the feel of Vex's body grinding against mine.

38
The Vow

CALLIE

It's been five weeks since the first Council of Eight meeting, and every single time I swim into the council chamber I'm still filled with nerves. I don't know what I'm doing. That's the truth of the matter and I can only hope the rest of the council can't see it.

I awaken, having been sleeping much more lately, because ever since the Goddess overtook my body, I'm always half present, half not. When I close my eyes, I revisit the night of the fight. The way I had seen Saturnus' soul shattered, the way I had enacted the second Tidal Kiss. It had been the kiss that had changed me forever and, in a way, I'm scared of forgetting. My mermaid memories are perfect, but I worry that the Circle will erase them because I know more than any mortal probably should of them and their magic.

I stir in the sheets; abandoning the night I had become Atargatis and relinquishing my hold on my dreams, allowing them to recede. I push my hands through the crushed velvet of the chocolate coloured sheets, nerves balling in my stomach at the thought of another meeting, searching for him. He's not there, so I sit up, looking around our expansive crystal suite in search of his face.

"Orion?" I call out; my heart beat accelerating at his absence as my voice echoes back at me. I float atop the bed, rising in the water and bending at the waist as I dive through the room, gliding over to where my crystal vanity stands.

There's a note atop it's flawlessly smooth faceted surface, which I pick up, my fingertips gently caressing the waxy pulp.

Meet me in the courtyard- Orion

I smile, laughing at the fact how he's signed his name. Like, who else would be leaving me notes in our suite? We have Jack guarding the door almost twenty-four hours a day, so it's not like some random stranger could just swim in here.

Spinning on the spot, I swim to exit the room, not even bothering to put on my tiara, sick of wearing it all the time. I know the maidens will probably be angry at me for not even running a comb through my hair, but I'm eager to see Orion, especially seeing as it puts a delay on whatever political debate I'll have to sit through, for hours on end, in today's council meeting.

As I hurry through the chasmic hallways and dive deep down the colossal spiral ramps of the new Alcazar, I think about everything that's happened in just five weeks alone. Oscar and Sophia have returned, telling me that my family are safe and that they want to see me as soon as I can make time. I have sat through mass funerals for the fallen warriors, having to say tear filled goodbyes to those I had loved and lost to the war that had changed everything.

Oscar has been working with Gabriel between the mer and Maneli forges too, designing new armour so that all the Kindred are wearing the same style. An important aspect in uniting the city under one banner.

In the weeks that have passed, I have also tried to get to know the vessels better, using their skills and strengths to try and make things better for everyone. In addition to this, Domnall, Casmire, Hironori, my father and Kaiya have been assessing how to move forward with the military as the leaders of their remaining men, looking to Orion and Cole for guidance, as both men take their new positions as military advisors for the entire army.

The Psirens have been unnervingly well behaved, even helping to dismantle the remnants of the Cryptopolis, which I had ordered as a show that this is truly now their home. Azure and Vex are avoiding each other, no doubt over something completely petty and juvenile, and Orion and I are trying to work out how to find the mer who are newly destined to turn after death, concerned that Azure's visions might be the only way.

499

On top of all this, I've been honoured in being asked to join the Sirena in their quests to help clean up the world's oceans, a personal dream of mine for so long, which may finally be realised. I think about the difference I can make with this many bodies and my heart swells, but then I pass the corridor which leads to the new council chamber, and my heart deflates again, realising how much needs to be done before I can even contemplate leaving the city for months at a time.

As I'm thinking on this, my stomach drops. The council meeting today, which is to finally decide who will stay in the Occulta Mirum and who will return to their prior states across the globe, is making me anxious. It's an important meeting, but one which will, undoubtedly, take hours longer than it should because nobody can agree on anything.

I sigh, running my hands through my hair as my stomach sinks, the thought of sitting in an uncomfortable crystal chair for hours on end too much to bear. I reach the double doors of the large cyclical entry hall of the spire and Cole opens them, greeting me on my way out with a knowing look of excitement on his face.

"What?" I ask him, and he laughs.

"Nothing. Can't I look happy, Your Highness?" He retorts, defensive, and I shake my head.

"Um… yes of course, and if you keep calling me that then I'm going to start getting pissy." I complain as I move past him and out into the centre courtyard.

"Catch ya later, Your Highness Queen Callie the Vessel." He says my whole title just to annoy me, so in very Azure like fashion I turn around and stick my tongue out at him.

"Well that's not very Queen like." The voice I've been waiting to hear reaches me in a cool and cocky rush. I spin to face where I'm going, only to see Orion leaning against the statue of Atargatis in front of me. I can still hear Cole laughing as he shuts the door behind me, and I roll my eyes, wondering if he'll start giving me the first name treatment, like he does Orion, without getting himself impaled first.

500

"What are we doing out here? We have a council meeting in…" I look down at my invisible watch, which doesn't exist, "Exactly the length of time it takes me to swim there." I conclude, laughing. He smiles, his lips curving up as he moves closer to me. I feel myself flush at his proximity.

"We're not going to any meetings today. We're playing hooky." He uses the expression and I can't help but exhale a flurry of bubbles, laughing.

"Playing Hooky? Who taught you that?" I ask him, suspicious, as I narrow my eyes.

"Ah, I can't tell you that. It will ruin my rugged facade." He jokes, kissing me full on the lips as I shrug, glad I won't have to go and listen to more whining for at least another day.

"Fine. Where are we going? Because if we're going to take off I'd rather do it now before someone else has a dire emergency that just 'can't wait'." I express my irritation at the ridiculous types of issue I've been dealing with over the last month. Housing, for a start, was turning out to be a nightmare. I had taken Atlas' knack for laying down the law for granted, particularly now the mermaids and Water Nymphs are in a clash to the death over the penthouse suites closest to the salon.

"We're just going for a little 'us' time." Orion holds out a hand to me, which I take promptly without looking back.

We soar above the city, hand in hand, our shadows flickering over the glistening, bottle clad streets below. Fish soar over the tops of surface scrapers like ocean trapped birds, serene in their colourful flurries of motion as the sun shines down upon the ocean floor, setting my surrounds alight with sparkle. We move out to the open ocean, swimming between two adjacent whirlpools, that will soon be helping some of the members of the pods return home. It is too easy for us to forget that every day we fight over who stays and who goes; there are corners of the ocean that remain undefended and vulnerable.

"Seriously though, where are you taking me Orion?" I whine, worried about everything I'm missing back in the council chamber. As much as I love him, I know I can't shirk my responsibilities so easily anymore.

"Relax Callie, I cancelled the meeting. If you ask me, the leaders and vessels will be glad of the break. Besides, I think it's pretty obvious nobody

501

really *wants* to leave the utopia built for us by the unearthly magic of Gods and Goddesses. The city, it's beautiful, comfortable, well stocked with everything we could need. They won't die staying one more night. I promise you." He vows, placing a soft kiss on my knuckles and saying exactly what he needs to hear.

"Alright. I'm sorry. I'm just... I'm wound so tight I'm finding it hard letting all that go. It's been a long five weeks." I admit, rubbing the back of my neck. I really need a massage.

"You can say that again." Orion agrees, floating on his back in the open ocean. "Lie here, relax. I'll swim us where we're headed." He opens his arms, beckoning me forward as I dive to him, enthusiastic in my speed as I plateau abruptly above his chest. I sink into the warmth of his skin and lay my head above his heart as we take off into the endless blue of the distance.

We arrive in the middle of nowhere, where nothing can be seen for endless miles on end, nothing except a very suspicious and somewhat familiar bolder. I gasp.

"Orion... I haven't been here since the day I turned...Not since the kiss that killed me." I reminisce and he looks at me, his expression curious and amused.

"Is that what you call it? The kiss that killed me? That sounds so romantic...Not! I'm not that bad of a kisser am I?" He says it sarcastically and I roll my eyes.

"Yeah. I know it's a little dramatic, but I being stabbed in the heart wasn't exactly a dull moment. In fact, I'm struggling to remember a dull moment between that event and now." I reply, absent, as I think back over all the events that have occurred since I awoke in the white marble chapel. Some of them had been calmer than others, but I definitely can't call many of them dull.

"God, I hate to think what you'll call this last few weeks." He jokes, smiling to me as he shifts the bolder in front of us and rolls it away, revealing a small opening in the sand.

"The politics that killed me." I laugh as he snorts, knowing what I'm saying is unfortunately accurate.

"That just somehow doesn't have the same ring to it." He admits, shooting me a sly smile and gesturing for me to enter the opening.

"You don't want to go first?" I ask him, as he floats, the masculine beauty of his features radiant under new sunlight.

"No. Go on. I'll follow you." He encourages me downward, gesticulating with one hand as I scowl a little.

He's so bossy. I sigh internally. *And he thinks I make a better ruler?* I smirk, wondering why he will never see himself the way I do, the way the Goddess had. I remember her sentiment, which comes to me in a rush of pleasure.

He is my gift.

I surface inside the cave, the glow of melancholy stars seeming not as sad as they once had as their constellations appear broken by the rippling surface of the water. I break it, taking a gasp of air as I do and grin as the sound of the small waterfall hits my ears. I turn in the water, suddenly realising that something is different.

As I gaze upward, stunned, Orion surfaces behind me.

"So… what do you think?" He asks me as I stare.

Above me, from the hundreds of painted algae stars upon the ceiling of the cave, a constellation I had never noticed before has been made, connected by lines of bioluminescent aqua in the dark. The words shine out, clear as a full moon in a cloudless sky.

Will you marry me?

I turn to him, this time there's no shell, there's no kneeling, there's just him, eyes aglow and holding a ring out to me which is clutched between two of his dripping fingers.

"Yes." My answer is simple, easy, falling from my lips like the breaking of a wave, inevitable and yet unrelenting in its power. There are no watchful eyes. There's no pressure. It's just him and me, bathing in the glow of the faux

503

stars, formed from the years we have waited to find one another. I don't even care about the ring, I just take a single, powerful stroke through the water and take him into my arms as his lips find mine, his hands clutching me to him and claiming me eternally as his. The kiss ends and I'm crying, breaking at the seams with emotion. This man, this ridiculously attractive, crazy, overly protective man is really mine. Forever.

"Here." Orion holds the ring out to me again, and that's when I realise it's not the one he had proposed with before. I take it in my damp palm, examining it in the eerie glow of the star mural above. This ring is different, unique, and I've never seen anything like it. It's a thin white gold band, holding a stone I don't recognise. "Do you like it?" Orion asks me, his eyes seeking my approval.

"I've never seen a stone like this." I whisper, bringing it up to the light.

It shimmers lilac in the shadow, but as I turn it toward the light the facets change to aqua. It's completely unique.

"That's alexandrite. Sophia helped me pick the stone and Oscar made the band and setting." He explains, nervous in his speech. "It changes depending on which kind of light it's in. It reminded me of you, because just when I think you're beautiful as you are, you show me that change can be just as beautiful too." He's babbling, so I decide to put him out of his discomfort.

"It's perfect." I breathe, slipping it onto my finger. It fits perfectly, as I knew it would, but I don't take any more time to examine it, I would rather instead place my hand on Orion's cheek as he gazes into my eyes.

"I can't believe you said yes." He breathes out, laughing and almost hysterical. "I was so nervous, oh my God. Look at me I'm shaking like a leaf." He holds his hand out, a tremor running through him before I place my hand in his, steadying him.

"You thought I'd say no?" I ask him, curious as I place my hand upon his heart, it's racing inside his ribcage. My lips silently curve, glad that he cares so much.

"You have declined me before." He laughs narrowing his eyes as his lips pucker. "I have to say I was less nervous this time than the first, but only because I already know the poker-hot pain of your rejection." He explains and I roll my eyes.

"Everything is different now. I've lost you. It made me realise that spending forever with you... well, it's what I want." I qualify, kissing him on the cheek as his gaze softens, melting at the sincerity of my words.

"We're getting married?" He asks me and I stare into his eyes.

"Yes, but you should know. I've already promised you forever. This just makes it legal." I admonish reminding him that marriage, for me, changes nothing. Nothing can ever change how I feel about him.

"There's something else." He says and I roll my eyes.

"More? I think my heart will give out!" I laugh as he nervously grabs something which is sat on one of the rock shelves that juts out of the wall. He passes it to me and I stare at it.

"This better not be a pre-nup..." I say, shooting him a suspicious glare as I slide my finger underneath the wax seal, admiring my new ring as I do so. It flashes from violet to aqua and then back again, gorgeous and subtle in every respect.

I pull out the paper that is folded inside, the envelope, tilting it and seeking light by which to read.

My Daughter,

I know you now. I have seen into your heart, into your desires. Thank you for giving yourself over to me, a Goddess, who until recently you have never fully believed in. I have loved you since I first saw your soul, blazing in the depths of the Crucible of Gaia which hangs above the Olympian Council Chambers. I have known ever since then that you and I are more similar than you might think, especially when it comes to loving men who are over protective, their love burning so bright it can sometimes consume, just like fire. I know you and Orion are to be wed. I have seen into you, and know this is something you want. I know he is your forever, just as Poseidon is mine. I will be watching none the less, ensuring that the two of you are blessed as you have done what few could manage, and because of this the Circle are forever in your debt. I am writing this letter, because I want to bestow upon you a gift in honour of your wedding. I know you love your mother and sister very much, as I know

505

you love your mer family. This is why I'm granting the Kindred of the Circle a single day in the sun. Your wedding day. It will be one where both your worlds may walk together as one, and so may you.

Be wed. Be merry. Live, but most importantly, love.

I will be watching,

Atargatis

I look up to Orion, handing him the letter. As he reads down the length of the page his eyes widen.

"Callie, this is unheard of." He breathes and I find myself wanting to cry because I'm so happy.

"Orion... my mom... Kayla... they'll get to see us get married." I can barely believe it. I hardly want to. I'm too scared it's all some cruel joke.

Orion picks me up, swinging me around in the water with a splash.

"Where are we going to find a minister who will marry us?" I ask him and he smirks.

"I'll sort all that. Don't worry." He kisses me on the cheek, pulling me close. Suddenly, I feel my heart fall through my stomach, sinking heavy.

"Orion... Marina. She would have loved this." My eyes well up as all the emotion of the last few weeks brims up inside me, uncontrollable as a storm.

"Hush..." He rakes his fingers through my hair, massaging my scalp as I cling onto him. "Focus on the good, Callie. You're going to be walked down that aisle by your father." He reminds me and a reluctant smile moves to my lips.

"Did you ask him?" I ask and he nods.

"Of course I did. I'm nothing if not traditional." He replies, squeezing me, comforting me as the joy of my wedding day brings with it equal grief, the hole left by the people lost to us more apparent now than ever.

"Does that mean I have to look like a giant cupcake?" I ask him and he frowns.

"I don't care what you wear. Just don't leave me standing up there like some schmuck. I'm done waiting." He says, eyes sparkling with determined happiness. I close my eyes, breathing him in as I realise that I too am done waiting.

The future, once more, spans before me in an unending torrent of days and nights lost in icy blue. As we hang there, beneath his question, the question for which I finally had an answer, I cannot help but smile. Knowing that I, Callie Pierce, have so much to be grateful for.

39

The Reunion

CALLIE

My little red vintage purrs as it pulls onto the sidewalk near a familiar, petunia lined front garden. A weeping willow sheds its branches like tears as they fall over the front porch and I smirk at the sight of it, remembering my escape, and how I had thought my problems were so big. Carl, my step dad, had seemed truly evil back then, but now, compared to the likes of those we have just overcome, he seems about as threatening as a cute little bunny named Daisy. I turn off the engine of my little red vintage, sighing and leaning back as I look up at the sky, a ridiculous smile plastered on my face.

"Happy?" Orion asks me, his eyes aglow in the dim light of moon rise.

"Very." I reply, leaning over and kissing him on the cheek.

As I pull away from him, I hear the front door open and turn as a woman in a comedy apron comes running down the front steps of what used to be my house. She's got Kayla in her arms and as she scurries down the front garden path I pull my keys out of the ignition. Tossing them to Orion to hang on to, I open my car door and step out, anticipation thrumming through me. As soon as I'm stood vertical my mother comes crashing into me.

"Callie!" She gasps my name, pulling me into her arms and crushing Kayla against me in turn.

"Mom! You're crushing me!" Kayla muffles with an indignant tone and I feel myself begin to laugh.

"Hey!" I laugh, looking down at her as my mom releases me just enough to give us all room to breathe. Kayla's large brown eyes find mine and she begins to laugh too. Orion moves around the shining red bonnet of my car and stands awkwardly like a spare part as, taking Kayla into my arms, I turn to him.

"Kayla, this is a very special friend of mine. His name is Orion." I say, introducing her with a smile as I look between them. Orion takes a few steps forward, dressed in light denim jeans and a white cotton t-shirt, he is heart-shatteringly beautiful. I can tell Kayla agrees with me as she takes one look at him and buries her head into my shoulder, shy as he is revealed by the stark white light of the full moon.

"Hi Kayla." Orion says, leaning in and holding out a hand for a formal handshake, clearly no idea what he's doing. I roll my eyes, passing her to him. He looks uncomfortable for a moment, holding her out at arms-length as she looks at him, fluttering her eyelashes that rim wide eyes. I watch them with interest as slowly, he melts.

"Well, aren't you adorable." He compliments her as she squirms to get closer to his chest. Pulling her close to his body, he carries her with ease.

"Well, I think so, but mommy always says I'm trouble." She scowls, looking accusatorily toward my mom as we all burst out laughing. I pivot in my sneakers to face her, raising an eyebrow as I see that she's got an apron on which portrays the figure of a much slimmer and bustier woman.

"Nice... Apron." I compliment her as she blushes.

"Well, I know we're supposed to be following you to L.A for the wedding... but I just, I couldn't help myself." She gestures for us to follow her inside with a mischievous expression plastered across her face and it startles me. I've only been gone a few months, but things have most definitely changed.

My mother is getting small wrinkles at the edges of her eyes, Kayla has grown at least three inches and her speech is more affluent. The petunia's might be the same, but the inside of the house is not in small but noticeable ways, and as I let the smell of home envelop me I feel strangely out of place. This isn't my world anymore.

"Come on!" My mom beckons for us to follow her once we reach the kitchen and I pull the loose white jumper, which hangs slightly off my left

509

shoulder, around me tighter, feeling a slight chill wriggle up my spine. I lead Orion, who is still carrying Kayla, through the kitchen and out the back door, where I'm instantly greeted by the smell of gas. I look around at our backyard, which is nothing like the beaten-up patch of dirt I'd left.

Flowers are blooming everywhere, and a small waterfall trickles into a pond at the very back of the yard near the back gate. There's a patio now, and small fairy lights are strung between the trees, lighting the paved space beneath where a table is set for four.

"Oh wow! You did all this?" I ask her and she nods, brushing a strand of hair out of her face and blushing. As she does, she smears charcoal which lingers on her fingertips up the side of her cheek by accident.

"Yes! The only problem is I have no idea how to barbecue." I roll my eyes, chuckling as I turn to Orion who is enraptured with Kayla's tiny hands as they gesticulate. She's talking to him about something he probably has no interest in, but he is none the less, fascinated by her.

"How about if Orion gives it a go?" I ask my mom as I turn back to him, "You're from the fifteen hundreds, you must be fairly decent at cooking over an open flame... right?" I ask him and his expression turns unsure.

"I don't know; I've never used a grill before." He admits.

"Come on, give it a try. We saved the world. You can't tell me that grilling a few burgers has you beat." I challenge him and he narrows his eyes as he sets Kayla down on the patio, much to her dismay I might add, before moving over to my mom and taking the apron from her. He pulls it over his head and before he knows what's happening, my mother has her arms wrapped firmly around his waist with her head on his shoulder. He looks to me, unable to help himself as he smiles, patting her on the back a few times.

After a few moments, she ends the embrace, looking to me with an excitable expression.

"I'll get drinks! What's everyone drinking?" She asks and Orion turns to her, authorative as always.

"Wine?" He asks and she looks suddenly worried.

"I don't know if I have anything... I'll go check, but I'm not a big drinker." She explains and Orion shrugs.

510

"Don't worry, I'll have what everyone else is having. Callie what are you drinking?" He asks me, picking up the spatula and inspecting it.

"Root beer, please." I say, leaning against the table and watching with amusement as Orion tries to work out how to turn on the grill. I would offer to help, but it's so much more fun watching him incapable when usually he is an expert at everything.

"Me too, please." He nods to my mom and she turns on her heel, calling Kayla after her.

"Kayla, come pour your juice, honey." Kayla gives me a cheeky grin as she turns and runs after my mom, her butt wiggling all the way through to the kitchen inside her denim dungarees.

"My sister loves you." I tease Orion, and he turns to face me, beaming.

"She's so cute." He comments, moving forward. That's when I notice it. He's wearing the apron, which is covered with a picture of a voluptuous woman's bosom.

"Nice... uh... boobs you got there." I gesture up and down to his apron and he looks down before exhaling.

"What a peculiar thing to put on an apron. I'm glad you approve though." He pulls it over his head; clearly deciding the curves don't suit him.

As he moves to drape it across the back of a chair, he grips around my waist, leaning in to kiss me under the dim moonlight. It feels odd, having him kiss me so frankly in my own space, in the place I had grown up. It is even stranger when I finally break the embrace and look left to see my mother watching us. She's got an odd expression and as she steps forward, with a tray of open root beer cans and half- full glasses in her hands, the edge of her flip flop catches a corner of one of the new patio stones and she goes flying.

Before I know what's happening, Orion is dashing forward, catching her in his arms. I cannot say the tray was so lucky, as it flies from her hands and crashes into the front of my body, splashing root beer all over me.

"Agh!" I cry out, feeling the sticky coldness of the liquid seeping through my clothes. My mom gets to her feet, Orion's arms still cradling her as she regains her balance.

511

"That was close." He says, looking to me as he lets out a sigh. I'm drenched in soda.

"Oh my gosh, Callie! I'm so sorry!" My mom gasps, looking me up and down with horrified eyes.

"It's fine… though I've looked better." I begin to laugh, knowing I've seen far worse as I stand, dripping on the patio with glasses and cans scattered at my feet.

"Why don't you go and change. You've got clothes upstairs still. Your room is just as you left it." My mom suggests. Orion's eyes light up.

"Callie's room?" He asks, curious like a small child.

"Sure, why don't you go with her. I'm sure you need to clean up." She looks at him and I can see now as he steps back that his white t-shirt is completely covered in soda too. "In fact, why don't I pop that t-shirt in the laundry?" She asks him as I narrow my eyes. Orion smiles, thankful, but I know her plan.

Orion whips the t-shirt over his head, the wave band tattoo adorning his arm suddenly exposed. His body ripples in the moonlight and Kayla comes out to see both me, and more embarrassingly, my mother staring.

"What you looking at?" She asks, plodding out into the garden before turning. Her eyes widen and she turns to me, affronted. "Callie, why is he all bulgy like that? He looks like a super hero!" She sounds incredulous as she interrogates me and I suppress a giggle. My mother looks mortified too as she steps forward toward us.

"Kayla, Callie and Orion are all messed up because mommy is clumsy. They're going to go and get changed while I try to get the grill working again." She explains as Kayla, Sippy cup in hand, suddenly looks excited.

"Orion, you *have* to see my teddies!" She demands, taking him by the hand and pulling on his fingers to get him to move. My mom takes the t-shirt from Orion and as I pass her I give her a sly glance.

"Hmm, pop that t-shirt in the laundry? Very nicely done, mom." I say, laughing as she looks blatantly offended and flushes red.

512

"Callie... I'm sorry, he's just... well, look at him!" She whispers as Kayla pulls Orion through the kitchen and toward her room. The poor guy doesn't know what he's in for.

"I know! I *am* marrying him." I remind her and her eyes shoot to my hand. I raise the ring up to eye level so she can see, still sopping from head to foot and getting stickier by the second.

"Oh Callie! It's beautiful!" She gushes and I nod in agreement as a shudder runs through me, the wind stirring around us as we stand.

"I know, Alexandrite I think." I explain and she moves my hand further from her eyes as she examines the sparkle of the stone. I watch her as she does so, knowing that I've seen more than I can ever express, that I've experienced more than I can articulate. I suppose though, we have all night to talk about it.

"You're a lucky girl." She announces it like I don't know already, but I nod, agreeing anyway. "Anyway, go and get changed." She pushes me forward and I move, feeling the sodden denim of my light-coloured jeans weighing heavy around my legs and making me miss the weight of my tailfin.

I walk through the kitchen and up the stairs, with memories of burnt toast, sleeping ogres and zombie-like mornings drifting in and out of my memory. With each step up the staircase I feel like I'm one step away from the girl who had last walked them. I had crept away in the darkness, afraid I would never return, and now I'm here, on the eve of my wedding day, with love surrounding me in every direction I turn.

I see Orion as I reach the landing, standing in the doorway of Kayla's bedroom and nodding enthusiastically to something she's saying. He hears my approach and pivots, still bare-chested.

"I've just gotta go and help Callie clean up. Okay?" He asks her. I don't hear her reply but he takes several strides toward me as I walk toward my bedroom door, exhaling heavily before opening it.

I step in and it feels too small, too ordinary, but I suppose that's to be expected, especially when one is immersed daily in that which is extraordinary.

I step over to the bed, which is scattered with quilts and blankets, and spot Bunnyboo as I flush with colour, hoping Orion doesn't notice.

"This is your room?" He asks me and I nod, blushing.

513

"Yeah, this is it. Pretty basic compared to the Occulta Mirum I know, but it was my fort in a storm for a long time." I say, realising I'm still dripping and standing, before walking toward the wardrobe.

"What's this?" Orion asks, looking down to the trash bin beside my desk. Next to the waste paper basket there's a crumpled-up piece of paper. He reaches down to pick it up, smoothing it between his fingers. I can't remember what it is, probably just trash, but I watch him with curiosity.

"Pros and Cons?" He raises an eyebrow as my eyes widen and my lips form an amused pucker, remembering the list.

"Hey, not my fault you came across like some kind of creepy stalker." I say and he scowls.

"These are pros and cons about me?"

"Meeting up with you. Yes." I explain, watching his face go from annoyed to amused and back again.

"I wonder what this list would look like now." He asks me with a sly expression, balling the paper up between two fingers and tossing it behind his shoulder. He, of course, doesn't miss like I had.

I strip the sodden and thin white sweater over my head and leave it in a pile on the floor as I open my wardrobe doors. Orion is behind me in a moment.

"I remember this one!" He says, fingering the black corset which I had worn in my escape to the beach oh so long ago.

"I bet you do." I roll my eyes, pulling out a clean t-shirt and a lilac sweater as well as my favourite faded jeans. As I do this, Orion turns from behind me, moving to the bed and sitting down amongst my blankets.

"Everything in here smells like you." He makes this assessment and I turn my head, looking at him over my shoulder and stood only in my bra and sodden jeans.

"Well, I did live here once upon a time." I remind him, slipping off my bra and the rest of my clothes before I set about dressing again.

"You are so beautiful, Princess." He uses my pet name and my stomach flips like a pancake.

514

"I'm glad you think so, you're the one who's going to be stuck with this forever. So, tough luck if not." I chuckle, pulling my bra straps over my shoulders.

"That is true. Tomorrow you're going to be a Mrs. My Mrs." He reminds and I grin, pulling on the rest of my clothes as he watches me with a loving gaze. Finally, I pull my sweater over my head and catch his gaze, falling to Bunnyboo.

"Who's this?" He asks me, picking up the raggedy-eared rabbit from the end of my bed.

"That's... uh... Bunnyboo." I explain as he puts the stuffed animal back down on the bed with a grin and moves across the room to me, placing his hands on my waist.

"I'm so in love with you, Callie Pierce. Everything about you." He kisses me quickly on the lips, eyes burning with unquenched desire.

"I can't believe we're getting married tomorrow." I confess, my heart fluttering in my chest with nerves.

"Are you nervous?" Orion asks me and I smile.

"A little. Mainly because I haven't got a dress yet." I explain and he frowns.

"Still? I thought Isabella was having something imported?" He asks me and I roll my eyes.

"How do you know about that?" I ask him; surprised that news of my dress had even reached the mermen.

"Well, it is my wedding too. Besides, do you realise how loud Isabella is when she's yelling down the phone at delivery men?" He asks me.

"Yes, I was *next* to her at the Lunar Sanctum when she made that call... I was deaf in one ear for a week." I remember her outrage at the shipping times because, in her words, the amount she was paying she expected the best.

I think back to the discussion with her about what I was going to marry Orion in. I had wanted something simple. Everything about my life had been so complicated; the last thing I wanted was to be wrangled into some monstrous contraption of a dress on the day of my wedding. But no, she was having none of it and I was too tired from all the meetings to argue. In a way, it felt right,

515

having her organise everything because I know Marina would have loved planning it with a fellow fashionista.

"Come on, we better get back. Kayla said something about a tea party." Orion says this like it's serious business and I laugh.

"You know there won't be any actual tea? It's make believe." I ask him and he looks disappointed as I chuckle. "Come on, let's go and get some food. I'm starving."

"Well, I don't think we did too horribly." Orion looks to my mother as he begins to clear plates away for us. She smiles up at him with dreamy eyes, making me glad he put his shirt back on.

"No, it was delicious." I nod in agreement at her reply and Orion moves, with the dishes, back into the house. Kayla is on my lap, almost asleep.

"Callie, I want to ask you..." My mom looks to me, her eyes now concerned.

"What?" I whisper, wondering what it is that's bothering her, but aware Kayla is almost asleep.

"Well, I wasn't going to ask, because I didn't want to really know. But... Sophia and Oscar, they got us to safety. Safety from what?" She looks to me with curiosity and I think about my answer carefully. Covering Kayla's ears gingerly as I move to reply.

"The Psirens, you know who they are right?" I ask her in hushed tones. She nods as the leaves of palm trees rustle, wavering in the light breeze as we sit in the glow of the heavy moon.

"Yes, I think I met one once." I raise my eyebrows, wondering who it was she had met. I look deeply into her eyes, cuddling the body of my baby sister who isn't so much of a baby anymore, and exhale, thinking back.

"The world was in danger. The Psirens, they got so large in number and they were raising this demon... The Necrimad. They wanted to take the magic out of it and become like super evil Gods or something. I don't know. It's all super technical." I explain, brushing over the finer details.

516

"So are the Psirens gone?" She asks me, worry still tainting her expression.

"Not exactly." I reply, not sure of how much to tell my mother. I mean, I still haven't mentioned the fact that she's destined to become a mer too, but somehow I feel like it's not my place.

"What do you mean? You stopped them though, didn't you?" She interrogates me as the fairy lights bathe us in orange and pink hue.

"Yes. We stopped the two main Psirens. The bad ones, but there are others. Like Orion's sister, Azure. Not all Psirens are bad. We've found they can harness the darkness for good." I explain and she looks to Kayla.

"Are they going to be at the wedding?" She still looks concerned.

"Yes, they will, but I promise, nobody will lay a finger on either of you. Orion and I would both die before we let that happen." I make her this promise, reaching out and placing my hand atop hers and squeezing.

"He seems so wonderful. You both do, together I mean." She compliments me and I exhale again, relaxing back into my chair.

"We've been through so much to get here. I just want everything to calm down for a little while. I just want us to have a normal life." I express my desires, feeling like I can talk openly with my mother now. It is funny, the things which have caused me to be frank and open when for so long I was closed to speaking the truth with her.

"I don't think you're suited to the normal life, Callie. Look at me... I mean, I love Kayla. I loved Carl... but did you ever feel like there's supposed to be more..." She looks up to the moon above and I smile at her, knowing that if I'm to tell her what will become of her after death then it should be now. I want to let the words out. I want to tell her she is chosen. But for some reason, I can't bring myself to say it.

I look down to Kayla, who sits in my lap, and I know she is why. I don't want my mother to long for a life she knows will come to her in time. I want her to enjoy the time she has with my sister. I want her to enjoy being a mother.

"I think Orion *is* my more." I reply, feeling his proximity as he returns to the garden through the back door.

"I think you're right." She replies quickly, smiling to Orion as he looks to us.

"What are you two looking at?" He asks, brushing his fingers through his hair in that way I love.

"Nothing." I say quickly, moving to stand and smirking. Now that the meal is over, the night draws on and we still have so much to get done.

"Come on, we better get moving." Orion says, gesturing for me to give him Kayla. I cock an eyebrow, surprised that he's offering to take her from me as I pass her to him and turn to my mom.

"You all packed?" I ask her and she smiles.

"Yeah, two cases and a hat box. I am the mother of the bride after all. Kayla's car seat is in the hall." She moves, rising from her chair and twisting around the furniture before moving in to kiss me on the cheek.

"Okay, I'll get Kayla's car seat." I say, walking from the patio in measured steps. My mom follows behind me, locking the back door after she's checked the grill is well and truly off.

"Are you sure all of this stuff is going to fit in your car?" My mom asks me, and I smile to myself, knowing that it definitely will not fit in my car. Kayla's car seat is bulky enough as it is, without the rest of the luggage to consider.

"Uh, actually kind of not. I invited someone to give us a ride." I say, not faltering in my response as we move through the kitchen and into the hallway.

As I stand, the doorbell rings and the hairs on the back of my neck rise.

"That must be him." I say, as she waits, expectant, at my back.

I take several strides down the hall, moving past the living room, luggage and car seat as I place my hand on the doorknob to turn it. I inhale, nervous. I open the door and the face I've been waiting to reveal stares not at me, but past me.

"Gideon." My mother breathes, her voice barely audible above the sound of my heartbeat, which rings in my ears.

"I hear you need a ride?" He says the words as though they have some significance I can never understand. His eyes are wide, taking her in as I move sideways and he steps over the threshold. Things then become awkward as

518

neither of them move, stuck in their places, as though time has changed everything. My father coughs, breaking the silence first.

"I see you kept my mustang." He announces, trying to sound cheery as he moves on to make small talk. I gape.

"Wait, my little red vintage… belonged to you?" I ask him, my eyes wide. My mother had never told me that. She'd told me she found a 'great deal' on it from a local garage.

Yeah right mom! I knew she'd never get that good of a deal on such a mint condition vintage car.

"Yes, I used to take your mother out cruising. We went everywhere in that damn thing." He says, looking between me and her, as she blushes scarlet.

"Well, anyway, we should get going. It's a long drive back to the house. I can't wait for you to see it, mom!" I gush. "Hey, on second thought, why don't you drive with me. Orion, you and my dad can take Kayla, right?" I ask him, pleading with my stare. I had thought my dad's visit would be a great surprise, but instead things were awkward. I kind of get it I suppose, there must be so much that's not been said, so many questions which have never been answered. I wonder if maybe inviting him here had been a mistake, but I had thought it would be better than them seeing each other for the first time in front of the entire wedding party.

"Sure, whatever you need." Orion moves to kiss me and Kayla stirs in his arms, sleepy at this late hour.

"Come on." I say, ushering everyone out of the front door. We pile out into the front garden and Gideon and Orion pack the suitcases and my mother's oversized hat box into the boot of the black mustang my dad has driven here. I have to help Orion put Kayla's car seat in place as Gideon almost implodes at the number of buckles, huffing and puffing as his giant hands cannot quite muster the finesse to fit it properly.

Job done, I kiss Kayla as I put her into the back of the car, watching her sleeping face and smiling as I close the door. With this, I move to hug my dad in the middle of the street.

"Thanks for doing this. I'm sorry if it's not what you hoped for…" I apologise, looking up at him with concern plastered on my face. He laughs, kissing me on the forehead as his whiskers tickle me.

"Don't worry about it Callie. It's been a long time. I'm sure it must be weird for her."

"I guess, I just thought she'd look happier." I sigh, shrugging as I step back.

"It's okay. It's complicated, but yes, I'll admit was hoping for a warmer response." He replies, mimicking my expression as he shrugs too.

"I don't get it either. I'll talk to her." I promise, moving to kiss Orion as he passes me my keys.

"I don't know when I'll see you next. So, if I don't see you before… well, just be there. I'm not getting all pretty for no-one." I tease him and he rolls his eyes.

"I've waited five hundred years for this. I'll be there." He whispers, holding me close to him for a few final moments before he rounds the front of the mustang to get into the passenger seat. Gideon gets out his keys and I turn away from them both, making light bouncy steps across the sidewalk and hopping into my car, feeling lighter than air with anticipation and excitement. My mom is already in the passenger seat and she looks stressed.

"What's up?" I ask her, hoping she's not angry with me.

"Callie! How could you not tell me that he was coming?" She looks at with desperation reflected in the luminous turquoise of her eyes as I hear my father's car start behind us before pulling away. I watch as they drive into the distance on the street I had once called home.

"Mom, I thought you'd be glad. Besides, it wasn't just me. He wanted to see you too." I justify the decision that had been entirely mine with a small half-lie. I had known my father wanted to see her again, but he just didn't want to admit it yet.

"He must think…" She starts as I put the key into the ignition and start the engine. I put the gearshift into drive and pull away from the curb, not wanting to lose my father and Orion despite the roads being extremely empty at this time of night.

520

"Must think what?" I ask her as she pauses and I press down on the accelerator, turning to her and looking behind me in the rear-view mirror as I do.

"He must think I look so…. old." She finishes the sentence and I want to laugh.

"Mom! Don't be so silly. You look beautiful! Besides, he's changed too." I remind her, knowing that my dad hadn't always had the long beard and thick white hair he does now.

"Yes, but he's still just as I knew him facially. I'm just… I'm greying. I'm an old woman. What would he want with someone like me?" I feel my hands tighten on the steering wheel, pursing my lips as I sigh.

"Look, I wasn't going to tell you this. Hell, I don't know why I am now." I exhale, anxious as I turn to the road ahead and turn on my headlights as we speed away from the house.

"What, what is it?" She asks, looking to me as she shifts in her seat, uncomfortable.

"Mom, you're his soulmate." I say, not turning to face her as we continue to drive on into the night.

"What do you mean? I'm not. I never was. It was always Alyssa." She says the word with hatred, and for a moment I feel like I'm in the car with her angry teenage self.

"Look, you know how I told you about the Psirens? About how we beat them back?" I say to her and she nods. I'm raising my voice now above the rush of the wind and the purr of the vintage engine, my heart racing.

"Well, okay, so I became Atargatis." I announce and she gapes.

"How?" She asks me.

"I'm her vessel. She came down to this plain for a bit, with the other Gods and Goddesses. There's eight. In a circle. It's a thing." I say, reverting only too easily to my teenage vernacular. I'm not Queen here; I'm just my mom's daughter. I'm just Callie Pierce.

"Okay…" she continues.

"Basically the goddess. She told me. Saturnus, he kind of lied to dad about who his soulmate was. It's super complicated, but yeah, basically you're dad's

521

soulmate." I explain it, skipping all the important details but not wanting to fry her brain. I feel like if I'd have known how complicated explaining this stuff to a human was I wouldn't have given Orion such a hard time when I'd first changed.

"But that means..." She inhales, getting what I'm really saying.

"Yeah, that's the thing. It's why I wasn't gonna tell you. Kayla needs you. So you can't let this change anything." I yell in short clipped sentences above the engine, feeling my heart race even still.

"Callie I... what happened to you?" She looks to me in awe and I take my eyes from the road momentarily to stare back.

"What?" I ask her, feeling mystified as to why she's staring at me like that.

"Callie... it's a long drive. Please. I want to know everything. Everything you've been through since you left. The truth." She pleads with me, her eyes brimming with tears.

I know it's horrible sometimes to know, but sometimes the agony of the unknown can be so much worse. So, I break. Deciding to spill my story.

"Okay mom. So, this is what happened after I left the house last time..."

40
The Gift
CALLIE

I pull my little red vintage up to the beach that Orion had bought for us. Our beach house stands bathed in a white glow as the waves crash upon the shore, and the wind whips my hair from my face. I sit back into the leather of my seat, finally done with my story. It's taken the entire journey, but my mom is finally up to date on everything that's happened. She's stunned to say the least, but as I turn off the engine of the car she turns to me and simply says, "I am so proud to call you my daughter."

Pulling me into her arms her words leave me speechless, which I appreciate after so much talking. I sit back from her, as she turns to look at the expanse of sand.

"This is our beach." I say, gesturing to the crashing waves.

"It'll be a beautiful ceremony tomorrow." She replies, her voice dreamy in its tone as though she's imagining the wedding right now.

"I don't know who is going to be officiating." I sigh, frowning. I know Orion is struggling to find someone to marry us, especially because the circumstances that surround us are so odd. We didn't want anyone too religious either, especially when we had very specific beliefs of our own.

"I'm sure Orion will have sorted everything. So, what about the dress?" She asks me, eyes bright with enthusiasm.

"Isabella, the Queen of the Water Nymphs, she's supposed to be having something imported. It still hadn't arrived at the Lunar Sanctum when I checked

523

last." I frown again, anxious. Surprisingly though, I'm not nervous about who I'm marrying. With Orion, I'm certain.

"Let's go up to the house." I prompt my mom as she exits the car and slams the door shut with a bang. Grabbing my keys and slipping them into my jeans pocket I realise I feel more like my old self in certain ways. I vow to ask Orion to hang on to these clothes, wanting to keep parts of my old life wherever I can.

As my mom walks around the bonnet of my car, she links arms with me and we climb up the sloping cliff toward my dream house. Everything is silent except for the sloshing of the sea, and as we approach the clifftop, where the house stands surrounded by the white picket fence of the tiny zen garden, the twinkling of fairy lights come into view and my mom examines her surroundings.

"Orion had this built?" She asks me and I nod as she ogles the building

"Yeah. You think this is crazy you should see the inside." I laugh, taking her hand and pulling her through my world. Suddenly, I hear my name called.

"Callie!" I turn, seeing Orion running up the cliff after me. With him is Cole, but my father is nowhere to be seen. Leaving my mother standing in the garden I take off down the slope once more, running to meet Orion and enjoying the jog on my way down the decline as my calves burn and twinge.

"Hey!" I reply, kissing him and glad I get to see him at least once more before tomorrow. "Hey Cole!" I wave at him as he catches up to Orion, carrying both my mom's suitcases and hat box.

"Hey, Your..." He begins and I narrow my eyes.

"Callie." He admonishes, before adding, "It's only because you're the bride. The mermaids are very quick to remind us men not to upset you. Something about running makeup." He chuckles, passing me the bags and rolling his eyes. "You got those from here?" He looks unsure as I nod, struggling at the weight of them.

Geez what did my mom bring, the entire house?

"Kayla is already inside with the mermaids. We dropped her off ten minutes ago." I grin at the thought of her driving them nuts.

"I'll meet you at the car, Orion." Cole waves goodbye to me and I return the gesture, hair whipped from my face by a small wisp of salty wind.

"You're going out?" I ask him, raising an eyebrow.

"Yeah, the guys are taking me fishing." He winks and I narrow my eyes.

"You know, I hope that means for fish and not for other scaled women..." I pout and he throws his head back in a chuckle.

"Your father is coming, so I hope not." He replies, face falling deadly serious far too quickly.

"Have you chosen a best man yet?" I ask him, knowing he was tortured over choosing before. He inhales, looking slightly worried as he breathes out to speak.

"Yes. I have. I uh... I chose Azure." He mumbles, looking nervous and I burst out laughing. I laugh so hard I worry I may be sick.

"You're serious? You got Azure to agree to this?" I ask, dazed. I think I'm still in shock.

"Sort of. She said so long as she doesn't have to wear a dress she's cool." He shrugs and I laugh again.

"Whatever floats your boat. How's Cole feel about this?" I ask him and he frowns.

"I asked him first, but he turned me down. He said he wouldn't feel right, because of Ghazi and all." He explains and I sigh out, heart hurting at the memory of Ghazi turning to sand in Saturnus' grasp. Realising that it's a memory I'll never forget. It's just too painful

"Okay. I understand. Have a good fishing trip." I say, looking to him. "Oh...and Orion, have a good sunrise." I beam to him and he curves his lips into the stunning arc of a smile.

"Oh I will, but I want my sunset with you." He sends a shiver through me at those words.

I turn away from him and begin my walk back up the hill, looking forward to watching the sun fall with him later as my lips spread wide. I beam, my stomach fluttering with anticipation.

My mom sees that I'm struggling with the bags and so comes to help, taking one off me in her left hand and gripping her hat box in the other.

525

"What have you got in here, the kitchen?" I ask her, huffing and puffing as I heave the suitcase through the gate of the front garden.

"Just a few essentials." My mom assures me as I knock on the front of the glass door. I hear a torrent of giggles, screams and watch shadows move behind the frosting of the glass before it swings open, revealing a gaggle of maidens. In the middle of them all, Kayla is being given a piggyback ride by Emma.

"Callie!" They all gush, helping me inside with the bags as they all begin to twitter about a million different things to do with the wedding. Isabella comes around the corner, magnificent in a black floor length robe as her raven locks fall, spattered with gold, down her back in a razor-sharp edge. She moves to greet me from the ice blue sofa on which she's been perched, her expression serene yet determined, like this entire wedding is business of the utmost importance. I look around, taking in the space, which is tiled in black twinkling, marble. The fibre optic effect leaves me stunned once more and I can't help but stare a moment, glad to be here. It feels so long since Orion and I last visited, too long.

"The bride is here!" Isabella practically sings, rushing forward and pulling me into her arms.

"Everyone, this is my mom!" I exclaim, gesturing back as she drops her suitcase on the floor. Isabella rushes forward.

"The mother of the bride!" She kisses both cheeks with Italian gusto and looks at her in the light. "Darling, you look exhausted." She sighs, tutting and shaking her head as the other mermaids gaze upon her, bouncing up and down on their balls of their slipper clad feet.

"Claude!" Isabella clicks her fingers as she raises them into the air. From around the corner, the blonde and incredibly Swedish masseuse, who I had met only once, comes into view.

"Take the ladies' bags down to the bottom floor." She commands of him as he moves forward, dressed all in white. My mom's eyes grow wide as she steps aside, sort of like she's possessed and allows the man past her. He grabs the bags as though they weigh nothing, gliding past her once more and taking them with him in one hand.

526

"Now, Callie..." Isabella turns, moving to me and placing her hands on both my shoulders with an expression that's deadly serious.

"Darling... what is happening with this place? I can't even find your bedroom!" She exclaims. "How can I fit you for this dress if you haven't got anywhere for you to change?" She asks me as my eyes widen and her lips creep up into a wide and glorious grin of triumph.

"Oh my gosh, it's here!?" I exclaim, relief flooding me. Well, at least I'll be falling down the aisle in style.

"Yes, darling. But this house is so... bare." She wipes lint from her shoulder with her long nails as I stride across the hallway to a simple table, that has white orchids standing on its flawless surface in a modern vase. Next to them I see the magical house remotes.

"Fear not! I have the house remotes!" I exclaim, being silly in my dramatic flair. I push one button, bringing the television down from the ceiling, then the fireplace as I hear Kayla's voice exclaim.

"Oh my god! Mommy! Did you see that?" She yells, clearly overly excited as she jumps and down with more energy than I expect at this time of night. I turn to the mermaids, my face faux angry.

"Okay, which one of you gave the five-year-old sugar?" I ask them.

Gingerly, Rose holds up a hand.

"She said she was allowed candy." She replies, looking meek. I know that the death of Marina and Fahima has taken its toll on her, especially since they had lost their lives so she could raise the signal. She was a lot less boisterous now, somehow having lost her fight.

"Hey, I'm joking. It's okay. It's a special celebration." My mom comes forward and scoops up Kayla, who is squirming like a mad thing, in her arms.

"I'm Patience. I know you're all special to my daughter. So, what are your names?" She asks, pulling focus. The mermaids each present themselves, smiling whilst stood in an array of pastel coloured silk pyjamas. I am glad now that I decided to throw this slumber party, knowing that I'm way too wired to sleep, especially because Orion isn't here. Isabella treads lightly across the marble floor, her feet soundless as she approaches, not wanting to interrupt, and pulls on my elbow.

527

"Callie, we really need to get into your room, darling." She is insistent, so I walk from the crowd. As I move across the space, Skye calls after me.

"Hey, where are you going? We still haven't made you a dress out of toilet paper yet!" She exclaims, annoyed. I turn back to them, sighing.

Well, might as well make it a group event. I hold up the remote.

"Who wants to come see my closet!!!" I yell, losing all sense of propriety. It's the night before my damn wedding and I'll party how I want to. The mermaids gasp and Kayla puts her hand up.

"Oooh oooh meeeee! I wanna play dress up!" She jumps from my mom's arms as the girls rush forward in a glossy stampede. Kayla leads the pack, her tiny legs and cute butt wiggling and waggling with such sass I could swear she was born to be a mermaid. We take a right at the icy blue sofas and stride across the breadth of the house until I come to the staircase, which descends downward in a precise spiral. I grin to my mom who is bringing up the rear of the group with Isabella. They're talking about something and, though I have no idea what, I'd bet its fashion related.

I descend, stepping out onto the cool chocolate marble of the bottom floor as I hear multiple pairs of feet padding down the stairs behind me. I stride through the pool filled room, climbing the bridge that rises high over the water beneath and walking toward the waterfall. I cock my hip, pausing for effect and loving the fact that I'm finally getting the mermaid's approval for something. If I'm not Queen material, then at least my house is fit for royalty.

I press the button on the remote, watching as the flow of water parts and splits into two curtains, revealing the door behind it.

"Oh! I should've known, darling. Waterfall door. Classy." Isabella shouts her approval above the sound of the rushing water and I roll my eyes, laughing under my breath at her response.

I look back to the faces of the maidens, whose mouths are hanging wide open in shock. I smile, smug, as I walk forward and toward the door that rolls open, revealing the master bedroom.

It looks remarkably different as I step inside. Now, the sheets have been changed from scarlet to white and the entire space is covered in white and pink fluffy pillows. The floor is also covered in sleeping bags and blankets and a TV has been set up in the corner next to a popcorn machine. I smile, knowing that Orion must have commissioned Georgia to come and prepare this space for my slumber party before-hand. He really is too good to be true.

Speaking of too good to be true, as I turn, I find a huge pile of junk food lying in the corner. My eyes widen and I realise I'm once again hungry after my homemade barbecue dinner. Striding across the room, I grab a bag of chips from the pile before pulling it open without pause.

"Oh my god. I love carbs." I sigh, crunching on a chip as Kayla comes in and face plants the pillows. I chuckle.

"Rose, how much candy did you give her?" I ask her, cocking my head and watching as Kayla tries to create a snow angel among the pillows, waving her arms and legs like crazy.

"Only like... a bag full." Rose admits and I continue to laugh as my mom picks Kayla up from the floor.

"Mom she's fine... she's just a bit... hyper." I protest, laughing as Kayla licks my mom's face.

"Kayla!" My mom exclaims as she drops the tiny monster. Sophia steps forward through the door as it slides to let her in, only just now joining us.

"Hey Sophia!" I exclaim, moving over to hug her tightly, still eating while I do.

"Hey Callie! Sorry I'm late." She pulls back from me, hair still damp.

"Oscar okay?" I ask her as my mom rises too, glad to see a face she finally knows.

"Yeah, he's okay. I just wanted to make sure. He's finally getting better about being on land I think." She replies as she steps over several pillows. The maidens are making themselves at home as they sprawl out over them, long hair glossy and luscious as it falls in glistening tresses over the blankets. "Kayla!" Sophia exclaims, picking up my little sister, before she too gets her face licked.

"Ew. Kayla don't do that!" I exclaim, giving Sophia an apologetic stare. "Sorry about that, someone gave her sugar." I explain and Sophia giggles.

"It's fine. I heard your dress is here!" She beams and I nod. Kayla pulls on my shirt as I continue to munch my way through the bag of chips as I look to the maidens. Suddenly, I have an idea.

529

"Hey... Kayla, if you go ask those nice ladies over there, I bet they'd help you play dress up." I nod to her, and shove her in the direction of the mermaids gently as I smirk at Rose. She gave the five-year-old sugar, and now she'll get to watch what happens.

Kayla sits down in the middle of Alannah, Skye, Rose and Emma, smiling her sweetest smile.

"Can you make me look beautiful. Just like you?" She asks, fluttering those lashes once more. I gotta wonder where she learned that trick, because I didn't teach it to her.

"She okay?" Sophia asks me, and I nod, snorting in the most unladylike fashion.

"As far as I can tell. She loves Orion." I chuckle and Sophia gives me a knowing look, her brown eyes so similar to my sister's that it's almost a little odd having them both so close together.

As I stand, my hand deep in my bag of potato chips, Isabella moves across the room, directing Claude, who is carrying a large box on one shoulder into the room.

"Callie, darling, where's the closet?" She calls to me and I step haphazardly over the stacks of pillows and sprawled blankets toward the wall that the closet is embedded into. The door slides open and the girls watch in interest, getting to their feet and ushering Kayla to follow me.

"Jeez. It goes all the way back there?" Sophia asks, suddenly at my side. I turn to her, grinning.

"Orion knows I like clothes." I admit and she shakes her head.

"You know I'll be borrowing all of these right?" She asks.

"Obviously." I reply, glad she's going to be on land and therefore needing clothes a little more.

"Make way! Italian Couture coming through!" Isabella's shrill tones cause me to move deep into the depths of the closet, way past the chaise longue and all the way into lingerie.

I had never, in all honesty, taken the time to look through all the clothes stacked in here, but now I was wishing I had. Some of the lingerie in this closet must be new; after all, it has *bridal wear* written on the tag next to the name of

530

an extremely expensive French designer. I examine some of the pieces, interested in the tastes of Orion, the man I am vowing myself to. None of it is whorish or tasteless. It's all just beautiful, creams and pastels, laces, satins and silks. I tilt my head, staring as a clunk on the floor startles me.

"Rise and shine, darling!" Isabella calls with a clap of her hands, marching deep into the closet and eyeing the bag of chips still in my hand.

"You want?" I offer it to her and she takes the packet.

"No. You're getting married at noon tomorrow… that means we only have like eleven hours prep time!" She exclaims, tossing the bag of chips to Claude who is about to leave the closet.

"Hey! I was enjoying that!" I exclaim, scowling.

"Darling, please! This is Couture. We don't alter couture." She rolls her eyes, turning and walking to the large white box now stood in the centre of my walk in. I watch as she takes a pocket knife from the depths of her floor length silk robe and slits the tape holding the box together. The box falls apart before us, revealing the gown.

All I can do is gasp, potato chips totally forgotten.

My wedding dress is something special. Something incredible. With a high waist, the bustier rises into a strapless, heart shaped, neckline. That however isn't what makes the dress. What makes this dress are the layers upon layers of organza netting. It's just big enough without being over the top and the underskirts are lilac and aqua, matching the ribbon tattoo at the base of my spine.

"Isabella… thank you." I gasp, walking forward, unable to take my eyes off my dress.

"Took its damn time getting here so I'm glad you like it, darling." She puts her arm around my shoulders as Kayla comes around the corner.

"Oh my gosh, Callie. Is this pretty dress yours?" She asks, looking to me with wide chocolate brown eyes.

"Yes, it is my little Kaylagator." I wink at her and she claps her hands.

"I love it! You're going to look like a princess." She sways, her hands clasped up like she's swooning. I wonder when she became so animated. She had always been cute, but she has seemingly adopted a flair for dramatics and the art of expression while I'd been gone.

"You'll look like one too. You're going to be my flower girl." I say to her and her mouth falls open.

"Really? Me?" She points to herself and I chuckle.

"Of course!" I reply and she runs to me as I bend down, reaching out and pulling her into a hug. She wraps her hands around my neck and then suddenly she's in floods of tears.

"What's the matter?" I ask her, my heart breaking at the feel of her tiny ribs wracked with her cries. My mother hears her sobs and comes bustling forward, parting the crowd of anxious maidens who are watching us with concerned expressions.

"I missed you sissy." She cries into my shirt and I chuckle.

"Okay, how about if I make a promise. What if I promise to come visit more? How's that?" I ask her and she snuffles, looking down to her feet and not responding.

"What's wrong with her?" My mom asks, her eyes worried.

"She missed me." I whisper, eyes welling too. I had missed them, but I was focusing on the gift. On this day that we had together. I wasn't focusing on the fact that soon I would have to leave again. Maybe that was because I knew it was too heart-breaking to bear.

"Kayla, baby, it's okay. Callie is gonna come visit us more, okay?" My mom takes Kayla into her arms and as I look up I see the maidens have welling, sparkling eyes too.

"What are you guys doing?" I ask them, standing and drying my eyes.

"We're just admiring your dress and, well, your family." Alannah speaks, walking forward as the rest of the maidens take that as an invitation to step fully into the increasingly cramped space with my dress.

"I miss Marina." Rose whispers and the others nod, sighing and taking pained breaths.

"I miss Fahima. I mean, I know she never said anything. But she made you feel, you know, safe." Skye reminisces.

"I miss my soulmate." Alannah admits, looking around to the other women who nod. That's when Skye takes a small step forward as a sad smile graces her lips.

"The thing is, I think I speak for everyone when I say I miss my soulmate too, but maybe, maybe we could be each other's soulmates?" She poses the question and then moves to explain. "I love you all. You're my sisters. I don't think anything can ever be more important. If it weren't for you, I wouldn't be here." She acknowledges the pain, looking each one of them in the eyes as my sister ceases crying and turns to look at us all. I move around the dress, careful not to touch it as I do, and over to them.

"You're all amazing women. Thank you for being my bridesmaids." I say, moving to hug each one of them in turn.

"You know how you can really thank us?" Alannah says and I cock an eyebrow, suspicious.

"You can make sure we're not in hideous dresses... and also give us the penthouse suites." She adds this little nugget in quickly and I scowl as I hear Isabella tutting behind me. She steps forward, rolling her eyes,

"For one, you're not having them, and for two, I'm dressing you darling. No crappy bridesmaid dresses under Isabella Fuliciano." She makes a small flourish with her hands and I turn to Sophia as the mermaids applaud with giggles escaping their plush lips.

"You up for being my maid of honour still?" I ask her and she smiles.

"Like you even need to ask that question." She replies and I place my arm around her shoulders, turning to look at my dress.

"I can't believe that's really my dress." I whisper as Isabella claps her hands, all business and no mercy.

"Let's get you in it then, shall we?"

The dim purples of dawn are beginning to show as I finally escape the depths of the beach house where I've spent the last few hours being poked with pins.

The maidens are in a flurry, their hair styling equipment and makeup everywhere. My sister and mom are snoozing on the circular bed which lies beneath the sky light and I've been getting plucked, waxed, smoothed and groomed in ways I didn't even know existed following my dress fitting with Gordo, the pushy Italian seamstress from hell.

Now though, I'm taking a moment for myself, a moment to bask in the sunrise. For I know it will probably be the very last one I see from this side of the ocean's shimmering divide.

I walk down the slope of the cliff, letting my bare feet kiss the cool concrete as the world's very first light gets nearer to breaking the horizon. I feel my heart ahce for those we have lost and yet my heart swells for those who remain. I let myself become lost in the moment as everything stands still and even the breeze dies promptly as I reach the edge of the beach, walking across the sand and letting the feeling of everything that surrounds me caress me like a blanket.

I feel the zing of salt air in my nose, the crisp breeze of the coast rustle through locks of my hair and I feel the taste of champagne, which I've been drinking all night, on my tongue as I look out over the ocean. I take a seat, plopping into the sand near the shoreline and sitting, waiting for the sun to hit me with its rays. It's been such a long time since I felt the warmth of the sun. The closest I had come to that kind of warmth being the boiling water surrounding the Necrimad and, as I think on this, I shudder, memories of bloodshed and of pain coming at me in an unending tsunami. The images rush through my mind, surfacing and clashing against one another. I bear it, the memories and loss. The feeling that Orion wasn't ever coming back. The feeling that I was going to lose everything, including my own life.

I feel a teardrop fall down my cheek as the darkness lifts and the sun breaks the surface, it's fiery magnificence blinding me. I raise a palm as I sit in the sand, my toes curling as its heat hits me, obliterating the darkness, the past, the memories of war.

It is a purifying light, and as it moves to cover me and caresses my skin I feel myself letting go. Letting go of what had been and allowing myself to look into what will be. Me and Orion, ruling over the Occulta Mirum, together,

534

Psirens at our side and not against us, connected across the globe with allies in every sea that covers this earth. Things had changed so rapidly, and so as the sun bathes me in the light of my wedding day, I let everything shed. I let everything that had been worrying me, everything I had feared, evaporate.

I hear my name being called a few minutes after the sun has fully risen. It's my mom.

"Callie… it's time to start getting ready, sweetheart."

41
The Long Walk
ORION

"Think I'll tan?" I ask Cole, as we lean over the bow of the small fishing boat.

"Knowing you, probably." Cole laughs, brushing his black hair back from his face. Jack moves up behind him and places his arms around his waist. Both men are wearing jeans and white shirts, with their hair styled flawlessly to suit their relaxed expressions. I watch them, feeling contented and then suddenly lonely.

"I can't believe Callie isn't here. She should be here. It's my first sunrise in like... four hundred and something years." I exclaim, wondering why I'd thought coming on this fishing trip was a good idea.

I've insisted we threw back everything we catch as well, much to Gideon's dismay. The Adaro I know had no problem fishing, after all they had mostly been Inuk once and therefore relied on the seas to feed themselves. I however, despite how I had learned to fish as a child on my father's boat, felt it unnecessary to hunt for pleasure and not return what I had taken.

"I can always cuddle you if that makes it better? I'm blonde, and quite curvy if you think about it. You'll hardly know the difference." Oscar quips, drinking down the rest of his beer. I'm sure he's drinking to compensate for his anxiety, but he's definitely more humorous.

"Urm, I'm good. Thanks for the offer though." I laugh as Gideon steps up behind us, making the entire boat shift as his huge weight tilts the wood beneath our feet.

"So how are you feeling about marrying my daughter then, Orion?" Gideon asks me, sitting down on the wooden seating inside the small vessel. He's wearing dark jeans and a blue t-shirt and his muscles are straining against the material. It makes me feel a little odd that I'm actually older than Gideon, and yet I'm marrying his daughter.

"Well, if that's not a loaded question then I don't know what is." Jack says, turning from the sky's bruised indigo dawn as he and Cole move to sit against the starboard side of the boat once more.

I look back over my shoulder, watching the stars above fade into the day. The sun will be up in a few moments and I wonder what it'll feel like. If it will be as good as I remember. I realise that while I'm thinking about the sun, the eyes of the men in the boat are resting on me. Waiting for my reply.

"I'm certain, Gideon." I state, turning back to him and deciding to keep emotion out of it. The reply is short but powerful and I can tell I've said the right thing as Gideon rises to his feet, causing us to waver again, as he holds out a hand.

"Good, but just so you know. You hurt her and I'll freeze parts of you that you didn't know could shatter." His gaze is suddenly intense as his mouth forms a harsh line and the wind stirs around us, causing his white hair to ruffle in the breeze.

"Yes Sir, I understand." I gulp, realising that I'm not the only one who would die to protect her.

We stand in the tiny boat for a few moments, still and silent, as the light around us grows brighter. We're quite a way from land, not that it matters because it's not like we can exactly drown and I wanted a full and uninterrupted view of the sunrise.

"It's time! Here's hoping that the Goddess actually comes through and that we're not about to become super attractive piles of sand." Jack crosses his fingers and Cole laughs, standing once more and looping his arms around his soulmate's neck.

We all turn to the horizon, the boat swaying beneath our weight, as suddenly the sun peaks over the ocean. The light is warm on my skin and bathes us all in its early morning glory. I look up into its burning imminence, realising

537

that perhaps the sun here is a metaphor for Callie. Almost too beautiful to behold, fiery and dangerous to harness, but beyond perfect. She had risen into my life, breaking the darkness apart and bringing a kind of warmth I couldn't describe to my every day existence.

"Well look at that." I sigh, closing my eyes and feeling the heat on my skin.

"How's it feel? First sunrise in almost half a millennium?" Cole asks me as I open my eyes and turn to him.

"It feels like… today is the first day of the rest of my life." I say, knowing that I'll be bathed in this heat when I marry Callie, that I'll get to see her in the sun.

"That's because it is." Oscar winks at me, standing. His green eyes glisten in the orange light of the sunrise and his expression becomes sobered.

"Yeah no kidding. I'm getting married." I can barely keep the smile off my face and Gideon slaps me on the back.

"Your father, I wish he could be here." Gideon says, eyes twinkling as he continues. "That's where I got the idea for your stag you know. I know Atlas would have wanted you to go back to your origins. I just know he would have brought you fishing. The sunrise just makes it all the more special. I can guarantee also that if he was here he'd have actually caught more than all of us combined." He chuckles, cracking open another beer with his teeth and spitting the bottle cap into his hand.

"Yeah. He was amazing at fishing. I mean, we sort of suck. We've caught what? One fish?" I ask and everyone nods, laughing.

"Yes and you made us throw it back!" Oscar exclaims with a hiccup, outraged.

"Somehow, I don't think Orion cares that we haven't caught anything." Cole rolls his eyes as I turn away from them, looking out to the horizon at the fiery ball of light casting its rays down on the day I've been gifted.

It was true though; it didn't matter about the fish. For I had already made the catch of a lifetime.

CALLIE

"Everybody out!" Isabella yells at the mermaids who are trying to clamber around the doorway to get a view of me. I feel like a Barbie doll in all honesty, with Water Nymphs flowing in and out of the room with flowers and announcements that the gazebo has finally arrived. Everything is getting busy insanely fast.

It's true, I had left most of the arrangements to Isabella, knowing nothing about wedding planning and not knowing enough people to easily plan something on this scale from the ocean, but I get the feeling she might have gone overboard. Especially since Claude keeps coming in and asking where the jazz band, harpist and DJ should set up.

My mother is the only one allowed in my room, under the decree of Isabella, and as the bridesmaids sit getting their hair and makeup applied in separate rooms and Kayla is getting fitted for her dress, I finally have a moment to breathe.

My dress has been moved so it's next to the bed and I'm stood, hair twisted up into a knot at the back of my head with curls falling down around my face. Seashells have been put into my blonde locks, and a fascinator of aqua sea netting adorned with tiny crystal lilac starfish is falling in front of my eyes. My makeup has been applied and I'm pacing the room in a white silk robe with lingerie underneath, listening to the cacophony of sound outside as I fiddle with my pearl strung bracelet.

"Me and Orion should have just run off and eloped in Barbados." I complain, stressing now that everyone has somehow ended up behind schedule as I move on to fiddling with the diamond teardrop pendant that I always wear around my neck.

How does this happen? We've been up all night and don't need to sleep, so how have we managed to end up behind? I wonder, looking to my mother and biting on a ragged finger nail as I pace around the room.

539

"Callie, don't say that." My mother looks to me, her hair in a half up-do as she peers out from under the widest brimmed hat I've ever seen.

"This is just. It's too much. I feel like I'm going to start hyperventilating." I say, flapping my hand in front of my face to try and get more air.

"Do you want to practice your vows?" She asks me.

I stop mid-step.

"Vows?" I ask her, my heart suddenly racing into overdrive as my nervous system floods with terror.

"Yes. Orion said he wrote his. You didn't write anything?" She asks me with a confused expression.

"Oh Goddess! I completely forgot…"

Now, I'm panicking.

"How could you forget?" She continues to look confused, as though I couldn't possibly have more on my mind than a wedding.

"Oh, I don't know mom, maybe because I'm the Queen of a mystical race of mer warriors? Maybe because I'm too busy making decrees about Psiren housing? Maybe because I'm eighteen and somehow ended up a freaking monarch?!" I exclaim as my mother leans back in shock at my reaction. I'm about to lose it and fall into a heap on the floor when I hear a sudden debacle occurring outside.

I can hear Isabella saying that everything is fine, and then another, less Italian and more authoritative tone retorting loudly.

The door to the cave-like room rolls to the left and Azure is revealed, hair up in a topknot and her slim, angular body clad in a black tux.

Damn. She can really wear a suit.

"I heard your distressed tones all the way out in the hall? What the hell is going on, Pierce?!" She asks me, cocking an eyebrow. "I have *not* gotten into a damn suit, which I look fabulous in by the way, to watch you go runaway bride." She folds her arms and my mother looks to her, startled as she storms across the room, "Who's this? Mother of the bride?" Azure asks me as my mother nods, stunned. I nod too, but too late, as my eyes widen and she walks straight past me toward my mother.

"Look, I'm sure you're very nice, but you gotta go." She shoves my mom from the room and turns on me.

"What's the drama, buttercup?" She asks as I stand, stunned silent.

"I don't have any vows. I sort of forgot. My mom is looking at me like I'm insane. I think she kind of forgot I'm busy ruling a mystical underwater city of mer people." I say, biting my bottom lip.

"That's it?" She sighs. "Jeez the way you were yelling I thought it was something actually *important.*" She rolls her eyes. "You know for someone who is the other half of my brother's *oh so romantic* soul, you shouldn't have a problem. If you can't come up with anything else just say, 'I will love you forever and put up with all your whining' Got it?" She looks to me as I take a step, my eyes still wide.

"Why are you helping me? I didn't think you cared about any of this stuff?" I ask her and she shakes her head.

"I'm gaining a sister, aren't I? Can't have my sister looking like a moron. Bad for the family name, that." She gives me an expression like she's torn between not caring and giving a damn. It startles me so much I stride toward her, putting my arms around her and pulling her into me before I lose my nerve.

"Thank you." I whisper. She doesn't push me away, like I expect, but she doesn't hug me back either. Instead she just hangs there, still, but letting me hug her.

"Can you get off now?" She asks as I laugh, stepping back.

"I'm freaking out. There's so much going on and I feel like it's not about me and Orion anymore. I feel like it's just… a giant circus." I breathe, looking down at my bare feet.

"Okay. Well then let's make it about Orion and you again. What do you need?" She asks me and I stare up at her, confused as to why she's being so kind. As I gape she rolls her eyes. "Well come on I haven't got all day!" she barks, snapping her fingers in very Azure like fashion.

"I just want to get ready in peace." I say, looking to her and sighing. It's true; I just want a few human minutes before I step outside this room. I don't want to be the bride, the vessel, Your Highness, someone's daughter, someone's sister. I just want to be myself.

541

"Okay. Well, one thing I am good at is keeping people good and far away. What about if I tell people to leave off? Nobody is gonna question me and if they do, well, I can throw a punch way better than you, and it doesn't matter if everyone hates me. They already do." She looks at me and I nod.

As I do, the door opens, revealing Isabella with my bouquet in her hand.

"Hi Isabella, yeah, it'd be great if you could well… bugger off." Azure announces as she walks over to her, using Vex's oh so effective 'push off' vernacular. Grabbing my bouquet from her hands, she gives her a tiny shove so she tilts back on her too high heels. The door slides shut and as it does Azure yells, "And STAY OUT."

Clapping her hands as she turns, she walks back over to me and hands me my bouquet. I stare down at it, surprised not to find flowers in the mix. Instead, hundreds of sea themed broaches are interspersed with aqua and lilac ribbon and the place where I'm grasping it is wrapped in dry seaweed.

"Azure. You're a pretty good sister." I say, grateful she's here. I need her in this moment, because on the day where everyone is on eggshells around me, when everyone is gushing about my bridal beauty, she's the one person who won't lie to me. If I look like crap, I know she'll be the first person to say it, whether I want her to or not.

"Yeah, yeah. Let's get you into your dress." She rolls her eyes and turns to look at the dress which is up on the raised platform next to the bed. Moving up to the bodice she pulls it up and off the dress form, ruffling the organza underskirts.

She steps forward making me a hole to put my head through as I let my silk robe drop to the floor.

"Ready?" She asks me, her expression mischievous. I know that expression; it's the one she gets when she's excited, or about to kill someone. I don't know which, because with her you can never tell.

"As I'll ever be." I breathe.

The sun is high in the sky as the procession lines up in the hallway of the beach house.

542

"Callie?!" I hear Isabella's frantic tones as she shoves my father, who is clad in a tux with an icy blue silk cravat tied around his thick neck, towards me. I look to my right to see my bridesmaids, all wearing aqua floor length gowns, simple and mermaid in shape. They carry tiny bouquets with purple broaches that shimmer in the sun, which is thankfully not turning any of us to sand.

My mother gives me final kisses before she makes her departure, teary eyed and stunning in a light coral dress. She's so beautiful, and I wonder how she can be so self-conscious around my father, as she moves to leave. Finally, I turn back to the crowd made up of my bridal party and father.

"I'm here!" I say, raising my bouquet in the air. The dress I'm wearing is huge, but amazingly I'm finding it easy to move in. The organza is light, far lighter than my coronation dress and as I feel my heart racing in my chest and my stomach squirming with anxiety, I'm glad I'm in bare feet beneath it all, despite the fact Isabella insisted I wear some sort of pearl jewellery around my ankle. The last thing I need is giant heels to trip over in.

I sort of wish Azure was still here, but luckily for me, Sophia is going out before me in the procession and she's close enough that I can grab onto her hand for support in my last moments as Miss Callie Pierce. My dad, who is at my side, holds out an arm for me to clutch onto as he looks down at me.

"You look so beautiful." He says, leaning down to kiss me on the cheek.

"So do you. Did you comb through your beard?" I ask him, giggling as he nods.

"Maybe I did." He grins at me, though I can tell the extra care in his appearance hasn't been taken for me. It's for my mother.

"How was Orion? You did bring him back in one piece, didn't you?" I ask him, cocking an eyebrow as he laughs.

"Yes. I've also warned him that if he so much as makes you pout I'll be freezing him solid." He grins to himself and I press my lips together, trying to stifle a laugh at that thought. Poor Orion.

"Are you ready?" He asks me and I nod, tired of so many people asking me the same question. I wonder if they thought I wouldn't go through with it, or that I'm too young to be making such a large commitment. Regardless, I realise that I don't care what any of them think. He's my choice.

I stare down at the white gold and alexandrite of the ring on my finger and smile because I know that soon there'll be one more.

"Procession, we are go!" Isabella calls as Kayla moves from the doorway. She walks down the garden path, a tiny basket of sea shells and dried starfish in her hands. Her flower girl dress looks like something out of the 1950's with a high waist and flared skirt. Her hair is in a tiny bun on the top of her head and her face is clear of makeup. She's so cute and I watch as she runs down the slope of the cliff to where the aisle begins. The underside of the aqua dress billows out as she moves, with lilac netting as an underskirt and her tiny feet, which pound the concrete as she skips, are left bare as are those of everyone else in my bridal party.

After her, the bridal party begin their descent down the slope as well, Sophia going last and leaving me to make my big entrance. I grip onto my father's hand, feeling his enormous palm clench mine as I lean on him, using his weight to steady me as Isabella kisses me once on the cheek and then gestures for me to step forward.

I hadn't seen what had been set up on the beach until now, mainly because I've been so busy getting ready, but as I step out and get a full view of the beach, I realise that I'm glad it had been a surprise. I'm getting the full view now, and it's really beautiful.

On the sand a large gazebo is set up at the back near the cliff, where tables and chairs are laid for the reception afterwards. The ceremony is on the open sand, and Orion and I are going to be married on the shoreline, right where the Ocean and land meet. The archway under which we will be wed is covered in sea stars and shells and the aisle leading up to it is marked out by thick lines of shells too.

I take step after step, and Daniella, who has travelled in for the day from Italy, announces my arrival as I reach the beginning of the aisle. The DJ, Paolo, who is playing 'Little Wonders' by Rob Thomas, lowers the volume slightly as she speaks.

"Please be upstanding for the arrival of the bride." She says from the sand beside me.

544

My heart goes pitter-pat as everyone's eyes rise to me and they get to their feet, a motion which is followed shortly by inhales and gasps at my dress coming from the female members of the crowd. The guest list has been made up of any of the Kindred who had wanted to attend, but I look straight past them.

It's not them I'm here for. It's him.

I find him, exactly where he's supposed to be, waiting for me at the end of the aisle. I stare at him, taking in his face before I'm distracted by the fact that there's no officiate standing behind him.

"Who's marrying us?" I ask my dad through my teeth as I smile at Orion.

"I don't know. Orion said he had it sorted." Gideon whispers back and my heart falters.

As I continue to take step after step, I feel like this is the longest walk of my life, but my eyes remain fixed on him. I don't worry about the fact I have no vows. I don't worry about the fact there's no one to marry us. I just look at his face, acutely angled with masculine beauty, and icy blue eyes, which are taking every single inch of me in. He glows, his skin a gorgeous, if not curious, tan under the direct sunlight.

Finally, when I think that the walk will never end, it does and I am here, in front of him. I look to him, my own eyes wide and confused. Where's the minister, or whoever it is that he's gotten to marry us?

"Callie, before we begin. There's something I want to tell you." Orion admonishes, moving in front of myself and Gideon. I stare at him confused.

"I should think so. Where's the officiate?" I ask him, my expression mystified and worried that I've gotten dressed up for nothing. I don't want to waste this gift. I want to be married. Today.

"That's the thing… she's right here." Orion turns and as he does, a bright white light appears under the archway. I shield my eyes as the back of my hand brushes against my fascinator and the blinding light forms a shape, before it dissolves, leaving her standing there.

"Atargatis." I breathe and Orion smiles at me, turning to the Goddess and bowing his head as the crowd behind us stand to stare at her.

"I'm so glad you came." He exhales, wiping his forehead as though he's been sweating with worry.

"Well, I did say I'd be watching." She smiles, her lilac hair and blue eyes vibrant compared to everyone else. I do believe this might be the only time ever when the officiate has outshone the bride.

"Thank you for coming." I bow my head, curtsying slightly and she looks to me and then my father, who is still arm in arm with me. I hear the crowd shifting, straining to get a glimpse of her around Gideon's wide frame and the poof of my dress.

"I was saying to Poseidon. We've already risked the walls between dimensions coming down. What can one more trip hurt, and what better occasion than the wedding of two of my very own Kindred?" She beams, her face radiant as her body stands covered in a deep blue robe, which falls way past her feet in a train that looks like the waves. I reach out to touch her, to lay my hand on her and she chuckles as my hand moves through her. I jump.

"I'm immaterial, here only in spirit, I'd have thought you'd have realised that no God or Goddess can have a mortal body in the lower plains, being a vessel and all. Well, unless you're my brother in law. Anyhow, I don't have much time. So, let's get you two married." She begins, looking to us with deep love in her eyes. "Who gives this woman to this man?" She asks my father and he beams, blinking quickly like he may cry.

"I do." His words come out gruff as he passes my hand to Orion. Orion takes it and nods to him, grateful. My father steps back to take a seat next to my mother, where she clutches his hand in hers, and I watch as Azure winks to me from over Orion's shoulder, before I turn to hand my bouquet to Sophia.

We stand there under the archway, with everyone's eyes on us, but I don't really care about the attention. Not as much as I thought I would, because, as he takes my hands in his, Orion's eyes are baring into mine, and even with a Goddess beside me, no one can compare.

"We are gathered here today to join these two Kindred souls in Matrimony." Atargatis begins, her lips caressing each word and her voice a melding of crashing waves and gentle surf. "We must recognise that these two people are the sole reason why this world remains safe today. It is my greatest

546

pleasure to make them merman and wife before you all and so I would like to ask that they each speak the vows that they have prepared for one another." I cringe internally at this, knowing that my mind is one blank slate. I should have prepared something. "Orion, you go first." Atargatis hands over the ceremony to Orion, who clears his throat.

"Callie, I had no idea how to possibly express what I feel for you in mere words. The only way I feel I can honestly say how I feel is by vowing to show you every day for the rest of forever. You have shown me what I can be, what the world can be. You opened my eyes, my heart and mind to the new, to the extraordinary. So, on this, our wedding day, the very first day of our forever, I want to vow to keep you safe, to support you, to love you. With everything I am." He looks so choked up as he speaks I wonder if he might cry. I'm dumbfounded. I hadn't realised how much the vows could actually mean.

He turns to Azure, who passes him my ring, before pivoting back to me and sliding it next to my engagement ring as I gulp, swallowing my fear. My wedding band is white gold, with the entire band encrusted with more alexandrite to match my engagement ring. As I examine it, Atargatis looks to me, expectant.

I open my mouth to speak, wondering what I can possibly say. I look to my mother, then to my father, to the two people who had waited so long to meet again in order to protect me. Then, I know exactly what I should promise.

"Orion. I didn't prepare any vows for today. I know that's probably disorganised of me, but here's the thing. I didn't know how much I wanted this until I got to this moment and anything not conceived from right now would have been a disservice to this. To what we have. I never realised how complete vowing yourself to another for eternity could make you feel. I know you waited for me, I can never forget that. But I want to vow never to make you wait again. I vow to be your forever, and to keep you strong even when things seem dark. I want to vow to never hold back. I want to vow to love you like every day is our last, even if we have a million more. I love you. Thank you for showing me this world. Thank you, for bringing me home." I speak the words and Orion smiles at me, his irises watering in the light of the high sun as I feel myself choke up too, my eyes prickling with my own tears. But I don't cry. I don't

547

want to lose an ounce of the emotion coursing through me to tears, because after all the sadness, and all the grief, I know now that it's far too precious.

I twist to Sophia who passes me Orion's ring. Holding the band in between my fingers I examine it quickly as I pivot to face him once more. It's simple, platinum with a wavy line engraved through the middle. It's supposed to represent the immortality of our love being like the endlessness of the sea, or something like that, but I really liked it because it reminds me of his tattoo.

I place the ring on his finger and Atargatis looks between us, her face excited as the next words dance on her lips. I wonder how many weddings she's been to, or if this is her first.

"I am very proud to announce that you are now merman and wife. You may kiss the bride." She says as Orion and I look to one another finally, our eyes, aqua and icy blue locking like two puzzle pieces which had been apart for far too long.

Orion takes a step forward, his eyes hooded as his eyelids close. His hand comes up and cups my cheek as his lips find mine. I feel a rush of heat scorch through me as the hairs on the back of my neck stand on end and his lips claim me. I kiss him back, bending backward as he wraps his arms around my waist.

The kiss ends too quickly and he pulls back, still looking at me with irises that blaze glacial. I look out to the crowd as they rise and begin to clap. I hold up my bouquet, which Sophia passes back to me, in triumph, unable to stop smiling as my mom and dad look to one another, long stale waters beginning a new rhythm between them.

We walk back down the aisle and Orion's hand clutches mine as we reach the end, looking back to where we've just walked to see that Atargatis is gone, and now only the bridal party, Oscar, Cole and Azure, stand by the archway. Then, as Isabella moves from the edge of the walkway, where she has been observing the ceremony, she speaks the words that truly puts the cherry on my wedding cake.

"The buffet is open!"

548

AZURE

I'm stood beneath the gazebo, looking dead snazzy in my suit, as I see an unexpected face moving across the dance floor. He, no surprise, has a cigarette in his mouth and as I'm perched next to the buffet table, taking my fill of the crab cakes, he decides, for some clearly stupid reason, to come over and try to talk to me.

"Nice wedding huh, Love?" He says, smiling in his leather jacket. He's got a tie on underneath, so I suppose he thinks it counts as formal. The sun is lowering in the sky behind us, and the stark orange light casts shadows across his face.

"I suppose. As far as weddings go." I reply, rolling my eyes.

"Look, I just, I want to talk to you about what happened." He starts, looking to me with wide eyes. I stare at him, a crease in my forehead appearing as I try to contemplate the pure density of his skull if he thinks I want to talk.

"Why? Are you a total moron? There's nothing to talk about." I snap, taking another crab cake and stuffing it in my mouth. Perks of not wearing a dress is that I don't even have to attempt to look like a lady. He coughs at my response as he places a hand on my behind. I shift uncomfortably, not moving to hit him, but only because there's children present.

"Right, so there's nothing to talk about?" He speaks slowly, his expression now dead as he takes another puff of his cigarette.

"Nope." I reiterate, crossing my arms across my chest.

"Nothing at all?" He asks me, as things start to become awkward. He puts his left hand in his pocket, finally taking it off my ass.

"That's right." I reply.

"Well uh right then. I'll leave you to your crab cakes." He says, dropping his eyes and slinking off across the dance floor once more. I watch as he goes, twisting around Gideon and Callie's mother who are dancing slowly together. Orion is dancing with Kayla next to Isabella and Domnall, who both look totally wasted, and Callie is sitting by herself, feet up on a chair and eating wedding

549

cake with a fork off a plastic plate. I walk over to her, bored of watching everyone else be sappy.

"Hey bridezilla, where did you get the cake?" I ask her as she rolls her eyes in retort and then points with her fork to a table with a cake that looks like a sandcastle, her mouth still full.

"It's weird it looks like sand right? It doesn't taste like sand though." Callie says as she swallows, shoving the fork in her mouth again with such gusto it's like she'll never eat again.

I walk over to the cake, cutting myself a slice from the bottom layer and being pleasantly surprised to find that the inside is chocolate. I turn around, plate in my hand, only to see Vex is directly behind me again.

I growl.

"You see here's the thing, Love. I really think we need to talk about..." he starts.

I don't think, I just act, wrapping my hand around my piece of cake and slamming it into his face. I smoosh the cake right in, making sure to get all the nooks and crannies. "Bloody hell!" He yells, and as he does the remaining guests turn to watch. I see Orion's expression turn comical as Vex pivots on his heel and storms from the gazebo and off into the distance. I smirk.

So that's his stupid ass taken care of. Who would have thought he'd get so upset over a piece of cake in the face. What a wimp!

"Azure. You might very well have just given me the best wedding present of today." Orion comes over and shakes my hand, handing me a napkin as he does so and laughing loudly. He's carrying Kayla, Callie's snot nosed kid sister, in his arms and she stares at me, her eyes wide as her head tilts, like she's not quite sure what to make of me.

Suddenly, she reaches out her chubby arms and simply says. "Up." Orion passes her to me as I stare at him like he's gone insane.

"Orion, take her back!" I practically cry as the little girl giggles at my horrified expression. Callie has turned, watching us and continuing to eat her cake, clearly not aware how much of a danger I can be if pushed the wrong way.

550

"Callie!" I call out, holding Kayla away from my body like she's the dangerous one.

"Hey Azure it's fine. She likes you. Besides, I have cake. I'm busy." She says, a cheeky grin crossing her lips as she puts more cake on her fork. I look to Kayla, then to Callie and then to Orion. I am *so* not a babysitter.

"You're very pretty." Kayla says, placing her hand on the side of my face. Her chocolate brown eyes are wide, her skull tiny and her hair is messy with short strands falling loose from her bun and curling.

"You think so?" I reply, not sure exactly what it is I'm doing as I get a wicked urge.

I let my eyes dilate to black, trying to scare her, make her go away so she no longer wants to cling to me. I watch as her eyes examine me. Instead of crying, screaming or doing any of the other things I expect, she laughs.

"Your eyes look funny." She giggles, leaning in and kissing me on the cheek. The small girl curls up in my arms and rests her head on my shoulder as my heart thaws. If only a little.

"She really does like you." Callie says, standing now she's finished her cake.

"She's not so bad, I guess." I say, not wanting to admit that the little girl is getting to me.

"Well, she's sort of your sister now too." Callie says with a smile. We stand together, Kayla in my arms as some kind of contentedness finds its way to me. Starlet might be gone, but I guess she wasn't the only one who could ever love me. After all, I'd saved Callie from herself earlier today with her stupid meltdown. I sigh out, vowing that I will learn from Starlet. I will be a better sister. I will try.

For just a moment, looking at Kayla, my half-sister, gives me a flicker of hope against my better judgement as I feel a sort of peace fall over me. I embrace it, knowing that, as always, it will only be temporary at best, but finding myself smiling anyway. After all, if a little kid like this doesn't think I'm so bad, then maybe, just maybe, I'm not so irredeemable after all.

551

42

The One

CALLIE

We walk, hand in hand, along the shoreline. Everyone is inside the house sleeping, preparing for departure, or back in the Occulta Mirum. It's been a long day, a beautiful day, and as most days like this are, it's also been tiring and yet over far too quickly.

I watch as the sun vanishes over the horizon, holding the hand of my new husband. I look down at his wedding ring, the small band claiming him as mine. As we walk, the moon rises, bringing with it a heady and intoxicating white light. The sand spreads out before us as we take slow and measured steps. Orion, who looks thoughtful and is dressed in pale denim jeans and nothing else, finally breaks the silence.

"I can't believe you're Mrs. Fischer." He says, looking to me with a goofy grin as his mahogany locks stand, tousled in that way I love and his glacial blue eyes bare into mine. I step closer to him, looking up into his picturesque and flawless face. I'm no longer wearing my wedding dress, but am dressed now only in lingerie and a white silk robe which comes only just to the middle of my thigh. I press my chest to his, laying a deep and passionate kiss on his lips as I take my time, enjoying myself.

"I can. I feel different." I reply, smiling gently as I lean away from him, letting my hair fall long down my back and expose my corset bound breasts.

"You do?" He says, cocking an eyebrow.

"Well of course. We're married now. Means I can legally have my way with you whenever I choose." I chuckle, "It's sort of liberating actually." I wink and his gaze turns feral.

"Well, if I'd have known you were holding back on that front I would have married you sooner." He jokes, lunging forward and picking me up before tossing me over his shoulder. I giggle as waves crash onto the shore once more, watching as his feet kick up sand, jogging until we're hidden behind a few rocks where he puts me down on the ground. Before I know it, he's on top of me.

"Callie Fischer. Hmm I like saying your name." He murmurs, kissing my throat.

"That's because it's your name." I reply, giggling as his kisses send shivers up my spine. I feel his hands clutching at my thigh, gripping at the garters which have been holding up my sheer tights and gaze at him, adoring the sight of him taking me as his. His expression is one of non-restraint, one of lust and love rolled into one. I watch him with seductive eyes as he rips open the corset top of my lingerie, his fingers running over my chill flesh as goosebumps follow in their wake. He kisses my ribs, my stomach, my thighs, staring up to me before he runs his warm lips across my skin, eyes blazing passion of every shade. I sigh, knowing that if heaven isn't like this I'll be sorely disappointed.

"You are far too delectable to be my wife." He whispers, moving up my body slowly and allowing his lips to glide up over my breasts before reaching my neck and nibbling on my earlobe with a low groan. I close my eyes for a few moments, surrendering to his touch and letting the tension leave me.

After a few moments of pleasure, I pull his head from my neck so he's facing me, kissing him passionately and feeling his lips caressing mine, needing him so desperately that I cannot contain my desires any longer. I suddenly feel tears leaking from my eyes and he stops, moving his arms so they're either side of my head. He leans over me, his silhouette cast by the moon which is showering us with pure white glow. A wave rolls up the shore, covering our feet as I tremble beneath him, crying.

"What's wrong?" He asks me in a hushed, breathless whisper.

554

"I'm just, I'm so happy Orion. How can this be real?" I ask him, tears falling slowly from me, like all the emotions I've been feeling today have come back all at once. I'm flush with colour, practically naked as I lie in the sand beneath his taut body and he stares down to me, eyes so full of wonder it's like he's looking into a galaxy. Like I'm his moon in a mortal body that's wanton, pulling him to the shore and keeping him grounded, bound by a force greater than either of us ever expected.

"Oh, Princess, it's real. You and I earned this. Every piece of it. So please, just enjoy it. I love you so much." He kisses me once more and my heart skips a beat as my tears dry and I settle back into the sand, hair strewn around me in a halo of blonde curls. Orion's arms cradle me and as the waves crash down over us and as the sea cools our rabid and aching hot skin, alight from the other one's touch. That's when I realise that this is what happily ever after could feel like.

I kiss him over and over, gasping for breath as the sea covers us like a blanket. I look up above to the stars as Orion kisses me, my body arching beneath his touch. I let him love me. I let him take me. I let him claim me. Like he's the sea itself and I'm drowning in the depths of his icy blue hold on me.

I think about our love, about the fact that he loves me for exactly who I am. That he sees me even when I cannot see myself. I had taken so long to get here, and as I watch his hair, dripping wet, and his eyes, blazing cold, as he moves in to make love to me, I know. I know as I think I have always known, exactly what it is that I am.

I am wild, I am free, I am calm, I am fierce. My heart is blessed with the clarity of the tropical shallows and yet my mind holds depths that one could drown in. Because I, Mrs Callie Fischer, am, and have always been, a mermaid.

CAEDES

Slithering. Sliding through the undergrowth like a slug. Like a tiny little slug. I thrash, spines broken. I am broken. Yet I am fixed.

Blood, need blood, but there is only water and sand.

The world is turning, burning, brothers gone, sisters gone. Everybody dead. The world is empty and I am alone.

So alone. Alone in my head. Except... for *him.*

CAEDES! Voice is in my head again. Get out. Bad man. I am a bad man.

CAEDES LISTEN YOU BLITHERING IMBECILE. I cover my ears. Try to make it stop. My body is not my own. Mind is so busy. Busy mind. So full with things one cannot see. One cannot hear. The ghosts in my head are real, but invisible.

CAEDES. THE FLAME. YOU MUST GET IT. FIRE. YOU SEE? The man talks in short words, thinks me is stupid. Thinks Caedes doesn't understand. Thinks Caedes is weak.

"Fire. Fire burns!" I let the words leak from my body like vital fluid. I speak to no one; the ocean is dark. Always dark. I am alone.

YES. I NEED YOU TO GET THAT FIRE. I NEED IT IF I AM TO RECLAIM YOUR WORLD.

Is it Solustus? Is it my Shepherd calling me home to his flock? Brothers dead. Brothers gone. Caedes has watched this come to pass. What if they cling on? Titus. Titus cling on, but no, how can this be? I have heard the voices forever. Since I was small and feeble. How can they be my brothers?

"Solustus?" I call out into the dark, a child, needing a mother on which to suckle and serve. Sanity. Like smoke. It evades Caedes. Blinding him. It is all an illusion. Just like me.

I AM NOT SOLUSTUS. YOU KNOW WHO I AM. I'M IN YOUR BLOOD. The voice tremors through me. A God who has fallen. My head hurts. The voices are too loud. Thoughts are scattered. Blood needs blood. Need fire. Flame. Burns.

THAT'S RIGHT MY CHILD. FLAME BURNS. Voice echoes and is gone. I collapse to the sand, watching tiny insects squirm in the dirt. I am a tiny insect too, the only difference is that I have a Shepherd. A Shepherd from a special place. He will guide me home. Like one brilliant star in the empty sky.

After all, Saturn and the Sun have all but flickered to ash. I have to follow my Shepherd, and he needs fire.

As I swim away, seeking that lone star, that flicker in the darkness of my head, I wonder why the voices need fire. After all, what can fire do but destroy?

END OF TRILOGY 1
THE TIDAL KISS TRILOGY

Acknowledgements

To everyone who helped make this trilogy possible, thank you! This book was my mountain, my Everest, and now I'm very much sat back enjoying the view. Thank you to my partner Mark, who is now entirely sick of mermaids, and one merman in particular! Thank you to my fabulous family, my mum, my dad and my Nanny to whome this book is dedicated. All of you listen to me moan and groan about how the book isn't done, and then get to watch my crash out after it's finally down on paper, lucky you! I also want to thank my editor, Jaimie Cordall, who believes in me when I don't believe in myself, and who is constantly teaching me new things, like how the word divot doesn't mean what I think it means. (Yes Jaimie, I'm still laughing.)

I also want to shout out to some very special people in particular, these being: 'The Incredible Dawn Yacovetta', 'The fabulous Emma Harrison', 'The Awesome Winters Rage' and 'The Wonderful Jessie Seloske Day', you are the best beta readers a girl could ask for, thank you for being brave enough to tell me when I suck, and when I'm doing things right (P.s. Yes, I'm totally officially dubbing you with these titles now. We need t-shirts!)

This last twelve months have been an incredible journey, and without every single one of you, I wouldn't be here, half a million words later, exhausted, but happy.

I hope you enjoyed the story and look forward to bringing you into new worlds with me!

Want more Tidal Kiss Trilogy magic?

BOOKS IN THIS TRILOGY
The Kiss That Killed Me
The Kiss That Saved Me
The Kiss That Changed Me

Follow the Trilogy @
Website: www.kristynicolle.com
Facebook: https://www.facebook.com/TheTidalKissTrilogy
Twitter: Nicolle_Kristy
Instagram: authorkristynicolle
Goodreads: Search The Tidal Kiss Trilogy
Photographs by the fabulously talented Trish Thompson

QUEENS OF *Fantasy*

Trilogy One - Book 3

ABOUT THE QUEENS OF FANTASY SAGA

Kristy Nicolle's Queens of Fantasy Saga is a collection of 3 trilogies, following the lives of three extraordinary women and their journeys, both personal and fantastical, into three unique but interconnected fantasy worlds. The first trilogy in the saga, 'The Tidal Kiss Trilogy', captures the fantastical underwater world of the Occulta Mirum and its scaly tailed residents as their world, which seemed stable for so long, begins to shift.

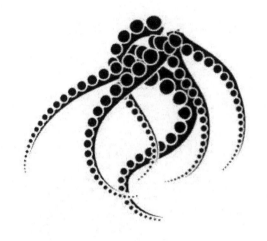

VEXED

WHY DOES HIS SUCKERED CLUTCH VEX ME SO?

SARCASM IS COMING...
WINTER 2017

IT'S GOING TO BE ONE
HELL OF A PARTY...

THE ASHEN TOUCH TRILOGY

THE OPAL BLADE
THE ONYX HOURGLASS
THE OBSIDIAN SHARD

CONVECTING TO A KINDLE
NEAR YOU 2017

THE TIDAL KISS TRILOGY:

The Kiss That Killed Me
The Kiss That Saved Me
The Kiss That Changed Me

TIDAL KISS NOVELLAS
Vexed
The Tank

TIDAL KISS SHORTS
Waiting For Gideon

OTHER QUEENS OF FANTASY TRILOGIES:

THE ASHEN TOUCH TRILOGY
The Opal Blade
The Onyx Hourglass
The Obsidian Shard

THE AETHERIAL EMBRACE TRILOGY
Indigo Dusk
Violet Dawn
Lavendar Storm

FOR PREDICTED RELEASE DATES VISIT
WWW.KRISTYNICOLLE.COM

Made in the USA
Charleston, SC
12 December 2016